That Certain Feeling

That Certain Feeling

X. V. ANTHONY

RARO

Copyright © X. V. Anthony 2008
First published in 2008 by Raro
Loundshay Manor Cottage, Preston Bowyer,
Milverton, Somerset TA4 1QF
www.amolibros.com

British Library Cataloguing in Publication Data
A catalogue record for this book is available from the British Library.

Distributed by Gardners Books, 1 Whittle Drive, Eastbourne,
East Sussex, BN23 6QH
Tel: +44(0)1323 521555 | Fax: +44(0)1323 521666

ISBN 978-0-9556082-0-9

Typeset by Amolibros, Milverton, Somerset
This book production has been managed by Amolibros
Printed and bound by T J International Ltd, Padstow, Cornwall, UK

To Ann

Contents

Prologue

For me it all began with a dusk. That warm, rosy, fumy dusk so long, long ago.

Before me a great traffic-filled open space. In and over it a haze of what seemed a fine pinkish dust. And seen through this, beyond it, a park, dim, sleeping, unfathomable. Into that warm evening haze there would emerge from time to time, with wonderful engineless electric glide and hum, a magical conveyance...perhaps the one we were waiting for. In the tender smoky pink half-light it was a more subdued red than by day – but the stars that its trolley-poles struck from the wires overhead were by contrast a fiercer blue, a sputtering sapphire. Echoed here and there across that space by others, they seemed to make visible an electricity coursing not just through wires and poles but through everything around me. And in the display panel above the driver's cab, the figures and letters of the route number and destination seemed to contain another, different message, tantalisingly hidden.

And oh, the petrol exhaust from the other traffic, its azure fumes hovering diffused, in places turning the Smarties pink of the sky to Smarties lilac. How richly *blue* the smell of that exhaust, that incense of the metropolis.

Ruby tail-lights studded the rosy dimness. And here and there, appearing, disappearing, other lights, a sweet red and orange, a mysterious peppermint green, seemed to be signalling another part of the elusive message.

Now and then I had the feeling I could decipher it, that message, if only I...if only...

One

Our two-down

Bexcray, where I grew up, was not so dark, closed in and oppressive a south-east-London suburb as some others, nearer the river. And Danehill Road, a row of terraces built at the turn of the century, stretching up an incline, had when I lived there something of the decorum associated with more middle-class areas. The bow-windowed frontages approached by short path and steps, the small raised front gardens, the width and quietness of the road lent those two-up-two-down, twopenny-halfpenny-scullery, outside-lav dwellings – the homes of bus conductors, hairdressers' assistants, gas fitters, booking-office clerks – something more of dignity than their poky, dingy interiors merited. And if the windowframes of many were neglected, their paint chalky and curling, their wood silvery and spongy, and if the gardens were little more than patches of rank grass, and if the railings were gone (sawn off in the war for munitions), their brown stumps corroding in the gums of the low retaining walls, well, these could have been simply the shabby element of a shabby-genteelness.

We lived at Number 33. Uncle Harry and Aunt Lil, who brought me up after my parents died, rented the lower floor only; the upper had been condemned. The focus of life there was the little back room, which served as dining room, living room and my bedroom. How cramped it was: the table (to which a faded brown-and-grey-checked oilcloth had lovingly, inseparably bonded itself over the years), the chairs, the sideboard, the put-u-up on which I slept, the hearth with its tin fender – together they took up, with Lil's clutter, almost all the floor space. And how damp it was, too: on one wall the blue-flowered wallpaper was peeling and islanded with discoloured patches (one had interestingly assumed the shape of a slowly expanding Australia), and on cold fireless days there was a pervasive smell of mildew. But above all how *dim* it was, that room: by day the light struggled in through a niggardly small window overlooking the back yard, and at night it glowered feebly from a naked low-watt bulb dangling from the ceiling, making the room then appear to be readying itself for some unspeakable crime.

'Mum and Dad'

On his days off from driving HGVs all over the country Harry was always coming home from the Prince Albert, our local, with eyes not quite focused and movements not quite steady, and he'd say to Lil things like: 'Well, what are *you* fucking staring at?' And then there'd be trouble. Like that incident with the broken glass... And the one with... Phew! It was just as well he was away so much.

Whereas Harry plastered performed the same tedious turn that all piss-artists keep putting on, Harry sober had of course a few more acts to offer. Like that on the Saturday mornings he had off, when he would sit with Lil at the table in the back room and study the racing page of the *Daily Warp*, that journal of relentless misinformation from which the pair of them took their off-the-peg opinions (and which at our place had, when torn into quarters and spiked on a nail, an additional, more useful function). In vest and trousers, braces dangling, unshaven, sipping a mug of bootpolish-brown tea and smoking, Harry would assess the form, taking powerful, 'thoughtful' draws on his fag, narrowing even further in his large white face his slits of eyes, less against the smoke than in what he thought of as canniness. Perhaps subconsciously he was imitating those underworld masterminds he'd seen in the movies, who, listening to a minion's report, evaluating it, would milk the full smoker's bit – lighting up, inhaling, exhaling, tapping off ash – to express authority or cunning or cool. And with Lil listening to him with that deference to their menfolk's opinions on all matters non-domestic that was automatic in most working-class women in the past, Harry, sending a 'pensive' stream of smoke ceilingward, would appraise the runners in scholarly fashion, pronouncing reconditely on underhandicapping, disadvantageously high numbers and suchlike, with what I then took to be, and admired as, astuteness.

That ostentatious, self-conscious, self-congratulatory manner of weighing up evidence and eventually coming to a verdict, how many times have I seen it since in other Harrys. In his case (and I have no doubt in many others), that manner did not spring from some pleased semi-consciousness of using his brain like a member of the professions: it was clear from listening to him that, vaguely, indiscriminately lumping together as 'posh' all non-manual workers, from ambassadors to salesmen, he was not even aware of the concept and term professions, let alone aware of the presumption that their members should use their noddles as a matter of course. No, Harry's manner derived from a typically cocky, ludicrous belief that his lengthy pondering, his shrewd (as he saw it) calculations, marked him out as someone exceptional. Though, to be fair, one could understand why he might be a victim of this fancy.

After all, he was surrounded, as an HGV driver and before that as a brickie, by workmates who, given little opportunity to display their brainpower, might have made him feel special; and in that era before the legalised betting shop, in which today so many students of form make so much use of so much research, he probably came across few other such scholars. Also, he was all too aware of Lil's grudging description of him as the 'brainbox of the family' (her term, too, for Mrs Smethwick's Dave down the road when he became a bank clerk). And finally, his reading confined to what passed for news in the *Warp* and to occasional dips into his two practical manuals, he never came across anything that might have opened his eyes to the actual composition of society.

As he puffed away with an air of discernment, Harry would study the form *narrowly*: a brain surgeon examining a CAT scan, a barrister a major brief. (And in fact later, when we got a telly, Harry, chucklingly empathising with smart-aleck counsel tripping up witnesses and reflecting on how easily he likewise worsted Lil in argument, would sometimes announce that he should have been a barrister and when asked by Lil in serious tones why he hadn't been would answer that he'd thought of it too late in life, an explanation that to Lil – and me – seemed perfectly reasonable.) Unlike those medical and legal inferences, however, his would not be based in the main on hard facts, much though he liked to think they were: so many unknown quantities bedevilled them – a horse's condition on the day, a jockey's confidence and health, other runners' improvements in training, the vagaries of the weather, interference on the track, not to mention the occasional bent stable lad. But each time he lost, it never entered his head that success had been out of his hands; he believed that there'd simply been a slight flaw in his complex chain of reasoning, one that he could remedy next time. Always that next time.

I would look at Harry and Lil engrossed in the racecards.

He ticked his selections in red biro, she underlined hers in blue. From time to time, the scientific spirit mocking the intuitive, Harry would grin derisively at Lil's fancy, dictated solely by the horse's name ('Ronnie's Tune, that sounds nice') or the jockey's mugshot ('That Gosling's a lovely-looking boy'): his lips would part in his lard-like face to bare decaying, 40-Weights-a-day-stained teeth, as Lil's white dripping when broached in its basin would reveal a substratum of brown. (Lil's liking for certain jockeys, though, was of the fickle kind. Should some blue-eyed boys of hers put paid to one of her dementedly optimistic Yankees, they would plummet from grace as suddenly as Elizabeth's favourites at court or Thatcher's in cabinet. None of their physical charms could save them from Lil's wrath in such a case. And ever afterwards she could never mention her one-time pets without damning them with her own Homeric epithets: just as much of an inseparable pairing as 'white-armed Hera' or 'aegis-bearing Zeus' were, for her, 'scabby-faced Gosling' and 'poxy-faced Hide'.)

Harry would make some facetious remark and Lil would respond with a playful shove and an affectionate 'Daft bugger'. And I would wish that such rare periods of contented shared activity, of harmony, could continue indefinitely.

Not a chance. Between Harry's placing of the bets and his return for dinner came a prolonged stay at the Prince Albert, and Lil, instead of ignoring his lateness, would curse and bang his plate down on the table and he would lurch up and grab her wrists and say slurrily, 'Don't you fucking come that with me.' And, as with a sequence in a horror movie seen before, what you knew was going to happen next was no less appalling, was perhaps more so, for being so foreseeable, so unpreventable.

I might have…

Harry and my father had a half-brother. Unlike the other two, he was the result of one of their mother's extra-marital flings – in this case with a wham-bam Sicilian barman called Dino. Choosing a name for her baby boy, she had taken his father's and Anglicised it to the one a singing Dino would later use in Hollywood: Dean.

Stocky and swarthy, Dean had small gleaming intelligent brown eyes, lank dark hair, an ample moustache and olive pockmarked skin. A less bulbous, more muscular Balzac. To look at he seemed unrelated to his light-brown-haired, whey-faced brothers, just as in certain pale-coloured moth species those forms industrially melanised to black seem unrelated to the rest. And he differed from them in another, more important way. Brought up like them in a world of low expectations and often even lower attainments, he'd managed unlike them to get on to one of the four traditional flights out (sport, entertainment, politics, commerce): after the war he started up as a street trader flogging American pulps from a stall, then with a partner, Vin Sharpes, he founded a small paperback publishing outfit, DV Books. Their line was snazzily dressed-up leftovers: at cut-price they bought the hardback crime, sci-fi, horror and adventure rejected by established, successful firms, had it printed cheaply abroad and, concentrating on packaging, splashed out only on classily come-on covers. Making a decent profit, they were gradually able to bid for better-quality titles, took the list more upmarket and renamed the imprint Spectrum.

When my parents died – in a road accident – Dean was laid low with flu in New Zealand, which he was visiting on a trip to expand Spectrum's market. I later learned that if he and his wife, Olivia (schoolteacher daughter of a literary agent), had been in England at the time they might have applied to foster me themselves: Olivia, unable to have children, had according to Lil already 'taken a shine' to me. After all, Harry didn't want me. It was only because to put an orphan into an institution wasn't the done thing in our class and because Lil, childless herself after two miscarriages, put the squeeze on him that he reluctantly took me, a five-year-old, aboard their stricken vessel.

Sometimes I found myself thinking how strange it was that, but for Dean and Olivia's absence at that time, I might have had a different upbringing, lived in a different house, gone to different schools... Even so, I've never *really* believed that that could have happened. Our early life seems to us so much the only one actually possible that, to me, growing up at 33 Danehill Road, Bexcray, has about it, with its commingled horrors and joys, a bitter-sweet inevitability.

To market

On Saturday afternoons Lil and I would sometimes take a trip to the market in neighbouring Blackwell. I went along to help carry the bags because Lil's back was usually 'killing' her, and Harry, when he was around, was rarely in any fit state to go.

We would catch a trolleybus in shopper-busy Artillery Row. On a fine afternoon, when the road quivered with heat and sunlight, resonated with bustle and traffic, I would love to wait at the stop, soaking up everything that pronounced this a regal occasion: the majestic blue above, the golden draperies the sun had hung on this façade and that, the rich silken frying odour from Champion Chips unfurling in the half-past-twoishness and the scarlet splendour of the trolleybuses.

Trolleybuses. The only fitting name for those magical conveyances, with their almost silent approach, their stylish fronts – flat, raked, engineless – their blue-sparking poles.

Coasting towards us, looming larger, the one we wanted would ease to a halt. Ah, that whiff you caught already, before getting on, that comfortable, modern, inorganic, urban smell raised by the warmth inside, the smell of rexine, moquette, tickets, electric current. Then the thrill of climbing aboard, of breathing in that smell in all its plenitude, of hearing and feeling, as we set off, not combustion-engine clamour, as in a bus or car, but a faint and unassuming hum, the thrill of luxuriating in, well, in what could only be called trolleybusness. The sun would slant in and there would glow on the back of the seat in front of us, where the pile was still clean and velvety, a rhomboid of fiery blue, and farther along the car another blue, faint, hazy, hovering, aromatic, would bloom into one rich and creamy. Ensconced in the warmth and fumes, I would sit back and let shops, pubs, houses unravel before my eyes; in that heat-drowsed-lizard state I seemed less to observe the ever-changing scene outside than merely to absorb it.

Like most kids, I would try to get a seat upstairs at the very front. There, raised on high above the world at street level, I now seemed no longer lost in that world but instead, god-like, to command it. Sometimes I would feel so happy, sitting at the prow of that top deck, as we sailed through one area after another, that I should have been content to stay perched there at ease indefinitely. And who as a child hasn't felt on certain journeys this desire never to reach one's destination, this desire to travel on, and on, and on...?

Plug-ugly

A garrison and industrial town, Blackwell was one of those sprawling, predominantly working-class suburbs that began proliferating without plan or form in south-east London during Victorian times, 'embryo slums' as one reformer called them.

With its ingrained grime, closed-in streets and absence of greenery, it was to me as a child depressing, menacing even, and once there all the Saturday elation I'd felt in Bexcray would vanish. Of course, sunlight would as readily drape and carpet that unlovely place as anywhere else, but the result then was simply that the grimy redbrick of a pub or chapel, which in dull weather you might not even notice, so absorbed was it into the overall gloom, was unable to hide itself when lit up by the sun to a grimy orangebrick, and in Docking Lane, which led down to the river, more ghastly on a golden day than the coal black of the sooty stonework on the sunless side was the ashy grey on the sunlit.

The *Blackwell and Bexcray Gazette* regularly reported drunken fights in the town between the squaddies stationed there (JILTED CORPORAL SLASHES RIVAL IN PUB BRAWL) and whenever we came across groups of them in their thick ill-fitting battledresses and clink-clanking metalled boots I would worry that we might get caught up in a flurry of jilted-corporal violence. Then there was the network of quiet, narrow, black-walled backstreets we took a short cut through to reach the town centre (getting off early saved us a few pence). Thieves and ruffians lodged there, I was sure, but even worse was the thought that perhaps… Some time earlier Lil had told me, in absolutely whizz-o detail, the thrilling story of Jack the Ripper, as she had become acquainted with it in the film *The Lodger*. Her account wasn't *quite* the full works: a merciful imprecision about the disembowelling, for instance, and nothing about what the victims were up to in those alleyways, but even so plenty of nice descriptive touches: the gas lamps, the fog, the dark looming figure with the medical bag, the screams, the blood trickling out of the alley. (I was to notice later how in this woman, and others I knew like her, who could as a rule barely give you an intelligible description of some everyday happening, the relaying of the unspeakable unexpectedly brought out a sophisticated narrative technique.) Yes, the Ripper. My awareness of manifest evil had been understandably minimal up to that point (Harry's drunken violence fell more into the category of the sordid, and the murders I read about in the paper generally resulted from greed or sudden loss of control rather than satanic urges), and there I was, tender soul, hurled into a confrontation with it in its very blackest form. The sheer terrifying depth of that moral blackness as it appeared to me then I can only compare to that of the physical blackness I found myself in some years later in the caves at Wookey Hole when without warning the guide turned the light out and demonstrated to me that until that marrow-freezing moment I had never truly known what *complete* absence of light was. Lil hadn't told me exactly where in London the Ripper had, in terms of moral light, kept achieving an identical absolute zero, so, whenever we made our way through that squalid area of Blackwell, I would wonder whether it mightn't have been deep within those uninviting passageways whose entrances we occasionally passed (and which at night would have been so dimly lit) that the shadowy figure *with the bag* had performed his unimaginable butchery.

The shopping centre of Blackwell had a grimness that was bang on. The main street, Cable Lane, for instance, was *impressively* begrimed and was regularly punctuated by what was only fit and proper to it: the boarded-up and the litter-strewn. True, there were the usual chipper enterprises that squared up to it – Dolcis, H. Samuel, that lot – but it was all flash stuff, that lightweight bravado that doesn't stand a chance against true heavies – and, boy, these didn't come any more plug-ugly than Cable Lane.

It was in that street, below a central island, that there lay what I later couldn't help regarding as a microcosm of the town: a noxious public lavatory. I never as a boy much liked descending into any underground Gents. Even their approach and entrance

I found disagreeable: the shoe-scratched, greyish squares of opaque glass inset into the pavement as skylights and, leading down into the depths, the iron-grille steps on which your feet clanged. Then, below, the wan light filtering down through those skylights, regularly pedestrian-darkened as though by passing clouds; the somewhat sinister susurration of the urinals; and, every so often, the jarring slam of spring-loaded cubicle doors. I also had an aversion – one of those many, strange, irrational aversions of children – to the penny-in-the-slot mechanisms on those doors. In that rarely, if ever, cleaned Blackwell lavatory, VACANT, already unpleasant enough to me in its tarnished brass housing, was the more so by association with what it often gave access to: pee on the seat, pee on the floor, and, in cubicles where the cistern was out of order, the raw stench of what low water had left fully exposed, to the excitement in summer of eagerly buzzing flies. And then there was the artwork and text that congestively covered every square inch of every markable surface of every one of those tiny galleries. A few graffiti could be seen in the school toilets, of course, before old Briggsy the caretaker scrubbed them off, but nothing remotely resembling this seething mass of dripping rockets, slashed pin cushions, twin balloons and medially conjoined puppets (few true draughtsmen operated here); of 'fucks' and 'pricks' and 'dicks' and 'cocks' and 'cunts' and 'cums' and 'spunks' and 'wanks' (even then I noticed the prevalence of the hard aggressive 'c' in so many of our four-letter words); of 9-inch boasts; of lusting, insatiable minors; of entire, door-panel-filling chapters of compulsive 'and then I...and then she...and then I...' narrative; of demonstrative arrows; of requests for assignations; of needs rigorously, remarkably specific... And for some reason, as unfathomable as my aversion to the brass penny-in-the-slot mechanism, what I found perhaps even more repugnant than the stink and squalor of that place was the *physical form* in which certain of its users' fantasies and frustrations were expressed: the *smeared blacklead* message on the wall, the *assiduously carved* phone number on the door.

We would reach the market, with its close-packed stalls and loud competing cries, and Lil would head for her favourite traders. In her weekly budget, food was what you bought with what was left over after your outlay on fags, drink, sweets, bingo, the pictures and the horses. Even when we were comparatively flush, that just meant there was more available for Lil's priorities, never better grub. So at the market she was always on the lookout for 'real bargains': bladderwrack bananas, black-skinned and springy to the touch ('at their best'); casualty-department tomatoes, all crimson puffiness and gaping wounds ('lovely and ripe'); pink-ruled-paper streaky bacon, lean more decorative than alimentary ('fat builds you up'); and various staples of unlabelled provenance ('tastier than them brand names'). What was more, once brought home, they had to be eaten up. In their entirety, every last scrap, like everything else. 'Waste not, want not' was one of Lil's mantras. And, unlike some of the others, such as 'If a job's worth doing, it's worth doing well', it was one that she put into practice. If someone refused a second cup of tea, 'Come on,' she'd demand, 'there's another two cups in that pot. I can't drink 'em both.' And she would belch loudly as though in part-explanation. But, on a second refusal, she would indeed drink them both. As compelled to finish everything up as those in *Cranford* driven to use up left-over butter on unwanted toast or as Mr Pooter to use up left-over paint on what didn't need it, she would pour both cups into a rebellious stomach, dyspeptically satisfied at having once more avoided 'waste'.

Lil reckoned herself a real savvy bargain-hunter but showed herself to be just another of the batty type: pursuing twopence-off-three when only one was needed and insisting on trips to the market when any savings she made there were virtually wiped out by the fares we paid to get there and the cuppa and orange squash she always insisted on buying us at Kenny's Mobile Snacks. I once foolishly began to give her the benefit of my deliberations on the matter: 'Mum, you know you saved sixpence on the fruit and veg, and fourpence on the meat, and twopence on the...' I went through my memorised list. 'Well, I was thinking, our fares...' Detecting my drift from the reflective tone that discomfited her whenever she heard it, she cut me off sharpish: 'You were thinking. You think too bloody much, you do.' (Another of the mantras.) I tried again: 'I only thought you could save – ' But she wasn't having it: 'Are you trying to tell *me* how to save money? *Me?* Are you? Cheeky little sod.' It was no good. I would have to wait until I left school before I could be given my head and put my obvious talents in the grocery accounts line smartly through their paces.

On those afternoons...

It was an unusually torrid early June and I was staying, for a whole week, with Dean and Olivia. This was when they still lived in a semi in Richborough, a commuter town in Surrey that had clung on to its heritage character: narrow streets, bow-windowed shops, listed buildings. On that visit, Olivia sometimes took me after lunch to the local park. Afterwards, we would amble home, lazily, sleepily. Walfield Road, where they lived, was short, quiet and, at such an hour, inky on one side, richly gilded on theirs. And at the farther end, on the sunny corner, resplendently dozing off in the Next-Collection-4PM heat, the bright red pillar box and the orange-painted post office were as gorgeously gaudy as birds of paradise... Beside me the low garden walls burned to the touch, before me the slowly moving stencils of ourselves on the pavement were a slaty blue. And then, still some way before we reached the house, I caught the first faint heady scent wafting from its garden in the heat and stillness. By the time we had turned through the front gate to see the wallflowers themselves massed around the lawn, the scent had become ampler, headier still. It may, this fragrance, have been less overtly sweet than that of roses, say, or of lilies, but for me the dull, dusky drowsiness of it, in which there was a touch of honeyed fruitiness, had a beauty more profound, it concentrated within itself, then and for evermore, the very *depth* of a regal summer afternoon as no other scent ever could. And how the rich warm dyes of those flowers, the throng of vibrant reds and oranges unbroken by any other colour, seemed to befit that fragrance: smouldering crimsons, some so deep they were almost black, glowing scarlets, ardent oranges, and all, at a little distance, looking velvety, or perhaps ever-so-faintly dusty, as though from flowering so near the road. Drawn to a particular clump of them, crossing the lawn, crouching the better to intoxicate myself with their smell, I could see just how sumptuous their colours were: some glowed with, if not the same hue, then the same purity of dye that gives anemones and poppies their intensity; others, equally fervent, combined two stains, causing an orange to blush or subtly suffusing one red with another, creating the loveliest colours of all. Up close, I could see too that what gave these flowers their appearance of velveteen or faint dustiness was the finest of naps on their petals – and that scattered in among them were clusters of tiny buds, a dull dark maroon, fittingly dusky companions. Immediately behind the close-packed bed, the old red brickwork of the garden wall, steeped in the heat, apricot in the unwaveringly benevolent light, wobbled slightly as though, like me, drunk with the wallflowers' scent, drunk with their heavy, slumbrous, depth-of-afternoon muskiness...

On those afternoons, in that still, beneficent heat, not even a whisper of what I would only come to learn later. That the dark serpent can slither in anywhere.

After tea, at that mellow hour on a fine summer's day when late afternoon is only leisurely preparing to become early evening, we would sometimes go for a walk through the leafy residential roads round about. Still lilting in my mind's ear would be the beautifully, absurdly carefree signature tune of a children's radio serial, tune and serial that transformed everyday life into an adventure, bright guileless voices and jaunty melodic music imbuing each garden and street and corner with the same romance as the story. What I was to remember most about those backwater tours was the stored warmth of the day lingering in every foliage-scented crescent, drive and close; the faint diffused bonfire smoke making aromatic that warmth, sweetly pervading the still daylight hours; children playing hopscotch, trailing long shadows behind them on a pavement of old gold; the comfortable whirr of an unseen lawnmower; the crests of privets and laurels caught by the declining sun somewhere beyond them, their aureoles disclosing the dance of midges; and, in one bower of gold and emerald hedge in an unmade lane, the already magical red of a telephone kiosk lit up to one even more so, a sumptuously fiery scarlet...somehow *significant*.

Held to Ransom

We had, as far as I knew then, three books at home. Two of them were practical manuals belonging to Harry, so heavy I could scarcely lift them: Mega Books' *Ultimate Guide to Wallpapering* and *Ultimate Guide to Lawnmowing* (Consultant Raymond Blight, NDH, FLS, a mythic figure who had *his own column* in the *Warp* and was head of a horticultural college). Crumbs, how they impressed me, those 1000-plus-page tomes. Though why Harry, who never once laid a decorator's finger on our little two-down with its stained, peeling paper and who used shears whenever, rarely, on some half-cut plunge into temporary dutifulness, he half-cut our overgrown grass back and front, why he of all people had acquired (certainly never bought) those giant volumes became for me years later one of those family mysteries that only ever strike us in retrospect and that we now feel we shall never solve.

The third book was a 1917 *Chatterbox* annual. (Where it had come from I'd never enquired, so much in our childhood do we unthinkingly accept as just *being there*.) A time came when, curious, I took that book from the cupboard where it lurked, unlovely and forgotten, and browsed through it. Then I began reading the first serial. And soon I found myself experiencing what I felt whenever I looked at a picture that hung on the wall beside the pantry door, facing the foot of the put-u-up. An Edwardian print of intended charm, 'cleverly' entitled *A Sea Urchin*, it depicted a little ragamuffin (sentimental pictorial favourite of the times), on an otherwise deserted shore, running towards a wave that reared above him, cold, green, glassy, seething at its crest. Age and fly-blows and the fine film of grease that overlaid so many surfaces in that room had made the scene more horrid still by darkening the original ochre of the beach to dun, the grape green of the sea to olive and the white of the foam to yellow. Because of its position, it had no difficulty at bedtime, that print, in overcoming my attempts to ignore it: it was more or less helplessly that I would gaze at that wave, that icy wall, and at the boy beneath it, all alone...and there would always then steal through me a strange unease. Now, reading that serial, I felt that unease in a more intense form that amounted, I suppose, almost to fear. Fear and yet a hateful fascination: after Lil, and Harry when he was home, had retired for the night to the front room, I couldn't stop myself slipping out of the put-u-up, switching on the light and taking up that story from where I'd left off. Merely as a material object, the *Chatterbox* annual was as disagreeable to me as the picture on the wall. Its unwholesome paper, time-jaundiced, foxed in places, singed at the edges and exhaling a fusty-sweet breath, and its wretched copperplate etchings, all scratchy halftones and inky black shadows, together cast a pall over everything in the book: just as in its physical self *A Sea Urchin* reinforced the effect of what it portrayed, so those very pages of *Held to Ransom* rendered even more horrid its story. Sallowed further by the sickly light overhead, they told me, their unwilling, intent reader, of the harrowing ordeals of two public schoolboys (virtual orphans I empathised with: mother dead, father abroad since their infancy) who set out for Morocco to find a hidden treasure with which to ransom that missing father, now in the hands of brigands. Stowaways on a scarcely seaworthy wooden barque, they were unable to escape from the battened-down hold when the ship was caught in a terrible storm, and their cries and bangings went unheard. In their sickeningly plummeting marine coffin they were plunged into pitch darkness. A compulsion to terrify the young reader surfaces every so often in children's fiction like a black running stitch and our author was at pains to stress repeatedly the stowaways' feelings of loneliness, cold and terror. The timbers were breached by a falling mast, the sea rushed in on them, the crew, still unaware of their presence, abandoned ship and the boys ended up at night in a leaky open boat on an ocean whose waves towered above them. The creator of *Held to Ransom*, who perhaps had himself shuddered at Coleridge's 'Alone, alone, all, all alone, Alone on a wide wide sea', pointed out how 'absolute and profound' the darkness was, how 'alone, alone' the boys were and how 'appalled by the horror of the sea', expressions which, like the dismally cross-hatched, graphic illustrations of their plight, etched themselves into my memory.

That special unease the story in the annual and the print on the wall induced in me was to visit me again and again over my early years – and in my reading I would come across others' experiences that were similar. Perhaps it was because these simply noted that fear and did not explore it, because it assailed me in different guises and because it varied so much in its intensity, perhaps it was because of all this that it took me so long to come to the underlying truth of it.

The Regal

Of the quartet of traditionally grand-sounding cinemas in Bexcray – the Regal, the Majestic, the Ritz, the Kings – it was only the Regal that truly lived up to its name. And whenever we went there Harry, the opposite of Lil in this respect, seemed to think our visit must be equally regal: whatever our financial state, he insisted against Lil's protests on getting the most expensive, front-of-Circle seats and lashing out on all sorts of sweets. I remember how, unaware then of masked balls at *palazzi*, millionaires' megabashes and suchlike, I supposed the front of the Circle at the Regal, Bexcray, to be the ultimate luxury in entertainment, a belief reinforced by Harry's smirk as he paid for those seats, his swagger as we mounted to them and his swank as we enthroned ourselves on them.

As soon as we entered the spacious vestibule of that temple, with its warmth, its gold and pastel rococo decor, its soft carpet, there flooded through me a sense of its opulence and comfort and security. How reassuring was its guardian, the commissionaire in his Regal maroon-and-gold. How voluptuous was its fragrance, that of the perfumed air freshener drifting into the foyer from the auditorium, fragrance that long before we had risen to cinema heaven already carried me up towards it. With each stage of our progress my contentment increased: watching the narrow perforated tongue of costly printed pink (stirringly differentiated from cheaper-seats green and blue) jerkily emerge from the brass ticket counter, our passes to pleasure, official, conclusive; stopping at the display of cigarettes and boxed confectionery, their cellophaned rectilinear packaging not only a guarantee of quality but the symbol somehow of something more, of the civilised, the agreeable, the secure; ascending the wide curving staircase whose milky-green-and-white-marbled rubbery treads exuded a de luxe rubbery odour, a faint secondary fragrance that mingled with the first and that seemed to me then the very meaning of luxury; gazing at the large framed photographs of the stars lining the wall – David Niven, Maureen O'Hara, William Holden, Doris Day – all with such pleasing, perfect faces (smiling perhaps from breathing in constantly the mingled incenses), remote from the mere mortals we all were (I could never have believed they had to pee and shit like us, had nightmares, got flu); and excitedly wondering, as we neared the Circle usherettes, what the mysteriously titled film, the usually, glamorously *American* film, held in store.

Entry at last into the inner temple. Buoyant interval music, all's-right-with-the-world music – resembling that which, less memorably tuneful perhaps but just as carefree (like that of the children's radio serials), you heard on the soundtrack of some films: all abounce and abubble, this would accompany some good-news-happy hero as he breezed from one scene to the next along a Manhattan thoroughfare of genially honking traffic, sparky newsboys and trouble-free passers-by, tipping his hat to some, who would exchange with each other smiles of delighted amazement. As well as the music, a third incense, the richest yet, that of cigarette smoke, headily aromatic. (How, in the same way as the most intoxicant of all those boyhood incenses, petrol exhaust, its visible form, soft hazy blue, seemed the perfect embodiment for it, as in cinema or trolleybus, at snooker hall or dog track, it hung sweetly on the air.) Then the lights going down. In the blackness the rustle all around of silver paper, the swirl up above, in the projection beams, of a filmy blue, and the glow down below, on a luminous digitless clock, of wedges of fruity green. And, after a while, appearing up there before us, vast, supramundane (even more so if in rarefying black-and-white), the Olympians themselves. How commandingly nonchalant, how *American*, the gods, with their tilted-back hats and loosened ties! How disturbingly vampish (early erotic stirrings), how *American*, the goddesses, outfits figure-moulding, sidelong glances inviting! How winningly casual, how *American*, the voices!

But after a time, when the 'So you're telling us your proxy had already given Anderson's attorney a duplicate of the conveyance?' plot had passed my understanding and when characters lowering themselves into chairs around a table warned of further fistless, gunless, Anderson's-attorney's-duplicate stuff to come, the initial thrill would wear off. Then my gaze would be drawn back to the clock. Reinforced in my subconscious by similar emeralds on a backing of black velvet – signals glowing in the night – the phosphorescent hours and hands would seem, like those lights, to be trying to convey something more than their ostensible meaning. But, as ever, trying in vain.

The racing page

I too made selections from the racecards – even though I wasn't allowed to bet on them (Harry, strangely moral, I think, rather than mean, in this respect, resisted all my 'Oh, come on, just sixpence' cajolings). I asterisked my choices with the lurid green chinagraph pencil I'd found on the pavement outside Woolworths and used at every possible opportunity. What with Harry's red ticks and Lil's blue underlinings, the racing page of the Saturday *Warp* acquired – like Stravinsky's red-, blue-

and green-annotated scores or like campaign maps marked with arrows and encirclements in various colours – one of those multichrome overlays that willy-nilly now make stimulating what had previously appeared neutral, boring. My best friend, Danny Glazier, made selections from his own paper. Helplessly male-competitive, we vied as would-be punters, seeing who could 'win' the more from our purely imaginary wagers.

Apart from the buzz of this ersatz gambling, there was the poetry of racing as I imagined it, particularly on the flat. I'd never visited a racecourse, we didn't have telly then and the few big races I'd seen on the news at the cinema were in black-and-white. So my fancy was free. I always saw, even on overcast days, the glamorous meetings – Ascot, Epsom, Goodwood (golden names) – as pulsatingly taking place, at those tracks which for me had no actual location but floated in some vague and wonderful beyond, somewhere Out There, I saw them as taking place in a great solid slab of sunlight, on a turf of gilded green that set off the jockeys' silks even more richly than the lamplit baize did the balls on the Prince Albert snooker table. As for those silks, their verbal contraction in the racecards – *crmsn and gold qtrs, crmsn cap; pk with mve arm hps, mve cap* – seemed correspondingly to concentrate their colours, to set them glowing even more intensely against their imagined background of emerald-gold.

But, in the same way that a simple black-and-white airline schedule may stimulate a traveller's imagination as powerfully as some full-colour holiday brochure, so just as magical to me as my multichrome reveries were the (pre-selection) colourless racecards in the paper. How, standing by their own in simple black, unembellished with any conjured up silks, the horses' names entranced me. Not just the splendid names, like PURPLE EMPEROR, or the evocative, like DESERT ISLAND, but even the mundane, like WAIT A WHILE, or the incomprehensible, like DEFERRED ANNUITY. For the thrill those names gave me derived not at all from their meaning or from imagining in physical form the runners that bore them but entirely from the printed names themselves, the unique collection of letters that composed each (their bold sanserif made the serif cards of other papers seem so prosaic that I could scarcely believe the runners were the same) and that summoned up not an actual horse, not a compact chestnut, say, or a strapping grey, but, in a demonstration of the imagination's unremitting striving towards the ideal, a *Platonically perfect*, disembodied horse (the 'whatness of allhorse'). Yes, a beautiful abstract horse, a kind of transcendent, non-signifying equine purple emperorishness or deferred annuityishness.

Just as a term like deferred annuity, thoroughly nondescript if encountered in lower case in its everyday meaning, whatever that might have been, could, if ennobled as a racehorse's name in the beautiful bold sans caps of the *Warp*'s cards, metamorphose into a thrilling latent force, so too could a group of four figures, so ordinary in most contexts, once it was used before the name of a horse to denote its most recent form. Not that the potency of the figures, any more than that of the names, had anything to do with their meaning – in this case, where that particular runner had finished in its last few races. No, as with the names, the potency of the figures stemmed from their *purity* as signifiers risen free from practical application. And those groups – 0040, say, or 1221 (equally fascinating whether indicative of success or failure) – also throbbed with something else, which the names didn't possess: the capacity to change, to develop after this meeting into a new group with a different resonance, an intriguing 0401, say, or 2213. Intriguing, though, not as an index of the horse's fortunes but in itself alone – once again, not as the applied but as the *pure*.

Ah, those purities, those Platonic perfections, that our idealising young imaginations are constantly spinning from the crude matter around us – beautiful they may be but what generalised trouble to come they constantly store up for us.

Travelling on

From time to time Olivia would take me on an outing. But, rather than the places we visited, it is the journeys to them that have rooted themselves in my memory.

Sometimes, when our destination was further afield than a trolleybus would take us, we might go by Greenline coach. Although red was for me the truly magical transport colour, how appealing too was that Greenline green, especially when you saw it on another coach in a leafy lane, green set in greenery. Then the note that the brighter, artificial green of the paintwork sang was a pure clear sharp, particularly when it was lacquered with rain and sun; the less brilliant, organic greenery was more a placid natural, a semitone below. How novel to me was this chromatic song. When young children, who naturally tend towards the direct and the obvious, first light upon the subtle, they relish what seems to them this unique discovery. And so, compared with the forthright consonant interval of red and green, the engaging perfect fourth, sung so diatonically by trolleybus amid summer verdure or, in reverse, by coach amid autumn russet, I found more intriguing that rare dissonant interval, that unresolved minor second, of green amid green.

And on mornings of bright cold sunlight and fresh breeze, the coach, as it drew up at the stop, then seemed besides, as a trolleybus would not have done, attuned to the whistle-clean and -keen air and light we would soon be travelling through, attuned to penetrating those roads where the foliage that brushed past would be of a green that more acidically approached its own, attuned to our whetted expectation.

Occasionally, when he was free, Dean would drive us, in the old Citroën he had then. I can see now his broad back in front of me as he sits solidly behind the wheel, gunning that car to a speed which Olivia finds excessive. When we made an early start, the morning would sometimes reveal herself as one of those lovely, still, warm, gauzy enchantresses that vaporise the end of a long stretch of sunlit, tree-lined, semi-residential road into a bluish haze. As soon as we entered such an avenue, the converging lines of perspective would irresistibly draw my gaze towards that veil of distance and sunlight through which sometimes you saw the smudgy lilac-pink transverse passage of a far-off bus or trolley, and I would experience again a happy expectancy. Seeing the road signs loom up, then flash past (their numerals further ciphers in some great mysterious message), breathing in the bouquet of fine-day petrol fumes, watching the bonnet swallow one by one the bars of pale gold and blue leading to the azure secret, I would thrill to the sense of approaching closer to it. Only to find that when we reached it the road, the trees, the buildings, the traffic were no different from those we had left behind. But no matter, we were travelling on, and soon we would be heading once more towards...towards...

'Scissors!'

Certain days of the week offered certain pleasures, had an appealing coloration, but for me Sunday was always an oppressive brown, and I'm unable to join in the hymns to it you come across in various memoirs of working-class life: 'A cosy day of late rising, a lunchtime session at the local, roast beef and Yorkshire, and a nice juicy murder in the paper'. I could never regard as cosy Harry's post-Prince-Albert lurches and snarls, Lil's waterlogged veg and market-bargain beef with its plenitude of warm, trembling, translucent yellow fat, and the assorted molestings, maimings and murders in the *News of the World*, which streaked the brown of the day with a troubling black.

We took that paper because it was suitably disturbing for Lil, one of those people who the more difficulty they have engaging with, coping with, accounts of wickedness find these beckoning the more irresistibly. Dinner over, the washing up done (by Lil and me) and Harry snoozing off his booze and heavy cargo of fat on the put-u-up, Lil sat at the table as tensely hunched over the paper as a pursued getaway driver over his wheel, staring at the page with the appalled fixity of one not simply reading the story of a dreadful crime but living every moment of it. How helplessly she was swept into the violence and gore, how vividly she saw the cruel blade, the ravaged flesh, the jetting blood, how piercingly she heard the cries for help, the pleas for mercy, the screams of agony. Sometimes, as glutted and stupefied as the snoring Harry a few feet away, she could take no more for the time being. She would look up in a daze and say, to my bafflement, 'With a pair of scissors! Oh, my God! Scissors!' And even hours later, preparing tea in the scullery, she would repeat: 'Scissors. *Scissors!*'

Obsessively drawn to the horrific wherever it put in its regular dark appearance, in newspapers, on radio or television, in films, in life, voicing genuine abhorrence ('I can't believe it, he kept putting a red-hot poker on its muzzle!') but never allowing herself to escape ('Leave that *on*, I haven't finished listening!'), immersing herself in one murky stagnant pool after another, she inhabited a world of pervasive malevolence where every stranger was a likely assailant, every knock at the door a cause for alarm. If the streets were dark when she and I were returning home, she would keep glancing fearfully over her shoulder, infecting with her apprehension myself, who sometimes half-expected, from various of her mutterings about the local soldiery, to see looming up behind us, clink-clanking, a *jilted corporal*, crazed and frustrated with jealousy and determined to take out his desperation on the innocent. And, once in the house, she would go through the ritual, whenever Harry was away, of looking under her bed and in every cupboard to check that some psychopathic intruder hadn't hidden there. As for venturing outside to use the lav, which with Harry home we would visit at night with the aid of a torch, that was out of the question. Whatever our need, we had to resort to the chamber pot.

Reflecting later on this black world which it seemed she had entered voluntarily, on other forms of masochism to which she was prone, on her general life-denial, I would wonder whether all her self-punishment might not have been dictated to her by that familiar old bully and more often than not con-man, Guilt. As to who he was working for in her case, the Mr Big who'd demanded atonement for the 'sins' he'd convicted her of, there was a clue. Lil kept on the mantelpiece a framed photograph of her dead father. A caricature Prussian martinet: scalp shaven, eyes autocratic, lips near-banished, downcurved in permanent censure; only the monocle missing. This was the Man, wasn't it? And hearing Lil's account of what she regarded as a model upbringing certainly did not weaken this suspicion. 'He was a wonderful father to us. He kept you in your place like fathers should. I remember if any of us so much as uttered a whisper at mealtimes he'd bring the back of his knife blade down on your knuckles something wicked. And he'd tell us we'd burn in Hellfire if we didn't do what we were told. That made us behave ourselves, I can tell you. You couldn't take any liberties with him. He was a real man. Not like today's bunch of ninnies. They let their kids do what they bloodywell like. Call themselves fathers?' (Though she surely excepted from this wholesale putdown her own Harry, who would belt you one as soon as look at you.) What filial devotion the truly appalling often inspire. Whenever Lil heard any of her dear daddy's favourite old songs on the radio, she would cry her eyes out.

Conundrums

Sometimes when I went to stay in Richborough, Dean, a puzzle addict, would, to entertain me, set me conundrums of various kinds. Soon I was hooked. I graduated to his books of problems, and eventually he lent me them so that I could grapple with their challenges at home. For the most part, I remember, they were set in a delightful fantasyland: *If Admiral Barnacle ordered 11 more destroyers than Admiral Bilgewater but 5 fewer cruisers than Admiral Bounty...*

Then Dean initiated me into the secrets of the cryptic crossword. I recall my delight as – sitting with him after breakfast on the dining room window seat, whose old cream paintwork diffused, as it basked in the early morning sunshine, a low-key, off-white, reassuring odour, one I forever afterwards associated with those earliest adventures into advanced wordplay – my uncle revealed to me the solutions to such ingenious clues as: *Chips, say, making a mess of the classroom (12)*. Marvelling at, in this example, the cunning of the initial word's hidden meaning that he explained to me and the rare beauty and appositeness of the anagram, I would, with his posh gold-and-green-moiré-cased ballpoint, eagerly write in the answer. Smitten by puzzles, by mysteries of every kind, I was well on the way to becoming a pushover for a certain book to which Dean would later introduce me, and which his own company, Spectrum, published, a book that was to have so profound and long-lasting an effect on me.

A particular impression

Once, shyly, I met the Spectrum staff – small in number – at the company's offices in Brompton Road. And then afterwards I saw some of them at the house in Richborough, which they occasionally visited on business-cum-social occasions. Three made a particular impression on me. (And much later, and in different circumstances, I was to come across them again.)

One was Vin Sharpes, Dean's partner. Bruiser's build, pencil-line tache, barrow-boy speech. A major decision, the speech, for the lowborn ascending: leave the accent or work on it? Better for one's game to retain obvious traces of the original as evidence of clever-dog distance traversed? Or, like Dean, to overpaint the lot to a 'classlessness' that will fool some and that will do nicely thank you for the rest? Not that Sharpes had done either. He'd gone, like certain celebrities from a similar background, for the regression thing, a Cockney far more glottal-stop and aspirateless than he'd started out with when flogging stuff from barrows, an aggressive, getta-loada-this East-End-speak intended to indicate careless confidence but in fact loudly signalling Insecure. Of course, I understood nothing of this then, and I actually found him an imposing figure. Especially in appearance. If the Regal was for me the last word in entertainment luxury, Vin Sharpes was the last word in style: the flash suits (spivvy hangover from his background); the ever-washed fluffy dark hair; the fixed tan; the regularly shot snow-white cuffs; the gold watch worn ostentatiously low, the gold bracelet ditto on the other wrist.

Unlike Dean, who was widely if haphazardly read in the manner of most autodidacts, Sharpes had never had any real interest in books. In fact, Dean once told me he doubted whether his partner had read a single one of their titles from cover to cover. But he was, apparently, a dynamic salesman and a canny scanner of a balance sheet.

Neal Easy was a general editorial bod. Where they got him from I've no idea. A slim, balding, wide-eyed man of about thirty, with an eager voice which heavy smoking had hoarsened, he approached everything with a schoolboy's oversimplifying zeal. Whenever, for example, usually unasked, he advised someone how best to tackle a problem, he always, no matter how uniquely tough it was, advocated with frank fourth-former's gaze and in keen husky tones exactly the same method. It consisted of nothing more than breaking the difficulty down into three clearly defined constituents – no matter whether it actually had five, a dozen or, it might be, none at all – after which, the idea seemed to be, the problem would somehow resolve itself, would vamoose. Each stage of his reductive process he demonstrated with an incisive karateist's downward chop of the hand and the appropriate accompanying vocalisation, a cross between a 'Whoosh' and a 'Phut' – a sort of 'Whut'. On one occasion he overheard me tell Dean that I wasn't getting on very well with a school project on Transport. With his sincere stare, he urged his usual panacea: 'Simple. Divide it up into Air, Sea, Land – whut, whut, whut.' (I'd already done this but didn't like to tell him.) 'Get books out from the library on all three – whut, whut, whut.' (That chopping hand again. He was as addicted to the manually resolvent triad as certain writers are to the epithetic.) 'Write up the main points, do some drawings, write captions – whut, whut, whut.' (I'd done this, too; it was the actual writing and drawing I was having trouble with.) 'And there you are.' Somewhat fancifully, I hear myself, daunted by this display of surpassing capability, reply with an ingenuous treble 'Thank you' like John Lennon's at the end of 'Ob-la-di, Ob-la-da'.

Walter Gudgeon was the Spectrum production manager. He was a tall man of forty-five or so, portly but in good nick: the whites of his liquid chocolate eyes had the faintly bluish clarity of health and his hair was still vigorous and free of grey.

31

Equally as strong and dark was his voice, a rich baritone with that oily, crumbly, winning timbre much used in commercials to sell cholesterol-rich food. This voice, redolent of fudge cake and pork sausages, was Gudgeon's pride and joy. He was as plainly in love with it as a body-building hunk with his torso, and just as the iron pumper augments the muscle bulk bestowed on him by nature, so by constant workouts Gudgeon had enhanced the splendid instrument he'd been born with, enhanced it in a particular way: he'd succeeded in investing it with such melody, such continuous, effortless, mellifluous changes of key, that listening to it was like being treated to a private recital by Fischer-Dieskau. It must, that magnificent baritone, have sounded even more magnificent to him than it did to his listeners, since for him the supplement of bone conduction would have given the sound waves added resonance. Not being in the kind of line he should have been in, one in which he could have flaunted that voice, that portamento, to his heart's content – on the stage, say, or in the pulpit – he grabbed every opportunity to show it off as lengthily as possible. So he never made a simple statement. Instead of 'Jennings rang me', he would say, to hear himself render gorgeously a whole lot more syllables: 'I had the honour this morning of a telephone call from our very good friend Mr Robert Jennings.' And whenever, by being asked to report on some production matter, he was given the chance to perform lieder, how joyfully he seized it: 'Time is absolutely of the essence in this matter, I feel, as I'm sure all of my most worthy and respected colleagues here would agree…' Gudgeon's colleagues were always most worthy and respected, whoever they might be, not because he was buttering them up, nor because on the contrary he genuinely believed in and wished to acknowledge their worth and entitlement to respect, nor because he was particularly fond of, for its own sake, that 'your obedient servant'-style hyperpolitesse of the old school but simply because it was only as most worthy and respected that his colleagues (and only as very good friends that Mr Robert Jennings and every other mere acquaintance) could provide him with welcomely extra relishable feet in his vocal line. 'At the moment, the idea I outlined to you last week isn't, I might say, completely foolproof in every single one of its aspects...' Each phrase was shamelessly modulated, each cadence lovingly savoured. 'But I think I can say that, all things being equal, and without making any hard-and-fast promises...' And so it would sing on, that voice, in all its splendour, while I would listen open-mouthed.

I suppose that if anyone had asked me then what sort of man I hoped to grow up to be, I'd have chosen an amalgam of those three jokers: a man who looked like Vin Sharpes, acted like Neal Easy and sounded like Walter Gudgeon.

A Gershwin tune

I loved to hear Olivia play the piano. I've no idea how accomplished a player she actually was but she always sounded to me fluent and expressive. She had, too, an eclectic taste that ranged from Schumann and Debussy to Rodgers and Kern. One day, as I sat with Dean trying to fathom the reasoning behind the latest answer he'd written into his crossword, Olivia went over to the piano, selected some sheet music from the top and began playing a piece which made an immediate appeal to me. Well, more than an appeal. The melody had for me that particular wondrous quality which, no matter how deeply we may respond to far greater music later in life, only certain pieces heard in childhood have for us, a quality of which, long after we've reached an age when we no longer regard those pieces objectively as anything so very special, we can still, down the years, catch an echo. What I was hearing was, Olivia told me, a piano transcription by Gershwin of one of his songs. (Though, because the composer's name meant nothing to me then, I wasn't as it were *truly* to hear Olivia informing me of it in that living room until much later, when the name Gershwin having by then become significant for me, I recalled it in one of those odd cases of purely retrospective recognition.) Certainly for me then that melody, in that slow, tender, reflective étude-like version, did have a wondrous quality, created for me as a boy, I now believe (I had no conscious understanding of it at the time), by that typically Gershwinesque alternation of the exuberant and the wistful, a joy in the present shot through, nonetheless, with a yearning for something other.

I heard Olivia play that piece on a few more occasions, and, along with other favourite tunes, it would sound in my head from time to time. Then one day, some time later, I came across it in a markedly different form. It was a hot weekday afternoon during the school summer holiday and I was making my way home from Bexcray town with some shopping for Lil. As usual I was dawdling and daydreaming through that somnolent residential labyrinth which constitutes the essential body of suburbia, which most of the castigators of it would call, rather, a corpse, but which I could never bring myself later to scorn because, the source for me of so many poetries and seminal experiences, it was always to some extent hallowed by them. I dawdled and daydreamed in the still heat, adrift in the empty mid-afternoon, the aimless Tuesdayish, Wednesdayish three o'clock that was so Big-Match-less unlike, so Big-Race-less unlike, the tingling three o'clocks of so many Saturdays. Then, as I idled along one road, I heard emerging from an open upstairs window ahead piano music. From the mastery of the playing and a certain abraded quality of the piano tone I guessed I was listening not to a live performer but to a recording of some age. I had no opportunity to hear more than a few bars before it came to an end. But then, after a pause, as I drew almost abreast of the house, the piano started up again...and now sent forth, loud and clear, cleaving the hot air, music that brought me to a standstill, enraptured by its beauty – one heightened by being so completely unexpected in that mundane hinterland. What I was hearing was a powerful, uptempo version of what Olivia had always played in its much slower, more pensive form, so that I'd assumed that was the only way the piece should be played. Punched out now into the hot, golden afternoon, what unbelievable drive it had, both the quicker-paced tune itself and the performance of it – what verve, what swagger, how proudly it knew just where it was going! How different, in the brio of this performance, it sounded to what I had known before. And yet, and yet... Still surfacing in certain notes, chords, harmonies was something of what I had heard originally: the tempering of the optimism and drive by something different, some strange longing.

The version I was listening to, I discovered later, was the composer himself playing the piece, at a tempo considerably faster than that of the original song, in a medley of his own show tunes. And the numbers that followed what I eventually learned was called 'That Certain Feeling' (for I carried on listening, I stood there motionless until the music had ended, transfixed in that sunlight on which the piano inscribed its glorious sounds, still holding Lil's shopping, not caring about her exasperation to come: 'Where have you bloody been all this time?'), those numbers too drove onward with an energy, an exhilaration, that I had never heard before, something far removed from the humdrum world of Bexcray. It was what I would later realise to be the spirit of twenties New York, of the pulsing metropolis, of the Jazz Age. But, more than that, in the unalterable rightness of what the piano was asserting, the inevitability of each crisp note and chord, its crystalline *truth*, I sensed subconsciously the workings of genius. And there was yet something else: prepubescent though I was, I obscurely apprehended the vigour, the bold forward momentum, the sure proud undeviating rhythm of the piano playing (especially in 'Do, Do, Do') – like that I was later to hear in certain performances of certain Beethoven piano sonatas and concertos – as an expression of the male sex drive, and in my response to it I seemed to catch a glimpse of my own to come.

Even so, within that torrent of dynamism there sounded through every so often what I had heard before, that same suggestion of yearning.

Danny

My best friend, Danny Glazier, was a good-looking boy with dark, almost black hair and dreamy blue eyes, colouring inherited from his half-Irish absent father. We sat next to each other in class at Elson Road primary school, and as he lived only a couple of streets away from mine we constantly visited each other. How competitive we were. In the tiny dank back yard at my place – enclosed on three sides and leading on the other, up a couple of steps, to the long, narrow, rising, untended garden – we played the most cramped and high-scoring games of football ever: insufficiently precise goal boundaries and the frantic confusing pace always led to sweaty, flushed try-it-on claims and counterclaims: '32-29 to me', 'No, it flippin' isn't, it's 31-30 to me'. And even, improbably, blowing bubbles (with soapsuds and two small white clay pipes, which, gripped between the teeth, felt – perverse pleasure – as hard as iron) had to be a *contest*. 'Cor, look at that one! What a whopper! Beat that!' Suddenly it would disappear, cease to exist – jus' like that. 'Yeah, but mine's still going, look.'

That obstinate old art director memory, so choosy about its effects, busy idealising here, there and everywhere, always insists that Danny and I blew bubbles only on wet, still mornings in the intervals between rain. Mornings when the shed roof drip-dripped; when the metallic-pink-gold-and-green globes, reflecting our surroundings in curviform miniature, wobbled off into pearly dampness; when the drowned chickweed in the runnel to the tinkling drain was a fresh bright green; when the tall cool fleshy leaves of the irises that flanked the steps leading to the garden, and the shells of the snails at their base, were decorated with transparent beads; when the domestic smell of the soapsuds in the bowl was joined by the strange, faintly pungent, indescribable smell of recent rain; when from the road there sounded only the occasional, unimportant, soothing swish of tyres; when the break-in-wet-weather atmosphere created that illusion we sometimes have that the day is in temporary suspension, that life itself is. Mornings when, like George Eliot's dreamer standing before Dorlcote mill, I was in love with moistness.

If bubble blowing always took place on wet mornings, then in the same way, whenever I used to set off from home to join a gathering at Danny's house to play Monopoly – with a happy anticipation that seemed to emanate as much from the scene around me as from within myself – it was always, I am led to believe, on lovely cold, still, expectant winter afternoons that were studies in powdery blue and rosy pink: streets carpeted with snow and canopied with a sky grown tender. And in the heart of the just declining day, in the heart of the blue and pink afternoon, there would hover in advance hotels of red and banknotes of orange and violet, establishments and currency of a world delightfully trouble-free.

'Uncle' Len

At one time we had someone staying with us (in those rooms that were too cramped for three, let alone four – though it's true Harry often wasn't there). This person, known to me as Uncle Len, wasn't in fact an uncle. Actually, I never learned exactly *who* he was. Years later, out of idle curiosity, I made some attempt to find out. But with Harry no longer around and Lil becoming increasingly vague about the past, all I could discover was that he was some distant relative of Harry's and my father's. But I also realised, as I looked back on him, that not only did I not know who Uncle Len was but I had no idea why he had been staying with us. Why had he suddenly appeared on the scene? Had he been invited, or had he invited himself? I couldn't recall Harry or Lil ever mentioning him beforehand or commenting on his presence while he was there. Had he paid for his upkeep? I never saw him hand over any money. If he was paying, was it out of the dole (he didn't work) or a pension (he looked considerably older than Harry and Lil)? In that case he would have needed to collect that dole or pension, but I never once knew him to leave the house. How long had he stayed with us: a few months, many months, a year, longer? I searched my memory but his lodgement in time was as vague as his identity. And finally, just as odd was his departure, as unannounced and unexplained as his arrival. One afternoon I came home from school to find his usual seat by the fireplace empty and that was that. 'He's gone,' was all Lil said.

In life and in print one sometimes comes across figures who are lightly referred to as men of mystery when in fact a considerable amount is known about them. For me, though, Uncle Len was the genuine article, the supreme man of mystery. Or rather, he became such in retrospect – like all the mysteries of our early years, which did not appear to us then as mysteries – because we begin as adults to reflect on those years with a brain overridingly concerned with cause and effect, concerned with that machinery behind the scenes of which the young are scarcely aware. No, as a child I did not find Uncle Len a mystery: like the ancient *Chatterbox* annual, he was just *there*. For all I knew, or bothered myself with, he might have parachuted in from some previously unsuspected kingdom in the sky to be greeted as imperturbably by Harry and Lil as those rascals in comics, crashing in through the ceiling astride a rocket or a cannonball, were greeted by their parents with 'Ee, lad, you're late for tea.'

He slept on the put-u-up, which I had to vacate for a camp bed squeezed into the scullery, and he took all his meals with us, except breakfast, which for him was simply a mug of tea and a fag. He had a jockey's build, a shock of grey hair and a thin, lined face of ashy complexion, probably the result of his lack of fresh air. After he'd had his morning wash in the scullery – and, once in a while, a shave – and pulled the braces back over his collarless shirt, he'd sit all day in the back room on one of the small fender seats by the fire, presumably because his circulation must have been poor. There he would roll his own smokes, cough a great deal, read the *Warp* and when I was around reminisce. These reminiscences were always of the same kind. They were accounts of an unbroken succession of sporting victories he'd achieved in the army – in the boxing ring and on the running track – all told in exhaustive, sports commentator's blow-by-blow or stride-by-stride detail. Many had tried to defeat him but he'd always managed to call up that little bit extra that is the mark of the true champion. 'I did have some framed photographs of meself with me trophies, Jackie,' he told me once. (He always called me Jackie, I've no idea why. Another of the mysteries.) 'But I mislaid them somewhere. And the trophies. Dunno where it could have been.'

He had in me a feeble captive audience. Whenever at weekends or on school holidays I was sitting in that little back room, usually because the weather was too bad to go out, whenever I was looking at a comic or was drawing or playing with my lead cowboys and Indians on the table top, I knew I would not be allowed to continue uninterrupted, I knew that at any minute I would hear Uncle Len's familiar formulaic introduction to one of his the-full-works stories: 'Did I ever tell you, Jackie, about the time...' Out of politeness I would stop what I was doing and look over at him.

You could tell that Uncle Len thought his narratives were as all-absorbing to others as they obviously were to himself, because he always recounted them in a would-be dramatic way, complete with preliminary scene-setting ('It was a thundery sort of day, Jackie, as I remember'), sketches of each competitor ('Whitey had a big conk on him and was taller than the rest of us; Pete Simkins, now he was a tough-looking little beggar...'), a full account of his own thought processes throughout fight or race ('Well, the bell rang for the fourth round, and I was thinking, if I can keep jabbing and block most of the big punches Millsy's throwing at me, I might be able to wear him down') and 'suspenseful' pauses at 'critical' junctures of the contest, even though you knew the outcome was never in any doubt ('So I come out jabbing, and quite a few of 'em get through, and I can see I've got him thinking, when suddenly it happened...') At which point he would break off and, to his way of thinking, tauten the suspense to an unbearable pitch – should I, I wondered, be committing *all* my cowboys to a frontal attack? – by not resuming until he'd rolled another fag, oh so unhurriedly: with what 'teasing' deliberation did he fill the Rizla paper with baccy, tamp this down, wrap over the paper, lick it along its edge, smooth the smoke into shape. Perhaps I should use *some* of them in a pincer movement. 'What I did, Jackie, was I made the mistake of taking my eye off him – that was because I could see Smithy signalling something to me at the side of the ring. Anyway, I never saw it coming. He caught me with a right uppercut.' (The fights, amateur though they were, featured as high a proportion of scientific blows – jabs, uppercuts, hooks – and manoeuvres –

40

ducking, weaving, clinches, feints – as characterises professional contests. Or those in ripping yarns.) 'That was the first time I'd ever seen stars. The ref counted. One, two, three, four, five, six...' Should I split the Red Indians into two groups? 'I managed to get up on seven, but I was still stunned. It was lucky for me I didn't have long to wait for the bell. Well, during the time-out, I started thinking I had to change me tactics...' Another of the 'unbearably' prolonged pauses, as he slowly reached up to the mantelpiece for the Swan Vestas, lit up, took two or more leisurely draws, and only then resumed: 'The plan I decided on was...'

The tales of the track featured canny slottings into position ('What I did on the sixth lap, Jackie, was tuck in behind Rawlings and Banksy...'), generously detailed commentary ('On the eighth lap, about a quarter way down the back straight, Banksy moved just ahead of Rawlings, and I could see Dobbo moving up outside me...'), momentous decisions ('That's when I thought it was time to make me move...')

These astutely contrived victories seemed to account for Uncle Len's entire time in the army, for he never so much as mentioned any other aspect of military life – the enormous number of his stories and their exclusively sporting content painted a picture of one who spent every hour of his service in the ring or on the track. When all this took place and where it took place was, when later I looked back on his narratives, to evade me as slipperily as any other hard facts about Uncle Len did: just as he appeared to have dropped into 33 Danehill Road from nowhere, so his highly unusual military service appeared to have taken place in some mysterious sphere outside space and time. And when I was no longer a credulous young boy, I did start to wonder whether any of it had ever taken place at all.

One autumn evening

One door up from us lived the Harnetts. Their son, Colin, was three or four years older than me and I never had much to do with him other than to swap comics over the fence of our overgrown garden. My *Dandy* for his *Knockout*, that *Knockout* in which Sexton Blake and Tinker were always thrillingly 'pitting their wits' against some 'evil genius', some mysterious bodysuited Central or Eastern European Vromm or Klamm or suchlike 'bent on world domination'. As each swap day approached, the longing to find out what had happened since the previous instalment grew more intense, as did that to soak up the front page once more, with its chunky masthead and enchantingly garish colours, and to enjoy the later exploits of every other hero or oddball in the comic. But one autumn evening as I waited in our garden after tea for Colin to fetch the *Knockout* from indoors, I began to feel in addition to that can't-wait-to-lay-hands-on-this-week's-issue expectancy another expectancy, of a different, stranger but by now quite familiar kind. The light was fading and a cold wind was bending the grass. The sky was red, a fiercer red than I'd ever seen it before, a great fiery vault over the gardens and rooftops in front of me. Next door, astoundingly, the dusk had turned the Harnetts' sheets snapping on the line to blue, a real blue, a clear deep blue like the laundry blue that might have been used in the washing of those sheets. And there it was, this pure blue, ever-flappingly-changing quadrilaterals of it, patterning that equally pure red. And nearer to me, the silhouetted nettles and burdock that in those overgrown gardens were taller than myself broke up the red and the blue with a black tracery, which had the effect of heightening their dyes as leads do those of stained glass. And from time to time, smudging the red and the blue and the black with a wispy azure, there swirled down to me on the wind, from a garden further up the road, bonfire smoke, burning-leaves-sweet, heady. Everything around me seemed to fuse with everything else, to fuse into one: the bone-chilling cold, the so-*Novemberish Knockout* to come, the restless grass, the red sky, the blue sheets, the black silhouetted plants, the smell of the tattered smoke. And together – like the elements of the primal rosy trolleybus dusk, from which this episode appeared to follow on like a thrilling story resumed – they seemed to be signalling, promising, that same strange something.

Out of focus

Did I never wonder about my true parents, when I was old enough to do so? Of course I did. From time to time I questioned Lil about them, though without ever getting answers as satisfactory as I wanted. I learned that my father, Vic, operated a bearings lathe at the Standard Metal Company in Canning Town. That's where he met my mother, Maureen. She worked in the canteen. The year they died coaches were as usual chartered for the works outing to an ice-dance show but my father decided to go on his AJS motorcycle, with my mother riding pillion. On the Rochester Way they collided with a lorry emerging from a side road and were killed outright. (The brakes on the bike were found to be defective, which the family considered slightly odd because my father apparently took good care of the machine.)

I gleaned random facts about them. Random, disconnected facts. My father: good at sport (ability I inherited), bad temper (like Harry), thriller reader, heavy gambler. My mother: dark (colouring I inherited), pretty (Harry fancied her and was jealous of my father), practical (she could run up a dress or curtains with ease), ballroom dancing mad. She particularly loved the Latin American stuff. Her fave was Xavier Cugat. That's who

I was named after. (Naturally, in a community of Daves and Billys and Petes, I was ribbed about Xavier right from the start, even by Harry and Lil. It was a bit of a pain at times, and occasionally I'd wish I was called something more ordinary. But then I grew rather to like the uncommonness of that name. And I felt a sort of distinction – unearned, true, but distinctions unearned are not that much less pleasurable than those earned – in being the only person I knew with the initial X. As Tristram Shandy's father said, 'Christian names are not such indifferent things.')

As for what I remember of that brief time when my parents were alive, well, a strange and universal law of memory decrees that from our very earliest years only incidents and places and atmospheres survive with anything resembling clarity, not persons – who for some reason are condemned to remain forever out of focus or even merely notional. So that, while in memory there still just about quivers with a sullen brightness that close, thundery day on which I stood with my father outside a shop on a slope eating ice cream, to know what he looked like then I have to consult not memory but the snapshots in Lil's album. And similarly a mental image of my mother twirling round the lighted room of a flat remains more stubbornly abstract than the curtained windows and lighted fire of that room until I attach to her the face captured in those small rectangles of often smudgy black and white that for most in those days constituted the only, poor salvage from lost time.

Lil told me that my parents and I lived in quite a few different lodgings in Bexcray and Blackwell. They were often in arrears with the rent and kept moonlighting. Later, when I was old enough, I tracked down the addresses that Lil could remember and visited them: the orphan's usual forlorn pilgrimage.

Film Fun

Every Tuesday I would set off from home to buy *Film Fun*, to which I had graduated from *Dandy* and *Knockout*. Once again, memory always presents these occasions to me in exactly the same light, the same atmosphere: lunchtime on one of those needlessly swaddled days of warmth so familiar to us British, just-breaking-sweat days insulated by flannelly off-white, the sun omnipresent yet nowhere to be seen, brickwork and flagstones lambent yet shadowless. Yes, it was always at that hour, always on those still, inert days, that I would yank the front door to behind me, with an uncivil slam in the silence, and start out for Randall's the newsagents.

As I hared down sleepy, deserted Danehill Road, there would impinge on me the steady uniform light, the bland burdensome air, the indolence of the hour, the soothing bourdon of some invisible plane on high, the warm drowsy lunchtime smell of cooking seeping out of doors here and there. Close, quiet, savoury Tuesday lunchtimes, very essence of the Danehill Road I once knew.

The cooking aroma so blended with the soporific midday, and the bleached light of this so harmonised with the lack of colour in *Film Fun* (it was black-and-white throughout) that they all seemed one, indivisible... Colourlessness, stillness... And yet, and yet, I felt somehow that they were not what they seemed, that they were in fact highly charged, were formed, like the pale apparently static blur of my old rainbow top when spun, from the high-speed whirling together of every colour in the spectrum (and that if you listened closely you could maybe catch the faint hum), that the invisible force that kept them in their state of tension had thrillingly in store, somewhere ahead, something more than *Film Fun*...

On the journey (which took me through a sedate residential enclave of Bon Repos semis posh with garages and proper front gardens), *Film Fun* characters – Laurel and Hardy, George Formby, Abbott and Costello – cavorted around me, announcing their latest adventures were now only minutes away. How I thrilled to their world of chortles and wheezes and oo-ers, of simpering heroines, all Marcel waves and splendid calves, of 'handsome' rewards and 'slap-up' meals (whole chickens and towering jellies); a sub-Magrittean out-of-joint world in which dressmakers' dummies, wardrobes, barrels, mirrors, packing cases, stoves, musical instruments were forever surrealistically turning up on street corner or esplanade, as so-convenient jape props or means of concealment; a world of unnaturally yet charmingly limited facial expressions and head positions almost as stylised as the unvarying profiles of Egyptian art; a world (in the Laurel and Hardy strips occupying front and back covers) whose white skies, silhouetted chimney pots, solitary dogs and no doubt silent, cooking-scented hours pressing on the almost vacant streets strangely echoed those around me.

But the deserted settings in the comic also sounded for me a mournful note. At first, it was only faint and didn't detract from the fun, but as time passed it grew more insistent: in my unfailing examination of each frame, as close and loving as that of a connoisseur of woodcuts studying every detail in a set of Bewicks, I found myself less and less happily absorbed by, say, the almost human grin on the dog or the curious failure of Olly's trouser pattern to follow the contours of his legs (just like the flat, non-moulding fabrics on the people in Masolino's frescos), and more and more morbidly attentive to the lifeless backgrounds to the action, so that when smirking Stan sat holding hands with coy Connie on a sabotaged log, the joke would be spoiled by the predictably barren park behind them, with its empty bandstand and lonely tree both standing in forlorn black silhouette against the blanched sky, and the discordance of grown men playing childish tricks, somehow acceptable in lively surroundings, became a little disturbing in those that were desolate. Yes, these melancholy mise-en-scènes, which seemed so inappropriate for the foolery in the foreground and which lacked any of that sense of something-round-the-corner that permeated the equally quiet route I tore along, undermined the comedy, brought it into question, induced in me a vague unease, a kind of rendition in a minor key of the disquiet I had felt when looking at *A Sea Urchin* and reading *Held to Ransom.*

Out of breath, I would round a bend of Southwood Road and enter the last stretch, leaving residential somnolence behind: ahead, transverse, was traffic-loud Artillery Row, with Randall's at its corner. Bursting with anticipation, I would pelt towards it. From Harry's boozer the Prince Albert, on the opposite corner, there would issue the mild, dull smell of beer, faintly metallic, not dissimilar to that of the muggy-day-moist coppers in my palm, and, wafted across with it, harmoniously, a reprise of what I had scented earlier, the mild, dull smell of traditional English lunchtime cooking. Sometimes today, on other streets, I inhale those same torpid pub odours, of beer and cooked food drifting out on to the pavement on a shadowless day of warmth and stillness, when they are at their most diffusive, and then, for a breathtaking moment, I live again those slack half-past-middays when *Film Fun* was almost within my grasp.

Into Randall's. In its cramped and dim interior I would at last take in hand, in mint condition, crisply black and white, masthead aquiver with promise, *this week's issue!*

Strange, in one way, that eagerness of mine to lay hands on it. For though each week's stories were apparently different from those I had seen before, they were all of them no more than variations on a few standard themes. One of these, for Olly and Stan, was competing for the favours of a 'fair charmer'. And if this week Molly replaced the Connie of a few issues back, if this week she said 'You are a one' to Olly not Stan, if this week it was Olly's 'bacon saved' by a so-handy discarded piano instead of Stan's by a 'just-the-ticket' diving suit (no less), well, such random, surface particularities no more changed the nature of the basic plot than, in a medieval mystery play, the incidentals peculiar to one city's version changed its essential outline.

But probably in this basic unchangingness lay part of the comic's (perhaps part of all comics') appeal; if I had been presented with inventive new storylines and characterisations, I may well have been unimpressed. I think that was all I wanted, the latest version of the comfortingly familiar. The latest it had to be though – nothing else would do.

Ah, the tyranny of the here and now. The same that rules me today when, hoping to watch on television some major sports event and finding it's been cancelled and some contest from the past is being shown instead, I switch off the set. I'm not interested. That combat of yesteryear – I may not know the result, the players may be all-time greats, the struggle tense, yet, just as in multiplication a whole string of positive numbers is converted by a solitary negative into a negative result, so all the pluses of that past event are cancelled by its single but overriding minus: *it is not taking place today*. In the same way, I would always have rejected the substitute of a past *Film Fun* I hadn't read for the current issue hot from the press. Purely by virtue of being that, the current issue, and for no other reason, it was for me superior to all other issues, splendidly irreplaceable. Until, that is, the following week, when it would pass like all its once similarly laurelled but far from hardy predecessors into oblivion.

A Bexcray boy

The streets, the stores, the cafés, the cinemas, the post office, the library... All those constituents of the place we grew up

in compellingly announce to us that in their unique form –
their particular names, characters, locations – they are somehow
so *fitted* to that place, so *right* for it, that they could have been
no other. It was to me a pre-ordained, unalterable fact of
existence that Bexcray High Street, for example, should be, not,
like so many high streets, level, straight and even-edged as a
ribbon, but gently sloping, winding and unevenly wide; and
that it should contain along its length the specific establishments
that it did contain and that these should be in precisely the
order they were in and no other. Sam Sports, emporium of
immaculate, brand-new-smelling, tangible promises of thrills
to come, if only you would buy them, if only you *could* buy
them – that ash blond willow, say, with sky blue rubber grip,
begging to make runs, or that cherry red leather embossed
with gold, begging to take wickets, or that white and bronze
leather, excitingly polyhedral, begging to bulge nets; a shop
that, sports crazy as I was, constantly drew me to it. Next door,
The Rendezvous coffee bar, magnet for Bexcray youth, all
espresso hiss, cigarette haze, jukebox pounding, callow raillery
and dalliance; where later I would hang out with Danny Glazier
and Billy Howe and fall for Claudia-Cardinale-lookalike Debbie
Lincoln. Smart Feller men's shop, dedicated to what was trendily,
enviably flaunted by older boys; where I would buy my first,
glaringly cheapo suit. W.H. Smith, which stocked *True 'Tec Tales*,
those picture-strip libraries with intriguingly muscular titles
like *Keep Your Distance, Pal* that Dougie Leonard read under
the desk lid at school; where I bought *Woman's Weekly* for Lil
but could never pluck up courage to take down and be seen
peeking at the girlie mags. Gowdy & Simpson's, the chemist's,
window aglow with lovely old flasks of red and green, and
behind the counter of the deliciously medicines-and-toiletries-
smelling interior its walnutwood cabinets containing mysterious
substances in drawers inscribed with letters of gold and black;
where I would get Lil's prescriptions made up and later

mumblingly ask for condoms. The public library, treasure-house for so many years... Ah, the library. Set back in a leafy, lawny surround, self-contained in Edwardian redbrick, it had that oasis-like quality that all peaceful enclaves have in the midst of a busy high street. As you turned off towards it, as you approached its detached greenery-fringed brickwork, it filled you with a happy expectancy. And inside how both calming and promissory were its profound library quiet, broken only by the occasional muted rubber-stamping or controlled cough, and its dry library odours, burnished only here and there by a hint of furniture polish or floor polish. And how often that promise was fulfilled on the shelves by some thrilling new find.

And then at the end of the High Street, if I gazed over the crossroads, with their traffic lights and diametrically opposed neo-Gothic Barclays and Lloyds, down the great stretch of King Street, I could see another decreed, unchangeable series. The Regal, palatial entrance into another world. Court's, booksellers and stationers, where I would buy my first paperbacks: Grahame, Chesterton, Queen, Carr, Nabokov, Scott Fitzgerald, Keats, Salinger, Waugh, Alain-Fournier. Pergolesi's ice cream parlour, speciality the Pergolesi Peach Sundae, another boy-meets-girl enclave, which I would frequent with that joint sexual explorer of my teens, that cruel inflamer, Linda Lorell. Valentines disco, pink façade, mock-Moorish (for no fathomable reason), and above the entrance a large scarlet plastic heart; the place where I was to meet my one true love. The main post office, monumental and imposing as an embassy... Ah, the post office. High-ceilinged and airy, it was another place that echoed to the comfortable *thump* of rubber-stamping. And how equably this and the pleasing, iodine-like, navy blue smell from the pen-holding inkwells on the long black rubberised worktop and the reassuring sense of post serenely, invisibly, continuously in transit were all suspended in the light that streamed in through the tall windows, a light that sometimes painted on the black worktop rectangles of warm golden-grey, symbols of a sunny afternoon that would seem to me then as a boy soothingly endless. And at blue dusk, seen from the High Street, beyond the traffic lights and the neon-lit Regal, the enticing rows of gold the post office windows inlaid into the blue suggested, at this distance, rather than an indication of what was actually coming to its dying-day end in the melancholy almost empty interior (that atmosphere type exemplified in later years by harshly lit rooms in which, a committee meeting or chess match over, only a few last stragglers remained), suggested instead the essential involvement of those golden rectangles in something electrifying and momentous, some tremendous adventure.

And then if, instead of going straight over the crossroads, you turned right into narrow Queen Street, there on the right-hand side was another sequence that could have been no other, that has embedded itself in me for all time. Lovat & Albery, the music shop, filled with instruments that you wished you could play; where over the years I was to buy or order so many records and cassettes – Gershwin, Schumann, Presley, the Kinks, Beethoven, Gene Krupa, Buddy Rich, Debussy, Franck, the Beatles, the Stones, the Beach Boys, Poulenc, Fauré, Little Richard, Aretha Franklin, Prokofiev, Fats Waller, Teddy Wilson – personal compendium emergent from that whole magical, diverse, glistening, multicoloured abundance of what in youth and early adulthood more powerfully than at any other time seizes our soul and transports it swift as electric current to other, more glorious worlds. Next door, the small Bexcray office of the *Blackwell and Bexcray Gazette*, to which I submitted, in a hopelessly offkey moment, a dreadful schoolboy essay on detective stories; where I would sometimes ask for an issue of the paper that I didn't want, simply to see and speak to the stunning Debbie Lincoln, the girl on the back numbers desk, who was shortly, alas, to become engaged. Pembertons department store, the largest and plushest for miles around, as much for me as a child the acme of stores as the Regal was of cinemas... Ah, Pembertons. Whenever you entered it, especially if from an outside world of chilled bus queues, Rapist Sentenced and scuttling litter, its warmth, its fragrance (Cosmetics department just inside the entrance) and its softness underfoot – the foyer of the Regal again – would enfold you in their comforting embrace. Then the effortless ascent to one great floor after another. Each so calm: sounds muffled, transactions leisurely, vistas never-ending. The merchandise, in the even light, the even warmth, so imperturbable: rolls of fabric, table lamps, dinner services, so fetchingly boring, content it seemed to display themselves for ever. The coffee shop polyphony, somewhere offstage, so inviting: tinkle, whoosh, clatter and murmurous hum. And the piped music, flowing gently through it all, so buoyant: melodies unfailingly uptempo, sprightly with xylophone and pizzicato: lollipops, or what, for some reason, I termed (in that private internal lexicon we each develop when young) 'orange' music. Music, like that at the cinema, whose confident gaiety banished darkness from the world, promised you that all was well.

And beyond Queen Street, past the fire station, where Artillery Row took over, yet another inevitable series. Champion Chips. Randall's. The Prince Albert...

Bexcray, so ordinary, so special, could you have been other than you were? Well, perhaps you could have been. Certainly the Residents Redevelopment Association thought so. But against logic I felt that you couldn't, that you were predestined to be exactly what you were, *the Bexcray I knew*. And could I, steeped in your streets, shops, cafés, cinemas, et al, have been other than I was? Again logic said I could have been and occasionally mused on 'I might have...' lines, but in my bones I felt that that wasn't really so, that, like the place itself, I was predestined to be exactly what I was – *a Bexcray boy.*

A new life

Lil had been feeling 'out of sorts' for some time. She complained of tummy aches, she was off that 'real-bargain' food of hers which usually she *tucked into*, and she was belching more than ever, particularly after one of the fat-freighted dinners. The pain got worse, especially at night, and her skin and the whites of her eyes turned yellow (Harry: 'You look like a bloody Chink'). So, finally, reluctantly, she saw Dr Grant, our GP, a large, bald, bearded, three-piece-tweed-suit man, one of those authority figures we held in awe. He referred Lil to a consultant, who said that it was her gallbladder, that the problem was serious and that she'd have to have an operation. But, if Harry was away so much, who was going to look after me? Lil was thinking it would have to be her sister Ada across the river in West Ham when Dean and Olivia offered to put me up for as long as was needed at the big new place they'd bought in Kingsdon St Mary, a village not far from Richborough. So began an unexpected interlude in my life.

Dean drove me there. Halfway down a hill he turned the car off to the left through a weathered stone archway that bore the name The Rectory. The tyres crunched over the gravel of a short, curving, laurel-bordered drive and we pulled up at the side of a large house. Dean led me to the front and I looked around with awe. The building, many-gabled, seemed to me enormous. (Years later, when I revisited it, it had – natch – shrunk and I recognised it as a standard Victorian rector's pad, roomy but not exceptionally grand.) In front of its lichen-encrusted redbrick extended a velvety lawn, surrounded by flowerbeds and dense shrubberies of predominantly rhododendrons, with at the end, its lowest branches sweeping the grass, a great monkey-puzzle tree, towering up in tiers like some dark green, spiny pagoda.

As for the interior of the house – why, the bedroom Olivia

showed me into that evening was bigger than our front and back rooms at home combined.

The different life I'd glimpsed, brushed against, on my visits to the house in Walfield Road I now entered fully, became part of. Much of it I found strange until I'd got used to it. At home I'd been allowed to stay up until all hours and I'd usually overslept (I was always late for school); now it was bed at eight every evening and up at seven. At home I'd picked at my food; now I looked forward to every meal. At home radio (on all day), comics and puzzles provided my amusement when I wasn't playing; now I feasted on Olivia's old children's books – to a few of which she had already introduced me. Partly in the hope of having children to whom she could hand them down, she'd kept all the favourites from her own childhood, mostly the familiar classics: *Peter Pan, The Railway Children, Black Beauty, The Secret Garden, Children of the New Forest, Swallows and Amazons*, the *Doctor Dolittle* adventures… (There was one Doctor Dolittle whose title it was, not the story itself – set in a fictional African country and rather disappointing – that enchanted me. *Doctor Dolittle's Post Office*. What made that title beautiful to me was its conjunction of the fabulous doctor's name and the ideal post office it conjured up, in which the sleepy orange sub-post-office at the corner of Walfield Road and the large airy light-filled main post office in Bexcray somehow, miraculously defying incompatibility – as so often happens in the synthesis of perfect dream worlds – became one. *Doctor Dolittle's Post Office*… Even now those syllables contain just a hint of the old magic.)

Olivia's books also included various annuals. Some were falling apart – the corners of the glossy pictorial covers scuffed to disintegrating grey card, the spines ajar or missing, binding reduced to fragments of brittle yellow paste and loose threads, sets of pages dangling from these or detaching themselves altogether and needing to be sorted. But what did this matter to me once I was lost in their contents. The *Daily Mirror's* Pip, Squeak and Wilfred (an impossible *family* of dog, penguin and rabbit). The *Rainbow's* Tiger Tim and the Bruin Boys (an impossible *gang* of carnivores and domestic pets). And Rupert Bear, in jaunty check trews and scarf. His adventures were a paradigm of a special kind of poetry: the startling emergence into an everyday setting of the exotic. Just as for le grand Meaulnes it was encountering it in a bleak winter wood that lent the fête such enchantment, just as for a mooching child it is coming across them in a dusty old hedge that makes the sky blue eggs so hypnotic, so for the reader of a Rupert annual it was their sudden appearance in a familiar English landscape of muted green that made rajahs or clowns or harlequins so especially magical.

Pip, Squeak, Wilfred, Tiger Tim, Bobby Bruin, Rupert, Winnie the Pooh, Peter Rabbit... How much of that seductive anthropomorphism there is in English children's fiction. And how easily some become sucked into and stuck fast in its sweet depths.

Blue and white

That stay at the Rectory also brought about other changes in my life. I arrived there in June and for the remaining few weeks of the school year I attended Kingsdon St Mary Primary. Why did I enjoy my time there so much? What had it got that Elson Road Primary hadn't? Well, there was the exciting fact that Olivia taught there – and that I was going to be in her class! Then there was the school's setting: it stood on what was more of a lane than a road, a lane sloping, winding, hedge- and tree-lined and bordered by grassy banks ornamented with pinkish-purple bells and rosy stars fascinating to a town kid: foxglove and red campion. And then there was the change in myself: a greater sense of well-being, brought about by that early bed, early rising and good food. I was now among the first to arrive at school – me! – and had time for pre-assembly cricket in the playground.

House martins built their nests of mud in the eaves of the school building and when you looked up at them at the start of a brilliant day, you saw the freshly whitewashed walls against the cloudless sky were, like that copy of a Della Robbia maiolica which Italophile Dean had brought back from a holiday in Florence, the purest white against the purest blue, state-of-the-art white and blue, the white and blue all other whites and blues, no matter how hard they tried, would find it impossible to better. (Even so, across that vault of serene unbroken blue, you sometimes, if you looked long enough, saw floaters drifting and darting around like pond micro-organisms under the lens, evading all your attempts to focus on them: early unwelcome reminder, though fortunately brief and soon forgotten, of the subjective self: the blue was situated not outside you but within.) And in the blue you might hear a delightful droning, its source *apparently* that glitter you could discern on high, hot-early-morning droning, resonant, seeming to promise endless lazy summer hours ahead. No, more than promise them: guarantee them. At that pre-school hour, the fine-day heraldry of blue and white heightened in advance the charm of what was to come – the hymns, the lessons, the afternoon story – and when you were in school, shut away from the open air, you were still conscious of it, that noble azure and virginal white, it hovered in the background of every element that made up the day: the warm mote-filled sunbeams slanting across the assembly hall and the smell of polish they brought out from the wood-block floor, a rich, strong, school-is-safe, summer-morning smell; the just-tuneful-enough shout of children singing 'Morning has broken, like the first morning', the matutinal freshness of high-pitched notes in perfect accord with that of the words; the lessons whose memory aids such as *Richard of York gave battle in vain* and *Columbus sailed the ocean blue in fourteen-hundred-and-ninety-two* would anchor themselves in your mind for ever, lessons which, at that age, like those at Elson Road Primary, were largely free of the oppressive tracts of boredom that would blight those at secondary school (tonnage of copper production at Broken Hill; pressure p is inversely proportional to volume V); the so-quiet sleepy art period, when Olivia and another teacher, Mr Carberry, would disappear into the store room to sort out books and you could lose yourself in your poster-paint daub At the Circus or In the Market. Yes, glowing in your mind through all of these, that blue and white insignia symbolised, constantly kept you aware of, the lovely day outside.

Intermezzo

The Rectory lawn was large and well-kept enough for small-scale cricket. On weekday afternoons when school was over, I itched to start a game with friends I'd made in my class (and sometimes, when they were free, Dean and Olivia) at any time the weather allowed (disappointment pierced me like a dagger whenever the sky darkened and I knew rain was on the way); but the call was most imperative on fine afternoons, which added a sort of glory to cricket in that setting. Then I would drink in the level expanse of half-past-four sunlight on the lawn around us and the shadows of the tall rhododendrons and the monkey puzzle that fell across it, shadows solid in their depths but at their edge, just before they gave way to unbroken sunlight, exquisitely openwork so that they appeared gold-parded. It must have been a very deep draught of those afternoons that I drank in, since ever afterwards I could never regard any domestic summer scene as truly idyllic unless it incorporated such a lawn, at such an hour, patterned in such a way; and that lawn in particular became an archetype, the original to which so many others, awash with gold and deepest green, would subliminally refer back.

And, on one such afternoon there sounded from the house, throbbing out over the garden, a beautiful music: the golden-light-and-deep-shadow-glorious, heart-of-chiaroscuro-mysterious Intermezzo from Act Three of Wolf-Ferrari's *The Jewels of the Madonna*, which was to become inseparably fused in my mind with that scene. (Later I was to ask myself: could it really have been so? Was it really there and then that I first heard that soul-stabbing music that seemed to me to emanate from another world? Did those lovely strains, which might almost have been written by the composer as incidental music to what I gazed on, really pervade it?)

Often, entering the tall, century-old rhododendron shrubbery to collect the ball, you would find yourself in a small dim recess with the thick Arthur-Rackham-gnarled stems of the shrubs round about, a soft carpet of old leaf and bark litter underfoot and, in decorative clusters on the dark leathery leaves, icing-pink flowers that showed in the gloom only palely except where, picked out by a stray shaft of foliage-piercing sunlight, they had the luminosity of flares.

Then you emerged to see everyone waiting for you on that sunlit lawn (into which, unbeknown to me, the dark serpent had already infiltrated, years before). They were turned towards you expectantly, motionless.

'The Open Road'

Each afternoon Olivia would read the class an instalment of a story. Looking back, I realise now that there was in this something of self-indulgence on her part; we might have been better occupied improving our own reading skills. But she read those books aloud because she loved them and she hoped she could inspire in her listeners the same love. Having finished Masefield's *The Box of Delights*, to whose final pages I listened as a late arrival without much understanding, Olivia went on to *The Wind in the Willows*, her favourite, which I hadn't yet read. A perfect June had yielded to a sultry July, and I shall always associate that book – in particular the chapter 'The Open Road' – with sweltering heat, with merciless dog-days pouring it on. The windows raised but the classroom no less torpid. Kenny Cottle snoozing off again at the back. Outside, the playground unusually bright, the stone walls around it doing the shimmy-shake. The elm trees beyond much too blue. The zinc drinking fountain greyly glinting as it tantalised us with what it had to offer. On the asphalt beneath the bike shed a dark rectangle, midnight blue, sharp-edged, a cut-out from one of those coloured sticky-backed papers we used to make collages with. And, hanging on the still air, just reaching us through the open window, raised from the boys' urinal by the heat, raised from the tan crust on its white glaze, a matured acidic smell, not, in its restrained bite, unpleasant on such an afternoon. (Many years later, on holidays in France, whenever there reached me on a similar afternoon a similar smell, wafted on the hot air from one of those outside *pissoirs* in some sleepy Clochemerle-like provincial town, I would find myself for a few moments back in that schoolroom as I gazed out of the window at that empty playground weighed down by heat and a vague melancholy.)

'It was a golden afternoon. The smell of the dust they kicked up was rich and satisfying...' Through the medium of Olivia's low, expressive reading voice (the magical sentences glimmering like precious stuffs in the relatively subdued light and heavy air), the slumbrous afternoon on the open road with Rat and

Mole and Toad and the old grey horse pulling the canary yellow caravan became one with the slumbrous afternoon in the classroom. You could almost see that 'golden afternoon' (which expelled from the world all that was dark), you could almost breathe in the 'rich and satisfying' smell of the dust, you could almost hear the leisurely clop of the hooves and rumble of the wheels. At your desk, heat-befuddled, drowsy, you idled along that road with those wayfarers, content, as on one of those roads you surveyed from the top of a trolleybus, to be travelling down it for ever...

Often, when reading or being read to, we find the busy stage director in the subconscious who furnishes us with the story's settings drawing them from our own world. So, as Olivia read us *The Wind in the Willows*, Toad Hall, with its 'mellowed red brick' and 'well-kept lawns', appeared to me as the Rectory; the Wild Wood, 'low and threatening', was Blackdown Copse, which lay on the horizon south of Kingsdon St Mary; and the railway station whose red and green lights caught the attention of the fugitive Toad was a station I'd seen, on a visit to a school sports meeting with Olivia one autumn afternoon, crowning an embankment beyond the darkening playing field. (Mounted on a sky of juicy strawberry and orange, like my favourite double-fruit-flavoured chewy bar, cut from a velvet as rosy black as a black rose, was silhouetted not only this station but a signal outside it set at red – and how beautiful that ruby cushioned in rosy black was – and a shunting engine, which, magical as any strange beast of romance, restively huffed and clanked and, against the fruity sky, raised aloft a plume of blue. And no silhouette of castle and forest illustrated in some fabulous tale could have enchanted me more than that symbol of the modern age that I saw before me. Symbol of the modern age, and one of quintessentially *suburban* magic...yet nonetheless seeming to me then not to belong to everyday life...to be a glimpse of the opening to another world...)

All that scenery from my own life more or less fitted the bill as settings for the story. But, because when we are very young there is only a comparatively small stock of it to draw upon, sometimes, unbeknown to us, the shadowy stage director is desperately forced to offer up as a suitable setting for a particular episode scenery that is no such thing. So, for the River, with its 'rustle and swirl, chatter and bubble', the only remotely appropriate river he could trundle out was a stream on the other side of the village, where I used to look for sticklebacks. Clear but slow-moving, bedded with dusky pink, slaty blue, and milky buff pebbles, overhung with alders and permeated by a faint odd sour smell, it had little in common with that stretch of the Thames that inspired Grahame. But the child's visualising imagination when it reads has little critical sense (not that the adult's in the same situation has much more), it will swallow anything. And so, as I listened to those chapters featuring the River, I accepted without a second thought the mental stage flats of the village stream that were presented to me, they no more lessened the enchantment of those episodes than actual stage flats poorly painted can spoil our enjoyment of a finely directed and acted play. As for the Open Road, well, among the avenues that had captivated me on car journeys with Dean and Olivia was one which we had travelled down on a baking September afternoon: leaving behind a suburb, we had passed between hedges tanned by the sun, decorated with blackberries of red and black and surmounted on our side by ripening apples; then, approaching an intersection, the avenue had suddenly offered up to us, had suspended just ahead of us at the end of our hedge, had set aglow there on high, above the foliage, in a delightful commingling of town and country, in an opulent addition to the natural fruit, a round, ripe, artificial fruit that commanded us to halt: a sweet hot red glowing disc (another of the lovely red lights), splendidly hot on that splendidly hot afternoon and soon to be joined by one of orange. That September avenue, with its golden hedges, its ripening berries and apples, its man-made fruits, took up within me, as such stunners tend to do, permanent residence. And it was that inappropriate stretch of avenue that my stage people wheeled on to represent the highway along which Rat, Mole and Toad kicked up the dust, the motor-car roared and the canary-coloured cart overturned into a ditch. But I wasn't in the least bothered that the avenue scenery depicted a metalled, far from dusty road, showed no ditch and, displaying traffic lights, was anachronistic. I mentally painted in a ditch and raised a cloud of dust, ignored the traffic lights and was perfectly satisfied with the result. In fact, it has remained my only image of that chapter ever since. So it pulls me up short to reflect that Grahame had nothing like my avenue in mind when he imagined his highway; that the book's millions of other readers have had nothing like it in mind; that they in turn have all envisaged it differently from the author, and from one another; that, in other words, for each one of us, far from its being the universal setting for the events of that golden afternoon, our Open Road is known to us alone.

An abrupt end

It was early September and the school summer holiday was almost over. The berries were ripening in the hedges, as on that drive I remembered, and the sun, though still warm, couldn't entirely dispel certain vaporous changes in the air. This made me even hungrier for the start of what the autumn term, in its name alone, had signalled in advance: a misty, smoky, frosty, russet excitement. October and November lessons would somehow be crisper, tangier, than summer ones, would crackle with a mysterious *extra*, some sort of promise, in a setting of bedewed cobwebs, country bonfires, ice that splintered underfoot, hips and haws, and red and orange leaves. I suppose I was tingling with the same 'Idea of Autumn' with which C.S. Lewis became enamoured as a child.

By autumn term I meant, of course, that at Kingsdon St Mary Primary. For I'd begun to believe that I was going to stay on at that school indefinitely. After Lil's gallbladder had been removed, an infection had extended her hospital stay, and then she had gone to her sister Ada's to convalesce. I had visited her in hospital and at Ada's but nothing had been said about when she and I were returning home. And children, who travel down the days without concerning themselves with the machinery that turns the wheels beneath, eventually imagine that persistent, ever-lengthening silence on something they don't want to happen means that now it never will, that it has somehow faded out of existence. So, without actually thinking about it much, as the weeks passed I was lulled into a subconscious sense that Lil and I were never going back to Danehill Road. That was why when Dean told me one day that I was going to rejoin Lil there at the end of the week, it came as such a shock. No more being looked after by Olivia, no more Rectory, no more Kingsdon St Mary, no more new school, no more afternoon stories. That unexpected interlude in my life, that experience of a wholly different world, had come to an abrupt end.

Olivia had said to me, 'She's had a hard time of it, your mum.' But, once back at 33 Danehill, I found Lil surprisingly unchanged from her pre-illness self. She seemed to have made a full recovery and she popped off to bingo and the pictures as regularly as before. She claimed though that she wasn't the woman she'd once been and that she was going to need much more help around the house. I wondered whether being waited on at her sister's had given her a taste for a lazier life.

In her absence Harry had cut down on the booze. Result: they were no longer yelling and fighting – for the time being anyway. But, more than that, he was showing her an unprecedented consideration. 'Can I get that for you, Lil?' 'Sure you wouldn't like another, Lil?' That the terrible rows had stopped was great, but I didn't much care for Harry's new solicitousness. I found it somehow unbecoming in one *so obviously unfitted for it*. That smile you now saw on his chops accompanying each fresh attention, that constant unnecessary use of Lil's name, that reasonable voice – they made me uncomfortable. There was something wrong. Much later we disovered what it was: after Lil had gone into hospital Harry had started having an affair with Peg Tumbrill, a woman he'd met in the Prince Albert. When it all came out into the open, I learned she was a trolleybus clippie who'd issued us with tickets on many a ride: a plain, bulky woman with cropped hair, a huge bum, which her shiny-seated navy blue uniform trousers moulded with unfortunate fidelity, and a voice of thunder (her 'Fares *please!*' as she swung heavily down the aisle soon scotched any idea you might have of fiddling them). Such was Harry's paramour. But it was to be a long time before Lil found out, and in the meantime she was quite taken by his unseemly pleasantness.

Our Christmas

The Christmas I was used to and loved was a gaudy, tinselly, wholly irreligious affair – but, even so, a work of art (one of the very few, actually, experienced by the masses in those days). A work of art which sometimes seemed to extend beyond the circumscribed intentional world of festivity and involve the world at large – for what, so it seemed to me in that holiday season, was a cerise or pink sky above ostensibly non-festive lamplit trees and white, red, green city lights but Christmas decorations on a grand scale?

But perhaps I loved Christmas even more in the anticipation than in the experience: no actual Christmas ever did or ever could match the idealised one. And I idealised the non-religious Christmas in the way most children (and some adults) do, by subconsciously combining elements from different sources: in my case, Hollywood films, popular music, comics. The films: a sunlit snowman, a great decorated tree, young people with a glow on their faces and romance in their eyes, presents in sumptuous Technicolor wrappings, a feeling of joy suffusing everything, *everything*, an American apotheosis of the secular Christmas so beautiful it was beyond anything you were likely to experience yourself. The music: the jubilant, winter-crisp 'Sleigh Ride', which portrayed in every jingling note a steamy-breathed exhilaration, the romantic, tender 'Have Yourself A Merry Little Christmas', theme music of some out-of-this-world party at which I would kiss a lovely, sweet-smelling girl under the mistletoe. The comics: 'Grand Xmas Number' (the tingle of those words!) above the masthead of *Dandy*, *Knockout* or *Film Fun*, snow mantling the masthead itself, paper-hat-crowned, cracker-pulling characters seated around an every-course-at-once-laden board featuring an enormous, spheroid, custard-capped pud, and, seen through a window beyond, snowflakes drifting down... O my! O my!

As for our actual Christmases, memory has ousted the worst aspect – Harry and Lil's brawls, whose eruption the stress of ill-organised catering in that cramped, steamy scullery and back room probably made inevitable – and fondly retained the child's standard delights: the decorations (paper chains magically transforming the seedy two-down), the tree (silver tinsel, covered in multicoloured baubles and lights), the presents (ah, the mysterious bulges and angularities of the pillowcase felt in the night), the iced cake (that even in the dim baleful light from above suggested, with its snowy top and silvery blue and white wrapper, frosty Christmas pleasures)... And something else, something of a different nature, something of an unfamiliar appeal: a certain carol we sang at school that in its words, and in the rather constrained, far from lilting setting of these, set it apart from the other, more heartily laudatory carols we sang:

> The holly and the ivy
> when they are both full grown;
> of all the trees that are in the wood
> the holly bears the crown...
>
> The holly bears a blossom
> as white as any flower;
> and Mary bore sweet Jesus Christ
> to be our sweet Saviour...

It gave me, as we sang it, an inkling at least of a Christmas poetry unlike any other I knew, in the image it conjured up of a wood, of greenery – of a Nature replete with religious symbolism, that Nature which, apart from the illustrated cut holly and snow on cards and in comics, and my fanciful view of skies and lights, I never really associated with Christmas, an affair for me predominantly of intramural artifice. I don't mean to say that the carol induced in me some truly religious awakening, made me from then on always see Christmas in its Christian light. Far from it: whenever I sang 'The Holly and the Ivy' its effect on me would be no more lasting than that of any other carol and Christmas would soon resume what was (if I discount my lovingly idealised version of it) its solely materialistic, self-indulgent character. No, what that carol revealed to me, even if only briefly, was not so much the spiritual as the aesthetic aspect of the Christian Christmas. But this, an example of a particular type of poetry, of which another early budding had been Greenline coaches seen in leafy lanes, was, like that other, far from unqualified in its appeal; it aroused in me conflicting feelings. I found the image in the carol of a massed greenery that, apart from its occasional beading of red and trimming of white, was austere, the image of a religiosity that was to me, at any rate, equally austere, I found them, these images, in comparison with the bright, multicoloured, irreligious, *straightforward* festive pleasures of Danehill Road, at once (strangely) beautiful in their purity and unappealing in their asceticism.

And I recall from those actual Christmases something else. Sometimes, late on Christmas Day afternoon, I would unlatch the scullery door, cross the tiny yard and walk up to the top of the garden. There, in the fading light and the silence, I would turn to look back down our garden and across the others on either side, lying damp, cold, deserted, all unChristmassy mud, cabbages and dead chrysanths (and as I stood there I would experience the child's amazed realisation that the rest of the animal kingdom *had no conception that this was Christmas Day*, that to that sparrow cheeping so sadly in a bush *this was an afternoon no different from any other*, that that moggy scrambling over a fence next-door-but-one *would not have the least understanding of fellow-moggy Korky's festive cheer*). In making this short excursion I was, I think, yielding to another prompting of that perverseness with which, along with acquired taste, the desire to be different and other deviations from the direct and natural, the child makes such a surprised and inanely self-congratulatory first acquaintance: that is, in this case, in a minor illustration of what Poe in 'The Black Cat' called 'the unfathomable longing of the soul to vex itself', I would, instead of obeying my natural urge to remain in the warmth indoors, with the carton of Rose's chocs and my presents, choose to visit and to remain outside in that chill and dreary spot, for no other reason than that I did not want to. This may, though, be oversimplifying matters. For there was, in this self-imposed exile of mine, as I stood looking down over those dismal gardens where there was no other soul to be seen, as I stood looking at the lighted windows of those houses where everyone else, absolutely everyone else, on this so-special, once-a-year day, was indoors doing Christmas-Day-afternoon things, there was in this disengagement a faint unearned feeling of superiority that I alone was standing up here, observing, discrepant, apart.

Everything promised it…

Boxing Day we usually spent at Lil's sister Aunt Edie's, in Sandbay. She and her husband Ivor, who ran a lucrative driving school, owned a largeish house, where we usually stayed for our summer seaside holiday (Edie was the one who'd 'made it' on Lil's side of the family). On Boxing Day they threw a party. I always looked forward to this because of a particular, delicious hope. It was that this year at last, at last, a pretty young girl, not at all like the only girl normally at these gatherings, Ivor's surly, boyish-looking niece Sheena (who was as indifferent to me as I to her), would be among the guests, that she would look at me in a certain way, that, making actual what was meltingly intimated in 'Have Yourself A Merry Little Christmas', I would get to kiss her under the mistletoe that hung in the hall, or during a game of a kind that we had never yet played but that *on this occasion someone would suggest*.

On our arrival at Edie's my hope would be initially dashed at seeing no sign of this girl. But in the cool and well-appointed bathroom, where you could hear coming from the warm hall below a repeated Boxing-Day-exciting sequence of sounds (ring at the door, loud effusive greetings, cold-nose laughter, 'Let's take your coats') that made you tinglingly eager to return to them, in that bathroom where, alone in a setting of detached, reflective porcelain, taps and tiles (so spotless at Edie's), you could savour the expectant mid-afternoon pre-party hour more purely, I would find my hope not only heightened by but, I don't know why, *seemingly rendered well-founded by* everything that impinged on my senses there: the pale golden-rosy winter light gently bathing the room, its source a sun that, low in a sky touched with nougat pink, was as easy to gaze at as a moon; the occasional squawk of an inland gull breaking the silence of the deserted streets; the too-hot running water that made you shudder with pleasure as you immersed your hands in it; and the scent of the soap that was the same delicate pink as the sky. Yes, all these, the pale winter sunlight, the gull's cry, the hot water, the scented soap – which would be what that girl's skin would smell of – seemed to *promise* that this year, entering the hall with her parents, rosy-cheeked from the cold, deliciously pretty, there would appear...

And, even regarded objectively, my hope was not entirely unfounded. After all, there had turned up on one occasion, emerging mysteriously from who knew where, some remote relations we had never seen before (though, admittedly, were never to see again either, as they returned to who knew where for good). So there was always the chance.

Mostly, though, the guests were the same old regulars, and the only kissing that got to be done was that contrived every year by Ivor's brother-in-law Jim. Stout and ruddy, with sandy hair and moustache, perpetually, securely pleased with himself, Uncle Jim, standing ostentatiously beneath the mistletoe in the hall on both his arrival and his departure, would announce, successfully passing off lechery as levity, appetite as ritual: 'Now if all the ladies would like to form an orderly queue... No shoving and pushing, please.' And he would give each of them a couple-of-beats-too-long smacker on the lips. Uncle Jim always insisted too that we play a game he had introduced called 'Teapot'. The rules were not taxing. Whenever it was your turn, you had to call out some property common to both a teapot and yourself – otherwise you were out. Every year, Uncle Jim's declarations included – I suppose inevitably – 'I have a long spout'. (Reflecting on what later sadly befell him, I cannot help recalling, perhaps unfairly, another Poe tale, with its observation that practically every insane asylum in France held someone who fancied himself a teapot, and, too, *The Rape of the Lock*, in which we hear of people permanently changed to living teapots.) I got really fed up with that game, mainly because the more notable characteristics which the teapot shared with ourselves refused, year in, year out, to spring to my mind. My impression was, too, that no one else apart from the instigator of 'Teapot' was exactly wild about it. But we always played it, every time, because Uncle Jim was one of those people whose determination to get their own way is never contested – well, never in the sort of company there was at Aunt Edie's anyway. Nor, apparently, does this wilfulness dent their popularity. Everyone fondly referred to Uncle Jim as 'a scream'.

An Argentine siren

In the front room at home, in a wardrobe whose rust-spotted mirror inflicted on you the sort of skin disease that Lil had, as far as she was concerned, inflicted for good on jockeys Gosling and Hide, she kept a stack of old gramophone records, many of them pre-war. Most of them were dance numbers and had belonged to my mother. Disregarding Lil's ban ('You leave them bloody records alone, d'you understand'), I would play them when she wasn't around, on the wind-up gramophone that stood next to the sideboard in the back room. Among them was one that I loved for a special reason. It was a tango, at once assertive – heavily accented sexual beat and full-bodied accordion surges – and yielding – wistful tune crooned by an Argentine siren. (And the scarlet and gold label of the record, a scarlet and gold which swam together as they revolved at 78 rpm, seemed the physical embodiment of that rich music, were part of its potent appeal – and blazed too in the very word tango itself. Not only in tango either. Thereafter any other word that began with the letters t-a-n-g acquired by association the same richness as tango. Tangerine, for instance, whether indicating a fruit or a colour, was for me more deeply orange, more of an opulent fusion of scarlet and gold, than any other kinds of orange, and had a sort of accordionish resonance they lacked. It also had in its very letters, I was intrigued to notice, a further, incidental link to that particular tango, that Argentine tango.) The special allure of that record, though, did not come until midway through it. Then the singer ceased singing and began speaking the words in a yearning, seductive, intimate voice. I had the wonderful illusion she was addressing me personally. It mattered not a bit that she was doing so in a foreign language. I had no need to understand what she was saying in order to understand what she meant. Her longing to know me, to be with me, awoke in me an echoing longing to be with her, to know her. (I was to experience something of the same feeling later when I first heard Melina Mercouri singing 'Never On Sunday' in so throaty and mysterious a Greek and so yearning a delivery, or, as Olivia explained it, rubato and sforzando.) And at the same time, something else awakened in me, something I had felt before when some goddess of the screen would gaze out at you in a certain way (at the hero really, but it seemed like it was at you), and also when you had longings to kiss a pretty girl under the mistletoe. That something was the first stirrings of eroticism, an eroticism more rarefied, more mysterious – and possibly more beautiful even? – in our earliest prepubescent experiences of it, at an age when we're not physically equipped to satisfy it, than it will be when we are. An eroticism that something in us has idealised – that old tendency yet again, and so habitual in childhood that one has to consider it innate. And apart from the exalted eroticism, the other feeling I had towards the singer, the wish simply to be with her – a form of devotion – was, too, an ideal. Certainly the fusion of affection, tenderness and sexual desire I felt as a child towards that unknown South American woman seems to me now an early model of the kind of love for a woman the grown man keeps before him as an ideal.

The Sandbay train

The year following Lil's illness we were, as usual, to take our week's summer holiday at Aunt Edie's in Sandbay. But when the Saturday arrived for us to travel down, Harry and Lil embarked on such a lengthy and stormy row (Harry's nice-as-pie stuff had long since petered out) that when we eventually set off for Bexcray station it was to catch, not our usual midday train, but an evening one.

The days of steam were not quite over on that line, and as we stood on the platform I eagerly awaited the arrival of the engine. But for me that station, beneath the warm, ever-deepening blue evening sky, throbbed with something else, too, something longer known, more mysterious. It seemed implicit, that something, in the beautiful sulphurous reek of dispersed engine smoke; in the encrusted, flaking soot on the trackside walls, which beyond the platform led into a tunnel (perhaps the tunnel at whose farther end the night train carrying Toad slowed down to let him jump off and escape the police); and above all else, in the signals down the line, glowing red and green, like those that had first alerted Toad to the presence of a station, softly singing the same message as a signal silhouetted against a fruity sky had once sung to me...the same message as that of the luminescent Regal clock...as that of the traffic lights at dusk seen across some darkening space...

Our train drew in, the locomotive looming above us, majestic, steam and driving-wheels deafening, cowing everyone. We climbed aboard. The only other occupants of our compartment were a middle-aged couple in a farther corner, each reading a book. After we were seated, Lil conveyed to us by quite clever facial expressions and eye movements that our fellow-passengers were 'posh'.

It was a warm evening. And soon that warmth brought out certain odours, particularly pronounced in the confined space. Lil looked at Harry, silently mouthed 'B.O.' and made dipping accusatory motions of her head towards him. I could tell from his glare of fury and hatred (the renewed glare of a furnace that the row had not burned out) that he would have exploded into scary violence if we hadn't had company.

The man in the corner opened the window. Lil took from her handbag a small bottle, a recent purchase from Blackwell market, of mysteriously anonymous manufacture like so much else she bought there, and said to no one in particular, '*I'm* going to try out my new perfume', as though others had announced different plans. She applied it so liberally that, with some ostentation, the opener of the window lowered it further.

After a while Lil produced a greasy brown paper bag. It contained the roast 'beef' sandwiches she had packed for the journey. The joint had been cooked the previous weekend, it had been a muggy week, and we had no fridge. Soon a new odour joined the other two battling it out for supremacy in the compartment. It was that of meat on the turn.

Lil, after a glance at the couple in the corner, offered the sandwiches to me with an uncustomary gentility of gesture and speech: 'Beef sandwich?'

I took one. But having raised it to my mouth, I wrinkled up my nose. 'That meat smells bad,' I timidly ventured. Timidly and *rashly*. Harry transferred the unquenched glare to me and I read fearfully in its white heat the certainty of pain to come.

'Bad?' exclaimed Lil as incredulously as if I had alleged the meat had just been singing. Which in a way I suppose it had – a line, say, from that number in *South Pacific*: 'I'm as...high as a flag on the Fourth of July.' 'What are you talking about, bad? That's fresh beef, that is.' Another glance at our travelling companions, then: 'Best quality, too. Terribly expensive.' I frowned. Not only at the whopper but at her curious manner of speaking. As Harry's brief spell of sweet talk had done, it sounded all wrong. 'Come on,' she urged, 'do take one.'

But I was determined to follow my instinct, I refused to eat those sandwiches, despite being subjected to what had now, above munching jaws, become twin glares. I made do instead with a couple of shrivelled, diminutive market oranges that Lil kept loudly referring to as 'Jaffas'.

Summer holiday

Our late arrival angered Edie. She'd prepared a meal for us and now it was wasted. Why hadn't Lil let her know we weren't coming that afternoon? Why couldn't she have rung her from Mrs Smethwick's? It wasn't right, it wasn't fair – and she was beginning to think it was typical. This so narked Lil that she launched into one of her tiresome screaming numbers. I went to bed that night to the sound of slams and thuds.

Next day was no better. For one thing, the weather broke. A mean wind started up teams of white horses all across the bay, then proceeded to lash them mercilessly. It was obviously on the lookout for trouble. Along the seafront it started crashing and banging around like Lil the previous night, and, as we misguidedly made our way along the esplanade, it set about us *with no provocation whatsoever*, cuffing us with its icy mitts and – in case we hadn't got the message, which was obviously Sod off – hurling the odd handful of sand in our faces. Then, in the afternoon, first Harry, then Lil, felt so nauseous that they heaved up, Harry in the town centre, right behind a bearded man in a wheelchair, who, quite excusably I thought, bawled out Harry something terrible, and Lil at the entrance to the Merrie England amusement arcade. Lil put it down to our lunchtime cod and chips having been served to us by a 'darkie', though she couldn't understand why I was all right. 'I think it might have been...' I began to surmise – then, an early learner, I decided not to pursue this idea aloud.

Neither of them was in any state to continue the afternoon. Or to eat the meal Edie had got ready. So, another one wasted. Edie said nothing but a certain look settled on her face, one of melodramatic self-righteous affront. I could understand why she might be a bit miffed but I found that silence and look, especially her persistence in it, as stupid and annoying as Lil's outraged yelling routine: two performances not only unnecessary but boringly hammy.

Upsets of this kind between Lil and Edie were not uncommon. Uncle Ivor, a model of composure, kept well out of them. He would carry on reading his paper, even if now and then turning and adjusting a page with rather more noise than necessary. Sometimes when I caught his eye, he would wink at me knowingly, to which I would respond with an uncertain, embarrassed smile. Whether his calm was constitutional or affected, I don't know, but I guess it was useful in his job as a driving instructor. There was only one thing that ever really bothered him, and that was a fierce disappointment from the war years which, whenever the subject cropped up, resumed chafing him. When, as a milkman in those days, he had been called up, he had enthusiastically applied to train as a fighter pilot but had been turned down on the grounds, he was told, of defective eyesight. This he could never understand. Eye tests after the war showed he had twenty-twenty vision – and even now he had no need of specs. (But Harry, who too had known failure, failure to become a QC – for which he blamed only himself – explained to Ivor, in his compensatory role as barrack-room lawyer, that if his vision was later found to be perfect then it must have improved after the war, since the Raff couldn't have had no other reason for turning him down, now could they? And if you'd told Harry that someone who'd served on a Waaf officer selection panel had admitted in a memoir that the panel automatically rejected any applicant who, when prompted, referred to the lavatory as the toilet and to a table napkin as a serviette, he would have replied with the stock Harry and Lil riposte in such cases: you didn't want to believe everything you read in books.) Ivor had *longed* to fly Spits, he said, to play an active part in defending his country, especially when through attrition fighter pilots were desperately needed. Instead, far from becoming a pilot officer, he'd spent the entire war as a real erk, a storeman. It was a regret that he had obviously, and, so some members of the family thought, absurdly, never really got over.

It took Harry and Lil's digestive systems only a couple of days to put down the rebel forces within. But then, no sooner had they recovered, no sooner had Lil dolled herself up again (lipstick, as ever, out of register like the mouth colouring in a badly printed *Dandy*), no sooner were they looking forward to going out in the better weather (the wind was taking time out from duffing up everyone and everything in sight, and the sun, plucking up courage as a result, was getting out and about more), no sooner had all this come to pass than Lil and Edie had another row – some rubbish about an alarm clock. Eyes bulging behind her specs, *Dandy* mouth distorted, Lil yelled,

'How dare you! How dare you speak to your own sister like that!' Then, in an appalling feral shriek that almost made the words unintelligible: '*I won't put up with it, do you hear!*' Oh, dear. The familiar nonsense. And finally, to Harry and me, she snapped, 'That's it. Come on, we're leaving.'

It was an order. Harry, who usually called the shots, seemed strangely lost. When sober, he was, like most bullies, easily intimidated by behaviour he was more used to inflicting on others than being subjected to himself. On this occasion, once we'd gone upstairs to pack and he'd recovered a little, he could manage no more than that tone of sweet reason and emollience that I felt so ill became him. 'Come on, Lil, there's no need for all that. Edie didn't mean nothing.' He flinched as Lil viciously hurled some shoes into a suitcase.

He was wasting his time. 'Get those sodding things into that bag,' Lil shouted at me, 'and get a sodding move on.'

Like the wind at Sandbay, however, her rage subsided as abruptly as it had arisen, and by the time we were on our way to the station she had calmed down. Observing her, I was sure she was regretting her impulsive decision to leave immediately, to break off, for the sake of a quarrel that could have been patched up (as countless others had been before), those traditional, corny amusement-arcade, cockles-and-whelks, Back-by-Popular-Demand, Kiss-Me-Quick days by the seaside that were her only extended break from life at 33 Danehill. But I was equally sure nothing would induce her to return to her sister's. Blown off course by her storm, she now found herself on one of those new courses from which, in the extremely wilful (who are always to some extent emotionally unbalanced), there is no turning back. No matter how cogently Harry reasoned with her, no matter how piteously I implored her to change her mind ('Oh, *please*, Mum'), she never responded with anything but a stony-faced 'I told you, we're not going back, and that's final.'

Then as we reached Sandbay station tears began to trickle down her cheeks. Harry had further words with her. It still wasn't too late. But I sensed she was determined not to forgo the exquisite torture of taking a step that once and for all would make the holiday irretrievable: having our return tickets clipped at the barrier. And when we were on the train and the guard's whistle pierced her with its note of finality, with its message that now it really was too late, I was sure as I looked at her tearsmeared face that she found her suffering as delicious as it was unbearable.

Guilt

One day at Elson Road primary school, before the summer holiday, Miss Knowles, our form teacher, had said as an illustrative aside when reading us a story, 'In the same way that *you* love *your* mum and dad.' How guilty those words had made me feel. I didn't think I did love the two people I called Mum and Dad (whereas I did think I loved Aunt Olivia and Uncle Dean). It's true I would have been hard put to it at that age, like any child, to say exactly what I understood love to mean. But I'm sure that if I had had to undergo then that foolproof though unwelcome test of knowing whether what we feel for someone is love, namely, our reaction to losing them, my feelings towards my aunts and uncles at that time would have been the same as they were later when one from each of those couples disappeared from my life.

Of course, since I knew that Mum and Dad were not my real parents, I sometimes thought that that excused the way I felt. But then I would remind myself of what they themselves had reminded me of more than once, especially when they lost their rag with me: that they'd given me a home, clothed and fed me, paid for my comics and sweets and holidays, all as though I had been their own son. Then, instead of understanding that this may have been a sufficient reason for gratitude on my part but not necessarily for anything more, I would feel guilty again. (I don't think, though, that in this regard I was ever quite so self-reproachful as some of those who have been unable to love a natural parent. Because he felt nothing for his father as a child, the young Stendhal said to himself, 'I must be a monster then...')

Much later, when I had left home to make a new life of my own, when reflections on my upbringing had taken a more sociological turn, I began to see my foster parents in rather a different light from when I had been living with them. In the first place, I realised more fully that they hadn't *had* to adopt me, that they could have got out of it (though it's true Harry had tried to). Then, too, I came to understand more clearly that life had not exactly been easy for them. I saw, if they themselves did not consciously see, the burden they bore: that of their anaerobic lives, starved of the oxygen of education, enlightenment, opportunity, prospects; of their hopeless marriage, doomed from the start when Harry was browbeaten into it by Lil's fearsome father because he'd 'got her in the family way' (with that child she lost); of their cramped, dingy, squalid two-down, which increased the stress of their daily lives. And I realised as well that some of what were Lil's faults in my eyes were not seen as such by many of our peers, that, for instance, in spending more on booze and fags and bingo than on decent grub she was doing no more than conforming to what was the norm in our class: giving the highest priority to instant 'good times' and 'treats' to make more bearable the crumminess of everyday existence. I came to feel a certain pity for her. Although that still wasn't love. But, then, I thought, when had she ever given me any real indication that she loved me? I mean, *loved* me.

Something

I was consoled for our aborted week in Sandbay when, a few days after we got back, Dean and Olivia invited me to spend the August bank holiday with them. They collected me on the Friday evening and over the weekend took me first to the Bluebell Railway and then to Hever Castle.

I don't remember much about the railway or the castle but I do remember that, driving away from Kingsdon St Mary, we would, every so often, as sometimes on other trips that took us into various parts of Surrey or out of it into bordering counties, plunge from full sunlight (on this bank holiday, tawny gold sunlight, the leonine splendour with which an English summer sometimes blesses us towards its close) into one of those greenery-enclosed high-banked tunnels of light and shade which so charm travellers as they leave town and village behind. The varying permeability of the foliage by the sun and the different types of leaves that comprised it together gave to it a wide range of colours and tones. For the most part it glowed as greens of diverse types – lime, apple, pistachio, sea, bottle – and of equally diverse translucencies; but where it was sheer it shimmered a top-note pure gold; and where it was massed and the light failed to penetrate at all it plummeted down the scale almost to black. In places, these different colours and tones encroached one upon the other in a pattern intricate and rich; most dramatically, there would intrude into an expanse of gold one of the clusters of jet silhouette, just as in certain of the Schumann or Debussy piano pieces Olivia played there would break into a rippling assertion in the treble, suddenly, thrillingly, a forceful comment in the bass. And sometimes I would see, in the depth of one of these glorious alleys, as some vehicle ahead of us slowed, twin red brake lights. Ah, those ruby gleams, transcending their mundane automotive source, as magical in the enveloping green, gold and black as tail-lights were in the enveloping indigo of dusk. The focal point in that tunnel, those signal fires, on which the vault of greenery, the leafy banks and the road were converging, to which they were so obviously leading, hinted to me that something wonderful lay just ahead, something quite distinct from our known destination.

It is, that something, for all of us when we're young, of the here and yet of the not here – throbbing in the heart of what's before us yet situated somewhere, somehow, just beyond. We can find ourselves hovering on its threshold anywhere, anytime: in my case, at dusk in a traffic-fumy open space or chill November garden or darkening playing field or smoky railway station, in the early morning on a sun-hazed avenue, at pearly noon in a quiet road... And each time we glimpse it, it appears to be on the point of materialising, almost as though by supersaturation with our expectancy. And despite its never yet having come to pass, we keep on believing at each intimation of it that some day, at last fulfilling the recurrent promise, it will begin.

Two

The pigeonholing tendency

When, the previous summer, Lil had fully recovered from her operation and I had had to return to Danehill Road, I may have been upset at having to leave behind my new life at Kingsdon St Mary but I'd soon got over it: the child's usual resilient renunciation of the past and renewed absorption in the present. And besides, I knew in my bones that it had been merely an interlude, that I was in essence a Bexcray boy, and that there were lasting Bexcray pleasures to plunge back into. Like those at St Luke's rec.

The rec lay at the upper end of Bexcray – the seedier, more Blackwellish part. The route there took you past the gasworks. Some inorganic smells that 'had something' were faint and subtle – that, say, of the sunbaked window seat in Dean and Olivia's house in Walfield Road – or, even if less understated, were still far from fulsome – trolleybus interior, post office inkwell. But there were others that on the contrary were rich and powerful – and that of the gasworks was one of them. Arising from the breakdown of coal, it was nothing like the dull, grey, faintly fungal smell of the gasworks' end product, that unpleasant smell that filled the scullery at home when the gas was left on unlit. The gasworks smell was, instead, bituminous, as dark and penetrative and intoxicant as that of a newly creosoted fence or a newly tarred road, and inhaling it, as them, was a raw pleasure. It seemed the fitting herald of the nearby rec, of its dark playing surface of asphalt, itself bituminous. No sooner had I caught the first whiff of this gorgeous industrial stink than my pulse began to beat faster in anticipation of the six-or-so-a-side game ahead, an anticipation heightened, as Danny and I ran down St Lukes Road past the tall blackened-yellowbrick gasworks buildings abutting it on one side, by the sound that reached us from the rec just ahead: according to season, the *pank* of an over-inflated football being punted or, in a game of cricket, the *thwock* of a peltless tennis ball being belted. And whenever – though rarely, in these less polluted, blander days – I come across that gasworks smell again, or something very like it, I fleetingly find myself running once more with Danny down St Lukes Road, inhaling deeply its dark deliciously mordant stink, eager for another of those rec contests with which that smell is so fused that the two are indivisible.

Keen on games, at which he does well, but surprisingly, in view of this, always in a dream. Form masters in reports from Sir Bernard Croucher Grammar School – which Danny and I had gone on to from Elson Road Primary – regularly expressed something along these lines about me. But I've never understood their surprise that sporting ability and mooniness could co-exist. After all, one of literature's great dreamers, Alain-Fournier, who embodied his dream in a masterpiece, was a keen and talented rugby player. But the pigeonholing tendency is, I guess, as impelling as it's universal. (I would, by the way, over the coming years, be made all too aware of it at work in myself.) As for that sport, playing football and cricket in school junior elevens, on the sedate, immaculate, extensive Sir Bernard Croucher playing fields, which had, so unlike the rest of the establishment, something of a public school atmosphere of serene privilege, gave me some of the keenest pleasures of my youth. In these pleasures the poetry of the occasion played as great a part as, and fused with, the exercising of a sporting skill and the thrill of competition. Mild October afternoons, smelling richly of gouged turf, peaceful beneath a soft sky, the sleepy houses on the horizon a damson-bloom blue, the expanse of still, lazy air setting off yet cushioning the thump of boot on leather, the call of a player, the beep of a whistle, the distant bark of a dog – an autumn repose so different from the nervous excitement that galvanised you as the ball, dully sky-reflecting, arced across towards you on the wing and you prepared to run hard with it. Sunny May afternoons, smelling of mown outfield, a faint breeze drifting the cumulus over the blue – a spring tranquillity so different from the nervous excitement that galvanised you as you saw the beautiful stumps and bails, honeyed white, that you would aim at with the beautiful ball, gold-stamped glossy red, first two fingers aslant its seam, to make it *cut*...

Danxavie

Dreamy I certainly was. ('Dozy' was Lil's word for it. Lil and me – the standard double act, Exasperated & Clueless: 'I thought I told you to...' 'Sorry, I didn't hear you.' 'Where's them matches you were supposed to...?' 'Sorry, I forgot.' How infuriating my eternal sorries must have been.) Half the time I was immersed in a realm that Lil knew nothing of, despite the fact that it was regularly in front of her eyes. Following in the footsteps of the young Brontës, the young C.S. Lewis and so many other precocious creators of alternative worlds, Danny and I had invented, mapped and populated a fantasy land and were writing accounts of the adventures that took place in it. Danxavie we called that land. I say that Lil knew nothing of our conspicuously visible project. But neither did Harry. The only awareness of it they ever showed was, during Danny's visits, a regular muttered curse as their feet became caught up in our maps and drawings and notes and manuscripts spread over the limited floor space. I dare say that if they'd heard me mention Danxavie, they'd have taken it for some new product, some superglue perhaps or chewing gum. And I dare say, too, that they believed, for the microsecond they paid any attention to the papers they trod on, that these must indicate they had a homework-mad academic weirdo on their hands.

Danxavie. But after a while that name seemed to Danny and me all too naffly like those similarly formed names we scornfully pointed out to each other on the semis in the 'posher' roads near ours – Lindalec, Arthada and, most dreadfully of all as I recall, Kenjeajac – constructions vainly intended by those who had proudly cobbled them together to be organic not synthetic, imaginative not obvious, fresh not stale. But, despite our embarrassment that we'd contrived our name along the same cruddy lines, we never got round to thinking up an alternative.

Brought up on the anthropomorphic animals that throng English children's fiction and comics (raffish lions in yachting outfits, avuncular badgers smoking pipes, and the like) and, in Danny's case, the hobbits and elves of Tolkien, we had settled our land with tribes of half-human animals, strange creatures of our own invention. One tribe, the Sprabs (a name thought up by Danny's five-year-old sister), innocents one and all, were fluffy yellow replicas of the eponymous hero of *Cheeky Chicko*, a comic for tiny tots and a one-time favourite of both Danny's and mine (though, in retrospect, we both now wondered why Cheeky was always so dashingly got up in pirate togs – stocking cap, belt, cutlass and sea boots – since, never once seen to board a ship, let alone set sail on one, he was, no question about it, a bloody *landlubber*, just like Sir Joseph Porter, Ruler of the Queen's Navee). Identical with Cheeky in all but their outfits, which included distinguishing forms of headgear, the Sprabs might almost have been his offspring but, as I now see it, must actually have been – in that land where, as in all others of its booted-chick, overalled-ostrich type, sex is unknown – produced by parthenogenesis. Very different from the Sprabs, the Vorks, a devious, treaty-breaking lot in the south, were purple and shaggy with quasi-human heads. Another bunch of bad news, the Tongs, aggressively expansionist inhabitants of a northern peninsula, were as black and glossy as blackbeetles. Whereas, suitably, the brave and idealistic Argos were sterling silver and wore armour to match. And there were various others, of similar freakish appearance.

These 'tribes' of what one might just about call members of the animal kingdom so differed from one another in every respect (size, shape, texture, physiognomy, colour), they so obviously were not simply different species, nor even different genera, nor even different families, but different *orders* of that kingdom, that when I looked back on them later, with the newly acquired no-nonsense 'when I became a man, I put away childish things' gaze of a young husband and father, I found them absurd, considered their communicating with one another when forming alliances, taking prisoners, and so on, as scarcely feasible and dismissed Danxavie out of hand. But then I reminded myself that I was only seeing our creation from the considered viewpoint of the adult, that in marked contrast the child will accept almost anything that appeals to it, that the chat between Vorks and Tongs, for instance, would be no more unacceptable to a young reader than that between, say, tiger and parrot in *The Rainbow* or between horse and mole in *The Wind in the Willows*. And if too the weird appearance of these creatures and their biological discordance both seemed in retrospect outlandishly, unacceptably extreme, well, I was to find physical traces of some of them in fictional characters that not only were far from scornfully dismissed but actually became some of the most famous and lucrative of our time, the bizarre, motley protagonists of *Star Wars* – the unbelievable lion-maned Chewbacca, sluglike Jabba, goblinesque Yaddle, et al; and I detect in the originators of these an unthinking childlike creativity unconcerned with probability or congruity not so different from that of the boys who so weirdly settled Danxavie.

The elaborate map of that land, which we had produced first, like Stevenson charting Treasure Island in detail before any notion of writing a story about it had entered his head, was as physically colourful as the characters: bottle green arrows (Dread Forest), lilac saw blade (Mystery Mountains), brown tipped-over E (Specter [sic] Castle), azure jigsaw piece (Heron Lake), pink pentagons (Argotown)... And here and there would appear a cross and an accompanying legend such as 'Vorks balloon landed here' or 'Where Crig lighted signal fire'. Some of these were blithely ambitious: inscribing them, we knew nothing at that stage of the events they located. And certainly there were quite a few whose easy promises of the dramatic never were fulfilled. For gradually Danny and I grew tired of that fantasy world of ours and eventually abandoned it in mid-adventure. Many years later, though, it was to have a surprising rebirth.

Full frontal

If the unknown woman on the tango record made an erotic appeal to my prepubescent self that was tender and idealised, some years later, after libido had climbed in behind the wheel and begun to drive me off on its usual fraught long-distance journey, another unknown woman exerted on me what was simply a nakedly carnal appeal. The difference was like that between romantic first love and a one-night stand. I have already said that only three of the four books that Harry and Lil owned were on display: the two practical manuals and the *Chatterbox* annual. The fourth was hidden, and it was some years before I discovered it, that *Home Medical Companion*, in the front room, Harry and Lil's bedroom, beneath some bedsheets in the chest-of-drawers. Since sex was to Lil a 'filthy' business and genitalia were unmentionables, the medical book was obviously not considered fit material for me to see. As it happened, I found it, on examination, most disagreeable. Published at the turn of the century, it had, with its faded brown board cover, its time-sallowed pages, its old-fashioned typeface and its copperplate illustrations, that same melancholy and somehow debased quality that the *Chatterbox* annual and certain other old books had for me then. But in this case there was something more. The graphic revelations by the *Home Medical Companion* of what I didn't really want to know about – beneath the flayed integument, our inner workings and the alarming ways in which they can go wrong (for communicating which that physically offensive book seemed so suitable a medium) – made it on many pages not just disagreeable but repellent even.

There was however one striking exception to these generally unpleasant disclosures. It was a black-and-white plate, a whole-page photograph – whose strict necessity in the book was not obvious – of a totally naked young female (innocent Eve to a postlapsarian Adam in loincloth a few pages on). Facing me full frontally, arms at her side as though at attention on parade, smiling (but faintly enough not to transgress Victorian and Edwardian respectability), she thrust straight at me her not inconsiderable pointed charms and made no attempt to hide the enticing contours of her loins. This literally laid-out-on-a-plate, come-and-get-it image inflamed me as a more seductive pose might well not have done. And whenever I had the opportunity, I would take the *Home Medical Companion* out to the lav – even, on occasion, when Lil was around, smuggling it there with difficulty under my pullover or shirt, one would-be-casually-held arm trapping it with difficulty against my body, progressing with unnatural, robotic movements towards the back door as I tried to keep my guilty side turned away from Lil throughout. Once I was alone and the book lay open on the floor at the right place – more or less of its own accord by now – actual sight of that stirringly forthright image would set aquiver and demand immediate relief for what had minutes earlier been initially aroused by the simple fervid, anticipatory thought of it. As I recall those early excursions into self-pleasuring now, I still catch a sense of how the eroticism of that picture was heightened by its twin unexpectedness: its isolated appeal in what was otherwise an expanse of the so-unappealing and its evidence that in what had previously seemed to me unsexy age-dinged 1900 or whatever there existed young women as enfevering as any modern pin-up.

The Rectory Christmas

The Christmas following Lil's bust-up with Edie was the first that we didn't spend at home and at Sandbay. Instead, we went to the Rectory, where Dean and Olivia hosted a considerable gathering that for the first time included Dean's side of the family.

Dean (magnanimous, ungrudging, reliable Dean) collected the three of us in his car. Driving southwest from Bexcray, he left the outer London suburbs behind. Listening to him telling Harry about the rest of the route he was taking, I suddenly caught the word Epsom. Epsom. A golden name, like Ascot and Goodwood, a symbol of glamour somewhere Out There, a source of daydreams. Was there a chance that I would now actually be able to see the racecourse? Could we drive past it? I asked Dean. And although it meant a bit of a detour, and although he may have been rather bemused by the desire of someone to see the place in winter, he didn't scoff (as Harry did) – he simply agreed to my request. It was a dreary afternoon: the light was wan, an evening chill was already in the air and a thin mist half-veiled everything. The racecourse came into view. Harry pointed out Tattenham Corner and spoke of low numbers being advantageous in races up to a mile. We drove past. And as I took in the desolate scene, as I saw the track, once sunlit and silks-bright, and the stands, once teeming and vibrant, now empty and silent in the cold mist, it was less disenchantment that I felt than a resurgence of an old obscure unease, the same that *A Sea Urchin, Held to Ransom* and certain frames in *Film Fun* had induced in me. It was more than an aversion to the forlorn. It was a disquiet that ran deeper.

I found Christmas at the Rectory very different from Christmas at 33 Danehill Road and at Edie's. Instead of the tree I had always known, silver tinsel, almost hidden by multicoloured baubles, Dean and Olivia had a real spruce which was hung only with festoons of gold, balls of red and orange, and candle lights of pinkish-red, which together less concealed the deep green they ornamented than emphasised it. As for the room decorations, instead of our Korkily Merry Xmas extravagance of polychrome paper and foil, with not a sprig of natural greenery to be seen (apart from that mistletoe in Edie's hall – probably put there by Uncle Jim himself), these consisted mainly of baskets of gilded pine cones and red and orange berries, and swags of holly and ivy that Olivia had gathered from the grounds, interspersed with only a few paper chains in harmonising colours.

Then there was what happened on Christmas Eve. Instead of watching telly in the evening as we did at Danehill Road,

Dean and Olivia attended as always a carol service at St Mark's, the village church. That year Olivia's father, her divorced sister, her sister's two teenaged sons and I went with them. The rest stayed at home. In that church we sat hunched against the cold, pulling our coats tighter as the candles guttered. Draughts knifed our ankles, as keenly as the voices of the choir in the minstrels' gallery cut through the candlewax- and old-oak-scented air. Many of the carols, parts of some of which, sung by the choir, were in Latin, I had never heard before: 'There is no rose of such virtue', 'Personent hodie', 'Tomorrow shall be my dancing day', 'In dulci jubilo'... To me they sounded tuneless, emaciated, boring, compared to what we shouted out at school, the memorable robust likes of 'Once in royal David's city' and 'God rest ye merry gentlemen' – although, as I've described, I found 'The holly and the ivy' something of a strange exception to these, nearer in spirit to what I was hearing on this occasion. As we walked home in the country dark, the sharp smells and muffled noises of a farmyard reaching us, Olivia remarked on how beautiful the service had been. Beautiful. I had found it, rather, with its chill, its hard wooden pews, its fitful candlelight and its relatively unmelodious, often incomprehensible carols, what I would have described later, when I was old enough to know the term, as austere. *But I pretended, not only to Olivia but to myself, that I had appreciated this 'beauty'.*

Then there was the Christmas afternoon walk, a traditional affair originally instituted by Olivia's father, which everyone except Lil and Edie embarked upon, even if in some cases with a reluctance that led to their turning back early. At home I'd imagined, on my solitary trips to the top of the garden, that such Christmas afternoon renunciations of befitting Indoors were rare, that I was unusual in undertaking them, rather as Harry, analysing racehorse form in depth, considered his cerebration as exceptional. But here were a whole gang of us walking into the countryside and not only that but every so often coming across others doing the same. I'd also imagined in the garden of 33 Danehill that, even if there were others who made excursions outdoors, they would, like me, not wish to prolong them overmuch. But this walk of ours, circular, taking us far beyond Kingsdon St Mary – in fact, right around Blackdown Copse – lasted well over an hour. Before we were even a quarter way round, I was tired of the unchanging vista of hedge, field and wood (despite the fact that the wood, 'low and threatening' beneath a 'hard steely sky', was patently the Wild Wood), and I couldn't wait to get back.

Even so, there was something about these strange new features of Christmas – the rigorous walk, the ascetic service, the reticent decorations – which, at the same time that it displeased and bored me, made a strange appeal to me. I sensed in a vague way that this ambivalent response was related to how I had felt when seeing a Greenline coach travelling through greenery, or when singing 'The holly and the ivy' or when reading of le grand Meaulnes embarking on his adventure in a desolate grove of firs.

As with the nebulous fear which certain experiences aroused in me, as with the faint melancholy I had experienced looking out over the playground on dog days, as with other cloudy feelings which pressed upon me, that ambivalence of mine towards the Rectory Christmas would recur over the coming years, and in response not simply to other Christmases of that kind but to so many other manifestations of the taste which that Christmas embodied.

Mosaic

How unforgettable was the moment when I found in a book, when I encountered *on the page*, there *in print* before me, the kinds of atmosphere and feeling of expectancy I had experienced myself but had not known at the time whether I was alone in experiencing. Now the thrill of discovering I wasn't alone, that there was at least one other who...

Olivia had introduced me to the world of books and now I'd become a voracious reader, one who swallowed all sorts of fare – though three kinds predominated. In the first place, I had joined Bexcray public library, which was not only to educate as well as to entertain me for so many years but also to charm me, in the way that all such detached peaceful greenery-embellished libraries charm the urban book-lover. And once a member, I'd begun gorging on the Boys' Adventure Stories section: *Treasure Island*, *Kidnapped*, the Lone Ranger, Biggles.

Then there were the books that Francophile Olivia had given me or lent me: *The Count of Monte Cristo*, *The Three Musketeers*, *The Little Prince*.

And finally, extending the lure of ludic digits and letters to that of the hidden clue, Dean had led me to a natural outgrowth of the brainteaser and the cryptic crossword: the detective story. As discerning in this matter as in so much else, Dean chose for me only the finest examples of the genre. He started with thoroughly play-fair challenges to the reader, exercises in pure logic: the early Ellery Queens. Next came apparently insoluble locked-room problems, exercises in lateral thinking: John Dickson Carrs. And then, and then, he produced the nonpareil, the most ingenious, the most poetic, the most mesmeric mystery story of all: D.E. Master's *Mosaic*.

Into the lives of many of us there has entered, at some time or another, *the* book. It is a book that seems to communicate directly, like no other, with something essential and precious within us, even though this something is usually at the time only vague and unrealised; a book that develops that dormant vision and in so doing changes our way of seeing the world; a book that in consequence can have as decisive an influence on us as any of the more obviously major events in our life; a book that, no matter how strong their rival claims, no matter how more profound they might be, no other books can or ever will displace. *The* book. (And permanently so. For even if changes in our personality, in our outlook, later cause us to turn away from that book, it will by that time have become over the years so fundamental a part of ourself that if, on the insistence of intellect, we tear it out of ourself, we then violate our very being.)

The occasion on which Dean introduced *the* book into my life – and so, unwittingly, changed it (for better? for worse?) – was one Easter Saturday at the Rectory. It was a balmy April morning – bathed in that soft spring light and warmth that seem to float deliciously among the very letters of the month's lovely name – and in the dining room the bay windows were open. I was sitting on the window seat, with nothing to do but gaze out over the garden. Olivia's tulips were in flower – a massed display, interestingly fringed or multi-petalled, and the rich colours of many variegated with green. She'd told me she always ordered them from a nursery, World of Tulips, and, dreamily idealising as ever, I'd seen this place as a great expanse of colour like that in Monet's paintings of Dutch tulip fields and tended by girls in lace caps and clogs. (Olivia had gardening in her blood. Her father had planted a large and beautiful garden at his place in Sussex; an aunt, Erica Hunter, had collected heathers from all over the world; and a second cousin, Pleione Bark-Chipping, was a noted orchid grower. How imposing I found Olivia's family. As well as the retired literary agent father and the plantswomen aunt and cousin, there was the amateur cellist mother, now dead, and the ENT consultant brother. It seemed, that world, very far removed from my own.)

As I lazily soaked up the sunlight that fell directly on me, as I luxuriated in early youth's glorious, all-too-temporary freedom from any responsibility whatsoever, I experienced the old familiar desire, the one I'd felt while riding on top of a trolleybus or listening to *The Wind in the Willows* on an afternoon of heat – and one similar to that induced by drink or approaching sleep – the desire to remain for ever in my present state of warm contented immobility. There hovered in my mind a vague and happy consciousness of the holiday: the Easter meeting at Kempton, with so many horses to choose from, their intriguing names on the racing page all bathed in that spring light in which I was now basking; the Easter fête that afternoon at the village school, promising competitive challenge (score more than twenty with three throws; guess the weight of the cake) and, who knew, a pretty girl who might look at you *in a certain way*... And this led me to re-experience an Easter feeling of old, an apprehension of an ideal form (one of the many such that the imagination keeps weaving, day in, day out, throughout our life). What I relived was how I used to feel reading an Easter issue of *Dandy* on a fine Good Friday morning at home. Lying in the long grass at the top of the garden, steeped in the sun's benediction, breathing in the subtle, faint, apple-sharp odour of vernal juices rising and volatilising in the warmth ('What is all this juice and all this joy?'), I would thrill to the promise of 'Grand *Easter* Number' above the title, to Korky's *Easter* escapade on the sunlit front page, to the *Easter*-bright primary colours in which it was portrayed. For it did seem, that page, that comic, truly saturated with Easter. A secular Easter, that is – the only kind I knew, in the same way that the secular Christmas was until recently the only kind I had known – one whose Good Friday, if it had a wonderful sonority to its name, possessed it with reference not to anything religious but simply to a welcome worldly holiday, to the allure of chocolate eggs, the Disney programme at the Regal, the fair on Bexcray Common. But more than all this, above and beyond it – as I obscurely apprehended something more than temporal – that front page seemed imbued with the spirit of some Easter of ideal form, neither secular nor religious. (It was similar to that spring of ideal form that was somehow, mysteriously, in a way not fully explicable by the words alone, distilled by the opening lines of a poem Olivia had read us, lines I loved to hear:

> Spring, the sweet Spring, is the year's pleasant king;
> Then blooms each thing, then maids dance in a ring,
> Cold doth not sting, the pretty birds do sing,
> Cuckoo, jug-jug, pu-we, to-witta-woo!)

Some Easter of ideal form. Fancy a *comic* breathing forth that. *Coo!* (as Eliot used marginally to note on rereading some of his magisterial essays). And I must say that seeing today one of those old issues of *Dandy*, I have to wonder at the power of the child's imagination which can, from no more than the somewhat sham superscription 'Grand Easter Number' (trumpeting what was merely, disappointingly, little else but the appearance in each strip of the stock beribboned egg) and the spring sunlight on a three-colour page, can, from no more than these, create something transcendent.

As I sat there, then, by the window, blissfully lost in the midst of an ideal Easter somehow projected from the usual worldly elements, Dean appeared and said, 'I've got another book for you.'

He was holding a fat paperback, one from his own company's list. A gentle breeze from the window played with his mane of dark hair and the strong sunlight exaggerated the pittedness of his skin. He handed me the book. The purple, lilac and old-rose cover, with the Spectrum rainbow in its upper right-hand corner, bore the title *Mosaic* and, below the author's name, two quotes. One read: 'A fiendish puzzle embedded deep within a city rhapsody...a breathtaking tour de force...' (I didn't know the meaning of this last phrase). The other: 'Quite simply, the greatest and the most beautiful mystery story ever written.'

I was often in the future to come across ludicrously overblown claims on the jackets of novels of every kind (never was an age so apparently blessed as ours with so very many works of virtual genius), claims that led me to waste too much money buying them and too much time trying to read them. But in the case of *Mosaic* I was soon to discover that what was vaunted on the cover was not hyperbole but the truth.

'Magic'

After they had fallen out on our summer holiday Lil and Edie failed, for the first time, to make up, and as is usually the case, the longer the estrangement was wilfully and self-piercingly persisted in by both parties, the more difficult it became for the untreated wounds to be healed. By the time our holiday came round again they still weren't having any truck with each other, so we had bed and breakfast that year at a boarding house. It stood on the eastern outskirts of Sandbay. Harry had insisted that, despite the risk of our bumping into Edie in the town, we shouldn't go to another resort: 'I like Sandbay and I don't see why we should let her stop us going there.'

Jayjay House, large for its kind, was run by an elderly Scottish couple, known to the regulars as Jamie and Jeanie. Jamie had the sort of long, dark, gaunt face – black bushy eyebrows, deep-set eyes, sunken cheeks, blue lantern jaw – that I associated with Saturday-morning-cinema castle caretakers of dour mien, who were usually up to no good. Not that Jamie was dour; in fact, no man could have been more amiable. Indeed, some might have thought him excessively so. We never passed him in the lobby or a corridor, for example, without his greeting us with as joyous a chuckle as if we'd just told him we'd made sure Jayjay House was booked solid for the next five years. And whenever he held a door open for us or gave us precedence in any other way, it was not the graceless Harry or Lil who thanked him but he who *heartfeltly* thanked us (and certainly with no trace of irony), an affable absurdity shared by his tiny, bird-like wife, who, every time she had dealings with a guest, kept trilling, in a high-pitched quaver replete with geniality, no matter what was going on (even if it were a guest's complaint): '…'kyou…'kyou…'kyou…'

Friendly though Jamie was, however, I found his presence uncongenial at table, where he served the breakfast which his wife cooked. His perpetually oily skin at this meal made even less appealing his hollow-eyed, dark-jawed face, and this, together with his showily displayed horsy grey false teeth, somehow made even more unpalatable to me the pale, undercooked, greasy egg, bacon and sausage he set before me with his usual show of overjoyed indebtedness. (Of course, young as I was and brought up in the underclass tradition of accepting what's dished out to you, I didn't realise I could have returned this food to be crisped up.) When I saw not only Harry and Lil but all the regulars attacking Jamie and Jeanie's anaemic, oleaginous fare with relish, and even in some cases, upon catching the eye of Jamie, signalling their appreciation, in mid-mouthful, with firmly grasped, raised, vertical knife and fork (a kind of extension of the thumbs-up sign, and a double one at that), I guiltily felt that I was indeed the 'finicky little sod' Harry and Lil called me.

At the end of our visit Jamie indicated to Harry, with chuckle and 'Thank you', the guest book with its awaiting 'Comments' column. I looked at what the most recent departures had said. I saw 'Nice one Jamie' and 'Spot on you rascalls you'. And then, higher up, a bouquet that took me aback: 'Magic'. *Magic*? This was a term I'd mentally reserved only for certain mysteriously beautiful things, separate from the everyday. And here it was being slapped on to a week at Jamie and Jeanie's, a week swimming in fulsomeness and oil! I'd always subconsciously believed, I suppose, that everyone used the same key words to describe the same key experiences. Now, for the first time, I realised just how mistaken I'd been.

Against nature

The degree to which being shut away from a fine day outdoors lowered my spirits in childhood and youth I now find remarkable. The call of the sunlight was so imperative then, to be out in it was so obviously right, that to be sitting instead in some gloomy room seemed to me to be totally *against nature*. Even the library, despite all its riches, could not escape this aversion. Both the great adults' and the children's lending rooms received no sun – though for most of the year I scarcely noticed this, when, artificially lit, artificially heated, the library was a cosy haven. Then how inviting the tiered books; how suspenseful the dry smell of the filing cards as you pulled out a drawer to search for a particular author; how soothing the library silence. But in glorious weather, when you became conscious of how disagreeably cool and sunless and deserted the library was, those books, that smell, that silence lost their charm, you wanted to leave as soon as possible. They seemed in their withdrawal from what glowed and throbbed outside as irrelevant and forlorn as that other perpetually sunless part of the library, which you could see beyond a short passageway off the children's room: a mystifying, ever-empty miniature garden of shrub-surrounded grass, looking, through the glass-panelled door, like one of those old disregarded botanical display cases in the corner of a provincial museum. So constant, though, was my search for reading thrills that no type of weather could keep me from the library for long, and in fact it was on days of high summer, when books were less in demand, that I found at last on the shelves certain long-sought-after Ellery Queens and John Dickson Carrs usually out on loan. But the cut-off-from-summer room, the deserted aisles, then gave to those detective novels a strange, slightly unpleasant new cast. They may have held out the same promise of mystery and ingenuity as before, but nonetheless this was now overlaid by a faint melancholy, as was their particular appearance, staidly, stoutly library-edition-bound in dull green or brown, and their particular smell, somewhat stale (appearance and smell which had been part of their charm in winter). Today, years later, those discoveries of Queen and Carr on such empty hot days return to me in a brief burst of joyous aching sadness – only to sink back soon after, like those one-off Boxing Day guests at Aunt Edie's, into an oblivion from which they will perhaps never re-emerge.

On one occasion I was away from school sick on a rare summer's day of splendour. Although little light of any kind ever entered our back room, I could discern the character of the day from what, as I lay on the put-u-up, I could see of the end of the garden: the Impressionist gold and blue of the sunlit crown of the apple tree and the sky. It reinforced what Lil had said to me before she'd gone shopping: 'It's a lovely day. Much too nice to be indoors.' She had 'as a favour' allowed me to listen to some of the old records, leaving them and the gramophone on the floor beside me. Bitter-sweet at any time, because they spoke with wistful melodiousness of my mother, who had owned most of them, and also of a faraway age, of the Long Weekend and the War, in which gaiety and anxiety, love and loss, were inextricably entwined, they were now, those in the main danceband recordings of popular numbers of the Thirties and Forties, as I played them on this afternoon of endless birdsong-punctuated sunlit hours outside, depressing – or, rather (for their actual notes were no different from what they had always been, from what I'd found enchanting on a winter's evening), it was listening to them that had become depressing. Those records, relics simultaneously of a lost mother and of a vanished era, now suddenly seemed, in a dingy, slightly chilly room shut away from the rich light and warmth beyond, futile, *unbearably alien to the day*.

To experience that feeling, I did not even have to be the one who was cut off from such a day. Occasionally, when I was making my way down some road in the neighbourhood, pleasurably soaking up the warm sunlight, inhaling the scent of gardens, I would pass a house in which someone was sitting in a north-facing front room never visited by the sun, a dim grotto. And whatever it was they were doing – reading, say, or watching television – seemed on such a day unutterably doleful, hopeless, *wrong*.

(Sometimes, when my route took me, on some tender summer's afternoon, through one of the leafier, more pleasant residential areas of Bexcray, I became aware of the immemorial nature of those sun-drenched suburban roads and avenues around me. The piebald pavements, the clumps of lavender, softly defined in the full sun, offering me over low garden walls their perfumed spikes, the stillness of the chestnuts, planes, laburnums and robinias beneath which I passed, the assorted bright dyes of the tea roses, the quieter rinsed pinks and blues of the hydrangeas on their bronzed foliage, the deep shadow cast by a privet – I knew that these typical dreamy-summer's-afternoon elements of Acacia Avenue, as residential suburbia would later be disparagingly docketed, had all, with minor variants, long predated my existence and would long survive it. This knowledge, that some poetic youth of Edwardian times, or of the Twenties or Thirties, many years before I was around, would have imbibed on some somnolent July afternoon or other more or less the same light and shade, the same warmth, the same sights, the same atmosphere, that I was now drinking in, and that, at some time in the next century, when I had returned to not being around, other such strollers would imbibe them, during summer after summer after summer, this awareness lent these scenes an even greater solidity than that furnished them by the houses, trees and dense shadows my eyes took in, a temporal solidity that reinforced the spatial one and that in so doing deepened the effect these scenes produced on me.)

I would even, somewhat absurdly it seems to me now, be troubled by the same feeling that to incarcerate oneself on a lovely day was à rebours when at the cinema I watched a character forsake some sunlit scene in which fountains sparkled and flowers glowed and enter a house or hotel or office block. When that happened, the intendedly interesting conversation that took place there, whether conspiratorial or romantic or amusing, was rendered by the shadowy room through whose window, beyond the talking heads, could be glimpsed the splendour of the day outside, was rendered, that conversation by that room – as the pages of a waiting-room magazine are rendered by the nervewracking suspense before a critical appointment – remote, dolorous, of no account, surreal.

An absolute shower

I can't say that I featured among the academic stars of Sir Bernard Croucher Grammar School (founded in 1938 by a wealthy Bexcray scrap merchant of that name). But then, to be fair to myself, hardly any pupils did. There is a fairly widespread belief that all grammar schools are 'learning centres of excellence' and that all those from the lower classes who attend them are eager to seize the opportunity to escape their background and to go on to higher things, a zeal in which they are just as eagerly encouraged at home. I wouldn't know whether that is a reasonably accurate picture today but it certainly wasn't in my time, and there could have been few more melancholy demonstrations of this than our school and its pupils. I wouldn't, in trying to convey some impression of that place, go so far as Martin Amis who described one grammar school he attended as 'practically Broadmoor' or the playwright Ian Curteis who spoke of his own as 'a tide of barbarity', but the suicide of three masters and two boys at Sir Bernard Croucher while I was there does I think give some indication of its general quality, tone, style, call it what you will.

Take the staff. If another writer, Roger Scruton, remembers that at his grammar school 'my physics master...introduced me to Beethoven' and 'the chemistry master...to Heine and Goethe', I remember that, rather less elevated in aim, their counterparts at Sir Bernard Croucher, 'Droner' Hill and 'Nasty' Naylor, introduced me to, respectively, catalepsy and an excruciating, previously unsuspected new physical punishment.

And what of the boys of Sir Bernard Croucher, what of them? Their academic bent, I mean. Well, in the year that I was in, if you left aside Clifford Jeavons, the Boy Genius ('Wouldn't you say so rigorous an argument smacks of a reductio ad absurdum, sir?'), who had his being on some plane so stratospheric that we simply ignored him, and Gavin Warlett, the Swotpot ('Could you give us a bit more homework on those theorems, sir?'), who was encouraged to study hard by his NALGO-official parents and was, I'm afraid to say, regularly dusted up by some of my fellow-pupils in an exceedingly unpleasant way, and perhaps Mike Lawrence and Dave Smith, B-Minus types who made an effort of sorts but well within the bounds of what was generally considered tolerable, if you left aside those, the rest of us were what Terry-Thomas used to call an absolute shower. For my own part, only showing any marked ability at art and sport, in class dreaming away, at home radio- and later telly-soused and as a result only feebly engaging with homework, I did no more than the others in that ruck of under-achievers in my year (not untypical of the school as a whole) to lift myself out of it.

Ah, Danehill Road...

After I'd heard that Gershwin piano music in the street one hot afternoon and recognised the piece Olivia had played I'd eagerly made enquiries and eventually discovered who the pianist was and what exactly he was playing. The record was unobtainable in this country but Dean ordered one from America for me and and I treasured it as I did my copy of *Mosaic*. (Some time later I heard for the first time the lyrics of 'That Certain Feeling', when it was sung show-tune moderato on the radio by a ho-hum husband and wife duo. I discovered that the words, of what was a love song, were quite banal, Ira having an off-day. A disappointment, but not a great one. By that time the wistful sweetness of the melody as I had first heard it played in Gershwin's own étude-like piano transcription and the then mystery of the title were both too fixed in my soul to be unsettled by listening to the original song.)

Since then I'd heard and fallen for two famous Gershwin orchestral works. *Rhapsody in Blue*: glorious, rich, beautifully proportioned melodies again. (And only loosely connected though these may be, and even to some extent interchangeable and scarcely fusing to create an organic whole – an 'episodic, fragmented, mosaiclike' work, to quote one musicologist – they have nonetheless ensured the piece an immortality that numberless compositions of faultless structure have failed to win.) And the *Concerto in F*: its highlight a section of the slow movement in which a stopped trumpet plays a noble blues melody, as serene and pure as a high clear blue sky, and then, taking over from this, the typically virile piano strikes out, at an almost insolently slow, deliberate tempo, on a bold new tune. I'd saved up and ordered from Lovat & Albery, the music shop in Queen Street, a record that included both pieces. Now, early one Saturday morning, I set off from home to collect it.

It was an autumn morning of frost, mist and sun. Before me in the bright haze, descending the slope of Danehill Road, a double file of silhouettes, giants with hair on end: pollarded wych elms, stationed at regular intervals along the white-powdered pavements, dissolving, with distance, like the yellowbrick terraces, to wraiths. Coursing through the frozen air a sudden brief warm current: the scent of bacon frying, tangy, convivial, inviting. From some opened door a familiar melody: the signature tune of *Housewife's Choice*, spurting out like a grapefruit its bright breakfast-time droplets, jaunty, reassuring, all's-right-with-the-world. And from higher up the road a muffled hum-rattle-and-clink: the milk float, sounding the cosiest of all suburbia's vaporous-morning music. A happiness flooded me, a subdued excitement, an *early-morning-frosty-misty-sunlit-Danehill-Road* feeling... At the bottom of the road, along Mountsfield Avenue, the mist lay thicker. And as I turned left into it I was immediately blinded by what seemed to be an incandescent golden smoke, the transfiguration of the mist by the great invisible sun straight ahead, a smoke through which a short distance away soft orbs of red and orange and green (modest miniatures of the sun) glowed in sequence, in which, beyond the changing lights, there was just visible the smudged golden-pink of a bus *going places* (trolleys had, alas, disappeared some years earlier), and into whose dazzle, further beyond still, the avenue was so absorbed that it disappeared altogether. And as I experienced all this, and as I was vaguely aware of around me Danehill Road, Mountsfield Avenue, Randall's newsagents, the Prince Albert, Artillery Way, aware of the particular route number of the bus, aware of the oddly sited pillar box just around the corner, aware of *Knockout* on the evenings of such days, aware of a certain indefinable atmosphere permeating all this that I knew nowhere else, I felt that old Bexcray-boy feeling again, I felt that, although I had known, had stayed in, other places – Richborough, Kingsdon St Mary, Sandbay – and although I had appreciated, even in some cases loved, what they had to offer, it was, if I got right down to it, Bexcray that was in me, in my soul, I felt once more that it was ordained I live my boyhood, youth, young manhood here and nowhere else. Ah, Danehill Road, I start in memory once more down your slope of terraces on a frosty, misty, sunlit autumn morning, I turn once more into Mountsfield Avenue, I head once more for the town through the golden haze.

Down Rosewood Road, then Chatham Street, into the High Street. The familiar shops now diaphanously veiled, some with lights on already. At the crossroads a right turn, into Queen Street. Lovat & Albery. Pianos, guitars, recorders, scores. It was with that pure, keen, almost painful joy of anticipation that only the young can feel that I asked the assistant for the record, took possession of it, hared home with it, placed it on the turntable before I'd even taken my coat off. It was with that obsessiveness that only the young bring to listening to music that I played it over and over again.

The book

At 668 pages in the paperback edition, *Mosaic* was a considerable read, but *The Count of Monte Cristo* had given me practice in tackling hefty tomes, and anyway I was entranced from the start, right from the opening paragraph set at torrid noon in Indigo City, an American metropolis athrob with *something about to happen.* Entranced, as I've already indicated, in a particular, amazed way. For the poetry that suffused the book, though more metropolitan-exotic (skyscrapers, streetcars, fantasias of neon) than any that I had known, nonetheless had so much in common with the urban poetry that I *had* apprehended. And in the same way that I had imagined events in certain other books as taking place in more or less suitable settings from my own experience, so when in *Mosaic* I read of, for example, the kidnapping of a character about to board a streetcar at dusk, my subconscious, hooking on to the soft warm twilight and the sparking-poled vehicle, set the incident in that rosy trolleybus dusk from my own childhood. This literary response to the poetry of the city or town meant the more to me because until then I had come across it in few writers, and even then merely as the occasional lyrical note. The most I would catch in them would be no more than charming snatches of song (such as 'a line of violet roofs and lemon lamps') when compared with Master's rhapsodies, so beautifully scored.

And then, too, the mystery with which the poetry was seemingly interfused, which sang softly, teasingly beneath every page, reminded me of my own intermittent sense of that special something ever about to reveal itself: so many skies, skylines, lights, signs, names, numbers, atmospheres appeared to be *significant*, so that when Rex Merchant arrived at the Pendragon Building on what was to prove a fateful evening and saw it silhouetted against what the author called, sending a frisson of troubled pleasure through me, an 'unearthly' sky of unnaturally bright green bruised with purple cloud, and when Bernie Law, waiting for Rex on Orange Street, found his gaze magnetised by the cerise neon of the 99 Club winking on and off, you felt that existence itself seemed to be signifiers of the secret, clues to its solution almost.

The characters who played out that great adventure were as strange and memorable as the poetry and the puzzle. Who could forget Rex, with his dark and intense gaze, his fur coat, limp and stick, his throwaway dicta, his kindness and cruelty, his great secret? Who could forget his mistress, the beautiful, quick-witted young lawyer Bella Ormandy; his minder, the Schubert-loving black belt Joaquín Ax; his benefactress, the virtually insane Duchess of Worcester; the mafioso Tony Torino; the sly, mountainous, corrupt police chief Reinhard O'Brien? And how could I forget the narrator, who kept trying to figure out what was going on, the handsome young writer Mark Estes, with whom, undoubtedly like every other young male reader, I identified?

Over the weeks of continuing enraptured reading at home (Lil: 'Have you got your head in that bloody book again?') I was torn between two irreconcilables: on the one hand I desperately wanted to reach the end of the story to discover the truth underlying what was so mysterious, yet on the other I desperately wanted never to reach the end because I realised sadly, with an early intuition, that once I had finished the book, once this magical reading experience was over, I would never find another like it.

And when, finally, the solution was revealed…! Oh, the thrill of it. The astonishing pattern, all unsuspected by me, which, once it was disclosed, invested so much in the book with a breathtaking new meaning. And from a purely technical point of view, how masterly had been the plotting that had achieved this, how exquisitely concealed the clues, all in such generous abundance, all so fair to the reader, and all together providing him with the keys to the mystery, if he had but had the wit to recognise them. There had been, for instance – as just one example among so many – that incident when Rex, in police custody, had been allowed by O'Brien to return the short story which Mark had given him to comment on. I for one had failed to see the significance of Rex's single, harsh, scribbled comment at the end of it: 'Improbable, son.' Despite the earlier evidence of Rex and Mark's anagrammatic games, I had failed to see – perhaps because that evidence was, with Master's usual artistry, so naturally, smoothly incorporated into the story – that what seemed to be a literary verdict, which initially depressed Mark, was in fact a message, that it indicated the thirteenth-century windows in Canterbury Cathedral known as Poor Man's Bible (Rex, like his creator, had a love and knowledge of stained glass). If I had seen this, I might then have remembered that Rex, in showing a reproduction of these windows to Mark, in company that had included O'Brien, had drawn his attention to one particular panel which showed three biblical characters sowing seed and had pointed out to him the remarkable double coincidence that Tony Torino's chauffeur (supposedly in O'Brien's pay) not only bore a striking resemblance to one of the sowers but also bore his name, Daniel. I would then have realised that this driver was the informer in Torino's organisation whose identity Rex had for some time been trying secretly to convey to Mark, as Mark was aware. (And there had been a second chance to latch on to it when, face to face with Mark, who stood outside his cell with beside him the habitually smiling, self-assured police chief, Rex laughed at every question and comment and, when Mark asked why, simply replied, to reinforce his written message, 'O'Brien's aplomb.' I had missed that too. But, buried in the narrative and not isolated and pointed up as it is here, all such cryptography could easily elude you.) If I had brought to light those tesserae, and the ones adjoining, which were discoverable from the marvellous Christmas clue and the one concerning the yellow Packard in the mist, equally fair, that might, *might*, have enabled me to glimpse *part* of the fabulous mosaic of the overall solution, and from there…

The poetry, the puzzle, the characters. And that was not all. Quintessentially American in its flair and pace, and with its diatonic excitement and purposefulness underlaid by chromatic mystery and longing, *Mosaic* seemed to me a literary approximation to that Gershwin music with which I had fallen in love. The correspondences I felt between them were such that in my *Mosaic* reveries I would, for example, picture the fare of a cab in the novel as Gershwin – brilliant, famous, but overshadowed so young by fast-approaching death – on his way to one of his shows, and I would hear his music, its vigour and optimism sometimes transposing to questioning (and, who knew, premonition?), as the theme music of the book. That added to *Mosaic* another allurement, one not intrinsic to it, one bestowed upon it by myself. (This is habitual in some, this daydream heightening of one art with another. For instance, if, at the time I started listening to serious music, I heard, say, the mysterious rustic shimmer of Ravel's *Le Tombeau de Couperin* on the radio, there might come to my mind the Cézanne print in the Rectory dining room, *Road at Chantilly*, with its tunnel of trees leading to and framing a country house, and this might summon up for me how the elusive manor house in *Le Grand Meaulnes* might have looked on a summer's day – to the reciprocal enrichment of all three, so that music, painting, book all swam together, the sunlight of France, the landscapes of France, the lyrical genius of France all fused in one heady distillation, *idealisation*, of the spirit of that country.)

Finally, there was the sorcerer's prose. On my first reading, I was not of an age truly to appreciate it. Actually, I never even distinguished it from the book's other qualities. They all merged into a single magic. (To convey this, though, when I urged family and friends to read *Mosaic*, all I could come up with was such schoolboy inadequacies as 'It's fantastic!' or 'It's great!' Perhaps I oversold it to Danny, because it was with amazement and disappointment that I listened to his verdict on the book: he was sorry but he couldn't see anything so special about it and had given it up about a quarter-way through.) It was only later that I discerned the precise elements that went to make up the quality of that prose: its easy fusion of the literary and the demotic, its sustained lucidity, its sure rhythms.

Yes, how I fell for that book! I knew of course that it had a legion of fans (well, there was even a D.E. Master Society). But I believed that my affinity with its author was more intimate, more profound, than those others' affinity with him. I felt that he was speaking to me, for me, personally. Such is the effect *the* book has on all its devotees.

Donna

Lil had patched things up with Edie – thus continuing the pattern I'd known for as long as I could remember – and we were to resume staying at her place when we went on holiday. Good, that meant no more Jayjay House, no more Jamie, no more eggs and sausages 'palely loitering'. I could now echo the words of one Jayjay guest: 'Nice one!'

We took our first holiday back at Edie's. And on it my daydream of falling for a pretty young girl there *came true at last* – though, as is always the case, it happened differently from how I'd imagined…and, too, it ended in a troubling way…

When the weather was good we usually spent part of the day on Sandbay beach. We always settled on exactly the same spot on those extensive sands – to the left of an ice cream kiosk, in front of the Starlight Ballroom – just as some railway commuters settle in exactly the same seat every morning. (And Harry and Lil became annoyed, as those commuters do, if they ever found that place occupied already, since it doesn't take long for what was originally selected utterly arbitrarily to become the fittest of all possible choices and then for the proprietary instinct, as ever, to assert itself over this 'ideal' spot.) Another family, a couple from Dagenham with a daughter a couple of years older than me, encamped in the same area and became regular beach neighbours. Harry, who with strangers slipped easily into a personable manner, got chatting to the man and discovered they'd both once driven for the same haulage company. The two families became quite matey, and I swam with the girl, Donna. She was blonde, quite pretty and already beginning to fill out her swimsuit, and after a few days I'd developed a painful crush on her.

It so happened that my birthday that year fell on the day before our holiday ended. Edie was making a cake and Ivor was going to arrange a few games and, oh no, do a bit of conjuring. On impulse, knowing that with only one full day of the holiday left there was no guarantee I would see Donna again, I invited her to my party. After some surprise, some hesitation, she accepted, and to my relief Ivor and Edie didn't object.

Already a crush – but now I was *felled* on the instant by Donna as she walked into the room. From the artless, lightly tanned, sand-encrusted, tousle-haired girl of the beach she had been transformed overnight into what I considered then a beautiful, sophisticated, stylishly dressed young woman: hair frizzed, face powdered, eyelids china blue as her eyes, lashes dark with mascara, lips glistening strawberry-ice-cream pink, almost obscenely tight dress and high heels matching those lips in colour and sheen. I was not quite stupid enough to give in to what I wanted to do, which was to gaze at her the whole evening, in an act of worship performed at as close quarters as possible – but my actual behaviour so betrayed what I was feeling that I might as well have yielded to that urge. My burning glances shot away much too quickly when detected, my hand shook visibly when I passed her a plate of sandwiches, some of my comments to her (such as thanking her for her present, a book, *Roddy Strang, Captain of Football*) I had to halt halfway through from breathlessness, and, most obvious giveaway of all in a healthy boy, I had no appetite.

Donna was friendly to me, as she had been on the beach, but I sensed in her nothing of the infatuation that was choking me and that filled me with a desperate longing to kiss the gleaming lips of this the most desirable young woman the world had ever known. I unhappily wondered too whether someone of such hitherto unsuspected sophistication hadn't been expecting a party to mean something a little more lively than this tame family do, whether she hadn't dressed up in anticipation not of Uncle Ivor's games and 'sleight-of-hand' but of some music and dancing and a few more young people like herself.

The time came for her to leave. No, I thought, she couldn't possibly walk out of my life like that. I insisted on accompanying her to the sea front, from where she would catch a bus back to her family's boarding house. I hoped to summon up courage to attempt a kiss and to suggest we write to each other. We walked to the bus stop. It had been an overcast day, too cold for the beach, and the evening was as dreary. Dusk was falling, the sky was dark with raincloud, the Sandbay wind was throwing one of its periodic tantrums and the waves were crashing in. As we waited on the almost deserted sea front, we felt the occasional smart of spray on our skins. We were both shivering. It wasn't exactly all systems go for a diffident boy – or even a lifelong roué for that matter – to make an amatory move.

Either the bus was late or Edie, no improvement on Lil in such matters, had got the service times wrong. After a while, Donna said, with that common-sense thinking and diction that come to girls so much earlier than to boys (though today her decision, in that spot, might not be thought so sensible): 'You get on back. No sense in both of us catching cold. Thanks for inviting me.'

Perhaps I sensed that she had no real interest in seeing me again, perhaps I just lacked enough bottle, but I didn't ask if we could write to each other, I didn't even express the hope we would see each other the following summer. I just sheepishly thanked her for coming, said goodbye and turned away.

For the rest of the evening, and as I lay in bed that night, I suffered all the usual pangs of the lovesick. But I was afflicted by another feeling, too. A return of the familiar obscure fear. It came upon me as I pictured Donna waiting at the bus stop. It had nothing to do with an anxiety for her safety (I was unburdened at that age and at that time with the 'Donna was last seen...' forebodings never far from the adult's mind today). It was all to do with the vision of that modern, prettified, dolled up girl alone on a cold, darkening promenade pounded on its other side by a hostile sea. It was all to do with her cosmetically heightened, scented, pink-garbed person, such a short time before ensconced in the warmth of Edie's place, now being stung by that chill, timeless, implacable element that seethed and crashed such a short distance away.

But I didn't know exactly why I found this image so horrid, I couldn't, before I eventually drifted off to sleep, understand why it filled me with quite such unease.

Messages

An epithet one critic had applied to Master stuck in my mind, as characterisations of one's faves often do. He called him the Great Sorcerer. Certainly, I can only compare my experience of reading *Mosaic* to a journey through an enchanted forest. And one which affected from then on the way I saw the world around me. But hadn't I myself, at privileged moments, already on occasion seen the world in a magical light? Yes, and although it is said of certain books – of which *Mosaic* was undoubtedly one – that they can bestow on the reader a new vision of the world, perhaps that is not strictly accurate. Doesn't there have to pre-exist between author and reader, before the latter has read a word, some sort of communion of spirit, some sort of shared vision (even if unequally shared)? Even so, it is only by the author giving eloquent and exact expression to what had previously been in the reader only mute divination that the reader finds, like someone for whom an eye operation improves his clouded sight, that that vision he shared to some extent has been amplified, purified, enriched. And after having had his vision enhanced in this way, the reader may forget after a while what the exact nature of that vision was beforehand, may even be deluded into imagining that he could at a pinch have written the book, or one very similar, himself – if he had had sufficient motivation…or opportunity…or time…or…

Of course, I realised that no more than in Chesterton were some of the seemingly meaningful poetries of *Mosaic* – the unearthly yellow-green sky, for instance, the winking red light, the promissory gold-embroidered snowdrift – truly significant, integral to the mystery. They had simply been more of the Great Sorcerer's tricks. Just as a stage illusionist makes use of stunning props to intensify the drama of his performance, to fool the audience into thinking that those props are intrinsic to the astounding feat taking place, so in the same way Master, enlisting equally stunning props, such as that sky, that light, that snow, intensified the drama of his story, made what was strictly speaking extraneous to the mystery appear essential to it. And as for those elements that had actually been significant, such as the hidden anagrams of Poor Man's Bible and the cerise 99 Club sign and the yellow Packard in the mist, that significance pertained to their being pieces of a design that, though ingenious, was no more than man-made. The messages quivering in various scenes throughout the book were, whenever they were actually messages and not the mirages of such, certainly not of that kind which in privileged moments the young seem to see throbbing round about them and to be on the point of deciphering, were not immanent fragments of some profound transcendental truth. No, they had served merely to unlock a puzzle that was in essence, and *necessarily* so as a man-made puzzle, no different from that of all other mystery stories: earthbound. Far more clever than them it might be, far more atmospheric, far more beautiful, but when all was said and done it still boiled down into the same familiar prosaic criminal elements that they did: a nefarious scheme, false identities, disguises, detection, retribution.

Even so, long after I had finished reading *Mosaic*, the sense of a greater enigma than that which had been resolved in its pages continued to permeate the book in memory. It sustained in me, *just about*, that old natural cabbalistic perception of the world that had been so strong in me from earliest childhood but that had waned a little in recent years. The skies, the lights, the atmospheres in the book that seemed to be on the point of revealing some hidden meaning of which they were the beautiful messengers made me explore again in memory those I had known myself; and, in that category of elements more obviously capable of yielding a meaning not just denotative but connotative, namely names and numbers, those in the book that did have a concealed significance revived in me the intuition that, at privileged moments, certain of them in one's own life, transfigured from the everyday to the seemingly numinous, might be further ciphers in some great overall message that was waiting to be decoded, the intuition that, as Baudelaire put it, all of the Creation was hieroglyphic.

If I finished *Mosaic* as one bewitched, I also felt a dreadful sense of loss in the knowledge that that wonderful reading adventure was over. I knew that I would go back to the book and delight in it again, perhaps many times, but I also knew that I could never relive the rapture of my first experience of it, when the journey ahead stretched fresh and unknown before me. What was more, whereas many who have fallen in love with a book can look forward to discovering the author's other works, I already knew that Master was, like di Lampedusa, one of a rare few among the literary elite: a one-book man. Having come to writing late and taken many years to produce his masterpiece, he had outlived its publication by only eighteen months. And although he had planned a sequel, he had left behind only notes for it, even more tantalising cryptic than Dickens's for *Edwin Drood*.

So began a search on my part for a work that would not be that dissimilar to Master's, that would satisfy, if only partly, the hunger for more that his had aroused in me.

'Lovely colours, look'

Always, like most young people, separating out so much of life into discrete, distinct substances and packaging each in its own clearly labelled, sealed container, I had placed Harry in one whose list of ingredients read: driving HGVs, gambling, boozing, smoking, rowing with Lil, reading the *Warp*, seeing the occasional film, watching TV. And that was that. No trace elements of anything else.

So when one Sunday evening I came home from the rec and found Harry reading a book that was obviously neither the wallpapering nor the lawnmowing magnum opus, and when I saw that the book was an *art* book and that it was *a profusely illustrated study of Gauguin*, I felt the sudden disorientation of the person who puts on a pair of those psychological-experiment spectacles that frighteningly turn everything upside down. I'm not saying that, in approaching Harry and his book once I'd taken in the title, I actually inched and groped towards him, but I imagine the expression on my face was not much different to that of one fearfully trying to cope with finding the ceiling beneath him. And it was in a kind of daze that I heard issue from him the comment: 'This one of the sands is lovely colours, look.'

I was as lost for words as I'd been at school when Mr Willis asked me, when my turn came, to speak for exactly one minute on Ballet, starting *now*.

It was true that my confident categorisation of my foster-parents had been a little disturbed once before when I'd heard Lil, who I'd never believed had any interest in football, make a not unknowledgeable comment about a match to Danny – in other words, when I saw in the container that bore her name an ingredient that should not have been there. But that incident hadn't really registered much of a reading on the fixed-category-shaking scale.

A little stronger had been the tremor I occasionally experienced at the cinema when some American big-city hood, some ruthless hardmouth, some urban man in extremis – who, no commuter, spent almost all his time in an entirely inorganic habitat of concrete, steel and glass and whose mental world was surely an exclusive one of bank heists, bars, crap joints and the rest – suddenly, in his so-befitting arid city prison, spoke of, showed he was *aware of the existence of*, a blackbird, say, or a rose, or, more than that, actually *expressed an interest in* one of those representatives of the natural world. That – in those days before I was aware of the Birdman of Alcatraz or the horticultural mafioso – was something in the nature of a small quake. But all that was as nothing compared to the matter of *Harry and Gauguin*.

I sometimes pondered afterwards on the mystery of how Harry had got hold of that book which *he had no right to have in his keeping*. That he had bought it from a bookshop or borrowed it from a library could be dismissed out of hand: he would no more have thought of entering either than he would an opera house. That he had acquired it through his job, in the manner he had acquired the 'surplus' cartons of cigarettes he sometimes brought home, wasn't feasible either: studies of Gauguin and the like, surplus or not, surely didn't feature in the loads he carried (did they, I wondered, in any HGV driver's?). So. It was a mystery indeed, deeper by far than the other one about Harry and books, why and how he had got hold of the wallpapering and lawnmowing tomes. And, even more than that enigma, to which I would at least come up with one or two possible, if far-fetched, answers, the Case of the Disturbing Gift was, as the result of a major change in our family life when I got around to investigating it, to prove insoluble.

But, vexing though it might later be, that mystery took a back seat to the fact that, regardless of how it came to pass, Harry was actually sitting in our little back room holding that book in his hands, was actually looking at its plates, perhaps even reading the text, and exclaiming 'This one of the sands is lovely colours, look'. That was major quake stuff, a reading way off the scale.

Master

Naturally enough, after falling in love with *Mosaic*, I wanted to find out as much as possible about its creator, to find out what sort of man it was who had written such a beautiful, ingenious and engrossing book. In other words, I was under that illusion – to which the young are particularly prone – that in an artist's life we can discover the same essence that has thrilled us in his work.

Bexcray library had in stock one of the biographies. Devouring it, I discovered that Dominic Edwin Master was born in 1893, the only child of an English surgeon and an American actress. He was educated at St Paul's and Trinity College,

Cambridge, from which he graduated, in Modern and Medieval Languages, on the eve of the Great War. Having served as a subaltern on the Western Front, he turned his back on a conventional career and spent some time – first in London, then on the Continent – writing poetry (very little of it published) and occasional articles, doing odd translation work or simply bumming around. In 1923 he emigrated to America. There two cousins asked for his help in setting up and running an arts magazine. But this failed after only a year, and Master, unable to support himself by his writing and translating, eventually secured a job as an editor at Scribners. There he met his wife, the Dutch-born illustrator Rosa Levy. He became a minor figure – though one noted for his wit – on the New York artistic and social scene. In 1928 he published a translation of fairy tales from the German, a book 'vividly if somewhat eccentrically' illustrated by his wife. Two years later his marriage broke up. He hit the bottle in a big way and couldn't hold down his job at Scribners. Then a substantial inheritance on the death of his father suddenly made it unnecessary for him to work; he dried out and settled down to write at last the book which he had conceived many years before and had never stopped planning and making notes for. When it appeared in 1937 *Mosaic* was immediately acclaimed as a tour de force. Eighteen months later, at the age of only forty-five, Master died of a stroke.

And that, basically, was it. The vision that had so entranced me during my reading of *Mosaic* was merely glimpsed in the biography, and then only rarely. The first occasion was when an early sensitivity by Master to the poetry of the town was revealed: a descriptive piece from his St Paul's schooldays that hymned Kensington High Street on a bright summer morning, a moving first sketch of a scene that would later be fully and splendidly orchestrated in *Mosaic*. Of other sketches the biographer had supplied only one tantalisingly brief example, an extract from one of Master's many notebooks. It was a picture of New York under snow on a winter's afternoon (as he saw it from Lemmon & Greenstock, the greengrocers of strangely apt ownership which he patronised). This was the raw material from which he fashioned the celebrated Christmas snow scene in the novel (incorporating *that* clue). I was sure there must be in the notebooks many more such descriptions that had been integrated into the mystery – and I could only wish that they had all been quoted in the life. All the biographer had had to work with, however, had been a limited number of transcriptions from the notebooks made by Master's second cousin, in whose keeping they now were. These extracts did, though, also offer enthralling glimpses of the maestro planning his work. There were ideas for plot developments ('Incensed with their treatment, Ritz staff lodge complaint') and clues ('Gerard's writer's cramp result of forging *entire* manuscript'), germinations thrilling for the aficionado, who until now knew only the full-grown trees in the enchanted forest. Ah, I sighed, if only I could gain access to those notebooks! How infinitely more fascinating those fragments would be to me than any fully-fledged new work by some other writer, no matter how highly praised.

The hero-worshipper is so eager to see his hero as his own self writ large, gloriously potentiated, that he will seize on any resemblance he comes across between the great man and himself. Any resemblance, however slight. So, how absurdly pleased I was to learn that at school Master, whose early years, so typical of his class, bore so little relation to my own in other respects, was, like me, a daydreamer, a bowler of some ability, a contributor to the school magazine. Yes, yes, that showed we were soul brothers, didn't it? Except that, so disappointingly, his other listed attributes included some to which I couldn't relate at all: his aptitude for languages, a short, thickset and powerful build, prowess at field athletics and an early interest in stained glass. There followed dismally unsuccessful attempts on my part at improving my French, bodybuilding, shot putting and appreciating the (admittedly doubtful) aesthetic qualities of the windows in our local churches.

But the greatest difference between us, and the one that set churning the deepest discontent, was in the quality of Master's juvenilia compared to mine. A school magazine article of his, written when he was fourteen, about a cultural tour of Europe he'd been on with his parents, read more like an English text for academic study than an adolescent's essay. How far removed its tone was from the usual schoolboy wrestling with the language, how adult it was in its concepts and vocabulary: 'the neo-grecian frieze a model of discretion', 'the opinionated philhellene querying the guide's pronouncements', that sort of thing. After reading the extracts from it in the biography, I uneasily took another look at my own piece in the latest issue of *The Croucher*, our school mag. Since it had appeared (in that organ more fitted to it than the local *Gazette*, which had rejected it with commendable alacrity by return of post), I'd gazed on 'Some Great Fictional Detectives' with fond pride more than once. But now, as I re-read it afresh, as this time I winced at the second appearance of the hob-nailed paragraph introduction 'Another great detective was...', as I compared it with Master's stunning debut, my main reaction was one of *shame*. If I could have wished it away I would have done. But there it was, there it so *inexpungibly* was. If only, at least, I had given myself a pseudonym (such as the one Vince Higgs had mysteriously chosen for his contributions on keeping rabbits and collecting stamps: Fabius Maximus) instead of so proudly and foolishly proclaiming my own name.

Then there were Master's schoolboy letters, to a favourite uncle and to a friend who was at Stowe. They were full of intelligent comments on literature, art, architecture, religion – and, of course, stained glass. I couldn't help making comparisons again, contrasting this correspondence with my own, the full extent of which, I reflected with shame once more, consisted of the occasional letter to Aunt Edie, thanking her for a nice holiday and it had been raining hard since we got back and I'd bought a bat second-hand and we'd been to the Regal to see...

Even so, such discrepancies between Master and myself were soon forgotten when I came across in the life further resemblances between us that I knew were far, far more significant: our shared liking for treacle pudding, for instance, and our common shoe size.

I so absorbed all these details – and those from the only other biography available, which I'd ordered through the library (ah, the thrill of seeing the green reservation card awaiting me on the door mat!) – that I ended up knowing more facts about Master's life than I probably did about my own and could have scored a *Mastermind* maximum on the subject. *At what hotel did Master stay when he visited Baltimore? The Cambridge. Correct. What did Master have for lunch – I've started so I'll finish – what did Master have for lunch on the day he completed* Mosaic? *Waldorf salad, pastrami and horseradish on rye, coffee. Correct. And at the end of that round you have scored 18 points, with no passes.*

Dog days

Into the school summer holiday there would sometimes heavily sink and settle a prolonged period of dog days. Then the sun, which usually meant so much to me, which was usually so benign in its radiance, issuing so irresistible a summons to go out into it and enjoy it, took on a different aspect, the light and shade into which it stylised the outdoor scene changed in character: the drop-dead vivacity of fine-day patterning, its greens, golds, blues and blacks often bestirred, set aquiver, by the softest of breaths, was replaced by a motionless chiaroscuro of intenser kind, which contrast made intenser still wherever that glare and shadow lay in neighbouring immobile slabs. These long sultry spells sometimes induced in me a torpor that was only partly due to the physical burden of the heat that everybody complained of, a heat that, no longer invigorating as on more temperate days when you soaked it up, now bore down heavily on you, smothered you, sucked at your energy. It had, that torpor, a more psychological cause. For the rest of the year the purposefulness with which those around me pursued their everyday occupations, and the resultant importance with which these occupations then seemed to be invested, helped generate, by a sort of electromagnetic induction, my own involvement with life, made me part of the vast invisible dynamo that keeps life on the move. So that when on dog days the oppressive, energy-sapping heat caused general activity to subside and the holiday season or a desire to keep indoors caused so many participants in that activity to disappear from view, and nature itself, instead of hinting at as usual an activity of its own, constant if hidden, seemed, in its new aspect of a series of photographs of itself (colours, shapes, tones fixed as they were at that moment for all time), to be in stasis, when all this persisted day after day, when, in other words, the dynamo, hum sounding ever fainter, seemed to be slowing almost to a stop, then my own life force, in youth too much at the mercy of everything around it, insufficiently self-generating, began correspondingly to slacken.

During such becalmed spells in the school holidays it wasn't, I think, so much heat lethargy as a sort of collective consciousness of the dynamo running down that induced in the usual cricket gang, faced with the almost deserted, shimmering rec, a general unspoken aversion to playing. I had then before me an early forcible example of how atmosphere can control events. What on sunny days of a different nature had, only a week before, in exactly the same place, involving exactly the same crowd, been engaged in so eagerly, been monitored with regular score checks so competitively, was now transformed, if a game had been started, into a listless exercise so obviously regarded by everyone as futile that any enquiry about the score would only be uttered in that apathetic tone that's the certain prelude to 'Oh, come on, let's chuck it in.'

Those empty, stretching, desolate days. Days when there was not just a tacit antipathy to playing cricket but to doing anything much at all. Days of boredom, of stillness, of constant oozing hairline sweat, of your spots more throbbingly impingeing on your awareness than usual, of masturbation more guilt-ridden than usual, of walks more aimless than usual. On one of these, well outside the town centre and at the most moribund hour of the afternoon, with scarcely a soul in sight, I passed a glaring white temple, the Ritz. Of the four Bexcray cinemas, it was the one that hardly ever showed anything you wanted to see, the one you knew would be the first to close down (it was). On this dead afternoon it was hopelessly offering something ancient, black-and-white, obscure. The building stood on an uninviting corner, its façade on a stretch of main road sloping down from the outskirts of the town, its side on a short residential road (a situation which made its name the more hollow and its death the more certain). I never usually noticed its bare whitewashed side wall, but now, in the pitiless light, in all its nakedness, it came to my attention and unhappily revealed its white skin to be suffering from both a scurfy scaling disorder and a green fungal infection, while melancholy dock and sorrel ran the length of its base. How inexpressibly doleful I found that scene – the stifling heat, the harsh light, the empty streets, the lifeless cinema, the old film, the disfigured wall, the forlorn weeds. As I stood there, I imagined someone actually entering the Ritz and I experienced a strange conflict of feelings. On the one hand, a dog-day instinct told me that an escape from the open streets, heat-cowed and sullen, into cooler surroundings, such as that cinema could offer, might be welcome. On the other hand, another instinct, that old one not to shut oneself away on a summer's day, told me that such an incarceration was against nature: the thought of someone steeping himself in the gloom of the auditorium in the middle of a sun-drenched afternoon, even one like this, was melancholy enough in itself; it was made doubly so by knowing that the film was utterly lacking in the appeal of a new release, was stale and irrelevant; and trebly so by knowing that the cinema would be almost deserted and that the few people sitting in there would have to be, according to my intolerant young lights, saddos to have chosen to be in such a place in such weather at such a time of day for such a film (how difficult it was to imagine any of them setting out from home, walking through the airless, burning streets, entering the silent foyer, buying a ticket, for that of all ends!); yes, it was a thought so desolating I found it barely supportable.

There was something else too. As I stood there – and indeed as so often when marooned on an isle of dog days – I was troubled by a more aching visitation of that feeling which had first stirred within me years before, on those sweltering July days at Kingsdon St Mary primary school when, as I listened to Olivia reading *The Wind in the Willows* to the class, I gazed out of the window at the empty, heat-distorted playground. Strangely, it seemed now, that feeling, to have something in it of what I had previously associated only with certain scenes of cold, not heat: the old unease.

Obsession

Mosaic wasn't for me simply a book (which was all that every other book, even the most enthralling, the most intelligent, the most beautiful, would ever be); it was a world in itself, a magical world that for so much of the time was more potent than, more significant than, the actual world I was living in. And as the creator of that world, Master had become for me a virtual demigod. I was in awe of his achievement. I was also in awe of another status he had attained to, one which is allotted to few artists: that of a genius loci. In his case, he had come, with Gershwin, to symbolise in the collective imagination the very spirit of the great American metropolis in all its energy and colour and poetry and pzazz. For, in the words of one critic, 'Bernstein's verdict on Gershwin could apply equally well to Master: "One of the greatest voices that ever rang out in the history of American urban culture."'

Love of Master's work, veneration of him, obsession with him... The obsessive develops a singular vision. Sometimes, when I was reading an article in the literary pages of a newspaper, my preconditioned eye, like that of a lookout peripherally glimpsing a far from obvious landfall, would spot out of its corner, some way off, in a neighbouring piece, the initial M of a name of about the right length, and, abandoning in mid-sentence the text before me, would involuntarily home in on that assertive capital to discover whether it began *the* name or some disappointing other, such as Mailer or Miller. If it was *the* name, the interrupted article could go hang, all I wanted to know was what this piece had to say about my hero.

The obsessive also develops a singular purposefulness. Entering a library or bookshop, I'd head straight for one of those categories in which there might be a work that mentioned Master – biographies, memoirs, literary studies – and, having chosen a likely title, turn immediately to the index. Sometimes I'd happen upon a lengthy entry – Master, D.E., 33, 63, 65-67, 74, 78-79, 96, 137, 142-43, 282-85, 301, 314-16. Such a string of page numbers would spark in me – as the bare stats of a sports event spark in the supporter who has not yet read the full account – eager anticipation. They trembled, those figures, with their promise, with an intensity of significance that someone who had no interest in Master would have been amazed they could possess. Perhaps this time, I hoped, before turning to the first reference to him, I'd find out *exactly* what sorts of pen and paper he used (so that I could get hold of the same – though to write what?) or *exactly* what remarks he had made that people had found so witty.

Once, in one of those books I made a beeline for, I came across the following: *Also present at the party were Dorothy Parker, George Gershwin, Lillian Hellman, Fred Astaire, Maxwell Perkins and D.E. Master.* Gershwin and Master! Together! I raised my eyes from the page and gazed into the Thirties penthouse where that gathering had assembled. So the link between my two heroes that I had previously supposed to be only spiritual was also, amazingly, social. I dearly wanted to know something of what they had said to each other. But there was no indication. Plenty of boring conversations reported between *others* who were there, but, *scandalously*, not a word of what had passed between those two. The list of guests at the party, by the way, threw into relief an authorial aspect of Master that I'd pondered earlier. It was that he had chosen, despite his long domicile in America, to initialise his forenames in that formal, reticent manner favoured for some reason by so many twentieth-century writers of his native Britain. H.G. Wells, D.H. Lawrence, T.E. Lawrence, G.K. Chesterton, P.G. Wodehouse, A.E. Housman, P.C. Wren, J.M. Barrie, R.C. Sherriff, E.M. Forster, A.J. Cronin, W.B. Yeats, A.P. Herbert, G.M. Trevelyan, T.S. Eliot, H.E. Bates, J.B. Priestley, E.V. Lucas, F.L. Lucas, F.R. Leavis, Q.D. Leavis, E.W. Hornung, P.H. Newby, L.P. Hartley, W.H. Auden, V.S. Pritchett, V.S. Naipaul… Unsurprisingly, no continental writers styled themselves in this self-effacing functionary's way and scarcely any Americans; in the midst of a list of full-blown transatlantic names, Master's (whose form of self-styling was duplicated only in a few other cases, such as Mencken and

Salinger) had the appearance of being chastely furled. I could only suppose that his choice had been subconsciously influenced by his early British upbringing. Not that I would have wanted him to have spelled out either or both of his first names: in another example of the complete ascendancy of the actual over the possible, the name D.E. Master had acquired so resonant a ring of rightness, of inevitability, like those other celebrated bank manager's names of literature, that just as I could never have imagined the creator of *The War of the Worlds* as Herbert Wells or of *Sons and Lovers* as David Lawrence so I could never for one moment have thought of the creator of *Mosaic* as Dominic Master. And I decided that if ever my own name should appear on a book, I would go for the initials style too. I had only one, but I would invent a second, perhaps adopting a V in memory of my father's name.

On another occasion I read in a collection of Edmund Wilson's letters: *One evening I bumped into Master in the lobby of the Strand Theatre. In that soft, low, almost diffident voice of his he spoke briefly of a novel he had almost finished writing...* Imagine. Wilson had not only seen plain the man who in a few months' time was to bestow upon the world the most beautiful mystery story ever written or ever likely to be written but he had heard of its existence from its creator's own lips! I tried to put myself in Wilson's place, to imagine my idol *actually before me, actually speaking*. I concentrated hard and eventually I saw someone, I heard him speak. But although he looked like Master, although he sounded as I'd read Master sounded, he was no more Master than the photographs and descriptions of him on the pages of the biographies had been. And how hard it was for me at that age to accept that, no matter how strenuously I might try to summon up his living presence, I never could, never would.

Linda Lorell

During my last school year, Danny and I started going out with two girls from Lady Croucher Grammar. We met them in the audience at our joint school play for that year, Enid Bagnold's *The Chalk Garden*. (What seemed to me the inherent tedium of this piece was not improved by standard school-production delivery – speak-your-weight – and movements – poker-up-the-arse – especially among the Sir Bernard Croucher players, but it was greeted at the end with excusably rapturous applause by the cast's nearest and dearest, in which, even so, the euphoria of relief must have played its usual part.) Danny and I were at this play not for the purposes of entertainment (we had heard rumours that in its mind-numbing qualities it, unbelievably, ran 'Droner' Hill exceedingly close) but simply to mingle with the crumpet of Lady Croucher, which these productions gave the boys a rare opportunity to meet en masse.

The girl I got off with – well, no, it would be truer to say that she got off with me – had, she told me, seen me drumming with a group who played at the Artillery Row youth club. Some months earlier I'd heard a Buddy Rich track on the radio and the almost superhuman power and technique of that virtuoso had blown me away. I began practising on the kit of a friend of Danny's, Phil Catt, who drummed for the group, and borrowed his Drum Tutor book. Then I bought and listened over and over to a Buddy Rich record (even though I was more into rock than jazz), marvelling at how the master's powerful relaxed rapid hands transposed from rolls to single stick work and back again so seamlessly that in that electrifying flow of percussion you scarcely knew where one segment ended and another began. One day Phil went down with mumps and I stood in for him a few times. Smashing at those skins, I revelled in what, I've decided, looking back on those thousand-decibel sessions – and a couple of others with a different group where I was again a stand-in – must count among the most enjoyable experiences of my life. I wanted a drum kit of my own but even second-hand this was way beyond my means. (Later, when I could afford one, the desire was no longer overriding, others had supervened.)

Yes, this girl had seen me drumming and had apparently taken a fancy to me. Taken a fancy to *me*! I experienced for the first time that incredulity we feel on learning that our so-defective person, which to us couldn't seem less deserving of romantic interest, has actually aroused it in someone. Her name was Linda Lorell. Skinny, pale, small-breasted she may have been but with her avid, slightly hard, sea-green eyes and faintly smiling, well defined, naturally deep red lips, to which her pallor drew further attention, she had the look of one whom, though I had had no experience in such matters, I instinctively judged to be more than normally intent upon self-gratification.

Mostly we went for walks together, at first in the company of Danny and his girl but later by ourselves. We never visited each other's homes (she lived with her divorced mother on Levington estate on the other side of Bexcray). Occasionally we went to Pergolesi's or the pictures. It was not long before kissing, at which she, with her lascivious carmine mouth, was proficient and I was a clumsy novice, progressed to other caresses and eventually, whenever we could find a deserted spot, to heavy petting – which brought an uncustomary cherryish glow to Linda's candlewhite cheeks and, for my part, drove me almost insane. (It was only some years later, in retrospect, that Linda's proficiency in this activity struck me as being suspiciously advanced in one so young, a suspicion reinforced by the marked lack of surprise I recalled in her at the nature of what she had taken in hand.) How I longed for us to go further, to journey to the ultimate goal. But this girl, who was morally bothered not a jot by what we were doing, had nonetheless decided not to yield up fully her unchaste treasure and refused all my impassioned urgings.

A bombshell

One day in May Harry left home. Buggered off never to return. He'd claimed he was driving to a boiler factory in Carlisle with a delivery of insulating material (I suppose the volunteered spelling out of his assignment in such detail should, since it was without precedent, have alerted us that something was up). In fact, he'd given in his notice to RGB Haulage a week before and had completed his last job the previous day. We didn't have to wait long to discover the truth. Two days after his pretended departure for the north we received a letter from him, postmarked Streatham. We learned for the first time that there was another woman, Peg Tumbrill. Lil, as a Prince Albert regular, knew well enough who she was. 'That fat-arsed cow,' she exclaimed through her tears. And she had only to tell me that the steatopygous one punched tickets on the trolleys for me also to realise who she was. (It appeared that she was something of a femme fatale. Two years earlier she had lured away Mrs Reddle's Greg, the plumber who lived at the bottom of the next road, only to ditch him a few months later – and before that Laurie Bodging, the odd-job man who lodged next door to the Prince Albert, had lasted scarcely any longer.)

Harry went on to speak movingly of our only having one life to live and of our 'having to grab happiness while we can, which is what Ive done and dont blame Peg, shes been a brick'. (I wondered whether Harry's action had been precipitated by the example he had read about, in the Disturbing Gift, of another free spirit, who had upped-and-awayed to the South Seas, leaving wife and kids behind, and I thought that, if this were so, it was an additional reason why Harry *had had no right to have that study of the French master's work in his keeping*.) Harry concluded courageously by saying that this had been a hard decision for him and that for a long time he hadn't been able to summon up the strength to take it, but that 'finally Peg [deleted] I found it in me to do it. P.S. Youll be wasting your time looking for us because were leaving the district to make a new life for ourselves.'

Bloody hell. This was a bombshell and no mistake. We'd had no warning of any kind. And, apart from the shock we felt, we realised that *from that very moment* our lives would never be the same again – yes, in such a way, I'm sure, did the more detached part of our minds, as we looked at each other in a silence broken only by the overloud clock on the mantelpiece, pitilessly highlight that mere fragment of time which otherwise was no ticking different from any that had preceded or would follow it.

Lil's reaction to Harry's clearing off was a wild disorder of feelings. Outrage, disbelief, pain, fury, mortification, misery. 'The *bast*ard! The *bast*ard!' one minute; tears the next. Was it that the man she had loved to hate had been all along, deep down, the man she had hated to love?

A reciprocal process

When we are young and such impresssionable dreamers there is often a reciprocal process at work in our reading: whenever we draw on our own experience to visualise the settings for a novel, whenever, in other words, the actual infiltrates the fictional, we may find that, in a symbiotic exchange between reader and book, the events of that fiction in their turn infiltrate our images of the actual scenes we made use of. So that if when reading *The Wind in the Willows* I pictured the Wild Wood that Mole so rashly entered as that copse which darkly crowned the horizon beyond Kingsdon St Mary, equally whenever I thought back on the occasions I had entered that copse I believed that I might actually have heard that pattering which had so alarmed Mole when he struck deeper into the trees.

Again, just the same interaction took place between scenes from *Mosaic* and scenes from my own life. When imagining Joaquín and the narrator entering one evening the great cavern of Lime Street railway station (its clamour and smokiness so brilliantly conveyed by Master and so cunningly slotted in as an essential piece of the mosaic), I saw this station as, suitably magnified, the more humble station at Bexcray on an evening when it had seemed to promise I knew not what; and, reciprocally, whenever I conjured up an image of Bexcray station, it was augmented by the blue vapour and echoing bustle of Lime Street station. Similarly, elements of my own primal dusk and of Master's key dusk – which despite the differences between their locations (between an avenue in an American metropolis and a confluence of thoroughfares in a London suburb) were similarly endowed with a gorgeous sky, an expectant atmosphere, pole-bearing vehicles of enchantment and a bejewelling of lights – exchanged places. In fact, there had now come a time when I could not be absolutely certain that some aspects of my remembered dusk did not originate in the pages of his book rather than in the pages of my experience. My imagination in these matters was becoming like one of those nations settled by a conquering power in which each civilisation, that of the settlers and that of the settled, becomes over the ages so fully assimilated by the other, to their mutual enrichment, that it is sometimes difficult in the modern culture to know which elements were originally native, which imported.

There was something else I could never be sure about. Would those moments of heightened awareness I intermittently experienced, which over the years had been decreasing in frequency and strength, as over the years the raptures of a once-passionate love do, would they soon have faded away entirely if I had not been introduced to and entered Master's magic world? How much of 'my' vision from that time on, I wondered, was just as much his as truly my own?

Anguish

One spring afternoon, when I met Linda outside the Lady Croucher school gates (I was in the habitual state of feverish sexual craving which just thinking about her aroused in me, so that I was forced to use my satchel as a cover-up), she told me that she was sorry but we wouldn't be able to go for our usual 'walk' (our shorthand for hot-footing it over to a disused pavilion at the farther end of the playing fields). What was more, she wouldn't be able to go out with me at all for some time to come. She was, she said, studying hard every evening and weekend for her mock 'O' Levels.

Studying hard for her mock 'O' Levels. As I watched and heard her telling me this, I knew that if she'd been taking Lying as one of those 'O' Levels, she wouldn't even have scraped an E for it. *Appallingly* low marks for style: she may have looked me straight in the eye, as conventional wisdom and teen mags had told her truthtellers did, but expression and tone of voice were all to pot. And, more importantly, a bloody great zilch for content: her story was *breathtakingly* bad, preposterous. For if from among those of my peers I knew well I'd been asked to choose the one academic loafer that I could *guarantee* wouldn't dream of sacrificing spring evenings and weekends to studying, let alone to studying for *mock* 'O' Levels of all no-account things, I think that, formidable though the list of candidates would have been, I should, from everything Linda Lorell had told me about herself and school, have had to opt for her.

So I knew right away that her story was bullshit, that she had lost interest in me. But despite realising this with certainty, that terrible certainty on such occasions which floods the body with a sickening feeling no words can convey, despite this, one part of me still embarked on that ostensible refusal to accept the situation which the desperate persist in even while they know it is doomed, that denial of the undeniable, the very act of expressing which somehow, subtly, cruelly, jacks up the anguish even further.

'Oh, come on, you don't have to go home yet. You've got masses of time.' (The pain of knowing how hopeless it was.)

'No, I have to go.'

'Why?' (The pain of *knowing*...)

'Because I have to.'

'You don't have to.' (The pain of *knowing*...)

'I do.'

'Well, can't I see you tomorrow?' (The pain of *knowing*...)

'No, I told you.'

'But —' (The pain of *knowing*...)

'See you.' With this, strictly speaking, nonsensical farewell, and with a piercingly polite smile, she turned and walked off.

The unbearable intuitive conviction that I would *never* be going out with her again. The fierce frustrated physical longing for her, for her so *Linda Lorell* green eyes, so *Linda Lorell* crimson lips, so *Linda Lorell* slim body, so *Linda Lorell* everything – which could *never be replaced*... The collapse of my self-esteem, which Linda's interest in me had virtually brought into being in the first place. Shock, from the suddenness of it all...

My God, however much we may regret the passing of all that youth has to offer, its glories and its joyous ever-welling hopes, there are occasions, looking back, when we feel like offering up thanks on bended knee that we no longer have to suffer the agonies of those days, the agonies of a sensibility unprotected at that stage by even so much as a rudimentary carapace.

Worse was to come: the misery of jealousy. The following Saturday, in the midst of a period so wretched that Lil and Danny thought that I was physically ill, I dragged myself into Bexcray town centre (with much the same appearance and gait as someone with flu). I was shuffling along King Street, which on this pale golden afternoon in spring was all mocking smiles, when I saw, some way ahead on the other side, the cruel beloved, in a heart-piercingly bright red dress, leaving Pergolesi's, heart-piercingly laughing as she heart-piercingly gazed up at a swarthy young man in black leathers and motor-cycle boots. Hitching up her dress in a heart-piercingly familiar gesture, she swung one slender leg over the pillion of his Yamaha to take up a heart-piercingly erotic straddle, and seconds later, to the accompaniment of an insolent explosion of sound and a blue billow of exhaust, heart-piercingly disappeared up the street with him.

Over the weeks that followed I kept making the rounds of likely places in Bexcray where I might self-laceratingly spot Linda and her new beau, and on various ocasions was all too painfully successful. Asking around, I discovered that she had become interested in the motorcyclist for some time before she had ditched me and that she was now 'crazy about him'. He had everything going for him: looks (I wasn't plain but I didn't have, as he had, what I *guessed* descriptions in cheap fiction meant by 'chiselled features'); maturity (he was *nineteen* no less – though with his precociously dark blue jaw and stocky build looked more like thirty); money (he worked as a mechanic at Lenley's Garage, just outside Welling); and of course transport. I couldn't compete.

The tortures of jealousy have been portrayed at length so often that there is scarcely anything more of interest to be said on the subject. All I shall say is that I suffered in the standard way: I kept picturing my inamorata gazing at her new flame with eyes insane with infatuation, adoringly doing with him what she had done with me. No, wait a minute...*doing more...yielding up the final prize...straddling him in the way she'd straddled the...* No, no, no, I couldn't bear the thought of it. But the thought came. And kept coming. I became almost suicidal.

Almost.

Jealousy was to torment me for months afterwards, until the merciful attentions of Time, reliable old Time, good-on-yer Time, began gradually to ease the pain, and then I was able to think of Linda and the man in black with no more than a dull ache.

'Earn your keep'

When Harry had done a runner, when, with Peg Tumbrill's connivance, he'd chosen to 'make a new life for himself', he had burdened his nearest – as free spirits are apt to – with the concomitant necessity of their having willy-nilly to make a new life for themselves too. And how. He hadn't sent us a penny for our upkeep, and he'd disappeared into thin air. Dean got Lil to obtain a maintenance order and he put a private detective on Harry's trail. A private detective! Shades of those Queens and Carrs that Dean had introduced me to and of those *True 'Tec Tales* that Dougie Leonard read! This gave me a real buzz – until the arrival of Harry K. Gumm disenchantingly revealed a plump, grey-faced, morose man with watery eyes and a tic in his upper lip. He asked us a lot of questions about his firstnamesake. But he asked them in what was – shockingly so at such an early stage – a voice devoid of much hope, and he had a sighing way of saying 'these cases' which made you wonder whether there was any point at all in his embarking on ours. There wasn't. Perhaps Harry *was* after all the canny operator that he liked to think he was and that I supposed him to be when I watched him studying the racing page with narrowed eyes – for he obviously had the old disappearing act well and truly wrapped up. Certainly Harry K. Gumm never sniffed out the least trace of him.

Without being asked, Dean chipped in to help us out financially (with a monthly payment whose amount Lil never disclosed to me) – otherwise we wouldn't have survived. Not that I ever heard Lil thank him. Just as she was always in the right, about every matter under the sun, so anything anyone did for her was no more than her due: to imperial omniscience was added the imperial right to tribute. But that was not all. She grumbled that Dean should be giving us more each month (though I suspected this would simply have funded heavier bets and boozes and not more eatable grub, toilet rolls and other such luxuries, as Lil termed them) – that is, she took ingratitude a grotesque stage further. Or was it a stage further? Wasn't it only logical that anyone who accepted favours as of right should feel free to criticise the nature of them?

As for Dean in person, we saw little of him at this time. Unbeknown to us, he had much on his mind: the possible sale of Spectrum to a larger company, and the foundation of several boys' clubs in that Deptford-Peckham-New Cross area in which he had grown up.

So, the breadwinner gone, embarked on his assuredly doomed 'new life' somewhere or other, and Dean's monthly remittance according to Lil falling short of 'what she needed', she started looking for a part-time job and told me that, at the end of the summer term, when I would have reached school-leaving age, I would have to find work too. Sharpish, and without too much regard to what it was. 'You've got to earn your keep, you have.'

This didn't surprise me in one way. After all, Harry had always told me I'd be leaving school at the earliest opportunity. But there was a difference between what he'd said he wanted for me and what I was now going to have to do. In mentorial mode, puffing away on his fag so very thoughtfully that it seemed to me an indispensable aid to sagacity, he'd said: 'I don't want you just going off and getting the first bloody job that comes along. Understand? You've got to get yourself qualifications. Then you'll have a better start in life than I did.

I started with nothing. Nothing. I made it *by my own efforts*. I don't want the same thing happening to you. *Qualifications.* That's what it's all about. When the time comes, we'll think what's the best thing to do.' Such promises, separated out from the groundless 'I Did It My Way' success story, had in retrospect, in view of his imminent abandonment of us, a hollow rhetorical ring. Of course, what Harry meant by qualifications was not GCEs, 'O' Levels, 'bloody bits of paper'. What he meant was 'learning a trade'. With some local firm of plumbers or electricians or whatever. That was the accepted summit to aim at in our world. Not that I'd ever shown any aptitude for practical work, any interest in using my hands to earn a living (I discounted sport, drawing and painting, drumming). But anyway, now even a trade apprenticeship was out of the question: it would, according to Lil, take too long for it to bring in enough money. So there was only one thing for it. I should just have to take the first job I could get.

Ken Day

At school in Deptford, Dean had been friends with a boy who'd taught himself jazz pieces and popular tunes on the piano and played weekend gigs at weddings and other functions. On leaving school he'd done odd labouring jobs and then, like Dean, managed to get on to one of the four standard flights out of Lostboysworld – in his case, on Entertainment. Developing his technique in pubs and clubs, he'd auditioned for and been taken on by the Joe Smart Sextet, whose pianist had recently foundered on a familiar jazz man's voyage. There then followed work with a couple of other combos. Dean had kept in touch with him, and from time to time they met up.

Once, when this pianist, Ken Day, had been staying at the Rectory for a summer break, I'd been introduced to him and found myself shaking hands with a man nothing like my advance romantic idea of what a jazz pianist should look like. In fact, if I'd been asked to guess from his lumpy features, coarse pink-chalk skin and squat figure what his occupation was, I'd probably have hazarded market trader or butcher or, like Harry, lorry driver. I'd also imagined a jazz man would be unconventional in his dress or, if not, at the least casual, but Day, in keeping – as I would discover later – with the dress tendency of most British jazz men of the postwar era, was Mr Straight: he wore on this occasion a 'smart' and none-too-well-colour-coordinated outfit that included a heathery sports jacket, stiff-collared blue-and-white checked shirt, red-and-yellow paisley tie and bright ginger suede shoes.

On my visit I'd heard him complain several times, with the bitterness of a spirit that wishes only to be free, of the constraints imposed on his playing by membership of groups. I'd felt sorry for him and hoped that he wouldn't have to wait too long to perform in public what he called his 'personal statements'.

Now, it seemed, Day had achieved his ambition: he'd struck out as a solo performer. And one Saturday, Dean took me to the Metropole Ballroom, Blackwell, to hear his old pal in concert.

Emerging from the wings, our man walked quickly to the piano, head bowed, frowning, apparently oblivious to the applause that greeted him. Seating himself, he remained silently hunched over the keyboard for a long time. A very long time. So long that I noticed that some in the audience had begun to stir restlessly. Then he launched, with an abruptness that made me jump in my seat, into a series of thunderous, tonally unrelated arpeggios. These ended with as disconcerting a suddenness as they had begun, and Day re-submerged into lengthy rumination. The outcome of this was a crashing discord, followed by another pause. Then another discord…and another pause. He then began, at a much quicker tempo, to meander chromatically up and down the keys, in, I couldn't help thinking, the manner of a student tentatively essaying a pastiche of some of that Debussy Olivia had once played for me. Another silence, before this time he embarked on several brief atonal runs, their hesitancy and his agonised look seeming to me to suggest a desperate attempt to quote once-heard, long-forgotten passages from various twelve-tone merchants, as Dean used, rather slightingly, to refer to Berg and Co. These must be, I guessed, the personal statements he'd been so keen to make.

The impassioned self-communing continued at length. After a while I began to feel guilty about what, as we were locked with the pianist in the dungeon of his soul, the lengthy incarceration was causing me to experience: a desperate longing for what already seemed a distant, carefree existence, a sort of golden age, the time when – I had to say it to myself – Ken Day was bloodywell not playing.

Sometimes one caught here and there in his performance a tantalisingly brief glimpse of a world outside that of the painful striving: a fragment of harmony and rhythm, pleasant-sounding, accomplished, unremarkable, almost an involuntary exercise of Day's fingers, which he could have played in his sleep, so ingrained in him was it after years of entertaining audiences with non-personal statements. But soon it vanished, as though, having momentarily, regrettably, let his fingers run away with him, Day had sternly recalled the serious intent of what he was about.

I should mention here that my knowledge of jazz piano at that time was limited. I'd liked and bought recordings by Teddy Wilson and Fats Waller, who respectively charmed and invigorated me, but I knew little of bebop, modernism, 'free style' – the jagged, the arrhythmic, the solipsistic – and had heard only snatches of Thelonius Monk ('gawky intervals and absence of swing', as Larkin characterised his playing), who I now learned from the programme notes was one of Day's heroes. And perhaps this unawareness and my fondness for Teddy and Fats had together led me unthinkingly to expect from a jazz piano concert something far less dissimilar to them than what we were now hearing.

At last – but only as denoted by a slight straightening of the back and a partial turning away from the keyboard and not by any musical sign, since we had thought we were in the middle of an as yet unresolved chord sequence – this particular piece was, we gathered, at an end.

The applause was thunderous. At the time, I couldn't understand why this should be so. It was only later, when I came across the phenomenon on other occasions, that I realised that applause is not always what it seems. And I told myself then, because for me Day's performance had been execrable, like that of a demented child let loose on the keys, that in this instance all that tumultuous clapping had probably arisen not from unrestrainable joy but from various other causes (embarrassment and mental discomfort, for which the loud slamming together of palms provides physical relief, pseudish pretended understanding of what Day was at, craven kowtowing to received opinion about him, the impulse to imitation in any crowd, and even an element of perverseness, a subtle pleasure in acclaiming what one has detested), and that eventually that applause, having become detached from its original causes, had, as it always does, fed on itself. Yes, I later told myself they were the reasons why Day had received such an ovation. But later still, in response to further events, I began to question whether I was right, and even, reluctantly, to re-evaluate my own reaction to this concert.

Dean and I sat through the rest of the first half, then silently agreed to leave. On the way home my normally voluble uncle said little.

144

Dazings, Cattalls

Lil wasn't long looking for part-time work – she got herself a morning job at the Prince Albert, scrubbing the floors, polishing the bar, cleaning the toilets. As for me, with the end of summer term, and with it school life, rapidly aproaching, I wondered whether I would be able to find something at Dazings, where Danny had already lined up a job. He was to be a packer, boxing up a luxury product unfamiliar to Lil until she had to use it in her job – Sanipan. The building of Dazings' giant factory at Blackwell had, despite its immediate heavy discharges of effluent into the river, been welcomed with an almost hysterical fervour by Lil and Colin Harnett's mum next door. They could scarcely contain themselves on hearing of the 'exciting promise of lots and lots of new job opportunities for *our* young people,' as it was put by Charlotte Colefax, Tory MP for Blackwell and Bexcray, who also proclaimed her pride in 'having helped to get the factory established *here*'. '*Our* young people...the factory established *here*' – Charlotte made it sound like she might have not just a political but a *personal* interest in the matter. For after all, Lil and Mrs Harnett said, wasn't she the mother of three of those young people *herself*, strapping young lads who, though at present boarding at various schools several counties away from the area, might be grateful, one day when they had to 'earn their keep', for the opportunity their 'mum' had helped set up in the area, a job at Dazings.

But there were no sits vac there for the time being. Instead, I spent a week at a cardboard box manufacturer's somewhere near Plumstead – filling in for someone on holiday but doing what exactly I no longer remember – and then got a permanent job at Cattalls, the construction materials merchants outside Blackwell. There, in a huge concrete storeroom of which I was the only occupant, my job was to count the nuts, bolts and washers of different sizes that filled a truly *va-a-ast* array of containers.

It may sound incredible to the reader but, do you know, it never occurred to me once – dozy sod that, as Lil rightly said, I was – it never occurred to me once to enquire exactly *why* I had to count all those nuts, bolts and washers, or why not a soul at Cattalls ever showed the slightest interest in, let alone took possession of, any of them during my (admittedly very brief) stay there.

Early learning

The effects on me of being cast aside by Linda Lorell had been in their gradually changing nature like those that take place after a severe physical blow. First there had been agonising pain, then the slow dulling of this to an ache more blunted, then an apparently complete disappearance of this, but one that in fact was only on the surface, for when the area of injury was pressed, as at the sudden unexpected mention of her name, it was still tender. But I had recovered enough to be on the lookout for other girls – in the discos and the coffee bars and the cinemas that I went to with Danny and sometimes Billy Howe.

Crushes. 'God, Danny, I just *can't* stop thinking about that Gloria Drew' (Billy's cousin's girlfriend). 'No, I'm not hungry, thanks – I just saw Veronique Thomson again' (an extraordinarily well-developed sixteen-year-old who lived two streets away from us).

Dates. I summoned up the courage to ask out other girls. Ignoring my physical self, its jelly knees and dry mouth, I forced it to act. What am I saying? *I* didn't force it to act, I had scarcely anything to do with the matter. Like some detached non-executive director, I just watched the chairman of the board of our conglomerate taking the tough decisions, in this case those that concerned Legs Ltd and Voice Systems, the locomotion and speech components of the business.

Before I met Sally, there were three of those post-Linda girls. April Holling, a canteen assistant at Cattalls I vaguely knew from Elson Road primary school days. Louise Parker, a friend of Danny's sister. And Rita Gameford, picked up outside the Majestic cinema as a dare. Randy Rita Gameford, who went all the way, transporting me to the ultimate ecstasy that Linda had denied me – the first time one evening in a park shelter, after that in a shed in her back garden. Rita liked to... But wait, these are details which, as a narrator not wholly in sympathy with the spirit of the age, I would rather not chronicle. Anyway, within a couple of months it was all over, because her mum remarried and the family moved away from the district.

Observing Rita when aroused, and, before her, Linda – the gleaming eyes, the flushed cheeks, the parted lips – I learned early, like many another lower-class lad of my time – and later considered myself lucky to have done so – how most girls express sexual pleasure. This spared me the fantasies of the cloistered or the backward who, having had no personal experience of genuine female sensuality and not being sure even that it existed but needing to envisage it to turn themselves on, absurdly exaggerated the reality, as all fantasists do. It was undoubtedly such daydreamers who were responsible for a genre of art on display in certain squalid galleries, like the one underground in Blackwell town centre, galleries that charged only a penny for admission. There you could view their pictorial shots in the dark – for you had to ignore their claimed autobiographical 'then I, then she' provenance – as to how the average female would behave on beholding and being penetrated by the astonishing equipment with which, to a man, these muralists were favoured: that is, with an almost demented frenzy – *besotted* with the phallus, *pleading* for a fuck, *deliriously* commenting on it. It must have been from these muralists' ranks too that there emerged another graphic specialist. This was the niche lettering artist, the finaliser of others' work in the field of poster advertising by means of discriminatingly applied speech balloons. On behalf of perfectly proper mums, sedately aproned and smilingly pouring out A's delicious gravy or doing the dishes with B's effervescent washing-up liquid, these balloons expressed for them, these mums, what they would otherwise have been powerless to convey: the lust by which, in the very midst of their homely activities, they had suddenly, helplessly, been overcome. It was a lust so uncontainable that they could do no other than lewdly beg for gratification of it at this very instant – by, these lettering artists doubtless dreamed, theirs truly.

None of those three girls I went out with was truly a girl*friend*: we shared almost no interests. With Louise Parker I did on a couple of occasions gingerly try to extend the conversation outward beyond film stars, pop stars, coffee bars and clothes, but there would then appear on her attractive slightly monkeyish face an apprehensive look. And, seeing this, and realising that the urgency of her every 'Right, right' signalled not intense curiosity but a desperate desire to escape, I soon clammed up and returned to the prime concern of those dates, the physical.

Fused into one

One evening, as I was reading in a life of Chesterton his account of his first meeting with Belloc 'between a little Soho paper shop and a little Soho restaurant', that undercurrent of obscure subconscious associations which ceaselessly surges beneath our reading bore to me on this occasion (I suppose 'little paper shop' was responsible) Walfield Road, with its sub-post-office-cum-paper-shop at the corner, on those tranced afternoons of wallflower-perfumed still heat when I returned to it with Olivia from the park, afternoons now emblematically fused by memory into one. It was almost like a dream to me now, that afternoon. It was *so* far away. But then I thought, wait a minute. *So* far away? Wasn't it in fact only ten years or so away? And ten years wasn't that great a stretch of time, was it? It was, for instance, only five years further away from the present than an afternoon at school that didn't seem far away at all, that stood out really sharply in my mind – the afternoon when we were told that shy, ever-flustered Mr Trig, the maths teacher, had hanged himself. But, despite this lesson from the intellect, that drowsy afternoon still seemed to me to predate the year in which rationality was trying to lodge it, in fact to predate the decade before that year, and the decade before that one, and the… Why, it seemed to predate even that Victorian meeting between Chesterton and Belloc, which, far from appearing remote and irretrievable, might almost, as I read of it, have been occurring before me now, so vivid was my picture of it and so contemporary did it appear. But why speak of decades, of Victorian times? That afternoon seemed to predate the entire modern world, *life as I knew it…* Yet still my intellect persisted, like a weary schoolmaster – like, come to think of it, poor Mr Trig trying to infix some facts in his wilfully resistant charges – in telling me that I'd got it all wrong, that in the context of the ages, that afternoon was as yesterday. Consult your birth certificate, it said. (As Chesterton himself autobiographically wrote: 'Bowing down in blind credulity…superstitiously swallowing a story I could not test at the time…I am firmly of opinion that I was born on the 29th of May, 1874…') Take a look at the postmarks on Olivia's letters of the time. There's the proof. What more do you need to convince you? And it won, that insistent voice of logic. Reluctantly I had to accept that prehistory could be pinned down to, of all things, a mere ten years earlier! I was discovering what every young person discovers at some stage: that past time as we experience it generally, in our daily lives (not as we might, rarely, experience it as Proustian-regained or apprehend it as Einsteinian-illusory), is not the uniformly coloured material we had always subconsciously taken it to be but is woven from two differently coloured threads that, as in shot silk, alternate in their predominance; that it isn't a single entity but is disconcertingly binary. And I couldn't help thinking how simple things were for us as kids, before the privileges inbuilt into just being a kid gradually fell away one by one. Then past time was just like absent space was. Absent space was simply the not-here: Sandbay sea front, the Rectory lawn, some country you read about in Geography. In the same way, past time was simply the not-now: yesterday, last week, last year, some age you read about in History. Yes, it was simple then: we hadn't got enough Time in for it to start revealing how tricksy it is, how, sometimes, scarily tricksy. How nice if it could have stayed that way, elementary and guileless. Did we ever *really* want to learn that past time is binary, that there's an 'objective' Historic Past that we conceptualise, that assigns all happenings to their 'proper' place, and a 'subjective' Personal Past that we experience, that stretches and shrinks the past in its own way like elastic? Did we ever *really* want to find out that the two are permanently locked in struggle, ready at any time to puzzle us with anomalies that we can never truly communicate to others and must deal with alone? Did we buggery.

In such a way, as far as that afternoon went, did I muse on the complexity of lived time. But after a while I began to wonder whether time entered into it at all. That afternoon, contemplated in daydream, seemed to me to exist outside time (like those involuntary resurrections of the past I would read of later in Proust), outside time and, for that matter, outside space, too: a sort of ideal form, a Platonic form. Those wallflowers, for instance, consisted of some substance which transcended that of the wallflowers I now occasionally came across; these were usually ordered in military rank and file in uniforms of unbecoming saffron and mauve instead of congregating en masse in the throbbing blacks, reds and oranges that were, that are, their only *true* attire (for what care I for Gertrude Jekyll's 'model' plantings of red, yellow, purple and ivory?). And whereas the wallflowers of today, I learned from Olivia, were biennials, which had to be dug up and replaced every other year, the wallflowers of that lost afternoon belonged to a unique variety that had apparently long been discontinued: everlasting, like the imaginary amaranth. (One thing, though, did link the wallflowers of Dean and Olivia's garden and those I saw these days: there lingered in the latter, even in the most regimental, the most vulgarly kitted out, a ravishing fragrance, like the ghost of that which once hung so gloriously heavy over that garden.)

And it was not only the wallflowers. If I gazed back at the pillar box at the end of Walfield Road, its scarlet coat aglow, nodding off in the heat of that golden afternoon, I saw a box whose Next Collection was never other than 4PM and in which no mail of known type – personal correspondence, football pools, income tax returns – was ever posted and from which no postman of known type – sweating, longing for a drink, hoping for a wage increase – carried out collections (just as no engine driver of known type had shunted that silhouetted blue-plumed engine I had once seen crossing a fruity sky and no printer of known type had produced that November *Knockout* I had once stood waiting to receive on an evening of biting cold). In the same way, if the corner post office, garbed in orange and just as drowsy as the pillar box, sold stamps – which I very much doubted, since I found it hard to believe that it actually sold *anything* – they were definitely not of the denominational, gummed sort you used for posting letters, since stamps of this sort would have needed to be paid for and licked by persons who had coins in their pockets and saliva on their tongues, and there would most certainly never have been any customers of *that* kind in *that* post office, that post office which would, for a wonderful, mysterious, unknowable purpose, always be Open.

Unless...

That search of mine for a book like Master's, a book that would satisfy some of the longing for more such enchantment – it met with failure. Dean and Olivia suggested various possible substitutes, but no matter how admirable the qualities of some they weren't what I was looking for.

In thinking about *Mosaic*, I kept wondering – as we often do when reflecting on a brilliant innovation in some sphere or other – why no one had hit on such a book before Master had. This was because my mind, too reductionist for its own good even then, had in a careful re-reading of the book examined word by word – an early, primitive, crude exercise in structuralism – the language used in its most magical effects and the structure used in its ingenious plot and had discovered, so it thought, a sort of blueprint for achieving these, which it considered should have been evident to previous writers, who could then have anticipated Master's work. Silly boy. In an all-too-easy anachronism I was making what was obvious after the event obvious before it. I might as well have asked why no one before Vermeer had fused a vision of the ideal with a masterly technique in quite the way he had, why no one before the Wright Brothers had realised exactly what was needed for flight. (And besides, in the realm of art at least, you could analyse a work as long as you liked, but you would never eventually be able to reduce the effects produced by genius down to a set of totally fathomable clear-cut constituents.)

Despite my jejune belief that other books like *Mosaic* should have been possible, I was forced to conclude with bitter disappointment that they didn't exist. And probably never would.

Unless...

The first faint wisps of an idea drifted into my mind.

Three

Sense of failure

Embarked at Cattalls on the mysterious solo assignment of counting the fabulous quantity of nuts, bolts and washers the company owned – plainly a lifetime's task – I had shortly entered into, had had the privilege of attaining to, in that monastic storeroom, a trance-like state of the kind we normally only learn anything of through the works of the great mystics. But soon into this religious experience I began to realise, with a sense of failure, that I lacked the dedication to commit my days to the exclusively contemplative life. I began to look around for something more earthbound. Lil was furious: 'That's a bloody good job you've got there. It brings in good money, and it's *steady*. Don't you go chucking that in for one of your wild schemes.' (Wild schemes. *One* of my wild schemes. I pondered hard, but no, I couldn't recall ever having engaged in any wild schemes. They weren't, regrettably, my style.) Naturally, I understood the importance to us of my being in a 'steady' job, but I did want to try one which in its steadiness was not quite so motionless, so becalmed, as the 'work' I was at present 'doing', that inventory which appeared to be purely, charmingly notional; I did want to try a job which would – requirement absurdly easy of fulfilment – be less unconditionally spiritual.

One evening I saw in the *Blackwell and Bexcray Gazette* that Lea & Lyle, the grocery chain, required an invoice clerk for their head office in Bexcray. Without telling Lil, I decided to apply. After a short simple test in mental arithmetic (these were pre-calculator days) given me by Mr Thrimms, the chief clerk (who had something of the look of Heinrich Himmler), I was offered the job and accepted it. Lil's initial shrieking fit subsided when I told her, first, that Mr Thrimms hoped my stay with the firm would be 'a long and happy one' (quietening Lil's fears on the steadiness score) and, second, that I had negotiated (that was how I put it to her) an extra five shillings a week more than I was getting at Cattalls (satisfying her on the income score).

Lea & Lyle

It was a fine summer's morning when I set off from home to begin my new job. I hadn't gone far when I was joined by a companion – a familiar figure, off for the day at the same time as myself – who with a gleam in his eye gave me a friendly impish grin. Chipper and cheeky, with unkempt brown hair, this was the district's stray mongrel. Having joined me, he wagged his tail briskly and after only a moment's consideration came to the decision to accompany me until his route would diverge from mine. We crossed Mountsfield Avenue together and turned off down a road of villas and robinias, and there, with a prankster's look of secret amusement, he played a trick on me. He turned up a path so that I should think it was the parting of our ways, only to take me aback shortly afterwards by reappearing at my side, the path having simply been a small crescent that arced around the back of a few houses separated off from the others. His grin this time was that of one who's pulled off a clever stunt. Then, near the end of the road, he actually did take his leave of me, and decisively so, his destination obviously determined on at the outset. This, it appeared, lay Elson way, for after indicating to me with a look, 'Right, this is where I leave you', he set off down a side road which led past my old primary school. I watched him pass this with stiff-legged, bouncing, resolute gait, then, perhaps conscious of my gaze, he slowed, looked back one last time with dark eyes shining and gave me a final panting grin before continuing on his way. Early morning, a slight blue haze at the end of the sunlit road stretching before him, a peacefully slumbrous cat on a wall, a faint smell of fried breakfast emanating from somewhere, his route planned well in advance, on course for his final objective, free as air, the whole pleasant day ahead of him – what a delightful prospect for that vagabond. No wonder he looked so happy.

The head office of Lea & Lyle occupied a small two-storey building halfway down Adelaide Street, a short, quiet side turning off Queen Street. Into that head office there flowed, from the managers of the chain's branches in Lewisham, Catford, Eltham, Woolwich, Deptford, Blackwell, Bexcray itself, Mottingham, Sidcup, Crayford and, well, practically every other suburb of south-east London and town in north-west Kent, the self-billing invoices of the groceries those managers had ordered. There, in the office, the cost of each item, ordered in varying amounts, was calculated, and then they were all totted up.

Three clerks dealt with this: Angela Adder, a dark young woman with a receding chin (and the first of many cases of so-called nominative determinism that I was to come across in my work); William Cogg, an elderly grizzled man who had worked in the office for many years; and now myself, replacement for some chap who had, as Mr Thrimms solemnly informed me, 'gone on to higher things' – by which he meant that, attaining to the same elevated level as Mr Thrimms himself, he had become chief clerk at Hopper Aylesford, the brewery at the end of the street. (At the other, busier Queen Street end stood a Kardomah café, which sold freshly ground coffee. So that, as I entered and walked down Adelaide Street, there would greet me, especially on a day of warmth that sent them wandering abroad and infiltrating themselves here, there and everywhere, first the aroma of roasted coffee beans, at once mellow and sharp, then that of fermented malt and hops, duller and fruitier, the two sometimes intriguingly intermingling. All's-right-with-the-world aromas, one stimulant, one relaxant, and, in that, olfactory counterparts of all's-right-with-the-world musical 'lollipops', which were also some sprightly, some restful. They were, those scents – like, say, in other settings, teashop tinkle or foyer cigar smoke – charmers that, suddenly slipping through a narrow opening in the tedious or abrasive fabric of the everyday, smilingly approach us, all and sundry, even the company director, telephone engineer, tax inspector and their no-nonsense like, and embrace us, sending our cares packing for a while and making us long for an existence in which they would be banished in this way forever.)

First thing every morning, Mr Thrimms, who operated from a half-glassed cubicle at one end of our office, would deposit a pile of invoices on the desk of each of us. Then it would be: Lewisham: 15lb green shortback – at 4s 11d per lb, that comes to £3 13s 9d; 55 cans Fray Bentos oxtail soup – at 2s 1½d per can, that's £5 16s 10½d – check that – yes, OK; 150lb sugar – at 1s 9d per lb – easy one – £13 2s 6d; 24lb butter at… Etc., etc. Grand total: £236 17s 10d. Next: Crayford: 20lb mature cheddar – at 3s 6d per lb… And so on for the rest of the day.

When my ambitious predecessor had left Lea & Lyle for the brewery, Angela Adder had, in that hierarchical establishment, been promoted by the SS leader's lookalike to replace him, to fill the post of Deputychiefclerk. And because, being a little hard of hearing, Thrimms avoided the interpersonal as much as possible, he had asked her to explain the job to me. Now, although I couldn't exactly call myself a whizz at figures, as Danny, for example, could, and although I cannot say that I was ever one of those who has felt helplessly, irresistibly drawn to the calling of clerk, I *had* grasped pretty sharpish that the principle of calculating each item on an invoice was to multiply its amount by its price. After all, it was an exercise I had successfully carried out several times at my interview. So I rather resented Angela Adder spelling out to me, in her dulcet tones, over and over again as to a child: '...so once more here you have *fifty-six* cartons of Rover Crunch and *each one* costs *two shillings and ninepence*, so again you *multiply* the cost, *two shillings and ninepence*, by...' Afterwards she announced that part of the 'task' that she'd been 'entrusted with' by Thrimms was to carry out spot checks on the invoices William Cogg and I worked on. And then, 'I have to warn you,' this whippersnapper informed me, with her sweet smile, 'that I'm an exceedingly hard taskmaster.'

I gave her what I had scarcely used on anybody before: the look. I'd been told by Billy Howe and Louise Parker that I sometimes had it. But I didn't know to what extent it was natural and to what extent copied from that steel-hard, don't-give-me-that-shit gaze that main men would periodically, splendidly switch on in great-stuff movie tosh. (These days, though, no one's 'the look' has the effect it might once have had: as a ploy, it's been sussed out too much, ribbed too much, that *self-conscious* piece of would-be intimidation by those who're sure they have 'the eyes for it' – take what horribly happened to that guy in *Get Shorty* when he tried it on. Though I dare say some gangland biggies still have naff recourse to it.)

William Cogg was a shy, polite widower, apparently one of those men born without a jot of ambition, content year after year to sleepwalk through the same humdrum old job. He was such a pleasant person, whom the accumulation of those tedious years had made even more wearily mild-mannered, that I found Angela Adder's treatment of him offensive. As far as I could tell, he was guilty of remarkably few errors in his share of our virtually non-stop, day-long computations, yet the 'hard taskmaster' would leap on any she happened to find with unjustifiable scorn. Unjustifiable because it appeared that Mr Thrimms, carrying out the occasional spot check on her own work, found about the same number of miscalculations in it as she found in William Cogg's. 'Mr Cogg,' she would say, 'you can't *possibly* have 36 jars of Epicure Pickle at 1s 6½d making £2 16s 6d...that's a *silly* mistake.' (Unfortunately for Mr Cogg, not one of his mistakes ever appeared to be of the far from silly, wholly excusable kind his chastiser perpetrated.) These humiliations were always inflicted on Mr Cogg (and on me) in the same unfailingly reasonable voice and with the same unfailingly winning smile. In fact, there was never on any occasion so much as the hint of a breach in that angelic demeanour of Adder's. That others apparently took this at face value disconcerted me. Mr Thrimms, in his buttoned-up way, designated her 'a most pleasant young lady' (but then, he was treated by her to oodles of honeydew-without-the-venom when she visited his retreat); her chief victim quite unironically spoke of her as being 'so nice'; and one of the two women who were always busily typing I never found out what in another half-glassed extension of our office described her as 'a sweetie'. Well, I loved puzzles, as you know. Mostly of course they appeared in the pages of books. But now I'd started coming across some in real life, and they were proving frustratingly difficult to solve. There was that business of why the jazz piano audience had so wildly applauded Ken

Day. And now this one, why the rest of the staff at Lea & Lyle considered Angela Adder a sweetie. That was a real toughie and no mistake.

Carmine

That idea I'd had on realising I would probably never find another book like *Mosaic* – it was to try to embody my own vision, or perhaps I should say my own vision revived and reinforced by Master's, in a work which even though it would be without the genius of his would at least be of the same kind as his, a work for all those who shared my love of it.

I decided to set this book in an invented city-state. The city: all-important urban locale. The state: all-important autonomous world. This setting would, I intended, mingle the most atmospheric elements of the London I knew with those of cities in America and Europe that my imagination had romanticised: New York, Paris, Vienna. The population, the architecture, the street names of this city-state would be truly cosmopolitan. I thought of calling it Carmine. Of course, this colour name was a bit of a pinch from Indigo, the city that formed the setting of *Mosaic* – but it did have a separate provenance, a connection with Dean. He'd told me that some years before, after much detective work, he'd discovered the identity of the Sicilian barman who'd fathered him. His name was Salvatore Vallone and he hailed from Taormina, where, until he'd left as a young man 'to seek his fortune abroad' (but in fact had found only his death: after a spell in menial jobs in Paris and London, he'd been killed in a nightclub brawl in Chicago), he'd lived in the lowly apartment where he'd been born, off the Piazza del Carmine. Carmine. I liked that name, especially in Dean's Italian pronunciation. And after all, I knew of fictional place names far more odd and far more curious in origin.

As to my story, I intended that it would centre on a quartet of individuals who would drive into the city. There they would find themselves caught up in some great mystery, the clues to which they would keep failing to discern. Until, at last...

The leader of this group would be a dark, singular, brooding, masterful man (looking back, I see now he was fundamentally Dean, with elements of Master's Rex Merchant and the Byron-Rochester literary template intermixed). Next, there would be the leader's son, handsome, brave, streetwise, heroic (again, something of a steal from Master's young protagonist, Mark Estes, and another example of what I and every other potential young male reader would have liked to be). Then there was this apollo's cousin, a dreamy-eyed visionary, fertile of imagination (who he?). And finally, the leader's young mistress, as intelligent and accomplished as she was beautiful (an idealised young Olivia?).

I could already visualise my opening scene. The light would be fading on a warm day in May. My four, as formidable in their own way as the celebrated comic-book Fantastic Four, would be entering Carmine by car. They would enter it as it smouldered in a dusk exactly like my primal dusk. And then...

When it came to me, the mystery – of which I knew nothing yet – would be, like that of *Mosaic*, suffused by the poetry of the city, ingenious, so difficult to fathom.

Mr Thrimms

I sometimes wondered why such a pipsqueak as Angela Adder had been placed in charge of us, especially why in charge of an experienced man like William Cogg. But I later discovered she was a dab hand at selling herself, and I guessed she had probably inflated her arithmetical prowess at her interview with Thrimms and regularly since then. The top Nazi's double might well have swallowed draughts of another's self-hype, for, a man more at home with sheets of figures than with flesh and blood, he showed himself on various occasions to be as typically credulous as his infamous original, that mistakenly supposed epitome of hard-nosed efficiency. (Not that I ever got to know Mr Thrimms any better than I did anyone else in that office. Seated all day in his observatory, from which he kept watch to make sure we didn't overrun our two five-minute teabreaks, he was what is commonly termed a Remote Figure.)

Occasionally, the owners of the firm, Charles Lea and Evelyn Lyle (or was it Charles Lyle and Evelyn Lea?), would put in an appearance, 'have a general shufti', as they used to say. Thrimms stressed to me that they must always be addressed as 'Mr Charles' and 'Mr Evelyn'. I took no notice of that, natch – despite Thrimms' exemplary demonstrations of the required style: he generously slipped in a 'Mr Charles' or a 'Mr Evelyn' after, I'd guess, about every fifth word. For their part, Mr Charles and Mr Evelyn just as undeviatingly addressed the ranks in the traditional manner.

'Hello, there, Thrimms.'

The man in the cubicle strained to catch the words (perhaps vanity had vetoed a hearing aid?). 'Oh, hello, Mr Evelyn. Lovely to see you again, Mr Evelyn.'

'Everything all right, Thrimms?'

'Severing all right limbs?' I'm sure that if this was how Thrimms, cocking his better ear bossward, had misheard the casual enquiry, he would, like the Levites killing their own brothers, friends and neighbours at the Lord God of Israel's command, have replied, 'I haven't been, Mr Evelyn. But if that's what you want, Mr Evelyn, I'll do it, rest assured, Mr Evelyn.'

Looking back now on Mr Thrimms, I find him, as I used to find Uncle Len, as we now find so many figures we merely brushed against in the past, scarcely real. (And I guess that, if by some offchance we ever briefly flit again into their consciousness, we might appear in the same way to them.) They were not *that* real at the time. We saw them only as cut-outs, restricted solely to that setting in which we came into contact with them, so lazy is our day-to-day imagination, so unwilling is it – or perhaps unable? – to envision them at other times, in other spaces, to lend them other, solidifying dimensions; 'WYSIWYG' is what our imagination shiftlessly fobs us off with. And then, receding from us down the vista of the years, those figures undergo that further stylisation, petrification, that time imposes on everything. Sometimes they then seem *so* unreal that we wonder whether they ever actually existed. Of course, now – oh, yes, *now* – imagination tries at last to pull its finger out, to instil some life into those pop-ups. *But it's much too late in the day.* We can't believe any of the stuff it now so tardily comes up with as we try to make out those ever-diminishing, blurred shapes. In this instance, 'Mr Thrimms was once a child, he played with toys,' my imagination babbles. 'Who you trying to bullshit?' 'He undoubtedly once read comics,' it continues in its doomed effort to add that third dimension, 'he turned the pages with interest, drank in the escapades of Desperate Dan and Keyhole Kate... You know?' No answer. Desperate as Dan, the imagination tries something different, the human-weakness line. 'Some mornings he probably overslept – er – swore to himself when he missed his bus to the office...yes, yes... And he may very well have left in the evening looking forward to – to – er – an Indian at The Oriental Garden and – and a Doris Day film... You know?' 'Now you listen to me, motormouth. I heard enough of this shit, okay? *Okay?* You get something straight in that knuckle head of yours. First, Mr Thrimms was never a child. Understand? *He was never a child.* Got it? What's that – how did he get to be Mr Thrimms then? Well, how the fuck should I know? I guess he just appeared in the world fully-formed like those Greek squaddies who sprang out of the earth when Cadmus sowed the dragon's teeth.

Something like that, don't waste my time. Next, get this straight: he *never missed* any bus to the office, because he *never took* any bus to the office, just as he never drove a car there or walked there *or travelled there by any other means*. You got it right in the first place, all those years ago. Yeah, yeah, I know, so how did he get to the office then? Look, woodentop, he *didn't* get there. That's the whole point. If you remember, he was always there when we arrived. Always. Every single day. Even that time when we misread the clock and got there incredibly early. I thought it was strange at the time, Inspec... Same thing in the evening. All that shit you now give me about The Oriental Garden and Doris Day. How could he have done restaurant, how could he have done picture house *when he never left the office?* You ever see him leave the office? You *ever* see him leave the office before we did, even when we worked late? Exactly. *He was always there...* Jesus, you still don't get it, do you, even though it was you who wised me up to it in the first place. Listen up, for Chrissakes. *Mr. Thrimms. Had. No. Existence. Out. Side. The office.* Now have you got it? Good. Well, then stop dishing me up those freaking unbelievable stories to the contrary, okay?

Gordon Bennett

Mosaic: The Delimitation of the Signifier. A new critical study of Master's book had just been published. It was by Professor Gordon Bennett – whose name, despite its owner's being the author not only of the present daunting work but previously of *Pound, Joyce and Eliot: The Logocentric Imperative*, resolutely refused for everyone, I'm sure, to shake off the connotation of 'Strewth!' A new book on Master. And with such an intriguingly unfathomable title, too. At Bexcray library I ordered a copy right away.

But why had a solemn logocentric-imperative-type academic decided to swivel his headlamp on to Master? *Mosaic* was not really considered to be one of the 'great books of the century', the books that enter, and once there for the most part lodge in, the established 'canon' (for what that is worth, the only canon that should mean anything to us being our own personal canon), and this was because Master had no interest in exploring 'the human condition'. (His book was, understandably enough, of no interest to anyone remotely Leavisian – though in the concealed truth that lay at the heart of its mystery and in the young hero's illusions that prevented him from discovering that truth, didn't it possess a certain significant symbolism?) Whatever claim to literary value *Mosaic* had, over and above the entertainment value of its superhumanly ingenious puzzle, was simply that of its being a beautiful, nigh-perfect work of pure writing, as, say, a Vermeer canvas is of pure painting or as a Mozart piano concerto is of pure music. (Perhaps one could say of its author what Laforgue said of Baudelaire: 'Neither a great heart nor a great mind; and yet…what a magic voice', and what Gide too said of the poet: that he owed his survival to 'musical perfection of form'.) A book like that will always split lit crit opinion as to its ultimate worth and its reputation will always ebb and flow. Currently, after a period of being becalmed, it was riding a towering wave ashore again, was enjoying 'rediscovery', was in academic vogue once more. Hence Professor Bennett's book.

Reading *Mosaic: The Delimitation of the Signifier*, or trying to read it, rather, was not a happy experience for me. One thing that Bennett kept doing was to take a passage of *Mosaic* that had presented me with absolutely no problems of understanding (since the prose of that book was, as I've said, so limpid throughout) and show me that I had not really understood it at all, that a seemingly quite straightforward description – for example, an avenue on a day of mist or Rex

Merchant's meeting with the Duchess – was not in the least straightforward, that it had a subtext, or, I should say, had in some cases, to my astonishment, *several* subtexts. Unfortunately, I had been unable to grasp the meaning of any of these, as Bennett explained them, and I realised that this must be due to a deficiency in my powers of comprehension, that I was struggling out of my depth in the waters of an intelligence far more profound than my own. One index of this to me was Bennett's vocabulary, so much more extensive and arcane than mine – and than Master's for that matter. When I kept coming across such expressions as *poststructuralist schemata* and such words as *oneiric* and *vatic*, I shrinkingly realised that I had stumbled into the big league where Bennett played and that I had no place in it.

But it was not just a question of subtexts and tough language. Even when, in cases where the professor was just paraphrasing a section of the novel and drawing conclusions from it and I understood all his individual words, phrases and sometimes even sentences, I was not astute enough to obtain a *true mental purchase on what he was getting at*, it remained resistant to my understanding; and then I felt the same frustration as someone who is sure he is carrying out correctly the instructions for assembling an appliance yet finds that it refuses to come together. For example, he would say 'Rex and the Duchess are both having and not having a barney here, and we can take that as we may, for in dispossession by stealth, certain ambivalences are the order of the day. We are made privy, in their exchanges, to a new grammar, that of the acquisitive slily masquerading as the munificent, and we salute in this regard Master's "syntactic" sophistication...' Reading and rereading this, I would take each phrase slowly by turn, and inwardly murmur my understanding of it – 'dispossession by stealth'...ri-i-ight...'a new grammar'...oka-a-ay... – but when I came to the end I would still feel as before, that, through a failure of my intellect, the signification of the whole had eluded my grasp in the slippery way a piece of soap in the bath does. I certainly couldn't believe that Bennett was in any way to blame for this, for in these cases the writing didn't particularly smack of academese. In fact, in using such expressions as 'having a barney', 'we can take that as we may' and 'the order of the day', it even had a rather conversational tone. No, I knew it must be me.

A magic carpet

Of course, there was a limit to how long and hard you could keep concentrating at Lea & Lyle on invoice sheet after invoice sheet of green shortback, mature cheddar, Rover Crunch, Britestar pineapple chunks, Daddie's Sauce, Jackaroo sherry, et al. Especially after lunch. And more especially on warm afternoons. Then, as I sat by one of the south-facing windows overlooking the street – in the silence of office drowse, with lozenges of sunlight idling across my invoice-laden desktop, the smell drifting in of coffee beans roasting or beer brewing or both, and from time to time, at the dusty junction of window pane and frame beside me, a heat-zonked metallic blue sunbather fumbling with dozy z-z-z to find an exit from his solarium – then, as I sat there, something I saw or remembered or imagined would float me off from that grocery office to another world, as though I had taken flight on a magic carpet.

Anything might launch me. An open page in Angela Adder's women's mag: an ad, an illustration of a trio of rosy-cheeked children eating bread and honey against a backdrop of sunlit lime green lawn and dark green hedges...Green Hedges, Enid Blyton's house...the children in *Sunny Stories* (Olivia's old copies of which I'd read at the Rectory years before) playing on a summer's evening in the environs of Walfield Road... Or it might be just an office memo: *Price reductions on tea: Horniman's Yellow Divi*...Yellow...the canary-yellow caravan, Rat and Mole on the bright summer's day the caravan would take to the open road, strolling across the 'gay flower-decked lawns' of the 'old house of mellowed red brick' on a thrillingly plot-furthering visit, as warmly pleasurable to the reader as the sun on their fur was to them...

And each of these voyages, initiated by some chance happening, might then lead into another. From the grounds of Toad Hall I might travel in enchantment to the garden of the Rectory on one of those summer afternoons when we played cricket and when over the lawn and in and around the rhododendron shrubbery and past the monkey puzzle tree and into the small copse beyond there throbbed, sunlit yet poignant, the strains of that intermezzo from *The Jewels of the Madonna*.

When I was lost in such virtually trance-like states, those memories and half-memories of the essential poetries of my childhood, together with various fancies that played around them, became fused by the great unifying power of the imagination into one single golden vaporous world. And at such times, instinctively, before intellect kicked in, I felt those poetries, those fancies, that world, to have been not simply created from my early years by first the privileged eyes and imagination of the child and then the idealising dreams of the adult but to have been *objective elements of those years themselves*, as though that was how everyone living through them had experienced them.

'Not very nice'

Lil continued to take the annual week's holiday at Edie's. For the last time, more from a sense of duty than for any other reason, I accompanied her on one of these visits.

As was so often the case, the Sandbay wind threw its weight around during almost our entire stay, getting stuck into everyone in sight, fashioning barbs from the icy rain and flinging them in the face, causing some to cry out in pain. This wind, by the way, presented me with another of those brutes of puzzles I'd now regularly started coming across. Rack my brains though I might, I just couldn't work out why, since that wind had been lording it over the inhabitants of Sandbay for as long as I could remember, since it was infamously a regular feature of the resort, why in that case the residents kept complaining, 'Terrible wind today', as though its appearance was a rare interruption of some halcyon climate they normally enjoyed. Yes, it was a teaser all right. And I couldn't help noticing that, whereas puzzles tackled in the pages of a book were fun, those that were now presenting themselves in real life were bothering me.

The weather was so bad that week, the rain so heavy, that Lil and I spent most of it under shelter: in amusement arcades, cafés, 'novelty' shops, cinemas, the Pavilion and, most of all, pubs (for Lil had been drinking heavily since she'd started working at the Prince Albert, the lunchtime booze-up in particular having become an indispensable component of her day). It was in these seafront pubs that I saw a continuation of certain behaviour of hers that I'd, unreflectingly, observed so many times in the past, often when we'd needed to ask directions to get to somewhere or other. On these occasions she would never approach an ordinary passer-by but would head for a bag lady, a beggar, a tramp, anyone down-at-heel, and if she failed to find one would seek out not a shopkeeper or a tourist information assistant or a policeman but the most menial of workers, a road sweeper or a lavatory attendant. Now, on this holiday, I saw the same thing happening. At lunchtime on the first day, we went into, or rather were hurled into, the Admiral Rodney pub, next to the Starlight Ballroom (and, I couldn't help noticing, almost opposite the spot on the beach where I'd played and swum with lovely Donna years before). We bought our drinks and then, with me, puzzled, trailing in her wake, Lil forced her way through the milling customers towards a couple she had spotted at the far end of the bar. I thought at first they must be old acquaintances, but that turned out not to be so.

'Better in here than outside, eh?' Lil said to the man.

He looked at her indifferently, then forced himself to reply: 'Terrible wind today.'

He wore a 'pale'-grey double-breasted jacket stiff with dirt and grease (once no doubt the upper half of a suit), and his bloodshot eyes kept flitting round the bar as though on the lookout for someone he didn't wish to appear.

'Gets busy in here lunchtime,' Lil persisted.

'Always does,' the woman said. The condition of her lank grey hair bore a marked resemblance to that of the man's jacket, her lower face was covered with eruptive blisters and she smelled strongly of an odour that once, in a different place and time, emanating from a tan-encrusted playground urinal, had bitten not unwelcomely into the torpor of a baking afternoon. I couldn't say I detected any of that quality in it now.

I was, as the result of what Dean and Olivia had instilled into me, too aware that human worth can be found beneath any exterior to look down on this couple socially or morally. But as I stood there, clasping my glass of bitter and forcing on to my face standard reactions of agreement, surprise or sympathy to the desultory remarks of the other three, I did wonder why, out of a whole barful of customers to choose from, Lil had set her sights on the most unwholesome-looking, most doubtful-looking characters on the premises. Now I know the answer. For all her bluster with me ('Are you trying to tell me how to...', 'Get out of it, you talk out the back of your neck...'), beneath it she must have possessed not an ounce of self-esteem. With a conviction of her own worthlessness so deep, so powerful, it was only with what society regarded as its dregs that she felt fit to associate; she gravitated towards them instinctively, she felt more comfortable in their company than in any other. This behaviour was all of a piece with her self-torturing immersion in the most horrifying of murder stories. And all of a piece too with conduct of hers at the Prince Albert that I'd recently been hearing about from Mrs Harnett and conduct of the same kind that I would shortly be observing in this bar for myself. What I'd learned was that she kept buying round after unreciprocated round of drinks for perfect strangers who were usually, so Mrs Harnett whispered to me, 'not very nice'. And what I saw now was that she was doing the same thing for our new-found drinking pals. 'You'll have another, won't you?' ('*Yet* another' would have been more like.) As for the nonplussed beneficiaries of this shocking largesse, well, they could scarcely believe their luck – they had never known its like before, they would never know it again. And I have to say that I too was shocked at the profligacy of this woman who was always claiming that we 'didn't have two ha'pence to rub together' and that the reason we always got the very cheapest food from the market, the fatty beef, the rank butter, the black bananas, the pulpy toms, the unnamed sweets, was that we couldn't afford anything better. Years later she was to exhibit an X-rated version of this behaviour after she unexpectedly came into a legacy from her sister Ada. I expected her to, I hoped she would, use this to buy herself the fridge-freezer she wanted, to replace the black-and-white postage-stamp telly she moaned about, to take the luxury cruise she coveted. But no. No way. Cashing the cheque she received, taking possession of a vast quantity of notes, which she toted around with her in a scuffed brown attaché case, she proceeded to blow her windfall in a matter of weeks on those inane Yankees of hers, their stakes now increased twentyfold, and on treating ever more strangers of suitably repellent appearance to ever more rounds. And perhaps too – for the money disappeared so rapidly – she was relieved of some of it in ways she knew nothing of in her pissed state: she was constantly opening the case in public to lay hands on a fresh bundle of readies, of which she who could always proudly quote to you every penny she had saved on this, every halfpenny on that, never kept an exact tally.

It could be said that Lil was simply following in the footsteps of a great Russian novelist who periodically blew whatever cash he happened to come into possession of, her variation on his work being 'Crime' and Punishment. For that was what it was all about. The lack of self-esteem that caused her to associate only with no-hopers, the self-mutilation of squandering her one-off pot of dough, they were all, weren't they, more of the work of her father's bully-boy emissary, the same one who ordered her regularly to put the frighteners on herself, that godawful Guilt geezer.

Poor Lil. One of the most pathetically unconsciously comic things I ever heard anyone say was what she sometimes used to announce before embarking on an evening out, a trip somewhere, a holiday. Out of the blue, this woman who had a positive talent for unhappiness would declare: 'I'm going to enjoy myself, I am.' She said it as if challenging one who had just made a prediction to the contrary, in a giveaway tone of unconvincing pugnacity, hopeless defiance.

Some mysterious adventure

Its bodywork still warm from the day's drive through the heat, the old black Citroën DS convertible, top open, clove the rosy June twilight descending on the city-state of Carmine.

The car entered the broad expanse of Princes Place, brimming and throbbing with dusk, traffic and bustle, and it seemed to Guy, at the wheel, that the occupants of the

173

Citroën invested the evening around them with a drama it would not otherwise have had, just as, in return, it heightened them with its flamingo sky and its red streetcars swaying through the dimming light, enchanted creatures of the urban sunset, humming, groaning, their antennae striking splintered blue ice from the overhead wires.

In the driver's mirror Guy could see a rhapsody in different blues: towers and spires and domes smoky indigos against the fireless antipodean sky. He caught sight of Leo in the rear seat. How masterful that reclining figure, hands loosely folded over the top of his stick, how compelling that natural authority tempered by the pathos of a limp, how reassuring the steady black eyes and decisive mouth. How glorious Leo's ripe young 'secretary', Candy, chocolate eyes kohl-rimmed, flawless skin palely powdered, kissable lips painted coral, all to please her artifice-loving lover. But Guy was conscious not only of how much he desired her, a lily all the more ravishing – contrary to the old sentiment – for being gilded, but of how much he admired her for her many talents and her passion for justice.

He glanced at Al, the young man beside him. Was he, with that fertile imagination of his that had produced the iridescent fantasy sequence *Aurora*, hatching something even more ingenious, some electrifying exploit?

Drunk with the dusk, with the rich fragrance of the traffic exhaust, with the power of the machine under his control, Guy watched the evening slowly darken around them, the tail-lights burn like red-hot coals, the neon signs flicker like a cascade of gems, the traffic lights glow like chemist's flasks, and it all seemed as if they were trying to convey something to him. But it was something that try as he might he was unable to fathom.

So read the opening to my book. I could only hope that it gave some idea of what my protagonist had felt as he entered the city, something of his sense of a mysterious adventure about to unfold. I knew as I composed this first scene that I had no idea of what the mystery could be, no idea of how my characters could become caught up in it, no idea of the nature of its solution. But none of that bothered me then, I was confident that in due course I should work it all out.

Not alone

Of the multitude of feelings we experience when young there are some, recurrent and strange, that we believe may be unique to us. Among them for me was the vague fear that had troubled me on several occasions. Then eventually my reading (the greedy, indiscriminate reading of a youth unconstrained by a course of study) revealed to me that I was wrong, that others had known that same fear in similar circumstances. The first revelation occurred when I happened upon the following passage in a collection of Flaubert's letters:

> I came across old engravings that I had coloured when I was seven or eight... At the sight of some of them (for instance a scene showing people stranded on ice floes) I re-experienced feelings of terror that I had as a child... I am almost afraid to go to bed.

An immediate recognition. People stranded on ice floes... Afraid to go to bed...

And then a little later I chanced upon this, in an autobiographical piece by Angus Wilson:

> My horror of the Polar seas came early in a picture of Golliwog's head appearing above the ice, entitled 'Golliwog at the North Pole'. And since then I have read all accounts of Polar expeditions...as others may read about psychopathic murders or the horrors of the supernatural...

That same recognition. The Polar seas...

Both of those descriptions recalled to me how I had felt on seeing a certain picture in a book at school: Shackleton's ship the *Endurance* trapped in the ice floes of Antarctica. She had been abandoned and was breaking up. I imagined the singsongs that had taken place aboard her, the warmth given out by her stoves, the hot cocoa or rum drunk by the crew. And as I saw her crushed by the ice that surrounded her as far as the eye could see, without heat, derelict, silent, the familiar feeling of disquiet invaded me once more.

The lone tot in *A Sea Urchin* about to be engulfed by a glassy wave...the two schoolboys in *Held to Ransom* all alone on a dark and bitterly cold ocean...Olly in *Film Fun* playing a prank on Stan in a desolate park...Epsom racetrack deserted on a winter's day of mist...Donna waiting for a bus at night by the cold sea spray...the *Endurance* abandoned in the Antarctic wastes... These may not have produced in me a distress as severe as Flaubert's 'terror' or Wilson's 'horror' but they had all brought about what was, in its mildest form (as triggered by the mildest stimuli), unease and, in its strongest, vague fear.

I could see of course that, disparate though they were in various respects, all these scenes had something in common with one another and with Flaubert's and Wilson's. I understood their nature and even, sketchily, why they produced the sort of effect they did. But, although the reader may well have done so by now, I still could not understand *exactly* why they produced in me *quite* the apprehension that they did. Even so, at least I realised now that I was no more alone in experiencing this than, as Master's book had shown me, I was in experiencing a feeling of a diametrically different kind. Reading had enabled me, as one of the blessings it can bestow, gratefully to begin freeing myself, like a drenched animal giving itself an initial shake, of some of the adolescent burden of 'uniqueness'.

Dream clues

Possibly because trying to hit upon a mystery for my book occupied so many of my waking hours, and possibly because in addition I had recently been thinking a good deal about my parents' death, about Harry's jealousy of my father and about the fact that he was the last person to call at his brother's place before the fatal accident, I experienced at this time a mystery-story-like dream concerning them all. In it, Dean and Harry and I were in the office where I worked at Lea & Lyle – only it had become domesticated with armchairs and pictures on the walls and was, unbelievably, Thrimmsless. Dean, who seemed vaguely to have become some sort of detective, spoke of various criminals he'd caught, one of whom was Mr Thrimms (which accounted I supposed for his unprecedented absence from the office). Dean was holding two books. One was a novel, *I, Claudius*, which, with a fixed look, he gave Harry, and the other was a play, *The Revenger's Tragedy*, which with an equally fixed look he gave me. The office then, in a trice, so effortlessly, so convincingly, became a cinema where Dean was reading with difficulty in the dim light a manuscript I'd given him. On the last page he wrote in capitals, instead of the Good: Distinction I was hoping for or the Poor: Fail I was dreading, FAIR: CREDIT. He spoke to me of my parents' death. Then he got up, signalled to the projectionist to stop showing the film and called to me, 'A *break*, a *break*!' so loudly that I woke up.

At first, in the suggestible mental state that immediately follows awakening from a disturbing dream, I believed that it was signalling to me the truth, that its message – the clues of the books, the anagrammatised mark awarded to my writing, the easily decodable homophone – must be rooted in fact. But then, as the dream faded, as fully rational consciousness took control, I dismissed it as absurd. I did, however – with an impulsive misplaced enthusiasm which I was to come to know all too well during work on my book – seize on those dream clues as possible elements in a fictional mystery. Until, that is, I realised that they were no more than adaptations of certain clues in *Mosaic*.

The divine madness

One evening in Valentines disco I was sitting out a few numbers, drinking, chatting to Danny, when my glance idly fell on a girl who was dancing with another. A most strange sensation of combined happiness and pain immediately flooded through me, as though I had been agonisingly pierced by an arrow tipped with some ecstasy-producing drug.

I was, perhaps, primed for falling: I'd been wishing for some time that I could meet a girl who had that 'special something' for me, and on this particular evening that wistfulness was more than usually strong. Then there was the singular nature of this girl's appeal: the fact that her exceptional good looks were disfigured by a marked scarring of one side of her mouth, a pale thin ribbon of dead flesh which ran from just below her nose, through both lips, and down into the chin, and which threw her sweet smile all awry. This marring of her fairness and the compassion it needlessly aroused in me heightened her attraction: I obviously had a penchant for that nineteenth-century Romantic thing, a beauty flawed, a beauty poignant. But beyond all this, and what prolonged the euphoric pain for the rest of the evening and over the days that followed, was some unique quality that girl possessed for me, one which, as is always the case, defied analysis.

The following Saturday I desperately hoped she would reappear. She didn't. A pang. The embedded barb given an excruciating twist.

The next time there was again no sign of her. I was distracted, unhappy (Danny could tell already I was a goner). Then, late, she arrived. At very sight of her, the age-old first indications of the divine madness struck, the at once wonderful and terrible madness: heart in loud overdrive, lungs mismanaging airflow, eyes locked on fixed-focus. The girl was with her companion of the previous week. No sign of a boyfriend. Glimmer of hope. I must ask her to dance. Soon.

Chest Group wanted to wait until its internal systems had self-corrected, were functioning at a slightly more acceptable level, if no more. But the chairman of the board as usual stepped in most decisively. Now there *was* a hard taskmaster if ever there was one (as distinct, I mean, from that self-proclaimed one, Adder). He got just as tough with Chest Group as he had done before with other components of the business (he wasn't numero uno at our complex conglomerate for nothing): 'I'm *very* interested in a meeting, with a view to a possible eventual merger – we're going to make the initial soundings right away.' 'But the airflow's still malfunctioning, sir, and the – ' 'Who's in charge of United Holdings?' 'You, sir.' 'Well, then, if I say we're making an approach *now*, we're making an approach *now*. Before some *rival concern gets in first.*'

So I, we, the whole outfit, whatever, went over and, in not too stable a voice, asked the girl for a dance. She turned and looked at me. The pain of my wound intensified cruelly. Up close, I saw how radiant with health she was, how gleaming her warm gold-flecked green eyes, how golden her skin. She smiled at me, loosing what felt like, in my suffering, an entire flight of the magic bolts. She accepted. As she turned to me on the floor, I became all too aware of both her body warmth and the light hyacinthine drift of her scent vaporised by that warmth. I felt, and had to restrain myself from giving in to, an insane urge, there on the spot, to gaze deep into those dear (so I was already terming them) eyes, kiss those dear (so I was already terming them) lopsided lips, cup those... Her name was Sally. It suddenly struck me – for the *very first time* – what a truly *lovely* name that was. I liked the way she talked: how terrifically *pleasant* she was without being in the least gushy. I liked what she had to say: how really *intelligent* she was without trying to... My God, I did have it bad. And so soon.

I danced with her once more. I returned to my seat. I wanted to take the next step, which was to ask her out. But there was a problem. The United Holdings research director, a canny but if anything overcautious bod, questioned whether there was 'any reciprocal interest in evidence to justify an overture out of the blue'. The chairman, however, who certainly didn't run the show on consultative, consensus lines, was having none of that. 'Good God, man, did we pussyfoot around waiting to find that out before the Holling, Parker and Gameford approaches?' 'But they didn't work out and —' 'I know, I know, they didn't fit in with what the company's all about, I accept full reponsibility for that. But that doesn't mean as a result we should now start retreating into our shell. So. Let's go for it.' The disco was ending. I went up to her while she and her friend were preparing to leave and, *with great difficulty* (as Voice Systems, too, had been cravenly warning), asked her if she'd like to see a film with me, the one we'd briefly 'chatted about' on the dance floor (I couldn't recall a word of what we'd said). This request took her by surprise, I could see that: for a few seconds she said nothing (it was a hesitation I wouldn't want to live through again). But then, with *that* smile which almost made me grunt involuntarily in anguish, she accepted.

During the days that followed, until the Wednesday I was to see Sally, I went down with the full-blown illness. I suffered all the classic symptoms: constant thinking about her, poor appetite, restlessness. As the hour drew near when I was to meet her, an almost physical pain tightened my chest and my heart embarked on the sort of steady pounding beat I'd once had to lay down on the bass drum for uptempo numbers. I could scarcely, I thought, have felt a greater discomfort if instead of being assured of seeing her I had learned that she had called the date off. If this discomfort had been the symptom of a physical illness I should have wanted to be rid of it as soon as possible. But because I knew that it struck only when, obsessively, my thoughts returned yet again to this girl, with her luminous green eyes and her traumatising asymmetric smile, because I knew that this objectively unpleasant feeling must therefore be one of the bodily manifestations of being in love, then I had no wish to be relieved of it.

Another sign that I'd fallen – plummeted, rather – was that everything I normally looked forward to had suddenly become, in some abrupt reversal that was scarcely credible, boring and pointless in comparison with *her*. How was that possible? piped up a more robust self, his tip-top immune system keeping him more or less free of symptoms. How could my book have glowed with an *intrinsic* fascination before I met Sally and now have dulled to an *intrinsic* dispensability? How could a competitive-betting evening at New Cross dog track with Danny, an engrossing biography, an important Big Match on the telly, how could they all become – overnight! – tedious, of no account? This wondering sturdier self in the background, reminded of how cricket in the rec used, with the arrival of dog days, suddenly to be transformed from riveting to hateful, thoughtfully proclaimed that love was an even greater alchemist than the weather, proclaimed this to the distracted smitten unwell self, which paid it as little attention as any physically feverish person would the consoling words of a philosopher companion.

We met outside the Regal. I had once at home, helping Harry mend a supposedly inactive electric fire that he'd forgotten to disconnect from the socket, received a mild shock. Feeling that current pass through my entire body in a flash had been a most strange sensation, one beyond the power of words to describe precisely. Now I experienced something very similar as, turning the corner on which the Regal stood, I suddenly came across Sally – not remembered Sally, not the disembodied Sally I'd been picturing to myself since I'd last seen her, but *actual physical Sally*, smiling at me, sending an instantaneous wave of something ineffable coursing through me. And, once inside the cinema, I was so intensely conscious of her presence beside me, overpowering my senses, that the old glamour of being in the Regal – faded somewhat over the years but still persisting – became no more than a background to the unbelievable bliss of being with her.

She agreed to see me again! Another date. And another.

Discovering shared likes and dislikes. An increasing absorption in each other. Misunderstandings, quarrels. Rapturouslyly making up. Lengthy necking sessions that then led to… Nuff said, as the captions would comment in *Film Fun*. ''Tis no way meet to bruit abroad the ecstasies Of voyages embarked upon with our true love.'

Blind swimmers

Sally lived with her parents – in Blackwell! – in a road off Cable Lane! Suddenly that benighted place palpitated with a sort of poetry, simply because *she* lived there. And my bus rides to Blackwell to see her, from the stop in Artillery Way at which Lil and I had once caught trolleybuses (long since discontinued) now re-acquired, in a new form, the thrill of top-deck journeys along that route years before.

Mr Banks, a beefy, red-faced man from whom Sally had

inherited physically only the colour of her eyes, was a train driver, on the electrified line that passed through Blackwell and Bexcray. Mrs Banks, small and pretty in a doll-like way, was a house-proud homebody. Sally herself, who had obtained some 'O' Levels, was a copy typist. She had, by something of a coincidence, worked at Cattalls, arriving a couple of weeks after I'd left. There she had typed from the handwritten drafts of the General Procurement Manager – well, she *thought* that was who he was – letters of which she understood scarcely a word, page after page of material like 'With reference to the order for 10,000 2½ in. 8-gauge countersunk, the procurement criteria has to be...' She typed these letters *in absentia*, as it were, rather as I had counted the nuts, bolts and washers in the storeroom. So it appeared that Cattalls had something rather special: a transcendentalising spirit that pervaded the entire place: what had worked its spell on me had not been confined to my department but had been more of a *genius loci*. Remarkable though this aspect of the company was, however, Sally had soon decided, as I had, that spiritual detachment wasn't really the most important thing one was looking for in a job, and she left after a month. That sprawling monster Dazings, which sucked in so much of Bexcray's and Blackwell's uneducated or only minimally educated youth, then swallowed Sally into its typing pool, where she was working when I met her.

Sally was bright. She could discuss what she read intelligently; she made incisive comments on the films we saw; she was later to show such a natural talent for learning Italian that in different circumstances she could obviously have been studying for a degree in modern languages (but then I would never have met her). Yes, she was bright and so, although audio-typing invoices for orders of Fresho, Safe and Glitter required greater attention than her previous job, even this interesting work palled after a while. She wanted... She wanted to... But, like so many others of her class and situation, she didn't know quite what it was...or how she...

Her parents were all for her learning shorthand. Shorthand-typing would be a step up in the world from copy typing; would enable her 'to cut more of a dash' was how Mr Banks curiously put it. Sally wasn't sure. She asked my advice. (She rather looked up to me. Perhaps it was because on a good day I could sound quite authoritative on the subject of *Mosaic* – which, my supreme test, she was enjoying – Gershwin's music, Krupa's and Rich's drumming, great sporting moments and, through the auspices of Olivia, some of the cultural output of France.) She asked *my* advice on what she should do. As someone who no more knew the time of day about the world at large than Harry and Lil, or the Harnetts next door, or Danny and his mum, or Mr and Mrs Banks, as someone who had no more idea than they did of the different levels of the social waters in which the likes of us so blindly swam as near-bottom-dwellers, let alone of what governed that stratification, and as someone who would have been astonished, even if he had been aware of this, to learn that it was all a game, knowledge of whose rules would allow you, even if you'd latched on to them late and even if at the depth you were you had little chance of rising to the big-winners levels, at least to ascend high enough to manage a consolation prize – as someone as clueless as this, who was I to advise Sally on what she should do with her life – apart from stick with me, that is? But I didn't, natch, wish to appear to my beloved as one bereft of all opinion on such matters, and so, in default of having the know-how to tell Sally – who, after all, was under no real pressure to 'earn her keep' – that the answer was night school, 'A' Levels, university, a degree, I opined weightily, for all the world as though I knew what I was talking about, as though I were offering a deeply considered judgment based on all the known facts, that I agreed with her parents that shorthand-typing seemed like a good idea.

'I'm afraid'

To avoid the risk of my besottedness with Sally becoming too obvious to her – which I feared might cool her feelings towards me – I knew I had to control my urge to see her as often as possible. So, if she told me that, for some reason or other, she couldn't see me for a couple of days, although this announcement would start up in me an almost physical ache (a kind of incipient semi-revival of the buried rejection-by-Linda pain), I would greet it with fake cool ('OK. Sure'); and I would even, inflicting on myself yet greater suffering (not in the least for masochistic pleasure but simply in pursuit of a higher end than gratifying present desires), occasionally tell her, on some invented grounds, that I could not see her on certain days myself. That was because I'd browsed through and mentally noted some tips in a primer on the subject: Stendhal's *Love*. Yup, those were the days when you could walk into Bexcray library and find on its shelves books like that, the days before 'pressure of space' forced them out (there even, unbelievably, came a day when in that place which had once been a repository of endless treasures you could search in vain for a copy of *Mosaic*).

What happiness then, after a break, to see her again. Apart from when we met at a rendezvous, this was always at her place. For I'd so far managed to prevent her visiting 33 Danehill Road, of which I was rather ashamed after seeing the Bankses' spotless house. But I was only postponing the inevitable, and one day I reluctantly invited her to Sunday tea. For this occasion Lil made a 'nice' ham salad and a 'nice' apple tart. ('Nice' was another of Lil's Homeric epithets, this one unfailingly applied to every one of her unappetising offerings.)

Sally acquitted herself well. With her natural good manners she forced herself to eat a heroic amount of the meal and with her natural charm made as favourable an impresssion on Lil as it was possible to make on that unpleasable woman. Afterwards I walked her to the bus stop in Artillery Row. When, curious, I asked her for her impressions of Lil, she was suitably polite. As for the state of our rooms, compared with the virtual asepsis of those she lived in, and our grub, compared with the palatable if plain fare her mother provided, she tactfully refrained from comment.

When I returned I asked Lil what she'd thought of Sally. Strange. I had long since ceased to take much notice of this woman's opinions on anything and yet here I was hoping to hear from her an approval of my girl, a verdict which I would then have taken to possess, exceptionally, some merit. Actors who have no time for the reviews of a certain critic will nevertheless, and no matter how intelligent they are, wonder whether they have not too comprehensively vilified him when they read in his column a favourable verdict on one of their own performances. In the event, Lil's response was: 'Seemed pleasant enough, I suppose.' This was strong stuff from her and gave me a satisfaction as absurd as it was rare in my dealings with her.

But this state of mind did not last long. Lulled by the uncustomary pleasure her words had given me into briefly forgetting who I was talking to, I mentioned that Sally was discontented with her present copy typing job and was considering learning shorthand.

'Oh, a *shorthand* typist,' said Lil with heavy irony and in what she imagined to be a posh voice. 'She wants to stick where she is. That's a bloody good job she's got at Dazings, by the sound of it.'

I made the mistake of telling her that it wasn't just the job but the inconvenience of getting to it. She had quite a walk from home to catch the 160C bus to Lower Docking, where she then had to change to a 163B.

Lil would have none of this. According to her, Sally could catch a 158B straight to work.

I told her this was definitely not the case. Sally had enquired at the bus station about the journey and found the route she took was the only one possible.

'Get out of it,' Lil exclaimed. 'Are you trying to tell *me* about the buses round here? She can get a 158B straight there, I'm telling you.'

With some weariness I fetched my bus-route map and pointed out to Lil that there was plainly no direct route from the centre of Blackwell to Dazings, whether on a 158B or on any other bus. She shook her head dismissively. 'I think you'll find they've got that wrong, I'm afraid.' (I knew that airy, patronising 'I'm afraid' well. I'd heard it so many times from her lips, more galling than any fiercer repudiation.) It was no good, no good trying to dent her iron certainty she was right, no matter how hard the evidence you produced to prove she couldn't be more wrong. Newmarket was in Surrey, and that was a fact. Dogs were more intelligent than cats, and that was a fact. Frankfurters were always made from beef, and that was a fact. I could get hold of a gazetteer, a study of animal behaviour, a fast food recipe book and show her that there, in black and white, in front of her, was the actual truth of the matter, but she would only say, witheringly (taking pleasure in throwing back at me the doubt I sometimes used to cast on the printed word, especially that in the *Warp*), 'You don't want to believe everything you read.'

Her wilfulness was so dynamic, her derision so imperious during these disputes that any third person as ignorant as herself who was present, such as Mrs Harnett, would assume that it *had* to be Lil who was right, surely, and would say to me or anyone else opposing her, 'I think you must have made a mistake, Xavier.' 'Course he bloodywell has,' Lil would confirm. The medieval church insisting that the sun revolved around the earth, in the face of all the astronomical evidence to the contrary, was not more immovable. When you took on Lil in a dispute over the facts, you knew you were in the ring with a fearsome opponent *who couldn't be beaten*. You knew that even if, reaching beyond whatever bit of text you were summoning to your aid, you had been able to assemble on the spot the world's leading authorities on the subject, who would present to Lil overwhelmingly conclusive proof that she was talking through her hat, she would, after reluctantly, scornfully hearing them out, simply reply: 'Sorry, you've got it all wrong, I'm afraid.'

A need

Into the unending continuous calculations the invoice clerks were engaged in at Lea & Lyle the only novelty, the only summons to be on the qui vive, was the occasional Special Offers which, for the duration of a week, would raise, let us say, Hyde's Golden Budgie Seed and Epicure Pickle from out of the ruck of other items and set them, savouring their brief spell of specially offering themselves, welcomely waving for attention whenever they were sighted by the glassy-eyed computator. So, in an occupation whose only highlight was a price reduction once in a while, it was hardly surprising that the daily start of my daydreaming, of my 'smoking enchanted cigars', as Balzac put it, inexorably retreated by stages, like the hour of the day at which the nascent alcoholic takes his or her first drink – in my case, from early afternoon to, at the last, early morning.

Daydreaming, like so much of our other mental activity when we are not actually doing something, is largely idealisation – the images presented to me by my reveries at Lea & Lyle were in the main ideal forms. Some were conjured up, usually for no apparent reason, by a piece of music. This was the case one winter's morning, when I had reached the stage of spending almost as much time daydreaming as reckoning. Just after the tea break there had re-sounded in my brain some wistful, lyrical, so-English music I'd heard on the radio that morning over my as-always-hurried breakfast: Elgar's *Serenade for Strings*. And as I heard it again, there suddenly – I have no idea why – surged ravishingly into my mind an 'Xmas' *Film Fun*, a mantle of snow draped over its masthead and flakes of snow drifting down its frames; and these then became part of an ideal generalised snow scene in which a pillar box, at the end of a road like Walfield Road, also wore its mantle of white. And, by association, my subconscious then summoned up a sweet New Year's image from *Cheeky Chicko* that had long since been crystallised by the idealising faculty in the depths of my mind: the yellow chick, the sun-gilded iced-cake lawn on which he stood, the cake-decoration snowman, casting on the snow an ellipse of pure and motionless blue, and duplicated on top of a water butt another ellipse of pure blue but this time ashiver – the whole tingling with a delicious sunlit chill, with the sense of the children's party Cheeky was going to host (though still, for no good reason, rigged out for a voyage of plunder on the high seas), and with the promise too that New Year always extends.

To most eyes a Christmas *Film Fun* may have been but a poor thing, all stereotyped figure drawings, feeble plot-lines and corny jokes, and a New Year's *Cheeky Chicko* but a col-lec-tion of pan-to-mim-ic strips that with the primitive illustrative and printing techniques used to produce them could not possibly have portrayed the sunlit snow and wind-ruffled sky-reflecting icewater I 'remembered' – but the idealising faculty, ah, the idealising faculty had raised them all into the domain of Forms, pure and perfect. And each had settled there, in its appointed place, fixed, unsullied, inviolable.

When *Cheeky Chicko*, all unbidden, quite unexpectedly, thus floated into my consciousness it was followed, as I reluctantly prepared to bend to yet more pounds and a half of this and half dozen packets of that, by equally idealised images of Mega Publications, the giant publishing house that produced the comic (and, among so much else, Harry's practical manuals and Dougie Leonard's *True 'Tec Tales* and Mr Harnett's *Fishkeeping Today*), and I wished that I could be working there instead of at Lea & Lyle (though Mega was, in its activities and renown, one of those worlds, like the BBC or MGM, so remote from my own that I would no more have dreamed of being able to work in one of them than I would have of being able to travel to another planet). I saw the offices in which *Cheeky Chicko* was produced as, somehow, prism-like, quivering with the rainbow hues of the comic, suffused with the reassuring cosiness of the mysteriously sea-booted infant bird's world and staffed by beings perpetually content with their work and no more truly corporeal than those movie stars who smiled so benevolently down on you from the walls of the Regal.

But we idealise not simply in reverie. Far from it. The idealising propensity is constantly active. Who doesn't idealise in advance every holiday? Or never mind holidays, who doesn't idealise in advance every weekend? Or never mind weekends, every *evening*? All those holidays, all those weekends, all those evenings that fail to deliver the idealised goods, that unapologetically hand us the rough-and-ready stuff that is all they have to offer. Who doesn't idealise in advance every major domestic task? All those do-it-yourself or gardening jobs that, self-presented to us beforehand in their model form so that we announce that we are 'just' going to do them, end up brazenly demonstrating that they have to be accomplished in real time, 'Good God, is that the time?' time. Who doesn't idealise everyone they fall for? All those upraised paramours who, to a man or woman, cannot help but totter on their plinths, poor things, whether they crash from them altogether or not. Who doesn't idealise day in, day out?

This propensity, it's so busily at work in so much of our

mental life that perhaps we should think of it as less a propensity than a need. And a need so profound, so constant, so shock-resistant (how soon it recovers, springs up again after every disappointment) that it must be fundamental to us. But what a Janus it is, how justified is our ambivalence towards it, that need which is responsible, in one of its guises, for uplifting hopes, noble achievements, works of art and at the same time, showing its other face, for pie in the sky, unavoidable disillusion, sickening plummetings to earth. Need at once innocent and culpable, at once glorious and godawful.

What a relief

One day in June I decided to pay Dean and Olivia a visit. With the calming realisation, as the months passed, that Sally loved me, the initial insanity of my own love had subsided sufficiently for me to be able to set my mind again to some of my previous interests. The desire to write my book revived in me, and I had a sudden urge to discover what Dean and Olivia thought of the idea, and more especially of the opening I had written.

I rang them and they invited me to lunch the following Sunday. I travelled down by train. It was a morning of cocooning warmth, fine soft drizzle and overhead a uniform expanse of white vapour. Yet you felt that at any time the sun could penetrate that vapour, since the white of it, seen through the faint feathery rain, was a white bright and throbbing. Soon we began to leave the straggling suburbs behind and enter the Surrey of the North Downs. The roofs I saw from the window were a clear but sub-topnote red in that suave, pulsing light and were backed by a horizon of undulating woods of a gentle blue (inescapably, even today, the mysterious Wild Wood), the red and the blue of some damply dreaming garden of wallflowers and forget-me-nots.

I had brought with me to read on the train the paperback edition of Professor Gordon Bennett's book on Master. I intended, with what I couldn't decide was commendable determination or deplorable obstinacy, to continue grappling with it after abandoning my first attempt some time back. (Of Auden's two kinds of literary critic, 'the documentor and the cryptologist', Bennett was definitely an example of the latter, who 'approaches his work as if it were an…immensely difficult text'.) Soon I came across a most strange passage that, rather than baffling me or eluding my grasp, took me aback. Bennett was discussing Rex's mulling over the idea of meeting Police Chief O'Brien in his attempt to get to the bottom of what had long been troubling him. Bennett had started by writing, in resumption of that style I had mortifiedly found glassy: 'Master here obliquely points us to Rex's problem, which is as much what he should *not* do as what he should. We are made subtly aware of alternative courses of action open to him, and around the decision he eventually takes we hear echoing, as it were, those he does not.' Then he went on to say, in elaboration – and this is what had pulled me up short: 'For example, by informing my partner that I am going to walk to the shops to buy some groceries and a newspaper, I am stating that I do *not* intend to run there, to cycle there, to motor there or to make my way there by any other means that would be quicker than walking. I am therefore indirectly conveying that *speed plays no part in my design*, that whatever may govern my aim of buying certain items it does *not* include any particular urgency in gaining possession of them. Such implied negatives can often as disclosures be valuable indeed.' I have to confess that initially, on reading this, lese-majesty struck. My first thought was how difficult those who knew him must find daily intercourse with the good professor; it couldn't be easy, I imagined, constantly having to second-guess all that he was getting at, to grasp all his 'implied negatives', to cotton on to the fact that, if he told you that, unable to fix something on his bicycle, he was taking it in for repair, what he was *really* getting at was that he was *not* going to suggest *you* have a crack at mending it, that *asking a favour played no part in his design*. Life with such a person might well be extremely fraught. My second thought, even more disrespectful, was that, under the strain of years of conscientiously investigating the deeper, hidden meanings of texts, of discovering in them implications that would otherwise have remained unknown to everyone else, the professor may, sadly, in the fastness of academe, have lost his reason. But then, as I studied the book as impressive physical object, looked at its imposing cover and preliminary pages, I was reminded again that it had been put out by *one of our most prestigious publishers*, that the contents were *the copyright of Gordon Bennett*, that its first part was entitled *A Deconstructed Telemachus*. Who was I, in the face of all this and of Bennett's professorship, to be harbouring doubts about him and his book? I wondered at my nerve. Especially so when I re-read the two quotes on the back of the book. One was from a review by one of the most esteemed female novelists and critics of our time: 'With stunning insight Gordon Bennett reveals to us aspects of *Mosaic* that we had previously missed, thereby enriching our understanding of and pleasure in the book. We owe a great debt to him for this wise, perceptive, urbane and elegant study, which takes us back to Master's novel with fresh eyes.' The other quote was from a Canadian professor of literature and simply said: 'Essential reading for all Master fans.' There we were. If you were a big league player, as these reviewers obviously also were, Bennett's book plainly offered unlimited rewards. If you were minor league, as I was, you had to reconcile yourself to not being up for it. A vague unhappiness touched me, as faint as the rain. I wanted to belong. I didn't like being unable to take part in the ecstatic applause for Ken Day's 'personal statements'; I didn't like being unable to share in my colleagues' appreciation of Angela Adder as 'a sweetie'; I didn't like being unable to join the celebrated novelist and the Canadian professor in their Bennett-led return to *Mosaic* with 'fresh eyes'.

The train rattled on beneath the damp white sky, beside damp green hedges, fields and trees. How bright the white, how bright the green, sadly lacking in Mediterranean blue and gold. And yet the bright whiteness palpitated with promise – and not just the promise of sun soon to break through and of the day with Dean and Olivia ahead but, echoing the pregnant colourlessness of those *Film Fun* Tuesdays of my boyhood which seemed like that of the spectrum spinning at speed, the promise of something else, the mysterious promise, the old promise.

After lunch, I told Dean and Olivia something about my projected book and showed them the opening I'd written. Olivia said she liked it. Whether she really meant it or whether she was just being kind, I didn't know. 'That feeling your Guy experiences,' she said, 'I felt something approaching that one evening in Vienna.' She looked across at Dean. 'Do you remember? I told you at the time. We were on a tram on the Ringstrasse.' (And, strangely enough, I had included in the composition of Carmine something of the atmosphere of Vienna – I mean of course the fairytale version of it purveyed in song, operetta, novel and film, the 'city of my dreams' of which Tauber sang on one of my mother's records, the Habsburg Empire city of high romance, in which spies mingled with beautiful women and dashing young officers at Strauss-melodic balls, in which rosy dusks, fantastic skylines and streets filled with snow portended an idealised intrigue, so unlike the real-life atmosphere of suspicion and fear that pervaded the city under the secret police of Metternich and Hitler.) 'I felt that we...' She stopped. She turned back to me. 'Well, just as you've described it...'

Dean, as I might have guessed, wanted some rather harder information than I'd given them on the actual plot of my book, as distinct from its atmosphere, from the vision I wanted it to embody. Why exactly were my four driving into the city? What exactly was the mystery to be? I had to confess, a litle abashed, that at that stage I didn't know.

Dean didn't put these questions to me aggressively, rudely – he wasn't like that. I'm sure now that, sensing more daydream than substance in my plans as I had outlined them, that eminently practical man was simply hoping to make me concentrate my mind more on fundamentals.

Later I handed him Gordon Bennett's book and told him how inadequate the reviews on the cover had made me feel as I tried to grapple with Bennett's ideas. He skimmed through the quote by the celebrated female novelist, and on reaching her name at the end he exclaimed, 'Oh, God, *her*.' I was rather taken aback by his scathing tone: she had won a couple of literary prizes, published a critical study of Tennyson, edited a bulky anthology of twentieth-century English prose, lectured in America, reviewed regularly for a broadsheet and appeared on television and radio as a literary pundit.

'She's almost certainly a mate of Bennett's,' he said. 'You mustn't be in such awe of *reputations*. You must be faithful to your own instincts in these matters. For instance. You love *The Wind in the Willows*, don't you? As I do. Well, OK, if you're looking at it as a work of literature as opposed simply to a magical narrative, you couldn't by any means say it's a *great* book – it's about *talking animals*, for God's sake. You couldn't call it a *great* book – any more than you could call *Mosaic* one. But then,' he added parenthetically, 'how many *great* British books have there been this century? Perhaps no more than a handful? By my count.' You could have been misled, listening to Dean, into thinking he'd read *everything* in the prescriptive canon. (Much, much later something else occurred to me. I wondered where Dean, who over the years had so industriously engaged in the business side of publishing and in charitable work – and who scarcely seemed, on the surface at any rate, to be a literary type – where he had found the time and inclination to do all the reading he seemed to have done. But, then, he was an exceptional person.) 'More to the point,' he said, 'is that *The Wind in the Willows* contains some of the loveliest passages of lyrical prose in the language. "Wayfarers All", for instance – the Sea Rat's adventures. There are some exquisitely written evocations of the South in that.' I sensed the Italophile in Dean speaking, spiritual brother of Grahame in that respect. 'Now you'd think a short extract from it at least might have featured in our friend's anthology, wouldn't you. But no. A whole crew of styleless plodders find their way in as *stylists*, can you believe. Whole pages of their stuff. Including some of her pals'. But no Grahame. So I don't think you need pay too much attention to what the author of that worthy, worthless tome has to say.'

Dean spoke with calm authority. Not the slightest hint that he might be mistaken. I loved to hear him when he was in such magisterial mode.

Then he turned, at my request, to Bennett's discourse on 'implied negatives', with its illustration of the author telling someone he was going to walk to the shops. And I was gratified, after Dean had laughed out loud at it – in an excusably artificial, point-making way – to hear him say, 'What you have here is a perfect example of two things. First, all this ferreting out of complexities that aren't there, this making the direct oblique, the graceful leaden, is what so often happens when the sterile uncreative academic mind attempts exegesis of the creative.' I made a mental note to look up *exegesis* – if I could remember the word when I got home. 'And second, it shows how such a mind, all mechanistic intellect, lacking entirely in intuitive intelligence, the mind of the tenured perpetuator of received opinions, can make such an ass of its owner when he fools himself he can in fact do Intuitive. The professor no doubt thought that it would be a good idea, that it would humanise him perhaps, to illustrate an argument in a more down to earth way than usual, to descend for a change from his usual' – he turned the pages in search of examples and found some – 'structuration, gestalt, hermeneutics, and so on, to descend from them to the everyday world of shopping for groceries and newspapers. But because he's not wired for Instinct, for common sense, he can only engage with that world in his usual rarefied, crackpot way, which defeats the whole purpose of his enlisting it in the first place.' He handed the book back to me. 'I shouldn't waste your time with it.'

Crikey, what a relief that was.

Classroom nightmare

One June morning over breakfast I picked up the paper, which Lil had just finished with. It was open at the racing page, on which, habit-driven, she still marked her selections in blue. I took in the fields. 0040 LOUIS QUATORZE... 1221 MARGIN FOR ERROR... 3300 RED FOR DANGER... Horses I didn't know – it was rarely I had a bet these days. In particular, I looked at those form figures that preceded the horses' names, trying in vain to recapture what I had felt when gazing at their like when I was a child: that they possessed the same sort of hidden significance as the names.

I glanced through the other pages, occasionally stopping at a particular story. One was headed CLASSROOM NIGHTMARE. I started reading.

A seven-year-old schoolboy was critically ill in hospital last night and a headmaster was being treated for a shoulder wound after both were shot by a masked gunman who burst into their school.

The attack took place at 3.20 yesterday afternoon at Kingsdon St Mary primary school in Surrey...

Kingsdon St Mary primary school!

Incredulous, horrified, I read on. The man had said nothing but had fired several shots at the headmaster, Roger Carberry. (So he was still there – but how lucky it was, I thought, that Olivia had given up teaching at the school some months earlier.) Of the shots that had missed Carberry one had hit the unfortunate boy in the chest. *Perhaps that very classroom in which Olivia had read us...* The attacker, whose build and colouring were described, had then fled. The police could establish no motive for the shooting.

I could scarcely grasp it. Memory and the need to idealise, combining creatively, had made of that school – as they had of Walfield Road, the Regal cinema, Pembertons department store, Bexcray post office, the Rectory garden and so much else – a place as safe as it was appealing, a place set apart, a place that could not be desecrated. Whenever I thought of it there came back to me the seemingly endless fine days of those two months I'd been a pupil there, the nesting of busy swallows in the eaves, the delicious drowsiness of listening to Olivia reading 'The Open Road'... Now into that image I had somehow, with appalled disbelief, to assimilate a mysterious masked intruder, a class petrified with fear, a boy and a teacher suffering horror, pain and shock.

The defilement of the sanctuaries had begun.

Notebooks

Never lose sight of the heightened awareness.

GKC on the mystery story: 'Essentially an art of the city, since the city itself has become a vast cryptic maze and an image of mystery.'

First you have to establish a context. My Four – where have they come from? – why are they driving into Carmine? Well, I think they could be returning there. Exiles perhaps? But an exile imposed by others or themselves? In either case, work out the reason.

Regardless of why the Four have been exiles, have decided that Leo wishes to establish a publishing house in Carmine. (One of its publications will be Al's *Aurora*.) Guy will work there.

To integrate, like Master, like Kafka, reality and dream.

I had started keeping a writer's notebook, devoted entirely to my book – for which I hadn't yet found a title – just as Master's notebooks had been devoted to his. The lit crit arbitrary renewal of interest in the author of *Mosaic*, not much different really from the ragtrade arbitrary renewal of interest in a particular colour, had eventually resulted in the publication of a new biography, which made use of manuscripts, notebooks and correspondence only recently released by the writer's family. This supplied information about how Master had written his book that had been lacking before, vital information I'd always desperately wanted to learn: *what writing materials he had used.* It turned out that he had written *Mosaic* with a Schaeffer fountain pen on yellow telephone-message pads – and that for several years before writing it he had jotted down all his ideas concerning the book with a 2B pencil (he wouldn't use anything else) in blue-covered pocket-sized faint-ruled memo books. Hey! this was *exactly* what I wanted to know. A Schaeffer pen. It so happened, by something of a coincidence, that some weeks earlier I had seen one in a second-hand shop. Now I went back there. It was still in the window. I snapped it up. (Once home, I found the rubber filler had half-perished, but it worked after a fashion.) But the yellow telephone pads – I searched everywhere for those without ever finding any. I had to make do with disappointing white ones. But I struck gold on the notebooks trail! In Court's I came across some that were almost a replica of those illustrated in the biography. And on the blue front of the one I bought I inscribed the same heavy black roman numeral I that Master had inscribed on the first of his. As for the pencil, easy of course.

I had known, from the hagiography, that Master's notebooks contained the rough drafts of certain scenes, plotting points, the germs of clues. Now, in the new life, extracts from them presented less godlike a figure, someone who scribbled the sort of mundane reminders to himself that you might to your own self: 'Don't forget to insert piece about translation in Bernie's trip.' 'Think up better reason for hotel's decline.' Sometimes, surprisingly to me, who previously had known only Master's miraculously symphonic prose, they were quite clumsily expressed: comments like 'Make Colombes more sinister – and also make Torino a bit more' shocked me rather. As did the desperation in such heavy-2B-pressure queries as 'What am I going to do about the chauffeur?' The handwriting (shown in facsimile) was, too, as the handwriting of genius always is, disappointingly ordinary, everyday.

These notes, this handwriting, no less mundane, unexceptional, than my own or anyone else's was, gave me the comforting illusion that Master was less awesomely different from myself than I'd previously believed. But then I thought:

how else should Master have planned his book other than by means of notes and handwriting just like everyone else's? How else should Bradman have demonstrated his genius at the wicket other than with a bat just like every other player's? How else Beethoven his genius as a composer other than with marks on sheets of staves just like every other composer's? I realised that the tone of Master's notes, the style of his handwriting, those commonplace attributes shared in varying degrees by every literate person, had in fact nothing to do with the inner powers of the man.

Even so, it was with an even greater sense of affinity with my hero that I confidently entered in my own notebook my own injunctions, decisions and queries.

Better than that

The latest company that Dean and Vin Sharpes had been negotiating with over the sale of Spectrum had been Mega, and now the deal had been finalised. I could scarcely believe it. I had always seen Mega, mighty and remote, and Spectrum, small and familiar, as having so little in common that to imagine the one being taken over by the other was as difficult as to imagine the newsagents on the corner of Walfield Road being taken over by a national chain. And how could I believe that on the cover of *Mosaic* the magical, so-fitting rainbow colophon of my uncle's company would be replaced by the ugly megalosaurus of its new owner?

Vin Sharpes had now become Managing Director, Mega Paperbacks (and Walter Gudgeon Production Manager), but Dean had retired from publishing. He wanted to spend more time establishing his boys' clubs in south-east London and working for his charities. It's only now that I realise how comparatively short his working career was. And, looking back on it, I find myself reflecting on his own attitude towards it. Like myself, like Danny, like some of my other peers, on leaving school this Deptford boy had found himself in the typically benighted world of his class: no qualifications, no money, no contacts, no awareness of the big picture, no prospects. But unlike us, he had had from an early age an interest in business, an entrepreneurial bent (he had bought and sold magazines even while at school), which had enabled him to take one of the flights out of his world, our world. This, allied to ambition, had brought him success. But – and this was one of the many characteristics of Dean that I admired – he had always been modest about that success. He had never regarded himself as cream rising to the top, never regarded his story as evidence of an attitude and qualities more commendable than the attitude and qualities of those boys he had grown up with who were in run-of-the-mill jobs or grinding jobs or no jobs at all. He once told me, when we were walking in the grounds of the Rectory, that he considered the main ingredient in his success had been merely a commercial flair as flukily in his genes as pianism was in those of his schoolmate Ken Day and as a powerhouse left foot was in those of ace soccer striker Malcolm Strimmer, another Deptford lad. But both Day and Strimmer (who transferred from West Ham to AC Milan for a record fee and then on retirement from the game acquired profitable chains of betting shops and discos) seemed to regard the instrument of their prosperity, one his hands, the other his left foot, as less a lucky inheritance than some sort of testimonial both to his character and to the enterprise culture. Day, so Dean told me, would sometimes fulminate against the 'work-shy' and contrast their 'attitude' with what had got him where he was, and Strimmer, as everybody knows, had become a way-out-to-starboard local Conservative activist and was adopted by the party at large as a self-dramatising 'I Did It My Way' advertisement for its philosophy. Both, in other words, flew the blue standard adopted by most disadvantaged lads who have *made it*, usually in one of the standard four fields of sport, entertainment, entrepreneurship, politics. But that blue was no middle-range blue, it was the arriviste's blue, deep and fierce, so much deeper and fiercer than that of those born to residence. No one more reactionary than your snooker-den-to-Crucible top cueman, working-man's-club-to-gameshow-host celeb, backstreet-to-High-Street tycoon, council-estate-to-Cabinet Tory bigshot.

Yes, Dean's outlook was very different to that of the stock no-hoper-turned-hotshot. But then, although he had the type's scalpel-sharpness (of course – how else could he have achieved what he had?), he atypically had something over and above and better than that, he atypically had not just intelligence but, what is much rarer, moral intelligence, *the* intelligence.

A controlled power

I hadn't, after producing an opening for my book, written any more: I still hadn't found the beautiful mystery that would envelop my four heroes on their return to Carmine – nor, for that matter, had I even hit on the reason why they had been away. *But* I had, already, most splendidly, almost filled my first working notebook with page after page of sketches, ideas, questions, reminders:

> The mystery as tangram? Seven pieces, meaningless in isolation, that can be assembled into several possible solutions?

> An icy wind swept through the streets and made the lamplight flicker. Guy felt a sense of excitement. Emil and the Detectives. Something about to happen.

> Who exactly is Leo? I mean, what is his background? What are his plans? What motivates him?

A thrilling blue dusk (dusk again!) in the old quarter of Carmine. Snow in the air. (Snow in the air. How tinglingly promise-laden I've always found that phrase.) The blue of that dusk gradated in stages. The intense, deep stained-glass violet-blue dye of the nearest buildings, the post office and law courts. Then, further off, the chalkier blue of the medieval west gate. Then, seen through this, the massed paler vaporous raincloud blue of the cathedral, closing off, completing, the perspective of the view. And inset into all this blue, the orange windows and orange crossing beacons glowing like Chinese lanterns.

'At the front of the Castle are the old General Post Office which was built in 1854, with its carved coat of arms, and entry façade to the old Evening Post offices...' – Swansea town guide. For post office in the old quarter?

The Evening Post makes me wonder whether I could feature a newspaper? Maybe, instead of Guy working at publishing house, he and Al manage to get on staff of only Carmine paper, propagandist, controlled by regime. At gunpoint they sabotage production.

Idea: Guy wants Leo to look in STOP PRESS. Secretly indicates this by crossword clue: Way to constrain fresh intelligence.

Overall design must be like one of those blown-up halftone newspaper photographs – meaningless scattering of dots seen close up, clear picture revealed when standing back from it.

Something incriminating found in newspaper waste-paper basket, à la Dreyfus case?

Perhaps Guy was born in Carmine, to which he is returning for first time since childhood. He has a false name, false identity. They all have.

As in Mosaic, the theatre could feature.

They entered Grand Parade, the main artery of Carmine, leading to its heart, silvered, gilded, bejewelled. Higher up, the tiny rectangular lighted windows of the massed skyscrapers competed with the pinpricks of sharp light in the vault above. Then soon they were in theatreland, whose multichrome neon completely erased the stars above it. Guy switched on the car radio. Music surged out into the dense, brimming dim air, the title song from the show Mosaic, whose venue he could see up ahead. How fitting it sounded to that young romantic at the wheel. Above an onward-thrusting beat swaggered the main phrase of the gorgeous Forty-Second-Street-type big tune. Mo-sa-ic. Proud of its joyful drive. Clackety-clackety-clack replied the loosely clattering feet of the tapdancing, cane-twirling chorus girls, top-hatted heads held high, acclaiming the melodious pronouncement like an ancient chorus acclaiming a hero, smiling at the audience broadways on. Mo-sa-ic. The tune repeated its title triumphantly, so brazenly he could scarcely refrain from keeping time with his hands and feet on the car's controls. Clackety-clackety-clack commended the feet again. The music drove on...

Yet now you could just hear in the background of its diatonic assertion, as you could behind the vibrancy of Master's opening chapter, faint yet unmistakable notes of chromatic unease and mystery.

Suddenly he felt a controlled power within himself, like that of the Citroën he governed – though in his case a power not in the service of some specific accomplishment but one diffused, generalised, all-encompassing, and one that was granted him simply by virtue of his being part of this evening, this scene, this happening.

Then:

Could I make Guy the narrator and have him fail to see the real solution to the mystery?

'Less than sixty'

At work, what with surreptitiously writing up these sudden ideas for my book, reliving the transports of the previous evening spent with Sally and wandering in the idealised world of imagination (though, since the recent contamination of part of it, wandering with not *quite* such happy ease), it was inevitable that my invoice-processing rate would fall.

Mr Thrimms did not fail to notice this. One Monday morning he summoned me into his office. I could tell it was to haul me over the coals, because for some time beforehand I had seen in the half-glassed box much unaccustomed darting of glances at me, accompanied by much tongue-moistening of the lips. (At the time, I am ashamed to say, I viewed these signs of apparent funk with some scorn, but today, having observed how none-too-coolly I have prepared myself to carry out a similar task at work, I feel more sympathy for my old boss.)

'According to my calculations,' he said, with a tremor in his voice and in his hands as he picked up a sheet of figures from his desk, 'you dealt with less than sixty invoices last week.' Foolishly, I glanced out at the other clerks at this point and so gave Angela Adder the opportunity to let me know, by means of one of her fainter angelic smiles, that she was enjoying my discomfiture. 'Now that simply isn't good enough, I'm afraid,' said Thrimms. 'I must ask you to pull your socks up, or...' Behind the berimless-spectacled weak eyes, beneath the shaking voice and hands, I became aware of a sudden steely Reichsführerlike resolve. It wasn't for nothing, I realised, that Thrimms had been created Chiefinvoiceclerk L&L.

Gormlessly I had always imagined that my job at Lea & Lyle was secure no matter what, and that if I left, it would be because I chose to, as at Dazings. Now, a little shaken, I took in that my job was on the line.

Dean's offer

And then, suddenly, it no longer mattered. Something happened. Out of the blue.

One evening of the very same week that Thrimms had issued me with a warning, Dean rang me at home (we had at last, at my insistence, had a phone installed) to ask whether he could call on me soon: he had something important to tell me. That visit by Dean has taken its place, alongside my first sight of Sally at Valentines disco, as one of those rare few occurrences in one's life that unmistakably, crucially determine its future course.

We sat in the back room on the old sofa. Lil asked Dean whether he would like a cup of tea and a 'nice' piece of bread pud. Attentive to the inner voice of experience, he politely declined. Then, without any small-talk preamble, in his usual direct manner, he asked me, 'Are you still unhappy in your work?'

'Er...yes.'

'What's the problem – *exactly*?'

I told him.

'And that's literally *all* you do all day long? I mean, you don't break it up with any other jobs?'

'No.'

'And even if you toughed it out, there's no possibility of promotion? To something a bit more congenial and better-paid?' He had as little idea of what the actual set-up at Lea & Lyle was as I had of that at Spectrum, as any of us have of that where others work. Hence those well-intentioned but hopelessly off-beam 'But couldn't you...?' suggestions from family and friends in response to the complaints about our job we all make from time to time. Unavoidably ignorant of the structures, the perspectives, the plans, the relationships, the enmities, the alliances that govern our existence in the workplace, they cannot help but picture it in some idealised, abstract, *tractable* form.

'Not a hope, as far as I can see.' I wondered where all this was leading.

Dean paused. Then he said, 'How would you like to work in publishing?'

I was dumbstruck, I simply stared at him. Now, even though I had this uncle who was a publisher, my lack of educational qualifications, my ropy work experience to date, my diffidence and the fact that Dean had never before so much as hinted at the possibility that despite all those drawbacks I might be employable in the world of publishing had together made the idea of it so remote to me that I think I would have been scarcely more taken aback if he'd asked me instead, 'How would you like to play cricket for Surrey?' I may once, in a reverie at Lea & Lyle featuring Cheeky Chicko, have *daydreamed* about working at (an idealised) Mega Publications but that was a far cry from ever entertaining a realistic hope that it could one day come about.

Meeting only with startled silence, Dean prompted me: 'Well?'

'I – Well, *yes*. But – '

'I don't like to think of you doing such a mind-numbing job as you're doing year after year. I don't think I could stand it for a week.' A week. The thought of Dean concerning himself with the prices of Chummie, Fresho, Feast O' Fowl and the rest for even an hour was surrealistic enough. 'Of course, you could find another job. But you don't have the qualifications to get anything much better – after all, what you were doing at Cattalls sounded even worse. You needed,' he mused, 'to have taken some sort of vocational course at evening classes.' This had never occurred to me. It had never crossed my mind that after I left school I should start studying again (or, to put it more accurately, should start studying), and certainly no one else had ever suggested it to me. 'Then you might have – ' He didn't continue. 'Forget it. I'm not here to tell you what you should have done. *I* should have got more involved, put you wise. Anyway, let's forget all that. What I'm here for is this. I think that, through Vin, who's now a director at Mega, I can get you a job there, as a trainee sub. It's obvious to Olivia and me that you can use words well enough.' He smiled faintly as he added, 'Not, though, that that seems to be an essential qualification for the job these days... Well, are you interested?'

Interested? Interested in leaving the tinpot grocery chain for the famous *publishing colossus*, in leaving invoices for *manuscripts*, the suburbs for *the big smoke*?

'Crumbs, *yes*.' Into these skimpy words, I tried to put all the enthusiasm, incredulity and gratitude I felt.

'Good. I'll get Vin to ask around at Mega, sing your praises – skilful young wordsmith, that sort of stuff – and see what he can come up with.' He rose from the sofa.

I was anxious to convey to him the full extent of my thanks. 'I really want to thank you, Dean – '

He cut me short with a compressed-lips 'Don't mention it' smile and half-raised-hand gesture of acknowledgment, then gave my arm a friendly squeeze.

After he'd left, I spoke excitedly to Lil, who'd been listening to it all in the scullery while engaged in some culinary preparations that I didn't much like the look of. Her main reaction to what she'd heard was the usual one. Jabbing a finger at me, she said, 'Don't you go leaving that job of yours till he can fix you up with something definite, d'you hear?'

She'd got the general gist of Dean's offer, but didn't know what a sub was. It wasn't until I tried to describe the job to her that I realised I didn't know *precisely* myself, and my explanation contained a large element of bluff. But what matter that, when the impact of Dean's promise kept striking me afresh? Going to work at Mega! Going to work at what would now be the publisher of *Mosaic*! Who could have imagined it? I kept recalling too the description of me that Dean wanted put around. Skilful young wordsmith. I repeated the phrase amazedly to myself over and over. In the same way that a young sportsman who has just won a title cannot take in that the word 'champion' he hears now refers to himself, so I couldn't believe, when I reheard in my mind's ear those three words of Dean's, that they had anything to do with me.

What others do

It was about this time that something happened locally which aroused disbelief in the innocent being I then was: as initially rumour had it and then the *Blackwell and Bexcray Gazette* confirmed, Mr Chark, who lived up the road from us and whose bonfire smoke sometimes drifted down to our own garden (as on that November evening imprinted in my memory), had been arrested with several other men for indecent behaviour in a public place. What in the first instance staggered me about this news was not that Mr Chark was homosexual – I had known nothing about him, he was one of those vague figures that, in the modern keep-to-yourself urban community, up-the-roaders always remain for us unless scandal or tragedy should strike – but that the venue for his sexual encounters was, of all places, the public lavatory in Cable Lane, Blackwell, that fetid underworld which I had loathed as a child and which, as a recent enforced visit had revealed to me, remained as squalid as ever. If I had been asked to name a location that could be guaranteed to snuff out all sexual desire I might well have settled on the stinking, soiled, unlovely-walled cubicles of Cable Lane Gents. And yet, apparently, erotic longing had regularly found its gratification there!

It was with the same disbelief that I later learned that Joe Orton had got his sexual kicks from cottaging at night in some public convenience's dim dripping dankness. And that at Dachau, after certain male inmates had been lengthily immersed in icy water as part of some murderous experiment and the half-dead survivors had then been warmed up by being placed next to naked women, some, in that nightmarish setting, had had sex with those women.

Disbelief and distaste. I must have forgotten what I'd done myself – fucked Rita Gameford in a damp, rotting, cluttered shed. I must have forgotten that I wasn't in the least put off by the fungi nastily sprouting from the timbers, the smell of decay, the unpleasant chill, the rusting bike and lawnmower, the mildewed boots, as, pressing Rita up against the spongy shed wall, I became singlemindedly, pleasurably intent on simultaneously freeing her left breast from her bra and thrusting my way into her. Well, never mind not being 'in the least put off by' my surroundings – the male sex drive is such a gross impervious imperative that I was *no longer even aware of those surroundings*. Gross impervious imperative. No longer even aware of. That was it, I guess, in the case of Mr Chark, Joe Orton, the camp inmates, whoever. If Mr Chark, who may well have been a far from crude and soulless man, habitually visited that Blackwell lavatory for sexual pleasure, then presumably it wasn't that he had to grit his teeth against what I found obnoxious there but that, helplessly in the grip of sexual compulsion, he'd ceased to notice it.

So, feeling disbelief and distaste concerning what I saw as the sordid sexual activities of others, why had I disregarded my own, which some – including perhaps Olivia, who I have reason to believe saw in me a sensitive, poetic surrogate son – would, if they had heard or seen them described ('They regularly had intercourse in a rotting shed filled with junk'), have considered sordid too? Why that disregard of mine? It could only be that, seeing the acts of others objectively, clearly, from a godlike overview – in which no amount of empathy can enable us to truly share their feelings – we see their surroundings in the same manner, and if these are unwholesome they contaminate those acts in our eyes; whereas when it comes to our own acts, seeing them not from an overview but, intent on fulfilment, only from within, we are so oblivious to any disagreeable setting they might have, or if we do notice this the force of its impingement is so much feebler than the force of our desire, that we are insensible to what might be considered objectively a defilement of what we are doing. In short, *and less from hypocrisy than from a difference in perspective*, it is always what others do, and never what we do, that is sleazy, even when the two are virtually identical.

Mega!

It was with a feeling that I was dreaming it that one fine spring morning, self-consciously natty in a new cheapo suit I'd bought at Smart Feller in Bexcray, I emerged from a street off Brompton Road, and saw, across the expanse of Regency Place, dominating the view, its Portland stone gleaming against the blue sky, the towering nine-storey bulk of Mega House. Mega! The mightiest publishing organisation in the land. So many divisions – Books, Magazines, Partworks, Comics, Picture Libraries, Paperbacks. So many publications. So many sales records chalked up. And soon, apparently, so my present dream would have it, I was to pass through the portals of this great building to become a *sub-editor. I*, Lil's boy from part-condemned 33 Danehill Road, the no-qualifications nuts, bolts and washers counter, groceries clerk.

Crossing the large circular central garden, its hub an imposing statue of some notable on horseback, how slowly I approached the stately edifice before me. Pausing at its threshold, how apprehensively I then pushed through one of the bronze and glass swing doors that gave access to it. How diffidently I crossed the vast foyer with its floor of repeated-gold-M-on-pearl-grey mosaic. How nervously I approached the glamorous female duo at the desk in the centre and told one of them of my appointment.

'One moment, sir.'

She made a call. How businesslike the procedure, how efficient her voice, how imposingly echoing the footsteps and voices all around. How utterly unlike safe, shabby, boring Lea & Lyle.

'Right, sir, if you'd like to take the left-hand lift up to the third floor, Mr Grout will meet you there.'

As I joined several others waiting for the lift, I considered with renewed fearful excitement what I was embarking on: a month's trial period in Picture Libraries, editing balloons and captions – on *True 'Tec Tales*! I was about to swap 3 dozen Rover Crunch at 1s 8½d a packet for he brought the butt of the Walther down heavily on the man's skull! For that was how I hazily remembered what I had seen of those tales at school – a world of Walthers and other gats and roscoes, of blackjacks and dames and punks, of tough American talk of the kind that had thrilled me at the cinema (though, just as I had been puzzled why manifest landlubber Cheeky Chicko always kitted himself out as a buccaneer, I had also vaguely wondered at times why, given the invariably British settings of *True 'Tec Tales*, its characters should periodically launch into the lingo of the transatlantic underworld). I found as well that I could recall some of the actual titles, the rousing hardboiled titles, of those picture-strip stories: *Stiffs Tell No Tales...Learnt Your Lesson, Doll?...*

As I rose in the lift – so *smooth*, so *silent* – my stomach churned slightly as I mentally regarded once more the commanding nebulous figure I had cast as the editor of those tough tales, the *boss*, a kind of craggy Mount Rushmore presence glimpsed through cloud. And then there were my fellow lift passengers. How *capable* they looked, how sophisticated. That grave, grey Scot, for example, with his head held so high, talking to that spruce, plump, apple-cheeked man. Why, they were in a different class altogether from the plodders I'd left behind at Lea & Lyle. An alarmingly different class!

It was, then, with some relief that, emerging from the lift into a corridor luxuriously soft underfoot with ox-blood red carpet, I discovered that Stan Grout was far from the intimidating figure of my imagination: the man in shirtsleeves who introduced himself to me was short, slim and balding with a toothbrush moustache and spoke in a voice that recalled that of Uncle Jim (he of the 'teapot game'), though with a slight, unsettling admixture of American accent. But I was soon telling myself that, unimpressive appearance and Uncle Jim voice notwithstanding, Stan Grout must, as *the man in charge* of a Mega publication, be several intellectual notches above his soundalike (though I did realise on reflection that that was not saying a great deal). Then, too, the forbidding size and complexity of the floor we zigzagged our way across – so many corridors, offices, staff – and, glimpsed through open doors, the dauntingly unfamiliar activities being carried on by that staff – mysterious work at typewriter, drawing board and light box, so distinct from, grander than, the tedious low-grade work I had been used to – all this, with the pressure of an anaconda, squeezed out of me the last of the small amount of bravado I'd with difficulty pumped into myself beforehand.

At last, after a route I was sure I should never remember, we came to the offices of *True 'Tec Tales*, and there I was introduced to the rest of the staff. The chief sub, Carlsen Purvis: unusual colour-uncoordinated platinum blond hair and slate blue jaw, hollow-eyed, restless movements, an impression of chronic insomnia, yet brisk-voiced, obviously go-getting. The other sub, Bertha Gurney: stocky, dark, plain, of indeterminate age, what looked like a Three Stooges black wig fringing her brow, deep no-nonsense voice, man's handshake. The two young lettering artists, Dave Watts and Andy Jones: most trendily and casually attired in muslin and denim, making me with my only-size-that-nearly-fitted new suit feel more aligned with square Stan Grout than them. The continuity girl, Clare Fern: pert, pretty, frizzy-haired, Dave's fiancée. And the secretary, Betty McDowell: angular, blue-rinsed, scarcely looking up at me from her intimidatingly rapid typing. I could never, I felt, have come across the likes of *these* people, these singular, impressive people, at piddly old Cattalls and Lea & Lyle.

Stan Grout showed me my desk, in the same office as the other two subs, and then produced several files of back issues of *True 'Tec Tales* and told me simply to familiarise myself with them. As I sat there all day, reading one story after another, studying at the editor's request the style of balloons and captions, I could scarcely credit that, whereas other youths and young men had had to fork out money to read what I was reading, I was *actually being paid to do it.*

Study in Cinnamon

Emerging that evening from Mega House amid a crowd of other staff, absorbing the busy streets and the rich smell of exhaust from the traffic, I was again conscious of the to me dramatic change in my daily life: I was now part of the great bustling metropolis, part of the great commuting swarm. At Knightsbridge I caught the tube, right away: plenty of standing room. But at Piccadilly, where I had to change, I was found wanting: I failed to board first one train, then another. Even pole position for the second availed me nothing, whereas some on only the second grid managed to get on to it. I was taught the first brutish lesson of my new existence, that if I was to make the grade on the track, that is, if I was to get home that night, I must, reluctantly, *abandon all normal civilised behaviour*. And so it was with much unprincipled cutting up, bumping and shunting, undoubtedly unpleasant to behold, that I made it on to the next train. And when I emerged at Trafalgar Square I felt, already, race-hardened.

At Charing Cross station, before passing through the barrier for the 6.23 home, I saw that most of my fellow-travellers were carrying an evening paper. Obviously a standard evening accessory of the seasoned commuter. So I turned back and bought one. It was some time after we were under way – clattering through junctions and past sooty house backs reminiscent of Blackwell – that as I looked through the Arts section of the paper the heading DAY RETURN and a picture of a familiar face caught my eye. I started reading. The Ken Day Quintet was about to embark on another tour of cities throughout Britain. One highlight would be an arrangement of a piece with which Day had opened his concert at the Metropole, Blackwell, and which he now called *Study in Cinnamon*. The tour would also feature other Day compositions: nocturnes and preludes (one of which, sounding much like his concert offerings, I had unsuccessfully tried to listen to on the radio). Then what I read next took me aback. The previous nationwide tour to which this was a follow-up had, the writer said, been a 'triumph'. Audiences had 'universally shown their appreciation' of a 'jazz genius', of his 'musical language', his 'remarkable eclecticism'. He had *wowed* several critics, he was soon to embark on a *European* tour...

I looked up from the page. I realised I was being confronted here not with a partial divergence from my own findings but with a seemingly universal, total dissent from them. Suddenly, as happens to everyone who finds himself, apparently, a lone voice, my belief in my judgment rocked and swayed like the train, disconcertingly shuddered and shifted at its foundations. It suddenly seemed to me scarcely feasible that I should be right and so very many others wrong.

True 'Tec Tales

The Picture Libraries department at Mega published six titles, each consisting of pocket-size, 64-page picture-strip booklets: *True War Tales*, *True Adventure Tales*, *True Horror Tales*, *True Love Tales*, *True Sports Tales* and *True 'Tec Tales*. Stan Grout had given me the last six months' output of his tales to read – quite a pile, since, like all the other libraries, they were published in monthly quartets. I began my studies conscientiously – even to the extent of working out and jotting down average balloon and caption lengths – but after reading a month's issues (well, even earlier than that, but I felt I ought to give them a fair chance) the disappointing truth sank in. I had allowed my feelings about going to work on the libraries to be coloured too scintillantly by what after all was only a callow earlier browsing through Dougie Leonard's copies (though, admittedly, before starting on my new job I had felt a quiver of uncertainty about the tales when I recalled Raymond Chandler's dismissal of the term 'tec as 'half-witted' and 'inane'). The fact was that *True 'Tec Tales* were the most dreadful tosh. (There was another point: in flat contradiction of their name, none of the tales were in the least true. Nor were any of the war, adventure, horror, love or sports tales true. It was an intriguing anomaly, a matter for some pondering, but one that I didn't like to raise for fear of being thought unworldly – and in that I think I was wise because in all my time in the department I never once heard anyone else mention it.)

So my disillusionment was deep. Despite that, however,

when, after I had finished 'soaking up the style' and had been shown by Stan Grout some rudimentary points of editing, I was then given my first script to tackle as a trial run, I felt absurdly thrilled. Hesitantly pencilling in suggested changes to plot, to speech balloons and captions, I could scarcely credit that here I was *editing*, that my diffident marks might end up *in print*.

The tales had a cast of eight 'tecs, each making a two-monthly appearance, as on a rota. I say 'tecs, in line with the tales' overall title, but, even though these 'tecs were exclusively British, like the settings, Grout invariably referred to them as 'eyes': he had a thing about what he would invariably call 'the US of A'. Hence that curious, tentatively Americanised accent of his, not so much mid-Atlantic as a sort of quarter-way-across-Atlantic, which I was already finding more disconcerting than if he'd gone whole-hog Yank. And it wasn't just the accent, it was the vocabulary: 'sock it to me' (to a sub about a script idea), 'get off your goddam butt' (to a writer who needed to do some research) – and all of it straight, no trace of cod. It was due to him that the 'eyes' spoke in that curious way I had noted years before. They would introduce into a formal, tight-arsed English already painful enough the most incongruous transatlanticisms, quite random: 'Yeah, buddy boy, so why does Chief Inspector Tattersall, who, as you are aware, has been placed in overall charge of the investigation, intimate that he heard you smart-arsing Big Eddie for Chrissakes?' Nor did the captions escape this excruciating idiom: 'Bert kept his eyes peeled for the next lay-by. And just outside Luton the trucker swung forty tons of big rig off the highway.'

Grout obviously reckoned that these fitful injections gave the tales more glamour, more drama, more life – since for him these were the exclusive province of the US of A. Most of the needle jobs he was responsible for himself: usually banging his head against a brick wall when he exhorted writers and editors to 'slick up this copy, goddamit', he would end up tetchily consulting the great database of Americanisms in his own head, culled from a thousand films, books and mags, and would inject the material himself, impatiently, haphazardly.

In his attempts to gee up those melancholy and apathetic souls, the stable of hacks who wrote our stories, Grout would often put to them, in his written responses to their contributions: 'Think again. What would Marlowe have said? What would Marlowe have done?' But from the evidence of what this prompting produced, it seemed that they were not too familiar with what the great man said and did. I have to say, however, that there was one thing they shared with Marlowe's creator (I stress one thing). It was in his casual admission, 'I'm one writer who never says I have a terrific idea for a story. I don't get ideas.' This summed up our chaps to a T. Their submissions were, distressingly – and in this they resembled life at large – recyclings of the same few tired old plots. Set and kept jerkily in motion by a bunch of grotesques – the grinning, square-jawed 'eye', the curvaceous 'chick', the pencil-line-moustached 'big wheel' – helped on their agonising way by periodic dollops of coincidence, vocalised in a language unknown to man, those stories of theirs must rank as possibly the worst ever written. It was understandable, then, that none of our hacks, in all my time at *True 'Tec Tales*, ever dared show their face in the office. And the only time they ever rang in was to enquire about their always criminally long-overdue payments. Talk about shadowy figures. Even so, I had a clear enough picture of them: men of drawn appearance and shabby wardrobe, bereft of all hope, rent- or mortgage-doomed to keep rolling the rock of those terrible tales uphill month after month, year after year.

Each new environment

If my opinion of *True 'Tec Tales* had soon changed, so had my perception of the staff. On my first day I had felt that the Mega people I was to work with could never have been encountered at tinpot Cattalls or Lea & Lyle. It had obviously not occurred to me that I exemplified in my own person the feasibility of dual citizenship and that my idea that it was impossible was therefore a nonsense – though a common one: when we try to evaluate the worlds we inhabit we never allot enough weight to the constituent that's ourself. I had forgotten too that on my first day at Lea & Lyle, when it had contrasted itself forcibly and favourably with Cattalls, I had experienced – if to not so great a degree – feelings similar to those that had overwhelmed me on entering the offices of *True 'Tec Tales*. It happens all the time in our impressionable youth, before the years have blunted our sensibility and homogenised the world around us. Each completely new environment that assails our senses as we enter it seems to consist, as would some strikingly original play we were seeing for the first time, of a *raison d'être*, an ethos, a cast of characters not only utterly unique, and therefore disorientatingly distinct from, unrelatable to, all those we have known before but somehow, strangely, *superior* to them. On first entering the offices of Lea & Lyle, for example, Angela Adder, William Cogg, the typists, the large wall clock, the beige and brown coffee machine seemed not simply more singular than the clerks, the typists, the clocks, the coffee machines I had become acquainted with at Cattalls on forays outside my monastic cell – and so much more singular as to appear almost to belong to another plane of reality – but also of higher quality, more agreeable, more efficient, more worthy. And it is in this apparent effortless excellence that the elements of our new surroundings, as we subconsciously contrast them with their commonplace counterparts from our past, daunt us, make us feel lost. It does not take long of course for them to become truly known, to reveal all their defects, to show themselves as all too like our own flawed self for our initial awe to survive, as all too like the familiar assembly of the imperfect, the ordinary, that has constituted all the other environments we have experienced (that imperfect, that ordinary, which those who inhabited those environments when we first entered them *had long since known themselves to reside in*). How could I, I used to wonder after I had been at Lea & Lyle some time, have been so initially impressed by Angela Adder, whose honeyed insolence soon became so evident, by William Cogg, who showed himself to be so feebly futile, by the typists, whose intermittently overheard small talk revealed them to be no different from so-ordinary Mrs Harnett or Aunt Edie, by the wall clock, whose overloud ticking seemed at certain times all too obviously to be counting off your days, by the coffee machine, which I discovered needed at times a good kicking to make it work?

And so it was at *True 'Tec Tales*. Stan Grout and each member of his staff and the offices they inhabited were gradually revealed, as the days passed, to be scarcely *qualitatively* different from all the other people and establishments I had known. Stan Grout's rather fatuous smirk of satisfaction whenever a new idea for a title occurred to him reminded me of that which used to appear on 'Nasty' Naylor's face in the chemistry lab when he prepared to inflict on a boy the latest of his unusual physical punishments; Clare Fern had a giggle and general outlook on life not dissimilar to that of my one-time girlfriend April Holling; the figures on the pay slips at *True 'Tec Tales* were no less unfathomable than those at Cattalls; the filing cabinets in our office had the same...

Later I would find myself wondering what the reason was for that disposition in the young to find so many novel environments superior to those that have gone before. And it seemed to me, on reflection, that the cause, yet again, is our helpless tendency, our profound need, to idealise, that when we are young our instinctive approach to the world at large, and by extension to individual worlds that are at first virgin territory, is a desire to believe the *very* best of them, of their people and their habitat, an involuntary investment of them with a worth that is unalloyed. It is, in short, an attitude of trusting generosity – and one rather touching as we look back on it down the perspective of the years that have gradually seen it wither away.

It

As one evening later that week the train carried me homeward, the view trackside of blackened terrace house backs and wasteland, most strangely *instinct* with my earlier reflections on Ken Day, brought me back to the question I had left suspended on that earlier evening: could I really believe that the many were wrong about him and I was right? And I came to the conclusion No. By this I don't mean that I began to convince myself that he must have had certain qualities I hadn't previously been able to discern. What I mean is that I realised the question, couched in the terms in which I had put it, was a false one. It wasn't a matter of being right or being wrong; it was simply whether you had an affinity with or an antipathy to someone's work. When I learned later that Poulenc extolled Debussy's music as 'oxygen' and Prokofiev spurned it as 'jelly', that Gounod thought Wagner mediocre and Chabrier thought him sublime, that Scott Fitzgerald (who wanted to be the Keats of English prose) hailed *Mosaic* as 'one long glorious poem' and Thomas Wolfe rejected it as 'meretricious', that Gide called Dostoevsky 'the greatest of all novelists' and Nabokov dismissed him as 'tedious and muddled', I understood that none of these men of genius was right or wrong in his strongly held opinion but was simply expressing a personal affinity or antipathy.

Affinities. In my case, one such was Schumann, whose musical language, whose lyricism, peculiarly his own, so different from that of other composers, was clearly transmitted on a signal frequency which my soul was one of those tuned to receive. (Schumann, who, incidentally, identified within himself a practical self he named Florestan and a poetical one, Eusebius – an internal separation that many must be familiar with and that I for one, in later circumstances, came to know all too well.) Sometimes in his music it was no more than a brief passage or just a phrase or perhaps merely a chord that spoke to me in that special voice. There was, for example, in 'Farewell' from the *Waldszenen* a passage in which the beautiful, wise, sad but indomitable melody in the right hand was immediately afterwards reinforced by a stirringly even more indomitable voice of affirmation in the bass, effecting in me one of those sensations which only music can produce and which no description can convey. Then in *Papillons* there occurred a particular phrase which induced in me an ineffably sweet ache. And in 'Romanze' from *Faschingsschwank aus Wien* a series of widely separated lone low notes sounding beneath the melody every so often, unexpectedly and so deeply, seemed to touch on a nobility equally ineffable, again supportive but this time quietly, like the measured confirmation of a god. All of these musical embodiments of the composer's psyche, lengthy or brief, had for me what I would have called in my more inarticulate moments that special *something*, or *It* – though, for expressing the inexpressible, these terms may not perhaps be so very lacking in eloquence after all – that something, or It, which evoked in my own soul a fervent response, fervent as that aroused in me as a boy by Gershwin and by Master. A response that makes us feel the composer or writer has spoken directly to us, that he or she has expressed for us something true and beautiful we have known or intuited deep within us but could never have put into such music or words ourselves, since we are, as it were, only geniuses *manqués*. We feel almost that, through their fully realised genius, those artists have returned us, with themselves, to a world we once shared with them. We feel as Baudelaire did when he wrote to Wagner, after being transported by his music: 'It seemed to me that this music was *my own*...I recognised it...' We feel, when we hear or read one of *those* passages, *those* phrases – passages, phrases indefinable and thus indescribable in their effect, perhaps bringing a smile to our lips or that stricken look to our face which is scarcely distinguishable from a look of cruelty – we feel that the composer's or writer's soul is linked to ours, we feel a fervent rapport with him or her, we feel we are members of the same spiritual family, of what the Elizabethans meant by 'the same kind', the kin linked by strong family feeling, members of the brotherhood Poe alluded to when, in writing to the editor who first encouraged his literary ambitions and whom he regarded as a fellow-spirit, he said: 'There can be no tie more strong than that of brother for brother – it is not so much that they love one another, as that...their affections are always running in the same direction...and cannot help mingling.' And Poe himself inspired such brotherly affinity in other writers who came after him.

Antipathies. To those whose work bores us or, worse, grates on us. Those to whose spiritual family we certainly do not belong. But I realised that, just as I had to stop thinking that in the great arena of more or less comparable artistic endeavour a particular response was right or wrong, so it would never do, in this matter of spiritual families I was considering, simply to swap one lot of evaluations for another – in other words, to suppose that the family to which we belonged was in any way superior to the families to which we did not belong; I realised that, just as we would not dream of justifying our love for our own parents, brothers, sisters, spouse and children, our preference for them to the others we know, by claiming they are objectively more estimable (indeed honesty would force us to admit that in certain respects they are all too flawed), so it had to be with our spiritual families. This was easier said than done, of course. I should find it difficult to renounce my natural attitude to what spoke most potently to me in music, books, paintings, an attitude developed over the years. For example, a certain ravishing, questioning chord in Gershwin's 'The Man I Love', a certain piercingly observant, startlingly imaged sentence in Master's *Mosaic*, a certain outlandishly beautiful passage in one of Modigliani's portraits of Leopold Zborowski all elicited from me that smitten, spontaneous, inarticulate 'Ah! This is It' – when by It I meant *the* truth, *the* essence, which their creators had intuited and I had recognised. (I had tried to examine the means by which those truths had been conveyed. But weren't all such reductive investigations pointless, really? When I asked Olivia about that chord in 'The Man I Love' and she told me, rightly or wrongly, that it was an inversion chord of B flat minor unexpectedly occurring after root position chords of it; when I analysed that sentence of Master's and pondered on the startlingly unexpected usages of certain words in it; when I studied that piece of portraiture of Modigliani's and noted the distortions, the palette, the impasto – where did any of that get me beyond the intellectual interest of the exercise? Weren't the truths expressed way beyond mere technique?) Yes, it had been my natural reaction to feel, when that chord, that sentence, that passage of painting pleasurably transfixed me, that this was It, *the* truth, *the* essence. But I had to recognise that this wasn't so at all, that what had delighted me was only one truth, one essence, among many possible others (which meant nothing to me), the truth, the essence, only of its creators and of those who responded to it. Having come across individuals who were devoted to artists who left me cold (Bertha Gurney at *True 'Tec Tales*, for example, was, incomprehensibly to me, a Benjamin Britten fan and made regular pilgrimages to the Aldeburgh Festival; later I was to work with an editor who, just as incomprehensibly to me, doted on El Greco), I had to understand that *these* artists expressed what *their* devotees felt to be It.

As a result of this train of thought, when a few months later I learned that Moisewitsch had called Schumann the greatest of all composers and Britten had called Brahms the worst and likened Beethoven's music to 'sacks of potatoes', it seemed to me that they should instead simply have expressed sentiments along the lines of, respectively, 'I have a special affinity with Schumann, I belong to the same spiritual family as he does' and 'I have an antipathy to Brahms and Beethoven, we belong to different spiritual families.'

And so to return to Ken Day. I knew now I had to accept that, of those who had acclaimed him on his tour, some had genuinely enjoyed his playing – though only some, the applause of others, I was certain, having had as little to do with authentic pleasure as I'd suspected the applause at the concert in Blackwell had. I couldn't understand that enjoyment, but I had to recognise it. I mustn't dismiss *Study in Cinnamon* out of hand, I had to believe that Day was a sincere artist (God, how difficult this was going to be) and that those who had taken pleasure in his explorations at the piano belonged to the same spiritual...(I gritted my teeth and forced myself to continue)...the same spiritual family that...(go on, you can do it)...that...he did...

'Your *real* duty...'

Sally and I were looking for a flat to set up in. If Stan Grout took me on permanently at *True 'Tec Tales* after my trial period, we could afford a reasonable place. But Sally hadn't said anything to Mr and Mrs Banks about leaving home nor had I to Lil: living together outside marriage was still regarded as sinful by many of our parents' generation and class. So when we moved it would be as a fait accompli.

Sally was sticking it out at Dazings. She had, to her surprise, taken to the shorthand classes. The challenge of the regular speed tests gave her a buzz. Loving and being loved, making progress towards eventually finding less uncongenial work, taking steps to becoming independent of her parents, looking to the future with that innocent optimism granted only to the young – all these together made this period of her life, as I sensed at the time and as she told me later, one of almost unclouded contentment.

Things weren't – natch – quite so simple for me. I too was happy – in my love for Sally, in the thought of living with her, of waking every morning to find her beside me; and in the expectation of earning more, which would help reconcile me to the nonsense of *True 'Tec Tales*. But, caught up though I was in romantic joys and financial expectations, I had a sense of something precious receding fast in my life. With reinforcements from *Mosaic*, it had for some time just about held its ground, but now, under the onslaught of 'I must get on to Dutton & Palmer again about that place we saw last week', 'Could I afford a season ticket from Dartford?', 'How will Sally and I have any time to ourselves tomorrow?', 'I must finish *Smart Dames Dump Punks* on Wednesday', under the bombardment of such heavy guns, it was now in full flight. Just occasionally, however, I would still sight it, hazy in the distance, where it had temporarily halted and encamped. One such occasion had been when I was walking past Ellison Park in Bexcray the previous summer. Small, devoid of sweeps and heights, domesticated, yet broken up here and there with a group of trees or modest shrubbery, it had never, when I'd occasionally played in it as a boy, yielded anything unexpected, interesting, special. Whether, on this pleasantly warm summmer's day, it was the presence of a fête that could be glimpsed through some trees, allied to a fruity orange potency the name of the park had acquired through an association with Ellison's Orange apples, I don't know, but suddenly, excitingly, briefly, that park seemed to promise something that it never had in the past and far beyond what the undoubtedly ordinary stalls would have to offer.

The only other, the last, time I had caught a glimpse of that something had been one Saturday back in early spring. Sally and I were spending the day in town and I set off from home to meet her on the train. It was one of those mornings fetchingly veiled in a fine-spun tulle of sunlight and mist. Tinglingly recalling similar mornings from the past, it seemed to charge with even greater excitement the day ahead, it wispily softened in advance, with its gauzy golden white, the sparkle and gleam of the great London streets and stores, the restaurants, the Astorias, Coliseums and Dominions that together in a magical metropolitan *mélange* enticingly beckoned. A morning full of promise to a young person setting out for a Day in Town. A morning full of wonderful surprises. Turning into Mountsfield Avenue, I marvelled at what I saw: approaching me along the bright pavement, throwing long shadows ahead of them, a young woman and a small boy, hand in hand, indistinct against the brilliance beyond, each outlined with light like a cloud stationed before the sun: around the red coat of the mother a nimbus of pink, around the blue coat of the boy one of azure, and around both their heads haloes of gold. They had taken on, these figures, an appearance scarcely of the earth.

Then at the station, waiting for the train on which I would soon, soon, soon be joining Sally, I found my gaze held by, down the line, in the mist, a green orb softly smudged, sweet as peppermint. The old strange message. Happily smiling Sally leaned out of her compartment, cheeks so morning-cool and kissable, eyes and mouth so gleaming and kissable. And once I was seated next to her, with those cheeks, eyes and mouth so near, the scent of her hair and skin so near, I could scarcely contain my intoxicated desire for her.

Later, in the West End itself, mist, if thinner, if more diffused, still partnered the sunlight in dressing the buses, the shops, their lights, the crowds with an almost ethereal charm. And through it all – walking down hazy memory-filled Danehill Road, approaching the aureoled mother and child, contemplating the crème-de-menthe signal, finding lovely smiling Sally on the train, making our way arm in arm along sparkling filmy Regent Street and Oxford Street – I re-experienced, even if only faintly now, that old feeling. But these days how fragile it was, even less substantial than the wisps of gilded mist through which it whispered whatever it was saying.

But even though it was taking its leave of me, even if so many urgent new concerns were hastening its disappearance, I still clung to the idea of giving it some sort of continuing and permanent life in the pages of a book, rather as a man who has been enraptured in his youth by his travels in a fabulous land, only to find over the decades that they have dimmed in memory almost to a dream, wishes to preserve what he can of them in some written account before it is too late and they vanish altogether. It was true that nine-to-fiving at Mega, looking for the flat, helping Lil with domestic chores and relaxing with Sally left me with little time for work on my book. But I knew that as soon as opportunities did come along I must seize them. For, after all, at the head of one of my noteboo

229

I had inscribed as a motto this admonition of Modigliani: 'Your *real* duty is to preserve your dream.'

Four

Beyond beauty

The last week of my probationary month on *True 'Tec Tales* was one of settled fine weather. As I gazed out of the half-raised window beside me at a quivering strip of gold, all that was visible of the tree-bordered lawn of Regency Place, as I felt the softest of warm caresses on my skin and saw trembling on an old sunwashed and therefore now pinkbrick wall nearby the redbrick shadows of some foliage offstage – signs from which the day at large could be read – I was filled with the same 'spirit of divine discontent and longing' that drew from Mole in his underground home a rebellious 'Hang spring-cleaning!' and that urged him up and out into the sunlight. I found it almost impossible to concentrate on the appalling script before me, the jerry-built plot I was supposed to reconstruct, the Grout-doctored speech of 'tec 'Slim' Marchbanks. Tedious before, that oppressive tale (it had the same atmosphere as childhood Sundays at 33 Danehill Road) became almost unbearable now. Seeing the vivacious rufous cut-outs on the pink wall, I longed to escape from whatever Marchbanks was lumberingly investigating in Bridlington and Thirsk, I longed to see other shadows aquiver, this time deep green and profusely massed on the gilded lawns of Hyde Park, such a tantalisin~¹

short walk away. I had to fight back a savage impulse to score heavily, with as thick and black a marker as I could find, through all Marchbanks' offensive spiel, to cast the entire script aside, to leave the office now, to walk out into the wonderful morning.

It is not, though, simply anticipation of the delicious experience of being out in the open on such a day – soaking up the sun, sighing the tension out, gazing into the infinite azure – that makes the day so sublime as we think of it. It is also all the happy associations it conjures up, some of them barely conscious: similar days glorified in favourite works of art and similar days from the past, which together blend into an ideal form. And these associations, this ideal form Lovely Summer's Day (which all that it may take to summon up over breakfast one morning is not even the glimpse of a promissory sunlight and shade outside but merely 'For the whole country it will be a fine day…'), augment, deepen, the particular lovely, even if impermanent, summer's day in the present.

When I itched to escape from the office during that week, I felt, intuitively, that this longing was well-founded, justified, a natural impulse, an instinctive need; that we shouldn't be spending the all-too-rare, precious golden days cooped up in offices like battery hens; that we weren't intended for that, it was perverse to disobey the summons of the sunlight, the trees, the sky, it was unwholesome; that the yearning I felt for a healthier open-air existence was atavistic. I was Kenneth Grahame, who in fine weather regularly made his getaway from the Bank of England as early as four o'clock: 'We chafe at every sunlit day that passes as worse than wasted.' I was Biff in *Death of a Salesman*: 'To get on that subway on the hot mornings in summer…when all you really desire is to be outdoors…' I was Blake's schoolboy: 'But to go to school on a summer morn, O! it drives all joy away.' In short, I hadn't changed as much as I thought from the boy who felt that shutting yourself away from the sunlight in shadow was somehow *wrong*.

I constantly wondered *to what extent* my colleagues felt the same. But of course that wasn't the sort of question people in offices ever asked each other. I had already learned that. The questions people in offices asked each other were of one currency, the 'important' larger denominations of which were exemplified by 'Is the copier working yet?' and 'Was that contract sent off yesterday?' and the small change by 'Did you watch Wimbledon last night?' and 'Where are you taking your holiday this year?' Questions about time or memory or sunlight were apparently considered foreign currency, useless for domestic trading and therefore pointless. Of course, someone might remark casually, on passing you in the corridor or drying their hands in the washroom, 'Lovely day,' but that told you nothing really, it was a coin from the same currency as, had the same value as, 'Have a good weekend', bestowed on you by people who, understandably enough, hadn't the least real interest in your weekend.

Trapped. But at least I could escape for an hour or so at lunchtime and join all the other uncaged creatures heading for the park.

I crossed the great foyer of Mega House, cool, echoing, dim, pushed through a swing door, and the full beauty of the day softly exploded over me. A stroll across the dappled garden of Regency Place, then along a couple of quiet streets, their stonework affectingly warm to the touch, until I emerged into humming Brompton Road, powdered ever so faintly blue by exhaust-tinged sunlight, a soft blue that symbolised summer day glory every bit as much as the pure darker blue above. Along Brompton Road, past the offices that once housed shabby interesting Spectrum and now smart sterile Sovereign Insurance Brokers, and into Knightsbridge. (A particular boyhood reverie of mine revived: the runners entering the starting stalls at Glorious Goodwood on such an afternoon, an image all blazing purple and pink, glistening chestnut and golden baize green

A pang at not being there.) Near Hyde Park Corner the usual mobile frieze of pedestrians, glinting cabs and wondrously geranium red buses unrolled today against a hovering blue background – less diaphanous than the exhaust – of sunlit tar fumes and drilled-road dust, and the usual music of roar, rumble and horns was now clatteringly punctuated by long bursts of percussion. But after you had crossed Carriage Road and entered the park, what had seemed all-encompassing clamour fell away with that same strange, unexpected suddenness and completeness as when you step from such a scene into a city church. And indeed the park was like some vast natural cathedral. The avenue of plane trees I strolled along was a nave lined by massive pillars with a vault of overarching upper foliage – translucent here and there like those tree tunnels one sometimes drove through on the road – ribbed with branches in silhouette. How shimmering today were the golds and greens of that vault, and in what a sharp and intricate jet the ribbing stood out against them! After a while I came to a path where the planes were joined by chestnuts. The lower foliage of these, far from appearing as one identical substance, took on different aspects according to its position: where it hung almost to the ground on the farther side of the tree, directly screening the sun, falling as a curtain of palest green, against which the trunks and lower boughs were etched with a particularly rich inkiness, it seemed liquid, at times vaporous, like a waterfall seen from behind its cascade against the sunlight; where it projected itself in front of the tree in occasional small sun-pierced clusters, it appeared as gilded rococo wood carvings, ornate and gleaming in the surrounding gloom; and where it sprouted directly from the sides of the tree as incipient shoots, the fringe of these, fluffy and yellow where the sun shone through it, resembled the halo of down around some cage-canary in a window seen against the light. Beyond the trees was a golden lawn, broken up and framed by the dark trunks and decorated with the bright dyes of summer dresses. And where on this grass the soft and velvety shadows of the foliage fell and at their outer areas instead of remaining solid became like openwork embroidery and instead of marking out their edges clearly and sharply did so indistinctly, the archetypal, the ideal summer lawn which the Rectory lawn had in memory become for me added density to this lawn in Hyde Park, just as the ideal form Lovely Summer's Day did to the day as a whole.

As I stood there imbibing this beautiful day, this perfect day, it seemed that in the unplumbable depth of its beauty, its perfection, it was permeated by a quality almost beyond beauty and perfection, a quality frustratingly impossible to grasp, to pin down. It was like that of those 'Golden Wings' yellow shrub roses that Olivia cut on summer mornings for display in the Rectory dining room, those roses as they looked when they first opened out, when they were at their most flawlessly radiant: orange-red and old gold stamens clustering at their heart and the petals cupping them rich warm yellow at their base, gradually lightening to primrose and finally at their exquisitely furled tips becoming palest eggshell yellow, every colour, every gradation, every texture the purest imaginable. In this, their first flush of youth, they were, these roses, a sort of apotheosis of fresh morning glory...and yet something more than this, something which no mental striving could attain to and define.

Whenever, rarely, I came across a description of such a scene as I saw before me now – for example, the paddock at a great racecourse on a glorious afternoon – it never contained any hint of that special quality I had sensed today. No matter how appreciatively the writer might fasten on the opulence of the sunlight, the bright colours it picked out, the depth of the shade, no matter how brilliantly he or she might conjure these up, they would still depict them in a manner no different to that in which they would any other appealing view. In just such a way might a painter portray the outward beauty of a village street or of a woman's face, without being aware of, let alone capturing, what it was in them over and above that beauty that had made certain men love them. Perhaps in music only had I sensed some expression of this indefinable spirit trembling in the heart of such scenes: in that intermezzo from *The Jewels of the Madonna*, for instance. And perhaps all I could say of what I saw before me now was that, in its transcendence of beauty pure and simple, in its mystery, in its incommunicability, its nature seemed to amount almost to the sacred.

Eyes, Babes, Punks

Such an oppressive air of unreality hung over *True 'Tec Tales* that I used to wonder: having read one of them, WHY WOULD ANYONE BUY ANOTHER? All right, so Dougie Leonard had occasionally brought them to school and I'd glanced through several – but we were young boys, scarcely out of short trousers. What amazed me was that recent Mega market research had shown that the (rapidly declining) readership of the tales was predominantly adult. When I read this, a failure of the imagination with which I'd become very familiar recurred. Just as I couldn't imagine anyone giving the book on Gauguin to Harry ('Fascinating, Harry, on his rejection of naturalism and his decorative use of pure colour'), so I couldn't imagine anyone handing over to a newsagent what was presumably *hard-earned cash* in order to take possession of a *True 'Tec Tale*. Or, rather – as in that other case – I could with extreme difficulty just about form some sort of mental picture of the event, but this image was so overcast by the same air of unreality that hung over the tales, was so deeply melancholy, that I quickly thrust it from my consciousness.

So why on earth *would* anyone buy a second *True 'Tec Tale*? After a while I realised the answer. It had to be the covers.

Especially the titles. Take, for instance, that leaden tale of insurance fraud in Swansea due out the following month, the one whose 'tec (Jed Burrows, a vaguely virile name that had been a decisive quickfire replacement by Grout for the hack's choice of Colin Simpson) had chickened out of everything remotely iffy. We were calling that, with cynical disregard of the 'hero' 's cravenness, *Eyes Don't Die Easy*. And another tale in the same batch, whose 'villainess' hadn't the bottle to put one across our 'tec – or even, you were sure, as much as jump a queue – that was going to appear as *Find Another Sucker, Babe*. Yes, it was easy to see the appeal to the punter – the true sucker in the case – of those formidably inapt Spillane-type titles. And once again it was The Man who was responsible. Grouty. In much the same way that Dickens compiled lists of characters' names for possible future use, our editor dreamed up titles in advance. I would sometimes see him, feet up on desk, jotter pad in hand, coffee by his side, gazing out of the window until inspiration struck, when, as additions to his already considerable store, he would then scribble down a 'One Big Mistake, Sweetheart', a 'Face The Music, Dummy'. (In the footsteps of Henry Green, Thomas Love Peacock and Ivy Compton-Burnett, who were one-, two- and three-word-title freaks respectively, Grouty was a driven four-word man.) Then whenever the day arrived each month for automatically discarding the lifeless titles submitted by our hacks – 'The Witherington Case', 'Blackmail in Leicester' and suchlike – the boss would dip into his stockpile and, with truly awesome disregard for what the tales were actually about, and like some Tinseltown studio head repackaging a bevy of young hopefuls, bestow upon them their glitzy and spurious new names.

The titles were the more important, I'm sure, but the cover illustrations too played their part in the shameless scam. They dramatised characters and events in Sheffield or Stockport or wherever at an unbelievably thrilling pitch. Much use was made in them of spurious reflected light. One half of a gat-toting 'tec's lean chops, for example, would fiercely mirror the red glow of some vast conflagration absent from our story. Babes, like gun barrels, often gleamed all down one side an electric blue, whose source was as mystifying as that of the red glow. All this was because the artwork was produced and allocated as arbitrarily as the titles: every so often Grout would commission our two tame cover artists to produce a considerable batch of suitable-style paintings for future use, then each month, feeling no need to consult the tales they were to help sell, he would choose four of those 'illustrations' at random. There was, in this *total indifference* to whether title, cover illustration and story possessed *anything* in common, there was in it, to my way of thinking, something of the sublime.

But I suppose that, in the matter of the mysterious buyers of our tales, it might be thought that the covers explanation falls short, that it fails to account for why those who were miffed to discover they had been conned by *Some Dames Love Danger*, say, should then hand over further monies for further deceptions. Well, this might be thought strange, yes, but only until we recall how often we have been similarly seduced into buying the same old junk over and over again. I remember how, whenever confronted in supermarkets with the mouth-watering representation on its packet of one of the latest 'gourmet experiences' put on the market by the fraudulently named Traditional Homebake (with which a new job was soon to give me a much closer acquaintance), every uneatable product I had previously tried from that unprincipled outfit would unaccountably vanish clean from my mind and, delighted with the promise held out by the steaming, golden-glazed, chock-full cross-section of Luxury Pie beaming from the box, I would inanely take this from the shelf and drop it into the trolley. (As to that picture of the pie, I was shortly to learn how it, as well as other pics, of casseroles and cream cakes and chocolate puddings, was probably produced – to learn of the extraordinary uses to which polyfilla, varnish, shoepolish and other DIY and cleaning materials could be put.) Then, once home and having heated up what appeared so bright and firm and generous and sprightly on the packet, I would – like D-Fens in the movie *Falling Down* grimly noting in a burger joint the difference between the item succulently illustrated and that served up to him – see on my plate yet again the wan, the drooping, the mean, the glutinous that was so drearily familiar and that seemed to sneer up at me, 'Surprise, surprise.'

When I was younger, I had been naively offended by such deceits. As a twelve-year-old I had found myself in sympathy with our English master, Mr Quest (who had left us after only two terms, following a nervous breakdown), when he expressed pained surprise that hardly anyone seemed bothered about the lies in television ads, they were just accepted. He quoted in illustration a catchy jingle all the kids were singing then, 'Three Toffofeasts a day Make you strong in every way.' This was in a lesson he foolishly (given the nature of his charges) devoted to pronouncements on Truth by Keats and Goethe. But when, soon after, I raised this in a class conversation with our religious education master, Mr Tungle, he convinced me that Mr Quest was simply showing a rather callow ignorance of the fact that the Lie is now Consensually Sanctioned. He put down our English master most cuttingly and disloyally (I couldn't be sure but I had the feeling he was implying his colleague's outmoded tenets and his breakdown were not unconnected): 'Come on, these ads he objects to, they're only *lies* for heaven's sake. The fact is,' he explained to me, as though to a simpleton, 'we're no longer living in the age of Keats and Goethe.' He isolated each name with derisory verbal quotation marks as though it were not genuinely the poet's own. 'Truth beauty? Do me a favour. *Dichtung und Wahrheit*? Wake up, boy!' He certainly knew how to make you feel small, Mr Tungle did, and I never broached the subject with anyone at school again.

So, to return to the readership of *True 'Tec Tales*, it is not so difficult after all to understand why those already taken for a ride by the come-on *No More Heists, Punk*, splashed above a real sharp couple of dudes sidelit in luminescent green, should allow themselves to be taken for another ride by the not dissimilarly illustrated *Eyes Don't Die Easy* or *Find Another Sucker, Babe* or – to cite another of the following month's titles, one of our U-S-of-A-crazed boss's alliterative masterpieces, with its fascinating echo of Steinbeck – *Of Gats and Gals*.

Gats did of course feature largely in our tales. But on one occasion Grout came down hard on our most senior hack, Hector Wills, for his overuse of them, for his excessive reliance on Chandler's useful dictum: 'When the plot flags, bring on a man with a gun.' Whether it was because it was only rarely that at any given point a Wills plot was not flagging, I don't know, but the fact was that men (and women) with guns had started entering his efforts with alarming frequency, about once every eight frames on average. One day I overheard Grout exclaim tetchily on the phone: 'For Chrissakes, Hector, go easy on the roscoes, goddamit.' And it wasn't just how often but also in whose hands the guns appeared. Bank managers in Cirencester, secretaries in Hull, housewives in Broadstairs seemed as readily able to lay an over-the-counter hand on them as they would in the US of A. The trouble with Grout's wigging though was that in response to it Wills, who obviously needed his regular fix of gats, developed severe withdrawal symptoms, as evidenced by the newly shaky signature on his invoices. I sometimes wondered whether this enforced cold turkey had been wise, in view of what happened next: he began mainlining on defenestration. An extraordinary number of characters – most of them quite harmless citizens, provincial stooges in Wills's stories – began getting the heave-ho from windows in high-rise offices or flats – all for the most part as a regular hopeless attempt to jolt some life into the barely twitching plot. It was eventually with a sense of foreboding that I would read *once more* in one of Wills's dreadful scripts the now familiar, chilling instructions to the artist: 'Place him by an open window.' And, impossible though it was to believe in one scrap of Wills's nonsense, I still felt an urge, like a child warning a goody in a pantomime, to call out to the innocent who was to be placed by that window, 'Look out! Look behind you!'

But despite my disillusionment with these stories, my detestation of them even at times, I worked diligently on them. I listed in a notepad all inconsistencies and improbabilities in the plots (a time-consuming, pages-filling job) and discussed them with Grout. I thought up more imaginative pic frames (an aerial view, a reflection in a hub cap) than the tired old succession of close-ups and medium shots given in the scripts. I livened up the balloon dialogue from time to time, though I could never truly overcome my queasiness enough to introduce into it the required number of 'punks', 'pals', 'dolls', 'goddamits' and the like, leaving this terrible task to the man who had initiated it. And the result was that when my trial period was up Grouty called me into his office and told me that I had passed it with flying colours. I was now a permanent member of the staff and my salary would be upped accordingly. He 'welcomed me aboard'. Pleasure and pain struggled for mastery within me.

That old idealisation

On rare occasions – it might be in the office or on the train or in bed at night – I would catch sight of what so many writers see before them from time to time, the perfect version of their book, a beautiful if vague abstraction. Like the ideal *Tender is the Night* that existed in Fitzgerald's mind but that he could never accomplish. Like the ideal *The Rescue* that Conrad dreamed of, 'lurking in the blank page in an intensity of existence'.

That old idealisation – which, even if nothing else does, makes of us all great artists, as we spin one delightful world after another from the coarse unpromising material around us – how persistent it is, over what a multitude of things it casts its wand. Certain London thoroughfares, for example: when I look back on those wonderful winter afternoons of playing Monopoly at Danny's, blue-snow pink-sky red-hotel orange-banknote who's-going-to-win? afternoons deeply imprinted in memory (though the identity of the other players apart from Danny and his mum are now completely effaced), I sometimes reflect on how the stylisation of roads and streets in that game as differing bars of colour has made the millions of us who've played it idealise them in that way ever afterwards. For us Northumberland Avenue, for instance, will always be what for non-players it has never been, a cheerful cyclamen pink, the Old Kent Road a robust plummy puce, both staying that way, perhaps, even after we have seen the one in all its actual solemn, lethargic pinklessness and the other in all its actual dreary, run-down pucelessness.

When, again, I look back on those wish-they-could-return afternoons of school cricket I recall how the scoreboard, the scorebook, the scorecard (local rag) all idealised, through the high abstraction of names and numbers, every game regardless of its quality, how they made of, let us say, such innings as

L.S. Nettley b R.D. Cotterman 17

and such bowling figures as

R.D. Cotterman O3 M0 R8 W1

something seemingly significant, worthy of preservation, to be consulted and, who knows, mulled over by some, even perhaps after they had seen as it physically took place what it was in this particular instance that that old rogue print had magickingly transmuted, seen the tedious, low-grade actuality of it, the scratched singles and flukily edged fours of rabbit Nettley's pointless innings in a long dead match, ended by the fortuitous daisycutter of oh-let-him-have-a-bowl third-change Cotterman.

And when I look back on those Saturday mornings of ersatz punting at Danehill Road, on the likes of 1221 PURPLE EMPEROR and 0040 DEFERRED ANNUITY (long since vanished from the racecourse, supplanted by generations of others), I remember how pure and disembodied were all those names and form figures in my imagination.

So with my book. But in this instance the ideal form that presented itself to me so radiantly was a frustrating one. It was like some ravishing houri glimpsed through layers of impenetrable diaphanous veils. If only, I thought, if only I could tear them apart and seize what smiled at me within! If only I could, as Master had miraculously succeeded in doing with *Mosaic*, actualise ideality!

Partings

Late one evening, after visiting Sally at her house (we hadn't yet found a flat we liked), I arrived breathless and sweating at Blackwell station to see my train pulling out. As we had been saying our farewells outside her back door, sexual passion had overcome me, had swept aside the querulous claims of ticking-away time and I'd delayed leavetaking that vital few minutes too long. These goodbyes I always found so painfully difficult. To wrench myself away from Sally required of me an exertion of will power so fierce and it saturated me with a sadness so acidic that I sometimes wondered whether I was a haplessly unique case, a sufferer from some previously unknown infirmity

– for the lovers' temporary partings I saw portrayed on screen or read about in books seemed to be accomplished, no matter how intense the lovers' feelings for each other, with relative ease.

But for me the pain of parting wasn't confined simply to partings from one's sweetheart. In a less severe form, more of a dull ache, I'd regularly experienced it on other occasions – whenever the time came to leave at the end of, say, a day spent with Dean and Olivia or an evening out with friends or a holiday. This had nothing to do with the curtailment of pleasure, with how enjoyable the visit or evening out or holiday had been – I felt more or less the same when they had disappointed me. It was the going away itself that brought on that generalised ache, the having to leave one settled state you'd become used to and being unable yet to re-enter another settled state. I even felt the same way when I simply saw the time to leave appear, massive and minatory, on the horizon, well before I needed to make a move. That hour or so – in the case of holidays, that entire last morning – before the point of departure was polluted with melancholy, dead time, in which it was impossible to lose yourself, to concentrate undistractedly on anything, to commit yourself carelessly to anything, because of what loomed ahead ever nearer. If it can be compared to anything else, that time, it is to equally dead surgery-waiting-room time. And then came the departure itself: the painful exercise of the will to make myself stand up and say, to others or myself, 'Well, I suppose I'd better be going'; the forlornness lapping darkly at me within, particularly if it was dark outside, as I put a coat on, said my goodbyes; the envying of my hosts or of the dancers who were still dancing or of the hotel guests who were staying on (even those being administered to by Jamie and Jeanie at Jayjay House!), who were not having to uproot themselves, who were Staying Put in a state in which they were at ease. Yes, saying goodbye was no problem for them, just as for me farewells at which I was not the one who was leaving caused me little angst; then the final hours before goodbye were not dead time; as others prepared to depart, the blue-black acid did not start to bite into my soul as it did when it was I who was about to leave; when they had gone I would sink back into the security of the oh-so-familiar – even if a little oh-too-familiar at times; I would switch on some music or television as *I* thankfully Stayed Put.

I wondered, as I said, whether I might not be alone in feeling such a corrosive dejection whenever I had to leave people or places behind. An understandable conjecture. Because I'd never heard anyone else talk about that feeling nor read about it. Just as the lovers' farewells I saw portrayed were far from prostrating, so the accounts I came across in memoirs or published diaries of people regularly leaving, late at night, friends they had visited or plays or concerts they had attended, and then making their lengthy way home, often by public transport, those accounts were always matter-of-fact and if they paid particular attention to anything it was to their hosts or to the play or the concert. 'It was a splendid evening and we promised each other we must repeat it at the earliest opportunity.' There was never any hint of 'I so hated those departures at that time of night and the journeys home that I wondered whether the purchase of a few hours of pleasure was worth it at that price.' I envied these untroubled leavetakers and night travellers. But it may be that their accounts were of that bland, skimming-over-the-surface type that is so common. You couldn't really tell. As is so often the case.

Years later I learned of someone else who found all partings painful, so painful that he avoided them whenever he could. It was Dickens, and in *Bleak House* he perhaps gave the reason behind that distress when he said that 'all partings foreshadow the great final one...'

The fear

After missing my train back to Bexcray that evening, I had a considerable wait for the next. It was a raw evening and I made my way to the interrogation cell, the torture chamber, the Francis Bacon *mise-en-scène*, that was, spot-on fittingly for good ol' Blackwell, the station waiting-room. My reaction to it echoed that of Walter de la Mare's to a waiting-room at Crewe: 'One can hardly imagine it to have been designed by a really *good* man!'; and Trollope's to one at Taunton: 'The mind wanders away, to consider why station masters do not more frequently commit suicide.' The ailing light of an unshaded bulb revealed in that unheated room bare wooden benches, punishingly rectangular; tall uncurtained windows, which the night had sinisterly japanned; an empty fireplace, coldly indifferent; drably distempered walls, grubby with the years. I was alone in this waiting-room, this surly silent waiting-for-one-shuddered-to-think-what-room. I sat hunched on one of the hostile benches gazing listlessly at a print opposite me. It was a Thirties advertisement for some English resort or other, a would-be irresistible vacational promise to whichever stricken occupant of the room might happen to let their unhappy eye briefly alight on it. Would-be irresistible because it seemed that once at that resort they would only find for company on the extensive, unpleasant burnt ochre beach, beneath the disturbing Prussian blue sky and beside the keep-away dark green sea (nasty mixture of the ochre and blue) that strangely lone duo of indeterminate sex (their ovoid heads featureless, their puppet bodies indicative of no gender) who in striped bathing costumes were running along the shore stiff-limbed and in perfect unison. They seemed, those robotic androgynes, that beach devoid of any other sign of life – as do the inhabitants, the settings, of so many depictions of the era that precedes our own – to belong, not to the comparatively recent in time and near in place, but to somewhen and somewhere unimaginably remote.

Whoever it was who had been assigned to extending a warm, happy, reassuring invitation to that resort had produced instead – a difficult trick performed with immense skill – a warning to any potential visitor to stay away or face up to a prospect disturbing indeed. I peered forward, looking at the bottom of the print, whose colours age and fly-blows had rendered even more dismal, to see if a particular artist I had in mind was accountable for it, if it was he who by some officials' aberrant judgment had been commissioned to produce it and had then turned out this new bad dream in the midst of painting all his others, such as that one of the railway train roaring out of a fireplace most disquietingly (I turned apprehensively towards the baleful grate beside me). But no, there was no sign of Magritte's signature anywhere. (Wondering who was responsible for waiting-rooms like this, who had allowed such antiquated Nightmare-by-Sea prints to remain hanging in them, I briefly enjoyed a fantasy of power. 'I've called you in, Paget, Murchison, to tell you that my first task as rail chief must be to relieve you of your posts as Waiting-room Planners. However, there are two vacancies currently available in which you might be interested. Do either of you know Lochluichart Halt or Upper Ardchronie? They both need a ticket collector, and I should be happy to recommend you.')

The print, the ill-lit room, induced in me an unease that was by now familiar. But, embedded in them, there was something more specific, something that for the moment eluded me... What was it? I tried to trap it, to fix it. But no luck. I gave up. I turned my attention to the book which Sally, because she had enjoyed it so much, had urged upon me that evening. *Jane Eyre*. It was a second-hand copy, an old, cheap hardback edition the original maroon of whose binding had mostly faded to a dingy pink and the borders of whose pages bore the scorchmarks of age. I began reading it, with difficulty in those cheerless surroundings and in that wan light that glowered down from above, and suddenly, as I read, the physical aspect of that book and the baleful light and the solitary couple on the shore facing me came together to fasten upon and reveal the memory that up till now had been evading me. I returned in a flash to the little back room at home as it had been in my childhood when at night, with the lone boy and glassy wave of the horrid *A Sea Urchin* ever before me, I had sat fixedly reading, by the light of a bare low-watt bulb, in an old annual with once maroon covers, the jaundiced and singed pages of the equally horrid *Held to Ransom*. And the unease I had been feeling in this waiting-room, while it may have been partially occasioned directly by what the present print on the wall showed and even by my own isolation in this bleak setting, had also been triggered, I knew, in my subconscious by the memory of the first occasion I'd experienced that unease, when it had been strong enough to have been called fear.

I wished I could get to the bottom of that unease, that fear, that had cropped up over the years in so many guises and that I had seen echoed in the pages of various writers. I mean, get *right* to the bottom of it.

I returned to my book. I read: 'I returned to my book' – a mirroring that I thought it would have been interesting to have had repeated in the book to which Jane Eyre returned (had that been a first-person narrative and not a scientific study), and then in a book to which the narrator of that book could have returned, and so on, endlessly, as in an infinite regression of reflections. I read on, and then, as I came to a certain passage, *everything suddenly became quite clear*, as Master would have italicised it in one of his scenes in which the truth is finally (and, in his case, thrillingly) revealed. Narrator Jane, having described certain pages in the Bewick she was reading that told of lonely haunts of sea-fowl on the coast of Norway, went on:

> Nor could I pass unnoticed...'the vast sweep of the Arctic Zone, and those forlorn regions of dreary space, – that reservoir of frost and snow, where firm fields of ice...surround the pole, and concentre the multiplied rigors of extreme cold.' Of these death-white realms I formed an idea of my own... The words...gave significance to...the broken boat stranded on a desolate coast; to...a wreck just sinking.

Death-white realms... Of course. That was it. I realised at last what lay, unacknowledged, behind the unease or, worse, the fear or, worse still, the terror (as experienced by Flaubert and Wilson) that can be induced by images of persons or objects abandoned in cold and silence. I realised that the observer obscurely senses that whatever has been thus abandoned, whether animate or inanimate – whether child or ship, for example – was once, as an *integral* part of a world of warmth, colour, movement, noise, so much a symbol of life that, seen now utterly alone in a frigid soundless stillness, it has become a symbol of death; and that, more importantly, this observer, having, with his own cherished animation and involvement with life, identified with this person or object as it once was in its heyday, then, by a logical extension, finds himself identifying with it dead.

As to why the feeling varies so much in intensity on different occasions, it seemed to me, as I thought about it, that this depended on the degree of each of various factors involved. An example of the unease at a very low point on the scale of intensity was how I had felt on seeing Epsom racecourse swathed in winter mist. Here the degree of one factor, identification with the symbol of life – the course with its stands – was low because the symbol in this case was inanimate. But the degree of a second factor, the past vitality symbolised – all the betting, racing and cheering that had taken place on the course – was high. Low again, however, was the degree of a third factor, the abruptness of transition from symbolic life to symbolic death (an abruptness that at its most extreme corresponds to death at its most capricious, when it arrives out of the blue and annihilates at a stroke) – the change that the course had undergone after the flat season was over had been gradual, it had, before it arrived at the chill, still winter antithesis to its ardent summer high points, passed through a period when staff were still around and the days were still relatively warm. Finally, the degree of a fourth factor, the symbolic death itself – the course and stands deserted, with however signs of life still around (passers-by in cars, like myself), on what was simply a cold, misty English day – was also comparatively low. Overall effect on me: melancholy tinged with unease.

Much higher up the scale of intensity had been the feeling induced in me when reading *Held to Ransom*. There the degree of identification with the symbol of life was quite high – the young heroes were schoolboys like myself – though that degree of identification could never be of the highest, because they were at a mysterious sort of school (it had a porter and a matron) with which I couldn't connect. The degree of past vitality symbolised – the social life of the school – was also well up the scale (though not as high as the buzz of the racecourse). But lower than that of the second factor was the degree of abruptness in the shift from the symbol of vitality to symbolic death: the boys' passage from familiar populated school to open boat on the ocean at night went through various intermediate stages. Very high, though, was the degree of symbolic death: the boys completely alone on an infinitely stretching expanse of black and icy water. Overall effect: fear.

As I sat in the waiting-room reflecting on all this, I was now able to understand why and how all the varied forms of the fear experienced by myself and others – such as my feelings as cosmeticised Donna, still warm from my 'party', waited at night for her bus on cold, spray-swept Sandbay promenade, or Flaubert's on seeing the picture of people stranded on an ice floe, or Angus Wilson's on seeing 'Golliwog at the North Pole' – occupied different points on the scale of intensity. And I was able to posit, by imagining circumstances that would raise each of the four factors I'd identified to the highest possible degree, the most dreadful form of the fear that would have been conceivable to me as a child. This would have been to identify, completely, easily, naturally, with someone of the same sex and age and background as myself, happily flushed with involvement in some carefree, lively festivity, transported on the instant, without a flicker of warning, all alone into pitch blackness, utter silence and extreme cold. But wait a minute. What experience was I describing here? It was – in a horrific ratcheting up of what had happened to the two schoolboys, and with only one factor, the abruptness of transition from one state to another, having a lesser intensity than in my extreme case – the imagined fate of a small boy in steerage on the *Titanic* allowed to stay up late one night to join in some adult merrymaking: finding himself less than two terrifying hours later in the dark and icy Atlantic. And, leaving aside my possible case, isn't it this general aspect of the disaster represented in acute form by that case, an aspect exemplified by hundreds of actual cases on that night (the first-class smoking room, for instance, crowded with card-players still playing well after the iceberg was struck), which chiefly explains the continuing horrified fascination of many with the sinking of that ship, rather than those aspects usually adduced, such as hubris (man's overweening designs), needless loss of life (messages not acted on, boats not lowered), courage (men sacrificing their lives) and cowardice (crew putting their own safety first), even though these may play a contributory part? And isn't the most horrifying of all the images of the tragedy, one with a particular chilling terror all its own, that of the great ship canted to the perpendicular above a sea 'calm as a pond', lights still blazing, about to slide down into the profound black icy depths? – isn't this image the most horrifying because the symbol of life, which, despite all the blazing evidence of that life and all the people still aboard, plunges so abruptly into actual death, is, as a 'floating town', more appallingly vast – short of an actual city upended and about to disappear into the abyss – than any other symbol could possibly be?

So now in that waiting-room I realised at last the real nature of those episodes of disquiet or fear that recurred throughout my early years, and those sometimes of horror experienced by others, when we were confronted by scenes of people or things abandoned in cold. Penetrating from time to time the comfortable insulation of the child's unconscious belief that it will live for ever, they had been the first, vague, troubling, unrecognised intimations of mortality.

'A painted ship'

If the spell of glorious weather earlier in the summer had wafted my spirits heavenwards – whenever, that is, I could escape from office confinement – the heatwave of mid-August kept them heavily earthbound. The dog days followed one upon the other in so prolonged and unbroken a succession that I soon felt the return of that old weariness of the soul I had known in the past during similarly afflicted school-holiday days when, robbed of cricket ('Oh, come on, let's chuck it in...') and Danny's companionship ('Don't feel like going today...'), I had aimlessly wandered the cowed streets and open spaces of Bexcray.

Grout was on leave (in, surprise, surprise, the 'US of A'), as was his secretary; and in consequence an emboldened Carlsen Purvis was finding himself on several days 'unable to make it' to the office as the result of a sudden indisposition or tradesman's call. Unfairly, I suspected the true reason was something vaguely horrid. This was because of a sexual proclivity he'd recently, casually, disturbingly revealed to me. During a coffee break chat he'd told me that he fancied a limp-looking girl of washed-out prettiness who worked on *True Love Tales*. 'She looks a really passive type,' he'd said, an appreciative look softening that ravaged Nordic face of his. 'Lovely. The more lifeless they are, the better, eh?' I said nothing, simply frowned a little. But, with the knowing smile of one seeing through pretended lack of interest, of one putting his finger on a universal laddish weakness, he insisted: 'Come on, surely every feller fantasises about making love to a dead bird.' *Necrophilia*. My God. As I stared at him, my frown gave way to the no-expression-at-all of deep shock.

Determined to shorten my own days on the tales while Grout was away, I took much-extended lunch breaks and sometimes caught a later train up than usual. Because of the season, because of the hour, the carriage would invariably be almost empty. It would also, despite the open window, be as uncomfortably warm as if the heating were full on. The train rattled through various deserted stations. The old familiar dog-day feeling tinged everything. Even the poetry of certain scenes. Such as that of Falcondene station, which I took in across the intervening downline track as the train rattled through it with a dismissive change of key and pitch. The underside of its canopy at the top, the waiting-room (with a green door) to one side, a store room (with another green door) to the other side, two green-painted iron pillars at equidistant intervals between them, and the platform at the base, all of them in deep shadow, together formed the sharply defined, tenebrous blue and bluish-green rectangular frame and dividers of a triptych whose panels were segments of a sundrenched scarlet-poppy-daubed golden green grassy embankment beyond. So profound was the shadow of the frame and dividers, so effulgent was the blaze of the panels, so devoid of life was the station, that they seemed the ultimate symbol of somnolent summer chiaroscuro. And then it was gone, the strange, silent, blue-green-gold-and-red, disused-slot-machine, aching beauty of that station. The train whisked it chatteringly away, as it did every other scene we passed, like some manic slide-changer.

In that stuffy, quiet carriage, its fulsome smell of warm dusty old upholstery so pronounced and unpleasant on a day like this, even the red stripes in the fabric of the empty seats opposite me, ignited by the sun to scarlet and travelling outside ahead of me as slender pillars of fire over every passing view, even they could not escape the diffusive dog-day melancholy.

During this holiday month, the entire palace of Mega was less populous than usual – you no longer had to wait for a lift in the foyer, fewer people passed you in the corridors, the carpet of these had less sound to muffle. The absence of Grout, the master of the good ship *True 'Tec Tales*, of Miss McDowell, the purser, and often of Purvis, the first mate, together with the becalmed state of the vessel, adrift on these torpid days, combined to create a sort of pervasive apathy in the handful of remaining crew. At this time I was supposed to be restructuring the 'plot' of Barry L. Horrey's 'His Wife's Best Friend' (a four-word title attempt, granted, but hopelessly lame and certainly due for the Grout chop on the great man's return; it eventually became some injunction to a sucker, punk or pal, I forget which). As a contributor, Barry L. Horrey was interesting, he stood out from the ruck, in that he had strong claims – even stronger than those of Hector Wills – to being *the worst writer who ever lived*. Trying to make something of the farrago that was his latest offering – so *criminally* negligent, I considered bitterly, as to warrant his arrest and summary execution – would have been torture at any time, but on mornings like this, with no breath of air to stir the sullen heat, without Grout or Purvis around to drum up any urgency about the job, without the machine-gun rattle of Miss McDowell's typing to seemingly corroborate that urgency, the task acquired a tedium so excruciating that I found it scarcely possible to continue with it. Of course, endlessly totting up the costs of groceries at Lea & Lyle had been far from enthralling, but at least after some weeks in that job an automatic pilot would see you through the worst times: while your thoughts, thankful to escape, drifted off somewhere or other, that trusty mechanical calculator in one room of your brain took over all the cheese and tea and chutney reckonings with perfect competence. But the curse of this *True 'Tec Tales* tedium was that no automatic pilot was going to help you with 'His Wife's Best Friend', with the terrifying job of trying to make sense of it all. No mechanical editor was going to allow you to think about Sally or your book while it took over the toil of remedying how the husband could have remained in ignorance for forty-two pages of something he must *necessarily* have known on page five, how the best friend could have shot himself after he had been dispossessed of his roscoe, how the wife could have been in three places at once. In the stretching hours of those days, the attempt to negotiate Horrey's 'tale', jagged, pothole-strewn, crevasse-riven, took on, as one kept sustaining sickening falls or sliding helplessly backwards, an aspect of utter futility.

The afternoon, of greater density than the morning as afternoons always are, and breathing even more pronounced a sigh of tristesse than those hours immediately after lunch often do, was even worse. In the airless cabin of a vessel 'Idle as a painted ship Upon a painted ocean', we floated motionless, becalmed. Yes, time appeared so to have slowed down that it was difficult to believe the afternoon would ever end. I had the dull, irrational feeling, as I stared at them, that the few sluggish disentanglements, rewrites, that I had achieved would never progress any further than my typewriter, that the tale itself would never – unprecedentedly – be published, that even if it were published no one would ever buy it, that I was working in a vacuum, that *True 'Tec Tales* was grinding to a halt, that Mega was, that the world was...

The price paid

I'd recently resumed reading a biography of Kenneth Grahame. I wanted to know more about the creation of *The Wind in the Willows*, that self-contained world so pure, so enchanting. And so rich in poetries. The spring morning on which Mole left his underground home and discovered the River Bank, a morning sunblessed, fresh, melodised by the gurgling river, had long since become for me the ideal spring morning. The summer's afternoon on which Toad, Rat and Mole set out with the caravan on the Open Road, an afternoon sunbaked, dusty, drowsy, was an extension of the ideal summer's afternoon I had known one wallflower-scented three o'clock long ago. The winter's evening on which Rat and Mole passed through a village on their way home, an evening snow-powdered, bitingly cold, lit up here and there with beckoning squares of dusky orange-red, was the ideal winter's evening. The South as chanted in a siren song to Rat by the wayfaring rat, the vibrant South of 'golden days and balmy nights', with a 'red and glowing vintage' at its heart, was the ideal South...

But perhaps it doesn't pay to learn too much about the genesis of the works we love. Perhaps we should let them shine on creatorless, transcendent, undiminishable. For in this case I did not like what I learned: that those letters first outlining the story of the book, which Grahame sent to his son, Alastair, to amuse the dejected boy while he was holidaying separately from his parents, failed to comfort him; that he piteously pleaded for a visit from them; that his pleas were ignored by the Grahames, who continued with their own holiday and left their son in misery. Alastair grew up a deeply unhappy boy, and in adolescence he put an end to his life by lying down on a railway track. There, unlike the propitious fictional train, delightfully sparking and swinging through the dark countryside, that his father had used, in letters to him, to bring about the delivery of Toad, there, on that track, an implacable, all-too-real train mangled him to death. So I learned that, since there might well never have been any River Bank and Open Road, any Rat, Mole, Toad and Badger, without those propitiatory letters, vain substitute for a longed-for, easily arrangeable visit, the price paid for the existence of those perennially enchanting places and characters was a high one: a boy's deep and lasting unhappiness.

But that was not all. The biographer went on to suggest that in the book the Wild Wooders symbolised the anarchic mob of which Grahame and others of his class were terrified, that the regaining of Toad Hall represented the triumph of the squirearchy, and that Toad himself, in his heedless pursuit of pleasure, his downfall and his imprisonment, was Oscar Wilde... Good God, could that magical story, outside of earthly time and place, set in a realm that knew nothing of class or sex, actually have its roots in a specific historical period, in a specific country obsessed with social distinctions and sexual propriety? Could it be no more than an allegory of real-life terrors and punishments? Suddenly a world marvellously supramundane and unblemished until now sank to our all-too-blemished earth, there to take its place alongside everything else. And although, from now on, whenever I thought of that book or reread certain favourite pages of it, those new aspects of it might recede, my mind would never fully cease to be aware of them.

Chiaroscuro

The morose heat, August's transformation from august to overbearing, continued. On one of those dog days I went at lunchtime to Hyde Park. I found it no longer glorious, resplendent in its finery, the ideal Hyde Park it had been on my visit earlier in the summer. Its scattering of occupants was keeping to the shade, and, seen between the profound sable silhouettes of planes and chestnuts, the baked lawns, stretching away in the blinding light, fading into an azure haze in which trees and pavilions showed as no more than smudges of faintly deeper blue, were now almost deserted. As on similar days in my youth, I felt that the vast invisible dynamo of life was slowing almost to a stop.

Sitting in deep shade, with my back against one of the great planes, looking out on the beauty of the lifeless chiaroscuro before me, Falcondene station returned to me, then the bluish-elm-backed, quivering, empty, cutout-shadowed playground I had gazed on from the schoolroom that July so many years before. I thought about the melancholy that tinged them all. And I recalled that it was not *entirely* absent from the sunlight and shade of any beautiful, still, deserted scene on a hot day, even one that was not uncomfortably sultry, that was far from a dog day. In such an unanimated spot, there would, in the steady static light and the pools of indigo ink lying motionless at the foot of everything – signs of that true summer for whose arrival I had earlier in the year been so impatient – there would tremble in the heart of these, like a worm in the bud, something that subtly troubled my spirit. And not only in actual scenes from my own life. It trembled too within certain works of art. In, for example, a particular piece of music – one emblematic of all that is most beautiful in the French genius – Debussy's *Prélude à l'après-midi d'un faune*. In this sublimation of a heat-soaked pastoral afternoon arrested at Mallarmé's 'fierce and tawny hour', the composer's notes of gold, green and black, palpitating in the 'proud silence' which they have interrupted but which at intervals, mysterious, heavy with some strange unknown meaning, resumes its resonance, notes creating so magnificent a tapestry, amid the trees and glades, of shimmering light and sonorous shade, are unmistakably underlaid by a subtle malaise, the composer's more eloquent conveyance of the poet's 'weary swooning almost unto death'.

Again, in a painting I loved, Monet's *Le Pont d'Argenteuil*, which, with its sleeping, suntanned, heavy-foliaged trees across the river, its bridge-house sweetened by the sun to the pink and cream of nougat, its idling boats of orange and cream, its cloud-wisped blue above, its scarcely ruffled water reflecting all this burnished green and brown and pink and orange and cream and blue, is drenched in the light of, saturated in the spirit of, a perfect summer's afternoon (intensified in this case by that aureole of a golden-age happiness with which our idealising imagination surrounds the Belle Epoque and all its works), I yet sensed, in the absence of a living soul, in the heavy sleep of the trees, in the motionless depths of the shadows beneath them and beneath the bridge, in the stillness of the whole scene, something of the familiar sadness.

It was there too in a great French photograph of 1871: 'Barricade dans la Grande Rue, au Bourget'. Framed by an archway, there looms in the foreground, viewed from a very low angle, like a shot in a modern movie, the barricade of the title, a street defence at the time of the Commune, a rubble of rocks and stones pale in the glare of the sun and, piled on top of them, striking in their rugged solidity and individuality, a number of barrels, big-bellied, disfigured, branded, stained, dusted with the dust of the rocks and stones. Beyond them stretches a wide, empty street whose buildings on one side cast shadows narrow enough to suggest that the blistering sunlight of that seized split-second of faraway time is that of midday.

Not a soul is to be seen. There is a beauty in the profound sunlight and shade but, again, one at whose heart there quivers a melancholy just as profound.

As I sat there in the park, I realised that the faint unease all those scenes induced in me must be connected in some way with that more full-blown disquiet (echoed in the work of various writers) whose truth had been revealed to me so recently in the waiting-room of Blackwell railway station. And yet in one striking particular these feelings were very different: one was induced by scenes of cold, the other by scenes of heat. Even so, the two types had something in common that was more important than that difference, something which showed that difference to be more apparent than real. What they shared was an absence of any sign of life, a pervasive torpor, which, as biologically, can be caused as much by heat as by cold. So that in certain scenes of heat, still and silent, there lurked something of that symbol of death I had found in certain scenes of cold, still and silent; it was the same intimation, this time in a minor key. (In the production of that vague disquiet within myself chiaroscuro strangely played its part. Ruskin believed that in the conflict between painters who were colourists and those who were chiaroscurists, the former had 'nature and life on their side', the latter 'sin and death'. And indeed – and making due allowance for the not untypical extravagance, some might even say craziness, of Ruskin's generalisation – in unpeopled summer scenes of extreme light and shade it was as though the harshness of a light that bleached out some colour and the depth of a shade that excluded it altogether – this character of each intensified by the severity of their contrast, the rigorous demarcation of their separate zones – drew attention to, emphasised, the *lifelessness* of a scene that might not so have impinged on your consciousness on more temperate days.) This form of the intimation was not quite so troubling as the other because – no matter that the Biblical representation of hell is a fiery furnace – exceptional heat is less unwelcome to us than exceptional cold. The symbolism of the sun plays its part too: we know that its light and heat were the necessary condition for life and that without them the planet would die. And then, also, the scenes of heat I've been speaking of were scenes of beauty – stained with the lovely dyes of flowers, of foliage, of sunlight – which the scenes of cold were not. In these ways, unlike the images of still and silent icy wastes that had filled me and others with unease, images of still and silent summer beauty had a certain ambivalence.

It bothered me, that note of disquiet, that intrusion into the diatonic and affirmative of a gently depressed chromatic key. But it would not be long before that response of mine to it would, like my response to so much else, undergo a considerable change.

Sally's town

Because Blackwell was Sally's town – she had lived there since she was seven – its aspect after I met her couldn't help but differ from the one it had always presented to me before. Although as dark and ugly as ever, it now seemed to me, in one sense, hallowed, simply because it was within *its* bounds, within *its* buildings and streets and no others that Sally had grown up. That particular house in Knightsbridge Road, *Blackwell*, that particular school in Hereson Road, *Blackwell*, that particular disco in Market Street, *Blackwell* (where, she told me, inserting a knife in my chest, she'd had a long-lasting crush on a certain Brett Bravington, who, partly I think because of his name, took on in my imagination a mythic quality that, since he had long ago left the district, could never be shattered by seeing him in his surely all-too-ordinary flesh), that particular coffee bar in Belmont Square, *Blackwell*, that particular swimming pool in Bexcray Road, *Blackwell* – those places and so many others had had the enviable privilege of witnessing the stages in her development from a young girl to a young woman, had had the wonderful good fortune to gaze constantly and clearly on the dear face and body of which all that my imagination, striving to conjure up pictures of her past selves, could afford me were mere intermittent and obscure glimpses. And Sally's presence in that sombre town not only modified my stylised mental image of it – which had been all sooty cheerlessness – it even had the same effect on the *name* Blackwell. How many of our apparently colour-fast mental images prove in the end to be nothing of the sort!

What's more, after rejecting a number of furnished bedsits we'd viewed in Bexcray, Erith, Welling, Eltham and elsewhere, and finding one that was pleasant enough, in a not too grimy area, here I was (I would never in the past have believed it) actually going to *live in Blackwell*.

The generational script

Thrilled though I was to be moving into rooms with Sally, I was concerned that Lil would now have to fend entirely for herself. She'd be more nervous at night without me in the house, and then there was the garden to look after. I decided I'd pay to have more secure door and window locks fitted and I arranged to call on her every weekend to see to the garden and do any other jobs that were beyond her. Try as I might, I couldn't *love* Lil, but I did feel some responsibility towards this woman who had housed, fed and clothed me.

A couple of days before Sally and I were due to move into our rooms I took Lil, at her request, to see them. As I'd expected, she found fault with everything. The walls and paintwork, in various hints-of, were 'wishy-washy'. If the landlord would let us, we should 'brighten things up a bit. You could paint the doors and windows a nice blue and paper them walls in a purple pattern. They've got some nice purply stuff in Pembertons. And you could do the kitchen a nice lemony green.' (A 'nice' bread pud, a 'nice' ham salad, 'nice' purply stuff, 'nice' everything she produced or proposed.) When Sally and I showed little enthusiasm for such an alarmingly Fauvist palette (which, I must say, I had never previously heard her advocate, either during Harry's desultory, wholly academic examinations of the *Ultimate Guide to Wallpapering* or, since his departure, whenever the subject of redecorating 33 Danehill put in a brief perfunctory appearance in our conversation), Lil would dismiss our objections with the contempt of a great colourist contradicted by crude daubers. 'You may have done all right at art at school,' she said to me, 'but when it comes to decorating you haven't got much idea, I'm afraid.' (That old familiar put-down 'I'm afraid' again.)

She didn't like, either, the arrangement of the furniture. 'The table would be better over there, and then you could have...' Nor was she much taken with the prints we'd chosen for the walls. 'No, sorry, I don't like them. Whoever done that fruit's done it all wrong, I'm afraid... And I've never seen a sky that colour before. No, sorry.'

But if Lil didn't like *anything*, Sally's mother liked *everything*, as she always did. Or did she? I sometimes wondered whether Mrs Banks had any genuine opinions, whether the approval she expressed for everything brought to her attention was not some free-floating material she invariably grabbed to fill in the void within her where ideas should have been – rather like Ken Day, during one of his 'personal statements' at the keyboard, having constant recourse to the same old crashing atonal chords when confronting in his musical imagination the – But no, no...I mustn't flout that conclusion I came to, break that resolution I made.

When it came to 'nice', Mrs Banks went one up on Lil. For her everything was *very* nice – though with her this unflagging approval was never applied à la Lil to her own handiwork, possessions or ideas but only to others'. So everything in the flat was 'very nice'. The curtains were 'very nice'. The pictures were 'very nice'. The cooker was 'very nice'. The telephone table was 'very nice', as was, I'm sure, the telephone on it. I'm ashamed to say that, in a spirit of devilry, I showed her the kitchen door as though I believed it possessed features that singled it out somewhat from other kitchen doors, a certain je ne sais quoi, and, yes, she found that too for some reason, or, rather, for no reason, 'very nice'.

Mr and Mrs Banks were of that pre-feminist generation – which manifested itself at its most extreme in their class – in which the approved gender roles in a marriage were something out of burlesque. And in their case they played these parts even more zealously, their performances were even more hammy, than the generational script called for. Take Mr Banks. Admittedly, there was nothing wrong with his portrayal of Breadwinner Man and Practical Man, other than perhaps a hint of self-consciousness; he was at home in the parts, he enjoyed driving trains, he enjoyed DIY. But Stoic Man – he really laid it on too thick when it came to that (not that I thought so at the time – I regarded him, rather, with awe). Once, a friend, another railwayman, had visited the Bankses with his wife and in the course of conversation had mentioned how a few months back he had heard Mr Banks groaning whenever he thought he couldn't be heard. This had gone on for a couple of days until his friend had dragged out of him that a fierce pain was stabbing ever more deeply and excruciatingly into his right upper jaw. His friend had insisted that instead of heroically fulfilling his roster duties before going to the dentist, Mr Banks should take time off to see one as soon as possible. It was an abscess in the gum. The friend gave this as his account of an event which he automatically believed Mrs Banks knew all about. But not only was this not so but neither she nor Sally had even been aware Mr Banks was in pain. By not so much as a wince or a whisper had he let on to them.

Mrs Banks' performance was just as uneven. She was spot on as Homemaking Woman – dusting, pastry-making, plumping up cushions. But Unpractical Woman, that was really over the top. OK, couldn't drive, couldn't replace a fuse, couldn't put up a picture, no problem, that was all in the script and her performance of those bits was perfectly acceptable if a little overdone. But couldn't change a light-bulb? Couldn't make out a cheque? Couldn't pay a bill? Surely those little touches of her own were uncalled for, ham-amdram.

In ways such as these Sally's parents made already far-fetched parts frankly preposterous. *But* as far as Mr Banks was concerned I want to say now how much I admired him in other respects. I have never come across anyone more prepared to help others or anyone more reliable. He it was who often drove Sally and me to view various flats, no matter how inconvenient the hour, no matter how tired he might be. He it was who transported all our belongings to our new home – and immediately after he had come off duty! And if he said he would meet you at six-forty-five, there he was waiting at six-forty-five, and if he said he would let you have that saw the following Saturday morning you knew it would arrive then as surely as you knew Saturday morning itself would. I couldn't help contrasting him with Harry, for whom the smallest favour was too much trouble and whose promises meant nothing. Sally's father had decided early on in life to be guided by certain moral precepts – perhaps of his own making, perhaps instilled in him by others – and had then followed them undeviatingly. (And atypically. It was, that stoical adherence to self-imposed duties, far more characteristic of the public school ethos than the state elementary school one.) He saw it as his duty *never* to hesitate to help someone if he could and to ensure that he *never* let down anyone who had placed their trust in him. It was to take me years to discover, through so many disenchanting experiences of others, that Mr Banks' principles were far from common, and it was not until after his death that I appreciated to the full those qualities of his I took too much for granted when he was alive.

'Character conferences'

Somehow or other, in what I felt should be commemorated in Picture Libraries as an epic feat of hardship and endurance – clearing massive rockfalls of coincidence, bridging vertiginous chasms in the 'plot' and draining swamps of soggy dialogue – I'd fashioned a just about saleable piece of real estate from the wasteland that had been Barry L. Horrey's script. (Barry L. Horrey. That name. I stared at it with loathing.)

On his return, our editor was full of praise for the scale and success of my heroic endeavour. He made clear to me that I was now a full member of the editorial team, on the same level as Carlsen Purvis and Bertha Gurney. And as such I was now to take part with the others each month in what Grout called the character conference (he considered it was characterisation not storyline that was really important in the tales). It had shocked me rather when I first learned of the existence of these conferences, when I first discovered how seriously my colleagues took the publications we worked on. Discussing the most recently published issues, the scripts now being edited and those just sent in by our hacks, they solemnly pondered the 'characters' of the robotic creatures that lurched and squelched through each over-signposted narrative, probed their 'motivation', their 'hopes and fears', their, yes, their *inner conflicts*.

266

The morning arrived for my first attendance at one of these sessions. Grout ushered me gravely into his room. The president inviting a new member of the administration to his first Cabinet meeting. When we were all seated around Grout's extremely large desk, he announced that he first wanted us to 'analyse in depth' the 'relationships' in a tale currently in production. It had already been illustrated but he still wasn't happy with it. And since it wasn't yet balloon- and caption-lettered, it wasn't too late for some changes.

'Right, listen up,' he began. 'Let's first of all take a look at the case of Gerry, emotion-wise.' Eh? Gerry was just another of our ever-grinning, clean-cut, square-jawed good-guy puppets. How, I wondered, could such as he present a case emotion-wise or any other -wise. 'I believe he has genuine feelings for Lynette, and he *has to lay them on the line*,' Grout opined. He addressed Gerry's love for Lynette as earnestly as an academic addressing Heathcliff's for Cathy or Mr Knightley's for Emma. 'I believe,' he went on, leaning forward with an intent gaze, 'Gerry's love is deep and true. I believe that after years of searching he's at last found a broad he can relate to. I believe – ' An old song began sounding in my head.

'Hang on.' Purvis cut off Grout's impassioned Frankie-Laine-like credo in mid-flow. 'I know he *says* he loves her...' Eh? again. If in-your-face Gerry said he loved someone, well, that was it, wasn't it? There couldn't be any two ways about it, could there? There couldn't be something *equivocal* involved, could there? But apparently there could. 'I know he *says* he loves her, but I wonder whether deep down he cares for her any more than Patterson does.' Ah, any more than Patterson does. Patterson, Gerry's rival, and distinguishable from him by the slightly larger check on what Grout called his sportcoat. The boss's eyes narrowed at this new slant on Gerry's soul. 'Carry on, Carlsen,' he said in the slow, deliberate voice of one who feels the team may be on to something real big here. Presidential concentration on Secretary of State Purvis's dramatic new take on the crisis.

'Well, he doesn't really react when she declares her love for him, does he?' Valid point, I supposed: Gerry's grin hadn't changed at all. 'And in that scene where everyone believes she's dead,' Purvis continued, 'he doesn't display much emotion, does he?' An abstracted look glazed his pale eyes in their sockets. 'She looked particularly attractive in that sequence, I thought.' He fell silent, seemed to drift off. I inched my chair slightly away from him.

'He *sort* of cares for her,' suddenly put in Bertha Gurney. She stated this without preamble and with great finality. Black-helmed, prognathous-jawed, fierce of gaze, equipped with a terrifying basso profundo, she struck fear I'm sure into the hearts of all who had dealings with her. 'His feelings are tugging him both ways. It's the same with Patterson.' I for one wouldn't have cared to dispute this finding, or any other, with her (though I did find myself wondering, perhaps unfairly, what she would know about it).

'Ah, now this is interesting,' the Chief mused, leaning back in his chair, steepling his fingers in a chin prop, swivelling to look out of the window, seizing any opportunity to escape the missile of Big Bertha's fearsome gaze, yet determined to remain in presidential control. 'You see...'

I became aware that for some time my mouth had been set as though in readiness to receive a considerable quantity of food. Because, as I had listened to the team investigating the subtle ambivalences in Gerry's and Patterson's thoughts and feelings, I had seen before me that pair as limned by our illustrator: musclebound, permanently overjoyed about something or other, touchingly cretinous, surely incapable of any but the most rudimentary of mental processes, and, if it hadn't been for those variant 'sportcoats', impossible, really, to tell apart. Despite that, I had made a great effort to take seriously the others' insights into the duo's alleged emotional turmoil, I had tried testing in my mind whether their unearthly euphoria and equilibrium *could* be disturbed: with a mental finger I'd given them as it were a psychically upsetting prod, tilting them over. But like those self-stabilising rubber figures that won't lie down, they'd simply sprung up grinning again.

Still, I decided, I had to pretend. During the seminar on Gerry's and Patterson's emotional states I had been incapable of speech, but by the time the discussion had turned from them to Gail, a young woman who was jealous of Lynette, I had recovered a little, I felt I should join in. I was suffering from the anxiety felt by many at meetings – that their continued silence will be taken for vacuousness. That wouldn't do. I needed my Mega salary. There was the rent on that flat. And there was an intuitive understanding between Sally and me that we'd be getting married. Yes, I had to join in. True, I had nothing more of sense to say about Gail than about any of the other 'characters', but then, I thought, this could be said to apply to the team as a whole. So I piped up, in a confident tone, with the first nonsense that came into my head. The vicious Gail, as nasty a piece of work, male or female, as had ever been portrayed in *True 'Tec Tales*, had carried out two murderous knife attacks on the defenceless Lynette until thwarted by Gerry or Patterson (it had been difficult to tell which), but, I wondered aloud, might there not exist within her a more gentle soul, one who had so far had little opportunity to display her better nature – her nobility even? Couldn't we, I continued to wonder aloud, show something of this more honourable Gail? I also wondered something else, though this not aloud: was that shameful tommyrot I could hear resounding in the incredulous air actually issuing from me?

Grout, Purvis, Gurney slowly turned their gaze on me. They had obviously seen through that drivel of mine, been shocked by it, they wanted the discussion brought back in line. But no, that wasn't it at all – it soon became clear that that fixed look of theirs was not one of appalled disbelief but of a different kind of wonder, wonder that one so young, so inexperienced, could at his very first character conference have come up with such a stunner! With great animation they seized upon my startling new idea and to my embarrassment – and shame – explored it, spoke for and against it, elaborated on it, reweighed it, until the boss, after much self-conscious the-decision-rests-with-me-I-know lip pursing and nodding, suddenly, resolutely announced he was gonna go with this baby.

Like Mr Banks

Change that we always imagine to be gradual sometimes turns out to be nothing of the sort. And just as the transition from one season to the next can, instead of being slow and almost imperceptible, announce itself suddenly, with a day markedly different from all those that have gone before, so a change in our personality can be equally abrupt. That was what happened when I ceased to be a Boy and became a Man. One day while I was grappling with a Barry L. Horrey special (my success with his previous stuff had horrifyingly led Grout to acclaim me as 'our troubleshooter' and to reserve for my exclusive attention all Horrey's harrowing work) an idea I'd never had before strode into my mind. I don't know why it chose to do so exactly then. Perhaps it was the realisation of how thuggish life was and how *unremitting* had to be the struggle to hold one's own against it – that and vague thoughts that, marriage probably in the offing, I wanted to show Sally I was an ultra-capable type who, in those then not so thoroughly feminist days, could 'look after' her...as Mr Banks looked after Mrs Banks. My idea was that I must toughen up, must develop and hone my practical side, must stop mooning and dreaming, must...well, become more like Mr Banks, I suppose. That was my idea, and characteristically I acted on it immediately. One week I was one person, the next another. Jus' like that.

With the fervour of the young and the newly converted, I took my transformation to extremes. Overnight, in a series of shockingly violent acts of reversal, I put away *Le Grand Meaulnes* and *The Shepherd's Calendar* as my commuting and bedside reading and replaced them with *Storm of Steel* and *Zambesi Quest*; I stopped sailing off with Schumann and Fauré and Poulenc to enchanted other realms by ceasing to listen to music altogether – just like self-hardening Lenin, who may have been considering the alarming warning of Plato: if a man yields to the enchantment of music, 'the sinews of his soul are extirpated'.

That was not all. Believing, with some justification, that, if the nature of the inner man has some bearing on the appearance of the outer, then conversely the outer man influences the development of the inner, I had my long wavy locks shorn to a crew cut, tempered my normally friendly and rather hesitant voice to a tone more terse and seemingly assured, and began adapting my naturally open, artless, dreamy expression to a cast more closed, 'canny', resolute, mainly achieving this, or thinking I achieved it, by a considered narrowing of the eyes and compression of the lips.

What my colleagues thought of the new me I never learned. Apart from the continuity girl Clare's 'You *have* had a haircut!' they maintained a judicious silence. But Sally was startled – as what lover wouldn't be? – when I sprang my disturbing metamorphosis on her without any warning. She wasn't overtly critical of my new persona, more nonplussed and wryly amused. It was only some time later that she told me that the boyishness, the openness, the idealism which I had never imagined featured for her among my plus points and which I was now setting out to quash so assiduously had all contributed to my appeal to her. So much for youth's take on such things.

Black shadow

My new reading being predominantly stories of real-life derring-do – that genre which, despite my love of fictional adventure in boyhood, I had never sampled before – it was only natural that it should encompass the Second World War. What particularly seized my imagination was the Battle of Britain. Natch. Young men of about my age (and of Uncle Ivor's at the time) performing the most heroic exploits imaginable, saving Western civilisation. I read illustrated histories of the battle, studied detailed records of the losses on both sides, devoured first-hand accounts. Then one day, in the course of this, I came across an incident I could scarcely credit. On a hot sunny August afternoon in 1940 a Messerschmitt 110 had crashed in Kingsdon St Mary, with the loss of its crew – and where it had come down was the coppice in the grounds of the Rectory! There had been an eye-witness who lived at the top of the hill, the daughter of the proprietor of the Bullers Arms inn (from which, at hot sunny August two o'clocks when I used to pass it during my sojourn at the Rectory, there would spill out from the saloon bar when the door opened on its dim interior a medley of voices and beery smells reminding me of those from the Prince Albert and stabbing me then with a strange pain-pleasure). This girl had been taking in washing when she had heard a tremendous roar and then seen a twin-engined plane, emitting smoke and flames, fly terrifyingly low over the garden. It had carried on down the hill, over the Rectory, then disappeared from view. Seconds later there had been the sound of an explosion and a column of smoke had risen into the air.

A family having tea that afternoon on the Rectory lawn, on the *archetypal summer lawn*. A wash of gold, fringed with openwork shadow...roses and irises and delphiniums in bloom around it...the old midge-haunted shrubbery, and beyond that the coppice...floating out of this the occasional muted birdsong...the lichen-ornamented redbrick façade of Toad Hall, I mean the Rectory, all mellow pink and old gold...up on high a vault of blue... An idealised image I had long borne within me of the magical summer I had spent with Dean and Olivia...quintessence of the English Elysian... And then, unbelievably, there bursts into the idyllic its very antithesis, suddenly appearing over the Rectory roof, horrifyingly on top of you, blocking out a tract of the serene blue with its dark bulk, pulverising the peaceful hour with its overpowering thunder, eclipsing the light on the lawn with its great black shadow, displaying in such close-up the sinister German markings, sinister not simply because they were the insignia of the enemy but because they seemed, that Nazi swastika and Balkan cross – unlike the colourful, debonair roundel on our Spits and Hurricanes – *intrinsically malevolent*. The shocking nature of this intrusion into the immemorially untroubled by the clamorous, black-crossed malign (which was all that impacted on my imagination then: I didn't even consider that airmen must have died, tragically young, in that crash) was increased for me, an insulated-islander representative of my generation, by the knowledge that it was a one-off, that before the war this village, like thousands of others, had dreamed on undisturbed for centuries and that afterwards it might well carry on doing so for further centuries: it appeared scarcely believable to me, that nightmarishly intimate meeting of Rectory lawn and Nazi warplane, it was the ultimate incongruity – or so I mistakenly thought then.

Now

Sally and I were married, one September afternoon, at St Augustine's Church, Blackwell. Driving there in a hired car with Lil, Danny (my best man) and Danny's mum. Sitting beside the driver, gazing out at the seething road ahead, the unbroken inky purple above. Listening to the most insistent evidence of how wet it is outside, the sound of the tyres. Then seeing the roadway and pavements calming down, no longer spluttering...and then, by the time we're into King Street, already becoming still and reflective, especially the puddles, now high-gloss, high-definition snapshots of the scene the wrong way up. Winding down the window and inhaling the fresh clean air. And then, as St Augustine's comes into view, seeing that sudden strange radiance with which the emerging sun bathes a scene on rainy days when most of the sky is still violet dark. As abruptly as though floodlights have been switched on, the nondescript ashlar façade of St Augustine's gleams with a becoming pallor and the foliage of the drenched chestnuts on either side turns a limelike green so magically bright and pure as to appear, like trees illuminated at night by an overhead street lamp, almost artificial. And since this light has made the raincloud behind the trees and church appear to darken to an even inkier shade – just as, in a colour change as instantaneous as that of a chemical reaction, switching a light on indoors turns the blue of the early evening sky seen outside to indigo – the scene seems to be displaying a photographic negative of its usual self. Strange, dramatic, almost unearthly radiance, you seem to be heralding a change in my life, in Sally's, in life in general, that will be as lasting as it is wonderful. Is it that, as George Eliot said, 'Nature at certain moments seems charged with a presentiment of one individual lot'? Or is the generous promise of this extraordinary golden light quite hollow, the pathetic fallacy indeed?

In the church, hearing the organ announce the bride. Seeing her slowly moving down the aisle on her father's arm, dazzling in creamy white and mysteriously veiled, shyly smiling paleness contrasting with Mr Banks' solemn beefy red. Making the vows and realising that now I'm no longer single, that's all in the past, I'm married. In this instant. Now. *Now.* Hearing the diapason of the organ's Mendelssohn filling the church and so thrillingly dramatising the occasion that my newly wrought music-renouncing toughness is no match for it. Standing in the porch posing for the album and gazing at Sally, at her eyes gleaming as greenly as the rain-glossed leaves outside, at her cheeks flushed the same pink as the rosebud bouquet she holds, at her flawless flawed lips. Stepping out of the church into the continuing smile of the sun, which, as the birds sing, sets the dripping leaves of the chestnuts beaming in response and the wet grass winking miniature spectrums. Experiencing all this in one of those rare privileged states from which the tedium, the fret, the shadows are *so* absent that – could it be possible? could it really be? – they seem to have vanished forever.

'A promising future'

Encouraged by the success of the hogwash I had desperately contributed to my first 'character' conference, and naturally enough wishing to continue playing to what I bemusedly supposed must be one of my strengths, I had now confidently, airily been tossing into these meetings for some time ever more outrageous new ideas. These my colleagues seized upon and chewed over with a zest that made me conscience-stricken as I sat there detachedly observing them. I was a little ashamed, too, when I saw that those of my fancies that were acted upon resulted on the page in the most dysfunctional puppets that ever jerked their way through a picture-strip story. Many readers of our tales, as happy I'm sure with a world of the reliably corny as I had been when reading *Film Fun*, must have felt completely at sea when some character or other upped and displayed a totally *uncalled-for* Jekyll and Hyde transformation of personality.

But Grouty saw this new 'depth' of characterisation as giving the tales a dimension that set them tellingly apart from the rest of the string in the picture libraries stable. Little wonder then that in a report on his staff he sent to Penelope Highe, Managing Director of the department, he referred to me, I saw, as 'a bright young hombre with an imagination out of left field and a promising future on our library'.

But in this prediction, as in so much else, our editor was wrong. Because, never mind about a promising future for me on our library, there was shortly to be no future of any kind for anyone on it. New broom Ms Highe had decided to sweep it out of existence. Reason: the *True 'Tec Tales* sales graph resembled the steady, inexorable line of descent of an aircraft's approach flight. Guiltily (natch), I wondered what part my introduction of characters that Grout called 'interestingly complex' but that I now considered clinically insane played in the library's decline. But, I reassured myself, this had started long before my arrival on the scene. I had had nothing to do with the deceitful titles and covers and the groaning plots. The boss was responsible for those. And he'd been particularly culpable in his failure to realise what a danger to the health of the tales those arbitrary fixes of his had been, those fitful injections of US-of-A-ese. Well, he was shortly to pay for that professional negligence, that dereliction of his duty of due care – to pay for it by being, as it were, struck off the register.

Ms Highe

Could *True 'Tec Tales* have been revived instead of being put out of its misery? Could a new editor with a new team of authors and a new approach have achieved a new sales take-off? Possibly. I wouldn't know. Not, I'm sure, that such an attempted revival would have featured strongly as an option for Ms Highe. Newly arrived at Mega from Pinnacle (or was it Zenith?), she came preceded by a stock reputation for being a 'tough cookie' and all too tiresomely was going to give just as stock a demonstration that it was justified, and how. She was a prototype of those models that would soon start rolling off the mass production line. Too early she may have been for the regulation Dallas power togs and regulation two-tone-crop coiffure (Ms Highe: slate grey suit, oyster blouse, natural blonde), but she was a trail-blazer in the regulation charm-school-smile ruthlessness – that willed ruthlessness which, although it's so trashily two-bit, every power-scene practitioner of it believes to be proof of an *exceptional* fibre and so regards with a secret, imbecile pride.

The closure of the library was to be a relatively speedy operation. The following month's tales had just been sent to the printer; a further quartet were nearing completion and would be printed; and so would another batch at an earlier stage. Everything else on the stocks was to be scrapped.

Carlsen Purvis, Bertha Gurney and I would only need about two weeks of our month's notice to finish editing the final four tales. So what then? Well, Ms Highe had promised to seek out, though without guaranteeing anything, other employment for us within the company. Late one afternoon, soon after the announcement of the closure (passed on to us by a pallid Grout, whose speech had been robbed by shock of its normal remarkable blend of two cultures), she called me to her office. It was a spacious, airy affair which she had had redecorated in pearl greys and charcoals, refurnished in tubular steel and glass and rehung with steel-framed abstract prints. Seated not at her desk but at a table, in one of the low-slung metal chairs, she was all hollow smiles, exposed thigh and, I couldn't help observing, wham-bam-thankyou-Sam-now-get-lost stares of icy lasciviousness that produced in me, one of tender years who had never encountered them before, some discomfort. She had, she said, received very satisfactory reports on my work so far (I found offensive her *de haut en bas* tone and headmistress-to-junior-pupil terminology) and was sure I could be employed usefully elsewhere at Mega.

'I have two possible openings for you,' she said, pausing with glacially brazen awareness of the double entendre. 'I can arrange for interviews for either or both – it's up to you. They'd both be paying roughly what you're getting now.' (Did I detect a faint contempt in the voice of this bigshot recipient of a salary that was, I imagined, about three or four times my own?) 'One's a sub's job in Partworks. A new arts series called *Vista*.' A new *arts* series! 'The other's in Magazines. A reporter's job on *The Swiss Roll Maker*. They need to replace someone who's leaving. You worked on a local rag before you came to us, I believe.'

Worked on a local rag? It was the first time, but it wouldn't be the last, that I amazedly found myself kitted out in someone else's past. I briefly thought of hanging on to it but decided it was too risky. But if I was to say it wasn't mine, I hoped that she wouldn't ask what I *had* been doing before *True 'Tec Tales* and that I wouldn't have to trot out my humorous-fob-off cod cv: Most recently, computation alternating with the exploration of ideal worlds, and before that the discipline of prolonged meditation.

'No. But I...' The slight narrowing of my eyes, compression of the lips, deepening of the voice were conveying, I hoped, Hardnosed Reporter Manqué.

'Oh. Some wires crossed somewhere. Well, I'm sure you wouldn't find the reporting side difficult – if you were interested.' She spoke of the job with the above-it-all hint of disdain of those too puffed up with consciousness of having long since ceased to be hands-on themselves, of being daily occupied instead with *meetings, lunches, decisions.*

Vista or *The Swiss Roll Maker.* At one time it would have been no contest. But today, with the advent of the new me, the Man not Boy, it was a different matter. I told her I would like to be interviewed for both jobs.

Print

There are times when a kind of acidic despair begins to eat into the soul of the hero-worshipper whose dearest wish is to emulate his hero. It usually occurs when a low reached by the one who is striving, an immense dissatisfaction with what he has to show for his efforts and with himself, coincides with the reappearance of his exemplar in all his glory, irradiated by the light of both achievement and renown. So it had been with myself and Master. Sometimes when I had still been struggling with my book, strenuously trying to find the pieces of what would be a marvellous mystery but once again ending up empty-handed, strenuously trying to write a paragraph that could begin to compare with one of Master's but in frustration crossing it through, sometimes on those occasions I would pick up *Mosaic* and happen at random on one of the finest pages, in which a brilliantly conceived and disguised key to the puzzle was embodied in the most lustrous prose – and then a terrible despondency would overcome me. And once, I remember, on the afternoon of one of these bleak days, I had come across in an *Observer* magazine series on notable writers of the twentieth century a potted biography of Master that referred to him in the familiar way as not only a literary legend but a symbol of an age, and it struck me even more forcibly than usual that, despite the fact that, as I saw it, we were soul brothers, there was nonetheless a vast chasm between us, between, on the one hand, the unsuccessful nobody and, on the other, *the literary legend and symbol of an age* – and this turned the despondency to almost a physical pain.

But since I had Become a Man (in one of the most rapid metamorphoses ever effected) this corrosive discontent had abated: I wanted to be as good a husband as I could to Sally, which meant, among much else, Staying on Top of Things; my disappointments concerning my book were only background noise all the time that that book remained, as currently, in limbo; and I was determined to relegate Master to a less dominant position in my mental landscape. Then, at about this time, a monumental new biography of him appeared that made the last detailed account of Master's life and work seem but a preliminary sketch. (I'd seen Auden's 'cryptologist' critic exemplified in Gordon Bennett, now the American author of this new book, Fuller D. Taylor, emerged as the epitome of the 'documentor', who 'with meticulous accuracy...publishes every unearthable fact'.) There followed within me a wrangle about whether I should read this book, a wrangle between Newly Emerged Man and Obsessive Fan, a wrangle that grew quite heated at times. Eventually, Newly Emerged Man prevailed. And when one day in Blackwell public library (surprisingly, to me, better stocked than the Bexcray one) I saw a just-returned copy of the book replaced on the shelf by an assistant, I withdrew it with no more than an understandable curiosity that was, I felt, *resolutely well-contained*. And although it had two invitingly thick sections of illustrations like a well-filled triple-decker sandwich and had an appetising garnish of footnotes clustering at the base of almost every page, luring the addict on with mouthwatering sidelights and elaborations,

I took the book to the counter only with just as resolute an intention of merely glancing through it at home.

The glance proved to be of the prolonged, all-encompassing kind. But strangely, as I began making my way through the book, what I read in no way weakened my resolve to become less fixated on Master.

The fifteen-year labour of an academic whom some might have regarded as verging on the demented in his exhaustive scouring for trifles, the biography was avowedly light on interpretation and evaluation and had as its chief aim 'the presentation of every verifiable known fact about Master, his world and his work'. It was therefore stuffed with those laundry-list minutiae (what someone who wrote about Gershwin's daily doings was comically pleased to call 'the statistical evidence of genius in its everyday life') which the general reader finds wearisome beyond words but which the loopy fan cannot get enough of. 'Do we really want to know what was in Master's suitcase when he followed his wife to Baltimore?' one exasperated reviewer complained. (The biographer had miraculously come into possession of his man's packing list on the back of an envelope.) 'Yes, yes, you bet,' replies the loopy fan, 'and what's more, do we know how *many* shirts he took?'

The book produced in me conflicting reactions. True, I was still bowled over by the *so-dense* and *so-shaped* life it created, which all the detailed research served to make *so much more impressive* than the unresearched lives of those like myself who read it. True, the formidable assemblage of facts on every conceivable aspect of that life (the mere printing of which, in such an authoritative typeface on such top-class paper, gave them significance regardless of whether they merited it in themselves or not), the histories of Master's forebears, siblings, wife and friends (who, as they stepped out of life into this account, took on the heightened quality of characters in a play), the weighty setting of Master himself in a historical, social and literary context, the investigation of his working methods, the facsimiles of his notebooks and manuscripts, plus of course the footnotes and the bibliography and the small-book-in-itself of an index, all that I found as clobberingly grand as ever. But at the same time, part of my mind now told me, which it had not in the past, that Master's life as lived had to be far less impressive, less daunting, than his life as condensed, fact-saturated, chaptered, footnoted, bibliographed, indexed. If I could have been granted the power to travel back in time and become involved in part of Master's actual life – something I would once have sacrificed a great deal to do – I would surely have observed so patent a difference between the lived life and the represented life. Seeing a man corporeal as any other, with thinning hair, enlarged pores and nicotine-stained fingers; seeing him as much a slave to the sartorial styles of his time as any other, wearing a type of collar, tie and suiting not thoughtfully settled upon by himself but arbitrarily decreed by fashion, a man caught up as helplessly in the despotism of the decadal as any other; seeing him consulting the time, climbing the stairs, taking a leak, checking his billfold, a man caught up as helplessly in the despotism of the quotidian as any other; seeing him meeting a musician friend so ruddily, corpulently, even perhaps halitotically less imposing in the flesh than his purely achievement-adumbrated counterpart on the page; seeing him signally failing to embody – since it was humanly impossible to do so – any of the impressively dense pages that helped to make his disembodied self so grand; watching him at any given moment, not as in the biography unfettered, airborne, ranging within a single paragraph, and during the thirty seconds it took me to read it, freely back and forth in time and space, but confined like us all to a particular circumscribed hour and a particular circumscribed place; seeing, if I had been able to travel back in time, all this, I would no longer, I told myself, have been so crushed by the awesome tomes about my hero.

As for this awe, it was due to a phenomenon that was constantly drawing itself to my attention: the spurious significance of print per se. All those exhibitions, plays, concerts, fêtes and other 'entertainments' to which Sally and I had been lured by a poster or newspaper ad or flyer that, merely by virtue of its *printed* announcement, itemisation and description of the event, lent attentionworthiness and the promise of value to what experience of it would soon reveal to be utterly unworthy of attention and devoid of any value. All those programmes, all those *tickets* even, that purely by means of *print*, bestowed dignity, quality, on what would turn out to be feeble in the extreme. If enhancement of information by the printed word is so great at such a basic level, on such trifling items of communication, how much greater is it in the case of a book: how much more significant, when I read about Master, was the *signifier*, the bulky, ramifying, imposingly supplemented text, than the *signified*, the subject's actual lived life, that alloy in which the base metals of the trivial, the unnecessary, the mistaken, the tedious play no less considerable a part than they do in the lives of us all.

There is an obvious hierarchy of authoritativeness in our forms of communication: at the bottom of the heap the oral; above that the handwritten; above that the various forms of the screened; above that the personally printed out (formerly the typewritten); and then, at the summit, wielding the real clout, the professionally printed, the ultimate medium, garbed in this or that dignified typeface and point size, uniform of authority that, like every other, may be masking the inept, the erroneous, the fraudulent, the iffy of all kinds, the ultimate medium that makes every first-time author, seeing it bestow the decisive seal of approval on what had often seemed before, well, a bit doubtful, beam with joy. And while I was reading Fuller D. Taylor's biography, I learned, from a newspaper interview with him, that, like the subject of his book, he wrote his manuscripts by hand, giving them to his secretary to type. And I realised then (especially as I had now seen the processes of text conversion at work in publishing – even if only at the sunken level of the dreadful *True 'Tec Tales*) that if I could have seen his book in handwritten, untidily corrected draft rather than in the print that had been so imposing it would have appeared quite mundane, would for me further have demythologised Master.

A haze dispersed

My new less romantic, more hard-headed attitude made me realise that the symbolism acquired by so many great artists after their death, the poetry woven around their very existence, were far from consciously embodied by them when they were alive, that they were far from appearing as demigods to themselves and their fellows, far from knowing that they would dazzle those who later gazed back on them. (At the other extreme, certain long-forgotten minor cultural figures who orbited around these stars and achieved comparatively little of note in their own lives were far from knowing that we, as we read about them – about, for instance, an unsuccessful small publisher whose constant meetings, constant journeys never seemed to lead to anything much – would, seeing of those lives only that bootlessness of which we read, keep thinking 'What on earth kept him going? Why did he bother? How pointless his life must often have appeared to him,' because we make the mistake of investing those figures with that same consciousness of the seeming futility of their lives that looking back on them across the years affords us, whereas, to them, wholly caught up in, fully engaged from day to day with, their plans and needs and desires, those lives never seemed other than important. As ours seem to us. Ours that, if they were ever written about when they were over, might arouse in the reader the same melancholy questions we once asked ourselves about those others: 'What on earth kept him going? Why did he bother?' It was that old business of perspective again.) The shimmering golden haze through which, when I used to read Master's book, I would see him in New York, a figure freed from the exigencies of time and space, hovering *encompassingly*, a presiding spirit, over that Manhattan of which he had been made one of the great twenties and thirties emblems, thinned out, dispersed almost, when I read that he'd started work on *Mosaic* in a shabby, airless apartment during a heatwave and suffering from neuralgia. I had seen Gershwin, another emblem of the New York of that time, through a similar haze and that too began to evaporate when I learned that *Rhapsody in Blue*, that stirring evocation of an age and later the unofficial hymn of the republic, did not come gloriously to him in some spontaneous blaze of inspiration but was an unexpected task in response to his reading in a paper that, news to him, he was 'at work on' something for a too-imminent concert. I realised – belatedly perhaps, but there we are – that these two men, famous and fêted in their lifetime though they were, had, when out in a New York avenue or street, no consciousness at all of being the transcendental symbols of that twenties and thirties metropolis the world later made them but, rather, as they waited at one of its crossing lights that checked them, as they walked or rode down one of its canyons that dwarfed them, felt themselves to be, like everyone else, an impinged-upon mere particle of it. Which was how the new, demythologising me chose to see them too. As for which of these ways of looking at Master and Gershwin was the more valid, as for whether either way, or any other, had any validity at all, it didn't matter. For what is any life to us other than what we choose to regard it as? Including our own.

Swiss rolls

The interviews had been fixed up. *The Swiss Roll Maker* first. Then *Vista*. Preparing myself for them was tough: they required such diametrically opposed presentations of my interests and abilities, such different distortions of my past.

The Swiss Roll Maker. As I psyched myself up for that one, it appeared scarcely credible to me that an entire magazine could be devoted to the manufacture of one particular type of cake, that enough material on this could be assembled each month to provide continuing interest to the magazine's surprisingly large number of readers in the baking trade. But apparently it was so. And no doubt, I thought, as I prepared to enter the office of Hugh Wynner, Managing Editor of Trade and Practical Magazines, I would soon find out how it was achieved.

With his floppy blond hair, rosy cheeks and head boy's steadfast handshake, Wynner seemed extraordinarily young for the position he held. With him was a much older man, with slicked-back dark hair and a handlebar moustache. Unlike Wynner, he shook hands with me silently and without a smile. And I realised this character had taken agin me on the instant. I didn't know why, it wasn't fair, but there it was. I'd come across this immediate, and therefore utterly irrational, enmity on only one other occasion. In my last year at Elson Road Primary a new boy arrived in the class, a fat boy called Chapman, and as soon as he looked at me I knew he had it in for me. His hostility never took dramatic form but constantly showed itself in small ways – so that, for example, in opposing playground battle groups, those groups that race around stuttering automatic weapon fire at each other at random, Chapman would never fail to single me out as an immediate casualty in that lethal crossfire through which everyone else around him was charging unscathed: 'You're dead! You're dead!' Now, after all these years, it had happened again. It was all the more disconcerting because, naturally affable being that I am – even if, in a sad development that remodels so many of us, no longer now quite so manifestly such – my initial relations with everyone else I'd met apart from Chapman had been amicable.

The man in question, the man who had a down on me from the start, was the editor of *The Swiss Roll Maker*, 'Lord' Eddie Kitchin, so nicknamed apparently because of his claimed resemblance to his famous First World War near-namesake, Lord Kitchener. I thought this notion was pushing it a bit but I suppose that on a dark evening he could just about have been taken for the 'Your Country Needs You' man. His sobriquet, like that of another ennobled in the same way, 'Lord' Ted Dexter, or like that of, say, 'Hurricane' Higgins, was obviously one of those in such common use that it ends by being uttered as naturally and unthinkingly as a given name. Certainly, Hugh Wynner, when wanting his colleague's opinion, would turn to him and say '"Lord" Eddie?' with not the least trace of self-consciousness.

Wynner said that he knew of my situation – but what had made me apply for this particular job? I shot him my prepared line: a professed longstanding interest in baking generally, though with no practical experience of it, and a 'certain' curiosity about the swiss roll making process in particular (I thought this cool *qualified* interest would be more convincing than one more impassioned). This went down well, better than I'd hoped for. With Wynner, anyway. Once more I was baffled. Why were my most outrageous pronouncements always taken so seriously? Why did no one ever say with a smile, 'Come off it'?

Wynner then gave me *his* spiel. 'I'm proud to say that Trade and Practical Mags is one of the most successful departments in the company,' he began. He blushed faintly (the sixth-former listing his school achievements), he pushed a hank of silky hair away from one eye. I knew it had to be an illusion but he looked to be several years junior to even my young self.

'And *The Swiss Roll Maker* plays a major part in that success,' aggressively put in its editor, with the *totally uncalled for* unspoken message that they intended to keep it that way. 'Its sales – '

'Absolutely,' Wynner cut in (he *was* school captain). If he was a litle curt in confirming his subordinate's claim, it was only because he was eager to get on with, not to lose the thread of, what was, it soon became obvious from its even flow, a well-rehearsed set piece. 'Now what keeps Trade and Practical Mags at the top of the tree?' he asked with a creditable attempt at spontaneity. 'Well, it's because we offer Joe Public much more than the competition does. Take one of our recent publications, *Mowing* – that's already outselling what the opposition has to offer.' He ticked off these rivals on his fingers. '*Mow, Mower, Get Mowing!, Great Grass, Greensward, Lawn News, Lawn Tips, Lawn, The Lawnmower.*' I wondered whether it was such command of detail that had overcome the drawback of extreme youth in getting him where he was. 'Why is it doing so well?' he asked. A pause. I frowned, readying myself to concentrate on why *Mowing* was outselling *Mow, Mower, Get Mowing!, Great* – 'Because it provides more of everything.' Further ticking off on his fingers. 'More product comparisons, more best buys, more where to buys, more experts' tips, more how-to diagrams, more pix, more snappy anecdotes...'

That thousand-page whopper, Mega's *Ultimate Guide to Lawnmowing*, came to my mind. I thought it could do no harm to mention that I was familiar with it. I did. And, while I was about it, I brought in the equally monumental *Ultimate Guide to Wallpapering*.

Baking, lawnmowing, wallpapering... I'd been expressing a somewhat nerdish familiarity with them all. A warning light flashed on. *Don't overdo it.*

'Two of Mega's most successful books *ever*,' Wynner said. 'Still in print.'

'Leaders in their field,' I said.

He looked hard at me for several seconds without saying anything, then continued: 'Swiss rolls. We have to admit it, most people take them for granted – though I know you don't,' he added hastily. Nevertheless, he still continued as though I did: 'Do they ever stop to wonder where they originated? Was it Switzerland or wasn't it? When were they first made? Are they eaten only in Europe? Or in the States, Australia, Africa, Asia?' I found this series of rhetorical questions, separated by challenging pauses, irritatingly needless. It seemed that Wynner, who had just acknowledged a certain prior preoccupation on my part with the subject, hadn't the mental flexibility to change course midway through his set patter and omit what had originally been aimed at candidates with no such previous interest. He was like those telly interviewers who can't think on their feet, who continue with all their prepared questions even after the interviewee has already answered some of them *en passant*. 'Do they ever consider which are the most suitable fillings for the different types and flavours of sponge?' Here he went again. 'Who makes the jam for them? What sorts of flour are most suitable for the sponge? What's involved in transporting flours for the big manufacturers, like Lyons and Traditional Homebake?' Traditional Homebake. Those frauds. I remembered well the swiss roll in their Country Kitchen range. Seduced by an exquisitely olde-world-illustrated, exquisitely olde-world-lettered box, which showed a charming bespectacled olde-world granny in an olde-world 'country kitchen' holding before her and contemplating with 'traditional homebaker' 's pride a fresh plump cylinder oozing with richly jammy jam, I had then found lurking lyingly inside the traditional-homebakebox a contemporary-factorybake object, curiously dry-yet-glutinous, tasting faintly of chemist's shop, its innards barely stained by something anaemically pink and synthetic. I remembered contemplating that box at some length before dropping it and its contents into the waste bin. Traditional Homebake. So I'd be having dealings with *them*.

Wynner said no more, letting his questions, which hung on the silence with tiresome resonance, and his still-raised eyebrows (the boyish face now looked foolish) make his point for him: that is, what boundless scope the subject of swiss rolls had for a reporter, what capacity to fill a thousand and one issues of the magazine. My impatience with his questions had now been replaced by slight alarm. For, although I tried hard, I simply couldn't imagine how, even taken all together, the answers to his passionate swiss-roll catechism could fill more than a single column of a single issue. However, I refused to let this failure dismay me. Nor did I allow myself to become disheartened by the realisation that his questions had been intended as mere examples of a vast number waiting to be asked and were not, as it had seemed to me, an already fully exhaustive list. No, I gave a compressed-lips smile of appreciation at the rich pickings awaiting any journalist let loose on such a lush field of enquiry.

'We've had an extremely good reference for you from Penny Highe,' said Wynner. His colleague, who maintained his hostile silence, seemed superfluous to the interview. 'She says that, according to your previous boss, Stan Grout...' He consulted a sheet of paper before him. '...you have an imagination out of left...no that's not it...where are we?...ah yes, you're always coming up with new ideas.' Always coming up with new ideas? I remembered the many days I'd sat staring at the excruciating scripts of Hector Wills & Co that I was supposed to rescue, staring at them with a mind so *completely* empty it sometimes disturbed me.

'Well,' said Wynner, contemplating me with a pleased smile, '*The Swiss Roll Maker* can certainly use new ideas. As many as we can get.'

Feeling some pressure on me to respond to his obviously great expectations, believing that I had a considerable unearned reputation to live up to, I began unwisely to muse aloud. 'There are interesting new ways of looking at almost every subject under the sun,' I intoned sagely. (No wonder he offered me the fucking job. It wasn't often that there walked through his door a bakery buff and a philosopher rolled into one.) Interesting new ways of looking at almost every subject under the sun? Were there? When was the last time any had occurred to me? Or, more accurately, when had any *ever* occurred to me? Still, I was now stuck with this line. 'For instance...' (Ah, m-m-m, ah, shouldn't have said that. Shouldn't have launched *SS For Instance*, shouldn't have cast *that* craft loose into a fog. Now you were committed to sailing it onward. I wished I knew where we were supposed to be heading.) '...couldn't we...' (*We*. Crumbs. Couldn't *we*. With what impressive confidence that I would land the job was I already using the pronoun of belonging!) '...sometimes look at things from...' (From what? Then out of the fog a landmark faintly materialised. Thankfully I swung the tiller towards it.) '...the consumer's point of view? The swiss roll *eater* as opposed to the swiss roll *maker*.' (They seemed not to understand the course I was setting, but the mist was clearing now and I could dimly sight my barren destination.) 'I know manufacturers do their own market research, but they can get stuck in a rut with their questions.' Can they? 'We could – er – we could do our own interviews with the public to find out...well...' (I'd entered a patch of fog again that temporarily obscured the view, but then I emerged from it.) '...ideas for new fillings...new twists on...old...'

Wynner nodded, looking interested.

Unfortunately, sudden sunlight distracted me at this point: entering through a window behind the preternaturally young executive, it turned a curl beside his ear to gold foil, set the ear itself glowing a translucent pink and knighted him on the

291

shoulder of his navy blue suit with a blade of sky blue. This painterly piece of solar work – of a type which not only brought to mind the technique of Vermeer but which for some strange reason I always vaguely associated with over-warm rooms, mote-filled beams and the aftertaste of a cooked lunch on the palate – brought back to me a similar scene I had...

Jesus, this would never do. I'd been letting my thoughts wander at the ship's wheel. At this rate I could run aground at any moment. That wasn't what Becoming a –

'There might be – er – there might be a line along those...' I heard myself slither into that verbal dislocation which the attempt to express abstract ideas not only produces, regularly, in Fowler-and-Prescott-type political blusterers but can produce, on a bad day, in almost anyone.

'Suggestions for imaginative new fillings,' Wynner mused. He turned to his subordinate. '"Lord" Eddie?'

'I can't see – '

'It's an idea,' Wynner said to me. 'Getting away from the old, time-honoured combinations, the plain sponge and apricot jam, the chocolate sponge and vanilla cream. Our respondents might come up with something really original. Coffee sponge, say, and...oh, I don't know...whatever...'

He was as short of a landfall as I had been.

'That sort of thing,' I said.

I was aware of Kitchin eyeing me narrowly. 'I see you worked on a local – ' he began.

'When would you be free to join us?' Wynner said. 'If we offered you the job, that is.'

Dusk

Sally and I, shopping one Saturday in Bexcray, had decided over lunch, despite our general dislike of going to the cinema in daylight, to see an afternoon film at the Majestic (still, miraculously, a cinema, as was the Regal – but not as was the Kings, now Casino Royale Bingo, and the Ritz, now an empty shell). It was into a slightly misty autumn evening that we emerged after the performance: the lights of the town, still busy with traffic, had lost exact definition. And fusing with, enriching, the thin mist was that fumy urban atmosphere I knew so well and which even now aroused a certain expectancy in me... Ah, we children of the city or town, how for so many of us it is *its* poetry, and not that of wood, field and stream, the kind we were set to study at school, that has entered and lodged in our soul.

> Mine is an urban Muse, and bound
> By some strange law to paven ground.

We made our way down a side road to where I'd parked the car. Against the sky the houses formed dark masses in which, behind the intervening moist black trees dripping in the gardens, soft orange rectangles glowed; and every so often my old faves, tail-lights, added further colour to that orange in the dim and dusky road, their red smudged and cooled by the vaporous evening to a softer, more mysterious cerise. Then something else, something sweetly aromatic, memory-laden: a whiff of smoke – probably, given the hour, the last smoke – from a bonfire smouldering in some nearby back garden. Suddenly, in a magical onrush, the houses, the gardens, the lights, the entire road, were suffused with the atmosphere of misty, bonfire-smoky November-*Knockout* six o' clocks of long ago, when the essence of that comic was indistinguishable from the essence of the autumn evening around it. And I re-experienced with a terrible ache the eagerness of the Danehill Road boy I had once been to hurry home through the dusk and take hold of that comic, to see the full-colour front page – a simplified, crude, yet still magical spectrum, subdued yet still glowing softly in the fading light of November swap-time (now the only one recognised by memory) – and to plunge into the latest wonderful exploits of Sexton Blake inside. I briefly re-lived the fierce rapture I had known on one particular autumn evening when bonfire smoke had drifted down to our garden and darkness was closing in, an evening much colder than this one, when a biting wind had set the blued sheets next door flapping on the line against the red conflagration of the sky, that evening when everything around me seemed to be promising, both within and just beyond itself, some…some what…?

At the same time, almost at one with this feeling, I felt a great urge to write about it. And, I believed, if I were to satisfy this urge I would be expressing for others the aching pleasure of their memories of almost identical experiences, those experiences for which I had a handy mental title: Autumn *Knockout* Dusks. In other words, I instinctively generalised that poetry of mine, embedded in the deepest layer of myself, I projected it – without at all being consciously aware of this – on to the screen of universal experience. And I half-thought, even, that a mere utterance of those three words, 'Autumn *Knockout* Dusks', would be enough to conjure up in anyone who heard them a particular known image – just as saying 'St Paul's Cathedral' would – and that they would then respond knowingly, happily, with 'Ah, yes, those old Autumn *Knockout* Dusks.' It wasn't until fully rational thought took over that I realised that, although others might perhaps have their own poetic memories of autumn (like Sally, for whom bonfire smoke brought back late afternoons in an uncle's garden in the country) or of *Knockout* or of atmospheric dusks or of certain mysterious intimations, nevertheless it was improbable that these would have been anything other than separate, dissociated and unfused into resemblances to my own. I realised that, contrary to what I'd always instinctively believed, I might be the only person on the planet who had known those particular dusks. Even so, I thought, if what we write about such experiences does not after all express for others anything truly comparable to what they themselves have known, perhaps it can sometimes be *just* close enough for a spark to cross the gap and ignite in them their own related special memories.

The formidable task

I postponed the *Vista* interview. That new partwork sounded too congenial. Becoming a Man meant, not indulging in some easy-peasy arts subbing, for heaven's sake, but shouldering the formidable task of becoming a reporter on a severely *practical* magazine whose editor had taken an immediate dislike to you. That was what Becoming a Man was all about. Hadn't choosing the most troublesome of two courses been what the sages of old had counselled? So when, a couple of days after my interview, Kitchin rang and in a toneless voice offered me the job (he'd obviously had his arm twisted), I accepted.

I worked out my last days on *True 'Tec Tales* and while I did so heard some shocking news. Ms Highe, in a further self-conscious exercise of the trashy five-and-dime ruthlessness, had more or less expunged poor old Grouty from Mega. Not content with summarily axeing his tales, his pride and joy, his reason for living, she had decided not to recommend him to any other department in the company (as she had everyone else on the staff) – and, for all I know, may even have, to use his own preferred mode of expression, 'bad-mouthed' him. He was on his own. I couldn't know for sure but I'd never got the impression he had contacts elsewhere in Mega and I guessed he'd find it difficult landing another job. Now it was true that his particular talents – the uniquely melded *For Chrissakes, punk...gorblimey, guv* style, the resourceful *Find Another Sucker, Pal* presentational skills, the ceaseless probing into the robotic psyche – were probably of limited use to most of the company's other publications, but I would have thought that the superbitch could have pulled a few strings to find a placement somewhere or other in that vast organisation for a man who'd given twenty years' service to it and who had an invalid wife to support.

I would like to tell you that the unpalatable Highe received her come-uppance and that the absurd Grouty was reinstated, but, alas, as is usually the case, that isn't the way things worked out.

Heavy Transport

'Go down to the Traditional Homebake Heavy Transport Division at Gribbleswade. And get the material there to write a four-page feature on it.'

Such were the terrifying orders given me as my first assignment on *The Swiss Roll Maker* by 'Lord' Eddie Kitchin, who in numbingly horrific emulation of his near-namesake and near-double pointed at me an imperative, unwavering finger. I *felt* myself blanch. Heavy Transport. *Four pages...*

'I want the lowdown on the entire fleet. Understand?' he demanded with undisguised detestation.

Determined to hide my funk from him, I took the mission on board with a swift, half-baked nod of instant understanding and a curtly competent 'Right'. 'All lorries, aren't they?' I said, essaying an easy, confident, knowledgeable tone. I had my tie loosened and my jacket hooked on one finger over my shoulder in dim remembrance of Yank newspaper 'leg men' seen long ago at the Regal.

'All lorries? All lorries?' Kitchin said quietly, in the so-very-reasonable voice he'd heard outraged men in corny movie scenes use, the all-too-foreseeable calm before the all-too-foreseeable storm. *'Of course they're all fucking lorries. What else do you think a fucking heavy transport division consists of?'*

I smiled knowingly as though to convey: Of course – I'd been but joshing.

He glared at me in the way that I remembered Harry sometimes did, as on the train to Sandbay after my suggestion that the meat in our sandwiches was bad. 'What I want, what our readers will want, is this.' He snapped out the requirements rapid-fire. 'Vehicle types (eight-wheelers, six-wheelers, articulated), roll carrying capacities, loading types (flat trailers, box bodies, low loaders), palletisation, typical consignments, destinations, scheduling, routes, drivers' rotas, maintenance… And I want that copy to sing. *Sing*. Understand?'

Could I remember all that? I doubted it. Nevertheless, 'You've got it,' I said smartly. Disappointingly, though, my voice was not entirely devoid of tremor.

An hour later he told me, in a studied insult, that he'd changed his mind, he wanted this job done well. He was therefore handing it over to the man I was replacing, John Brown, whose last week on the magazine was overlapping my first. Brown, who was showing me the ropes, was a burly thirtyish Yorkshireman who before his four years on *The Swiss Roll Maker* had previously worked on another Trade and Practical publication, *Fixtures and Fittings*, but was now leaving Mega altogether to start up a new mag at Zenith (or was it Pinnacle?): *The Pipe Layer*. (Obviously, someone who had found in the field of swiss rolls a seam of ore so rich he'd productively mined it for years on end was ideally suited to embark on a similar venture in that of pipe laying.) He was a pleasant, helpful chap who explained clearly to me how he set about obtaining the news stories and regular features that made up the bulk of *The Swiss Roll Maker*. (The features included Masters of the Rolls, celebrated swiss roll creators past and present; Roll Models, young lovelies who worked at roll-making firms; and Roll Players, roll-makers pursuing interesting leisure activities.) The rest of the mag consisted of fillers produced by a sub, mainly from PR puffs; and an editorial written by Kitchin.

I took conscientious note of Brown's info and tips, and in my new persona of Hardnosed Reporter I felt a matey empathy with this practical, no-nonsense colleague into whose shoes I would soon have to step. But then one lunchtime a couple of remarks he made revealed to me out of the blue how unspannable was the chasm between his mind and mine. (It had happened to me once before, on that occasion when without any warning Carlsen Purvis had apprised me of his distressing sexual proclivities.)

Brown and I had gone for a drink to the Falstaff, one of the two local pubs favoured by Mega people. Walking back to the office, we passed a small newish redbrick block of flats. And my companion said to me: 'Wonder how many bricks it took to build that.' It wasn't simply a mind as empty of supposition on the subject as any mind can be that kept me silent, it was also stupefaction and, I have to say it, a certain *resentment* at the question. The second remark came after we had turned the corner at the bottom of the street. There a sunlit bus, geranium red, stood throbbing at a stop, and as we passed it I caught a whiff of its warm rexine-banquette-and-tickets interior that momentarily, for no more than a second or two (since outside the pages of fiction and the cinema screen such associative memories are never other than fleeting), sent me hurtling back to the long distant past when I used to climb eagerly aboard a trolleybus. 'How much d'you reckon one of them RTs weighs?' sounded in my ear. It was the voice of one who had completely misread my lost gaze at what stood beside us so redolently scarlet and aromatic.

I could see why Kitchin had decided to switch the Heavy Transport article to 'Capability' Brown. To sort out those eight-wheelers, those box bodies, those low loaders he preferred the safe hands of one who voluntarily, helplessly, quested here, there and everywhere after aggregate and tonnage. Reluctantly, I had to grant Kitchin sound judgment in the matter.

Standard stuff

Within how short a time and in how unforeseen a way can our life take on a totally new cast. When in the years after I left school I lived at 33 Danehill with Lil, how unbelievable it would have seemed to me, as I vaguely peered into the immediate years ahead, that they would see me living in *my own flat*, with a *wife*, reading *war books*, taking on a tough job on a *practical magazine*, published by *Mega* – and learning, as I had just done, that I was going to be a *father*. Not that when Sally told me this it was exactly a surprise. She had decided some time ago she wanted to start a family as soon as we were married, and I had gone along with this. Standard stuff in those days for the likes of us: marry young, have children young, wife stays at home, husband wins the bread. Almost everyone we knew did that. And we all thought we were acting freely in the matter. We all thought, as we embarked on our near-identical journeys, that the route and the destination were our own independent choice.

Unenlightened at that stage, Sally thought she wasn't interested in a career, as opposed to looking after a home, on no other grounds than that she hadn't found the shorthand-typing jobs she'd done as a temp much less tedious than copy-typing at Dazings. Perhaps if she'd realised that that needn't necessarily have been the end of the story, she would not have had children so young, would not have followed in her own mother's footsteps. On the other hand, perhaps she still would. But then that would have been a real choice and not the illusion of one.

Kramm Pyes

'Schench rrrets.' Such was the mysterious pronouncement, just audible, of the tiny, bald, bespectacled, wizened man who sat hunched behind his desk opposite me, little more than his head and shoulders visible. Kitchin had sent me down to the little town of Bunton to see the bosses of Kramm Pyes flour mill. He wanted a feature on it, another four-pager for the next issue. It was my first assignment as a *reporter*, my first solo assignment (I'd earlier accompanied John Brown on a couple of jobs). Kitchin: 'You *should* be able to manage this one on your own.'

Dr Kramm nodded. 'Schench rrrets,' he repeated. I had just asked him, for want of anything else entering my head, what the most important factor was in buying wheat – which was the subject I *thought* he'd been holding forth on in a hoarse undertone for the past few minutes.

Schench rrrets. Jeez, what on earth could those be? 'How do you mean exactly?' I asked him. This question with its phoney terminal qualifier implying that only a shade more information was required for full understanding was a desperate formula I'd already used after each of Kramm's 'answers' to my previous three questions. But I was bothered that he might start finding my endlessly repeated ploy vexing.

I looked down at the first page of my brand-new Kenmere Reporter's Notebook, so proudly toted along to the interview, and as I saw there my scrawled, scarcely legible guesses as to the meaning of Dr Kramm's faint, rapid, riddling assertions, I felt decidedly uneasy. From such scribbles was soon supposed to emerge a *four-page feature*, an article that had to *grab and hold the attention of swiss roll makers all over the country*. Which suddenly brought home to me a dreadful disadvantage I was labouring under – one greater even than my inability to understand a word of what Dr Kramm was saying – namely, the fact that I hadn't the faintest idea of what the article was supposed to be about. Of all the handicaps that may threaten the success of a reporter on an assignment none can be greater than that. I cast my mind back to Kitchin's orders. 'At Bunton,' he had thundered, pointing the commanding forefinger at me, in ludicrously lordly imitation of his 'lookalike', 'you'll interview Dr Kramm and Professor Pyes.' At the time, it had seemed, in the way such things do to the inexperienced, reasonable enough. Interview the two supremos, right. It was only when I actually sat down facing Dr Kramm (Doctor of what, I wondered – and, incidentally, where was Professor Pyes?), that I thought: interview them about what? It was with an unpleasant groundswell of alarm, truly physical in nature, that I realised this was rather a late stage in the game to be asking that question.

Through the windows behind Kramm I could see across a large yard some of the mill buildings, their impassive chimneys and the disconsolately waving treetops beyond silhouetted against the unbroken white cloud like a skyline in *Film Fun*. There was no sign of life anywhere. The office block we sat in was strangely silent too.

'Schench *rrrets*,' repeated Dr Kramm yet again. Had his voice taken on a hint of tetchiness? It had certainly become unusually loud and clear. But then it subsided to an even lower volume than before. I leaned forward, straining my ears to catch an occasional baffling fragment of what was presumably an elaboration on his mysterious opening shot: '...vmus ...zy...byin...hvl...rrrets...schench...sks...'

I narrowed my eyes, fighting against the full-works panic that now surged through me. Where *was* Professor Pyes...? With a name like that, *he* must surely speak English. At a break in Kramm's virtual soliloquy, I politely asked him whether I would be seeing his partner soon.

'Nfr...sks...Pyes...frnserg...' He looked apologetic, then resumed where he had broken off. 'Schench rrrets...znyforbl...'

Then, at last, a light appeared. Schench rrrets. Schench rrrets. Perhaps… Could it be? *Exchange rates*? I wrote the words down, eagerly, with a simpleton's delight, as I saw them shine out like a beacon in the surrounding murk, the one intelligible phrase on the page. But soon my pleasure ebbed away. Exchange rates – well, yes, but what about them? To find out, I would have to ask Kramm, and the mere thought of another of his 'explanations' made me inwardly shudder.

'Und…mlvskchv…rrrets…'

I'd given up, in a most un-Becoming-a-Man-like way. In a suddenly detached state, I self-pityingly wondered what I was doing with this scribble on my knee, in the offices of a flour mill, trying to make something of the unplumbable pronouncements of an exchange-rates-obsessed Czech or German or Swiss or Hungarian or whatever he was. Yes, what the fuck *was* I doing here?

But then I heard the voice of a self who'd come to rescue me. After easing my inner tension with a bit of mock-mockery delivered in bright and breezy tone (he was of a Puck-like jesting kind, this helper, speaking in the general style of a Kipps or Polly that might have annoyed some but that I could just about put up with) – 'What're you doin' 'ere, ol' chap, what're you doin' 'ere? Why, you're Becomin' a Man, that's what you're doin' – he told me to forget, to get shot of, the source of the intermittent faint burbling, as of a distant rill on a country walk, that could still be heard in the background, and to ask it to introduce me to some of the senior mill staff. 'They may be able to help, ol' chap, you see.'

So I met the mill manager, Rob Baines, a hearty, ruddy, self-confident middle-aged bloke with small bright brown button eyes and a big friendly grin, who conducted me around the place and explained to me enthusiastically and in readily understandable terms the milling process. And with the same gusto, that of a small boy describing an all-absorbing hobby, he told me about the various types of flour produced and their different uses (I eagerly noted a terrific piece of info: those used for cake-making, *and therefore swiss-roll-making*, were designated turbo-milled cake flours). As I looked at Rob Baines' animated features and listened to his animated tones, I marvelled, as I had done at *True 'Tec Tales* listening to the excited script discussions of Grouty and his team, that anyone could experience such fervour about such an activity, and I felt too, as I had done then, a touch of envy. Actually, I felt the same whenever, upon seeing in Bexcray or Blackwell vans or buildings proclaiming on their sides Acme Plating & Processing or PNJ Ventilation Services or Phoenix Bill Brokers or Alex Ashford Pressure Vessels, I fell to realising that certain individuals had voluntarily and presumably enthusiastically set up these businesses. What was it, I wondered, that got anyone, presented by life with the million-and-one lines it was possible to pursue as a living, what was it that got them *so taken by* plating & processing or bill broking (whatever either of them might be) that they chose to devote their working life to it? What was it about ventilation that had so enthused PNJ that he was determined that that was the thing for him, nothing else, not heating, not insulation, but *ventilation* – yessir, he'd set up a *ventilation business*? What was it about *pressure vessels* (whatever they might happen to be, too) that had induced in Alex Ashford that inner certainty as to vocation whenever he thought about them? What lucky blighters they all were.

After I'd watched the flours being made and packed (the process was largely automated, hence the scarcity of staff), Baines introduced me to the chief chemist, plump, dark, moustached and with a rolling gait, who demonstrated how the quality of both incoming wheat and outgoing flours was checked. She wondered whether I would like some literature on the delivery, milling and packing operations. I gratefully garnered every available booklet and leaflet, preparatory to leaving.

Then Baines said, frowning, 'Don't you want any pictures for the article?'

Pictures. Of course. How could I have forgotten them? I had the little Instamatic I'd inherited from Brown in my pocket. What a dozy sod I was. Ah, there was so much more to this Becoming a Man business than I'd imagined. How difficult it was to concentrate on it non-stop, every minute. One lapse back into moony Boy and you were in trouble, trouble that no crew cut, compressed lips and newspaper man's loosened tie could get you out of. That mask of competent adulthood you had fashioned and wore, while it enabled you to be accepted into the company of true Adults, who took you at face value, while it enabled you, as false papers and a convincing second language enable a wartime agent, to infiltrate an alien world, it was of no use to you, that mask, when it came to the crunch. Just as the agent in enemy territory feels the chill of danger when asked a question to which only a native would know the answer and desperately tries to bluff his way out of trouble, so I sensed that my cover was about to be blown and had to resort to pretence.

'Pictures, yes,' I said casually, simulating absent-minded preoccupation with pocketing my bulky reporter's notebook. 'I was just going to have a word with you about them. I've left them until now because I wasn't sure which ones would be most suitable for the article.' Would that do? Not really, would it, but…

'Perhaps you don't need to take any,' said Baines. 'We've got quite a stack of our own publicity shots. Pictures of the operations we've been showing you. Would you like me to sort some out and post them to you?'

'That would be great. Thanks.' I paused. 'I'll just take a couple of pics of you, Rob, if I may?'

Rob didn't need asking twice and smilingly posed, arms folded, mill-manager-style.

Gazing down

Since I'd been working in London I'd been able to have the odd lunch with Dean. We met at Piero's, a little Soho restaurant he favoured – Italian, natch. (A little Soho restaurant. I could never hear that phrase without the meeting of Chesterton and Belloc I'd read about automatically, absurdly, flitting into my mind.) Now, one cold December day, we met there again.

Just before I'd reached Piero's I'd been charmed to see down a little side street, against a weathered, yellow-lichened brick wall and overhung by the bare branches of some planes, an old telephone kiosk glowing a subdued red in the cold pale winter light, like a low-burning but welcome fire. Then outside the restaurant, beneath a sky of paper white, the red, white and green striped awning, the scrolled name Piero's and the miniature bays in tubs, a Christmassy dark green – all infused with a fairytale quality – extended a cordial greeting to everyone who approached. As did, inside, the warm dining-room, the lighted orange-pink wall lamps, the reflective cutlery and the palest of pink tablecloths and napkins.

When we'd ordered, Dean questioned me about myself, Sally and Lil – not vague generalities of the order of 'How are you keeping?' but enquiries about specific matters he thought important. To do this, he consulted, as another exemplary man, the equally conscientious and forethoughtful Roman emperor Augustus, used to do at every meeting, even with his wife, a list of notes he had drawn up beforehand. I could see why Spectrum had been such a success. On hearing of my doings at Mega, he understandably raised his eyebrows at the new job I'd chosen. But, after I'd described my shaky start and confessed certain qualms about the future, he simply said, with such matter-of-fact certainty I believed him, 'You'll manage.'

Then he told me about himself, about an important decision he'd come to since retiring from publishing: he wished to enter politics. A long-time member of the Labour party, he intended to apply for adoption as a parliamentary candidate. He went on to spell out his political philosophy: a full-blooded socialism. At some length. And as I listened to him, to this highly articulate and persuasive man, I found myself undergoing what occurs only rarely in most lives, and never at all in some: a profound and permanent change in one's outlook on the world.

I had always proclaimed myself to be apolitical. And in reply to a question from Dean I told him this. His response was that the self-proclaimed apolitical usually fitted into one of three groups and I was no exception. (That Dean was a compulsive categoriser there was no doubt – he knew it himself and confessed it – and I wonder whether his former employee, the triad-obsessed whut-whut-whutter Neal Easy – who had apparently left Spectrum after its takeover by Mega and was now working on a mag called *Showbiz* – whether he hadn't been influenced by the sorting, tabulating tendency of his boss, though he of course had corrupted it into a fixed and facile all-purpose tool. I have long since noticed in myself as well, in the course of investigating what interests me, a compulsive need to classify my findings – and who knows whether I too didn't subconsciously acquire this from Dean. He was, after all, what is often called 'a forceful personality', compelling in the expression of his strong opinions, one of those far from common men who influence almost everyone who comes into contact with them.) Dean's three categories of the apolitical were: those who mistakenly believe that the life they lead is independent of the social structure within which they lead it and believe that therefore they have no need even to consider political matters; those, more enlightened, who are fully aware of the nature of that structure and what part they have played in it, but who have become so 'disillusioned with the political process' that they have 'washed their hands of it'; and those who have long since withdrawn from society altogether, to support themselves alone in some island retreat or highland fastness. I obviously belonged, Dean said, to the first group, those who, he added apologetically, don't know the time of day. I thought, didn't I, that my world, which revolved around Sally, my family, literature, my book, earning a living, music, sport and one or two other interests, had no connection with politics. I thought, didn't I, that the social structure, or what little I knew of it, was of no concern to me.

He was right. And I knew that in this attitude I'd been reinforced by what I'd read about my hero, Master. He had never shown the slightest interest in politics – indeed, he'd once admitted that he'd never even voted. Idolater and naïf that I was, I had wished to follow in Master's footsteps, along as many paths as possible. Besides, it wasn't only Master. So many other artists I admired who, like him, had created magical new universes, among them Debussy, Poulenc, Monet, Grahame, Nabokov, had remained practically aloof from politics, most never expressing anything other than a desire to retain the status quo – though in some this shaded into a more pronounced conservatism. I mentioned this to Dean and he said that I'd failed to realise that this lack of interest in, this desire for no change in, the social make-up of the world they lived in was only natural in those born, as they all to a man were, into a comfortable middle-class stratum of it, within whose cushioned support they could create beautiful new worlds while choosing to ignore whether their own should have been propped up in the way it was. I had failed to realise that what I imagined to be on my part a comprehensive empathy with them was no more than an aesthetic one. From the social aspect, I had scarcely anything in common with those artists who, even if they had no time for the typical *cultural* values of the bourgeoisie, nevertheless, owing so much to having been nurtured by it *socially*, never thought of questioning the class structure that had given rise to it. (Throughout this lunch it was, as much as any of the facts he cited, the typically matter-of-fact tone in which Dean explained everything to me – no different really from that in which he would have described the route I needed to take to get somewhere – that convinced me that what he had been saying was true.)

Looking back on earlier conversations I'd had with Dean before this one, I can see now that certain of his comments when he had discussed my upbringing, my situation, my work had been obliquely political but that I had not cottoned on to this. Now, though, he went on to describe the composition of and the prime moving forces in British society – class, education, money, big business, networks of various kinds – so fully, so explicitly and with such direct references to my own life that, as though gazing down on the topography of it all from an aerial view, I couldn't but make out in it for the very first time the place I occupied.

An optional extra

I sat in my office at *The Swiss Roll Maker* (which I shared with the sub-editor and Kitchin's secretary) staring at the pages of jottings in my reporter's notebook and at the various brochures and leaflets I'd been handed at Kramm Pyes. Then I looked at the impressive four-page centrepiece in the previous month's issue of the magazine, a report by John Brown on a new swiss roll manufacturer, Auntie's Kitchen (its logo portraying a woman startlingly, preposterously, similar in appearance to Lil – whose own auntie's kitchen it was best remained a family secret). I could see no way of turning the first, my scattered raw material, into anything resembling the second, a professionally crafted article. And there was no help at hand. Brown had left. Kitchin was away at what seemed an inordinately long cake-making magazines conference (pride, anyway, would have prevented me from consulting him). And the sub was at the printers. I was on my own.

Where did I start? I began to study other features in back issues. And I noticed that what they all had in common was an attention-nailing opening, slightly oblique in its approach. I also noticed, though, that, as a tuneful song in a daft show disarms the listener, makes him tolerate the tedious non-musical business that follows until the next song, this breezy intro seemed to dispense the succeeding text from any need to sing, as Kitchin put it.

An imaginative opening. I mentally abandoned my previous hopelessly pedestrian lead-ins: 'Among the flours that Kramm Pyes mill produces are turbo-milled...'; 'The turbo-milled cake flours you use are supplied by...' These direct, guileless, styleless efforts, so uncomfortably reminiscent of my school-mag 'Another famous detective was' manner, certainly wouldn't do. What then? Well, I asked myself, what had been my reaction to the actual mill when I entered it? What had been its most notable aspect? Answer: it hadn't been anything like my idea of a flour mill at all. Nor presumably anything like our readers' idea of one either. Well, that was the opening, then, wasn't it? After a struggle – numerous attempts, crossings out, rewrites – I eventually came up with:

> A sterile, brightly lit space...row upon row of ceaselessly humming machines...an occasional white-coated figure carrying out random checks... Some great medical laboratory? A nuclear power station? No, we are inside Kramm Pyes flour mill, suppliers of the turbo-milled cake flours you use to make your swiss rolls.

How surprised and pleased I was that I'd managed this. Now I could start on the slab of facts about the mill's activities and staff that would form the bulk of the article. It would be an adaptation of Kramm Pyes' own handouts (an exercise I would later discover was gratefully termed by experienced hacks a bread-and-butter piece). So:

> Flour milling has now become a fully automated process, in which...

When I'd finished typing out a fair copy, I was aware that I'd produced for swiss roll makers everywhere a clear enough account of how the flour they used was milled – if that was what Kitchin thought they wanted to read. But I was bothered by how short the piece was – far too short, it seemed to me, to fill four whole pages.

The next morning a flushed Hugh Wynner entered the office to tell us that 'Lord' Eddie's wife had just rung through from Harrogate: our editor, who had been due to return the following day, had been taken seriously ill with food poisoning. 'Tommo' Thomlinson, the sub, would have to take charge of the mag until 'Lord' Eddie's return.

Tommo was a plump, florid, round-faced, bespectacled chap of about forty who was always rubbing his hands together busily. He had, in contrast to his physically mature appearance, a curiously boyish persona – which, of course, I could empathise with. His speech was punctuated with the 'Oo-er', 'Cor' and 'Crumbs', the 'pesky', 'diddle' and 'snaffle' that, as regular usage, I'd previously only come across in the comics of my boyhood. He even sometimes, disconcertingly, lapsed, as Kenneth Grahame did in letters to his wife, into baby talk. 'Whassa' 'en?' he would say, his eyes round behind his specs, when confronted with a piece of copy he couldn't immediately identify. This strange infantilism, combined with the natural diffidence that had prevented him over the years from aiming higher than sub-editorship on a small magazine, resulted in his saying to me, after Wynner had made him acting editor:

'Oo-er, mate. Fancy pesky ol' me bein' in charge. Crumbs.'
Then, reddening to an even riper tomato hue, he puffed himself

up, with all the innocent, exuberant pride of a small schoolboy unexpectedly made monitor. 'Still, why not? Why not is what I say.' And he trotted next door and sat in Kitchin's chair and swivelled in it and held his head high in pantomimic lordliness.

Flaming idiot Tommo may have been in this respect but, in a certain dichotomy of character that is not unusual, he was red-hot at his job. It opened my eyes to see the treatment he and Phil Upman, the sombre, chain-smoking layout man (who took umbrage if he were ever referred to as anything but a designer), gave to my piece.

First, Tommo considered my heading for it, the pathetically straightforward, workaday KRAMM PYES FLOUR MILL, so archaically 19th-century, *Gentleman's Magazine*-ish in its literalness. 'Cor, mate,' he said, 'we gotta do sumfink about that – let's 'ave a ickle fink.' And in a flash he came up with the thoroughly modern, cleverly punning, splendidly meaningless FLOUR POWER. I was both impressed, doubting that I could have discovered this in a whole week of trying, and horrified, finding the title as dishonestly baseless in what it promised as were, each in its own way, the names True 'Tec Tales and Traditional Homebake.

Then Tommo and Phil tackled the article itself. 'Flippin' 'eck, bit short, innit?' Tommo said, glancing rapidly through my copy. 'Still, not to worry, not to worry. No problem.'

Coo, what they did to that first effort of mine to make it fill the four pages! The glad rags they dressed it in! First, Tommo inserted masses of cross-heads – Whispering machinery, Took samples, Different sacks, and the like – which, with the white space around them, distended my piece as popcorn and wind will distend a tummy. Then what *liberal* use Phil made of the pictures I'd received from the mill. And several he blew up to an extraordinary extent, which they certainly didn't merit (though, fearful of having otherwise to write considerably more copy – about *what*? – I kept quiet): two stevedores unloading a bargeful of wheat, which consisted mostly of a great desert-like sea of grain in the foreground; a rear view, which I would not myself have used, of the tubby chief chemist bent almost double over a machine; and the obvious dregs of one photographic shoot, a casting-around, using-up-the-reel shot of a single stark bag of flour.

Next the ingenious pair hived off sections of my copy into self-contained boxes of info that were thus made to appear necessarily supplementary to the main text (but that in their content were in fact nothing of the sort); and each of these boxes had its own space-eating head and cross-heads. They also invented diagrams with fascinating arrows and dotted lines showing, for example, wheat and flour flow directions within the mill (a graphic demonstration that in this case was quite useful). Then, learning that I could draw, they persuaded me to do a stylised pencil sketch of the mill, to which Phil appended arrows labelled Turbo-milled cake flours – broad curved arrows this time, very, well, very impressive-*looking* if nothing else – leading out from the mill to Traditional Homebake, Auntie's Kitchen, J. Lyons & Co and other swiss-roll manufacturers... Wow, all these heads and cross-heads and photographs and captions and boxes and diagrams and illustrations so elbowed their way on to the pages, so took them over, that there was no longer the slightest danger my piece would prove inadequate for its role. Indeed, so agreeably intriguing in appearance were the busy results of Tommo and Phil's stratagems that, as in all such cases, they relegated reading the text simply to an optional extra.

I had received, with this example of the designer's art, my second lesson (and it was certainly not to prove my last) in that ubiquitous, exponentially expanding, unstoppable proceeding of modern times: Tarting Things Up.

New heroes

An indirect effect of Dean's talk with me over lunch was a shift of emphasis in my reading, and, through this, in my plans for my book. The true action stuff I read now was about political action, in particular that of courageous individuals who fought for honourable causes, who strove to end tyrannies. Castro starting off with only a handful of men to overthrow Batista's regime of 'repression, assassination, gangsterism, bribery, and corruption.' Che struggling to bring democracy to Bolivia. Stauffenberg trying to rid Germany of Hitler.

I thrilled to the deeds of these determined men. They became my new heroes. My old idol, Master, had shrunk just a little when I reflected that he was almost certainly a conservative and that the events of *Mosaic* seemed to occur in a social and political vacuum (but 'so what?' I think today). I intended for my book a new dimension. I wanted the band of comrades in it, who until now had been tacitly 'apolitical' like Master's, I wanted them to have a political mission. (I was the poetic young man who has reached a time when he becomes less besotted with the beauties of the inanimate world around him and is caught up instead in the great dramas being played out in the world of men: an exchange of one romanticism for another. I was at roughly the age that Wordsworth was when he became politically aware in revolutionary France and for the first time made Nature 'subordinate to' Man.)

The city-state Leo & Co would now enter would be ruled by a fascistic junta headed by a homicidal tyrant (a ratcheting up of the plight of Master's Indigo), and their daunting mission would be to remove it and to establish in its place a socialist democracy.

So the ideas I jotted down – in what was now Notebook III, no less – took on a new slant:

The coup that brought about the dictatorship – Leo had seen it coming for a long time. He left the country before it happened. In exile he thought and planned.

Try to get hold of *The President* by Miguel-Angel Asturias – 'Nightmare fears of a city enmeshed by an evil dictatorship.'

Leo to make contact with people he knows to be sympathetic. The need to recruit resistance members, arm them, set up cells, etc.

My four, returning, have false identities.

Pushkin: poet *and* political activist – under police surveillance. Investigate.

They travel *at speed* of course. But this not the druggy thrill of travel, of velocity, for its own sake, that desire for *perpetual* forward motion of Marinetti and the Futurists and of Toad bombing along in a stolen car ('the miles were eaten up under him as he sped he knew not whither, fulfilling his instincts, living his hour'). [I could have added here, if I had read Kerouac and Tom Wolfe at that stage, the Beats on the Road and the Pranksters on the Bus.] Not that powerful thrust forward to... to... No, Guy at the wheel will be burning rubber only because the urgency of the heroes' noble aim, the restitution of democracy and justice, brooks no delay. My alter ego will be *gunning* the car, as I will be gunning the story.

Action and speed were obviously to replace observation and ratiocination, the thriller to replace the detective story; perhaps I could recreate some of the excitement I'd known when drinking in those pre-*Mosaic* boys' adventure stories so many years earlier. Even so, there was still to be a mystery of sorts: a traitor in the midst of the resistance whose identity had to be discovered. But this mystery would of necessity be only one element of the story, it would not permeate the entire narrative as that of *Mosaic* so gloriously did and as I'd originally hoped that of my book would. The poetries of the city were also to feature after a fashion: those with which Guy (who was to perform an act of great gallantry at the end) renewed contact on revisiting the scenes he remembered from childhood. But, again, the poetry would need to be intermittent and localised and not systemic as in *Mosaic* and as I'd always previously wanted in my book. And the mystery and the poetry would, it seemed, generally be discrete and not, as ideally, fused, one.

In other words, my book was becoming even less of a vehicle than before for what I wanted to express. But I was still determined to write it, to commemorate my almost lost vision as best I now could.

Five

Civically active

Another effect of my new political awareness – and with mine, Sally's – was that we joined the Labour party and became more civic minded, more involved in local affairs. We were now rather self-righteously critical of what we saw as the apathetic majority and rather too forgetful of how recently we had, quite untroubled, belonged to it ourselves. Becoming active in the polis – which, having just discovered the ancient Greeks, was how we now thought of the community in which we lived – included attending meetings with such titles as 'Whitehall or Town Hall?' and 'Urban Planning of the Future'. On dark, shivery, wind-racked November evenings, when the bleak, balefully lit south-east-London streets we drove through almost persuaded us to turn back and rejoin the 'civically inert' behind drawn curtains, we heroically forced ourselves onwards, out to some open meeting in Blackwell or Bexcray or further afield, there to enter, as at the Labour party meetings, an unheated hall or room as bleak and balefully lit in its own way as the streets we had left behind, to sit on hard wooden chairs and, far too often, to listen not to what had seemed to be promised on the posters but to what were no more than an accumulation of abstractions (for the young, further sad eye-opening evidence of the chasm between what print pledges and what actuality serves up).

While attending these meetings I noticed a curious phenomenon they had in common: hardly any of the questions from the floor were genuine. By genuine I mean motivated by a spontaneous desire for understanding or information, that natural curiosity of the kind which, say, when someone tells you he is off on holiday automatically makes you respond, 'Where are you going?' Most of the questions at these meetings had on the contrary an air of contrivance, of having been thought up with difficulty by people whose last motive in putting them was a need for enlightenment. Some questioners were, to judge from the inordinate length or complexity of their 'questions', chiefly interested in hearing what they themselves had to say. (Once, on a different sort of occasion, I witnessed the puncturing of one such questioner. The film director François Truffaut was discussing his work with an audience. One member stood up and launched into a long smart-arse analysis of what he claimed to see as the profound symbolism of one particular film, not bothering by any more than the perfunctory preface 'Does Monsieur Truffaut agree with me...?' to disguise this extended would-be peacock's display as a question. To which the director simply replied, to widespread appreciation, 'Non.') Other questioners, a surprisingly large number, had some sort of nervous ailment or speech defect, and their 'questions' appeared simply to be, by providing practice in public speaking, a means of helping them overcome their problem. Yet others were those who haunt such meetings for the opportunity it gives them to keep airing their obsessions about some unrelated matter. And there was always present as well at least one of those unfortunate crazies who appear to attend from some need to gabble nonsense in public.

I noticed, too, that many questioners would, while receiving a polite, forced 'answer' to their 'question', attempt to lend credence to the fiction that the latter was genuine by adopting a ham attentive pose, occasionally nodding their head ostentatiously for all the world as though they had some real interest in what was being said.

One of these meetings, 'The School in the Community', was held in the geography classroom of my Alma Mater, Sir Bernard Croucher Grammar. How strange it was to find myself sitting at a desk in that room again, with the same old Mercator projection on the wall beside me, its colours now faded by years of boring-afternoon sunlight, and the same old smell of chalk dust in the air, that room in which I had never concentrated enough on January rainfall in Kweichow province and fishing catches in Venezuela to achieve exam success, that room which still carried the echo of Mike Lawrence's 'Sir, what's a ginkgo, sir?' during a lesson on the Cretaceous, one of those random, insignificant, pointless memories that sometimes, inexplicably, are all that have survived of a segment of our past that we feel should have preserved something more interesting and worthwhile. How strange it had been beforehand, on this return, to switch on the lights in empty corridors, to peer into dark deserted classrooms, to sniff the dull heavy unpleasant smell of gas lingering in a lab, the ink-like stimulating smell of poster paint in the art room, smells that generously restored to you in a flash, *but all too briefly for you to be able truly to reinhabit it*, the beautiful rendingly sad essence of that world you had once inhabited so casually. How strange it was, when you looked at group photographs on the corridor walls, that mere smudges of black and white no more than a couple of millimetres square, indistinctly representing boys you had scarcely known at the time and had never thought of since, *instantaneously*, as though by some magic independent of your brain, presented you unfailingly with their names, one after the other, names you would never have imagined your memory had retained – Moulton, Straker, Golding, Hillman, Nash…

In the 'The School in the Community' meeting itself the speaker wafted us through a vaporous realm of 'two-way processes', 'integrations of interests', 'establishments of dialogues' and the like, without once telling us what 'the school in the community' actually *was* – I mean, in the sense that you would expect to be told by someone speaking on 'Financial Services in the Retailing Outlet', for example, that in concrete terms this meant an in-store bureau able to arrange for you investments, savings schemes, etc. No, seen only on the misty horizon of a cloudscape of abstractions, 'the school in the community' remained at the end of that lengthy speech as vague as it had been at the beginning, a thing of mystery.

Afterwards an atypical questioner elicited from the speaker a lone hard fact. It was that parents would visit 'the school in the community' on certain evenings. But this was just an aberration before the typical questioners started up again. And the first was a young woman who seemed to combine all the various types of these in one. Thin, dark, tense, hair scraped back in a bun and for some odd reason barefoot on this cold autumn evening, she 'took up' the issue of parents' visits. Addressing at full volume the speaker she was so near, she first informed him in a significant tone: 'My name's Penny Voles.' The speaker flinched slightly. Then: 'Don't you think there's a risk of *uncleanliness* and *infection* in parents coming into the school in the evening?' Her fingers curved into claws as she spoke. '*Vandalism*. You know. Leaving cigarette ends and sweet papers all over the place. Leaving drinks stains on the children's *nice clean* desks. Generally making a mess of the classroom.' (I felt like adding chips to the unlikely litter. *Chips, say, making a mess of the classroom.*) 'Don't you think there could be bother from that sort of *unsociable* behaviour, and it could be difficult to control? I mean, the parents would have to be told...' (A man next to me, whose head jerked violently and alarmingly every few seconds, and who had for some time been consulting a grubby handwritten note he held which I guessed was a 'question', was obviously growing impatient with how long Ms Voles was taking to paint her improbable scenario, because he kept half-standing and half-lifting a powerless hand.) 'Don't you think you have to bear that in mind if parents are to be invited into the school? There must be a considerable risk involved, surely? It could lead to – '

The speaker interrupted to 'answer' her 'point', which he did by means of further, soothing 'two-way processes' and 'establishments of dialogues'. During his 'answer', the firebrand assumed a preternatural calm as well as the stock attitude of great interest – leaning forward, elbow on desk, chin on hand, gazing up at the speaker like a student listening to the elucidation of a text by an adored tutor, nodding gently the while...

There were too many meetings like that, but I would still, once we were returning home from one, find myself taking a certain satisfaction in our having attended it. This, however, I was rather dismayed to discover, was in part perverse. For I could separate out from a feeling of self-esteem at having conscientiously spent the evening doing something high-minded instead of going to the pub or seeing a film or reading a book, I could separate out from this another, more questionable feeling, one that if the dutiful evening had been spent listening to a stimulating talk in comfortable surroundings it would not have yielded, one that derived from the very boredom and discomfort of the meeting. And I sensed that this was somehow, obscurely, tied up with certain ambivalent feelings I had known in childhood, and with others experienced since, and even with other, seemingly unrelated matters, a mysterious entanglement I felt it would be tough indeed to unravel.

Jammy

During my third week on *The Swiss Roll Maker* I interviewed the head of the Mr Kipling sales force about a major swiss roll export drive in Sri Lanka and Papua New Guinea; took pics of and obtained caption info for that month's Roll Model, a glam Sales Secretary at Auntie's Kitchen; at the same company questioned a Sponge Mixer about her job; researched, on beaming, chair-swivelling Tommo's 'orders' (he was revelling in his new position while Kitchin was away), a Roll Players feature – the footballing success, in the London Bakery League, of the Lyons Swiss Roll team; and, on receipt of a press release from Traditional Homebake about a new raspberry jam filling they were introducing into their swiss rolls, paid (with understandable reluctance) a visit to their factory. I was determined that when Kitchin returned – which couldn't be far off – he would find the greater part of the issue already written.

It was on the last of the above stories that I learnt a journalistic trick, one that was to help me so much in my work that I would use it over and over again. At Traditional Homebake, a Thoroughlymodern Productionline outfit, the Factory Manager and Production Manager told me that they were adopting the new jam because it had both a fruitier flavour and better spreading qualities than the one they'd used before (remembering my one experience of the old jam, I felt like responding with a caustic 'You don't say'). This business about the improved jam would not, I'd realised in advance, be enough for an article of any length. What was needed to fill it out – and this was a policy of the magazine, based on a survey – was the views of the men and women on the factory floor. The problem, though – from my experience so far, anyway, as with the Auntie's Kitchen Sponge Mixer I'd 'interviewed' – was that they might have very little at all to say about their work.

The first Jam Spreader I spoke to was a pallid, puffy-faced, plump man with sensual, swollen red lips, whom I suspected, probably unfairly, of taking home and eating rather too many of the free samples he was allowed. When I asked him for his thoughts on the new jam, all he had to say, quite unsurprisingly, was: 'All right, I s'pose.' Another Spreader was even less forthcoming; he simply shrugged his shoulders. Although I knew these were men who mainly expressed themselves through their work and not the spoken word and therefore couldn't be blamed for their reserve about their preserve, I nevertheless felt a certain understandable exasperation with them as I wondered how else I could bring in the shop floor side of the story. It was then that I hit upon the solution to the problem. This was, although I didn't know it at the time, an already existent journalist's (and cross-examining barrister's) sly technique: the leading question.

Introducing myself to a third Spreader, a perky, cheerful-looking man with bottle-bottom glasses, I asked him, 'Would you say this new filling is a great improvement on the old?'

'You could say that.'

'But would *you* say that?'

'Yeah, s'pose so.'

'Would you say that it spreads more smoothly yet it's solid enough not to disperse too much or soak into the sponge too much?'

'Yeah, you could say that.'

'But would *you* say that?'

'Yeah, why not?'

'As for the flavour, would you say that it's a little sharper, a little less bland, than what you were using before?'

He frowned. 'Well, I...'

'Can't you taste some now?'

'Not s'posed to, chum.'

I dipped my little finger into a great aluminium bowl of

the stuff and held it out to him. Darting apprehensive glances to either side, he reluctantly licked some off.

'Well?'

He hesitated. Then: 'Yeah, it is a bit, I s'pose.'

Next I went back to the pasty-faced man.

'Would you say,' I asked him, 'that the new filling definitely enhances the overall flavour of the roll? That it's a winner in your opinion?'

He looked at me blankly, morosely, seemed to be making no effort at all to focus on the question.

Perhaps I should *goad* him into an answer? 'After all,' I hazarded tentatively, 'I imagine you've eaten more than your fair – '

He didn't like that. And who could blame him? 'Listen, squire, I don't know what you're getting at, but if it's what I think it is – ' The puffy face had become menacing. 'Anyway, I've got work to do.' And he turned away.

But I put the same question to yet another Spreader and this time I got the agreement I was angling for. A few more questions on the same lines and I had what I wanted. Jammy. Back in the office, I was able to write, with a clear conscience – well, clear enough:

After some reflection, Vernon summed up the new filling's qualities. 'I'd say it's a great improvement on the old. It spreads more smoothly yet it's solid enough not to disperse too much or soak into the sponge too much. As for the flavour, it's a little sharper, a little less bland than what we were using before.'

And Jam Spreader Billy Bower went even further. 'The new filling definitely enhances the overall flavour of the roll,' he said. And added: 'It's a winner in my opinion.'

From then on the spoon-fed opinion, the ghosted interview, became my standard fall-back for producing any story that featured staff. And, returning to the different factories again and again as I did, I would occasionally come across some Vernon or Billy or whoever holding open a copy of the magazine and proudly pointing out to an incredulous colleague – who was used only to hearing listless monosyllables from him – his lengthy, judicious pronouncements on this or that aspect of his work.

One offshoot of acquiring this new technique was that I was never able again to read newspaper interviews in the same light as before, particularly those in which known inarticulates soared on this occasion into a previously unsuspected eloquence.

No longer knowing

The approach of Christmas always instilled in me a vague happiness: its stirring admixture of the religious and pagan festive, its indefinable excitement that quivered even in the letters of its name, never failed for me to triumph over its notoriously tacky modern aspects, never failed, for the incorrigible idealist I was, to transcend all that.

Sally and I were spending Christmas Day this year at Dean and Olivia's. (Lil had been invited, but her one experience of Christmas at the Rectory, years before, had been, in her own words, 'no bloody fun at all', and since then she had always spent the entire holiday at Edie and Ivor's.) We were then to go on to Sally's parents, where the family gathering would be smaller and quieter than usual: Mr Banks, who had recently been in hospital with a heavy nosebleed brought on by high blood pressure, was to take things easy.

Christmas at the Rectory was the same as ever: a real tree which reached almost to the ceiling; plenty of natural greenery, brought in from the grounds; a certain restraint in the decorations; predominantly religious cards and a religious Christmas Eve; the long Christmas afternoon walk.

Traces of the mixed feelings I had first experienced as a child towards this sort of Christmas, so different from the kind I would re-enter on Boxing Day at Sally's parents', still remained. But now I leaned more favourably towards the Dean and Olivia Christmas than towards the Edie and Bankses one, I had 'acquired taste' for it.

Acquired taste. Into what subtleties, oddities, hypocrisies, complexities this leads us, as opposed to the comparatively straightforward simplicities of our first tastes in childhood. Then our desires were only for the sweet and the bright, the tuneful and the colourful. But so unadulterated and frank a preference didn't last long, sooner or later we experienced the attractions of flavours and harmonies more strange and rarefied: the chromaticism of the Greenline coach in the leafy lane, the austere coloration of 'The Holly and the Ivy'. But they jostled with our primary inclinations, which had far from vanished. Hence at that early age our ambivalence towards them.

Most of the child's more 'sophisticated' tastes, though perhaps equivocal, are genuinely come by; those of mine that I've already described were. But some, since affectation is not unknown at even this early age, are insincere. Once, when I was no more than seven, I was so taken by the seductive ruby glow of Dean's claret in its glass that I asked to try it. Perhaps it was because Dean insisted that I wouldn't like it that when at last I was given a sip I pretended to enjoy it (and was gratified to hear delighted surprise at so precocious a taste in one who was supposed at his age only to enjoy the sugary and fizzy). My just desserts were that whenever Dean and Olivia drank wine in my presence after that I was always given a small amount 'as a treat' and had to continue with my charade of appreciating it. But there came a time when, still a child, having grown used to it, I no longer objected to it, and then a time when, scarcely out of childhood, I positively enjoyed drinking it. Persisted in, that taste originally feigned became as natural as any I first knew genuinely. In the same way, I may at the start, as a child, have sometimes affected an appreciation of this or that aspect of the Rectory Christmas for the worst of reasons – either perverseness, in acting counter to my natural leanings (that perverseness whose sere breath I had, after 'The School in the Community' meeting, felt upon me so recently), or snobbery, in pretending to myself that I enjoyed the customs of those I obscurely apprehended to be a cut above Lil and Harry and me – but the result was that, these 'preferences' being maintained over the years, they ended up becoming true preferences, second nature.

But that isn't always how it works out. Persisting in, say, an attempt to appreciate artists whose work we didn't much care for at first – that persistence turning them into as marked and permanent a feature of our inner cultural landscape as any that we always liked – sometimes results in our no longer knowing what we truly feel about them. We no longer dismiss their work, we strain to enjoy it, until at last we *think* we've begun to see something of what others claim to see in it, we tell ourselves that what we are feeling is no longer boredom but a refined, higher pleasure, a more subtle form of enjoyment – because we know that that is the course that acquired tastes take. But no, can we *truly* say it's appreciation? Though...perhaps it *is*... Or is it? We no longer know exactly what it is we're experiencing as we listen to this music, stand in front of this painting, read this poem. That was how I ended up feeling about, for example, most of Poulenc's late work, and Monet's. And I wonder whether this is not the reaction to the *Ring* cycle eventually reached by those who, simply because to go there is the done thing among their class, have been dragged to Bayreuth year after year to listen to works that originally bored or irritated them.

But in many instances – perhaps most? – the years bring not even this response to what we disliked, or detested even, at the start: no amount of repeated listening or viewing can overcome our antipathy. No effort on my part can ever make me respond to, for example, the music of Messiaen, the paintings and etchings of Goya, the novels of Henry James. And nothing, no dash of snobbery or of perverseness, was ever able to make me genuinely enjoy those Christmas Eve services at the little church in Kingsdon St Mary, with their carols which were always confined by the vicar, through what I suspected might be a snobbery and perverseness on his part, to the least known and the most tuneless, and with their icy draughts knifing in through a never-fixed door. But what about Olivia? She had, I knew for certain, genuinely deep feelings for so much that was beautiful in life and art. But was she being absolutely honest in her proclaimed enjoyment of those church services and the more austere of Poulenc's religious works? Or did she, as I say, in her heart no longer know?

Florestan and Eusebius

On a cold afternoon in January I squatted on the bare boards of an unfurnished bedroom, surrounded by a bloody-minded collection of objects all wilfully keeping stum about their exact role and place in window world: sections of curved rail, various types of bracket, small blocks of wood, different kinds of screw and some oddly shaped metal things. The bedroom was in the maisonette to which Sally and I were shortly to move from our too-small flat: the baby was due soon. (The maisonette was one of twelve built around three sides of a court, in an area Lil considered 'posh'. 'You have gone up in the world,' she said when she saw it, though in a tone that sounded more disdainful than complimentary. She, who gravitated naturally, compulsively even, to the seedy and disreputable, considered perhaps that, as a member of her family, I was 'getting above myself'.)

The assorted items around me were apparently the components of a bow-window curtain rail and pelmet support that had been removed and never replaced as promised by Hi-Class Property Maintenance, Craftmanship Guaranteed, in the course of his unacceptable two-shot redecoration of the room. (When I'd had to recall him after his first attempt, he'd said as cheerfully as if he'd just been praised not criticised for his work, 'You're right, that undercoat's still "grinning" through. Yeah, well we'll soon see to that. Don't worry about it... What, d'you reckon the paper's skew-whiff on that wall? Could be. Well, we'll get that sorted soon enough. Don't worry about it.' He kept warmly reassuring me I was not to worry about these things in the tone of one generously forgiving shortcomings of mine that he had selflessly to remedy.)

Having examined and fiddled with the crabbily tight-lipped bunch around me for the third uncomprehending time, I looked up and saw at that very moment, on this day of bitter cold when you'd given up hope of the sun paying a call, that it had turned up after all: on the house opposite, against a sombre backdrop of grape blue raincloud, the tiles and the chimney stack, on whose cowl perched a fluffed-out sparrow, suddenly glowed a fiery orange. As I saw this instant ignition of the winter afternoon before me, this burst of resplendent flame against the gloomy indigo, I felt surge through me a poetic response to the world I had not known for some time. I heard, for no reason I could think of, some beautiful chords from Schumann's *Papillons* – and simultaneously there suddenly returned to me a scene from *Mosaic* in which, as one side of the towering Burckhardt Center glowed in a similar light against a similar sky, there came to Mark, the narrator, the first thrilling inkling of what he thought the great puzzle of the book might be all about; and I relived the wonderful excitement I had experienced with him at the time. And there was yet something else – a vague memory of reading a certain section of the book on several cold afternoons at the Rectory when the lovely sad radiance of the declining sun, flooding in as I sat on the dining room window seat, seemed to soak the pages in an atmosphere that, though it was unconnected with their content – which was all hopeful spring sunlight, busy traffic and intriguing turns of event – augmented this not in the least incongruously, so that whenever I thought of those pages both atmospheres came back to me superimposed. And all these, the sudden glow in Beacon Court outside, the poetic feeling it induced in me, the similarly lit scene of Mark's apparent incipient enlightenment, the tingle it had given me, and the light which magically saturated part of the book seemed to merge into one blissful whole. Nature, Master's poetry, my poetry all seemed one, and I was briefly lost in them – I mean truly lost, plunged in the way we are on rare occasions into an atmosphere that has no point in common with the everyday one we have just left behind. When this brief ecstatic voyage came to an end, however, the return brought with it first a painful discontent with my present practical task and with my working lot on *The Swiss Roll Maker* (which I'd imagined for some time I'd Manfully come to terms with) and secondly a disappointment that, despite my belief that I'd more or less withdrawn myself from the seductions of Master's world, it was still apparently deeply rooted within me.

A painful discontent. Yes, but Becoming a Man meant fighting that off, making sure Schumann's Florestan had the upper hand over his Eusebius, banishing the poetry, getting down to the task in hand. And half an hour later, much to my amazement, I had worked out for myself what each one of those surly incommunicative bits and pieces around me were about and exactly what their heights above and widths beyond the window recess should be and was well into the job of putting them up, despite the problems of doing this alone.

While I was engaged on this task, however, I experienced another, stranger feeling. I apprehended in me, not for the first time, the presence of two selves that must be familiar to many. Separate, diametrically opposed selves. One was hopelessly unpractical, was definitely the senior of the two (a sort of elder brother) and regarded himself as the rightful boss within me, my 'essential' self. As the other, younger self double-checked measurements and marked the wall with due care, reshaped a wood block that had split, drilled holes in the wall and overcame the difficulty of putting in screws a hand-cramping fraction of an inch below ceiling level (I was certain now that Hi-Class Property Maintenance's double failure to do the job was a 'Sod that for a lark' dereliction of duty), the detached 'senior' self looked on in astonishment, kept wondering how that other self, to whom after all he was so closely related and with whom he shared the same living quarters, could be engaged in an activity from which he, the 'essential' self, was so unbridgeably alienated, which he had always thought of as the exclusive domain of D-I-Y-ers. He obviously considered that the principal self he claimed to be was an observer self, a writer self, and writers were cack-handed, weren't they, they didn't sort out fragmentary curtain rails and pelmet supports, did they? After all, Master, for one, was Mr Unpractical. The 'essential' self obviously considered that the other self, the Becoming a Man self who was currently engaged in being a handyman, was getting too ambitious, was trying, like several royal younger brothers at various times in British history, to usurp the throne from the legitimate ruler.

The day ahead

My reportage for *The Swiss Roll Maker* took me far afield as I visited roll makers at work and at play here, there and everywhere. When fine weather came I enjoyed those largely motorwayless morning drives out of London into the green belt and on into the byways of the home counties. First, on the fringes of outer suburbia, there would be the avenues, semi-residential, where town began to give way to country. They were particularly beautiful, some of them, on sunlit May mornings after rain, when, freshly washed, the luxuriant foliage and candelabra of the chestnuts that lined them were drenched as much with light as with moisture. Driving down these, relishing the onward thrust of the old red Renault, as its weathered-to-pink bonnet ate up the dark reflective steaming asphalt, I would be much taken by the pzazz of a road sign sailing towards me, red border singing against the luminous wet golden-green and creamy white of the chestnuts ahead, singing as cheerfully as the melodious expanse of blue above the dripping trees and as the newly vocal birds within them; much taken, too, by, beyond that sign, where the artificial suburban invaded, integrated with and beautified the natural rural, a flickering scarlet and azure deep within the grotto, signifying a bus and its exhaust passing through dappled light; and by, further beyond still, a touch of that haze which, even on mornings that glitter and gleam, so often veils an avenue's end.

Then on minor roads there were the tunnels of greenery, rich patterns of emerald and jet and gold, sometimes with an intermittent ruby glow in their depths.

In those avenues, in those tunnels – both of which the regular traveller off-highway comes pleasurably to recognise as type settings of such English drives – I felt just a hint, the merest whisper, of that old expectancy I had known in them long ago.

As I drove, I would idealise the day ahead, the next in what had become by now a considerable succession of uncongenial assignments. I would idealise it because I'd been duped both by that incorrigibly selective memory which forgets the regularly all-too-flawed that has gone before and by that equally incorrigibly sanguine anticipant which apparently keeps on believing in the possibility of the unflawed. Together they simplified and smoothed out in the imagined future what had invariably been so knotty in the past: they substituted for the specifics of these visits, for the problematic statements and activities of certain individuals I would see at, say, the launch of a new swiss roll – the Product Manager I had an appointment with and the Head Chef and the Ingredients Mixer I would undoubtedly be trying to put leading questions to – which together with various chance unanticipated happenings would actually make up the gnarled preponderance of the day ahead, they substituted for these a bland, trouble-free abstraction – New Product Launch – in which a presentation pellucid in its clarity was made by model spokesmen in perfect accord with one another and in perfect amity with myself (as incorporeal really, these spokesmen, as those movie stars whose portraits smiled down on you at the Regal and as that enviable staff I had when young imagined working in the offices of *Cheeky Chicko*) and in which associated photographic and interviewing sessions would pass off as smoothly as those of a staged royal event. In producing this immaculate picture, the two incorrigibles, selective memory and sanguine anticipant, working in tandem, blanked out all the tiresome contingencies – the absence sick that day of an essential interviewee perhaps, or, with no immediate relief available, my desperate desire to pee – which were the very stuff – as one of my selves, also apparently absent sick on such airy journeys, well knew – of reporters' assignments in real life.

On the face of it a foolishness, this idealisation of the day ahead, might it not be, though, in the result it produces – that of ensuring that we keep optimistically engaging, on each fresh occasion, with tasks, people, situations that have been far from easy in the past, in the underlying, scarcely conscious trust that all will be well this time, in short, that of ensuring that we keep hopefully pressing on with our lives – might it not be one of Nature's various ruses for realising her objectives, part of that blind life force which sweeps along in its powerful current even those most troubled by a sense of the futility of existence? (I couldn't, by the way, help marvelling as I thought of everyone else waking up each to his or her own stylisation of the day before them, every stylisation with its own unique perspectives, colourings, modellings, emphases, most bearing scarcely any relation to what would actually be experienced. Around you all these millions of different, false representations of what lay ahead...)

A succession of uncongenial assignments. Yes, that's how I found my reporter's tasks on *The Swiss Roll Maker*, the actual experience of them. Deep within me, in that part of myself I was trying to stifle, I loathed that little magazine and my work on it. And a few years ago, when browsing through the autobiography of Arthur Machen in a second-hand bookshop, I happened across a surprising anticipation of how I had felt about my job: 'When I plied my sorry trade of journalist, I disliked most things...but I hated my occasional missions to the Hôtel Splendide and the Hôtel Glorieux...to find out, say, the exact method employed by the new chef, M. Mirobalant, in cooking red herrings...' Pleased to make the acquaintance of another malcontent in that line of work, I murmured to myself, 'Yes, I know exactly how you felt, Arthur.'

Even so, even so, I have to confess that when the first few issues of *The Swiss Roll Maker* that I worked on came out and I saw what had been my often unhappy scribbles so impressively transfigured into *print*, saw paraded across the spreads those tarted-up news stories – Thrilling filling – and features – Les Baker, the baker's baker – which not so long previously I could scarcely have believed I would play a major part in producing, there was intermingled with my amazement (and horror) a certain feeling of satisfaction. If a thing's *not* worth doing it's worth doing well. It seemed that this negative twist to the old saying (the one pressed on me as a child by non-exemplar Lil) was what motivated so many when faced with disagreeable commissions (which gives the lie to another of Ruskin's questionable dicta, 'Nobody does anything well that they cannot help doing', and which is demonstrated, to provide just one other example, by what Primo Levi noted in Auschwitz: the inmates' compulsion to carry out to the very best of their ability even those jobs given them that were harmful to their own people). And, in the matter of earning a living, it is such out-of-register pride as I showed in the successful accomplishment of an uncongenial task that so often reconciles those capable of better things to what they actually find themselves locked into doing.

And Kitchin? His reaction to my output? Well, he never praised a word of it, it's true, but on the other hand he never slagged any of it off either. Though as malevolent of gaze as ever, he simply appeared to accept, grudgingly, that I just about passed muster. And I had to count that as a sort of victory.

Macho Man

One evening, returning home from an especially taxing day on *The Swiss Roll Maker* that had included a spiky session with Kitchin, an unsuccessful interview with a surly Sponge Mix Supervisor and the tedious fashioning of a Masters of the Rolls piece (on a certain Harrington Moody, apparently the most likely originator of the chocolate filling), weary too from standing all the way on yet another late train, and for hours undergoing, so it seemed, the ever-increasing compression by a vice of the top of my skull, I began unburdening myself of my troubles to Sally.

Now during my apprenticeship in Becoming a Man I'd considered myself wimpish when tempted to behave in this way. I kept ever before me the shining example of Mr Banks, that Man writ huge. Could you imagine him beefing to Mrs Banks about problems in the driver's cab or raw deals concerning his shifts? Course not. Why, not a word of woe had escaped his lips even when the pain of that tooth abscess must have driven him almost insane. So, returning home, I would invariably, no matter what my day, greet Sally with a comic-book hero's smile that announced God's in his heaven, all's right with the world.

But then came that nosebleed that put Mr Banks into hospital, and with it the diagnosis of a ragingly high blood pressure – and that changed my thinking. I have said that in a world not exactly teeming with good men, Mr Banks was unmistakably one of them: honest, reliable, selfless. (Just as everyone referred to Uncle Jim as a 'scream', so everyone referred to Mr Banks as a 'brick' – though maybe the term also contained the hint of a subconscious secondary association: Mr Banks' colouring, a clue perhaps to his underlying physical problem.) But I now realised that he had a fatal flaw. He *would* strive for something more than the knightly qualities he genuinely possessed and admirably demonstrated, he *would* strive for yet more, in particular a tolerance and patience *absolutely boundless*: in a word, sainthood. And he was not cut out for that onerous calling. Not cut out for it because his temperament was fundamentally choleric. It wasn't difficult to guess that the combination of darkly rubicund complexion and compressed lips was the outward sign of something far from equable within. Of course, he had a wonderful *crack* at the sainthood. Sally and I used to marvel at how firmly he contained what must have been an accumulating head of exasperation at Mrs Banks' inanities (he was considerably the more intelligent of the two) and of anger at her extravagances: she seemed to spend half her outdoor existence and certainly far too much of their modest income in Pembertons' and Summerhills' fashion departments and in Bon Marche, A La Mode, Sylvia's, Spoiled for Choice, Marjorie Spooner's, Just for You and Belinda's Bargains, where, while she held up before her throughout the passing hours a seemingly endless succession of garments in pastel shades, to all of which she applied her portmanteau 'That's very nice', a silent Mr Banks remained outwardly placid, patient. At most, his lips would compress themselves ever so slightly tighter than usual and he would pant through his nose ever so slightly louder than usual. But that was all. At home, too, subject to what some might have considered intolerable irritations and provocations, he *never*, Sally told me, raised his voice, lost his temper, slammed a door. 'Nothing ever bothers him,' Mrs Banks would say, cast for ever in the role of ingénue. (Only those marginal changes in the lips and the breathing, together sometimes with a certain look that came into his eyes and, *rarely*, after a passage of 'good-humoured' digs at his wife, a sudden quiet bladelike insult, startling in its studied thrust – only these would hint at what lay beneath.) A formidable demonstration of tolerance and patience, yes – but, I came to realise, one too good for his own good. All that superhuman control of the stoked-up scorn and rage, all the years of it, caused pressure to build up within him like the steam in the stoked-up boiler of those engines he drove early in his career, until that day when for the first time the boiler burst.

(But what Mr Banks *had* once briefly obtained relief from was his role as Macho Man, as distinct from that as Saint, shedding it, as I had recently learned, in what was to me the most astonishing way. Sally and I were at her parents' place and were leafing through their family scrapbook. On one page was the programme, opened up, of a panto performed by the NUR Southern Region Benevolent Fund. And there, looking out from a photo of the cast, was a just-about-recognisable Mr Banks as Widow Twankey, coyly simpering in standard wig-rouge-and-bustle grotesquerie, Cupid's bow lips pouting. *Mr Banks as panto dame!* He was unexpectedly good in the part, Sally said – he had all the right expressions, gestures, walks. But it was the only time he ever did anything like that. His one acknowledgment of and paroling of the feminine component of his nature before he slammed the cell door shut on it, this time for good. Even though I knew that there was to a greater or lesser degree that component in every heterosexual male, it still came as a bit of a shock to me to see it evidenced so extravagantly in that photograph, thrusting itself so without warning into my previous – utterly unrealistic – image of Sally's father as Mr Masculine, Old Style Unalloyed.)

After the torrential nosebleed, then, I began, as I've said, to change my mind about Mr Banks' suitability as a roll model – I mean role model (having to use that idiotic pun in my work so regularly led to an unconscious habit that I've since found it hard to break). My admiration for his fine qualities continued unabated but I now considered foolish the extremes of his stoicism, his refusal to allow any release for what was troubling him. When tried beyond endurance, he should occasionally, I felt, have blown his top – perhaps should even have done so with (surrealistic image) the piercing shriek with which the steam trains that he used to drive blew theirs. I didn't want *my* blood pressure ending up like his, so on coming home from work, I would now from time to time take a break from square-jawed fortitude to give my frustrations, my unhappiness, an outlet – and Sally would commiserate with me, murmur soothing words, give me a hug. And when she was feeling down I did the same for her. That was all fine, straightforward enough. One who's feeling OK comforting the other who's not – simple stuff. But when neither's OK, when neither has the mental and emotional vigour needed to make a good job of comforting the other, then even experienced couples, who pride themselves on do-and-say-the-right-thing know-how, even they can feel out of their depth. One of us would sometimes, under the pressure of our problems, begin to unburden ourself too intensely and at too great a length for the other, who was perhaps tired or in a bad mood, to be able to take any more, to remain buoyant enough not to sink into the same despondency. When that happened, the one bemoaning their lot would feel a pang of guilt at having made the other feel worse, because they would be aware that scarcely any load is actually so crushing that it cannot if necessary be borne alone – they would indeed then find that the still unrelieved portion of it which had so recently seemed unendurable could in fact easily be supported unaided. I say a pang of guilt. But with me it was sometimes much more than that: it was a self-contempt that left me feeling wretched.

But later another, wiser self, aware of how difficult can be the decisions we have to make about burden-bearing, would reassure me that we each needed for the sake of our wellbeing to avail ourself of as much support from the loved one as possible, not testing this to its extreme limit admittedly but at least, if our need was great enough, to the point at which it showed the first sign of giving way; and that, because it was sometimes difficult to know when that point had been reached, we shouldn't feel guilt (or self-contempt) when it was. That was what loving partners should expect from each other, that was how to avoid the fate of Mr Banks.

Like so much other theory, easily formulated away from the arena itself, this was very persuasive. But when it came to the actuality, as on this particular evening, it was a different matter. I hadn't long been telling my troubles to Sally, who was now heavily pregnant, when I noticed she was having difficulty concentrating, was offering me little comfort, was in fact grimacing now and then. She'd apparently had heartburn and backache all day, felt tired. Suddenly, all theory about this sort of situation vanished as completely as though it had never been and that feeling of shame I had told myself I had no need to feel I did feel; it surged through me, as unpleasantly as the onset of nausea or flu. Here was my pregnant wife, my dear girl, feeling rough and here was I thoughtlessly complaining of, etc. What sort of feeble, etc. And yet, and yet, I felt lousy too… I was rather like the famished man who bemoans the fact that he has not eaten a proper meal all day, is then shamed into silence by a newspaper picture of a starving child, yet, after all, still feels famished.

I embarked on a genuinely felt but low-grade commiseration with Sally. But she, feeling guilty in her turn that I who was not in much of a fit state for it was addressing discomforts she had after all managed to survive all day, interrupted me, summoned up enough animation for her own substandard expression of sympathy.

We were floundering. But we needed these difficult roles. Otherwise, having smugly succeeded in the doddles of parts we'd played before, we might foolishly have begun to think we'd got this marriage thing all sussed out.

Books

One day, over lunch at Piero's, soon after I'd become a father for the second time, Dean told me that Vin Sharpes, his old partner, with whom he still kept in close touch, had moved from the managing directorship of Mega Paperbacks to that of Mega Books. Sharpes had big plans for his new fiefdom, had already started increasing the number of books to be published and was looking for extra staff. If I'd had enough of *The Swiss Roll Maker* – on which I'd now been working for a couple of years – I should give him a ring. Mega Books. Crikey, was it possible I might actually work for that household-name publisher, producer of so many monumental best-sellers? Hold it, I told myself. What had my time at Mega Picture Libraries been other than one of utter disillusionment? What had my time at Mega Trade and Practical Magazines been other than an experience which, though I had Becoming a Manfully persisted in grappling with it, had proved to be even more uncongenial than I'd feared? Why should Mega Books turn out to be any different? After all, what did I really know about that organisation? I may have kept coming across its titles in the press and in trade mags, but I had never bought any myself, there had been none in the Mega offices I'd already worked in, I had never hefted down from its shelf at the Bankses Mega Books' doorstopping *Patio Companion* (there was no patio at their place in Knightsbridge Road, that row of grimy Blackwell terraces not untypically named – parallel to it ran identical Belgravia Road – but Mr Banks did, I think, hope to have one some day), and so the only Mega Books productions I had ever actually looked at, examined, had been those that Harry owned (and took with him when he embarked on his improbable 'new life'). Well, even though I might know little about them in their modern manifestation, they *were* books, weren't they, and books, of all kinds, had been among the most important things in my life. So if I were offered the opportunity of working on them, I should certainly take it.

Heat

Reading about the Second World War had given me some ideas for my own book. Permeating it, I hoped, would be that experience-intensifying sense of danger that Sartre described constantly feeling in wartime Paris. Leo, setting up the resistance movement in the city-state, would be modelled in part on the celebrated leader of the French Resistance, Jean Moulin, a heroic figure, dynamic and uncommonly brave. And Guy would have something in him of Claus von Stauffenberg, the young German army officer who had attempted to assassinate Hitler and lead a coup to overthrow the Nazi regime.

We all assemble during the course of our life a personal pantheon of heroes. And I had now added Stauffenberg to mine. This choice was not surprising: he epitomised not simply the hero but the Romantic hero. He was driven by a burning moral imperative (he even carried with him a copy of a poem that he hoped would convert others, Stefan George's *Anti-Christ*); he bravely committed himself to the bold and dangerous enterprise he felt that imperative demanded; he was intelligent, gifted, possessed of exceptional powers of concentration and clarity of expression, physically tough as well as mentally, remarkably handsome, and a natural leader. One of his superiors described him as having 'the qualities of genius', another as being 'magnetically attractive'. And this charisma, pronounced enough already, was given an added dimension, after he had been severely wounded in North Africa, by the Romantic skew of physical disability: he lost an eye, an arm and two fingers on his remaining hand. Despite this, he insisted on returning to army service to pursue his plan 'to save Germany'. Colleagues spoke of his unfailing cheerfulness and indefatigable resolve.

One particular aspect of that momentous day, 20 July 1944, on which he attempted the coup made a deep impression on me: *the sweltering heat.* Even as early as six in the morning, when Stauffenberg leaves his house in a staff car, bound for an airfield, the day is signalling its intent. And at seven, when he boards the plane, it is already sultry. At ten the plane lands at Rastenburg. A nine-mile drive to the Führer's headquarters where Stauffenberg is to make his military report. In the briefcase of his accomplice beside him are two bombs. The car has to halt at several SS checkpoints. The tense wait each time before the car is waved on. By the time he has arrived at headquarters the temperature is approaching ninety, the air is stifling. Unendurable delays before the conference starts. With fifteen minutes to go he requests a place in which to change his sodden shirt – and to transfer the bombs to his own briefcase and activate them (he manages only one). Entering the conference room, he places the case beneath the table, as near as possible to Hitler. He makes an excuse to leave. The explosion. The race to Rastenburg airfield. Bluffing his way past the checkpoint guards. The urgent return to the other conspirators in Berlin, who have been waiting for him, sweating with tension and the heat. They hear the coup is on! And then, fired up, none of them feels any trace of dog-day oppression. (And isn't, in a city, the heat of high summer, as in Berlin on that day, aesthetically the most fitting setting for high drama – historic, heroic, bloody drama? Don't the *monumental* beauty of great slabs of golden light and inky shade – the intrinsic melancholy of their stasis counterbalanced in the city by the roar and thrust of the traffic and the variegated scene – and the *intense* beauty of vivid colours made more vivid by the concentrated sunlight – flowerbeds, summer dresses, streetcars, foliage, draped flags – don't they together, in their extremes, accord with events equally extreme?)

Those accounts of the July plot changed my customary response to dog days, that period defined in dictionaries as one of stagnation and inactivity and unhealthiness and in whose effects I had already discerned the symbols of death. That response had been one that was natural and widely shared: a sinking of the spirits, a slowing down of the dynamo as one saw that of the world around one slowing down. Now, as I read of Stauffenberg's exploits, I saw in them – apart, obviously, from the major theme of courageous resistance to tyranny (no matter that Hitler lived, that the coup failed and that Stauffenberg, poor brave man, was summarily executed that night) – I saw in them a subsidiary theme of personal interest to myself, that of the human spirit impervious to nature's effluvia, of a historic undertaking carried out in conditions that I'd always instinctively dissociated from endeavour. Even though I knew it was the momentous, adrenalin-pumping nature of Stauffenberg's actions that made him utterly indifferent to the energy-sapping effect of the heat on a weakened body and metabolism (though, since one must never underestimate the capacity of the ordinary to draw attention to itself during the decidedly out-of-the-ordinary – the dandruff-sprinkled shoulders in the row ahead, the smell of dogshit on a nearby shoe unwantedly impingeing on the notice of someone at a stirring ceremony – it may have been that on occasion even his relentless concentration was briefly diverted away from his historic task on to, say, just how drenched that heat had made his shirt), I knew also that even if it had merely been some routine business and not a heroic mission on which he had been engaged that day, he would simply have used his will to overcome the effects of that heat (after all, what were these to a man who had dealt with the agony of his injuries by fortitude alone, without recourse to any pain-killing drugs, and who had insisted on coping with everyday tasks unaided). I too, then, would from now on triumph over the lowering pressure of dog days, would rise above them. (It later dawned on me that, as is commonly the way with young people, it had taken an illustrious example for me to find a lodestar for my future actions, when all around me there had been many more humble but just as compelling examples: firemen, policemen, medics, who in heatwaves raced to fires, hold-ups and accidents no less purposefully than they did in milder weather.)

So it was that Sally, who was accustomed to seeing me, even since I had started Becoming a Man, leadenly dragging around on days of oppressive heat, now amazedly found me on such days tackling with drummed up vigour such strenuous jobs as hacking away at Lil's overgrown garden, and persisting in them until, coming to an end at last, I looked as though I had just emerged from an overheated bath. In just such a way, I thought, reflecting on what I had read about him, must the young Stauffenberg, building up strength and will on the estate where he grew up, have brought in the harvest so energetically on days of heat. And (I might have added if I'd known of it at the time) in just such a way too, to the amazement of the natives, must the young Napoleon in Egypt have worked in the fierce heat, uniform buttoned to the neck, twelve hours a day.

But it wasn't just to dog days that my attitude changed. It was to fine weather as well, whenever I was shut up in an office. I now smothered that old 'spirit of divine discontent' that spontaneously arose within me at such times. I addressed homilies to myself: OK, if you think that the life of modern working man is unhealthy, that being cooped up indoors in such weather is against nature and that we should all be free to work in the sunlight, who do you propose is going to man the utilities on which we all depend, who is going to look after the sick in hospital, who, even, is going to print the newspapers and books you want to read? I chastised myself mercilessly: You and your 'spirit of divine discontent'! Stop gazing at that tender sky, those gilded leaves, those gently trembling shadows, and get your bloody nose down to writing that piece on Homebake's new ovens.

Whatever there was of the poet in me still had some sort of ebbing life left in him, I suppose, but it wasn't long before I could sit in the offices of *The Swiss Roll Maker* for azure day after azure day and work as undistractedly as Kitchin, Tommo and the rest.

Plumpford

Mega Books was not a traditional non-fiction publisher. That is, it did not publish books by individual authors, whose idea they were in the first place, books generally temperate in length and modestly illustrated. No, Mega, like Pinnacle, Zenith and Patten Paige, to name but a few, first chose its own subject and approach for some mammoth, highly pictorial work of reference, then decided on its page length and designed its general layout, and then commissioned copy and photographs or illustrations from a number of sources to fill this layout. Not that I knew anything of this at the time I rang Vin Sharpes. To me Mega Books books had always been, well, just *books*. How they might actually have been created I had never considered.

Sharpes didn't see me himself but arranged an interview for me with his Managing Editor, Bob Plumpford. I took a lift down to the second floor, the domain of Books, in which I had never set foot before. The same intimidating maze of corridors, the same vaguely perturbing deep red carpeting. Bob Plumpford turned out to be very Bob Plumpfordish: Bob's-your-uncleishly dismissive of problems and Plumpfordishly plump. He had rosy apple cheeks, a beaming smile and glacial eyes and was, Sharpes told me, 'as 'ard as nails and as cunnin' as a wagonloada monkeys – but a bloody good editor'. He would, Sharpes had warned me, try to screw me down to as low a salary as he could get away with. 'But don't you 'ave none of it.' And he told me the going rate for subs at Books – which was roughly the same as I was getting as a reporter on *The Swiss Roll Maker*.

At the interview I gave an adequate performance of a not very demanding part. The only weakness I was aware of was the scene where I went on rather about my long-standing desire to work on *books*, about *books* being what I felt I was most suited to, not picture libraries or trade journals, about the less ephemeral nature of *books* compared to... At that point Plumpford interrupted me to broach the matter of a salary. He mentioned a figure. 'How,' he said, with one of his winning grins and the air of one who had so taken to me that he'd decided to do me a special favour, 'does that grab you?' Briefed by Sharpes, and knowing that, as a favour to Dean, he'd plugged me to Plumpford in advance, I was able to reply – with a civil smile – 'It doesn't', and to tell him what I expected. The merry look vanished – only fleetingly, but for that single second *absolutely*, as with certain professional smilers on telly immediately they think they're off-camera. Then he obliquely inclined his head a little in wrily smiling acknowledgment that I had his number. He felt more respect for this hard nose than for the sap who'd gone on about his yearning to work on *books*.

He offered me a position as a sub-editor on the spot and, having agreed terms with me, told me that, once I'd worked out my notice on *The Swiss Roll Maker*, I would join another sub on an *exciting* new project that had just started. It would be, he said, declining to name it, quite a *challenge*. 'Exciting'. 'Challenge'. These were words I would be hearing regularly throughout my years in the department. They were, I was to discover, a sort of incantation that marked out all true 'Mega Books people'.

Like Toad

Looking through what Mega Books had produced over the previous decade, I'd soon realised that there'd been a revolution in the nature of its publications since the old days of the Ultimate Guides. Though amply illustrated, these had been text-not design-led: those who'd produced them had, whether with full awareness or not, subscribed to the precept of such influential typographers as Stanley Morison: design must always be the servant of text, never its master. As I leafed through an office file copy of *The Ultimate Guide to Wallpapering* (and what memories it brought back of the dingy damp never-repapered back room at 33 Danehill Road, where it sat on a shelf scarcely ever disturbed, like its companion *Lawnmowing*), various aspects of it drew my attention: some pages, because what they were saying required no illustration, remained therefore without illustration; on those that were illustrated, the step-by-step line drawings, because each required a different amount of caption, received therefore varying lengths of caption; on the right-hand pages the last sentence, because it was not always able to end at the foot of the page, in those cases ran its natural course over to the next page...

Then, somewhere along the line, the books changed. Designers were given more of a say. Text still held its own – but pictures or diagrams, whether necessary or not, began appearing on every page and white space began to spread. Eventually, it became no contest. Like Toad in the car in which he had been given a lift, design had with affected diffidence asked for a turn at the wheel, then, revealing its true colours, had gradually increased speed and taken over full control. The subdivisions of a book were now no longer determined by editorial, and each no longer ran continuously from one page to the next until it reached its natural conclusion; instead they were decided upon by design, and each was unvaryingly made up of self-contained pages or spreads (miniature replicas of which were pinned in sequence on the office wall to form something like a movie storyboard). And the amount of text on any given subject was, again, no longer determined by editorial, on the basis of what information was essential or appropriate, but by design, on the basis of how much space should be filled with words on purely visual grounds. Larger-type headlines, deeper intro blurbs in bold, bigger pictures, longer captions, proliferating diagrams – together, these grabbed more and more space at the expense of text. In addition, captions now had to be of equal length, regardless of how much needed to be said about each illustration; widowhood increased, since, whereas on a newspaper, and initially at Mega Books, a widow was simply a short end-of-paragraph line that had to be filled if it unprepossessingly appeared at the head of a column, now it was a short end-of-paragraph line that had to be filled wherever it was; and a sentence could never as of old run over to the next page but had always, with implausible constancy, to discover, even in a continuous two- or three-spread piece, that it had luckily *just* managed, phew, once again to finish saying what it had to say on the last line of this page.

In other words, these books had ceased to be what I had always known books to be and imagined they ought to be, and they had instead, as assemblages of hundreds of extravagantly designed spreads, become giant colour supplements. And exceedingly successful ones.

The particular giant colour supplement that I was to work on, the exciting new project, was the *Complete Illustrated Family Guide to Marine and Freshwater Fish of the World* – or, as Plumpford would insist on calling it, Cifgmaffow, which he pronounced 'Sifgermaffow', to rhyme with 'cow'. This consisted exclusively of self-contained pages: each fish got *exactly* one page to itself. Surely the biggest or best-known or most intriguing merited a spread? Surely the tiddliest or most obscure or most boring required only half a page? Nope. A page for each, no more, no less.

So what was the challenge that Plumpford had promised me? It was to join another sub, a man with three years' Mega Books experience, to help edit what constituted the great bulk of the book, entries on a thousand fish. Not nine hundred and forty-seven? Not one thousand and thirty-six? Nope. A thousand, no more, no less.

Mike Mallarmé was a half-French young man who claimed descent from his illustrious namesake. His spoken English still retained some accent (he hadn't come to this country until he was thirteen) and was marked by a curious compulsive foul-mouthedness of an inordinacy I'd never come across before. But I was to discover that his written English – informed by a feeling for the language greater in some foreigners (Nabokov and Conrad illustrious examples) than in most to whom that language is native – was impeccable, unrivalled in the department.

Together, Mike and I had to remove from the submissions of a team of ichthyologists every last trace of what project editor Willie McStutt termed 'subjective guff' (that is, anything that lent the slightest scrap of interest to 'our subaqueous friends', as McStutt invariably called them) and to strip the information down to *exactly* twelve items on each: colouring, length, girth, weight, eye diameter, number of teeth, fin size, feeding, egg production, habitat, geographical distribution and world population. And if the contributor failed to supply any of these twelve facts, it was up to us to make good the default. As my colleague, professed descendant of the man who gave us *La Mort de l'anti-penultième*, *L'Après-midi d'un Faune* and *Les Noces d'Hérodiade: Mystère*, so succinctly put it, with that faint French intonation of his: 'Fercking arse'oles, you evair known such a fercking bastard job?'

One by one...

The accumulating years, increasing the possibilities of this or that happening, and my more extensive adult consumption of news, increasing the possibilities of my learning about it, together ensured that the defilements of the childhood sanctuaries now came thick and fast. For 'he that increaseth knowledge increaseth sorrow'.

Pembertons, with its soft carpets, snoozing merchandise, pizzicato melodies in the background... Television newsflash: an IRA bomb exploding on the second floor, killing two, severely injuring others, blowing the arm off a small boy, screams, gouting blood, sirens...

The main post office, vaulted, airy, cosily echoing to the thump of rubber-stamping, safely permeated by the navy blue smell of its ink-wells, patterned on its worktops with rectangles of golden-grey... The *Blackwell and Bexcray Gazette*: a hold-up just before closing time, a balaclava-and-sawn-off-shotgun pair bludgeoning unconscious a counter clerk who tried to foil them, the terror of the last customers...

The Regal, that haven of security, with its stately commissionaire, marbled rubber stairway to the stars, perfumed warmth... The morning papers: a racist gang, under cover of darkness and surround-sound, attacking a black youth in the back row, blinding him in one eye...

And it wasn't just cherished places that became inexpungibly stained, it was also certain cherished things. Cigarette smoke, an aromatic cloudy blue, whose ritzy fragrance had bewitched me at the cinema as it wisped and eddied in the projectionist's beam, and on a trolleybus as it swirled creamily in the sunlight... It had now been established beyond doubt that it was carcinogenic; it contained, I learned, aromatic polycyclic hydrocarbons, aromatic not in the aromatic-cloudy-blue sense but in a different, menacing, chemist's sense; and these would send millions – one of whom would be Uncle Ivor – to a painful breathless early death...

And little did I realise as a child that there would come a time when another seductive impalpable thing, the most sublime of all, sunlight, the great radiant beautifier and gladdener, which transmuted green to gold, lent splendour to so many dyes, stitched such glorious patterns of light and shade, laid so warm and kindly a touch upon your skin, when it too would take on a different aspect; when it would become, through man's impairment of the natural order, ever more radiant not in the radiant-beautifier-and-gladdener sense but in a different, menacing, physicist's sense; when, increasingly stimulating skin cell division, it would become increasingly lethal...

One by one...

'Challenges'

Following the instructions of Willie McStutt on how to treat our contributors' submissions, we were stripping away the 'subjective guff' as pitilessly as whalers flensing their catch, until we were left in each case with what we hoped would be our twelve-item piece of gradgrindery. Hoped in vain on so many occasions, our ichthyologists' contributions all too often turning out to contain only a fraction of the facts they'd been asked for. And here I came across yet another of those unfathomable puzzles that life kept annoyingly devising for me: since the brief to our fish men had been so starkly explicit, why in so many cases had they made no attempt to carry it out? It was another real brainteaser. Of course, sometimes, as one could appreciate, the information was hard to come by – especially diameters of eyes, numbers of teeth and sizes of girths – but much of it could be dug out with a bit of effort and, as Mike stated in his trenchant way and charming accent, they *were* 'fercking ichthyologists, for ferck's sake', and, as such, did have 'access to all the right fercking specialist data', and they were being 'fercking paid for it, for fercking arse'oles' sake'.

It was not infrequently, then, that our contributors would pass the parcel on what they should certainly have either known or been able to discover – geographical distribution, say – and would do so with a totally unacceptable 'Not generally known' ('We fercking know it's not *generally* fercking known, you lazy fercking sod, but you're fercking supposed to be a fercking ichthyologist.') or, worse still, an utterly disgraceful 'Can range considerably' ('You evair fercking 'aird serch fercking shit?'). (There was when Mike was 'on song' a lovely rhythm and rounded rightness to some of his blank verse which made me veer away from believing him merely to be a possible case of the Tourette's towards accepting, on the contrary, his claim of kinship with the father of French Symbolism.) In such cases the pair of us would have to research the matter in a number of musty old London Library books, on which we were sometimes the first to lay a borrower's hand in more than a century.

To make matters worse, design had decided on a five-line entry for each item. Not too difficult to comply with for colouring, egg production, habitat and one or two others in the list. But five lines on fin size, for example? That was a real toughie. No way out of it though. We pleaded for a reduction on some items to the senior designer on the project, Wayne Flatley (the first person I ever saw with the now ubiquitous designer stubble, back in those days when it just looked like got-up-too-late-to-shave), but he took his orders from above and would have none of it. Some of those five-liners – 'strewth, they almost drove us to the point of insanity. What also incensed us – particularly Mike, because he'd had to put up with so many of them on previous books – were one-time-*Showbiz*-assistant-editor Plumpford's regular scribbled queries on our copy. On the porbeagle shark: 'Are its teeth longer than the blue shark's?' On the dace: 'Is world population increasing or decreasing?' On the clingfish: 'Roughly how many in a school?' Questions as arbitrary as they were unanswerable, or, if answerable, only by means of an impossible amount of research – one of Plumpford's inquiries on an earlier book, the *Canal Companion*, 'How many barges were operating on 17th-century canals?', had taken up many hours of Mike's time, fruitless hours, and he'd ended up furiously inventing the answer. Questions irresistibly reminding me of John Brown's 'Wonder how many bricks it took to build that'. Questions that seemed to form the sole basis for Plumpford's rep as editorial hotshot at Mega Books, which had evidently been overimpressed by the advent, into its (still, just) bookish editorial practice, of the pop-mag journalist's gee-whizz approach, dementedly out of control though this was in Plumpford's case. To me they came to symbolise, those questions, the enviably cushy life of one who had little to do in his office but mindlessly scrawl them on the page.

Plumpford also made light of all sub-editing difficulties when these were drawn to his attention as reasons for delays in the department's punishing schedules, dismissing them with an amazed, uncomprehending 'What's the problem?' He was one of those bosses who is now, on high, above remembering the trials of the toiling shop floor on which he once laboured himself and as a result self-deludingly euphemises them – in his case as 'challenges'. Challenges. Whenever I caught sight of Mike's dark Latin face warped into fury by another of the irresolvable random queries and heard him explode, 'What sort of fercking stupid bastard question is that, for ferck's sake?' I felt that, in the midst of all those ten-a-penny so-called challenges bandied about by Plumpford and his like, Mike personally faced a genuine challenge: how long could he hang on to his marbles?

Red threadwork

One fine day in late September, weary of the struggle to give the latest batch of fish their Mega-style ID, I left the office earlier than I needed to for my lunch with Dean. Finding myself in Soho with plenty of time to spare before we met, I strolled through the narrow streets around Piero's. By this time of year the warm sunlight, now of a gold that was full-toned, had become more sleepy and in the afternoon actually needed to take a siesta, which it did on the red, white and green awning of Piero's, on the tubbed bays outside the restaurant, on the fruit in front of a greengrocer's, on the provisions in the window of a delicatessen, lending them all a Caravaggio mellowness of colouring... And it induced in me, as I soaked it up, a lazy contentment in tune with its own.

Heading back from my brief tour in the direction of the restaurant, I turned down a short side street – something of a backwater, with its lack of paving, its rustic wall, its plane trees – and there, just ahead of me, stood the telephone kiosk that I normally caught sight of from the other end of the street. Set in a sort of alcove formed at a bend, backed by the crumbling, lichen-yellowed redbrick wall, which was now smiling a soft orange-pink, and overhung by, framed in, the luminous, yellowing but still green foliage of a couple of the plane trees (beautifiers of so many city streets), that old red kiosk, responding to the sun's greeting, glowed vermilion.

Seeing it there, so engaging, so suited to its setting of orange-pink and yellow-green, I caught an echo of what the sudden hoving into view of one of its kind had meant to me as a boy, an echo of the unlikely magic which that utilitarian object once radiated – for example, the one that so appealed to me in its nook of greenery in the environs of Walfield Road, especially when the summer evening sun set it afire. A magic shared by the telephone kiosk's cousin, that other familiar red denizen of the streets, the pillar box – which in certain settings and lights had inspired Chesterton to touch on its charms, the young Master to do likewise in his early prose-poems and Orwell to speak of its 'entering into your soul'…which was an integral element of my idealised heat-soaked Walfield Road…which, capped by snow and only notionally red, had featured in certain of my *Film-Fun*-based reveries (ah, Ollie or Stan posting a letter to rich great-uncle Chester Cash in one such box, amid the gently drifting snowflakes)… How heart-warming, how for some reason promise-laden, signifying more than its mere function, one or other of those two red presences used to appear to me in my impressionable boyhood when, walking along a street or travelling on a trolleybus or bus, I suddenly caught sight of it – perhaps (double pleasure) accompanied at a distance by its cousin – either vivifying what until then had been a monotonous vista (scarlet urban counterpart of those stray poppies that enliven roads lined with tracts of cornfield) or adding its sanguine livery to other colours in the heart of a town, painting into the view an essential finishing touch. (Little did I know then that red telephone kiosks, those enchanting artefacts I had always thought of as being a permanent feature of the English scene, were in fact an endangered species.)

But the pillar boxes and the telephone kiosks were only two strands in what is a vivid red threadwork running through the tapestry of England, red threadwork that for some stands out in their early years as a particularly enchanting motif. Certainly for me so many of the everyday things which, detaching themselves from the multitude I saw as a child in Bexcray and Richborough, chose to smile at me with such a special smile, so many of them were red. Trolleybuses, buses, mail vans, pillar boxes, telephone kiosks, tail-lights, traffic lights at stop, railway signals at stop… At dusk the reds of some burning or smouldering…in the sun flaring…in dappled light flickering…in snow glowing…in mist modestly blushing… Set off by indigo, or by azure, or by green, or by gold, or by soft white… Symbols of the vanishing magic of boyhood. Vanishing, yet even so, because they were once among the signifiers of the magic, still by association blessed with a lingering trace of its essence. So that even today, yes, even today, when life has for the most part been reduced down to a tedious collection of Things Known, and in some cases, worse, Things Contaminated, if, as I did during this September hour when I was to meet Dean, I round a corner and see before me one of those fondly remembered reds – the singing scarlet of a bus on a sunny afternoon, say, or the sweet vaporous cerise of a traffic light on a misty morning, I apprehend once more, even if only briefly, a throb of that old magic.

'A winning formula'

It seemed absurd to me that Mike and I were being forced to discard almost everything of interest from the Fish book. No mention, in the entry for the Weeks' bichir, for example, of its remarkable ability to survive on land for hours on end – yet five lines allotted to its belly measurement. Couldn't we add to our list of twelve 'essential' facts another, Special Characteristics? And to make room for it couldn't a few other items be shortened, Flatley's ukase repealed?

I decided to tackle McStutt on the matter. Mike told me, wearily, that I was wasting my time. But I went ahead.

Our project editor, a short, stocky Scot with a box-like head topped with corrugated grey hair, kept me waiting a studiedly considerable time before he looked up from his desk. Looked up – that is, tilted as always his head right back, as though preparing for treatment in the dentist's chair or for an old-fashioned shave in the barber's – the better it seemed to sight you down the sawn-off double barrel of his gnomish retroussé nose. At that point his small mouth, characteristically touched by a faint smile, began repeatedly to pucker up as though in readiness for an imminent kiss – a tic which over the years had etched deep lines all around his lips, like those at the opening of a drawstring purse.

'What can I do for you?' McStutt, who hailed from Edinburgh, uttered his refined Morningside vowels in a precise croak. He regarded me in autocratic fashion, mouthed a few incipient kisses.

'Something's bothering Mike and me. It's the information we're having to cut out of...the Fish book...' (Try as I might, I couldn't bring out the term-of-belonging, 'Sifgermaffow'.) 'Some of it's so much more interesting than all the statistics we have to put in. I was wondering whether – '

'You were wondering whether we couldn't retain some of it, to paint a fuller picture of our subaqueous friends, er-heh-heh, er-heh-heh.' He was given to these periodic emissions of small, dry laughter, usually for no apparent reason. 'Let me tell you, as an old stager to a young tyro,' (how prissy those croaked *o*s and *a*s sounded) 'it never does to change a winning formula. So I think we'll leave things as they are.'

'But if I can just give you a few – '

'It never does to change a winning formula, er-heh-heh, er-heh-heh.'

So that was that. There was to be no let-up in the megagradgrindery.

Those benumbed days at Lea & Lyle when, longing for escape, I'd daydreamed of working at Mega! Now, already disillusioned by the falsity of true 'tecs and the indigestibility of swiss rolls, here I was trudging through month after month of *Length: After three years, adults may reach 15-18in...* that was essentially no different from month after month of *40lb green shortback at 5s 2d per lb...*

Rising stock

Books, not unnaturally, was the most prestigious of the Mega departments. Whereas no Julian or Sebastian or Ginny or Polly would have dreamed of working in Trade and Practical Magazines on *Fixtures and Fittings*, for example – unless it were, like Hugh Wynner, to take overall charge – or in Picture Libraries on *True 'Tec Tales*, or in Comics on the repulsive *Socko* or *Whizz*, he or she was fully prepared to work in Books on anything. Not that they wouldn't have preferred to have gone to a company with more cachet – a Cape or a Chatto or a Weidenfeld, for instance. No doubt Mega had been a destination of last resort for many of them (some perhaps with only a third from, despite their schooling, a third-drawer university). Nevertheless, it was still publishing. And besides, Mega Books' stock was rising. Traditional publishers had once looked down on the company (as on all such outfits). They considered its synthetic productions – as opposed to their own organically grown ones, as it were – as unspeakably vulgar, just as they did the Mega advertising style (of which more shortly). But gradually the huge sales notched up by Mega, which had profitably tapped into the universal weakness for good looks (no matter how shallow the personality beneath might be), together with their own dwindling share of the illustrated reference book market, made traditional publishers rethink. While perhaps having been in the past a little too sweet on text and insufficiently willing to accept that in certain cases 'one picture is worth a thousand words', these publishers, swept off their feet by the hoydenish newcomers with their dressed-to-kill, frantically winking spreads, all come-on and often not much in the way of true satisfaction – in short, like all prick-teasers, a self-regarding end unto themselves – now switched from one extreme to the other. They adopted the philosophy and techniques of Mega and its lookalike rivals for their own wares. And it being in the nature of things that the perceived vulgarity of others' beliefs and activities miraculously ceases to be such once oneself and one's own kind have espoused them (cheering on the Gunners or the Blues or chucking darts in a pub no longer a coarse pleasure to the upper-middles once they have taken to it themselves), Mega-style Tarting Things Up, from once being considered by the gentlemen of publishing as something they wouldn't dream of soiling their hands on, now, as it played an ever-greater role in the production of their own illustrated non-fiction, became, somehow, 'rather exciting' and its end-products 'rather splendid'.

Not one 'widow'

At one of the pub lunches I used to take with Mike he had introduced me to William Faulks-Lockhart, an editor he knew from a previous project. Large, bespectacled and with a head of cherubic golden curls, he was a privately educated Oxford man of about thirty who as a minor littérateur had among other things reviewed for a couple of literary mags and written pieces on Waugh and Isherwood for some British Council pamphlets. Having fallen on hard times – as occasionally even public-school Oxbridge Faulks-Lockharts may do – he had, through a contact, the son of DeVere Lyttelton, our chairman, and with understandable reluctance, obtained a job at Mega Books: working on the *Canal Companion*. On the completion of this, he had moved on to *In Search of the Unknown*, a three-volume series on the supernatural. When, six months after Faulks-Lockhart joined the project, the series editor left – for a senior position at Pinnacle (or was it Zenith?) – the newcomer was chosen to replace him.

The credulous approach of the series (Milkman Foresaw Pearl Harbour), the amorphous, unresearchable nature of the material ('unfortunately no records of the meeting survive'), the penny-a-line prose ('The Hubbles couldn't believe their eyes, their hair stood on end') – this entire enterprise, which must have made the scholar in our littérateur wince in anguish and on which he had previously been only an unenthusiastic ancillary, he now, on being put in charge, had to advance and keep decked out in the same style.

The first volume of the series was now ready for publication, and one lunchtime, over beer and sandwiches with Mike and me in the Falstaff, Faulks-Lockhart produced an advance copy of it. As he gazed at its handsome cover and imposing bulk, riffled through its hyperdesigned pages and told us that he had managed to ensure, after many tribulations, that everything now fitted, that not one 'widow' remained – of the unique Mega type that mattered not a jot in literary mags or British Council publications – that every illustration was now correctly (three-line) captioned and every 'fact' correctly indexed – as, in other words, he basked in the knowledge that we, like everyone else in the department, could see how successfully he had brought to completion this glittering gewgaw, he displayed a satisfaction with his achievement as great as if it had been something of genuine worth. And this man who a couple of years before would have treated *In Search of the Unknown* with contempt, who would have wittily picked it to pieces among his friends, now managed to find justifications for its existence. Between swigs from his pint, he told us, in an earnest voice, 'No, I think it's a good read and a thought-provoking one' and, I was rather shocked to hear, 'There are more things in heaven and earth...'

And I recognised in him that same out-of-register pride, that same dishonest reconciliation of oneself to the third-rate, that same ropy rationalisation that I'd experienced myself on seeing in print the first of 'my' issues of *The Swiss Roll Maker*.

Killer

Condemned to continue on the Fish book exactly as before, as Mike had prophesied, we two editors carried on producing our lists of stats, all too often having to spin them out to get them to fill their unwarranted linage. Week after week, month after month it went on. In our darkest days we tried to console ourselves with the notion that some there might be, out there, eagerly awaiting that information we were scraping together. But who, we sometimes asked ourselves, who could they possibly be, these mysterious beings agog to learn the eye diameter of perch and pike, the egg output of swordfish and smelt? Nah, Mike and I knew that we were kidding ourselves. We knew that, as with all Mega Books productions these days, when it came right down to it, the text could go fry itself. All that really mattered was: did the book *look* good?

So, did the Fish book look good? Hey. Does Nicholas Soames get enough nourishment? Can Andrew Lloyd Webber pay his water rates? The Fish book look good? Man, it was *killer*. Blinding. Those designers. Mensch. Forget the pathetic hacks' contribution of Mike and myself – 212 teeth, size 9 fins, tributaries of the River Don, all that rollocks. Instead, imagine if you will (to use the terminology of Mega Books ads) a page for each fish that, beneath a spiffing great colour painting of the 'subaqueous friend' in question, gave you: a *woodcut* of its habitat; a *gouache* of its spawn; a *pencil sketch* of its dissected eye; *pen and ink drawings* of its skeleton seen from *three different angles*; a *watercolour* of its distribution area and migratory patterns, complete with broad *curving* arrows of *different hues*, nicely *fading at their base*; and all sprouting a *profusion* of labels which, if far from necessary, certainly gave a *convincing impression of being so*, and of being so in an essential-information-*saturated* way. Imagine if you will the cumulative effect of page after page of *that*.

Models

I was trying to hammer and screw a plot together for my book. And how difficult I was finding it! But, I told myself, after the inspiration of his brilliant basic idea, Master had then had to devise the details of his wonderful plot, hadn't he – and how intricate were their ramifications (and, I thought painfully, how scarcely mortal his ingenuity). Yet somehow his plot, apart from being so original, had also been of a complexity so light and graceful, of a symmetry so apparently exclusive of any possible other (that illusion of inevitability presented by all works of art), that comparing it to mine was like comparing some elegant suspension bridge of soaring span to some primitive low-slung mortar-bonded affair. This plot of mine, far from being clever (for, incapable of artful design, and 'civically' committed to a political story of resistance against tyranny, I was now trying to write primarily not a mystery but a thriller), was being laboriously assembled from various standard prefabricated blocks. Leo, like Jean Moulin, was to be betrayed to the secret police by someone within the resistance leadership. He would be arrested, tortured and killed. Guy was to have as mistress a beautiful co-resistance worker, Zoë, who would meet the same fate as Leo. Feigning sympathy for the regime, Guy was to join the secret police. From within he would discover the identity of the traitor and avenge Leo and Zoë. And to further the movement's plans for a coup, he would provide it with inside information about the movements of the president, the military dictator. Finally, like Stauffenberg, he would, on a day of burning heat, play a major part in the coup and lose his own life.

Other characters, too, would incorporate aspects of actual people, in these cases people I knew. In the president's surface affability and inner ruthlessness there would be something of Plumpford. The Minister of 'Justice' would have the same moues and croaking hauteur as McStutt. And for the sadistic secret police killer of Zoë, Carlsen Purvis, the hollow-eyed blond necrophiliac of *True 'Tec Tales*, would provide some physical traits. I had to have recourse to such models – I had no interest in that one-hundred-percent-invented-character stuff I kept coming across in round-up pocket reviews of thrillers in the broadsheets: 'Rumanian albino glassblower Carol Antonescu fingers dodgy Burmese transvestite antiques collector U Ne Win, then meets gruesome end. In her third outing, feisty wheelchair gynaecologist sleuth Rhiannon Multiple uncovers blackmail, murder and treason in high places.' You just knew that, cosmopolitan sophisticate though author Lavinia Coutts might be (and she had the stock Bond-Street-gallery-owner-to-St-Moritz-ski-instructor-type cv on the book jackets to prove it), nevertheless the mandatorily outré figures she manipulated in her intrigue were figments of the imagination so pure that not the faintest whiff of reality had ever touched them. No, that wasn't, couldn't be, for me. I was too reliant on real life.

This reliance would, though, I thought, provide me with an unexpected reward. The fictional roles I'd allotted to Plumpford et al would undoubtedly invest their everyday office selves with a new aspect, one entertainingly dramatic.

Mike's yellow

At last the blissful day arrived when, helium-filled, breaking away from our earthly moorings, Mike and I made the final marks on the page proofs of the Fish book. Our suffering was over. Even so, Mike had landed himself in trouble. Plumpford had pencilled in on the page proofs a few more of his inane – and in this case impossibly late-in-the-day – queries. 'Does the girth of the porcupine fish include its spines?' – that sort of thing. Instead of following our joint policy of ignoring these, Mike had crossed each one through and scrawled against it: 'Who gives a fuck?' By rights, these pages should never have been seen again by our managing editor. He always took it for granted that someone would set himself to answering these last-minute whims of his, these lightly dreamed up and cavalierly appended absurdities (mark of 'what had got him where he was'), in whose answers he understandably took no interest at all. He therefore never felt any need to check whether they'd been attended to – and by the time the book was published, Mike said, they'd always vanished clean from his mind, so smitten was he by the thing of beauty he beheld in his hands. They would only be seen by the printer (McStutt had already cast his perfunctory eye over the proofs), who, according to Mike, would in this instance just have a good laugh at the way they'd been dismissed. But on this occasion, by some mysterious process (one that Mike and I never got to the bottom of), the pages found their way back to Plumpford's desk. Appalled, incensed by Mike's lese-majesty, his entire face now as glossily red as his display-apple cheeks, the 'chief' (as he was known by some, who did not include Mike and me) had demanded an apology, ordered Mike to address himself to the queries (which he soon did 'answer' by means of various vicious – though never, to my knowledge, rumbled – inventions) and threatened him with the sack if he stepped out of line once more.

I never discovered exactly how much Mike was bothered by this business and by the knowledge that, under Plumpford, he would certainly never be promoted. But I did notice that immediately after the event he scaled breathtaking new heights in his incantatory use of the obscene.

The throne room

One Saturday morning at home I began tackling an accumulated pile of bills, bank statements and unsolicited financial advice. One item of junk mail was from Mammoth, the investment outfit. 'Want a bigger slice of the cake?' it asked. A great wodge of pink-icing-topped cream-and-jam-filled sponge – captioned *Its your's for the asking* – more or less filled the front page, and inside there was a splendid assortment of slices of gateaux, flans, bakewell tarts, lemon meringue pies, fruitcakes, you name it, all just as big as the piece of sponge and all there to help you decide – in the absence of much financial detail (no room left) – whether to take up the Mammoth investment offer.

Soon after I'd started working my way through the pile, I glanced away abstractedly, reflecting on some upcoming expenses, and caught sight of a book that Sally was reading, *The Man Who Was Thursday*. Picking up and browsing through this strange novel I had so enjoyed in my youth, I found myself drawn once more into its lurid dreamlike world. When eventually I surfaced from it I felt a tinge of guilt at having abandoned what I considered my necessary paperwork for what I considered an unnecessary immersion in fantasy. (It reminded me of what I had felt as a boy when, reading *Mosaic* in our little back room, lost in it, I would be startled out of it by Lil banging a broom around my feet and angrily ordering me to do a household job I'd forgotten all about.) That immersion in Chesterton's novel, it had been total, it had excluded during my reading all consciousness of everything else, including what I had been doing beforehand and what I planned to do afterwards. And as I pondered this, it seemed to me that what it meant, whether I liked it or not, was that my state of consciousness during my reading of *The Man Who Was Thursday* had been – forget my guilt – as *valid* as that during my financial brooding – or as that at any other time. Valid. What, I wondered, did I mean by that? Obviously I didn't mean 'valuable', because how could reading a fanciful adventure story count for as much as sorting out our money problems: I had to consider the reading state of consciousness as self-indulgent and profitless, the finances-considering state as dutiful and useful. No, by the two states being equally 'valid' I must mean something else, a bare truth that the draping of practical and moral clothing over one of them concealed. Then I realised that by 'valid' I had understood that, *in their essential nature*, stripped of any apportionment of comparative value that a practical and moral adult might dress them in, both states were of equal weight – in the same sense that two substances, one of which man has decreed precious, the other base, may be of identical physical weight and would in that case be indistinguishable to one who hefts them only: to the blind man gold has no more evident value than any other metal. After all, in a hypothetical life untroubled by problems of any kind, physical, mental, emotional or financial, the extensive reading of, absorption in, favourite literature could come to seem to that person living that life as having equal weight with any other aspect of it, just as on holiday we may well regard our sightseeing and leisurely dining as having equal weight with our work and the work of those we see around us.

But later that morning a less happy extension of this train of thought was to strike me. Having returned to domestic paperwork and cleared it, I was trying hard to work out the details of a plot development in my book when Michael came running in to ask me to look at a butterfly on the balcony at the rear of our maisonette. It was a painted lady that had settled on one of the geraniums I'd planted in an urn. We crouched some distance away observing it, absorbed in the unfolding and folding of its wings, like a book being regularly opened to reveal two beautiful colour plates within, then shut. But soon

Sally appeared to tell me we had a problem: the fridge had conked out again. I rang Ice Warriors Refrigeration, who had charged a considerable amount to 'fix' it to a state 'as right as rain', and concentrated on what the exact wording of my complaint should be. Then, as I hung on to the call, waiting, waiting, waiting for someone who was 'just being fetched', I found myself, in a semi-detached state, considering the past morning. First, the Mammoth sweet-trolley nonsense, utility bills and a precarious bank balance had *commandeered* my consciousness; but then *The Man Who Was Thursday* had *sent them all packing*; only for them to return unabashed to *take over fully again*; then preoccupation with a sequence in my book had *banished them in their turn*; then absorption with Michael in the painted lady had *utterly ousted* that preoccupation; then determining what to say to bloody Ice Warriors had just as tyrannically *taken over full control*; until, supplanted by this spell of reflection, it too had been *dismissed out of hand*... One by one, each had been slung out. Suddenly it hit me (I'd been only vaguely aware of it before): how absurdly hollow and ephemeral is the reign of each one of those conscious states in the noddle's throne room, a sequence which is all that constitutes the waking life of any one of us, whether you, me, Florence Nightingale, Mister Motivator, Ottorino Respighi, the postman, Martina Navratilova, Michael Portillo, that woman who runs the launderette round the corner...; how illusory is the sovereignty of each incumbent, which, in the same way as it gave the old heave-ho to its at the time seemingly equally sovereign predecessor, is in its turn shortly going to be unceremoniously booted out by its successor.

If I'd 'known' all this before, it had been only in a superficial, theoretical Philosophy for All way. Now that I'd been brought into its actual presence by its minder, its facilitator, 'Mr Muscles' Reductionism, it slammed me full in the breadbasket. For, once freed from having to put on its civilised act in the pages of a book, it can now reveal itself for what it actually is. As finally do so many previously bland-seeming abstractions. Infinity, for one – as Musil's Törless alarmingly discovered looking up at the sky. Jealousy, for another – as I agonisingly discovered when Linda left me for the man in black. You blithely imagine you know them, those abstractions, when you meet them on the printed page, where they're so polite and innocuous; you may carelessly discuss them with others from time to time; but it's not until you run slap bang up against one of them in person, when they've cast off all their fake urbanity, when all your book knowledge and informed chat count for nothing, it's not until they wade into you, rough you up, rub your sophisticate's fizzog in the dirt, it's not until then that you really *know* them.

So. Your life as fundamentally no more than a string of largely disconnected... One in which whatever happened to be the current, seemingly pre-eminent consideration would shortly itself... Bloody hell. I wasn't exactly mad about it, as I guess most of those who've been dragged by 'Mr Muscles' down into the cellar to meet one of his bosses aren't about what they experience there. But fortunately, with one bound Jack was free. I scrambled up above ground again...

And as I did so, I began to toy with what would once have seemed to me a disgraceful idea. In my own stumbling fashion, I had tried over the years to pursue the unremitting search for truth first enjoined on us by Plato and ever after by life guides of every shape and size. Now I began to wonder whether, for most of us, that search shouldn't be...(could I bring myself to say this?)...whether it shouldn't be...well, *selective only*...

The Overjoyeds

Dolled and painted up to the nines, last-minute titivation over, the Fish book was now ready to strut tartily out into the world.

Ads appeared in the tabloids, in TV mags, on telly itself. These had been produced well in advance before actual printing and showed only dummy volumes with the title on their spine. One, in the *Warp*, was a heartfelt testimonial to the stunning quality of the book by a frank-looking, £1,000-will-do-nicely ex-cabinet minister. Holding the blank-paged whopper before him, fixing the reader over his specs with the unmistakable gaze of integrity, he proclaimed: 'Turning the pages, I have been deeply... Without a doubt, the finest... I do most strongly...' (Despite my recent reservations about a no-exceptions commitment to the truth, how shocked I was when I came across such a flagrant flouting of it. But then there returned to me from the past the reassuring words of Mr Tungle, my old religious education teacher: 'Come on, they're only *lies* for heaven's sake.' And I seemed also to hear again the wise, equally reassuring pronouncement of Big Daddy in *Cat on a Hot Tin Roof*: 'Mendacity is a system we live in.' And my disquiet passed.)

Other ads featured a flawless family of four. In one they sprawled on a rug gazing with amazed delight into the empty pages. What seemed to be firelight was reflected in their eyes as they embarked happily on that 'entrancing exploration of the seas and waterways of the world...the magical journey of a lifetime' that yesterday's man of straw had promised them. That expression of theirs, that amazed delight, brought back a memory of those Hollywood films I saw as a boy in which preposterous pedestrians exchanged similar looks as the elated hero jauntily strode by.

Those who bought certain of Mega Books' wares I couldn't help seeing as facsimiles of the models who blissfully examined them in the ads. Unwarranted, I knew, but it was a picture that stuck. All the takers for the Fish book, for example, I saw as the Overjoyed family, exponentially replicated, as in some virtual world. More particularly, it was Mr Overjoyed – not pretty, pert

Mrs Overjoyed, wiping flourcaked hands on apron as she eagerly peered at the new purchase over his manly shoulder – it was hundreds of thousands of copies of him, that grinning thirtyish chap, that I saw having made the decision to fork out for the 'entrancing exploration'.

Some of the later ads showed actual sample pages from the book in miniature, which intensified their busyness, and this was increased yet further by superimposed demonstrative arrows and encirclings. Mr Overjoyed, who gazed at them in ecstasy, was, I thought, overimpressed by their hyperactivity, by their 'real moneysworth' stacks of stats. He was too elated as he was asked whether he knew that the rudd spawned from April to June, that the dab was rarely longer than 15in. His eyes widened in too happy a surprise as he learned that the Overjoyed family, he and Jean and little Jimmy and Julie, would at last be able to identify with precision and peace of mind each of that tremendous variety of fish they kept coming across, time after time, in seas and rivers and streams and canals and lakes and ponds. Yes, too elated, too happily surprised *by far*. I thought that as, a little later, in virtual time and space, that overexcitable young man sank, with all his replicas, into the common armchair from which he was supposed later to embark on his Fish-book-induced Arabian Nights travels, some of the glee might disappear from his well-chiselled chops, he might fall to more sober reflection, might ask himself, as he pondered that essential guide, whether any of the Overjoyeds had on their travels ever actually seen a live fish or were ever likely to…if they did see one whether they'd note with any accuracy its eye diameter and number of teeth…if they did note these whether they'd be able to retain a mental note of them until they could consult the guide…if they did consult it whether this would afford them an unequivocal identification…if it did afford them an unequivocal identification whether they could give a… I imagined that, across the room (which like other

Overjoyed families' rooms clearly displayed a compact library of other Mega Books publications), the young man might well catch sight of and quickly avert his eyes from the long-neglected, the scarcely opened *Great Illustrated Family Guide to One Thousand Ferns Around the World* (or 'Gifgotfaw' as Plumpford invariably called it). I doubted whether Mr Overjoyed would be able to bear its reproachful gaze or that of its sisters on the shelf. 'After all,' this harem would pitiably protest, 'you chose us, you bought us, you must have fancied us once. But now you don't even so much as touch us up.'

But then winsome Master and Miss Overjoyed, who had been ultimately responsible for the purchase of the ferns book, would burst in. 'You bought it, Dad. Cor, look at all them smashing pictures, look at all them fish eyes and eggs and things!' would cry that cherubic pair. Dad would be touched and feel rewarded by their flip-through-today, cast-aside-tomorrow eagerness. He would recall, too, the marine-and-freshwater-fish-guide-as-an-*educational*-tool pitch of the advertisement of which he himself and his family were the stars, he would recall its subtext: 'You will never forgive yourself, Mr Overjoyed – and worse, JIMMY AND JULIE WILL NEVER FORGIVE YOU – if you should be churl enough not to purchase this guide, this guide that NO ONE CAN DO WITHOUT.' (Who, I wondered, could have stood firm against such a message? Only perhaps men of far greater steel than the irresolute Mr Overjoyed – probably further and incurably enfeebled by so much replication.) And so then this unfortunate soft touch would tell himself he had done the right thing, would feel much better, and a grin would return to his collective dial.

That was how I saw those multitudinous heads of household, yes: identical personable young fellows, bright enough in some respects probably, but weak, weak, weak.

An eye-opener

'If a primary tumour can be removed, a secondary tumour in the eye may be destroyed, or the eye can be removed.'

I looked up from the page: Eye Disorders in Children by Mr Ivan Orbit, MB, FRCS (Mr not Dr, as the so-English form of distinction had it). It was no good. I'd read that testing sentence five times. It belonged to that glassy kind of statement on which, as though you were one of those Sisyphean insects that continually slide back down the slippery sides of a container, you can never gain any true purchase. *If* a primary tumour can be removed. That implied that if it couldn't be, nothing was done about the secondary tumour, the one in the eye. Surely not. And then: the secondary tumour *may* be destroyed? Only may be? Surely not – or was it pointless to consider seriously, as it was so much else in the copy, Orbit's comparative use of *can* and *may*, as though they were intended to express some exact differentiation in possibility and intent? And then, anyway: *destroyed*? Destroyed how? Parents would want to know, wouldn't they? And then: *or* the eye can be *removed*. That casual alternative.

Finished with fish, I had been drafted in as editorial help on a family medical guide. (This was until I was to take on the following spring a mysterious 'special new role' Plumpford had earmarked me for, an – I waited for it – 'exciting new challenge'.) Now, having just completed a titanic struggle with Orthodontics, I had, for my pains, been landed with something even worse.

Not that my colleagues were having an easy time of it. Chris Alexander, one of the hottest subs in Books, was struggling with an account of the mechanism of emphysema, by Mr Barrington D. Eyre-Waye, MB, FRCS, that bore as much relation to the consensus of every other account in the literature as Stan Grout's titles did to the contents of *True 'Tec Tales*. And

Ruth Marks' man, Mr Denis Capsule, MRCP, FRCS (a telly wheel-on), obviously believed, in his 'comprehensive' survey of rheumatoid arthritis, that it would be, well, somewhat crass to mention pain in the joints – how else explain his not alluding once to this symptom that lesser mortals would have thought it impossible not to address, a feat of breathtaking virtuosity. 'On top of that,' Ruth said, 'the inconsistencies in his copy are absolutely staggering. *And* there's a medical error. *And* there's no logic to the way any of it's organised.' She sounded shocked.

It was with similar incredulity, I suppose, that the world learned that certain merchant bankers allowed their venerable institution to be wiped out by a lone trader; that certain historians were duped by the transparent fraud of the Hitler diaries; that certain art evaluators were similarly bamboozled by the dreadful daubs that purported to be Vermeers... And certainly such incompetence was an eye-opener to me, who, as a working-class Bexcray boy whose attitudes and opinions were so largely based on those of Harry and Lil, had been brought up to believe that doctors, lawyers, architects, professors and all the AB rest were superior beings far removed from ourselves.

Sometimes a contributor did deliver the goods – the accurate, the logical, the clearly expressed. And when that happened, you found yourself *exaggerating* that contributor's merits whenever you spoke of them and *fastening on* any opportunity to do so – from a mixture of genuine gratitude for such unexpected excellence and the more self-conscious savouring of pleasure in being able to go overboard for once.

Gicbog

Two thousand pages. *Fifteen pounds* in weight. It was true that the case history of Mega Books' megalomania, of its wild-eyed determination to produce, on every practical subject under the sun, the impossible last word, went back a long way and included the production of some mighty tomes, but even it had never essayed before anything quite like the *Great Illustrated Comprehensive Book of Gardening*. I remember how, when the assembled editorial and design quartet were acquainted in Plumpford's office with the specifications for this work, our gazes became as fixed, our figures as immobile as the sight of some awesome, chilling spectacle of nature might have made them. Senior designer Simon Flimby, normally so hyped-up, now looked strangely cowed, as did his assistant, Karen Lee, an innocent fresh from college. McStutt, it was true, tried with head thrown back to maintain smiling seigneurial assurance but it wasn't long before he began – tell-tale sign – to mouth his habitual kisses with an unprecedented rapidity.

Plumpford, on the other hand, could scarcely contain himself, he found himself rising from his desk as he poured out the planned contents of what he was inevitably already calling 'Gicbog': 'There's gunnabe undergrounddrainage hedginggreenhousegardeningshowbloomswallfruitrockgardens fishponds – ' (soaring higher and higher, he seemed now, from what he listed next, to see below some extensive landscaped estate) ' – woodlandgardensfountainswaterfalls – '

'O stop, stop,' we cried.

'It's gunnabe so huge that Production reckons it'll need a revolutionary new binding technique.' He was drunk with the enormity of it all.

Then, with the would-be demonstration by the half-cut that he still has his wits about him, attempting to convey a switch to sober realism merely by a greater widening of the eyes, he warned us: 'Not that it doesn't have to be produced fast, real fast.' (Natch.) 'We've got just twelve months to do the whole thing.'

He went on to speak of the rewarding times ahead for those who would be privileged to work on such a back—, such a groundbreaking new venture. And as he elaborated on these, I allowed what he was saying to slip out of focus while I studied with horrified fascination his flushed, fleshy, neat-featured face and demented voice, no longer thick with, but risen above, that molasses mateyness with which he asked you in corridor or men's room whether you were finding such-and-such an exciting challenge or with which he pontificated in pub or staff restaurant on sports cars, whisky brands, golf handicaps, property prices and passing females' bums. His physical being seemed the ideal embodiment of what he had outlined to us on more than enough occasions: his 'rise to the top' – from *Showbiz* assistant editor (where he'd known Neal Easy) to Zenith (or was it Pinnacle?) project editor to Mega Books managing editor.

When I refocussed on his actual words, he was concluding a feverish enlargement on the monstrous scope of the new book. Then: 'And guess what,' he said. '*Guess what.*' I shuddered. 'The copy isn't gunnabe produced like normal – contributor writes it, sub smooths out the wrinkles, and that's it.' Smooths out. Wrinkles. He was ensconced in some cloud-capt realm from which what the subs actually struggled with was conveniently hidden from view. And, so that he could continue serenely to inhabit it, at progress meetings he would refuse to listen to project editors who cited the state of the raw copy as the reason for missed deadlines, and in pubs he banned all shoptalk in his presence.

'No,' he said, 'that's not how we're gunnado it. I've got a surprise for you.' He paused, beaming. It was the sort of pause and beam suited only to an announcement that we would soon be seeing pleasing changes on our payslips. *'We're* gunnawrite the text for Gicbog. Every job, from tree-felling to building a gazebo, is gunnabe demonstrated by experts and we'll take notes and photographs on the spot. Then in the office we'll write it all up and select the best shots to illustrate it. *That's* how we're gunnado *this* book.'

I wondered why he'd been looking at me for most of his speech.

'Yessir, that's the picture,' he said. 'And I want you, young Xavier, to spearhead the reporting team on the book.'

So this was what my 'special new role' was to be. I guessed that the combination of mythical newspaper experience that had followed me around on my company cv and my actual reporting job on *The Swiss Roll Maker* had made me the obvious choice for this horrifying new task.

And where was this reporting 'team' I was 'spearheading'? Apart from McStutt, who was obviously not to be a member of it, there were no other editorial persons present.

As if he'd read my thoughts, Plumpford added: 'There'll be others joining you as soon as they're free. I'm expecting one'll be Chillingford Flint when he's finally finished on Gifgerhupmaubmisk.'

Did I protest? I who had about as much interest in horticulture of any kind as McStutt had in the line-up of the Buddy Rich Big Band. Did I express to Plumpford what I felt about my role in his ever-more-grandiose careerist schemes: 'Hang on a minute. What makes you so certain I'm willing to assist you in your repellent plans for world domination?' Course not. Rebels spring but rarely from the pushchair-in-the-hall brigade. Instead, I simply stared at him emptily for several seconds as one might initially at a bobby who has just stopped one in the street with the words 'I am arresting you for the murder of Roger Ackroyd'. But then, with my breadwinner's look – that shrewd-eyed, firm-lipped, forthright number – and breadwinner's voice – steady, measured, low – that I'd now learned during many a pretence-filled year at Mega to assume at will, I replied, 'Right...Bob...' (it was with difficulty, as always, that I managed to mouth the name). 'Sounds an interesting...' Did I actually say that? *Interesting*? Yup, 'fraid so. But no amount of effort could produce the next word, *that* word.

'Challenge?' prompted Plumpford. 'Yes, Gifgerhermeeaw, Sifgermaffow and Gifgerhupmaubmisk were tough,' our acronymaniac boss admitted, in a stunning display of articulative facility, and in one of his rare concessions to reality, 'but Gicbog'll be even tougher. It'll be a *real* challenge.' He spoke in the satisfied tone of one who contemplates what a feast of others' suffering he has contrived for himself.

Thrills and spills

On a fine morning in early May, a morning warm, diaphanous, tender, I parked my car outside Simon Flimby's flat in Regent's Park. We were to visit the World of Tulips nursery in Surrey, there to pioneer the reporting and photography techniques that would be required for the Gardening book. World of Tulips...World of Tulips... Something stirred vaguely in the recesses of my memory.

The morning was the lovely realisation of another of those moving breakfast-time radio promises: 'It should be a fine day throughout the south, with temperatures reaching...' Ah, that 'throughout the south', ah, that *with temperatures reaching...'* Promise of a rare benison. Memories of open-top drives with Dean and Olivia, the smell of blue exhaust hanging on the balmy air, an outing to...somewhere or other...somewhere or other Out There...

Spring, the sweet spring, is the year's pleasant king.

Approaching the flat, I soaked up the warmth, the light, which had redecorated the broad sweep of classical terrace around me in fresh pastel washes. In the contented air, the faint, comfortable hum of middle-distance traffic reached me: unseen traffic, OK traffic, accident-free traffic, ideal traffic. Vague reverie of the start of the school cricket season. In the morning, well before a match would begin, the ground languorous, the same placid traffic murmur beyond it as now, the farthest trees blue in a slight haze, the scene softly athrob with the play to come.

I mounted the steps and rang the bell. How, I wondered, could Simon afford this place. Certainly not on a Mega Books salary.

I was about to ring again when he opened the door. He was, I thought, a rum cove and no mistake. Dressing loose was more or less statutory for designers, yet Simon clothed his willowy frame in sober suits of beautiful cut, formal shirts of snowy whiteness and silk ties of dark opulence. His hair he pomaded and brushed flatteningly back above his jug ears to a patent leather which almost matched in sheen his toecaps, and there sat incongruously on the top lip of his slim, delicate-skinned, fine-boned face a full black tache. Then there was his curious lingo – an incessant maiming of standard phrases, malapropisms, painful unintended neologisms – speech rendered even more opaque by not only the standard vowel clipping of his class but in his case the excision of whole syllables – all this delivered helter-skelter. And on top of this his strange eager boyish manner – sudden short-lived flushing pothers and enthusiasms, which consorted so oddly with the debonair Guards-officer-in-mufti appearance.

'Hello, Xav. Bit r'lief, 'sidering if I didn't know whether to start to th'office.' The 'explanation' tumbled out. In Bexcray High Street I sometimes saw a poor soul with Parkinson's disease tottering along at some speed, leaning too far forwards, overbalancing from time to time and recovering only by 'losing' a step or improvising some corrective movement. The compassionate bemusement I felt watching this unfortunate ataxic chap I now felt again, listening to Simon.

'Wasn't 'solutely sure hadn't bodgered it. Anyway, all cracking to go.'

He patted the photographic gear he'd just slung with difficulty over his shoulder. Its expeditionary bulk took me aback. Surely snapping people doing things to tulips would be a straightforward enough affair. Yes, but mundane reality wasn't what Simon was into. Take the business of his car, which was in for repair. I'd guessed the problem couldn't possibly be of the boring blocked-carburettor or leaking-radiator kind that afflicts the rest of us but had to be due to *yet another sensational occurrence*. For the life Simon led away from his perfectly ordinary office existence was, as related by him, an action movie without end. Yes, as we drove off, he recounted the latest breathtaking episode. It had taken place in the byways of rural England, an uneventful enough setting in the experience of most of us but one that had acquired in Simon's claimed ordeal the threatening tone of the Scottish moors in *The Thirty-nine Steps* or of the American prairies in *North by Northwest*. Returning to town from a country weekend by minor roads, he had been pursued, for no understandable reason, by a gang of bikers – as the motorist in another movie of dark and inscrutable menace, *Duel*, was pursued, for no understandable reason, by a truck. Relentlessly, they had chased him up hill and down dale through one county after another.

'Scary bloody crew, Xav, can swear for it, I can tell you.' He said this with the muted bitter half-laugh of one who believed himself to be recalling unnerving fact.

Ravaging a few more standard phrases, he explained that eventually he'd managed to shake them off with a combination of cunning and wristy skill at the wheel – though not without several nasty encounters with junction boxes, walls, trees and the like. The repairs bill would be heavy.

"Sincred'ble, really was,' he exclaimed, eyes bright, fine skin colouring. 'Was in one heckle of a state, don't mind telling you. But I dealt for those buggers in the end,' he concluded on a note of triumph.

Listening to this latest of his tales of thrills and spills, I was inescapably reminded of Uncle Len's endless dramas of track and ring, and I was reinforced in a conviction that had grown in me over the years that our mysterious lodger's exploits were of the same nature as I took Simon's to be.

A rushed and incomplete breakfast had left me feeling hungry, so I bit into a Mars bar. I didn't offer Simon any – I knew that the strangest thing of all about this strange being seated beside me was that he did not eat. By his own account, he never had breakfast; no one at Mega Books had ever known him take time off for lunch (another Thrimms); at office parties he never touched the snacks; and in his stories of unfailingly dramatic evenings and weekends there was an equally unfailing absence of any reference to meals. As Chris Alexander had remarked recently, you would have expected in these highly detailed accounts to have heard an occasional such reference simply as a time placement ('after dinner', 'before supper'). Instead it appeared that Simon stepped into his extramural world of adventure directly upon leaving Mega House and that there was no need anywhere along the way for the normal stop to take on fuel. That was it: difficult though it was to comprehend, extremely difficult, he had obviously, by some marvellous, if disquieting, process, ceased to require what the rest of mankind requires to sustain life. It seemed that all he needed for continued existence was a series of regular jolts to his nervous system, self-induced if need be. So, on the journey to the nursery, he deliberately conjured up the hassles and panics which the monumental, understaffed, cruelly scheduled Gardening book probably held in store for us.

'G' lor', Xav, what on *earth* d'you reckon on this r'dic'lous project?' he asked in 'impassioned' tones. 'Look what time the buggers've put it down to! And staff 'located us! 'S bloody r'dic'lous! *Bloody r'dic'lous!*' His voice had risen almost to a shout. I winced in the confined space.

He was so gorging on that 'anger' he'd set bubbling on the hob (the hot kitchen work, as it will, had brought the blood welling up beneath his fine skin), so gorging on his cooked-up substitute for material sustenance, that it was possible, I thought, he might therefore have strength enough to continue until lunchtime without further helpings. I certainly hoped so.

'Yes, it could be tough,' I said, with that affected composure that was earning me a ludicrous reputation for cool, and taking another bite of my Mars bar.

'G' lor', you are a calm bugger and no mistake,' Simon said with an admiring smile. His 'fury' had vanished with as disconcerting a suddenness as it had flared up. Disconcerting too had been his production of a normal sentence. But then:

'Would take a lot to make you in a flap. How d'you manage it, on earth's sake?'

Conviction

I managed it because of my essential detachment from the Gardening book, like that from the Fish book, from *The Swiss Roll Maker*, from *True 'Tec Tales*. I gave of my best to each of those publications, but I could never take any of them seriously enough to get in a lather, as some did, about the problems that inevitably developed on them and that were just as inevitably always resolved. I was convinced my *true* working life was writing my book. I felt this even though lack of time made my work on it intermittent and even though this work was currently nothing but research – reading book after book on dictatorships, paramilitary and secret police forces, resistance movements, coups.

As for that research, it was only from the hard detailed information it provided – the key strategic installations that must be seized if a coup is to succeed, how a Gestapo-like organisation is recruited, trained and run, and so on – that I could construct the strong armature needed to support the narrative. I knew, though, that excessive background reading has too obviously taken over far too many novels – especially those by compulsive literary masochists: 'worthy' fictions in which the strenuously hewn has squeezed out entirely the intuitively imagined or the personally apprehended. (Another example, it seems, this adopted literary asceticism, of the perverse at work again. I've always thought that it is some such savouring of what is against nature that in the English theatre, for instance, has been behind certain relentlessly minimalist, arid productions and certain rigorously schematic, arid plays of the past forty years; and that whatever success they may have achieved has been due not to any genuine enjoyment of them by theatre-goers but to a corresponding propensity in many of these for cultural self-laceration.) Not, I told myself, that I would ever allow my own research to displace too much of what had been the original inspiration for my book, its essential justification.

On the ropes

We arrived at World of Tulips. World of Tulips. Suddenly it came back to me. This was the nursery that Olivia used to order from, whose fields I had once dreamily imagined to be like those in Monet's paintings and tended by girls in lace caps and clogs. (I didn't know it then but the nursery, which produced no other bulbs but tulips, had been ailing for some time. Owned by the Gunn family, it was only to become a commercial success when a marauding Dane acquired it the following year, subjected it to some pitiless knifework and broadened its output.)

We headed for the firm's offices, set well back from the road. They were housed in a converted redbrick mansion, half covered with the fresh young greenery of a Virginia creeper. In the sunwash the façade was a Cézannesque golden pink and golden green, and the golden green stirred lazily in a sweet-tempered breeze. My pace slowed. It slowed against my will, as though this delicious May morning, with its warm embrace, its shy caress, were some sorceress with the power to seduce me from my purpose.

But I shook off her charms, I stepped out decisively again: I was here to make a start on an important task, to embark once more on unremittingly practical reporting, asking all the right questions, filling pad after pad with notes, turning it all into authoritative instructional text, anonymous anodyne text, Mega Books text...

I was peeved to see that the nursery owners' secretary, who met us in reception, was exceptionally, distractingly desirable. Notably uxorious, difficult to please, I didn't come across that many truly devastating young women, so why, I angrily put it to fate, why on today of all days, when I needed single-minded concentration on tulips and not (the comic-book pun came irresistibly to mind) on two lips that – there was no denying it – were so provocative that they virtually *demanded* to be kissed, why had one such young woman been placed slap-bang in front of me? Why, in the corny idiom of *True 'Tec Tales*, was she so 'hot' a 'number' with 'curves in all the right places'? Moreover, why was she (as I'd learned from McStutt's correspondence with the nursery) possessed of so cruelly apt a name? Miss *Pierce*.

The print dress she wore, vermilion-spotted gold and green and blue, was far from modest, was tantalising in its part-disclosure of what she could bestow. And artifice had heightened her natural charms: a touch of synthetic coral her lips' allure, some fragrant dabbed-on chemical her skin's, and, it could just be glimpsed, snug yet skimpy upholstery her body's. The exhibition lily, not gilded but rightly, enticingly touched up here, adjusted there. And unfortunately, the confined vestibule, further cramped by large cardboard cartons and Simon's Scandinavian-backpacker gear, forced her to stand disturbingly close to me. The whole caboodle rushed, in unsporting combination, straight to my head. How overpowering the impulse to reach out a hand and place it on that warm, fragrant, sunripe flesh, to lean forward and taste those lips! You'd be doing no wrong, would you, it couldn't possibly be considered 'sexual harassment', could it, you still loved and desired Sally, didn't you? In some ideal existence, you...

First, in the tone of one commenting on a strange coincidence, she told us that her father owned several of 'our' books, those books that were to be found in so many households.

Then: 'Are you the writer?' she asked me.

The writer. Rather grand term, I thought, for my role on this project. (Had McStutt described me to the nursery owners thus?) But, shamesouledly, I discovered that I had no intention of disabusing The Girl Can't Help It of her notion, of forfeiting the glamour that that term writer, even when vague and unqualified, automatically seemed to possess for the unsophisticated.

'Yes,' I said.

Her lovely lips parted in a shy 'knockout' of a smile. (Quite astonishingly, that *True 'Tec Tales* terminology for limning 'chicks' and 'babes' that I'd once inwardly mocked was proving to be hole-in-one: Miss Pierce's smile *was* concussive. And I wondered whether some of the tales' other favoured expressions were quite so derisory as I'd once thought – whether, for instance, a villain might not sometimes after all 'snarl' defiance or 'hiss' revenge.)

The comfortable stuffiness of the lobby, the mote-filled shaft of sunlight hovering athwart it, the nearness of this girl, her drowsily provocative scent, the happy stupor induced in me by her sucker-punch smile, all murmured to me to linger dopily on the ropes. The session hadn't even started and here was my impaired brain having the gall to suggest to me how pleasant it would be to stay here, to chuck away my preparatory notes, to take a step even closer to She Was Meant to Please and...

God, this was intolerable. Intolerable. I clenched my jaws, summoned up Sally and the boys, demagnetised this temptress by deliberately, caddishly imagining her so-kissable lips opening only to emit a malodorous belch followed by a witch's cackle, and, as she led us to the office of one of the Gunn family directors, the man who was to demonstrate tulip growing to us, averted my eyes from her unreasonable rear.

World of Tulips

Pelham Gunn, who was seated behind a large Victorian mahogany partners' desk and backed by a wall hung with the obligatory set of sporting prints, was a short, gaunt, rigid stick of a man, whose small darting eyes and compressed lips, surmounted by a pepper-and-salt moustache, were set in a head that quivered throughout our visit, perhaps from some nervous disorder, perhaps from perpetual repressed fury at the modern world, perhaps from exasperation that he'd been saddled with what he saw as a chore. He certainly regarded me about as welcomingly as if I were some jobbing gardener who had ventured into the inner sanctum unbidden. For Simon, with his 'an officer and a gentleman' look and, what with the pinstripe, gleaming shirt front and dazzling toe caps, apparently dressed more for the boardroom than the tulip fields, he perhaps had greater hopes.

Straightaway he snappishly asked us why we needed to take photographs – what was wrong with using existing drawings as reference?

Hadn't McStutt told them, as he was supposed to? Well, that wouldn't be unusual. I explained to Gunn that our express instructions were to take photographs, which would either be used themselves or serve as reference for artwork – it hadn't been finally decided yet. Gunn replied that he really couldn't see why we couldn't use illustrations they already had. I told him again this wasn't on and why. He said that he knew of some drawings that would be just the job. They were, he said, in a gardening manual, and he took this from a bookcase. It was a late-nineteenth-century publication whose disagreeable sallow pages and copperplate etchings immediately brought back to me the *Chatterbox* annual of my childhood. Full of pictures of defunct garden tools and machinery, it was steeped in the aching melancholy of all things long since abandoned. Gunn started pointing out to us, briskly, as though this forlorn object were hot off the press, some illustrations in it of repellent line and shading (that densely cross-hatched stuff I hated in *Held to Ransom*) depicting riveted, armoured-vehicle-like watering cans unpleasantly sprinkling murky parterres, the setting for some dismal Wilkie-Collins-type skulduggery or other. (I could see later why the business had been so infirm before the Dane brutally revived it.)

'Ideal!' Gunn barked.

Undoubtedly once Major Gunn: the regimental tie, the Dunn Bros tweed hacking jacket and twill trousers in shades of khaki, the plain-uppered utilitarian brown shoes, the ramrod bearing, the greater predisposition to action than speech, the jump-to-it tone, the snap judgments. Another well-trodden path: forces career, statutory early retirement, then automatic directorship of a family firm, for which the scantest knowledge of the business would serve.

With a look of painful striving, occasioned by the task of trying to frame a true sentence, Gunn then said: 'May I – ah – ask – who you have as a – ah – as a – ah – to help you with – ah – '

'Our consulter, you mean?' prompted Simon.

'Your consulter – exactly. Ex-*actly*.'

'Veronica Budd,' I told him. 'Apparently she's published – '

'Budd?' A shot from a Lee Enfield. 'Never heard of her.'

Hoping to find her unrepresented in the nursery library and thus prove to us her absolute nullity, he summoned – oh, no – Miss *Pierce*. With a slow, stiff turning of the head towards her, like a gun turret that needed oiling, and with an exaggerated raising of the brow, a tartar's ham rendition of casual, he said: 'Miss Pierce, find out – ah – whether we have any – ah – books by a – ah – a – ah – Veronica Budd.'

For a moment Miss Pierce turned her shining gaze on me (She Mesmerises Every Mother's Son) before mercifully leaving the room.

A silence. I searched for an intelligent filler but, like those 'questioners' I'd heard at public meetings, could only think up phoney enquiries in whose answers I wouldn't have had the slightest interest. Unlike them, however, I had no intention of putting any of those 'questions': 'How old is the nursery?' 'How many tulips do you reckon you grow?' (John Brown). I briefly considered 'Do you have a large library?' but rejected it as being as barrel-scrapingly wretched as the others.

Gunn said: 'I suppose – ah – you fellows drove down.'

'Yes', I was surprised to find, was all I could come up with. But Simon, hungry again, I was disappointed to observe, seized the tendered opportunity of elevenses.

'Came down A30,' he said. 'Pretty clear on traffic, wasn't it, Xav. Not like last time I – Bloody hell. Drivin' down for Bagshot, tooterin' along, like you do. Got to Sun'dale, p'lice cars all over, right chokeup it was. Could you b'lieve it, bank raid. Bloody *bank* raid. And they'd got those buggers housed up in a shoot-up.' It was an event that I couldn't recall ever having been reported anywhere. 'Bloody 'munition richettin' all over.' His eyes widened and he smiled in retrospective – and, I felt, understandable – incredulity. 'Made sure on keeping my cover, I can tell you.' Whatever expectations Gunn may once have had of Simon it was obvious from the way he was now regarding him that they had vanished. 'Got out of there in pretty damn flash, can tell you. Lost my route... But today just through Cam'ley, wasn't it, Xav, turn off for Sandhurst, past 'cademy. Then...'

At this point She Got Lots of What They Call the Most returned, followed by an elderly male dogsbody (improbably addressed by Gunn as 'My man'). Each carried an armful, no less, of Budd's books on tulips.

The fair one, or rather the unfair one, repaid Gunn's perfunctory thanks with a smile of ravishing beauty, without this time – I felt a pang – glancing at me. How pleased, how sad, I was to see her disappear again.

Gunn was visibly flummoxed by the magnitude of Ms Budd's work. Seventeen books! (And tulips were such simple-seeming plants too.) He had dismissed as a nobody one who was evidently a doyenne in the field (extremely limited though that field might be). But he recovered quickly. Having riffled disdainfully through a couple of volumes, he delivered judgment of a thrilling severity (and of a remarkably unequivocal kind for one whose examination had lasted no more than a matter of seconds): 'Scissors and paste jobs!'

(As it happened, my own later detailed inspection of Budd's oeuvre did tend to show that that particular stray shot in Gunn's aimless fusillade of instant opinions had uniquely struck somewhere near the mark. Although it wasn't strictly accurate to apply the term scissors and paste to work that had originated with the author – if you gave her the benefit of the doubt on that one – it had to be said that Budd's stupendous output, issued by six separate publishers, *was* nothing more than a recycling exercise, a model example of how to present exactly the same material in seventeen different guises. Not that the blurb for each version failed to claim it as both a new approach and a leap forward – the definitive work. 'The one book every tulip grower...' 'Here at last...' But in an industry so sopping with a supersaturation of practical books such whoppers can perhaps be forgiven.)

This would never do, I thought. We weren't here to discuss Budd and her life-work. The morning was well advanced, we needed to get started. I told Gunn so. Reluctantly, with a frown, he led us outside.

The tulip fields were nothing like those in Monet's paintings – they were far from extensive and colour-saturated (only the later-flowering types were in bloom) – and not one quaintly dressed Dutch girl was in sight. Instead a solitary toiler of the fields awaited us, shirtsleeves rolled up and leaning on a spade. Strawy hair and eyelashes, sun-averse pink face and arms, concave white chest, hand-rolled fag stuck to lower lip, smile of generalised effrontery, smart-aleck corporal to Gunn's snappish major.

'Right,' I forced myself to say, in a let's-get-cracking tone. 'Growing tulips. Simon and I have to take pictures and make notes on every single stage from start to finish.' At 'every single stage' I gazed fixedly at Gunn and his subordinate, who introduced himself as Den. 'So, what's the very first thing you need to do before you plant your bulbs?'

'The – ah – the – ah – very first thing – you – ah – you – ah – need to *do*,' Gunn began, head raised high, addressing the assembled ranks, 'before you – ah – before you – ah – plant your bulbs is to – ah – '

During this transparently temporising rubbish, I saw to my annoyance impatient Den, squinting against and inclining his head back from his fag fumes, rapidly digging a patch of soil as though in a race to find buried treasure. And now he was smoothing the earth over before Simon had even finished unpacking his gear (which in view of its size and complexity was naturally taking some time) or before I had even taken my pen and notebook from my pocket. So much, I thought, for having spelled out to Den beforehand the rules of the game.

'– is to – ah – make sure the – ah – the – ah – *soil* is – ah – '

Jesus.

'– is – ah – up to *scratch*.'

Up to scratch? I waited for some elaboration on this. But Gunn said no more: he'd dealt with that point, now what was next?

'Yeah, well this soil's already up to scratch,' said Den with heavy mock patience, chafing to get everything over with as quickly as possible. He just hadn't got the point, had he? 'It's alkaline.'

Alkaline, alkaline. Chemistry with 'Nasty' Naylor. Litmus paper turning...

'So what if your garden has acid soil?' I asked.

'Lime it first,' said Den.

'Right, we ought to show that,' I said.

Gunn, eagerly grasping at action to avoid the burden of thought, even if it meant forfeiting the opportunity of ordering his NCO to do the job, barked out that he'd get some lime from the store room and marched off.

Den, exhaling smoke, said with his insubordinate's grin, 'Store room? Store room? We haven't kept any lime there for years.' He directed the grin my way, an invitation to share his contempt for his 'betters'. 'It's in the shed!' he called after Gunn.

'While we're waiting,' I told him, 'we'll take some shots of you digging the soil over.'

'I've already done that.'

'Yes, I know, but we need pictures of you doing it.'

'So,' said the wise-guy, taking a last, heavy draw on his fag, 'you don't reckon your readers know how to dig a bit of soil without being shown it, like?' He grinned at Simon this time, shamelessly recasting the role of ally already.

'Well, whether they do or not, our instructions are to record every stage of cultivation, simple or otherwise, and make no exceptions,' I said, more sharply, laying the official-speak on thick, hoping this might prevail upon him where simple language had failed. And, too, I fixed him, reluctantly, almost ashamedly, with 'the look'. I've mentioned before that, as far as I can see, that intended ace only triumphed unfailingly in the old days; imitative overuse seems to have ensured that most receivers of it today return it easily and early, staying in the point. With Den, however, I was surprised to see, it was a clean winner: he tamely averted his gaze and shuffled over to a new patch – though not, I have to admit, without a subdued mime of long-suffering weariness.

As Den redug the soil, in an exaggerated, unnatural way, hot-stuff Simon clicked and whirred away with this lens and that, this filter and that, and from a hundred and one different positions and angles: on tiptoes, crouching, squatting, screwed sideways. It seemed a little excessive. As did the fashion photographer's praise and encouragement for Den's humdrum activity, the simple turning of soil: 'Lovely... Hold it... S'perb... One more time... Lovely...'

He changed film. A whole reel? Already?

'Just few more shots, Den, with fork through... Lovely... S'perb...'

By now Gunn had returned with a bag. He handed it to Den, who immediately scattered some of its contents over the newly dug soil.

'Hang on.' It was Simon's turn. 'Is that lime?'

'Well, it isn't peat,' said Den, grinning at me, in another brazen reordering of his cast. I ignored him, and, reckoning that we certainly needed to know how much lime you would use per square yard, I unthinkingly, foolishly, asked the major.

'How much – ah – how much – ah – lime – ah – per square yard – ah – '

I realised I couldn't put up with much more of this. It was not so much the cluelessness of one who had earlier styled himself a 'technical expert' on tulip growing as his obvious inability to admit it.

'You would – ah – require – ah – not a large – ah – not a large – '

'Three to four ounces,' said Den.

'Exactly,' snapped his commanding officer. 'Ex-actly.'

We got Den to repeat his lime strewing, which he did with all-too-foreseeable ill grace. Then over the next couple of hours, we managed, every so often prompting Gunn, reining back Den, to deal with bulb planting, watering, fertilising and dead-heading – to my astonishment, all the jobs we'd hoped to cover that morning. Simon took the most stirringly unexpected of shots; and I scribbled page after page of notes I fervently hoped I would be able to read the next day.

'Encompassed by nature'

At lunchtime I drove with Simon to a nearby pub. In the sunny garden behind it we found some seats. (The hedges surrounding this garden were of the dense, rich green kind which those around Enid Blyton's house, Green Hedges, had been in the imagination of every child who read *Sunny Stories* but had decidedly not been – so I had recently learned – in real life: there was but a single hedge there, and that a scrawny, dusty, dingy thing. And as for supposedly cosy Green Hedges itself, life within it was certainly far from domestic bliss.) While I pretended to listen to Simon's lunch – some heated account of how he had fought off two would-be muggers on his way home – I actually attuned my ears to the comforting chatter and laughter ebbing and flowing around us and fastened my eyes on the motionless azure shadow a shrub was casting on a nearby white wall. As I did so, I found myself free of all ontological unease, free of all concern with the great dichotomy in our life: that alternation between, on the one hand, an unquestioning, unconcerned absorption in the daily round, in the so *disarmingly specific* everyday elements that make it up, such as what I could see and hear around me now (playful shoves, tilted glasses set aglitter by the sun, 'Oh, you'll love Amalfi!'), and, on the other hand, a not quite so unconcerned mindfulness of the profound currents swirling along beneath them. Unusually, I now felt as serene as that blue shadow on which my gaze remained fixed; all awareness of the deeps was lying doggo. But on another day, in this very same place, there might well have intruded into all the sunlit gaiety a realisation of, say, how all this is slipping unceasingly, ungraspably away from us with every passing second.

As your standard-issue Troubled Being, I considered an apt metaphor for this journey through our days to be skating on thin ice above dark, unplumbable depths. But I had no doubt that for many, for most of the time, the ice appeared happily thicker – though whether naturally so or only as the result of a willed myopia, it wasn't always easy to tell. When, for example, I was drinking with Mega people in the Falstaff or the George, occasionally, very occasionally, someone (though I have to say it was never me) would let fall on to the otherwise smooth, undisturbed surface of the lunch hour one of those whacking great metaphysical stones such as 'But how can we be *absolutely* certain we aren't dreaming it all?' and when that happened it was difficult to know if the unfailingly negative reaction to the crash by spokesmen for the group – whether sidesteppingly flip ('Dreaming it all? Well, in your case, Henry, you're always in a bloody dream') or edgily serious ('Philosophy's banned here, mate') – was the result of a complete lack of interest in that or any other metaphysical stone, through their being 'caught up in and encompassed by nature, the totality of things', as Schopenhauer described it, or was, on the contrary, the result of 'a more luminous moment', in which, unexpectedly, unwillingly detached from 'nature', these spokesmen became 'almost terrified' at the sudden glimpse they had caught of 'the totality' and determinedly turned away.

Today I joined them. As I finished my beer and prepared to leave, I was content not to have experienced on this occasion any luminous moment but instead to have been encompassed by nature.

Back at the nursery, we 'discussed' with Gunn the jobs to be demonstrated that afternoon. The three of us were leaving his office when from a door at the other end of the passage The Girl Can't Help It emerged. I suddenly realised I hadn't thought of her once since our arrival. But now, seeing her again in all her uncalled-for splendour and heading straight towards us, I was again stricken. More of that disconcerting old discontinuity.

As she approached, I felt a need, as urgent as it was absurd, to attract her attention. It so happened that dating back to adolescence one of my inane intermittent daydreams, usually brought on by reading of the sexual conquests of the powerful, had been of myself in some similar position of authority – heading purposefully somewhere, surrounded by obvious acolytes – bestowing upon some ravishing girl chanced upon en route a gentle smile, that of a man kindly for all his consequence, which, tincturing sweetly and potently what was already the aphrodisiac of his obvious power, so overcame her that she was struck by the thunderbolt and was his. Now, I thought, a little beerily optimistic and recalling that to the secretary I was that apparently esteemed creature 'the writer', now was my chance. As soon as I gauged her to be within earshot, I began, in a voice unquestionably louder than necessary, to lay down the ground rules for the demonstrations that were shortly to take place in the fields. I spoke with authority: 'What we simply must avoid... I need to stress...' (As to what needed to be avoided or stressed, I made hasty use of some half-digested scraps of Veronica Budd I'd sleepily forced down me the previous evening.) Ostentatiously prescriptive and emphatic – while affecting such an absorption in what I was saying that I was only vaguely aware of her approach – I wished to convey to Miss Pierce that I would exert on the proceedings that afternoon the grip of a born leader. What's more, as she drew near, I granted her that faint, masterful, absent-minded yet gracious smile I had granted girls before only in reverie.

She gave me not a glance.

Afterwards I was to wonder what she had thought of my absurd posturing – if, that is, she had even so much as noticed it. But as I was never to set eyes on her again – thankfully so, I later thought – I was never to find out. Twice suddenly, powerfully invading my non-consciousness of her, she would, like so much else hankered after for a brief while, soon sink back into the void.

That afternoon we covered lifting, storing, replanting, propagation. With some surprise I realised we'd wrapped it all up.

'Take It Again'

Having long since revoked the ridiculously extreme denials and changes I had forced on myself at the onset of Becoming a Man, I no longer looked like a squaddie in mufti, I had resumed reading fiction and poetry, and, since I was not in training to become one of the guardians of Plato's ideal republic, I was listening to music again. That evening, in nostalgic mood, I put on a record. The first Buddy Rich disc I'd bought, when I was still at school. I played a track I particularly enjoyed. 'Take It Again'. 1943. Listening to the master storming away, thrilling to the rhythm driving through your inner being, you could almost imagine yourself to be Buddy, thrill to the selfsame adrenalin ride (and who knew what other kind) that was powering him through that number, exult to the magisterial command regulating every beat. Suddenly I recaptured the joy I had felt listening to that track with Danny and his drummer friend years before. Joy at the virility, the almost preternatural skill, the perfect rhythm (the same joy at the same qualities I'd recently re-experienced when watching Gene Kelly clatter-dancing on roller skates in *It's Always Fair Weather*), joy that set my stickless hands throbbing with the feeling that they were producing that seamless surge of sound themselves. It was another of those identifications with genius at full throttle – like that I'd experienced reading certain pages of Master – that are so absolute, exclusive and profound that they give you the fleeting illusion of possessing genius yourself. As I sat listening entranced once more, I wished that that track, extensive though it was already, would never end. Who hasn't on certain journeys felt...?

Temporarily inspired in this way, and recalling my own highs on the drums in the past, I began to wonder: might I not be following the wrong path in trying to write, might I not be lacking in the necessary talent (that is, the *special* talent that lifts you out of the ruck and justifies the struggle), might not my real ability, if I possessed any, lie instead, who knew, in that driving, pounding activity that was now so galvanising me?

Office Cobblers

McStutt glanced up briefly from his desk at my approach, then continued with his ostentatiously rapid pencilled comments on the pages before him. He kept me waiting a good half minute. The usual fatuous I-boss-you-minion routine. Eventually he put his pencil down, then went into his other favourite number: the thrown back head and faint smile of hauteur. I told him I'd completed my first batch of copy. I placed it on his desk. Tulips, my fourth and final draft. Conscious that it was to be the prototype for future text and captions, I'd worked hard on it, whittling down my raw material to as clear and succinct a why-and-how-you-did-it as the designers' usual cavalier constraints and deformations of space would allow.

'I've tried to cover everything you need to know, as concisely as possible,' I said. 'I'll leave it with you.' Since it was an important test run, McStutt would need to study it, gauge this aspect and that, query this point and that, before deciding whether it fitted the bill or not.

I was about to turn and leave the room when I saw him pick up the copy and start to whizz through it. Somewhere along the line he'd come to believe he was the possessor of an exceptional mental gift: the ability to appraise any piece of text in a flash. *Any* piece – no matter what its subject matter, its form, its complexity. He considered this as much his special forte as Plumpford considered startlingly pertinent queries his. Ah, self-delusions. And so outlandish are so many of them (not least our own) that who knows where they could possibly have originated? What, for example, could first have given McStutt of all people the idea that he could *gut* copy? Perhaps it was implanted in his brain in the way these fancies quite commonly are – by some soft-soap sycophant ('Whew, Willie, you sure do get to the nub of a piece in no time!'); and, pleasurably surprised by the idea, enamoured of it, McStutt had fed and watered it until it was now the monstrous thing it was. Who knew? Who cared?

Unwilling to watch another self-conscious demonstration of his special talent, I made for the door. But, reaching it, I wasn't decisive enough – against my better judgment, I glanced back. I was still too young to realise that *you scarcely ever get away with against-your-better-judgment stuff*, you've got to be on the ball *non-stop*. McStutt, once more ready to be shaved, sighting me down his snub barrels, kept slowly, melodramatically crooking a forefinger at me to summon me back, to the accompaniment of the familiar croaked 'er-heh-heh, er-heh-heh'.

I returned and he resumed his lightning 'assimilation' and 'assessment' of each detailed page of text and captions. I was almost on the brink of cutting short his performance with a peremptory 'Next!' when I was distracted by a view that a half-open window gave of an inner courtyard below. The light, the shadows, the reflections in this cloistered place had often acted for me, gazing down into it from the windows of other offices, as a guide to what sort of scenes the world beyond it – Regency Place, the surrounding streets, Hyde Park – would be presenting at that moment. Now, in mid-morning, it did so again, with various pointers: on the side opposite McStutt's office a weathered yellowbrick wall – not really yellow at all but of subtly variegated pale ochre, dun and mauve – was now beaming over at me, the pocks in its face heartwarmingly casting tiny shadows within themselves; then, at the foot of this wall, twin green wooden-slatted polygonal tubs, each containing a lollipop bay (for whose compact, leathery-leaved charms I'd always had a soft spot, especially those outside Piero's), demonstrated, by their unusually pronounced tonal changes from slat to slat (ranging all the way from lime green at one extreme to near black at the other), just how strong the light probably was Out There; then, even if less dramatically – with more muted greens and smoother transitions from light to dark – the two loose cones of bay leaves above the tubs repeated the demonstration, confirmed the glad news; and finally, the windows in a shadowy side wall exhibited, in a row of midnight blue rectangles touched by a few wisps of iron grey, a series of snapshots which, though profoundly underexposed, captured as faithfully as if they were not – and somehow more pleasingly – what was barely visible from my viewpoint, the serene cirrus-brushed azure on high.

It all added up to a reading today of Set Fair.

These signs of what lay beyond, together with the warm current of air wafting in through the window so deliciously, bringing with it vague memories of comics lazily read on similarly balmy mornings, seemed further to mock McStutt's posturing – and, come to that, all Office Cobblers. How reluctantly I returned my attention to the man with the razor-sharp intellect. He'd finished with the copy already. He'd evaluated in a trice its approach, its comprehensiveness, its consistency, its entire content – on a subject he knew as little about as I once had – and was about to pass judgment. First pouting a few kisses at me, he proclaimed, the *o*s and *a*s even more prim and proper than usual: 'An old stager is pleased to inform you that – er-heh-heh – this is' – he lightly tapped the copy with two knuckles of an upturned hand – 'a creditable first attempt – er-heh-heh, er-heh-heh. But I think it needs a little more work, more elaboration of various points – er-heh-heh.'

'More elaboration?' I tried to manage an even tone. 'The designers haven't allowed any room for that. I've had to – '

'And some of the captions need to be more explicit – er-heh-heh – and others, I feel, not quite so explicit – er-heh-heh.'

'Well, there again, you must know that every caption has to be exactly the same length. So that you have to cut some bits of information to the bone and pad others out. It's not what I'd – '

'Yes, well, have another crack at it and let me see it again.'

Let me see it again. Well, now. Well, now... I remembered what I'd done on the later stages of the Fish book when he'd made the same demand: I'd resubmitted the material unaltered. McStutt, assessing it with the usual masterful rapidity, had pronounced it a marked improvement. I must repeat the same trick. And in the meantime I could be getting on with real work, the next of the fearsome number of assignments stacked up ahead.

Out There?

One evening, when Sally was at her Italian class and the boys were in bed, I decided to play some of the record collection I'd built up over the years and then abandoned for so long. I made an initial selection from records I'd bought in my youth, those records that not just in the music they release but in their very physical appearance – sleeve design, label colour, even the width of ungrooved vinyl at the centre – can poignantly return to us the very atmosphere, indescribable in words, of the time when we first played and kept playing them.

Looking through them, the pop, the rock, the jazz, the classical, I couldn't decide what to put on first. Perhaps Poulenc's *Les Biches*, whose lovely evocation, in some of its movements, of an Arcadia in the age of the Sun King helped form, together with such pieces as Ravel's *Le Tombeau de Couperin*, Debussy's *Petite Suite* and Fauré's *Masques et Bergamasques*, that foolishly idealised France, la Belle France, in which, as well as in other daydream worlds, I had once mooned so happily. Or should it be 'Krupa's Wail', that superhuman performance on the drums whose power, invention, electricity and technical mastery had once driven me almost crazy with excitement and envy? Or one of those Schumann piano works – such as the *Six Canonic Studies*, simple, beautiful, with that grand bass again, especially when heavily accented on forte pianos – that had been among my first loves, windows into a soul at once noble, sweet and painfully vulnerable? Or that Gershwin piano medley replete with exhilaration yet longing I'd first heard in the street one hot afternoon... Or a Beatles, Stones or Beach Boys single? The magnificent hymnal 'Penny Lane'? That stirring fusion of sexual drive and wistful melody, 'Let's Spend the Night Together'? The celestial 'God Only Knows'? Finally, I decided on that intermezzo from *The Jewels of the Madonna* which I used to believe, but could never be sure, I had first heard late one summer's afternoon at the Rectory. I wondered again: could it really have been there and then that I first became drunk with its magical strains? If so, had I heard them coming through one of the open windows? From a radio or gramophone someone was playing? But if so, who? I now thought it possible – probable even? – that I had first come across that music at a later date, that my subconscious had found it a fitting idealised-late-summer-afternoon, light-and-shade-saturated, glorious-yet-mysterious accompaniment to my memories of the Rectory garden and had steeped them in it and that forever afterwards the two became one, the version incorporating the Wolf-Ferrari taking over from the original, as the musical adaptation of a play sometimes supersedes in popularity the original drama, which then ceases to be performed.

I lowered the stylus and immediately, as soon as the first notes sounded, I entered again the enchanted world for which that intermezzo was the unique and, so it seemed to me, the only possible musical setting. Indissolubly fused with the patterned light and shade of the Rectory lawn, shrubberies and trees, throbbing with hot golden sunlight and dark velvety shadows and, above this, wistfully proclaiming something beautiful, wise but sad about the depth of that sunlight and that shade, something with a hint in it of age-old sylvan myth, something I was tantalisingly unable to discern, that music pained me with its beauty. (It was a beauty, however, that received no mention whenever, rarely, the piece was played on air or written about in record guides, so that I realised with lonely surprise that this music was far from special for everyone – a realisation of that kind to which we find every passing year brings fresh sad reinforcements.)

As this intermezzo continued to transport me away from the everyday, I noted at one slightly less displaced moment that it seemed to have no connection at all with its source, the disc rotating before me, to have transcended such mundanities, to have broken free from and be floating above what had brought it into being. You had the illusion it had acquired self-contained independence, an independence permanent, inviolable and – as, lost in it, you forgot everything else – sovereign.

A world independent, permanent, inviolable, sovereign? A world that had some sort of objective reality, even if one scarcely glimpsable? A world beyond the life we knew? Something that was Out There? Or a world which had no existence outside the envelope of the self? A world whose only being was within our head, where it had been created? Just something that was In Here?

That was the big question. A very big question. And this seesawing between one viewpoint and the other – the intellectualisation of two conflicting yet equally potent intuitions – chafes every thinking person. When Proust's narrator, for example, explores the effects upon Swann and himself of Vinteuil's music, he seems to have faith in the real existence of a 'divine world', a 'realm of angels' from which the music has descended like some 'supernatural creature'; he speaks of 'the joys of the next world'. But elsewhere, in a vaguer passage, his thoughts confront him with 'the other hypothesis, the materialist one, that of nothingness'. However, in what is more or less his last word on the subject, he seems to reassert his faith in the 'invisible reality' of the music when he speaks of 'its mysteries whose explanations are probably to be found only in other worlds'.

At first while I was listening to that piece from *The Jewels of the Madonna*, I too *felt* with all my soul that it emanated from a world that existed independently of me, a lovely world in which the music and the sunlit pre-infected Rectory garden that returned to me were one. I *felt* this, yes, but then, at a certain point, my familiar old reductionist self stepped in and argued otherwise. That world was, wasn't it, despite what I *felt*, not self-sufficient at all but dependent on that labelled vinyl disc I could see before me, which in its turn had been dependent on a group of ordinary men and women playing instruments in a studio, on a tape that recorded the sound signals they had produced, on a process that transformed these signals into grooves on a master disc, on a subsequent process that had involved silver nitrate, electroplating, nickel shell, sodium dichlorate and heated PVC plastic before the actual record I was playing could be manufactured, and which was now, that disc, dependent on the stylus, turntable, inner wiring and speakers of my record player. From this perspective, the musical world that seemed to transcend the mundane specifics that had brought it into being was on the contrary utterly reliant on them.

These musings did not last long however. There came a particularly ecstatic bird-like trilling on the flute and, all my severely rationalist reflections now forgotten, I was swept back into the world of ineffable mysterious beauty from which that call sounded...

Then, with disconcerting suddenness, the music stopped and the room was plunged into darkness. A power cut. My previous thoughts returned to me, this time with added force. The music had ceased *on the instant*, in mid-phrase; the silence, more complete, more importunate, than it would have been if it had not been preceded by the music, and accompanied by an equally abrupt blackness, had a quality almost of malevolence: beauty banished, supplanted by mocking emptiness. That world that had seemed at the time sovereign, far above all temporal concerns – why, a mere interruption in the flow of electrical current had been enough to extinguish it. Not, of course, that it had even needed a power cut to do that. I could, if I'd wanted to, have deliberately switched everything off myself and achieved the same physical and psychological effect, with the additional proof that, far from the music holding sway over me, I held absolute sway over it. It was that same effect, that same proof, as when, alone late at night watching a lively television programme whose colour, movement, chatter and laughter so proclaim at that moment its dominance over us, over our surroundings, we rise and suddenly switch it off in mid-flow. Then how easily and swiftly that bright animated world, that had seemed so established, self-sufficient, secure, collapses into darkness, is dispatched into the black void, how shocking is the absoluteness of its absence and how unhappily we are made aware of its essential impotence.

So, I reflected, not only might the world I'd briefly re-entered listening to this music have been completely without substance, existing not in the least Out There but only In Here, but the music that gave rise to that world, whatever the nature of this, was itself all too vulnerable.

And yet, when the power was restored a few minutes later and the lights came on and the music, after an initially groggy, growling resumption from where it had left off, sounded forth clearly again, I soon, forgetting the unwelcome interruption of a short time ago, re-entered its world once more and found myself scarcely able to believe that one so beautiful and inductive to such intense feelings could not have some independent reality, found myself wondering once again whether, by some means my rational mind could not fathom, it did indeed, this world, transcending all the mundanities that appear to govern access to it, lie beyond them.

Orchids

Underground Drainage, Rock Gardens, Lilies, Cold Frames... Simon and I were scampering from one demonstration to another, I filling notebook after notebook with scarcely decipherable scrawls, he getting through an almost obscene quantity of film. And so far only Tulips had emerged as final copy. Coping alone, we were apparently still 'pioneering the necessary techique'. Plumpford, seeking to impress Sharpes and the rest of the board as the meanest budget-whittler ever known at Mega, was keeping on hold the rest of the 'team' we were 'spearheading'.

During the Rock Gardens assignment I experienced again what I had occasionally known on the Medical book. The Underground Drainage demonstrator had been brusque and inarticulate, and before him I had had to deal with incompetent

Gunn and bolshie Den. So how pleasurable it was to find Edmund Stolon such an amiable, helpful man. As Simon said at the time: 'G'*lord*, Xav, what a turn-up if we could get more dem'stators like that Rock chap.' Yes, indeed, what a turn-up and I felt towards 'that Rock chap' both fondness and gratitude. But, as I'd done before, with those medical contributors who had, exceptionally, cut the mustard, I then, speaking of him to others, heaped on Edmund Stolon laud more befitting a candidate for sainthood than simply an accommodating plantsman. In this I observed in myself something of that counterfeit that you saw full-blown in Simon's 'rages'. But even arrived at this self-awareness I persisted – because, as I've noted before, a curmudgeon doesn't give up lightly his rare opportunities to over-enthuse.

I had now, interrupting my third draft of Underground Drainage, to embark on another reporting job, Orchids. And I had learned that the demonstrator was to be none other than Pleione Bark-Chipping, that imposing-sounding horticulturalist second cousin of Olivia's I'd heard about at the Rectory years before (a name like that couldn't fail to stick in your memory).

Pleione Bark-Chipping. Yet another example of that possible nominative determinism I'd noted at Lea & Lyle in the case of Angela Adder. There had also been, in Blackwell, an A. De'ath & Sons, funeral directors; in Bexcray, a Maggie Flowers, florist; at Traditional Homebake, Les Baker, 'the Baker's Baker'; on the Fish book, Roger Wrasse and Andrew Stingray; and on the Medical Book, Ivan Orbit, Barrington Eyre-Waye and Denis Capsule. And now, on the Gardening book – and reminiscent of such notables of the past as Roy Hay and Alan Bloom – there were Derek Seedtray, the annuals man, Trevor Tortrix-Moth, the pests and diseases expert, Edmund Stolon, and this latest addition, Bark-Chipping. Even so, as we know, this apparent auto-suggestion, this apparent subconscious urge to befit one's name, only affects some. Statistics, I'm sure, would show that in fact there are, for instance, far more Seedtrays, Tortrix-Moths, Stolons and Bark-Chippings who have not taken up gardening professionally than those who have.

About Orchids I had some misgivings. I had discovered from preliminary research that they are a vast, a complex and, as Beerbohm said of the Oedipuses, a tense and peculiar family, one likely to make life difficult for any hack chronicler of their upbringing. For a start, there was the size of that family: *25,000* species, *100,000* hybrids! Then there were the strange tribes they're split up into: some, it's true, are simple folk of the soil, but others hang about in trees, while yet others camp out on rocks. And then once you've adopted them and have to lodge them under glass you're dealing not with simple eager-to-please creatures like tulips but with the awkward squad: some insist on this type of house, others that; some this amount of light, others that; some this way of feeding, others that; some this sort of grub, others... You get the picture.

What's more, some of them were not just ornery, they were downright sinister: 'nasty things' whose 'flesh is too much like the flesh of men', as the General in *The Big Sleep* put it, whose 'perfume has the rotten sweetness of a prostitute' (boy, for someone who chose to grow them, he sure did hate them); monstrous things, too, in some cases, like that cypripedium Des Esseintes in *Against Nature* disgustedly likened to the underside of a tongue attached to a glossy pocket case oozing viscous paste. All right, so some of them were lookers, but I was sure they were bad-news lookers, Delilah lookers, Helen of Troy lookers, *Some Dames Spell Trouble* lookers.

And when Simon and I visited Bark-Chipping at her Sussex home and asked her to demonstrate to us how to grow her preposterous charges, it soon became obvious that she would be of little help. Sweating profusely in the near-lethal temperature of her vast greenhouse, wild-eyed behind her specs, wild-haired, constantly distracted by the grievances of her 'little darlings', her little terrors ('not enough shading', 'compost too moist', 'compost too dry'), who dangled from the roof or watched us from staging or crouched in baskets or clung freakishly to rafts of fibre, she resisted all my efforts to wrench her exposition into some coherent order, or even into something I could make the least sense of.

To Simon, of course, none of this presented any problems. He snapped away as enthusiastically as ever, capturing Bark-Chipping on the move from one mysterious task to another, while I, swabbing my brow and envying matt Simon (it wasn't just he had no need of food, *he didn't sweat either*), at one moment attempted to differentiate odontiodas, odontonias, odontocidiums and odontoglossums (to all of which she made abstracted, fleeting, vague reference) and at another interposed a half-hearted 'But I thought you said dendrobiums flowered on jointed stems' or a weary 'But you're leaving *six* pseudobulbs on that one'. The tone of those remarks told its own story, as did my pencilled notes, which had become (as on my very first, tyro's reporting job) increasingly sparse, disconnected, *faint*.

Plumpford, it may be remembered, had decreed we base our entire text on first-hand observation of the experts, on watching them propping, cropping and lopping, clipping, tipping and stripping, sowing, hoeing and mowing (cripes, I must take a firm hold on myself, fight off these attacks of the mechanical rhyming triad, so beloved of Mega Books and resurgent once more as I relive those days). Any other method of producing the copy was absolutely out. Well, OK, reportage was fine as long as it worked. But in this case it obviously didn't. So Plumpford's categorical ban had to be given the boot (I visualised his pop-eyed outrage): since Bark-Chipping had been unable to provide intelligible information verbally, I must ask her to send me it in writing.

The most devastating

One morning during a coffee break, while McStutt was at a meeting, I was looking through his *Telegraph* when downpage a glimpsed 'Richborough' drew my attention.

GIRL MAY HELP
FIND BOY'S KILLERS

Police in Richborough, Surrey, are appealing to a young blonde girl in a grey duffel coat to come forward to help them with their investigations into the murder last Thursday of Zack Trennell, 16, a clerk, of Parkland Avenue, Richborough.

They believe the girl must have seen a group of four youths who followed Trennell and his cousin after they left a friend's birthday party. The two parted about a quarter of a mile from Trennell's house.

Trennell was found lying dead in a pool of blood on the pavement in Walfield Road, less than...

Walfield Road.

He had been stabbed repeatedly in the back, chest and neck. A resident of Walfield Road heard a cry at about...

Walfield Road.
Wallflowers, sunlight, heat, Olivia, a golden stillness...
Walfield Road.
A relentless knife, agony, terror...

The shooting at Kingsdon St Mary primary school, the Nazi warplane crashing in the grounds of the Rectory, the IRA bomb explosion in Pembertons – all defilements of what had once seemed pure, but none had been as devastating to me as now was the pollution of this murder. This murder committed perhaps on that very pavement that always received the afternoon sun, in view of that pillar box and post office that glowed on the corner…perhaps right outside that garden whose wallflowers sent out such fragrance.

I sat there staring at the page. And it was some time before I could break away from the images that confronted me and return to my work.

Topsy-turveydom

The comprehensive written account of orchid growing I'd requested from Pleione Bark-Chipping lay open before me on my desk. To my horror, I'd discovered that the wild-eyed one's musings in the study were just as impenetrable as they'd been in the greenhouse. As I gazed at this latest 'challenge', as I unhappily considered the labour that would be needed to try to make something intelligible of 'Orchids for the Amateur' (memories of the scandalous offerings of Barry L. Horrey and Hector Wills on *True 'Tec Tales* returned to me), the task seemed similar to that of reconstructing a public garden laid out by a lunatic: an attempt to re-lay paths that kept doubling back on themselves, to hack through deeply impenetrable hedges that sealed off key areas, to resite or remove signposts that gave conflicting directions or sometimes pointed to nowhere…

Gradually I lapsed into a state familiar to me from my pre-Mega working life, those days spent counting nuts, bolts and washers at Cattalls and totting up columns of grocery prices at Lea & Lyle. My hand and the pencil in it long hovered motionless over our orchid expert's surrealist work, and anyone observing me would have been alarmed to detect in me no apparent sign of life.

Suddenly I realised that, mesmerised into immobility, I was allowing myself to remain trapped most unManfully in Bark-Chipping's topsy-turveydom. I had to do something sharpish.

Summoning up all my strength, I jerked up my head and hurled the manuscript away from me.

There was only one thing for it. On Monday, his regular day for coming into Mega, I would have to seek help from the recently appointed general consultant on our book. Raymond Blight. *That* Raymond Blight, whose august designations on the title page of Harry's *Ultimate Guide to Lawnmowing* and his column in the *Warp* had so impressed me as a boy. A mythic figure who bestrode horticulture's remotest peak. Crumbs, I could never have imagined when I lived at 33 Danehill Road that one day I would be picking up the phone, as I did now, and leaving a message that I wished to book a meeting with the great man.

I wondered whether...

I sat on the balcony of our maisonette, relishing the genial morning that had succeeded heavy overnight rain, hearing the Saturday midday time signal on the kitchen radio squirt out, like droplets of juice, the same certain if unspecified lunchtime promise as when I used to hear it as a boy. I'd slept well; admired over breakfast Sally's tone, her glowing skin and gleaming eyes; experienced, as I played with my sons, a daddy's doting pride in them; managed to replace a defective bathroom light switch and ceiling rose all by myself; and savoured the prospect of being free of Mega for two whole days. I was brimming with that young man's boon (insufficiently valued at the time, natch): a scarcely containable animal vitality. So brilliant did I feel, as brilliant as the morning around me, that, like the hero of my book driving into Carmine, I had the illusion I could achieve almost anything I wanted to.

I had brought a pad and my notes for that book on to the balcony with me. My mental zest would undoubtedly enable me to tackle at last that early chapter about the junta setting up a paramilitary police force, the SPO, to crush all opposition to the regime. Feeling as brilliant as I did, how could I write it other than brilliantly and at speed?

But half an hour later all that I had before me was a several times rewritten opening paragraph that I would probably scrub anyway. Despite all my efforts, I was finding it impossible to fuse the mundane details of organised resistance and political repression with the heightened awareness of a poetic vision and the pervasive sense of an underlying mystery. Well, it *was* impossible, wasn't it? But no, it wasn't. Of course it wasn't. Because, if you substituted a setting of municipal corruption for one of city-state tyranny, *that fusion was exactly what Master had achieved.* So why couldn't I achieve it, no matter how hard I tried?

Turning aside, looking down over the balcony (the maisonettes were built on two floors and ours was on the upper), I found my gaze drawn for the third time that morning to a neighbouring garden, to a sort of bower that lay at the end of it. This was formed by the crumbling rear wall of the garden – old, rustic-looking red brick, weathered here and there to rose and limy white – and by two flanking apple trees, gnarled and equally rustic-looking, whose upper branches met in a canopy. When I'd first come out on to the balcony this alcove had been, with the sun directly behind it, in deep shadow, but at noon, as the sun reached its highest point above it, first the mossed masonry on top of the wall had flickeringly lit up, then the edges of those upper bricks not perfectly flush with the rest had become slivers of luminous pink. Now, as I looked again, with the sun past its zenith and penetrating the crowns of the apple trees, more and more of the brickwork was illuminated, its vaguely ruddy dimness daubed with an increasing number of peachy patches, which oscillated gently, as every so often a soft breeze stirred the drooping foliage. Ah, sheltered, sunlit, basking brickwork, ever since I first saw you as quivering backdrop to the wallflowers in Dean and Olivia's garden so many years ago, how you have always been, of all the visible signs of warmth a languorous day displays, one of those I have cherished most.

As I sat watching its slowly changing patterns of light and shade, this rural-seeming arbour, which contrasted so markedly with the urban scene beyond it, exerted a tremendous charm on me. I felt a strong desire to capture it forever in paint, a revival of an urge I'd known first at school and then at intervals since. I wondered whether perhaps that was what I should have been...a painter...

Reluctantly, I returned to my police state, tried once more to bring it to life in a paragraph infused with that special Masterian 'something'. But as I looked away from the page again, this time to ponder a dull detail – the kind of file the SPO might keep on suspects – I found my attention distracted again, this time by what I could see before me on the balcony. Most of the overnight rain on its uneven surface had by now been dried out by the bright sun and breeze, but in a hollow beyond the red geraniums in a central urn the largest puddle still remained. Shrinking only slowly, dark and glistening in what around it was pale and matt, the rainwater (like those shadowy windows overlooking the inner courtyard at Mega) reflected the cloud-wisped sky almost colourlessly, like a black-and-white print – though one that now and then trembled and lost its resolution ever so slightly, as though still in the developing tank – a monochrome reinforced by tiny daggers of silver flashing from the wet leaves and grit at its edge. The geraniums were flowering, flaring, midway between that puddle and myself. Their petals, of the purest vermilion and, because the sun was full on them, devoid of any modelling, seemed cut from some richly dyed silk. This vibrant colour and its cool, classical colourless background, each intensifying the character of the other, formed one of those contrasts used in photography to maximise interest in an outdoor scene, the one commonly seen on picture postcards: for example, in the foreground a crimson azalea ablaze, in the distance a soft blue bay asleep. I felt I should get my camera and try to capture the vivacity of that contrast. A photographer? Perhaps that rather than a painter?

In what I saw before me it wasn't just that particular contrast I found pleasurable. Focussing my eyes on those red petals, so that they were clear-cut and their background a blur, then voyaging visually beyond them, to find a new focal point in the puddle, now in its turn sharply defined, with the flowers just smudges, then making the return journey to render once more the flowers distinct and the puddle indistinct, I took a conscious enjoyment in that faculty we normally exercise only unthinkingly, that stereoscopic vision with which nature has endowed us, which enables us to locate so swiftly the depth of objects in space. A cinematographer's enjoyment rather than a photographer's...? I wondered whether...

Underminings

The door opened narrowly and Lil's face appeared.

'Oh, it's you,' she said. 'Come in. I thought when I heard the knock it was some more of them bloody charity collectors. Bastards. War on Want or some sodding thing. Pictures of all these darkies. They look better fed than what I am.' I followed her down the dingy hallway, whose matting, worn when I was a kid, was now threadbare. 'There's only one of 'em I ever give to and that's the RSPCA, bless 'em.'

Tibbles, the cat Lil had acquired just before I left home, appeared. Sometimes he refused to leave the house on a cold night. Then Lil kicked him out hard: 'Get *out*, you bastard.' He now swept his flank against my leg with sensuous firmness.

'He remembers you,' Lil said. Then, solemnly, as though revealing a profound personal discovery, not reciting an old biddy's bromide: 'They're better than human beings any day, cats are.' She picked up the squirmingly resistant Tibbles with difficulty. 'He loves me, he understands me, he does.'

'He loves – ' ('He loves your Kit-e-Kat, he understands your boot' was what I'd been about to say, but I checked the cruel truth just in time and scrabbled around for something else) ' – attention,' I finished, not very plausibly, considering the ferocity of Tibbles' struggles.

But Lil was oblivious to this. 'He *does* love attention,' she said, as he finally escaped and ran off.

We went into the back room. Every time I re-entered it, that familiar old oh-so-33-Danehill-Road smell of damp assailed me and awoke so many memories – memories that were a strange amalgam of the sombre and the radiant.

I sat down on the cat's-hair-covered put-u-up and asked Lil how she was, how her job was. I was just going through the motions. Her story was always – not unlike one of those basic *Film Fun* plots – the same old story. In her case, though, the same miserable old story. She'd had a hard life, I knew, but did *everything* have to be a grievance, a trouble, a pain? As refracted through the darkened prism of that mind and soul, I suppose it did.

This week's issue: 'That little swine next door, the racket he kicks up... Me back's absolutely killing me... Another bloody darkie's moved in at number twenty-five...' (no doubt 'lowering the tone' of Danehill Road, which these days had broken out in a rash of pebbledash, carriage lamps and brightly coloured new front doors). 'That bloody meal at that do last week, it give me the runs. I got caught short and...'

Knowing that this woman who had so often informed me 'You're not sensitive like I am' would always try to paint you as faithful a picture as possible of her many disorders,

416

conscientiously seeking exactitude when it came to the details, I swiftly switched her on to another track with some questions about the Prince Albert. New brewers had taken it over, it had a new name, the Cat and Powder Monkey, and Lil now worked for a new landlord.

'Oh, him, the sod... He's the brother of that bloody Marge whatsername, who tried to diddle me out of me proper change last week... Anyway, he ask me to polish the counter twice yesterday, twice, the bastard. So I...'

I tuned in again a few minutes later, as the detection device still somewhere at work in such cases informed me that the litany was nearing its end.

'...so why can't sodding Herbie Bolitho do it hisself?'

'Exactly. Why can't he?' I commiserated. I had no idea who Herbie Bolitho was or what it was he should, or possibly should not, have been doing himself. 'I'd have a word with him.'

I passed through the scullery into the sunken little back yard, where Danny and I used to play basketball-score football and blow bubbles. The reason for my call was to see to the shed – its roof was leaking. Inside was the familiar old hoarded junk: the rusted, the mildewed, the broken-limbed. From behind a seized-up mangle, its cogs stained orange-tan, I tugged out the roll of bitumen felt and clout nails I'd bought a few years back to carry out a similar repair. In doing so, I knocked over a lidless cardboard box behind them, and various bits and pieces fell out. As I bent to put them back, I noticed among them a small tarnished steel trophy cup and two small wooden shields.

I crouched down on the floor to examine them. Engraved on the cup was: FLYWEIGHT CHAMPION 2nd BATTN THE BUFFS 1925 L/CPL LEONARD AMES, followed by two further engraved dates, 1926 and 1927. And on the inlaid steel plate of one shield: MILE WINNER 2nd BATTN ATHLETICS CHAMPIONSHIPS 1926 L/CPL L. AMES, and on that of the other the same inscription for the year 1927. The name Ames was unfamiliar to me, but the Leonard had to be Uncle Len, didn't it? And if that was so, then his saga of unchecked sporting prowess had been true after all. And he had lived not in that mysterious atemporal aspatial sphere in which I had always situated him but all along in the known world that the rest of us inhabited, the world of actual places, actual dates, actual events. And the challengers to his titles, Millsy, Rawlings, Banksy, Dobbo, previously such notional wraith-like creatures, now also acquired solidity, took on panting bodily form, settled themselves in a specific location at a specific point in time.

First Mr Banks, in his manifestation as panto dame, confounding my long-held image of him. Now Uncle Len, in his manifestation as sporting-trophy-winner, doing likewise. What next? Gauguin-sands-appreciating Harry as a Sunday painter? Simon actually embroiled in one electrifying drama after another? McStutt on alto sax leading the McStutt Five into another rousing number? It was another of those tremors, those intermittent underminings of impressions, beliefs, judgments that previously seemed to us so stable.

But if these trophies were indeed Uncle Len's, what were they doing here in this shed? After I'd finished repairing the roof (to which Lil's only response was a complaint that the felt strips weren't absolutely straight), I asked her.

'Oh, when he went back to Sid's,' (Sid?) 'he didn't collect all the stuff he left with Molly.' (Molly?) 'When she went into the home she ask me to take it and he'd collect it later. But that was years ago. I don't know where he is now.'

The figure of Uncle Len now acquired for me an unexpected pathos, that of the lonely impoverished bachelor, haplessly shifting from one take-you-in-for-a-while distant relative to another.

Etc., etc.

Lil put the kettle on for tea and while we waited for it to boil she began ironing. She tested the heat of the iron with a wet finger and there was a faint hiss.

A faint hiss. I lay in bed on the put-u-up, blanketing out the sickly light overhead. Lil was ironing. After a while we heard a key scratch uncertainly at the front door. It continued so long that I started giggling. But I stopped sharpish when the door slammed loudly shut and heavy, uncertain footsteps sounded down the hallway. A fumbling at the doorknob. Then he lurched in, smeary-eyed, face even pastier than usual.

'What time do you call this?' Lil demanded. 'Never mind the sodding money you must have been pouring down the drain!'

'Listen, that's *my* money.' He tapped his chest, kept tapping it. '*I* earn it. And if I want a fucking drink, I'll have one.'

Oh, no.

'A drink you call it? A drink? You stay in the sodding Albert all sodding day – ' Then with that bloodcurdling inhuman shriek which I'd learned to dread and hate as the inevitable prelude to violence, and which my child's mind considered so unnecessary, wilful, gratuitous even: ' – *and you call that having a drink?*'

'Now listen,' he said with obvious menace, swaying slightly. 'I'm not putting up with any of *that*. D'you understand, you cow?' He advanced towards her.

'Don't you come near me or I'll put this iron on you.'

'You wouldn't fucking dare.' He faced her across the ironing board, finger jabbing at her.

'Wouldn't I, you *bastard*?' The stressed syllable was an even more insane screech.

She thrust the iron at him.

Oh, no, you shouldn't have done that, you shouldn't have done that.

Drink-dulled, he didn't withdraw his hand in time. There was the faint hiss of hot metal on flesh. He jerked the hand to his mouth.

'*You fucking cow!*'

He sent the ironing board flying. She staggered back and dropped the iron. Almost falling himself, he grabbed her wrists and gasped, 'I'll kill you for that, I'll fucking kill you.'

He swung her off balance, and she crashed to the floor, etc., etc.

Etc., etc.

I drank my tea.

'How're you getting on these days?' Lil asked perfunctorily, holding up a flannel nightdress to see if she'd pressed it enough.

'Fine, thanks.' I got up to go. 'You must come round to our place again soon for lunch or tea.'

'I will. But don't get any of that bloody smoked stuff – Polish, was it? – you got last time.'

'No, OK.'

We exchanged 'byes and pecks on the cheek. I left.

Blight

When Simon and I reverentially entered the office of Raymond Blight, it was to find a man who bore an unsettlingly close resemblance to the elderly Arthur Askey. Reclining in a chair, with brass-buttoned blazer draped over its back and his feet up on a pulled-out desk drawer, he was drinking tea, eating cake and doing the crossword in the *Warp*.

The room, wood-panelled, expensively furnished, was part of the directors' suite, given over to Blight's use on the odd days he came in. The desk top looked remarkably, enviably clear: just a telephone, the tea things, an empty In tray and an Out tray containing a single sheaf of typewritten pages. It was a carbon copy of Bark-Chipping's orchids 'article' that I'd sent Blight by internal mail. On the top page I saw to my astonishment the simple scribbled pencil comment, presumably by Blight: 'OK'.

Our consultant seemed in cheery mood, understandably so for one on a rate of, I estimated (working from his reputed daily fee and with the expertise of a former 24-pkts-Spratts-Ovals-at-1s 9½d man), two quid a clue. (Or, to be more accurate, those were my thoughts later. At that moment I was far from harbouring such lese-majesty.)

'Come in, you chaps,' he said airily, in his light Welsh singsong, remaining at semi-supine ease. 'Take a pew. Call me Ray, by the way – I'm no Mr High-and-mighty. Well, what can I do for you?'

He appeared then to have forgotten already the note I'd attached to the Bark-Chipping pages? And my telephone call checking that he was still free for our appointment and informing him briefly of what it was about? Odd. One wouldn't have said it was due to pressure of work. Respectfully, I reminded him that we needed the answers to a great many questions on the subject of orchid growing.

His brow rose in surprise, he indicated what was in his Out tray, said, 'All there, isn't it? Nice piece, I thought.'

Nice piece. Nice piece. He couldn't have read it. Could he?

'Well, there are various points in it that aren't completely clear to Simon and me,' I explained euphemistically. 'And we need to get them cleared up. Urgently,' I added, seeing no change in his posture, his expression.

His response was a pensive look, silence, then a decisive reaching for the phone, the dialling of an internal number and, after an impatient wait ('Come on, come *on*'), the summoning of further refreshment. He spoke of what excellent tea and cake the Mega directors' Betty made, of how it beat hollow Amy's at the Meridian Gardening School – of which, he added as an apparent afterthought, he had been honoured to have once been the principal. I had a reluctant suspicion that, just as many a mystery story writer conceives his solution first and only then invents the plot leading up to it (that, apparently, was how Master had written *Mosaic*), so Blight's seeming supplement about his principalship had preceded in conception his doubtful tale of Betty's teatime treats.

Tea and a whole jam sponge arrived. Blight summoned an extra cup for me (Simon, of course, declined). The sponge was remarkably slab-like in appearance, with that dark heavy wet undercooked interior into which a jam filling readily bleeds (so I noted with the expertise of a former swiss-roll-maker man), and the tea turned out to be standard issue. My suspicion was strengthened.

Our consultant's attention apparently taken up exclusively by the 'sponge' (he was one of those people who examine closely the foodstuff in their hand before each mouthful), I made a determined attempt to get us started on the questions and answers:

'Well, first – '

'Did you see that programme about hair dryers last night?' Ray immediately interrupted.

This was a dazzling strike, a real stunner and no mistake. As far as I could make out, the remark hadn't the least relevance to orchid growing, or, for that matter, to anything else that could possibly interest us. But, but, there was a devilish cunning behind it, and that gave it a sort of audacious artistry, d'ye see.

'No, switched off,' said Simon. 'But saw some of *your* little programme 'forehand – 'bout the grasses.'

Ah. So that was it. Talk about baffling the reader – it had been another masterly manoeuvre by one obviously possessed of a mystery writer's mind, a brilliant demonstration of the oblique approach, worthy of Master, Queen or Carr.

'Saw you planting away there,' Simon added with that smiling, knowing, mock-accusatory tone he might have used if Ray had been caught out in some naughtiness. So there he was supplying a straight-man cue as obligingly as if our consultant were indeed the 'Hello, Playmates' man himself.

Ray seized on the feed as avidly as, at the same time, he bit into a third, sizeable wedge of Betty's creation. 'Oh, you saw me then, did you?' he asked sheepishly, indistinctly, for all the world as though he actually had been caught out in some minor misdemeanour. 'Yes, well, I couldn't very well get out of it. The producer of the programme – nice young chap – said he had to have me at all costs, no one else would do.' The Welsh lilt had become rather more pronounced. 'Well, I am the world's leading authority on grasses...' (This was, however, far from the ranking later accorded him by our Grasses man, author of the highly acclaimed *Helictotrichon Handbook*.) 'So what could I do?' he appealed to us.

''Xac'ly.' Simon obliged again.

'Anyway, they were extremely impressed with what I did, said they'd never had anyone so professional on the programme,' Ray resumed, with a return to his quiet, disarmingly direct, full-blown conceit.

How rapidly the fabulous figure that had once commanded a distant, hazy height (Consultant, Principal, Columnist), how rapidly it had tumbled down from the summit, and how shocking it was to see it before me now as the preposterous thing it was – its narrative craftsmanship notwithstanding.

'So they've asked me back to do another – on rhododendrons and azaleas, on which I'm also something of a world authority.'

Natch, Ray, natch. But what has all this got to do with ye fucking Orchids, may I ask?

He proceeded to tell us, via dazzlingly circuitous lead-ins, and with Simon whizzo as stooge, that he had the finest collection of Kurume azaleas in the country, probably in

Europe, that local authorities were panting for him as a consultant, that he was currently advising on some major planting scheme out Farnham way, that his garden had recently been featured in *Town and Country*...

'So, there it goes, you see...' It was the simple conclusion to an unsolicited account of the most successful of lives. (I was beginning to entertain another suspicion, later confirmed by the Grasses man: that Blight's principalship of the gardening school, a stuffy privately run organisation, had been a simple case of Buggins' turn.)

'Right,' I said, making another attempt. 'First. Monopodial epiphytes. They don't have pseudobulbs, so the copy says, so you propagate from offsets. Yet – '

'My old grandfather used to grow orchids. That was just outside Llanelli. Many years ago now. He had this enormous greenhouse. I remember walking round it as a boy – '

' – for Vandas we have – '

'Vandas. Lovely plants. Saw them in Burma when I was lecturing on grasses. I was the very first person from Meridian to be invited to lecture abroad. A very great honour.' He consulted his watch. 'Good heavens, I don't believe it. You'll have to excuse me, you two. I've got a very important appointment with your chairman chappie, Mr Lyttelton. He wants to grow some pampas grasses on his new estate, and of course what I don't know about them isn't worth knowing really.'

Gold and black

So much of what had once seemed to me inviolable was now tainted – by so many kinds of dark incursion. Perhaps not destroyed by them but so infected and weakened by them that they could never be restored to their original purity, just as those who recover from certain debilitating diseases sometimes never regain completely their old strength. (Time of course as well as place was involved in these contaminations. Most, such as the shooting at Kingsdon St Mary school and the murder in Walfield Road, had occurred later than when I had known and cherished those places in childhood. A few, such as Alastair Grahame's suicide and the Messerschmitt crashing near the Rectory, had pre-dated the cherished time. And yet others, that I was soon to consider, actually occurred at the cherished time but not in the cherished place.)

It had been the child's poetic vision, innocence and need for security that in combination had first made those worlds – which to others at the time probably appeared quite ordinary – magical, hallowed, safe; and later, in youth and early manhood, it had been selective memory and the innate need to idealise that had reinforced them as such and gilded them. And that gold was unsullied then. Of course I had long known from an early age, as most young people know, that dark forces are constantly abroad in the world, and there had been occasions when they had emerged horrifyingly to the forefront of my awareness – Jack the Ripper, child murders, the Holocaust – but I'd never dwelt on them for long; repulsion and fear had consigned them to the shadowy outer regions of my mind, from where they hadn't impinged much on the central consciousness of the idealising, beauty-seeking, reverie-prone young man I'd been. (But then neither apparently had the idea of death much obtruded into the thoughts of certain shepherds in their land of bliss until they came upon the tomb inscribed *Et in Arcadia ego.*)

Now, though, through my own particular experiences, my own variation on one of the universal themes of discovery in the young, I had gradually seen over the years that what was gold was not hermetically sealed off from, was not proof against an encroachment of, the black, that the two, seemingly incompatible, could intermingle. Perhaps the Greeks symbolised at least the possibility of this conjunction by making the Elysian Fields and the entrance to Hades close to each other instead of far apart.

A simple pirate

Orchids. I'd done my best, hadn't I, to get information straight from the horse's mouth. And not one mouth but two. And look what I'd ended up with – from the first a tale signifying nothing, from the second Songs by Toad. There was nothing for it but to forget them both and write Orchids from my own research.

Writing from your own research. Well, now. A tricky business when it came to instructional material. The first problem was the difficulty, sometimes impossibility, of finding a natural-sounding, succinct alternative to the often spot-on words of your source. As I set out on my task, I teetered constantly on the brink of what that source might construe as plagiarism (I knew that legal actions were not unknown in the ever-sideways-squinting world of Mega and its competitors). Was there, for example, any sensible, readable rephrasing of 'In March sow seeds 1in. deep in pots of John Innes seed compost'? If I rejected such translated-from-the-German or demented-Welshman forms as 'In pots of John Innes seed compost seeds 1in. deep in March sow', the only course was to sacrifice both active voice and concision and say something like: 'Seeds should be sown during March. Sow them 1in. deep in pots, using John Innes seed compost.' Since this was comparatively inelegant and space-consuming, I knew that McStutt, only too eager to give me an 'old pro' 's lesson in editing, would rewrite my rewrite as: 'In March sow seeds 1in. deep in pots of John Innes seed compost.' Circular journey that if repeated often enough would bring a view of Lawsuit on to the horizon.

The second problem was that, surprise, surprise, the sources sometimes conflicted. Take the feeding of orchids. Here was Sir Herbert Dibber in *Orchids for Pleasure* recommending that for these scandalously finicky creatures you make up your own inorganic liquid feed: 42.5% calcium nitrate, 22% ammonium sulphate, 11% ferrous sulphate, 11% potassium phosphate, 11% magnesium sulphate, 1% manganese sulphate. (Even if you could lay hands on all that lot, how, I wondered, did you measure out amounts equalling such specific percentages? And anyway, how come 1.5% had been lost along the way?)

Well, that was the Dibber formula, but here was Dr Heinz Blumentopf in *You and Your Orchids* (his finger pointed accusingly at you from the cover, reminding me unpleasantly of 'Lord' Eddie) proposing something very different. He was pushing this: 42% potassium nitrate... (Potassium *nitrate*, whereas before we'd had potassium *phosphate* and *calcium* nitrate. So were these...? Yet again I found myself summoning up 'Nasty' Naylor and the school chemistry lab. But on this occasion to no avail. Why *are* you bothering, dear boy? I heard an inner voice shockingly exclaim.) And 21% ammonium phosphate (whereas before we'd...), 21% ammonium sulphate (wow, snap! more or less what Dibber had), 14% calcium sulphate (my momentary high spirits subsided) and 2% ferrous sulphate (a five-and-a-half times harsher ration than the obviously more indulgent Dibber allowed).

Then there was Joy Peduncle in *Flowers of Every Hue: Orchids Revisited*, who, in keeping with the vague, 'literary' title and nature of the work as a whole, feebly suggested some unspecified foliar feed. And finally, Mega rival Patten Paige's *A-Z Practical Gardening* stipulated liquid manure. Still, best not to take too much notice of *them*.

So what, I mused, was a simple pirate to make of it all? And that was just feeding. There was so much more ahead.

Still, I pushed on with the drudgery of this lengthy exercise in disguised filching – of which the most hair-tearing aspect in fact was not trying to reconcile so many conflicting 'expert' views but trying to find an unnatural new way of putting every single phrase – and somehow or other, with much sweat and many a curse, I managed to grind out a full account of the family at large and a step-by-step guide to every aspect of raising and increasing each tribe. When, by the way, it came to feeding them, I went for Blumentopf. With his doctorate, his reassuring square-rimmed specs and goatee, and his confidence-instilling frown as he measured out ammonium this and ammonium that in his hothouse in Wittenberge I think it was, he got my vote every time. Oh, and I liked his cruel-for-your-own-good attitude to the ferrous sulphate allowance – from his severe cast of feature you'd have expected nothing else. I backed him against the broadly smiling Sir Herbert, smacking too much of the light-hearted dabbler to be fully trusted (that missing 1.5%!) and far too lenient to those in his care. True, the Wittenberge man's general horticulture was far from aesthetically pleasing, rather clinical-Teutonic (his herbaceous borders, seen in the background of some of his pics, were rigorous blocks of arctic whites, pinks and blues), but then you can't have everything. He knew what he was up to test-tube-wise, that was the main thing. I was a little bothered on the plagiarism front about pilfering his exact chemical quantities – so to be on the safe side, I knocked a couple of percentage points off this amount, added a couple to that, and so on. I have to say, though, that the seeker after truth in me, despite being less dedicated than he once was, still winced at these 'adjustments'. However, I told myself, who could say that this new formula of mine wouldn't prove to be just the job, wouldn't gee up the inmates of orchid houses all over the country into ever more owner-gratifyingly monstrous colours and forms.

The final result was an account so authoritative-*sounding* that it might for all the world have been penned by a virtuoso in orchid nurture. Not, I knew, that it would give me any satisfaction to see it in print. And when eventually o'er the published piece my eyes began to roll, it was certainly not in pleasing memory of all I stole.

Simon and I visited Bark-Chipping again and directed and filmed her in a role which, as *auteur*, I insisted be free of any attempt at improvisation and adhere rigorously to my shooting script. At the end I just stopped myself saying 'That's a wrap.'

A postscript. Later, when Bark-Chipping was sent the proofs (a mere gesture – we at Mega *never* took any notice of contributors' 'corrections'), proofs of a piece that contained scarcely anything of what she had submitted, she nevertheless in her reply referred several times to *her* article – and in the book she was in fact credited as the contributor. Was there, I wondered, any connection between this credit and the fact that soon afterwards this previously unpublished horticulturalist was commissioned to write *Orchids My Way* – which turned out to contain verbatim great chunks of what I'd cobbled together for the Gardening book? (She went on to become the wheel-on media orchids expert – and later a rentaflusteredscatterbraingoodforagiggle chat and game show celeb.)

As for Plumpford and his insistence on nothing but reportage, he never got to learn how Orchids had been produced. His only query on the copy was: 'If a bulb of every species and hybrid was laid end to end, how far would they stretch?' I took a leaf out of Mike Mallarmé's book and off the top of my head gave him three miles for that one. It seemed feasible enough, give or take a mile or two.

No problem…

In the switchback ride that, like so many other marriages, ours was, Sally and I were currently riding a crest of mutual infatuation again. We hadn't quarrelled for a good three weeks, we had each forgotten, with that subconscious (rather than unconscious) amnesia characteristic of most functioning partnerships, just how stupid and impossible the other had appeared during the last upset, and we had each remembered, again subconsciously, only what was finest in the other. In other words, we'd begun – yes, here we go again – we'd begun *idealising* each other once more. And so our current affection was zealous, sanguine, *unqualified*…smiles and kisses so very tender…

That idealisation had of course its downside. Such as Sally's attitude to me as a breadwinner. Although, whenever over our evening meal I had a grouse about my latest 'exciting challenge' at work, she would agreeably interpose – in more or less the right places, and with those unquestioning echoes of our own exasperation we need to hear at the end of a bad working day – a splendid 'God!' or 'How ridiculous!', I was never too keen on her standard, calmer, more considered follow-up: 'I'm sure you can do it, though.' Yes, when she was idealising me, she believed me capable of more or less anything. 'I had a meeting with some representatives from the energy industry this morning. It's unbelievable, Sally, they want me to…' 'Yes?' 'They want me to… You won't credit this…' 'Yes? Yes?' 'They want me to…*design a new breed of nuclear reactor.*' 'God, *no!*' But then, after the usual thoughtful pause, 'I'm sure you can do it, though.'

Partly responsible for that touching faith of Sally's, which could not I suppose be accounted for entirely by the idealising factor, must have been that 'capable' persona I'd been cultivating ever since my decision to Become a Man. That 'Leave it to me' number. Why, I'd been working on it for so long now that I'd almost perfected it. And that look, that tone, not only fooled others, they were in danger of fooling even me. As one of my faves, La Rochefoucauld, put it: 'We are so accustomed to adopting a mask before others that we end by being unable to recognise ourselves.' A mask. There were, then, signs already that... But how could I have...

There are those among us who would have done well not to have so decidedly attempted to convince the world at large that we were Capability Brown, Smith or Jones – because those who over-compensate for a deficiency in the 'No problem' department can if they're not careful acquire so much more convincing an outward appearance of proficiency than the naturally capable that they end up being nominated over them for burdensome tasks. So it was that, in my role of Mr Competent, looking and speaking the part as though typecast for it, I found myself saddled with this and that unwanted position I found it difficult to refuse: chairman of a sub-committee of the local Labour party, and Books representative on non-unionised Mega's ineffectual staff association. Ah, if only I hadn't, like an animal shedding one skin for another, replaced my old outer self with a new, if only I'd stuck with my natural look and voice of moony incompetence, I could have remained in the ranks of those who always escape being chosen as 'just the man for the job'.

Sharpes: revised version

Simon and I were a few minutes late for a meeting in Vin Sharpes' office, and when we entered, Plumpford and McStutt were already there. Even so, I thought the pointedness with which Plumpford raised his wrist on high and gazed at his watch was as totally uncalled for, as well as infantile, as Aunt Edie's prolonged martyred silences had been when Harry, Lil and I arrived late on a visit.

This was the first occasion at Mega I would be observing Sharpes at close quarters for any prolonged period, but my opinion of him had already changed considerably from when I was a boy. The ever-washed, fluffy thatch, now tinged with grey, the Cecil-Parkinson-style vast, deep-winged collars of his hand-made shirts, which so imposingly dressed the neck and like an Elizabethan ruff made almost a dais for his head, the opulent silk ties, the sedulously maintained tan, the enormous expanse of cuff, the unnecessarily-low-on-the-wrist watch and bracelet and the ostentatious gold signet ring were no longer what they had been for me when I was young, the admirable last word in style, but now simply signified flash and self-regard, an impression heightened when I saw how his glance lingered on his own wrist and hand whenever he extended it to take hold of a page or to point something out.

He also presented to me now a rather incongruous figure. He may have worn Savile Row suits with a handkerchief in the breast pocket and Jermyn Street striped shirts like the other male members of the board (Ms Highe was the only female on it – a fact to which she did not however respond with feminist indignation but with an all-too-obvious smile and prance of achievement) but whereas you expected to see these men, with their narrow heads, rangy frames and privately educated voices, dressed in this uniform, which they wore as casually and unthinkingly as a long-serving army officer wears his, it never looked quite right on Sharpes, with his squat boxer's build, predatory, forward-jutting head, spivvy moustache and that barrow-boy accent he had deliberately done nothing to modify; and indeed he somehow *wore* it differently from his fellow board members – with a self-conscious, cuff-shooting pride, the conspicuous satisfaction of one commissioned from the ranks.

Apart from his reputation at Mega for 'spotting a winner' (it was after his successful Erotic Classics and True Crimes series at Paperbacks that the Chairman had decided he was just the man to take over at Books and beef up the sales even more), Sharpes liked to get involved at the shop-floor level of projects and was renowned for the obsessive, quibbling interest he took in such details as the right face and size for a body type and the most suitable shades of colours for a diagram. If he thus usurped what would normally have been the business of Design and Production, it was because he believed, like many self-made men, that his commercial acumen (demonstrated with Dean in the days of their joint paperback venture) was only one aspect of an unerring judgment that could be extended indefinitely to any field you cared to think of. Whether, in fact, such decisions as changing 9 pt Monotype Times to 'something a little bit wider' and changing ochre to 'something a bit more darker' had the slightest effect on the sales of any book could of course never be known, but that did not prevent many from being certain that those decisions did, that Sharpes had a rare, mysterious, priceless 'flair' for the look of a page and that this was an essential factor in Mega Books' growing success. (And even some of those who weren't at all convinced still subscribed to the idea in public, bandied it about, since in the office it isn't just dramas and scandals that help quicken inert days.)

Naturally, Sharpes knew of this reputation and ostentatiously demonstrated his celebrated 'eye for detail' on every possible occasion. As now.

Although this was principally a Gardening book meeting, Simon had also brought along at Sharpes' request some line drawings for another project, the updated *Conservatory Companion*. 'Just in,' he said. 'Haven't had time for proper examine.'

'Pass them over, laddie,' Sharpes said. With the careless

433

insolence of an 'I Did It My Way' vulgarian, he addressed almost everyone in the department thus, even Plumpford. The three exceptions were grizzled McStutt, whom he called Willie; Gudgeon, who, for old times' sake, as a former colleague at Spectrum, remained Walter; and myself, for whom, in deference to my status as nephew and protégé of his former long-time partner, he seemed to think 'son' was less high-handed than 'laddie'.

Having lightly passed a hand over his crown of down, he then extended it to accept the artwork, taking in appreciatively the exquisite juxtaposition of dark cloth, dazzling linen, nut brown skin and gleaming gold. There followed an extravagant 'assessment' of each illustration, showily 'astute'; it was a cabinet minister on camera 'mastering' the contents of a red box, it was McStutt 'gutting' copy, it was Harry 'sussing out' the racing page.

'Don't like the hands,' he said at last. 'Fingers too long.' That unique eye had spotted again what had passed others by. 'And them pot things need to be a bit narrower. Not much,' he added, 'just a bit.'

'Isn't it about time you got a grip of those artists of yours, Simon?' said Plumpford, venomous put-down conveyed, as always, and so cornily, with joky voice and rosy smile.

'You really do have a remarkable eye for detail, Vin,' McStutt enthused, the inevitable 'er-heh-heh' follow-up transposing on this occasion from the usual meaningless verbal tic to an affected chuckle of admiration.

Simon took back the illustrations, a certain familiar look on his face telling me that he was savouring what was shortly to be his first square meal for almost two days, an imminent outburst of 'rage'. 'Let's have a look. You're right. *Bloody* little nuisance! *Bloody* little fool! Whole work *ruined!*' (Half an hour's minor adjustments would surely see to what would have passed as just the ticket at any other publishing house, one without our special directorial touch.) '*Bloody* little idiot!' Each furious rebuke, separated from the last by a short pause, was like a fresh shovelful of coal he was hurling into the stove, 'cooking up' his 'anger'. A suffusion of blood flooded his face like a pink dye (in which, at temple, jaw and neck, rivulets of what looked like blue ink showed just beneath the fine skin). But the fire he had stoked up was not burning fiercely enough yet. Searching around, with his inventive imagination, for something else to throw on it, he came up with: 'He did a job all wrong for me last week, y'know – did a whole rough *complete* opp'site for what we s'missioned!'

Even without knowing that the illustrator was skilful and experienced, I would still have detected that Simon was fibbing, because a particular giveaway sign had appeared on his face: while he was castigating the almost certainly innocent artist, there would persist in hovering over his lips, at odds with the vehemence of what he was saying and his beetling brow, the ghost of a smile. Simon's incensed words, tone of voice and frown sometimes came close to convincing him that his simulated rage was genuine, but they were never able to defeat that faint smile, which represented an irrepressible self within him that did not believe a word he was saying and was actually quite amused by it – and, like a small military force resisting all attempts by a larger one to wipe it out, entrenched in its small but significant pockets of resistance, it would not budge from the little hollows at the corners of his mouth. It is the bad actor's smile, and you used to see it, varying in intensity – now trembling on the brink of extinction, now reviving and gaining the upper hand – on the lips of various male epic-movie stars, who, as a tragedy reached its climax, would cry out in anguish, 'My God, what have I done?' while seemingly appearing to find their plight not entirely without its comic side.

'Wait till I get hold of him!' Simon 'exploded', subtly smiling.

And then, as abruptly as ever, his 'fury' was at an end, his nutritional need satisfied. For it was with a quite disconcertingly sudden calm and reasonable tone of voice that he showed Sharpes, who had asked to see it, the work of two possible new illustrators.

Sharpes glanced rapidly over the offerings of each, snapped out in one case, 'Forget him' – *Forge' 'im*; in the other, 'Take her on' – *Take 'er on*.

These matters disposed of, Sharpes got down to the serious business of the meeting. This was to inform McStutt, myself and Simon of an important decision that had been made about the Gardening book: in view of the vast amount of work in the field and in the office that remained to be done, the logistics entailed for such sessions as waterfalls, fountains and gazebos, the time it would take even with the imminent transfusion of new staff – hey! – and the severely limited schedule and budget for the project, in view of all this the big construction jobs were to go. The book would now consist mainly of the more usual, accessible gardening jobs – though there would be the same extensive range of these, covered in the same detail. As a result, Gicbog was now to make a 'more modest' 1800 pages and come in at 'only' 13lb.

He and Bob had reluctantly come to this decision, said Sharpes. He and Bob? Listening between the lines, as it were, and observing Plumpford's uncharacteristically subdued expression, I didn't have much doubt who had really made the decision – the decision to rein in our managing editor's original wild ambitions, his *megalomania*.

But none of that mattered. The tasks ahead slashed, and help on the way, that was what mattered. I could almost feel physically that lightening of the book's bulk and the distribution of its load.

A terrible beauty

At the Rectory there was a Japanese painted fire screen (Olivia was into chinoiserie and japonaiserie). Against a background expanse of gold stood a flower-laden handcart of black. The gold shone out more richly, its beauty was heightened, through the invasive contrast of those black wheels and shafts. And that was the strange effect that defilement had begun to have on so many of my personal golden worlds. For instance, the dark serpents that had slithered into the enchanted domain of *The Wind in the Willows*, to take up permanent residence there (for even though those intruders might sometimes disappear from sight whenever I thought of or reread parts of that book, my mind would still be half-aware of their lurking presence), had, in some ways, impure ways, intensified the loveliness of that world. (The elements of the incursion were sometimes reversed, of course, producing an intensifying contrast of the opposite kind, as when the sun shone on Blackwell and seemed to deepen its sooty squalor.)

Perhaps, in my new attitude towards those havens of childhood of which the memory had happily and sometimes comfortingly persisted in me for so many years but which had now been contaminated, I had been seduced, in an example of what Mario Praz called the romantic agony, by 'the supreme beauty of that beauty which is accursed' – though not those melodramatic nightmarish versions of it indulged in by so many nineteenth-century Romantics and Decadents (a synthesis of beauty and pain which in some cases shaded into sadism), but rather my own version of it (one which I was certain was shared by others), in which poetries pure and innocent had been transformed now and forever into poetries complex, powerful and strange. So for me now the murder of Zack Trennell (whose name – unlike the names of certain people I had once actually known – I was to find I would never forget) had brought a strange new dimension, a sort of Yeatsian terrible beauty, to the golden idealised image of Walfield Road that had for so long lingered in my mind. For me now, the vibrant dyes of the wallflowers that had so duskily, muskily throbbed in a garden of that road would always be associated – some might think fantastically, I suppose – with the death of that poor young man, as though, in an odd reversal of time, they had acquired their deep hues from his spilled lifeblood, just as in Greek myth anemones sprang from the blood of the dying Adonis.

To aestheticise thus the intrusion of the unspeakable into the beautiful was, I knew, questionable. But in some ways it seemed unavoidable. Particularly for the artist detached in time and space. We've only to think of how many great paintings have depicted the truly horrendous taking place in a setting contrastingly delightful, and of how many viewing them have been more enthralled than appalled by the terrible beauty of such works of art.

Flint

Three days after Sharpes' announcement, two-and-a-half new arrivals joined the Gardening book 'team'. One, as reporter/sub, was Roger Taylor, an affable Rip-Kirby-like hornrimmed-specs, leather-patched-sports-jacket man, who had a reputation for calm competence. (If I don't have occasion in this narrative to mention him much, or other amiable and talented colleagues such as Chris Alexander and Eileen King and Richard Robbins, other than to pay my respects to them here, it's because, as is well known, the agreeable and the capable must in any work with the least claims to entertainment take a back seat to the frauds and the piecans.) The other whole help was Camarra White-Spacey, a photographer/designer, a skinny blonde six-footer who'd apparently done a spiffing job on the revised updated wallpapering guide.

The half help was none other than the long-promised, mysterious Chillingford Flint, a sub who *still* hadn't completed his work on the equally mysterious Gifgerhupmaubmisk. (They were, some of these Plumpford acronyms – only he appeared to have the articulative skill to use them all – as much of a mouthful as, and syllabically reminiscent of, those to us ugly and scarcely pronounceable place and character names in Dostoevsky, those Skotoprigonyevsks and Svidrigaïlovs.) Flint was to divide his time between that book and ours, on which he would help clear an accumulation of subbing tasks. Long spoken of but never yet seen – no one had been able to point him out to me in foyer, corridor or lift – he had acquired for me that curiously potent identity, compact and of a piece, which all those who have long been spoken of but never yet seen take on for us. His, based on what seemed a valiantly long stint on Gifgerhupmaubmisk and McStutt's praising him as a 'most willing, able and charming chap, er-heh-heh', was that of someone industrious, efficient and personable.

On the day Flint was to start giving us his afternoons, McStutt was away with 'a touch of flu' – whatever that meant – and rang in to ask me to show Flint that morning the editorial style of our book and the nature of the subbing required.

Flint had insisted on the phone that I visit him rather than he me, and so it was in the offices of Gifgerhupmaubmisk that at last the mystery was replaced by the reality. I entered his room and saw sitting at a desk facing me a heavily built man in his late thirties. Sandy hair and eyelashes, a cold and torpid eye, an unlit pipe clenched between his teeth.

I went through some sample pages with him, then gave him the proofs and layouts he needed for his first subbing job.

'I see,' he said, taking the pipe from his mouth. 'So if the pics sort of, you know, look as if they...' He spoke in an iron-toned drawl. '...if some cretin of an artist has, you know...then you...yes...'

The telephone rang. It was someone returning a call.

He listened for a few seconds, then demanded belligerently, 'Look, d'you have any Pilkington pipes or not?'

'Some cretin,' he said after he'd slammed down the receiver. He fixed me with his stony stare. 'I know these shop types aren't, you know... I mean, we wordsmiths can't expect them to, you know... But, I mean, ye gods...' He took a small penknife from his pocket and began scraping dottle from the bowl of his pipe. It was an activity I was to become increasingly familiar with, occupying as it did so substantial a part of his every day. 'Anyway, everything has to be...every, er...'

'Yes, as usual, the designers – ' I began, thinking to refresh his memory or help him in his efforts to communicate.

'...*everything has to be...*' he repeated, talking me down, raising his voice to that of one who has no intention of putting up with interruptions, thank you very much, '...thoroughly... So we have to...yes...' He knocked dottle into a wastepaper basket, replaced the pipe between his teeth, prepared to rise from his desk. 'Let me have those other, you know, this afternoon...' he ordered me. 'I'm popping out in a sec...before the shops get too, you know...' It was half past eleven.

Somewhat narked as I left him, I told myself that next time, instead of commanding me to deliver it, Flint could himself collect whatever he needed to do the job. The job which now, I felt like reminding him, had at least as much claim on his time as his old one.

After lunch I took the further sample pages he wanted to his office.

'Is Chillingford around?' I asked a young woman sitting at a paper-strewn desk, a junior sub who looked scarcely out of school and who it appeared from the unfinished sandwich in front of her had been too busy to eat out.

'No, he's not back yet.'

It was five to three. (This, it must be understood, was before the days of 'presenteeism', 'the long hours culture'.)

'But,' she added brightly and easily, as though three-and-a-half-hour Flint lunch breaks were standard, accepted, happily sanctioned even, 'he shouldn't be too long, I expect.'

Danxavie redux

A few years earlier Danny Glazier had married and moved away from Bexcray, and we now kept in touch only sporadically. It was one of those school friendships that distance and new priorities eventually test to evaporation point. We did, though, at rare intervals, still write to each other (we were at the fag-end of that period when people still sometimes swapped news by picking up a pen instead of the phone). Danny had long since left Dazings. He'd become a salesman with WelFit, the double-glazing outfit, and then after his marriage had become manager of the Reading branch. I'd sometimes idly wondered what had become of certain of my other classmates at Sir Bernard Croucher. After leaving school I had, at first, occasionally bumped into some of them in Bexcray, but with the passing of the years that happened less often. Now Danny wrote to tell me that he'd been rung by Gavin Warlett, the Swotpot, who had characteristically, and laudably, been trying to track down his fellow-students (Danny had given him my number and I'd be getting a call soon) with some aim of a class reunion – he who had been so unmercifully beaten up in that class.

Clifford Jeavons, the Boy Genius, had gone up to Cambridge. He was only the third boy in the history of Sir Bernard Croucher to make it to Oxbridge, so the whole school had been given a celebratory afternoon off. He was now in the diplomatic service. (Try as I might, I couldn't see him at this planned gathering, mingling with the likes of Gary Fripp, now a grease monkey in Blackwell – or, come to that, with Danny and myself.) The only others who were known to have gone on to further education were Gavin Warlett himself (Sheffield University; now an accountant) and Dave Smith (a poly somewhere; present fate unknown). Billy Hines, who'd been a talented artist – spot-on caricatures – had joined the police, and Alan Diplock, a whizz at languages, was working in his dad's greengrocery. As for Derrick Grassingford, who'd never needed to study maths, because he could solve any problem in a flash, faster even than Mr Holmes, well, he was facing charges of flogging stolen watches and lighters, and, as far as the reunion was concerned, it was doubtful whether he'd be able to make it to any place of his own choosing for some time to come.

Danny also told me that about a year ago, his mind turning to children's stories (he had a three-year-old daughter), he'd thought again about that fantasy world we'd invented together as boys. He'd kept all our maps, drawings, plot outlines and unfinished drafts – those remnants of an idea I'd long since 'grown out of' – and had fished them out. Rather taken with that bizarre and colourful world of ours he'd rediscovered, that world of the Sprabs and Vorks and Tongs and Argos, he had selected one of the stories that had originally been his idea, had been writing it up in detail and now intended to send it off to a publisher. He had, naturally enough, discarded the name Danxavie, something we'd never got round to changing all those years ago. But he hadn't come up with a replacement he liked and he asked me if I had any suggestions.

Overview

The gold infiltrated by the black, heightened by the black, richer and stranger than that of the pure unalloyed gold of adolescent reverie, now dominated my imagination. Just as the person who has recently been impressed by some little-known book or piece of music or place, say, that he has discovered for himself cannot help feeling that he has a special relationship with it, so it seemed to me that I had the same special relationship with the idea of the gold and the black as I have described it – as a strange and powerful poetry, as a particular form of the Romantic agony, as an insistent leitmotiv in life – a sense increased by its surprising absence as an explored phenomenon in the creative works I knew.

Evidence of how insistent the theme had become for me was the widening of my imagination spatially. It now increasingly acquired a satellite-eye view, one which took in the entire globe and was aware of a limitless simultaneity – which inevitably included incongruities of a horrifying kind. So that now, when revisiting some treasured aspect of my past, I would deliberately call up to my mind – to create what I thought of as poetically a disturbing chiaroscuro, ethically a necessary corrective to a heedless happiness and philosophically an enlightened overview – something dark that I either knew had taken place at the same time or could be reasonably certain had. So if, for example, thoughts of the woodland garden I had visited on a rhododendrons assignment for the Gardening book should summon back to me the sun-pierced shrubbery at the Rectory, I no longer just contentedly reimmersed myself in that past as I once had done but told myself that, at the selfsame moment that I stood before the gleaming sunlit flowers (and heard the notes of a certain lovely music?), another child, somewhere or other, and possibly not that far away, was in the throes of terror and pain. And then I would experience what, in music, Mahler conveyed in his First Symphony – a sinister shadow falling across a sunlit landscape – or Ives in his Fourth – a disquiet ever-increasingly, insistently, entering a hymn of joy. In fact, I had produced my own version of this theme: there had been such a spate of child murders recently, and some of them had taken place in surroundings of such pastoral charm, that one evening I set to work to update Nash's 'Spring', that poem I had loved as a boy:

Spring, the sweet Spring, is the year's pleasant king;
Then blooms each thing, then maids dance in a ring,
Cold doth not sting, the pretty birds do sing,
Cuckoo, jug-jug, pu-we, to-witta-woo!

A girl and boy, in a wood, dash with joy
Past Hell's envoy, whose mission's to destroy,
A knife his toy, its steel he'll soon employ,
Eyes crazed, while birds do sing, to-witta-woo!

Midst light and shade, the two so unafraid,
Through violets wade, when he brings down the blade;
They scream for aid, as their life stains the glade,
Eyes glazed, while birds do sing, tu-witta-bloody-woo!

Or if, to take another example, a pale rosy-gold three o'clock winter sunlight and the squawk of gulls should charmingly bring back to me Boxing Day afternoons at Ivor and Edie's, I would remind myself of what I had later learned, that on that festive day one year a fishing boat had been lost off Iceland, that at what might have been the selfsame moment that, paper-hatted amid family jollity, I was downing Tizer, several despairing lost souls, struggling in the dark tumult of the waves, were helplessly taking in mouthfuls of something horribly different, mouthfuls of what would soon icily choke them.

Not that I confined this new overview to my own experience. I sometimes irresistibly applied it, historically, to the poetries, or even merely the pleasures, of others. Reading, for instance, of a woman taking a day return to London in the late thirties, to shop in Oxford Street and see the latest

Cole Porter musical, I would reflect that at the very moment she was comfortably considering buying some tableware or was chatting and laughing in some crowded foyer, at that very moment, someone perhaps known to her or to a friend, fighting for the International Brigade in Spain, might be dying alone in some waterlogged foxhole or smoking ruin: while admiringly she examined a piece of Spode he was feeling the cold hand of death on him. (A mind-set, this new compulsion of mine, the exact opposite I supposed of that of those young women at Mega Books I never heard speaking of anything but the cosy world of Bond Street, horse trials, Gstaad et al in which they were cocooned.) And conversely, I could now no longer read about or see photographs of the slaughter on the D-Day beaches without being aware, in appalled amazement, that as, in that maelstrom, young soldiers in agony realised with terror that both their legs had been blown off or their guts were spilling out, a few miles away on that June morning, across only a narrow stretch of water, a housewife was having a joke with the baker, an old gentlemen was whistling in his allotment, a schoolboy was practising his offdrive...

The new overview was making me see everything now in a different way. Listening to, say, that Buddy Rich number, 'Take It Again', recorded in 1943, imagining a live performance of it taking place in some American ballroom during a tour by the Tommy Dorsey Orchestra, I would now insist on telling myself that elsewhere at the same time a guard in a gasmask was dropping canisters of Zyklon B through hatches in a roof. As, in the ballroom, hazed and fragrant with tobacco smoke, Buddy happily embarked on some phenomenal solo, to the delight of the afficionados in the audience, the inmates of a 'shower room' were inhaling fumes of an appallingly different kind, were stampeding towards the massive, hermetically sealed door of the room in panic, to the indifference, or perhaps pleasure, of whoever was observing them through a peephole, were screaming, clawing at one another, piling up in blue, bloodied pyramids of flesh.

Yes, once I'd arrived at it, then this view from the stratosphere, which the reluctant god that is information-saturated thinking modern man must accept as his burden, changed for ever my pictures of the past.

Exact location impossible

The weather that Gardening book summer was standard British allsorts of mostly inferior quality: torrential rain, which made outdoor jobs impossible, jeopardised the schedule and exerted pressure on the reporters to do even more when fieldwork was possible; drizzle, which, however, was regarded by no one as a bar to getting out on assignments; biting wind, which, as it bowed the plants in nursery or garden and set notebook pages clacking, made you goosepimplingly intolerant of standing around any longer; *Film-Fun*-white-skied mugginess, which, in the context of getting out and about, I termed like everyone else fine weather (though inwardly I felt 'a languishment for skies Italian'); a single visitation of dog days (over which my will had now completely prevailed); and only occasional passages – northerners' rations – of true summer. But when these days of languorous heat, pure blue skies and the most gentle conceivable of breezes did bestow their benison upon us, how I appreciated my good fortune in being able to escape from the office; then I felt part-compensated for what else on the book I found so burdensome. On one such day, in a fruit garden, I saw beyond a yew hedge a stand of faintly stirring, bluish trees, which nebulous thoughts of Robin Hood, *The Wind in the Willows*, a host of forgotten children's adventure stories and who knows what unidentified else so imbued with a mysterious promise that I felt briefly, with Keats (passing over the Italophile proviso above that he added to his lines):

> Happy is England! I could be content
> To see no other verdure than its own;
> To feel no other breezes than are blown
> Through its tall woods with high romances blent.

After one long morning spent with Simon on a fruit farm in Berkshire – strawberry layering, raspberry spraying, currant pruning, etc., etc. – we drove to the large country house of Mega chairman DeVere Lyttelton. It had been arranged that we meet Ray Blight there. He was organising the planting of ornamental grasses in the grounds and wished to take this opportunity to 'correct', by demonstration, one or two 'errors' made by our Grasses man, Peter Panicum.

I shall not describe this session – it would simply be, in terms of the parts played by Blight, Simon and myself, a reprise of what has gone before. I only mention the visit to the Lytteltons' property because it provided me with further illustrations of a phenomenon I have already recorded.

The first instance of it on this visit was the sherry that Mrs Lyttelton offered us (her husband was in town, chairing a board meeting at Mega) before we went out into the extensive grounds. A manzanilla of the same palest straw colour as Mrs Lyttelton's writing paper, this was unlike any dry sherry I'd ever tasted before: it was *bone* dry, as in 'bone bleached dry in a barren land'. A fraction of aridity more and it would have ceased to be sherry at all. Then there were the house plants. As well as the tall green foliage shrubs and ferns growing in jardinières at floor level, there were, as smaller pot plants on higher surfaces, only various *green*-flowered cymbidiums, orchids I vaguely remembered from my sessions on the plants. (In a fatuous attempt to impress Mrs Lyttelton, I identified the plants and dropped Bark-Chipping's name in a manner that implied a closer acquaintance with her than I'd had or desired. To which the mistress of the house, a willowy woman of fifty with piercing blue eyes, replied: 'Oh, we know Pleione quite well. How's she keeping?' And with a new shamelessness that surprised me, I found myself lyingly responding: 'Very well.') And then, when we entered the garden, immediately behind the house, I saw the theme repeated: massed foliage of different greens, amid which bloomed, again, only *green* flowers. No others, just those green-flowered spurges, lady's mantles, angelicas and perfoliate Alexanders – which our hostess named, almost to herself, as we passed by them. (These green flowers amid all this green foliage... Something stirred in the recesses of my brain – only for my attention to be diverted from it by a most-cleverly-led-up-to piece of Blight bragging.) Then, when we returned to the house, there, beside the hi-fi, were, no surprise really, recordings of Britten operas: those works which, whatever their other qualities, are without a single melody and whose composer was once heard miserably to wish that he could write 'just one tune'.

I couldn't help wondering. Could these tastes, for the driest of wines, the most colourless of gardens, the most tuneless of music, could they really be *natural* tastes: a heartfelt enjoyment of these things that was innate? Or were they perhaps *acquired* tastes: a genuine transition from an original antipathy to a long-maturing appreciation? Or were they *perverse* tastes: a masochistic bent, particularly among a class educated at Spartan institutions, towards the stripped-bare, the bleak, the chill (exemplified by Britten himself not only in so much of his music – described by some fellow-composers and critics as 'thin and churchy', 'drab and penitential', 'thin-blooded' – but in his self-imposed domestic regime: cold baths all winter in windswept Aldeburgh)? Or were they *sham* tastes: so great a snobbish contempt, learned during upbringing, for the sugary sweet, the garishly colourful, the cloyingly melodious favoured by the likes of Harry and Lil that, in wishing to distance itself from them as far as possible, it pretended to desire their polar opposites? Or were they sometimes neither one nor the other alone but a subtle amalgam of several?

And what about my own tastes? Some years later I almost convinced myself, after Olivia had lent me her recordings of them, that I enjoyed the austere a cappella works of Poulenc (and in so doing recalled the preference of that ultimate contrarian des Esseintes for 'emaciated' medieval monastic music and the 'stark nudity' of plainsong) as much as, even if in a different way from, his full-bodied, golden-reverie-inducing earlier secular pieces – *Les Biches*, the *Sinfonietta*, the *Suite Française*, the *Concert Champêtre*, the flute sonata. I almost convinced myself, too, that I enjoyed cool, limpid, restrained classical fiction, such as *Exile and the Kingdom* and *Strait is the Gate* as much as I did rich, freewheeling romantic stuff, such as *David Copperfield* and *Lolita*. But I say 'almost convinced' because I would sometimes ask myself whether I was truly, hand on heart, enjoying those pure unaccompanied choral works and those pure spare tales, and I simply could not be certain, could not be certain whether I had 'acquired a taste' for them or not. But surely, I thought, I *ought* to be certain, I *ought* to know beyond doubt in every case what I enjoyed and what I didn't. As I did when I was a boy.

But it was no longer possible to know…beyond doubt…in every case… Past a certain age, it was as though in this matter of tastes – the natural, the acquired, the perverse, the affected, the combination of several, where one subtly shaded into another – you had entered an area analogous to that where several counties meet, inasmuch as, with no lines of demarcation to guide you, exact location was impossible.

Cheeky Chicko

From time to time at Mega I'd meant to visit the Comics department, up on the sixth floor, to see where *Cheeky Chicko*, en-chant-ing com-ic of my in-fan-cy, was produced. I had of course long since outgrown the foolish daydreams of adolescence, when I imagined that the fluffy yellow sea-booted rascal emanated from an editorial space as rainbow-coloured and cosy as the comic and inhabited by simple happy beings scarcely physical. That was why I'd kept putting off this visit: I knew I should find the *Cheeky Chicko* offices no different from any other. But rational knowledge is one thing, nostalgic curiosity another (which is why, despite our knowing full well that the magic which certain places possessed for us in childhood was only that which we infused into them at the time and that the person with that animating imagination has long since ceased to exist, we still have the desire to see them again). So one afternoon I decided to take a short break from knocking my Blackberry notes into shape and to satisfy my curiosity at last.

It was an arctic day in August, the sort of day that induces in you an unseasonal desire for hot drinks, stodgy snacks and a book like *The Count of Monte Cristo*. As a result of the cold and so much tea drinking, I needed to relieve myself before taking the lift up to Comics. The men's room, large, high-ceilinged, was deserted. With its emptiness, its silence broken only by an occasional sluicing, its harsh even lighting, its white tile and sink glare reflected in a row of mirrors, how strange it was, set down in the midst of rooms that were so different – peopled, coloured, noisy. When you were in it alone, it made – as I was sure it did for the rest of the male staff, even the least meditative among them – the bustle of the world beyond its self-contained white stillness recede immediately – a dismissal underscored by a sudden cool swishing in the indifferent urinal

– recede, temporarily, yet prefiguringly, to that same aspect of unimportance that world would assume, this time permanently, when you had left it behind for another job, for retirement, for...

Returning to the world of activity, to the populated corridor outside, I saw coming towards me, in quiet conference, DeVere Lyttelton and Vin Sharpes. Lyttelton had one arm draped across Sharpes' wrestler's shoulders, and to be seen thus, to pretend in public to treat this still rather spivvy-looking character as an equal, undoubtedly gave him one of those 'sophisticated' pleasures that those of conventional intelligence like to cultivate. In the same way, when he introduced Sharpes to someone at a party it was as casually as, it was outwardly no differently from, when he introduced any of his other colleagues, who were all more or less urbane and articulate; and he liked to be seen with Sharpes at these gatherings, glass in hand, head lowered and gently nodding, listening with apparent attentiveness to the crude utterances of this man he would never have dreamed of inviting to his house for the weekend or including among his true friends.

I took a lift up to the sixth floor. Exchanging the occasional hesitant nod with Comics staff in the corridor, who vaguely assumed I was there on editorial business, I passed the offices of the unpleasant *Socko* and *Whizz*, which visits to Randall's newsagents in Bexcray had shown me to my dismay were among the successors to the defunct *Knockout* and *Film Fun* and which, with their uncouth characters and crude graphic line, bore about as much relation to those stylish comics of my childhood as Cable Lane, Blackwell, did to Regent's Crescent, Richborough – but which, I sadly accepted, my sons might well be buying a few years later. Eventually, at the end of the corridor, I came to a half-open door whose pebble glass bore the inscription Cheeky Chicko. I walked in. It was a small office with only one occupant, a plain woman of about thirty with close-cropped carroty hair and blue-tinted specs, whom I took, from the sanctum-like nature of the room, to be the Ed. She was speaking aggressively into the phone with a broad Glaswegian accent: 'Listen, mein Herr, that copy's now three fucking weeks overdue...' She glanced over at me briefly, looked away. 'Well, that's scarcely the point now, is it?' I caught a glimpse of a dusty bulky back-issue file of the comics in a corner before I went through into a larger, shabbier office: scarred furniture, discoloured walls, threadbare carpeting (how privileged, I suddenly realised, we were in Books, with our spruce decor and deep pile). Bent over a typewriter, scowling as he bit into a cream doughnut, was a prematurely balding young man, most certainly physical, indeed some might have said excessively so. A girl with bulging eyes who was carrying an armful of artworks towards the door halted at my entry and said, 'Can I help you?'

The true reason for my nosing around was the least unconvincing one I could come up with: 'I've got fond memories of *Cheeky Chicko*. From when I was a little kid. I was just curious to see where it was produced.'

She looked at me doubtfully. Intruders had filched wallets and purses from various unattended Mega offices a month earlier, and I felt the customary guilt of the innocent in such situations. Having cast a pointless nodding, smiling look around the room, I left, not as casually as I would have liked.

When, while musing at Lea & Lyle about alternative ways of earning a living, I had idealised the world in which various comics were published, how little I'd realised that working in an office at the great publishing corporation of Mega, from which one of those comics issued, would in so many ways be little different from working in an office at that grocery firm. But those outside Mega who heard what I now did for a living saw in it such a contrast to what I had once done (and often, by implication, to what they still did): 'Lucky you. Much more fun than that grocery job – all those dreary cheese and dog biscuit prices.' It was the error of the onlooker, who, not living the life glimpsed, ever-ready to idealise, builds up from fragments of information (in this case the so-variegated list of editorial subject-matter I would mention to them – fish, medicine, the unknown, the conservatory, the garden – and a few glossy phrases – 'discussions with the author', 'consulting with the designers') a whole fascinating world of work. And even if the onlooker should enter that world for a while this does not necesarily shatter the illusion. In fact, it may heighten it. So the school visitor may find the squeak of chalk, the smell of textbooks, the essays awaiting marking – which to the one who experiences them a thousand times, day after day, symbolise only a Mr-Perrin-like tedium and problems – redolent of a charming, enviable, Mr-Chips-like existence.

Supercharged

My preoccupation with the theme of the gold and the black, my personal victory over enervating heat and the heroic exploits of Stauffenberg had in combination decided for me the penultimate chapter of my book (even if, apart from the opening and some rough-and-ready heavily researched early chapters, the rest of it still remained in limbo). And I wrote this near-ending without the tedious struggle those earlier parts had caused me. Engaged with its themes, attuned to the supercharged narrative, aware of an intuitive mastery over the controls, I drove that chapter forward with a speed and ease I'd never known before. And it was with only a few minor changes that my first draft became my final, from which the following passages are extracted:

Reception Day. Guy awoke to the alarm at seven. He pulled back the curtains and saw that it was going to be hot again. Already a heat haze lay over the city, and the trees were perfectly still...

At 12.40 the telephone rang. It made them both start, even though they were expecting the call. Marcius picked up the receiver.

'...Good. So the party's on. We'll be leaving right away.'

In the underground garage it was cool and dim. Guy slung his tunic into the back of the car and, getting in beside Marcius, who was driving, placed the briefcase out of sight behind his feet. Up the ramp and they suddenly emerged into heat and glare. It struck them like a blow. The buildings and roads ahead shimmered, and the blue of the sky was deep and fierce. The air flowing past them in the open tourer brought some relief from the torrid assault, but it resumed when they stopped for the lights in Phoenix Street and had to sit a long time waiting. The fiery reds seemed an added cruelty on a day like this.

Cooler greens flicked on and they were off again, entering now a more built-up area – blue canyons where the heat was less intense.

At the end of one of these a dark-uniformed figure waved the car to a halt.

'It's OK,' Guy murmured. 'Routine ID check.' Even so, he was uncomfortably aware of the briefcase.

Guy produced his SPO card and the man snapped to the salute. They sped away again...

Across Palace Square and into The Parade. The park began unrolling alongside them, its chiaroscuro of deep green and gold more intense than ever today. But it appeared to Guy slightly unreal, as though he were viewing it in a waking dream. The sundrenched leafage of the plane trees beneath which he and Zoë... On the other side of The Parade, beyond upsloping lawns whose flower beds were a blaze of colour, the backs of the colleges soon appeared. Vacation-deserted, so it seemed. Guy saw that nothing showed at their windows as yet.

The car stopped at the bend, just before Nova College. Marcius and Guy looked at each other hard, grasped hands. Marcius said, 'Good luck'...

Guy sat on the bench, sweltering in his uniform, pretending to read the newspaper he held up before him, his gaze fixed beyond on a certain high window in Nova.

The tension mounted inside him. He looked at his watch. 3.28. Due in twelve minutes.

But as those minutes ticked by, there was still no light in the window, still no sound of the convoy.

He tilted the paper away. Its glare had become dazzling. His watch showed 3.47. Still nothing. Seven minutes late. The merciless heat, the waiting, the concentration on the window, the stretching of his nerves were beginning to test his strength.

As the minute hand of his watch moved towards 4.00 he began to think the opening of the headquarters had been cancelled, that the General...

A light sprang on in the shadowy blue wall.

He was on his way.

Hands steady, he lifted the papers in the briefcase, pushed the towel aside to reveal the sandwich box. He prised off its lid, felt with his fingers beneath the greaseproof packages until they encountered the metal of one of the grenades. Hand hidden by the flap of the case, he grasped the grenade, lifted it from the box and placed it beneath the papers at the top. Then he did the same with the other one.

Two minutes later he heard the distant wail of sirens and the thrum of engines. From an alley of the park a little further down, Emmanuel, his back-up, appeared, wheeling a dustcart that contained more than dust. On the ground floor of Nova two windows were raised.

The blood began pounding in his ears.

He stared along the shimmering length of The Parade, waiting for the first sign of the convoy.

For some time the road was empty.

Then he saw them. The first dark shapes, wobbling in the road-reflected heat.

More shapes came into view, joined the others in one formless quivering dark mass.

The mass grew steadily larger.

The noise of the sirens and engines was loud now and he could make out the individual shapes of the motorcycles and the leading car. The car of the General, the tyrant, the butcher. His target.

He wiped the palms of his hands on his uniform.

The wail and roar now shattered the blazing afternoon. Limos and escort emerged distinctly from the heat blur. White helmets, glinting handlebars, flashing windscreens.

He made no move yet.

The note of the engines changed as they began to slow down for the bend.

Slowing down further. How real, how clear, they were now, but again it seemed like the reality, the clarity, of a vivid dream.

Suddenly a noise like the amplified clatter of a sewing machine. Joined by another the same. *The LMGs.*

Two motorcycles swerved, the riders toppled.

Heart thudding, palms wet, nerves screaming, he forced himself still to hold back, to wait.

Then two loud sharp reports. *The tyres.*

Now he flipped back the top of the briefcase.

Rubber screeching, the General's car glided into a seemingly endless skid that sent flying another of the motorcyclists, who had drawn his pistol. The car behind swerved, also went into a skid. The convoy was disintegrating as it loomed ever nearer.

Now he grasped the grenades in his hands.

And now, not only is the scene still dreamlike to Guy, it seems as well to be taking place very slowly. The General's car slews, as the driver fights to keep it under control. Guy rises, keeping his eyes fixed unwaveringly on the car, paying no attention to the continuing machine-gun clatter, to the splintering glass, the shouts, the screeching tyres. He sees the car slowly, gracefully even, swing broadside on towards him, paintwork and glass adazzle, juddering to a halt. He lifts the right-hand grenade to his lips. He sees the rear door of the car open. He glimpses the General starting up, familiar tungsten eyes now wide with fear. He pulls the pin out with his teeth. A bodyguard emerges raising an assault rifle. Guy aims and lobs the grenade as he has been instructed and sees it bounce and roll beneath the car and knows he will not need the other grenade and at the same time is aware of the bodyguard staggering as Emmanuel gets him but still aiming and firing at Guy and as Guy starts to throw himself down a sudden blinding light, thunderous roar and explosion both without and within and...

'Mr Essence'

'To train blackberry canes on wires...'

Blackberries on a wayside hedge. In the sun. Black and red. In the car with Dean and Olivia. A hot September afternoon...

'...stretch 10-12 gauge wire between posts...'

As I set about describing this procedure, that old detached I, he who regarded himself as the 'essential' I, put in another of his intermittent appearances. This time he couldn't believe, as he observed the working I typing 'Set the wires 12in apart, to a height of 5ft', that he, 'Mr Essence', could have any connection with that efficient young man concerned with wires and posts. How, Mr Essence wondered, could the pair of them apparently be one and the same person?

Undoubtedly it was this detached I who had been responsible, not exactly for my continuing fretfulness at Mega – for even without him I would still have told myself I was in the wrong job – but for the extent of my discontent. Bored by, alienated from, so much of the quotidian specific, this detached I had such unrealistic ideas: he seemed to think there were occupations out there that had freed themselves from that fetter. It was he who throughout my time at Mega had kept wondering how others could become so *immersed* in the subject-matter of their days, in, for instance, the psyches of robots, the consistencies of swiss roll fillings, the vital statistics of whitebait; how they could become so *vexed* about insufficiently enlarged prints, overdue captions; how the other, working I, his blood brother, could *bother* himself so much with 'We need to show *every* stage of cultivation.'

It was certainly he too who wondered how power-hungry Bob Plumpford, who had so distanced himself from the day-to-day concerns of his underlings, was yet apparently okay with the so ordinary constituents of his position: reaching his office by a mere *lift* and *corridors* no different from those the tea ladies used; sitting at a *desk* and using a *telephone* no different from anyone else's; having meetings about nothing more important than *Mega Books* for God's sake. If he had such bloody big ideas, why didn't he forget Mega and try for something 'truly interesting', truly ascendant, enter that idealised world of power which in all its vagueness was not tethered to such commonplaces as lifts, corridors, desks, telephones, book schedules, but consisted instead of...of...of what exactly?

When, additionally, that detached I had wanted a 'truly interesting' job for me, he hadn't had in mind those glamorous escapes from the world of conventional work on which some sail off: cultivating a vineyard in Provence, botanising in South America, making a documentary in China. (He knew anyway that most young people from my background did not have the wide horizons, the easy expectations, the precedents that would ever lead them to consider those options and that, even if they were to consider them, lacked the know-how, the confidence, the contacts to realise them. I dare say that when they were girls there was little in grace and agility to choose between

Chillingford Flint's sister and Linda Lorell, star of her school's gymnastic display and such a lissom mover on the disco floor, but whereas Ginny Flint went on to dance for the Royal Ballet, Linda Lorell, in those pre-ballet-classes-for-every-girl days, went on to help run the local Doughty's newsagents with hubby Jock Hoddle, alumnus of Sir Bernard Croucher, who as manager of the shop was considered by Mrs Harnett, who knew his mother, to have 'done really well for himself'.) No, what the detached I had desired for me had been a 'truly interesting' something which, while it might fall into the category of orthodox occupation, somehow did not limit its practitioners to no more than a concentration on the rigorously specific and circumscribed. He had forgotten, that detached I, that such a concentration on the rigorously specific and circumscribed was for human beings the only mode possible for engaging in any endeavour, even the greatest; had forgotten that, when it came down to it, all that my literary hero, Master, had done when he produced his masterpiece had been – far from creating it in some sort of enviable supramundane existence – no more than to make mark after mark after mark with pen or typewriter on paper in exactly the same way as – when, to take an example at random, I inserted into Apples a long list of varieties – I did in my to me unenviable all-too-mundane editorial existence; had forgotten that, though the actual conception, development and accomplishment of *Mosaic* may have been uncountable times more interesting and rewarding than the writing up of Apples, the concrete means of its realisation were little different; had forgotten what his more realistic brother had long ago apprehended about Master and Gershwin, and what was after all a pretty simple obvious truth, that their worlds consisted of the same basic material as everyone else's, were subject to the same unwelcome contingencies, were not in the least less existentially limited.

The working I dismissed him, that detached, incorrigibly

idealising I, went on with 'Alternatively, train the canes up supporting posts and...'

'Unbelievable!'

I may, in Becoming a Man, have made myself more weatherproof than of old but I sometimes found that overlay less impervious than I'd thought. Particularly during those rare spells of true summer that paid a visit on office days. Then, lunch break over, with what a dull aching reluctance I walked back to Mega House, pushed through one of its great bronze and glass doors, as I did now on a glorious August afternoon, and left the splendour behind outside. Whereas when you moved from the sunlit clamorous city streets into Hyde Park the sudden cathedral-like quiet that enveloped you was soothing and uplifting, by contrast when you stepped from the sunlight and bustle of Regency Place into the Mega foyer the sudden dim hush, broken only by echoing footsteps across the mosaic floor, had a *lowering* effect. That silent, sun-shunning atmosphere, which swallowed you up so completely once the door had swung to behind you and which compared so dismally with what lay without, had a peculiarly unpleasant quality all its own: it seemed almost palpably laden with the long hours of problem-filled, tedious, uncongenial work that stretched ahead, those heavy hours when you keep saying to yourself, 'God, is that all the time is?', those banged-up hours from which there is no escape. Even after years of entering that lobby, I still felt on such days, as I crossed its expanse, a sinking of the spirits, even sometimes that physical stone-in-the-pit-of-the-stomach, your-turn-next-in-the-waiting-room thing.

After giving Angie and Jill, this year's glammed-up receptionists, a smiling nod, the easy smiling nod of a 'Mega person' looking forward to the afternoon ahead, I made for the stairs (four flights to the second floor – kept you fitter than the lift).

I was halfway up the third flight when the detached I, who was certainly on a roll these days, brought me to a sudden halt, transfixed by an attack of that ontological incredulity which visits us on rare occasions: the incredulity that, in the limitless extent of eternity, of which the span of our existence accounts for such an infinitesimally minute portion – even less than, say, in a great ocean the amount that one atom of one droplet of water accounts for – it is a moment of that infinitesimally minute portion, as opposed to any of the inconceivably vast number of moments when we didn't exist and will not exist, which, could you believe it, *just happens to be occurring NOW*. In other words, a trillions-and-trillions-and-trillions-(keep adding the noughts)-to-one long shot, that makes a bet on the Lottery look like smart money, *has come up*. Perhaps this abrupt glimpse of something as disturbing as it is astonishing is an unsophisticated nothing in comparison with the profound (yet, even so, at base, bootless) investigations of modern theoretical physics into the origins and nature of the universe, time and space, but nevertheless, to me, taking it in the guts as it were, it –

At that moment, the swing doors on the floor above me burst open and Jerry Langham, honcho of Accounts, with a bulky folder in his hand, called angrily over his shoulder 'Tell him it bloodywell *has* to be done today', then bounded down the stairs, exclaiming to me as he passed, with a shake of his head, 'Unbelievable!'

But it seemed, whatever it was, a very minor matter for unbelievability compared to the fact that in the brain-zonking immensity of time he, Jerry Langham, just happened to be existing *now*. Then, as I climbed the remaining stairs, the detached I graciously retreated and allowed the working I to take over at the controls again, to re-engage with Megaworld.

Scarcely a trace

Violent death in the depths of a beautiful afternoon. A few days after writing it, I re-read the penultimate chapter of my book – and laid it aside with distaste. How strange it is that we can be *so* contemptuous of what *so* pleased us *so* short a time ago. I was unhappy on two scores. In the first place, I was aware that I'd melodramatised the existences of those who resist tyranny in real life, melodramatised them in the manner of one of those highly coloured, selective biopics, and therefore falsified them. And it wasn't just the ending of the book I'd treated in this way – I now realised, looking through the rest, that there'd been that tendency all along. The real Jean Moulin and the real Claus von Stauffenberg, my part-models for Leo and Guy, hadn't found resistance romantic. Moulin had undertaken many tedious journeys to attend many difficult meetings, had become embroiled in organisational in-fighting, been accused of abusing his power, struggled to cope with at least five different Resistance factions each with its own political agenda. And there were always doubts about what his own was, what exactly he was up to. At the top, even more than on the ground, resistance in occupied France was a complex, often frustrating and dispiriting business. Where was any of this in my book? All I'd done was to present Leo as one of those wise, strong, laconic, father-figure leaders wheeled on in movie thrillers to deal masterfully with every situation. He was never bogged down in anything boring or intractable. And those around him were all united. Stauffenberg, too, as a career soldier, a colonel in the Wehrmacht, had, like Moulin, been caught up in a web of doubts, hesitations, disappointments. And the German Resistance, like the French, had also been riven by dissension. Again, where was any of this in my book? Guy, driven as much by vengeance as a fight for freedom, was some stock Byronic hero unhindered by the trammels, often so unromantically squalid, that beset the real-life man of action all along the way. It was true that after the war both Moulin and Stauffenberg had been mythologised in their own countries and that anyone who enters the pantheon of his nation's heroes is burnished in the public imagination to an unrealistically dazzling, flawless sheen, but if you were writing about a political resistance movement, even if only in fiction, the reality of it all could not – or, rather, should not – simply be brushed aside.

But apart from all that, more importantly, what had that climactic chapter, what had so much else of what I'd written, to do with the book I had always wanted to write, the beautiful book inspired by *Mosaic*? Through, first, a deficiency in inventive powers, then a decision that heroic action would largely supersede numinous mystery, then, via the theme of the gold and the black, a seduction into melodrama, I had ended up with what was simply a piece of hokum, something that possessed scarcely a trace of my original dream.

Six

Potts

The small office was warm and stuffy on this September afternoon. Beans: Broad, Dwarf, Runner. Working on runners, I typed: 'Spray the plants in the evening to help the flowers set.' But no need on evenings when the sky was threatening, when it was indigo, such as those when the rain began to fall on the back gardens of Danehill Road and the sun, suddenly breaking through at the same time, lit up the silky orange flowers of the Harnetts' runner beans next door. Then, while a rainbow 'faded in' from only-just-visible to a luminous spectrum against the purplish backdrop, the leaves of those beans, each emerald or jade according to whether the sun had made it translucent or not, would create a constantly shifting pattern as they danced to the rain's silvery tattoo. And, in places perched on top of the leaves, in others peeping out from under them, those orange bean flowers, where they caught the light amid the wet variegated golden and dark green, would glow and flicker like flames…

I came to. As I'd ponderously set about transforming my reams of field notes into copy that morning, Beans had felt more than heavy enough. But now, this afternoon, as though they were feeding on the soporific after-lunch fug, they seemed to be increasing in weight by the minute. Willpower. Willpower. It could enable you to triumph over any...

I was interrupted in my renewed determination to push on with my task by a sudden awareness of how remarkably the only other occupant of the room was behaving. This was Barney Potts, a sub working on the update of the *Conservatory Companion*. I had recently moved in with him: office redecorations and more and more new projects starting up meant that staff were constantly being relocated; an earnest young office manager with a clipboard was to be seen here, there and everywhere, arranging it all. In my case, this room was temporary accommodation until a much larger one had been made ready to house the ever-growing Gardening book workforce in one place.

I looked across at the figure facing me at his desk. Whereas I had thought of myself as, among so many other possibilities, a photographer *manqué*, Potts, it was evident, much more interestingly thought of himself as a *photographic negative manqué*: for some profound, unknowable reason, he strove to emulate physically one of those unearthly beings who gaze out at us from the strips of film the processors return with our prints. Flaxen hair; hilariously deep, almost ebony, sunbed tan; George Raft togs: pale suit, dark shirt, pale tie (today pearl and navy). As for that behaviour that had attracted my attention, it was some weird telephone stunt. Having just made a call, he had lowered his head and the receiver down to the copy on his desk (Conservatory Potholder Tips) and with thumb and forefinger was sound-effect rustling and crackling the pages of this near the mouthpiece to simulate heavy-duty work on it, while he murmured sham-distracted 'M-m-m's and 'Ye-e-es'es and 'I se-e-e's. He couldn't be...? Surely not. He couldn't be trying to prove to whoever was at the end of the line that he, Barney Potts, was some high-powered two-brains much too busy to break off from work during telephone talk but easily capable of managing both together anyway? Well, yes, on past evidence, that was probably what he was doing.

A man approaching forty, with a rather haunted look beneath the acquired subcontinental duskiness, Potts was a roofer's son who hailed originally from Bermondsey and had left school at sixteen. I knew all this because he hadn't bothered to conceal anything from one whose background he had discovered by persistent indirect questioning to be not that dissimilar to his own. He'd even admitted to me that he'd bluffed his way into Mega, laying claim to A levels he didn't have and to authorship of two publicity brochures he didn't write – for the insurance company at which he'd been a clerk. However, he had been able to produce at his interview something he actually had written – of which more shortly.

Potts had attended to his accent, acquiring like Dean a passably 'classless' one, which, erroneously to most who hear it, places its owner in a social limbo. He had also met and married a young woman who worked at a stockbrokers, daughter of a Sothebys auctioneer, ugly to an unusual degree but blessed with a generous allowance. And he had bought a property in gentrified Islington. In short, he had been ascending. His successive base camps on the climb he pointed out to me with barefaced directness, and usually out of the blue. It was, for example, apropos of absolutely nothing at all that he would volunteer that he was now banking at Coutts or acquiring an Aga or growing old shrub roses or buying some Meissen or giving another large dinner party (at which the guests appeared to be predominantly his wife's old chums). And he was as oblivious of the actual effect each announcement had on me as some tyrant's blinkered propagandist is of the actual effect his all's-well bilge has on his impassive audience. His political allegiance was, natch, of the regulation deep blue colouring adopted by most of his kind, and how tiresome it was to keep hearing this Johnny-come-lately roofer's son's predictable demands for punishment of the 'work-shy', slashing of 'nanny-state' benefits, and tax-axing for the 'wealth creators'.

But Potts and I didn't just have similar backgrounds. He was also another wannabe writer. Potts, though, as I've mentioned, had actually had one piece of fiction (if you could call it that) published (if you could call it that) in a newspaper (if you could call it that): a short short story of his entitled 'The Startled Cat', chiefly notable for its particular mandatory 'twist in the tail' having clodhoppingly given away what it was to be as early as line three, had appeared, several years before Potts joined Mega, as one of those single-column fripperies in the Teatime section of the *Warp*. Having it printed had obviously acquired a monumental significance in his life: I lost count of the occasions on which a visitor to our offices would find the subject of cats mystifyingly introduced into the conversation (à la Ray Blight) by Potts, who then casually made appear out of nowhere, as a conjuror might, one of his many photocopies of his minimalist tale.

I have to say, though, that in one of his aspects as wannabe writer no one could have been more unlike me than Potts: his prolific output. He produced his novellas (his curiously preferred genre) at a rate that I felt put to shame my laborious cranking out of fragments of my own fiction. But, other than the Teatime trifle, which first gave Potts the idea that he could make it as a writer, nothing of his stupendous output had so far found a taker.

So, Beans heavy, I sat regarding this singular being bending his head down to desktop level, scrunching sheets of paper near the mouthpiece of the phone and dementedly mouthing 'abstracted' acknowledgments and agreements into it. On his desk I espied three fresh novellas. He had, it was clear, become, as Grouty would have put it, 'a goddam novella-producing machine'. And as to who had to take the blame for first setting that machine in motion, the finger had to be pointed unwaveringly at the *Warp*. Yes, I couldn't help thinking that the decision to accept 'The Startled Cat' with a straight face, to lend it the dignity of *print* for heaven's sake, had to be regarded, from a responsible standpoint, as almost criminal.

As well as his background and his literary ambition, Potts shared with me a dissatisfaction with working at Mega Books. But whereas, for political reasons, I did not sound off about this a great deal, Potts constantly cursed his lot to anyone who would listen. And, too, whereas my aversion was to the particular type of work I seemed to be trapped in, that of Potts seemed to be to any job at all. Day after day he would harp on about his need for a legacy, a premium bond jackpot, a windfall of any kind – not in a tone of wry regret that such good fortune is rare but in the querulous voice of one who thought he was being unfairly denied his due. 'Other people seem to strike it lucky,' he would complain, citing the odd case he'd heard of. This bonanza would liberate him from the demeaning business of earning a living and apparently enable him to devote himself full-time to his unusual line of literary endeavour. (Of course, I too had the common fantasy of coming into unexpected liberating riches. But mine, unlike Potts', which was simply grounded in a highly unlikely reality, was true fantasy, which I knew to be outrageous, impossible, laughable: some millionaire, who would enter as suddenly and mysteriously into my life as one of those super-rich distant relatives did into the lives of 'our heroes' in the pages of *Film Fun*, would offer me a vast sum of money if, for example, I could complete the task I was engaged in *within one minute from now*; or if I could bring myself to eat something *unspeakably vile*; or if... He was, this shadowy millionaire, a strange personage, given as he was to these sudden arbitrary, misplaced, pointless bouts of largesse, from which he himself appeared to obtain not the least benefit. A figure of fantasy indeed.)

I sometimes wondered why Potts had chosen that particular form, the novella, to work in. I believe – though I have never tried it myself – that it is a demanding discipline to take on. Like the 800 metres. Neither a sprint nor a distance event. Great judgment required. Tough. (Perhaps he felt, mistakenly, that it had a certain cachet.) Anyway, the difficulty of it made his supernaturally prolific output even more astounding. As for that output, well, just as unbridled philandering is sometimes due less to actual superstud virility than to a desperate attempt to prove possession of it, perhaps that spewing out of novella after novella, which might to some have indicated enviable literary assurance, actually denoted deep literary unease. There was further support for this idea: Potts kept thrusting his work on me for my opinion and no amount of contrived cool on that troubled face could hide its owner's anxious attendance on my lying verdicts. What's more, he also solicited my opinion of his editorial work – a unique case in my experience. What bolstering he'd needed on the Fish book (on which, as author of 'The Startled Cat', he'd been brought in late to produce short 'creative' intros, as distinct from the stodgy text that Mike and I were lumbered with). Not that self-esteem ever allowed him openly to admit he was seeking my help. No, whenever he asked me what I thought of one of his efforts – 'How's this, d'you reckon: "Laying their thousands of eggs, the salmon's breeding takes place in the north in gravel in fresh water"?' – the note he struck was offhandedly rhetorical, he affected scarcely more to require an answer than if he had murmured, 'Lovely day, isn't it?' Or sometimes, more directly (though then typically unaware of the self-defeating near-insolence of his remarks), he would, again at the dictate of pride, belittle in advance any suggestions I might make by opening his request with: 'As a nit-picking so-and-so, what's your opinion of...?' This relegated my role to that of pettifogging copy editor to his creative writer, or, more specifically and fantastically, to his

Scott Fitzgerald, with whom – partly on account of 'Scotty's' weakness in spelling and grammar, to which he, Potts, made unnaturally regular reference – he startlingly claimed affinity. At first I tactfully suggested some changes to the pieces he 'nonchalantly' read out, but eventually, weary of his gall, I lyingly approved them all and let him take the consequences. Whenever, for instance, I heard yet another example of his favourite idle, specious, all-purpose 'while' construction ('The conservatory bridges the house and garden, while tender plants can be grown in its warm atmosphere'), which he may have picked up from its arch-exponent on the Fish book, the terrible Roger Wrasse, I would okay it with a 'Fine, fine.'

It was not only aspects of photography – the negative – and of the modern industrial process – the fully automated machine – that Potts demonstrated in his person but of cybernetics too, in the form of the self-regulating circuit: he sedulously instilled in many people the idea that he was a writer; they then tacitly treated him as such in their dealings with him; this then reinforced in him the idea that he was a writer; he then the more confidently instilled it further in those others; and so on, in a perfectly functioning closed loop.

His literary standing was highest among non-editors, who saw his outbursts against Mega Books as the understandable frustration of a creative soul enmired in a philistine world. Karen Lee, Simon's assistant, had said to me, 'We all feel it's such a shame about poor old Barney. It must be so difficult for a really creative person who's had his stuff published to lower himself to this level.' So it was always Potts, and none of the many other available subs, they chose to consult on any literary matter. Corinne Marchant, a designer on the *Book of Britain*, had approached him the previous week and said, 'I know it's none of my business, really, but one of our people – no names, no pack-drill – has written these captions on the Lake Poets, and they seem feeble to me. As a "literary bod", Barney, what do you reckon? You know how to play around with words.' (Potts as *ludic* master.) But, apart from some mumbled cobblers about Keats, Potter, who'd once told me that he'd read scarcely a line of poetry in his life, could come up with nothing but the silence of the nonplussed. He rallied, however, and, peering at her over his half-moon specs (he'd swiftly acquired a pair after the Chairman had taken to wearing them and never let an opportunity pass to lower his head and sight you over them with headmasterly gravitas as Lyttelton did), he reassured her with an avuncular: 'Leave it with me – I'll see what I can do.' I never learned what it was he later saw that he could do. To tell the truth, I went out of my way to avoid learning it.

Apart from his Mega work and the three novellas, there were also on his desk neatly stacked notebooks of various formats, together with serried rows of ballpoints, pencils and felt pens in a wide range of colours; and into the drawers of that desk one would see him regularly stow reams of typing paper, plastic envelopes, cardboard folders and ringbinders, all of different 'classificatory' hues. For Potts was, among other things, a stationery freak. Scarcely a day passed without one of his raids on the stationery store, and each time that he returned with an armful of fresh items it would be with the contented smile of any addict who has just had his fix. (I think of Stu Laine at school. He had this attaché-case-like walnutwood box full of brushes, pens, pencils, inks, pastels, fixatives, sprays and God knows what else, the envy of the rest of the class. He couldn't draw or paint for toffee. I think of Mickey Boyd at the rec. Unlike the rest of us, he was always accoutred in the full works: replica shirt and shorts, shin pads and the latest boots. He was always the last to be picked.)

At last, with a final extra-fierce rustling of a page in the mouthpiece, Potts' obscene call came to an end. Then he resumed work with the matter-of-fact air of one for whom conducting phone conversations with mouth at desktop level was nothing untoward.

After a while he said in an offhand way: 'I was talking to Geoff Green in Sales at lunchtime and he told me something quite interesting.' (Sales was one of his areas of assiduous – yet, as it turned out, largely fruitless – networking.)

I looked up, swallowing this casually floating, innocent-seeming fly.

'Yes, he said that Sigmerfaffow' – a typical Potts error, but Sifgermaffow, Sigmerfaffow, Sigmerfaffoff, who gave a toss? – 'has just passed the fifty thousand mark.'

Painful disbelief as the hook dug in. 'You're joking.'

This was what Potts had been angling for: he'd long known what I thought of the book. He attempted to tug on the line, to fix the barb more excruciatingly: 'Yes, and they reckon it might reach a hundred thousand by the end of the year.' But too cornily mock-innocent a voice and look gave the game away (well, what else could you expect from the author of 'The Fucking Startled Cat'?), and, determined not to gratify him further, feigning resignation, I confined myself to 'Well, there you go.'

He returned to writing a new page heading for the *Conservatory Companion*, but soon it was obvious his old unease about his efforts had resurfaced: he 'carelessly' offered me another of his 'on approvals', this time a sort of deliberate compilation it seemed of his most favoured desecrations (broaching it with the usual self-defeating cheek): 'What's the pedant's view of this? "Proving an essential item for every conservatory, the use of potholders is a must, while highly ornamental jardinières lend a splash of charm."'

Was it perhaps in some dim remembrance of the appreciative diners at Jamie and Jeanie's that I gave it the *double* thumbs-up?

The Mega *Mosaic*

Pushing through the great swing doors of Mega House, I thankfully left Beans and Potts behind me. Ten to six. But not your usual end of summer ten to six. The leaden brightness, warmth and stillness were more pronounced, more obviously expectant, than is usual before the weather breaks. I crossed Regency Place and headed for the tube down a street of solid mansions and office buildings. Soon there sounded from on high several low thumping noises as of heavy furniture being dropped on to a carpeted floor. At the same time, large dark spots began leisurely to pattern the pavement, pattern it at random, and simultaneously there was a faintly pungent odour in the air, bringing with it memories that were elusive: the quiet roads and gardens where I sensed I'd inhaled it on mild dull afternoons in the past, as the first full warm drops hesitantly fell, were as vague and unidentifiable as so much else I 'remembered' these days. Subtle, odd, far from fragrant yet delicious, this leisurely-onset-of-rain smell, soon joined by that of damp fabric from those around me and now a glistening on the pavement up ahead, transformed that everyday street to one touched with enchantment...

On to a packed tube train. Near me a young man strap-hanging was just about managing to read with one hand. As he swayed I caught a glimpse of his book. It was *Mosaic* in its Mega Paperbacks reincarnation. When it had appeared the previous year I'd examined it and found that the magic of the edition I knew and loved had now vanished. In fact, the whole list and presentation of what had once been Spectrum had plummeted downhill under its new imprint. For one thing, when Vin Sharpes had been in charge he'd jettisoned many outstanding titles (though, at Dean's insistence, he had retained Master's masterpiece); they were 'clogging up the list', as Dean told me his old colleague had put it. Sharpes' policy, continued by his successor, had been to take on a cargo of commercial shoddy – puffed up books of surface glister, possessing not a trace of true poetry or wit or insight or comedy or tragedy or mystery or exploration or style or anything else that would explain why their authors had bothered to write them or why anyone should bother to read them. In addition, the covers had become cruder: representational illustration had taken over from the stylised and the abstract, and in some cases, reminiscent of *True 'Tec Tales*, the scene depicted bore no relation to anything in the book. Replacing, for instance, the original purple, lilac and old-rose design on the front cover of *Mosaic* – which for me had always suggested one of the 'significant' skies in the novel and had even become an element in the book's essential atmosphere – was, as I now saw again before me, a narrative painting, in repulsive high-gloss detail that showed every hair and every crease, depicting O'Brien, the obese police chief, hammily gloating over the recumbent form of an inaccurately fair-haired bozoish Mark, a scene which was certainly not in the book. And the back-cover blurb was the hopelessly off-beam hard-boiled: 'In Indigo City a lot of scum have risen to the surface. But scummiest of all is Police Chief Reinhard O'Brien…' Faced with this cover, hesitating over whether to buy the book or not, someone who knew nothing of its true nature would have had no inkling that they were hesitating at the entrance to a uniquely magical world.

But it wasn't only the cover of *Mosaic* that had changed drastically. So had the physical appearance of its contents: a new, thicker, whiter paper, to bulk the book out more, and a different typeface in a slightly larger size, set with wider margins, to increase the number of pages (all to provide an even bigger doorstop to justify a hoick in the price). And just as a new interpretation of a favourite piece of music or play can seem actually to alter its very substance, so the new form in which the text of a favourite book is presented to us can, amazingly, seem to affect its very quality. The words are exactly the same, and yet they have become, according to how we react to the paper and type and margins, either more or less evocative, profound, eloquent, enjoyable than before. There have been familiar books I have come across in American editions where the alien typography, un-English spellings and odd page smell have made me feel I am reading a different, less congenial, inferior work. So it was with this Mega *Mosaic*. Almost unbelievably to me, in this new edition the actual appearance of the individual words and the disposition of their massed ranks on the brighter, thicker page had somehow contrived to make the book rather less impressive. Favourite passages I re-read, physically of lower relative density as it were, had suffered a corresponding reduction in literary potency.

I looked at the young man and wondered, as we do when we see someone reading a book that has meant a great deal to us, how he was reacting to it. Perhaps, if he'd thought he was buying an Elmore-Leonard-mean thriller, he was feeling nothing but disappointment.

An 'old hand'

No more than I could bring myself to use the term Gicbog for the Gardening book could I bring myself to refer to our spacious new office by the popular name it immediately acquired: the Allotment. I felt about this as I did about the names with which some eating-place chains at that time tarted up their unexceptional fare. Ordering from the waitress in one of these, I found myself unable, my vocal cords physically unable, to ask for 'A Whole Hunk O' Pleasure and a Bottomless Cup, please' and, uncomfortably aware of how obvious was the circumvention, could speak only of apple pie and coffee. In just the same way, if Plumpford's miniskirted secretary Bunty (whom, he claimed to male colleagues, he'd taken on for her 'world-class arse') came skittering down the corridor to ask where her boss was, I would find it impossible to mouth the succinct 'The Allotment' but would resort awkwardly to 'The Gardening book room' – to which she would reply, 'The Allotment, do you mean?'

Despite the fact that I was still so busy, attending one reporting session after another and trying to get it all written up – and written up, that is, to accord with the inflexible demands of the designers – despite this, when McStutt was asked to select one of his staff to give editorial training to a young woman who wished to enter publishing – Cindy Lyttelton, a niece of the Chairman – he fastened on me. In private, I protested to him, telling him I couldn't possibly fit this into my already taxing workload. What about Flint, who was now 'working' full-time on our book? Constantly 'popping out', without the least reprimand from McStutt – indeed, with his reluctant acquiescence: 'OK, Chillingford, er-heh-heh' – to 'see about' another pipe or lengthily attending to one of those he already had, he was spinning out his job on Shrubs to an extent I wouldn't have believed possible. Patently, he could have accommodated the tuition of half-a-dozen trainees into his Edwardian gentleman's day. But McStutt insisted to me: 'No, no, you're just the man for the job.' That wasn't the reason, of course. The real reason was that McStutt so feared Flint, was so anxious not to incur his stony-eyed displeasure, that he wouldn't dare try to 'burden' him with another job. Well, I persisted, what about someone from another project? Chris Alexander, say – and what better mentor?

'No, I believe from what I've heard that Chris has more than enough on his plate already. He's just started doubling up on the *Conservatory Companion* update, er-heh-heh. Barney Potts' work on that needs some fine tuning, shall we say, er-heh-heh.'

OK, what about another project editor coming up with someone under less – ?

'No, the Chairman has asked me personally to find someone.' He leaned back, adopting the familiar ready-to-be-shaved position. 'And we must keep the Chairman happy, er-heh-heh, er-heh-heh.'

Well, in that case, I had to warn him that some of my allotted tasks would inevitably fail to hit their deadlines.

'No need to worry yourself about that. Chillingford may be able to help out, despite all the hard work he's putting into Shrubs.'

I had found a new solace when the likes of McStutt, Plumpford or Flint were riling me: it was the pleasurable imagining of them asleep, the pleasurable knowledge that those who took such obvious enjoyment in exercising what they believed to be the absolute primacy of their decisions and will were for up to a whole third of their lives impotently adrift in a world of chimeras, delusions, metamorphoses, dissolutions of space, reversals of time, a nonsensical world in which colleagues' illogical arguments (somehow, even though spoken, developing line by line in italics, in that typically notional-yet-horribly-ineluctable dreamscape way) trounced their own, an uncontrollable world of whose elements they were, far from being complacently in charge, on the contrary at the mercy. What a pity, I thought, that that night-after-nightly phantasmagoria that trashes us all had no apparent lasting effect on them, never seemed, once they were awake and in blithe unchangingness pomping it once more in the offices and corridors of Mega, to instil in them a drop of humility, of acceptance that they were no less *essentially* vulnerable than the rest of us.

So I began to 'train up' Cindy Lyttelton, or, rather, I went through the motions of doing so: it soon became obvious to me that she was little more fitted to working with words than Simon was and that she would never make an editor. But then I remembered Barney Potts...and then the nepotism of my own entreé into publishing...and I thought again. As I sat there, explaining to this brash young woman some of the bare bones of editorial work, that incredulity stole over me that steals over all youngish 'old hands' in such circumstances: how short a time ago, it seems, we were tyros ourselves. Why, it was so clear in my memory, that occasion on which Stan Grout sat down with me to prepare me for making my very first editorial pencillings on paper, to show me what I had to do with his appalling scripts. And now here I was...

That afternoon, while I was consulting Simon about Heathers, there was a call for me on an outside line. Ironically, it was Stan Grout reversing our previous roles, asking for my assistance. He wanted to know if there were any editorial vacancies in Books. I'd heard rumours that he'd had a hard time since *True 'Tec Tales* had folded, barely scraping a living as a freelance for this outfit and that. Remembering his invalid wife, I felt sorry for him. Otherwise I wouldn't have done what I did. I knew the *Lay-by Companion*, a monumental tome, needed another sub, so I told Grout I would recommend him that afternoon to Manny Van White, the editor, and suggested he ring him the next day. I felt like saying, 'But whatever you do, if you get the job, lay off the goddam "truckers", "gas", "autos", "big rigs" – for both our sakes.' (After all, how did I know I might not have to apply to Van White for a job myself one day?) Instead, I merely said, in response to his effusive thanks, 'Not at all. Hope it works out well.'

Effaced

I may have retained clear images of my early days on *True 'Tec Tales*, but there were certain slivers of my past working life which had already become unreal to me. My very first job, for example: that week at a cardboard box manufacturers somewhere outside Plumstead. When I'd worked there, I was in my mid-teens, a time by which, I would have thought, memories would start being firmly laid down. But no. I could no longer recall anything about that job. The name of the firm, where it was, who I worked with – all lost. I couldn't even be sure *what I did there*. Wasn't it something to do with putting labels on the boxes? Or was it stacking them? Or both? I could remember the full name and address of Danny's married sister, a young woman I'd visited with him only once, I could remember some of the essay subjects Mr Cowper-Crabbe, another English master at Sir Bernard Croucher (who shot himself), had set us, but I could remember nothing about my first job. For a whole week of my life I had caught a bus to Plumstead, I had walked from a bus stop along some route or other, I had with a fully functioning consciousness entered a building, spoken to people there, engaged for four hours in the morning in a particular activity, eaten lunch somewhere, worked at that activity for another four hours, walked back to the bus stop – and it had all disappeared without a trace. It wasn't like those hazy segments of our past, islets glimpsed upstream as we travel away from them, that may be misty but are still discernible – like my time at Cattalls. No, that week had been effaced from view as though by an impenetrable fog that would never lift. How do I know then that it ever took place? Well, I don't *know* it, that's the alarming thing. I only 'know' it: that is, I have to give the benefit of the doubt to that archivist in the brain who, without supplying any supporting evidence, any pictures or sound recordings, simply informs us of the the bare, brief, unsubstantiated 'fact' that such-and-such a thing took place in our life. We're not convinced – his arid information could as well apply to the life of someone else for all that it means to us – but we have to take this character on trust, or where would we be?

Vanished for good, that week? *That entire week?* Yes. No associative memory – no smell of cardboard boxes, no canteen odour – is ever going to resuscitate those days for me. They're lost as permanently as a bubble that has burst is lost. And so such days seem no more real to us, even though they have formed part of our own life, than do certain incidents in others' lives that we cannot *really* believe ever happened (in my case, these include, for some reason I'm unable to fathom, the Futurist Marinetti dropping rabble-rousing leaflets from a plane over Venice). How scary this realisation can be: that segments of our past that we lived through at the time, no less normally, fully, than we are living through our present days, seeing, hearing, speaking, washing, dressing, eating no differently than we are doing today, have been so totally expunged that from our present standpoint they might as well never have existed. And the more that we try to peer back at those irretrievably lost tracts of time, tracts of what we mistakenly believed was a life we *own*, the more disturbingly, saddeningly ghostlike they become.

No matter how much we may read about Time in the works of philosophers, scientists, poets, novelists, no matter how intelligent and vivid their explorations of it, their descriptions of its effects, their lamentations about its tyranny, none of it can prepare us for, or provide solace for, our own terrifyingly unique experience of its monstrousness.

'Carefully maintained ignorance'

About that time I came across, in the stimulant effect a certain book had on Flint, a further example of a phenomenon I'd first become aware of in the underground Gents in Blackwell. Mega Paperbacks had started including soft porn in its list, and one of its recent offerings had been a novel about a classful of leching schoolgirls. According to Flint's account of the book to Simon, Roger Taylor and myself at one of those rare middays when he was still to be found in the office, the girls were *longing* for sex with the boys of a nearby school, and after various misadventures they fulfilled this desire to the great enjoyment of one and all. As Flint told it, this seemed to constitute the totality of the story – which indeed it may well have done. The novel was obviously aimed at those who fantasise about lustful schoolgirls – as did, for instance, in their correspondence, two notable English men of letters. And to give itself more credibility and thus its readers a greater thrill, the book broadly hinted at being autobiographical: the middle-aged stockbroker who it was discovered later had penned the work and who, rather like those who self-publish on lavatory walls, had presumably done so to share his fantasies of nymphos in gymslips with others, had used a female pseudonym and provided as authorial photograph and cv on the jacket those of a young woman. In the same way, and for the same reason, John Cleland's *Fanny Hill*, with its narrator's gasping paeans to the phallus, purported to be 'the memoirs of a woman of pleasure'. Perhaps for the one who can only fantasise about female sexual desire supposed schoolgirl lust is the most thrillingly convincing indication (convincing because adolescence is an age when desires and behaviour tend to be more genuine and spontaneous than in adulthood) that that female carnality which he would love to encounter but never has encountered is innate. Given the nature of Flint's education and his early marriage to a woman who when she called into the office did not give the impression, with her voice, eyes and general demeanour that matched his own, of one who might be hot stuff in bed (though you could never be completely certain, I suppose), I thought I was fairly safe in assuming that he had not been exactly surfeited in his life with evidence of female sexual passion but, rather, belonged to that generation of public school men who, at that time at any rate, as Wayland Young said, 'were educated in a carefully maintained ignorance of the fact that fucking is pleasure for both parties'. Certainly, he was so agitated by that tale he had just read, he so wished others to read it and share his turmoil, that it stimulated him to an unprecedented animation, disregard of his pipe and completion of one of his sentences: 'Well, I tell you, it... These randy bloody girls are dying for some of the you-know-what. Ye gods. And they want it with these young lads so much they decide to, you know... And it's obviously all based on this hot-looking bit of stuff's own, you know...'

Disquieted remembrance brought him to a halt.

Gudgeon: revised version

It was an October morning of mist and sun. Because of a tube strike (Potts: 'They should sack the lot of them'; Flint: 'The idle buggers get paid enough already'), I was taking a bus to work. Sitting on the top deck of a No. 9, at the front, gazing down on everything around me, travelling through London at leisure, freed for a day from the confines and the press of the Underground, I felt at happy-go-lucky ease, I wanted this bus journey to continue indefinitely, I recaptured something of the old feeling I'd known as a boy at the prow of a trolleybus. And then, too, as we passed Green Park, the transfiguration it had undergone on this morning of mist-softened autumn sunlight added further lyrical chords to the happiness I was feeling. Up until now, this sunlight, creating noble tableaux from the façades, arcades, crowded pavements and crawling traffic it bathed in its powdery gold, had been a glory diffused, but here, beside and below me, in the park, it was a glory channelled, concentrated, by the spectral yet still material and mediatory trees between which it had to pass, into separate shafts of light, broad shimmering shafts that, carving themselves out of the surrounding haze, looked far more solid than the trees did and that came to rest on the grass in circles of soft luminous green. These beams revealed, too, the presence of drinking fountains you might otherwise not have noticed, sending, from their dull zinc, sudden subdued glints winging through the mist. The sunlit haze, the bustle, the red buses, the slow progress – I felt, in my contentment, less on the way to work than at the start of a never-ending holiday.

Brief bliss. In the office I prepared to write up Tomatoes. The usual disinclination and blank-page inability to get going. And, since the move into this large room, a further hindrance to work: a level of distracting noise and activity, like that of one of the busy streets I'd recently passed along, which I'd not known in previous offices. At last I made a start but no sooner had I done so than I was interrupted by the arrival of Walter Gudgeon, Dean's old colleague, who was now Production Manager at Books.

I had first encountered Gudgeon again, after so many years, in the foyer of Mega House when I'd been working on *The Swiss Roll Maker*. I had thought then how little he'd changed, even though he must now be nearing retirement. His hair may have been grey, his face more lined, but the canine eyes still gleamed and he was apparently still brimming with energy. In the old orotund way, he'd expressed delight at seeing me again, reminisced about my being only a small boy when we'd first met at Spectrum, and wished me well in what he was 'sure would prove to be a long, happy and illustrious career in the service of our most worthy employers'. Since then our paths had occasionally crossed again, always briefly and at some distance: I had never been involved with production matters. But the favourable impression I'd had of him as a child was fading fast. That voice, that mellifluous purveyor of rococo nothings, was, the more I heard it, beginning to annoy me. At this moment he had trapped McStutt at his desk and was singing his captive listener a long song about the schedule, a song which the occasional interruptions of McStutt turned into a duet. Despite my efforts to shut it out, it would persist in entwining itself among my greenhouse tomatoes tied to canes.

'Time is absolutely of the essence in this matter...'

'Quite, Walter, er-heh-heh.'

'As my esteemed young assistant, Peter Jamieson, brought to my attention late yesterday evening, it would appear, I'm afraid, that in certain areas the schedule is falling behind to a degree that, in the circumstances...' (Despite my exasperation, I had reluctantly to acknowledge the exquisite phrasing and modulations of that rich baritone in every line.)

'Quite, Walter, er-heh-heh.'

'So it would, I think, in more ways than one, be of advantage if...'

At last, after what seemed to me a full hour, but was perhaps no more than five minutes, Gudgeon's performance, intended as much to enthral the room at large as to communicate a message to a single individual, drew to a close. But then I was perturbed to sense, rather than see (I refused to look up for fear of catching his eye), the Fischer-Dieskau of publishing advancing towards me. He reached my desk. Placing on it the clipboard that he carried with him everywhere as a symbol of efficiency but that I never once saw him actually consult, he picked up at random (I saw from the corner of my eye) one of the various books on greenhouse gardening I was using as reference. Despite his constant assertions that time was of the essence, Gudgeon always appeared to have an extraordinary amount of it on his hands. He was undoubtedly yet another of the great army of the Bored, seeking out his distractions where he could find them. In this respect, the office recitals obviously meant a great deal to him.

'Xavier.'

Forced to acknowledge this address, I looked up. But though sung as a greeting it had actually been no more than a determined commandeering of my attention. For, having raised the book to eye level and gazed at its cover for some time, in the manner of one evaluating an *objet d'art*, he had nothing more to convey to me than – as though I might be at a loose end and in need of entertainment – a slow, lingering and beautiful rendition of title, author and publisher: '*In the Greenhouse*. Andy Slats. Twining & Trellis. H-m-m.' H-m-m indeed. Now clear off, please, there's a good chap, and let me push on with blossom end rot. But becoming even more profligate with that essential time he spoke of so often, he then began an aria from the jacket blurb: 'From choosing and erecting your greenhouse to equipping, managing and selecting the right plants for it, Andy Slats takes you through...'

The voice sang on, magnificently and pointlessly. With a contrasted pointedness, and a philistine disregard for his bel canto, I made an obvious show of continuing with my work. But this clear message had no effect. '...expert advice on heating and ventilation...hydroponics... refreshing commonsense approach...' At last, at last, after a dramatic pause and on an equally dramatic note of finality, he sang the triumphal closing phrases: 'This is, without doubt, the one book beyond any other that every greenhouse gardener needs.' (Again that claim to some special last-word quality, one repeated by every other book in the pile on my desk.) A silence of some length ensued. Was he perhaps expecting applause? Then: 'H-m-m.' Then, as if the book were a novel: 'Interesting?'

Not only was he the uninvited performer, he was also the asker of the unanswerable question. I had come across the type regularly throughout my life. The first occasion I remember was when as a boy I had called at Dr Grant's for a repeat prescription for Lil. Scribbling away, the doctor had asked me: 'And what does your father think of it all?' I racked my brains. What did Harry *think* of it all? Nothing, it seemed, if one were to go by his total lack of discernible reponse to whatever was wrong with Lil. But I could scarcely offer this as an answer. I was reduced to a flummoxed 'Well...' and a nonplussed expression, which, as I ran to Gowdy & Simpson's, the chemists in the High Street, I kept scornfully telling myself had been feeble in the extreme. But when, despite all my efforts, I was unable for the rest of the day to devise a reasonable reply, I began to think that Dr Grant's question hadn't actually had much point to it: even if Harry had expressed himself on the subject of Lil's illness, what could he have come up with other than some such conventional sentiment as 'Hope she gets well soon'? And reporting this would surely have been fatuous.

Others of Gudgeon's remarks were born of that compulsion in certain individuals forever to be trying to find something witty to say. It is a current affliction of two radio presenters, one of pop, the other of classical music, in whom it takes the form of such announcements as: 'The Naked Truth will be in concert there on Friday...' Then the boringly inevitable 'drily witty' follow-up: '...fully clothed we'll assume'; or 'The Vesta Trio will be performing live for us this evening... when they'll be welcomely striking a light in the darkness, I'm sure'. Comments always as contrived as unamusing, as insincere as sterile. I had chanced on one of Gudgeon's the previous Christmas. In the Medical book office a secretary, in a token seasonal gesture, had decorated a few desk lamps with tinsel.

Stately Gudgeon approached Ruth Marks' desk, minimally prettified in this way. I waited for the laboriously 'resourceful' remark. Here it came. In 'jocund' vein and deep mellifluous tones, Gudgeon asked her: 'Is all this finery inspiring you in your work?' Ruth was temporarily at a loss, as who wouldn't be? So though she would I'm sure have preferred to ignore the banal one, she politely searched for a reply and came up with the equally bogus, aridly 'clever' 'Well, I hope it's giving it a little added sparkle.'

As for Gudgeon's present 'Interesting?', it was obvious that the book contained the same practical information on staging, heating, shading, etc. that every other greenhouse book in front of me did, and that by its very nature it couldn't be some unusual stimulating read – especially if you weren't even a gardener, as I wasn't and as Gudgeon had told McStutt he wasn't. Less concerned than Ruth not to offend Gudgeon, I ignored his 'query'. The message of my non-response was, I hoped, clearer this time: bugger off. Not that much clearer apparently. For Gudgeon remained by my desk and riffled through the pages of the book with a speed that made the already senseless activity even more so. But he couldn't let his visit tail off in this limp manner, he needed a conclusion of force. So – when he shut the book, it was with a loud decisive thump, when he deposited it on my desk it was with a 'H-m-m' more lengthy than usual, more doubtful, more suggestive of magisterial judgment suspended, and when he left the room it was *with measured tread*.

True Horror Tale

From time to time, in lifts, corridors, foyer or the streets round about, I would see people I had worked with before joining Books. Once, unwelcomely, I found myself face to face in a lift with Kitchin, who fixed me throughout the descent with his unpleasant stare (only matched for malevolence by that which Manny Van White now gave me every time I passed him in the corridor). By contrast, ever-jolly 'Tommo' Thomlinson would always stop for a chat, and we had the occasional drink together. 'Ta muchly,' 'Tommo' would always 'warble' when I handed him his pint. I told him of my work on the Fish, Medical and Gardening books. 'Crumbs, mate,' he 'gurgled', with a mixture of childlike glee and awe, 'you're becomin' a flippin' encyclopedia, you are, and no mistake. Tee-hee! You'd really be able to kerflummox "Lord" Eddie these days, you really would.'

Former colleagues I never saw around I would occasionally check up on in the Mega directory, a bulky publication in itself. Bertha Gurney, that formidable *True 'Tec Tales* sub, was missing; she'd obviously left the company. But not so Carlsen Purvis (with whom I never exchanged other than a cool nod). Far from it: browsing in the directory one day, I happened on the entry for him: 'Purvis, Carlsen, Managing Director, True Tales Libraries, Ext. 974.' How amazed I was to read this. I had judged my necrophiliac ex-colleague to be a confirmed ranker (as one might say), without ambition. I'd obviously been wrong. And this was confirmed one lunchtime. I was eating a sandwich on a bench in Regency Place when I was joined by Dave Watts, the young *TTT* designer (now on *True Horror Tales* and married to Clare, the frizzy-haired continuity girl). He told me that the general opinion in True Tales Libraries was that Purvis had slagged off Stan Grout to Ms Highe, the production-line supertoughiebitch, hoping to take his place. When, instead, catching Purvis as unawares as the rest of us, *TTT* had folded, he'd moved on to *True Horror Tales*. Soon afterwards, the editor of this, closeted in conference with the corpse-fancier, had had a heart attack and died on the spot. Purvis had succeeded him. Sales of *THT* had increased under its new overseer, and when thigh-revealing Ms Highe was promoted to much higher things – Deputy Chief Executive of the company, only next-but-one in line to the Chairman! – this sequence of events, the only *True* Horror Tale the department had ever actually produced, culminated in Purvis being chosen to replace her. Well, who would have thought it? Apparently not me. And this misreading rather took me aback. After some initial puzzles and surprises as we blunder our way into the big world, we begin to think we're at last sussing it out – which includes, among much else, who's going to make it and who's riding for a fall. Then the completely unexpected sticks a foot out and sends that 'susser-out' sprawling, and we realise he'd been growing too big for his britches by far.

Easy: revised version

But now someone from much farther back in the past than Purvis reappeared on the scene, the third of that trio I had originally met at Spectrum: Neal Easy. A recent *Warp* casual currently looking for work, he had been brought in as another sub on the ever-growing Gardening book team, owing the job no doubt to his old Spectrum colleague Sharpes or his old *Showbiz* colleague Plumpford, or perhaps both. Unlike Sharpes and Gudgeon, Easy had no recollection of me, but, despite the more marked change in his appearance than in the other two – fully bald now, vinous-nosed, tired-looking, sixty-a-day hoarse, prematurely aged – I would immediately have recognised him, without knowing his name, by that old 'incisive' chopping motion that accompanied so much of what he said – though less vigorously now – and that had apparently become, by overlong usage, mindlessly involuntary. Warmly referred to by Plumpford as 'a real pro', confidently recommended by him to McStutt as one who would 'burn rubber', he in fact brought to his odds-and-sods-ing on the book – writing heads and captions, cutting and filling – a *Showbiz/Warp* approach that proved disastrous. On those first mornings when I saw him at his typewriter (he did everything before lunch, that segment of the day when he was capable of work), I was disconcerted to see him, fag drooping from his lower lip, squinting against the smoke à la Harry, hammering away at the keys at breakneck speed, churning out material at a rate that made the rest of us look incompetent or idle – or in Flint's case even more idle ('Ye gods,' Flint drawled several times, observing him in intervals between cleaning his pipe and 'popping out'). However, what dazzles us initially is often seen after the novelty has worn off and under examination to be nothing much after all, perhaps even, amazingly, worthless, like a glittering gem revealed to be paste. So it was with Easy. As soon as the results of his mornings-only snap-crackle-and-pop became apparent – the *Showbiz/Warp*ish sub-heads ('Watch that branch', 'Shoots up in a jiff'), fact-fudgings and sheer inventions – the rest of us felt a great calm flow sweetly through us. We knew that, ex-ragmag man though Plumpford was himself, he understood that such tabloidese would never do for the world of books, not even for Mega Books.

Easy hadn't changed in wanting to bestow on others at every opportunity his 'expertise', to teach granny to suck eggs. On the eve of one of my reporting jobs he 'advised' me hoarsely: 'Get him to show you the different stages of pruning – whut, whut, whut...' I no longer found the no-nonsense whut-whut-whutting in the least impressive. No, as with Sharpes' vanity and Gudgeon's fruity recitals, I now found it simply irksome, and I wanted to repeat to Easy that instruction of Hamlet's to the players: 'Nor do not saw the air too much with your hand.' (So all three of those childhood models – of appearance, speech and manner – had come crashing down from their pedestals. And I could say with Charles Lamb, when the mantle of veneration he had cast over certain figures as a child was in later years torn away: 'Fantastic forms, whither are ye fled?... Why make ye so sorry a figure?')

Easy also liked to give the impression of one for whom native resourcefulness could ferret out any facts at all. Flirting unreciprocatedly at the coffee machine with Corinne Marchant – who was now working on the *Complete Illustrated Family Guide to River Banks and Seashore* – he advised her how to identify marine life *in situ*: 'I always ask the locals, Corrie.' (Although the use of first names was as standard at Mega as in most offices, I had never come across anyone who took to using the chummy abbreviations of those names quite so instantly and insistently as Easy. Within the first minute of joining us, he was addressing me as 'Xav' and Flint as 'Chilly', a diminutive no one else had ever dared use.) 'I ask them, what's that in that pool? They'll tell you. Get hold of a local, Corrie. They know the rock pools like the back of their hand.' (I doubted there was actually much evidence for this. Certainly I'd never come across the least hint of such familiarity with rock pools among the natives of Sandbay.) It was the same with identifying shipping (he seemed bizarrely to imagine this young designer as roving seaside reporter): 'Get on to a coastguard, Corrie. They know these vessels like the back of their hand.' I found my thoughts straying along the same old lines: had Easy really ever consulted a local about the inhabitants of a rock pool or a coastguard about a vessel? With difficulty I forced myself to visualise it. And, in what had become one of the leitmotivs of my apprehension of the world, this picturing of the to me scarcely credible was once again suffused with a truly horrid surreality.

Unfortunately for Easy, the trenchant cure-all chopping would appear never to have met with any success when applied to his own affairs, since he was the stock Street soak of that time: his soppingly liquid lunches left him stupefied in the afternoon, scarcely in a fit condition to sub, his third marriage was falling apart and he was scarily deep in debt (his presumed 'advice' to himself along the lines of 'Do your weekly stint, bank your monthly income, note your balance – whut, whut, whut – ensure your standing orders, household expenses, drinks money don't exceed this – whut, whut, whut – and there you are!' had obviously failed to do the trick).

Poor Neal Easy. After his fill-in on the Gardening book even Sharpes refused to find him more work at Mega (and Plumpford had left by then). Eventually he became more or less destitute and the third wife walked out on him. The whut-whut-whut approach to dealing with life's difficulties – never I think *entirely* convincing to me as a child – had revealed itself for the sadly inadequate thing it was.

Mike's red

Mike Mallarmé had moved on to the *Book of Britain*. Atypically simple Mega title (grinningly referred to by Plumpford as 'Bob'), typically immodest Mega aim. Here, in 1500 harrowingly overdesigned, overillustrated pages, was, as the ads would later have it, a 'comprehensive overview' of British geology, geography, landscape, climate, animal and plant life, history, science, invention, industry, politics, the arts, popular entertainment, the armed forces, costume, sport – which is but to scratch the surface of its subject-matter.

Looking through the pages that Mike showed me had so far been produced, I saw that every 'coo-ee dearie' one of them bore witness to the fearsome power of design's hand and the palsied feebleness of editorial's: a pic of Marty Wilde dwarfed the text on Oscar...the sand mason worm loomed larger than the horse... 'cut 8' had slashed George and Robert Stephenson down to seven lines while 'fill 6' had pumped 'Nobby' Stiles up to eleven…and in a literature caption the Keats goofily invoked by Potts in Corinne Marchant's presence one somnolent afternoon had as a result found himself dazedly in the company of the Lake Poets.

Still, Mike had buckled down to his new subbing task, even if cantankerously. But then soon a stream of Plumpford's 'editorial-hotshot' inanities ('How many Top Twenty hits did Marty Wilde have?', 'What's the diameter of the sand mason worm?', 'What was the total cost of the Stephensons' London & Birmingham railway?') began to tip him over the edge again. He considered sabotage. Now that was something that, not unnaturally, had occurred before to Mike and me (to the two young curmudgeons that, after an initially affable and accommodating approach to life, we had eventually and at so early an age become). I, for instance, partly inspired by Max Beerbohm's splendid jape of painstakingly substituting a convincing apostrophe for every aspirate in a copy of a contemporary's work, had been possessed on the Gardening book by a scarcely controllable urge to change every *is* and *are* to a *be*, to make every *of* an *o'* and every *-ing* an *-in'*: 'Where shoots be growin' vertically and be challengin' the central leaders o' trees…' And, if I had ever had the chance, I should have liked to append beneath the book's title, with a nicely judged fatuity: Written by *Real* Gardeners.

A scarcely controllable urge. Should have liked. But I almost certainly pram-in-the-hall wouldn't have followed it through. Whereas Mike, irascible, self-destructive Mike, who had no dependants to think about, did begin to sabotage the *Book of Britain*, or at least to vandalise it. When the project editor, Deborah Gradd, went off on her holiday and unreflectingly left him in charge of the Entertainment section, he went to work on it. He'd told me that the television entries already written had been based on no more than publicity puffs put out by the television companies and these often presented the most unremarkable of their contract screen regulars as 'icons', 'legends' no less. This reminded him, he said, of what his great fellow-countryman Montaigne had complained about in one of his essays: that the epithets 'divine' and 'great', which had once meant something when restricted to one or two men deserving of them down the centuries, had been devalued by being indiscriminately applied to any old nonentity. 'Nothing changes,' Mike concluded. What he'd done was to scrap all existing entries of the familiar vacantly grinning Mega Books kind and substitute his own versions. And these acerbic new appraisals of certain 'stars', which Mike felt more truly defined them than lazily perpetuated cant, he *saw into proof*. My! What a squealing and a squeaking and a screeching filled the air when Gradd, a jittery, humourless woman, returned from her hols and when Plumpford heard from her what had happened. It was all up with Mike then. He'd already had a yellow, now he was shown the red.

We had a drink together on his last day. He hadn't yet found another job, his situation was serious. But you'd never have guessed it from our mandatory non-emoting masculine cool – so unlike Mike's incandescent outbursts over text. The nearest he got to anything remotely resembling an effusion was: 'I'll be glad to leave the fercking place.' Then he added, in matey insult, 'You, poor sod, I wouldn't be surprised if you're sterck there for the rest of your days.'

'No way,' I said.

Ubiquitous and relentless

Flint was still 'working' on Shrubs. To effect this model demonstration of how the constitutional man of leisure should approach the demands of employment he had, I'd observed, needed to augment the pipe cleaning and the 'popping out' with a deal of pencil sharpening, telephoning his wife ('Did you make sure you bought two tins of the – you know – ?' 'Can you give that idle cretin a ring – and tell him he's got to – you know?') and visiting Accounts in some never-ending to-do about, one gathered, his payslips. McStutt's only response to this blatant dereliction of duty consisted of an occasional timorous 'Shrubs must be almost finished now, Chillingford'. To which Flint, removing his pipe from his mouth and fixing McStutt with a fearful opaque and frigid eye, would merely reply, with adamantine drawl, 'No, some way to go yet.' 'Right you are, Chillingford, er-heh-heh, er-heh-heh.' In the circumstances, a chuckle in more than usual poor taste. Five minutes later, Flint would rap the bowl of his pipe against his wastepaper basket, slowly rise from his desk and announce calmly, to nobody in particular as usual, 'Just popping along to Accounts, OK? They've made another cock-up of my – you know. Idle bloody cretins.'

The decree that all the information in the book must be based on expert personal demonstration had long since been revoked; and it had nothing to do with my already having flouted it on Orchids – problems of time, manpower and logistics had seen to it. Some major sections were now being produced in the old way, as commissioned material. The next such section I had to tackle was Greenhouse Gardening, a great slab of copy, in itself the size of one of Books' smaller tomes. It would require much mind-numbing toil to put it right and, to a lost Romantic soul such as myself, was overhung by a pall of tedium: God, the number of pages there were on siting, staging, heating, watering, damping down, ventilation, shading, compost-making, fumigation... It was obviously another Orthodontic Appliances, only worse. True, that particular Medical book copy, with all its excruciatingly arid technical detail of dental plates and springs and wires and screws, had settled as heavily on me as some succubus – but the task that squatted massy and malign on me now was ten times more monstrous! What, I thought despairingly, had all this electrostatic shading paint and 150ft cable and 14,500 BTU per hour and thermostats and BHC and sterilising bins – mere sight of which at a later stage would send the wellied couples in our ads into raptures – what had it all to do with me, lover of *Mosaic*, would-be author of a work as magical?

My mood wasn't improved on Flint's return, when, learning of what I'd had dumped on me, he drawled a toneless 'Hard luck' with not even a pretence of sincerity. And as he murmured, 'Glad I kept clear of that one,' there hovered on his face a 'subtle', self-satisfied smile, for all the world as though his avoidance of Greenhouse Gardening had been due to some Machiavellian cunning, some fly manipulation of the situation, instead of mere dilatoriness, mere gall. (In fact, as is not uncommon in those who pride themselves on canniness, he could be as credulous as a simpleton. Just as he had unquestioningly accepted the authorship of the lusting-schoolgirls fiction as female, so he had been taken in – unlike William Faulks-Lockhart, who had been similarly approached but had suspected a scam – by a cold-calling Old Etonian crook who was selling some 'quick-profit' commodities investment. Flint had sent him a cheque and never heard any more.) Yes, it had been mere gall on his part. But wait a minute. *Mere* gall? Gall could scarcely be characterised as mere, could it, while it was increasingly being revealed to me what a formidable force it was. First, there was what it could achieve for its possessor. Certainly, allied to a stony imperviousness to what others thought, the two in combination creating a tip-top unpleasantness, that gall had done Flint proud at Mega (and, I had no doubt, elsewhere): why, through it, he was able simply to swan around the offices, to lead unchallenged a life of relative ease. And, thinking about this, I had actually begun to envy him that world-class unpleasantness of his, that confident, overt, *successful* unpleasantness. How feeble and literally unrewarding in comparison seemed the basic pleasantness of so many of the rest of us. As a result, I was already trying to become more unpleasant myself – take my curtness towards Gudgeon, for example, and the obvious hostility I'd shown towards McStutt. In this I was trying to emulate not only Flint but a biggie I'd studied in my men-of-action phase, Napoleon, who as much as proclaimed No More Mr Nice Guy when he said: 'I am compelled to defend myself against this natural disposition [to please men] lest advantage be taken of it.' And I had, I suppose, achieved some success. But don't get me wrong – I was under no illusion as to just how far I still had to go, just how much more work I had to put in before I could pull it off, rise to anywhere near the Olympian heights of Flint, *better* myself. Of course – I had, a little discouragingly, to admit it – he had the boon of having been born with an innate talent for unpleasantness. I should have to graft, to make up through practice and willpower what I lacked in inborn ability – as a Cliff Thorburn had to, compared with a Jimmy White, a Geoffrey Boycott, compared with a David Gower. It would be tough, very tough, but that was no excuse for not taking up the challenge. And I should, having been allowed to work alongside Flint, accept the heaven-sent opportunity to study a master at work, his techniques, his methodology, any new wrinkles he might introduce.

The second aspect of gall revealed to me was its powerful, smashing impact on the lives of others. In this particular it was as much up there in the big league as those two other high-scoring pulverisers of all that is reasonable and proper, namely incompetence and malevolence. Earlier in my life I had been under the unthinking misapprehension that the more positive, the finer human qualities of others must attract more of our attention, play a greater part in our lives, than the negative, the baser ones. For example, I had automatically assumed, because Lil was so boneheaded, ignorant, secretive, bigoted and often ill-willed, that what she said and did must impact far less on my life than what, say, thoughtful, open, generous, tolerant Sally or Olivia said and did. But experience kept demonstrating to me the exact opposite. I discovered, too, as we all do, that it is not the official who deals with our case efficiently and discreetly who impinges much on our consciousness, it is the one who makes an unnecessary difficulty of everything; it is not the pleasant friends of our child who take up any of our time and energy but the vicious one who with a single act sets in train distracted visits to doctor, hospital, police, school.

Yes, I belatedly, reluctantly recognised that, contrary to what I would have liked to believe, there is no direct ratio between the worth of the people we know or have dealings with and their effect on our life. As Nietzsche's Zarathustra lamented, a man's life is so at the mercy of the unreasonable that 'a buffoon may be fatal to it'. This is a crass aspect of life we try to forget; it offends us; we go back to our ideal world, that world in which our interactions with others, our treatment by them and the results that flow from it are those that we consider befit us. Hence our resentment when we're brought down from that ideal world to an abrasive reality in which we have to 'waste our time', as we angrily put it, in dealing with the words or actions of the stupid, the insolent, the indolent, the malicious, who inconveniently have no conception at all of the kind of behaviour to which we think we're entitled. Or we may be equally foolishly offended that the 'rightful' order of things is 'out of joint' when we learn of the unearned troubles visited on others, when we learn of, say, in an extreme case, the great creative artist being forced, no differently from the mere mortal, to wear himself out in coping with the misdeeds of a ne'er-do-well relative or the harassments of some

Dogberry. Such is our forgetfulness of how ubiquitous and relentless a force is the ratshit in life.

Even they

For some reason (perhaps not too difficult to fathom) I hadn't considered that, just as such poetries of childhood as the village school and Walfield Road, once so seemingly safe, had become infected, so too could what I'd always felt to be the ultimately immune: the special intimation, the experience in which everything around me had seemed to fuse into one great message and promise combined. But there came a time when even that happened, when the defences of the primal dusk itself were breached. The soft blue urban incense of that warm, charged dusk, the intoxicating essence of it that I had once breathed in so ecstatically and that throughout boyhood whenever I caught a whiff of it would continue to entrance me, was, I learned one day, *intoxicating* in a very different, older sense of the word than the one I'd used to describe those fumes (just as two other Circes, cigarette smoke and full sunlight, were respectively *aromatic* and *radiant* in uncommon, scientific, ill-omened senses of those words): it contained particulate hydrocarbons, a hazard to the lungs, and particulate lead, which messed with young brains. And perhaps, I now thought, perhaps while I had so ecstatically inhaled the incense of that dusk and others when I was a child, that lead had messed with *my* brain. Perhaps, who knows, it had prevented me from being clever enough to emulate *Mosaic*, to write what I had once longed to write.

But that wasn't all. The world of Master, still so closely linked for me with that world of *Mosaic* he had created, which was itself inseparable from those presentiments I had experienced when young, because it had not only echoed them in its own way but had ended by becoming indissolubly fused with them, that world, too, now gave up its purity. Purity, yes, because, although I may to some extent have deglamorised that world – and the associated world of Gershwin and his music – during my musings on it, although I may to some extent have demythologised my heroes, even so, the ardent idealisation of youth refuses to vanish completely, jus' like that, and much of the golden haze still lingered around my conception of the lives lived by that so-special writer and composer in twenties and thirties New York. When I read of Master taking a cab to his apartment on Eighty-sixth Street or having tea with his agent at the Plaza Hotel, or of Gershwin partying at the Palais Royal nightclub or playing at Carnegie Hall, and especially if, temporarily unManned by alcohol during this reading, I reverted briefly to a state of dreamy romanticising, that world, whose topography was always pervaded for me by the spirit of scenes from *Mosaic* and passages from Gershwin's music, as though these were its only natural, only possible, accompaniment, that world still throbbed with the seductive, exhilarating appeal, the magic, it had possessed of old. But now it too became infected. And in this case, it was not by the means now familiar to me – that is, by an element from the world of darkness entering a seemingly secure world of light – but by a reversal of this normal process: an element from a seemingly secure world of light entering the world of darkness. Diametrically opposed movements, virtually identical effects. Once again it was reading – necessary, unnecessary, blessed, cursed reading – that brought it about. And once again the defilement was darkly spawned in the Second World War.

At that stage of my life that world of Master and Gershwin (my first loves among writers and composers and retaining that special place in the memory that, even after they have been outgrown, all first loves do) was, like most idealised worlds, homogeneous and self-contained. Each of its elements was necessary to it and belonged to it alone. That was true even of the minor elements. Such a one, among many, was Master's wife's half-Dutch cousin, Jan Levy. A man of letters – to use the term of the time – he shared with Master a keen interest in, a fascination with, Poe (they admired him as a supreme exemplar of what Ellery Queen called the affinity between the poetic and the ratiocinative mind). During Levy's brief sojourn in New York, in the early thirties, the two went drinking together, and it seems that the author of *Mosaic* confided to his cousin-in-law some of his first ideas for the book he hoped to write. Jan Levy played only a small part in Master's life (after his stay in New York the two never met again), and even in the monumental biography he occupied only a couple of paragraphs in one chapter. Yet for me he was, in this subsidiary role, no less integral an element of Master's biographied world than any other. He was, in those intriguing binges and literary discusssions he had with Master in various bars, hermetically sealed into that unique world, almost as though he had no life outside it (like all those delimited, contingency-free, consequently slightly unreal people who exist for us only in the niche that is all we know of them). And there was something more: he also, by virtue of once being at the same party as Gershwin (that link again!), had his small place in the wider poetic Master-Gershwin-Manhattan world. How could it be then – as, during research for my book, I now discovered – that this man had met his end in a concentration camp? If this question I put to myself had required an answer of literal fact, that answer would have been: in an act of brotherhood some might have regarded as foolhardy, others as admirable, Jan Levy had left behind his comfortable life in America to join his fellow-Jews in Nazi-occupied Holland, the land of his early upbringing, and once there he had eventually, under the dread regime of Seyss-Inquart, been deported to Buchenwald, there eventually, after many months of degradation, to be shot. But my question didn't require bald explanations of this kind, it wasn't a question at all, it was an expression of disbelief. Disbelief that a man who had inhabited the world of Master and Gershwin, who in cosily lit bars had been privileged to hear at first-hand from the writer about magical key episodes in his book, who had been in the very same wisping-smoke, clinking-glass room as the composer, amid so many glamorous guests, and had perhaps heard him play, as he often used to at parties, a medley of his own wonderful show tunes, that this *so Master-Gershwin-Manhattan* man was to find himself in another time, head shaven, in rags, and no longer a person but only a number, stumbling through a hell of murder and torture and starvation and despair. How could the poetry of Master and Gershwin possibly be linked, no matter if only indirectly, with, of all ghastly places on the face of the earth, Buchenwald – Buchenwald, where poetry, in a similar fashion to those 'enemies of the Reich' consigned to Nacht und Nebel, had vanished without trace? How could a man who had been linked, no matter if only briefly, to this poetry, who bore within him the memory of it and the warm civilised surroundings in which he had heard it (fragments of a lighted room, voices, music, returning to him from another world amid the stench and fear and misery he was now immersed in), how could he now be so hellishly distant from it? Even more distant than it would at first appear. For, if reading about Jan Levy's fate brought about a contamination of a previously unspoiled world, it also brought about another of those strange wrenching dislocations of time, those that turn upside down our bland everyday experience of it. In this way. Whenever I read passages from Master's marvellous mystery, whenever I listened to that recording of Gershwin demonstrating his brilliant pianism, they seemed, the book and the music, with the timeless appeal of all true art, to belong as much to the present as to the past: certain scenes from *Mosaic* so echoed scenes from my own life that, as I've already described, I could sometimes scarcely be sure, in recall, which were which, and as I listened to Gershwin playing 'That Certain Feeling', the immediacy of that playing, in its sure rhythm and persuasiveness, was such as to give me the feeling that he was in the room with me. Whereas over the Nazi death camps there hung so black a pall, they were such embodiments in themselves of night and fog, that they seeemed to belong more to the Dark Ages than to our own times. So that those camps have always had the semblance of an anachronism even in a century which knew the Somme and Hiroshima and the gulags, and I have always had the curious illusion, in the face of what the history books tell me, that there was no way they could have postdated Master and Gershwin, that they had their existence *long before* that time (just as the unspeakable doings of the Ripper in a Whitechapel of seedy doss-houses and dimly lit alleyways seemed to have taken place in a light-denied region long anterior to the light-filled worlds of, for example, Rossini's music and most Impressionist paintings, which actually predated those murders). Therefore, it seemed to me that Jan Levy, that man who was once, enviably, Master's confidant, had, far from travelling forward in time to his eventual doom, been hurtled backwards, like so many other poor souls in those camps, far beyond the happy normality he had once known, backwards into some terrible distant past. And because of this, the realm of gold that was Master's world could never be the same again, could never be a true sanctuary of the imagination any more. Perhaps for some who knew of these same facts it could be. 'But not for me'.

The '*Showbiz*' card

One morning Vin Sharpes called the entire staff of Mega Books into his vast office to announce 'a bit of a bombshell'. Bob

Plumpford was leaving the company to become editorial director at Pinnacle (or was it Zenith?).

'As I don't need to tell you, Bob'll be a hard act to follow' – *a 'ard ac' t' foller* – Sharpes told us. 'A very hard act to follow. But we're very lucky in having someone of the capabilities of Willie McStutt to step into his shoes. Willie will become our new Managing Editor. And I know he'll do a splendid job. And to take over from him as Editor of Gicbog we've appointed Chillingford Flint. Chillingford is someone who gives you a hundred and one percent, a "Mega person" through and through, and I'm happy to put Gicbog into his capable hands…'

Jesus.

After it was over, a buzz of Waughian chatter filled the corridors.

'Don't know much about Flint. Just a name to me.'

'Very capable man, I believe.'

'Fancy, Willie Managing Editor. Is he up to it, do you think?'

'Mmm, I wonder. I know one thing. Bob's going to be a hard act to follow.'

Whenever some biggie left the company (obviously it hadn't happened on Mike's departure), the design department would supplement the conventional leaving card with one of their own, some novelty they'd concocted, collectively signed Everyone in Design. In the case of Plumpford it was to be tabloid-sized – complete with a special envelope for him to take it away in – and 'themed' on the mag he'd once worked on. Beneath a *Mega Books* masthead modelled on that of *Showbiz* the front of the card would show our boss in a considerable variety of 'roles' or 'moods', with some vague intention I suppose of depicting him as protean – some versatile actor, perhaps, as he might have appeared in Plumpford's old paper if, that is, it had ever concerned itself with anything meaningful.

First, without letting Plumpford know exactly what was going on, a photographer would capture him in various posed attitudes. Then, in a common jokey illustrative technique, the heads would be cut from the prints and stuck on full-length cartoony drawings of Plumpford. Finally, these would be humorously captioned.

Unfortunately – or fortunately, according to how you cared to look at it – someone then decided that the ideal team for this undertaking would be, as photographer, Simon; as artist, Willard Rumple, a burly, bearded, choleric-looking designer known to doodle caricatures and cartoons in his spare time; and as caption-writer – because the words accompanying the pictures needed to be contrived with some wit and therefore someone 'creative' from editorial must be given the job – Barney Potts (who, after an emissary from design had nervously put the proposition to him, had with supra-semilunar peering solemnly accepted it).

What this 'unholy trinity', as Chris Alexander termed them, came up with was, I think, considerably removed from what the originators of the idea had had in mind. The trio's take on it was an intendedly tongue-in-cheek, inoffensively waggish guying of our boss. But this seemed to me, in the hands of those setting out to execute it, distinctly iffy as an Ave atque vale, Bob. To bring it off, if indeed it could be brought off, needed nice judgment, spot-on realisation. And it was Simon, Rumple and *Potts* who were attempting this? There could be only one outcome, and what Simon later secretly showed me of the half-completed card proved it. He had snapped Plumpford in many different poses and with many different switched-on 'reaction' expressions – as well as at different angles and in different lights (I visualised him in familiar fashion-photographer mode: 'Lovely, Bob…now at left…S'perb…') But a number of the shots he'd taken, or perhaps, rather, those selected from what would undoubtedly have been the reelfuls he'd taken, showed Plumpford straining too hard to come up with Authoritative, Amused, Kind, etc., and looking instead either in severe pain or in some cases deranged. A few pics were OK – Thoughtful Bob, for example, showing him chin on knuckles, softly sidelit, was a commendable close miss at depicting in him capacity for true thought. But the rest... In Amused Bob, for instance, the eyes were even more glacial than usual and made the excessively laughing mouth a Bacon-like thing of horror. And, as for Kind Bob, well, in its preposterous concept and over-the-top realisation, it reminded me of nothing more than Harry's 'niceness' towards Lil when he was having it away with Peg Tumbrill.

Those were the mugshots. Then came the coloured figure drawings to which they were appended. In these, hard-case Willard Rumple had, with uncalled-for savagery, I thought, portrayed Plumpford as exaggeratedly plump, almost obese in fact. And in one, topped by a manic, leering face (originally shot, Simon told me in all seriousness, as Imaginative Bob), the vicious artist, commemorating Plumpford's numerous acts of sexual harassment over the years, had shown him with one hand clutching the bum of a distraught female in cheeks-hugging jeans.

And then, and then, there was Potts' contribution. The captions. Potts specials. 'Side-splitting Bob seeing the joke' (the horror-movie shot). 'Intellectual Bob thinking up another shivery query' (the chin-on-knuckles one). 'Legal Bob laying down a decision' (Plumpford scarily lit from below and wagging a finger at the camera). But there was something worse than the cack-handedness. It was, in certain cases – and perhaps then influenced by Rumple's drawings – the excruciatingly offensive tone. 'Day-dreaming Bob dreaming of being as powerful and rolling in it as Midas' (a shot in which camera movement – deliberate? – had smeared the icy eyes into a look that might possibly have passed for reverie as their owner bemusedly contemplated before him in the ether a pile of what looked like assorted gold tableware). And worst of all: 'Harrasing Bob being too "cheeky"' (the groping one). I winced. Lads can get away with outrageous kidology, because they always then deflate it with a guffaw and some statutory 'straight-up' compliment (those telly-interviewed sportsmen on the subject of a fellow-team-member: 'What do we all think of Gary? We think he's a bossy, loud-mouthed bighead.' Horselaugh. 'No, seriously, he's a great guy...'). But on the page there could be no laugh or retraction to bounce everyone over the ill-judged too-nasty insults. Rumple was bolshie, I suspected, and may have had in him a streak of that self-destructiveness I'd sensed in Mike Mallarmé. But Potts? From what I knew of him, he was quite the opposite. No, those captions of his were simply the hopeless miscueings of one who didn't know his arse from his elbow.

Simon earnestly asked my opinion of the work in progress. 'Bit near the knuckle, isn't it?' I understated.

'G'lor', Xav, you really think it's near? I did wonder. Still, prob'ly get away with it. Ol' Bob's got a sense of humour, hasn't he? And we're too far down what's possible now to back it up.'

Well, it was none of my business. After all, what did I care what went into either of Bob Plumpford's leaving cards? Besides, this 'Showbiz' one would never make it to the finish, would it: someone in overall charge (that was a point, who *was* in charge?) would put the kibosh on it, wouldn't they?

The Fatuous Four

I suppose I really knew it was all up with my book when I began helplessly indulging in put-downs of my band of heroes, turning the whole thing into a comic opera. I found myself presenting Leo now as a self-dramatising Quixote, who, to tell the truth, was slightly mad: at moments of suspense or danger, he would comment on them in a Southern drawl and would always preface his dramatic, half-baked, doomed decisions on how we should respond to them with a cocksure 'Instinct tells me...' Candy had become a ludicrously overdressed floosie smitten with her sugar daddy, whom she saw as a charismatic man of consequence. Guy was now a brutally pragmatic Sancho Panza, who kept trying to shoot down his uncle's absurd plans and get him to behave sensibly. And Al, who had now become the first-person narrator, had turned into a naïf every bit as foolish as his leader, to whom he was blindly loyal. Even the old Citroën DS convertible had now become a send-up Benzo-Hesperides.

The Benzo purred onward. Soon, at last, we were to meet V.

Ahead a large greystone building appeared on the right. 'Sweetie,' said Candy, 'isn't that the SPO training college over there?'

'The S...P...O...' Leo mused. 'The Speycial Poh-lice Ohganahsation. Yeah.' He paused. 'An' instinct teylls me we hayve to show theym mothafuckas they ain't so speycial.' And he broke into a chilling laugh.

At these words I saw us superimposed by main titles and heard a low, portent-laden music start up and impel us onward. But obviously Guy didn't. He ruined it all. He withdrew from an inner pocket an extract from a Second World War French Resistance paper and angrily pointed out to me the following injunction: 'Practise an inflexible discipline, a constant prudence, an absolute discretion... Never boast...'

'Them sonsabitches gonna wonder whah they eyvah – '

'Leo, can I ask you something?' Guy interrupted insolently. 'Why the fuck do you have to keep speaking in that stupid fucking voice?'

Leo was obviously taken aback by this. And who could blame him? I looked at Guy. Leo, why the fuck do you have to keep speaking in that stupid fucking voice. What sort of question was that? Where was the sense in it? What had it to do with the cause we were embarking on? You know, despite Guy's many fine qualities, I had my doubts about him. It seemed to me he could well be the fly in the ointment of our splendid mission. For instance, there was the way he chided us about quite unnecessary things. Like how we needed to buy a street map of Carmine. A street map! When we had Leo, who'd told us I don't know how many times that he knew the city like the back of his hand. OK, so we'd lost our way on two or three occasions, but so what? No, the fact was, Guy was becoming a bit of a pain.

Not only was Leo now seriously off the rails and a blabbermouth (that Resistance paper: 'Beware of lightweights, those who talk too much...'), he also had the most unheroic fits of petulance, as displayed in a scene in his apartment.

'If the SPO do already suspect you,' said Guy, fiddling with the controls on Leo's new hi-fi, 'your cover – '
'Leave that alone, can't you.' Leo knocked Guy's hand away from the expensive equipment. 'Do you have any idea how much that cost me?'

And perhaps worst of all, he would sometimes when talking to one of the others in the apartment interrupt what he was saying with a somersault, *between syllables.*

'If you think we should see him to dis – ' (he sprang, pressed and flipped upright again) ' – cuss the matter, I can arrange a meet – ' (he did it again) ' – ing.'

Another thing – I found myself, in the persona of my fatheaded young narrator, writing the action scenes in boy's-own-paper style. At one point, as he and Guy were walking down a quiet narrow street, two thugs leapt out at them from an alleyway. But 'quick as a flash' Guy 'drove a powerful left to the solar plexus of one and followed up with a vicious right to the jaw of the other'. And they left 'the two bruisers squealing with pain'.

How I enjoyed writing those scenes. I hadn't had such fun with my book for a long time. A very long time.

But why had I transformed my Fantastic Four into a Fatuous Four? Why had I holed the project below the waterline in this way? The answer was simple. The dream, the one that a certain motto had proclaimed it was your *duty* to preserve, had by now receded so far into the distance as to be almost lost to view.

Seven

So farewell, Bob

Plumpford's leaving party, a crowded affair, took place in the Gardening book office, the largest in the department. (The office: that 'realm of the fantastic', as Kafka called it.) The sipping, nibbling, chattering prelude, then Sharpes rapped on a desk for silence. His opening sentence was of the way-out-indirect kind favoured, expected almost, on such occasions. It told us of his uncle's advice on how best to check the condition of a second-hand car. There then followed an extended motoring metaphor, whose relevance to the occasion I couldn't quite follow. Then at length Sharpes cut to the overt eulogy: 'You, Bob, have worked wonders... We been very lucky, Bob, to have had the benefit of your great ability... If it hadn't been for you, Bob, Mega Books would never have been the great success it's been...'

Looking at the beaming, wine-flushed faces of those around me as Sharpes *marvelled* at the stature of the man soon to leave us, I was annoyed to discover that I had on my own lips the same daft, contagious-as-a-yawn smile as everyone else.

That paean of Sharpes'! As Toad's saviour, the engine-driver, did with his coals, so Mega Books' managing director did with his praises, 'piling them on, shovelling furiously'. It was certainly something to hear. In fact, so prodigious grew the homage that we began to think we were saying goodbye not to a man but to a demigod.

Sharpes then presented Plumpford with his leaving gifts – a complete set of golf clubs, a pair of golfing gloves and a hip flask – and two cards. After a creditable-enough show of wonderment at receiving the gifts he had chosen himself, Plumpford looked at the first card, read some of the messages, smiled, thanked everyone, then picked up the second in its giant envelope. I'd been amazed to learn from Simon that this had not been ditched but had *made its way unmodified to the final*. And I was, therefore, agog to see how Plumpford would react.

He pulled out the card and then, for the first and the only time, I felt a certain empathy with him, a twinge of sympathy, as he was forced, under the full onslaught of the collective Mega Books gaze, to take in the representations of himself on the card. And there was something else, subsidiary to this: as I studied him, I had once more reluctantly to admit that those shadowy men who'd written for *True 'Tec Tales*, those whose work I'd once cursed and derided, the likes of Wills and Horrey, had actually been acute observers of the human being in the grip of strong emotion. For a certain facial reaction they sometimes used to describe shock or outrage, 'his face stiffened', but whose actual existence, never having come across a hint of it myself (any more than I had the 'snarl' and the 'hiss'), I had scornfully dismissed out of hand, well, that was precisely what I saw now, as I looked at Plumpford staring at the '*Showbiz*' card: *his face stiffened*.

Plump with belief in his own worth, generally sufficient unto himself Plumpford may have been, but I guessed that even such a one, even one surfeited moreover with so recent a display of approbation and goodwill, was, faced with what he now saw before him, no less assaulted than so many others would have been by the terrible suspicion that all the praise and affection bestowed upon him might have been a cruel sham, that this could be one of those classic cases, dramatised in movies, of a hated boss finally receiving his come-uppance, finally learning his staff's real opinion of him.

But no, thought Plumpford. Vin's speech, the applause, the golf clubs, the smiling faces... No, this bloody '*Showbiz*' card thing had to be a joke. A piss-poor one, to be sure – by Christ he'd like to get his hands on whoever was responsible (I saw in his narrowing eyes a look I'd once seen enter them in the corridor when I'd begun to question the excitingness of a challenge) – but nonetheless a joke. One he had to pretend to take in good part. So he simply gave the 'unholy trinity''s scandalously screwed up frolic a smiling headshake as he examined it again. *Harrasing Bob being too 'cheeky'*? What insolent sod had drawn that and what illiterate had written it? And what was this incomprehensible shit about 'intellectual' Bob 'thinking up' another 'shivery' query? And who'd chosen that fucking terrible pic where he looked certifiable? And *Bob dreaming of being as powerful and rolling in it as Midas*? Who the fuck *was* responsible for it all? Christ, if he ever found out... Once more he shook his head and smiled in 'rueful appreciation'. Then, putting the card back in its envelope, he told us, his impossible role calling now for gratitude and humility, how touched he was to receive such parting gifts, how he didn't deserve all the praise heaped on him, how, etc.

It was perhaps understandable that my attention should drift away, that it was drawn to what, at this darkening November hour, I could see outside through a window that looked on to Regency Place: thirst-quenchingly fruity above rooftops of damson blue and netted in the bare trees' rosy black branches, an expanse of strawberry and apricot – just like the one that had entranced me so long ago above a dark skyline of station, signal at ruby stop and shunting engine. I was just thinking that each interstice in the network of ruddied branches resembled nothing more than a capsule of the sky's sweet red and orange juice when some change in the cadence of Plumpford's voice told my subconscious, which was still listening to him even if 'I' wasn't, and which, as I returned, now re-established my 'Mega Books person' rictus, that he had entered upon his peroration. Yes, he'd come to treasured memories.

'And so I'll never forget the exciting challenge this job has been for me. I'll never forget the great teamwork you've all shown over the years, the wonderful times I've had working with you on our great books, and what a great bunch of folk you've all been…'

The applause at the end was resounding – and I clapped as loudly as anyone.

Caged beast

During those few weekdays between the Boxing Day and New Year's Day holidays when Mega staff had to turn up for work (this was before the Christmas break unofficially became in the world of commerce the entire last week of the year); those days when post-indulgence low was brought lower by the sense of the old year's lingering death; those days on which the lassitude lying heavily on offices throughout the land grew even more leaden as the light faded from the sky at an impossibly early hour; those days when in employees who'd been required to return to the grind the realisation that others hadn't bred a sullen sense of injustice (despite the knowledge that doctors, nurses, policemen, firemen, entertainers, footballers and so many others were all working as normal); those days at the fag-end of the year when grocery invoices, *True 'Tec Tales* scripts, Masters of the Rolls bios, of little interest at the best of times, would lose, in quiet offices half-emptied by 'sick' absentees, any vestige of meaning, consequence; during those days as I experienced them now, on the Gardening book, a pervasive torpor made the stretching slough of Greenhouses seem more impossible than ever to flounder through, so that, resolutely mindful though I was of how I had made myself triumph over that other torpor, of dog days, and Manfully though I clenched my teeth until I set the jaw muscles rippling, even so I sometimes felt I would be sucked down long before I reached the other side.

Being under the thumb of our new editor, Flint, didn't help matters either. In his new position he developed his gall into an even more fearsome weapon than it had been before. Watching him, returning after a 'popping out' extended to a couple of hours or more, stroll bleak-eyed across the office and, withdrawing his pipe from his mouth, drawl to Roger Taylor, a comatose Neal Easy and myself that we had to finish the copy we were working on that evening, *without fail* – he who would have stretched out work on it for days, weeks even – you couldn't help admitting he certainly had something.

As I waded through those days with heavy heart, I savagely put to myself the same old questions. What was I doing at this place? Why was I lurching, with so deep an ache in my soul, through Greenhouses, of all things? Why couldn't I get an interesting job in some other line? But this question paper, like that set at most furious self-examinations, was one to which the sitter already knew all the answers. I knew I was no more able to escape from Mega into something more congenial than Kenneth Grahame was able to escape from his bank into the careers he coveted. In his case it was, as he periodically complained, lack of a degree that held him captive; in mine it was lack of any qualifications at all (unless I tried to remedy that by – dreadful prospect – slogging away, after those taxing days in the office, at evening study). Yes, I knew all the answers. And so the bitter self-demands were simply the regular, ritualised snarls of the caged beast everywhere, indulged in for no other reason than that, if they weren't, the beast might go mad.

Angst

A January evening. A wind with a blade, out and about in the edgy darkness. I headed home up a slope of terraces not dissimilar to those of Danehill Road. A vague unease fretted me. In the objectionable light of a sodium lamp, an unknown figure appeared, face daubed horror-flick sallow and mauve. Shadows lurched, litter scuttled. Darren was last seen leaving the corner shop... That was it: amid the generalised angst a more specific troubling, one imprinted deep in the modern consciousness, imprinted by the long succession of bad-news years, of was-last-seen years, one that informed you that at that very minute a sample of the sick and the sable were slowly prowling the streets at the wheels of their death traps, sweeping methodically with Asdic eyes, on the lookout for the lone child returning from errand or visit, snatchable with little risk beneath the blanket of evening. I felt a sudden twinge of fear. Irrational (there was no way Michael and David would be out in the street at this hour, and certainly not alone; they and Sally would be safely ensconced indoors). Irrational, but the seemingly plausible irrational that fear is so good at.

That disquiet which sometimes seeped into me these days... Dean, that Camusian pointer up of Mediterranean light and Northern darkness, had several times informed me that it was far from universal, that I would not have experienced it in Italy, for example (natch). In Venice, which he had recently revisited with Olivia, crime against the person, he said, was practically unknown (perhaps that was so in the present, but even though he couldn't know the city was heading for a Mafia-contaminated future surely he couldn't have forgotten its internecine past); and on those October evenings when he and Olivia set off for a restaurant through a myriad *calli* and *campi*, at an hour when most English parents have long since withdrawn their children from the streets, there were, he told me with the Anglophobe's bitter pleasure in presenting fresh evidence for his claims, little ones at play everywhere in the gathering dusk, scampering, sometimes alone, down dim and deserted alleys or across the shadowy corner of some empty square, squealing, giggling, as heartwarmingly unafraid as the parents who far from irresponsibly allowed them to roam free.

Just ahead of me now, as I neared the top of the road, lay our horseshoe of maisonettes, Beacon Court. From some way off I'd seen an *unfamiliar* car parked in the road outside, *well beyond* the street lamp, *lurking* in shadow. Now I could just make out in the driver's seat an *unrecognisable* silhouette, bulky, hunched, *suspiciously still*. Kildare had kept watch on the court for several evenings... I drew nearer. At that moment an elderly woman emerged from the maisonette next to ours, crossed to the car and got in. So, the driver was only Jack Tuttle, bronchial, lame, pleasant, helpful, sad. And the car was obviously the replacement he'd said he was getting for the clapped-out Escort. And all he'd been doing was waiting patiently for his Dot, who was always, always 'only going to be a tick'.

I let myself in and climbed the stairs. From the boys' bedroom a greeting: 'Hello, Dad.'

'Michael, aren't you asleep yet?'

Then David's less formed voice, enunciating each word with as much difficulty as I'd had addressing Plumpford as 'Bob'. 'Michael...played...with a...ball.'

I put my head round the door. 'Did he?' I forced a light, cheery tone of gratified surprise at the unremarkable news. 'See you both in a minute.'

Sally was in the kitchen. She turned and smiled at me. Over her shoulder as we embraced I saw open on a chair an Italian textbook. At that moment I stylised her thus: a good mother, who had bathed the boys and read them a story; a fine cook, who was preparing an undoubtedly enjoyable meal; a natural linguist, who had acquired considerable fluency in a second language; a lovely young woman, whose gaze could still pierce me. At that moment that was Sally in her entirety: exclusively virtuous, talented, desirable. Yes, yes, yes, I was at it again, I was in that old idealising groove again, its insistent riff had me under its spell. So compulsive, persistent, tireless, resilient is that urge to idealise that it has to be as fundamental to us, as atavistic, as, say, the need for social bonding or dispelling the dark.

A bedside lamp shone softly on the boys. As I greeted them, I marvelled afresh at the angelic beauty of bedtime children newly bathed. The diadem of downy hair, the rosy skin fragrant with soap, the large clear eyes gleaming. Oh, boys, can't you stay like this forever?

'Story, Dad,' said Michael.

'Hasn't Mum read you a story?'

'Yes, but – '

'Well, then – '

'But we want another one.'

We? I hadn't heard a word from David about it.

'Sorry, it's too late, Michael. My meal's almost ready.'

'Tell us about your books, then.' Your books. That was how Michael always referred to what I did.

Well, perhaps I had time to acquaint them with just one of those Amazing Facts of Nature that only bar-room bores recount to other adults but that children love. Delving, I retrieved from memories of the Fish book an outlandish creature of the deep that even the reductive Mega approach had been unable to rob entirely of its grotesque fascination.

'I'll just tell you quickly about these very strange fish. They live deep in the ocean, where it's really dark. They've got these very big mouths with all these sharp teeth like needles, and they can swallow fish as big as themselves.'

I saw that David, all unconsciously, in unresolved response, was at once wrinkling up his nose in loathing of the dreadful creatures and opening wide his mouth in a sort of empathy with their feeding habits.

'And guess what – do you know how they *catch* their food?' I simulated awe.

Their eyes widened, their 'No' was one of genuine awe to come. A faint sadness brushed me. These sons I never wished to deceive had no idea I was faking it all. How easy it was to fool them, how vulnerable they were.

'Well, they've got little fishing-rod things on their heads, with little lanterns at the end – and these lure their prey...' Lure. Prey. David wouldn't understand. Did Michael? Better reword. 'These lanterns make fish come to them so they can catch them and eat them.'

Michael was obviously unsure how to treat this preposterous piece of information. He started by hazarding disbelief. 'Little fishing rods and lanterns...' he said with scornful voice and smile, though not a scorn really of any great conviction. Which was proved when, seeing that his dad remained serious, he abruptly changed course halfway through what he was saying, as only children and double-take movie mutts do, and, smile now gone, tone now solemn, concluded: '...on their heads.'

From the kitchen Sally called me to our meal.

'What are they called?' Michael asked.

'Angler fish.'

'Ang...' David's attempt at confirmation quickly petered out.

'Why do they call them angeller fish?' Another question from Michael, partly genuine, partly a familiar detaining ploy.

Thinking of Sally's summons, I wondered whether I should say goodnight now (press button one) or whether I could *just* squeeze in a swift explanation of angling for Michael (press button two). Which did I...? Press now! Right, perhaps I – PRESS NOW! 'Well, an angler is someone – '

Sally's voice again, impatient this time, annoyed – to my mind, disproportionately annoyed. So, I thought, jabbed the wrong one again, another bloody no score. I suddenly resented Sally's tone. But not simply because I thought it unfair. No, just as much because it had caused a faint crazing to appear in the glaze of Ideal Sally, the figure I'd recently recreated so happily and with such foolish devoutness. Unfairly on my own part, I was taking exception to her unwittingly damaging a vessel so exquisite and fragile I should never have fashioned it in the first place.

'I must go, boys.' I kissed them goodnight.

As I was leaving, Michael said: 'Dad, they're more clever than people, those fish, aren't they?'

'Well, in some ways perhaps they are.'

Ever-proliferating

I lunched with Dean at Piero's. Except that it wasn't Piero's any more. The eponymous proprietor, a slight, quiet, elderly man with a friendly smile and sad eyes, had died, and the restaurant had a new owner, a new name, Da Francesco, and, I noticed on the menu outside, new prices, their novelty of a kind that made me wonder whether Dean, not short of a penny though he was, might resent them and turn away. However, after a grimace and some initial hesitation, he decided to go in.

Francesco, plump, fortyish, somewhat resembling Annigoni, the Queen's portraitist, unpleasantly got up in frilled lilac shirt and tight black velvet trousers, greeted us with an ecstatic amazement which wouldn't have been out of keeping in the painter himself should he have been unexpectedly visited by further royals requesting a sitting. I missed Piero already.

Over lunch Dean asked me how I was currently finding the Gardening book. Although, with rare exceptions, I didn't beef at Mega about my work, outside the place it was different, and to Dean I always unburdened myself as though to a father. My groan about Greenhouses took in, natch, the designers. For they were still like coach horses out of the control of the coachman (Flint, so ready to use the whip on his editorial stableboys, showed no more sign than McStutt of trying to rein in those headstrong steeds *a little*, of trying to prevent them from trampling *all over* the text, of warning them, 'Whoa, there, Tarty and Flash, m'beauties, you stop getting ahead of yourselves now, or I shall have to teach 'ee a lesson!'), they were still making an intolerable job even more so. 'Add 47 lines on shading paint.'

'It seems to be a bête noir of yours,' Dean said. 'That hyperdesign, as you call it.'

Yes, I supposed it was. And what was responsible for it was that incorrigible old idealising self in me, wasn't it, wilfully refusing to accept the so-imperfect real world, to accommodate himself to it. I had always unquestioningly accepted that self's values, his outlook, his aims, his will, but perhaps, I now reflected (for the very first time), I should no longer automatically allow them to prevail.

Francesco was now in front of us, cooking our main course at table, something Piero had never done. To this end he had for some reason adopted an athletic stance, legs apart and braced, trunk leaning forward slightly from the waist, a pose which further, unwelcomely, tightened the velvet trousers. He now poured some oil into the chafing-dish, exclaiming the while, '*Mama mia*'. I missed Piero even more.

'Surely you realise, Xav,' Dean continued, 'that all that design serves a valuable purpose. It seduces large numbers of people who never normally buy a book into acquiring knowledge they wouldn't otherwise acquire. Take the *Book of Britain* that you and your mate Mike are always having a go at.' (He'd met Mike but didn't know he'd been sacked.) 'OK, so it probably is a load of cobblers in many respects, from all you tell me – the designers giving Marty Wilde more space than Oscar, a not exactly stringent control of the facts... But it's *still* acquainting people with *largely* accurate information on a wide range of subjects they wouldn't normally read about. Without all those hectic overpictorial pages, do you think most of them would even look at such a book, let alone buy it – regardless of whether the text was of the quality you want or not?'

I listened to Dean amid a double distraction: Francesco's antics, which had become increasingly athletic; and the conversation of a couple at a table across the room whose voices so carried to us that they might as well have been sitting at our own.

'It cuts me up terribly to leave poor old Spot behind,' the man informed us. 'He was barking fit to break his heart when we left.'

'That's because you're such an old softie, darling,' the woman explained to us.

The man was about to make a decision. And he didn't, as most would have done, keep it to himself – he considerately let us in on it: 'I think I'm going to have some more cheesecake.' There was a certain, unnecessary it seemed to me, defiance in his tone.

He beckoned Francesco, during a break in his dramatic activities at the spirit-lamp, to serve him a second helping, as well one of his beefiness might, since the restaurateur, an artist with as delicate a touch as his lookalike, could confidently have challenged anyone to subdivide further the segments into which he had cut the dessert.

Francesco obliged. 'More of Francesco's speciality,' he lilted, with an implausible variety of notes and profusion of stresses in the 'Italian melody' of that brief phrase. He deposited another sliver of the cheesecake on the man's plate with a grand flourish.

'Marvellous, Francesco, marvellous,' boomed the man.

The couple smiled up, Francesco smiled down.

'Irresistible, no?' (No, thought Dean when he sampled it himself later and pronounced it to be just one of those mass-manufactured cheesecakes bought in by many restaurants without the pretensions of *Da* Francesco.) 'And cream, rich cream fresh from Jersey?' He poured it from a considerable height, once more exclaiming '*Mama mia.*' He was certainly, with all this rhetoric and mummery, making a grand job of disguising from the broadcasting duo the unexceptional nature of his fare and the paltry helpings of it, for it was with beaming delight that they watched him.

'Buon appetito.' He made a circle with thumb and forefinger and, the other fingers raised, half-tossed it towards them, a delicate darts-ace flick, fitting accompaniment to the exquisite nature of his 'speciality'. I now began to wonder whether this performance, rather than being, as I had at first thought, a hideous misconception of, and misjudged playing of, what he considered was expected of an Italian restaurateur in this country, might be instead a deliberately, brazenly outrageous self-parody; whether he might actually despise those patrons of the restaurant seemingly enamoured of his menus written, unlike Piero's, exclusively in Italian ('the real thing, darling'), his exorbitant prices ('you pay for quality') and his 'brio' ('so Latin'); and whether, if that were so, his self-guying insolence might be affording him a perverse pleasure that agreeably supplemented the simple one of getting rich quick. I wondered, but I couldn't be sure. Though there was one thing I could be sure of – two at least of his customers would not be paying a further visit.

'You don't think, do you,' Dean said, 'that most people are much exercised by how great a part hyperdesign now plays in books or any other form of communication? Correction. You don't think, do you, that most people even *notice* it? Even otherwise observant, thinking people. I'm afraid, Xav,' he added with a tired smile, 'yours is a bit of a voice in the wilderness.'

I always took notice of what Dean said. He was right, I supposed. I must wise up, get smart. We were in at the birth of a new phenomenon. One that would keep proliferating, reach to the remotest corners of the communications industry, manifest itself in practically every piece of printed matter produced by practically every organisation and enterprise throughout the land. One that would even, eventually, invade serious television and get into the driving seat there as elsewhere ('The chancellor's upping the stakes.' Lengthy sequence shot of poker-playing actors moving chips across baize).

Yes, thinking it over, I guessed I had no wish to be a voice in the wilderness.

'I think you imagine,' Dean said, 'that what offends you in your work is peculiar to that line of work. Believe me, that isn't true. That high-mindedness of yours, that desire for substance *always* to take precedence over glitz, that *rigorous* insistence on certain principles – ' Like so many who see intelligently into our condition, Dean hadn't got it *quite* right, had black-and-whitened it a little too much, and I wanted to tell him that I'd long since ceased to be as intellectually pure, as unswervingly committed to the truth, as he was painting me and to give him examples of how that had creepingly come about, but I had no opportunity to break in. ' – you'd find them frustrated in whatever you happened to be doing – industry, finance, academia, law, politics, you name it. About the only field where you might have been happy earning a living is scientific research. Though, I don't know… Even there… Ever read *Arrowsmith*?'

526

I shook my head. I'd never heard of it.

'Sinclair Lewis. We published it many years ago. Medical research and *Illusions perdus* – to lend the book someone else's title. You've got the same theme with Lydgate in *Middlemarch*, haven't you? Though perhaps today...'

Lydgate. Ludgate. Ludgate Broom, the Shrubs man. The laughably infelicitous Balzacian metaphors in his planting lists (let through unchanged by Flint!). The calceolarias with heads of rounded orange flowers 'like the contents of several tins of baked beans'...the dwarf almond that formed a cluster of pink flowers 'like a brightly coloured dressing gown that had fallen off the line'... All this passed through my mind in a flash, in one of those ephemeral associative distractions that, like droplets of spray, die almost as soon as they're born...

'It's always been that way,' Dean continued. 'Read your Swift, your La Bruyère, your Juvenal. You can almost see their contempt for so many aspects of the world around them withering the page. But of course they had the consolation of being *creative* outsiders, of being able to express their scorn in some artistic form.'

Creative outsiders. I felt a pang.

Sublimation

Switching off the alarm, heroically relinquishing Sally's warmth to plunge into the glacial atmosphere of our bedroom (central heating playing up), I drew back the curtains and, shivering, saw, not as expected, the court outside, but instead, immediately before me, on the window, the work of some master craftsman: an intricate diamond-point engraving on rock crystal of cluster upon cluster of acanthus leaves, their every fine line picked out in silver-gilt by the pale sun they screened (materials echoing those of certain reliquaries in Venice Dean had shown me reproductions of: masterpieces of Islamic engraved rock crystal mounted in silver and gold). Hugging myself against the cold, I studied this work of art in amazement at its complexity, precision and beauty – though with the usual frustration of knowing there was nothing more you could do than *look* at it. Other than, that is, if you wanted to see outside, *vandalise* it, which, goosepimpled, breath steaming, I proceeded to do: with a thumbnail I chipped and scraped away some of that thick glittering translucent foliage and through the crude aperture I'd made I gazed out. A dusting of white over everything, as of a fall of fine snow...a frozen silence broken only by an occasional muted dispirited cheeping...outside the court, in the road beyond, a filmy veil softening houses, gardens, parked cars...rooftops chalked a powdery blue...above them a sky of dog-rose pink...and, hanging low in this, the clearly outlined, platinum, almost lunar disc of the sun... Behind me, that sun was bathing the bedroom wall in a light of delicate rosy gold and casting on it shadows, including my own, of an equally delicate lilac blue. This fragile February radiance, this arctic air, this foliated window, this tenderly lit wall, newly sweet-pea-tinted, awoke in me such a medley of memories: the light of a similar sun in a similar sky at the other end of the day, a light palely illuminating Edie's bathroom late on a Boxing Day afternoon, when, in the silence before the arrival of the other guests, and pleasurably shuddering as I washed my hands in the too hot water, I would inhale the fragrance of her pink soap that echoed the colour of the skyline...the gelid charm, in a memory idealised, of a New Year's *Cheeky Chicko*, white lawn gilded by an icy sunlight and Cheeky animated by a New Year expectancy that was no doubt simply my own...the mornings of frost, mist and sun, punctuated by the hum-rattle-and-clink of the milk float, the savoury escaping scent of frying bacon and the friendly, lilting signature tune of *Housewife's Choice*, when I would set off down Danehill Road

528

to walk into the town, perhaps to buy a record at Lovat &
Albery, or, at a later date, to walk to the station, where, gazing
along the line at the soft nougat pink or peppermint green of
the signals in the mist, I would wait to join Sally on the train
for a day out in the West End...

And because these memories shared, in varying degrees,
elements with this morning that I was experiencing now and
with one another, they all fused into one vague but lovely
generalised whole that was, more than a rendering of reality,
a sublimation of it.

'But what then?'

On the train, unusually, I found a seat. Opposite me sat a middle-
aged couple, very spick and span, not off to work but, like Sally
and me on those trips on this train that the morning had earlier
brought back to me, off for a day out in town. After a subdued
discussion of where they intended to go, the man produced
from his wife's bag the *Daily Warp*. I saw that he handled and
regarded it with what one could only describe as a combination
of reverence and self-gratification: before he and his wife began
to read it, he placed it on his lap as fastidiously and devotionally
as a pious old maid might have placed in hers a bible or a
hymnal, yet it was with the self-indulgent postponement of a
pleasure the better to enjoy it that he and his wife first cleaned
their glasses at inordinate length, blew their noses, adjusted
themselves in their seat and hitched up their immaculate trouser
creases before they would allow themselves finally, actually,
to lay hands on the hallowed pap. Even then, the man's patting
its already trim edges square with his palms and his delaying
an intensive read with a lingering general scan of the front page
were all carried out with an expression as solemnly devout and
sensuously anticipatory as mine had been long ago on sitting

down with the latest issue of a far, far superior publication, *Film Fun*. After a while, and after the man had several times, preparatory to reading a left-hand page, folded it back with the same firm, careful, even pressure along the crease that must have been needed to produce the knife-like edges on the couple's trousers, the woman extracted the Teatime section: the deeply considered astrological conclusions of a tubby beaming man on a pleasing new retainer who reminded me somewhat of Plumpford...one of those single-column 'sting'-in-the-tail feuilletons of which 'The Startled Cat' had been a particularly gruesome example...a truly shocking vindication of avarice entitled 'Gold-digging Can Be Fun'...

My eyes fixed, now unseeingly, on one of these Teatime pages, I began to reflect on another, quite different vindication, Dean's recent one of all-conquering design at Mega Books and elsewhere. Had he convinced me? Only in part. I should have mentioned to him the cases where that out-of-control design was, not merely idiotic or exasperating, but truly pernicious, as in that first-aid pamphlet I'd seen when working on the Medical book, in which an image of a great roll of bandage had left no room for that full explanation of binding different types of wound that any first-aider would want to have, or as in that monthly mag, taken by Ivor, for sufferers from...

At that moment my musings were interrupted by the arrival of two ticket inspectors. On production by the couple opposite me of their day returns and by myself and the other passengers around me of our season tickets, the inspectors replied with their usual, mechanical "kyou, sir...'kyou, madam...'kyou, sir...' But to my surprise, upon coming to one man on the other side of the gangway, whose grey longhorn moustache and embroidered waistcoat gave him some remotely Wyatt Earp appearance, one of the inspectors, when this man showed him his season, responded with a heartfelt 'Nice one, boss'. I peered across at the season, as unobtrusively as I could, but it appeared to me to be in format, colour and printing no different from mine or anyone else's. There was obviously something particular about it that the inspector admired, but what could it be? Neither could I see what it was about the sketchily and, I suspected, self-consciously Nevadan aspect of the man himself that, given the absence of any accompanying air of authority or insignia of office, warranted the deference just shown him. But again I was undoubtedly missing something, for as the inspectors continued on their way down the crowded carriage they did so only with their standard "kyou, sir...'kyou, madam...' without once favouring any other passenger with the respect and acclaim bestowed on the 'lawman' and his season.

Nice one, boss. It was yet another tough puzzle, one as tough as the toughest in that book of toughies Dean had given me as a boy, *Something to Think About*.

I began to grapple with that puzzle – but just then the train, drawing away from a station, came to a halt again. I gazed out. At this later hour and this farther point up the line there was no trace of the frost that had sprinkled its white dust over Bexcray, and the peaceful February day outside looked almost soft enough to have been plucked from spring. In a siding some old railway sleepers were being burned against the backcloth of a Victorian redbrick school, a pinkish tan in the wan sunshine and flanked on one side by two great elms clad in ivy, the *sunlit dustiness* of whose green frills possessed for me, as always, a charm I could never quite explain to myself. Between and around the burning sleepers there wavered flames of an orange so pale and transparent in the sunlight as to be at times visible only as wobbles in the redbrick and the ivied elms. The undersides of the wood had split into cubes of an almost translucent, fruity red, to which the creamy blue that smudged them here and there, before it rose to haze the tremulous sunlit trees and walls beyond, seemed an almost gastronomic accompaniment. How soothing it would be to sit here in this backwater and let the charm of the scene soak into one all morning. The train seemed equally entranced by the prospect, for it hadn't budged for some time. Aware of the more than ordinary pleasure this view outside was affording me, wishing I could capture it in some medium or other, my thoughts began to enter a familiar channel: perhaps I should have been... In this, I now think, I was rather like the composer Halévy, who kept wondering whether he wouldn't have been better suited to something other than writing music – one day he'd decide he should have been, of all things, a general, another day a geologist, another day... Well, no, on second thoughts, I was, having created nothing, not at all like the man who gave the world a great opera.

Throbbing, the train valiantly roused itself from its happily dreaming state and we at last moved slowly off. I gave up on the Case of the Sheriff's Season, baffling beyond solution, even, I would have guessed, for Ellery or Father Brown. In no mood to read either my newspaper or my book, fed up with deciphering upside down the distressing pronouncements of the *Warp*, which now lay awry on the laps of the couple opposite as they dozed open-mouthed, I began considering my situation at Mega. Confounding the doubts of many, the Gardening book now looked on line to meet its completion date, less than two months away. (But how, it may be asked, did an outfit like Books with such an admixture of shirkers, clowns, sots and malcontents manage it? In the same way, I suppose, that governments riddled with incompetents manage to govern, that armies led by donkeys manage to win wars, that theatrical companies run by scatterbrains manage to stage productions. Things Get Done.) As always when the end of a book was in sight, I felt that same happy expectancy that the schoolboy feels as the end of term draws near. But as always, too, unlike the schoolboy, I heard intruding into the soothing melody of that expectancy the uneasy notes of 'But what then?'

Who could say?

Wallflower (*Cheiranthus cheiri*) Biennial. Height 8-24in, spread 9-15in. Lance-shaped leaves, 2in long, and spikes of four-petalled flowers in many colours, appearing in spring and early summer. Outstanding are 'Harpur Crewe' (yellow) and 'Bowles Mauve'.

I was returning a book to the vacant desk of Chillingford Flint, taskmaster and fainéant extraordinaire, when I saw on it the proofs of Selected Annuals and Biennials and read that entry on the wallflower. I knew that, as with other individual plants, this listing would constitute the only information on it in the book. A Latin name, some measurements, a leaf shape, a petal number, a flowering season and the highlighting of those two to me sickly varieties that so often paraded unharmoniously together in municipal beds. Not a word about the poetry of velvety, sunsoaked, deep-dyed red and orange varieties, drowsing on some burning afternoon, sending out wave after wave of dusky, musky fragrance into its depths.

When Flint eventually returned to his desk, I went against my general principles at Mega Books and took the matter up with him. All I wanted was to introduce a mention, no more than a mention, of the smouldering kinds of wallflowers and their heady scent; I felt I owed it to those 'blood walls of a lucious smell', as Clare called them. But Flint, natch, found the entry perfectly adequate as it stood. So, as usual, that was that.

By that gaunt, leaves-2in-long, yellow-and-mauve entry I was disconcertingly made to realise once again how so many of our poetries, our affections, our ideas, so many of the essential furnishings of our mind, that we have automatically, without giving it any thought, assumed to be shared by others, are in fact entirely unknown to most of them.

Thinking again about those wallflowers I had known in Dean and Olivia's garden in Walfield Road and then, by association, reflecting on the Platonic ideal form they and other elements of that road had assumed for me over the years led me to wonder whether all the poetries of boyhood that intermittently returned to me, the special intimations included, had not also been such forms. An ideal Post Office. An ideal Cinema. An ideal Department Store. An ideal Library. An ideal *Cheeky Chicko, Dandy, Knockout, Film Fun*. An ideal Trolleybus Dusk, Railway Station Dusk. An ideal Morning Avenue. An ideal Tree Tunnel...

But so many of those poetries had been contaminated, hadn't they, in one way or another. Even so, hadn't it been the sources of those poetries that had been blighted, rather than the poetries themselves? Could I then perhaps think of the sources of those poetries, all too helplessly impinged upon, impacted by, the cruel realities of everyday life as they were, as being, if one were to pursue the Platonic doctrine of forms further, no more than smudgy, binnable copies of the original patterns, the pure, unchanging ideal? Could I perhaps think of those ideal forms as transcending what had since been contaminated – and as transcending even, in addition, the new poetry of this contamination, the earthbound poetry, the gold and the black, the Romantic agony? It seemed, as I considered it, a somewhat fanciful idea. It implied that, in the first place, those ideal forms had some sort of independent existence, beyond the terrestrial one of the copies (a concept which philosophers after Plato struggled unsuccessfully to accommodate), and that, in the second place, we have a privileged apprehension of them as children ('trailing clouds of glory').

Whereas perhaps it was simply the irrepressibly idealising predisposition of the imagination that had created those forms. Who could say? It was like the question concerning another seemingly independent, autonomous world, the one that we enter when listening to certain music. Who could say likewise whether that world existed outside of ourselves or was simply an illusion born within us and destined to die with us?

The great gap

'We might see some foxes – or a badger, look.' Mrs Banks pointed to a page in a book. Michael and David peered at it. 'Or if we don't see a badger, we must look out for its footprints. They look like this – can you see?'

It was a fine Sunday in April and we were driving to Oakleas Wood, a few miles outside Bexcray. The spring air was limpid, its smile gentle, and with its annual alchemy it transmuted everything around: a weathered, warped, brittle old board fence basking in the sun was now the fetching pale lilac-grey of a pigeon's breast, and the sun shone so full, so directly on it that not one projection or indentation in its danger-of-splinters roughness pencilled in a shadow of itself.

Sally's mother was in the back seat (Mr Banks had stayed at home resting, after another nosebleed), showing the boys the Spring section of *What to See in the Countryside*, which she had bought by mail-order. Put out by Mega rival Patten Paige, it had a selling pitch of the usual kind: instead of simply strolling around the countryside, contentedly taking in the pure air and peaceful surroundings, letting your children romp about, while stopping occasionally to point out to them a beech tree, a squirrel or a clump of crocuses, why not get a grip on yourself, take your chequebook out and lug this 850-page tome around with you so that you could identify exactly all the many amazing things you might *just* conceivably come across but undoubtedly would not?

'Then we might see some pretty fun-jee in the woods, like this pretty yellow one. What is it? Oh yes, the velvet foot. Isn't that nice? We might see one of those. You can eat some fun-jee. Did you know that?'

'Mum! Michael, David – you're not to eat anything you find in the woods. Do you hear me?'

'Yes.'

'That's right,' Mrs Banks confirmed. 'Some of them are poisonous. Like this other pretty yellow one. The sulphur tuft. You must leave that one alone.'

'Leave them all alone,' I put in more testily than I'd intended.

'Yes,' said Mrs Banks, 'and you must stay away from hornets' nests, like this one. "Hornets make paper nests from chewed wood and often build them in hollow trees."'

I glanced in the mirror. Our sons were gazing at the page wide-eyed. I was pleased that Sally's mother was both educating and amusing them on the journey but I did wish she would treat the mendaciously named *What to See in the Countryside* as the armchair book it actually was and not as the indispensable everyman's field guide it claimed to be, raising so high the boys' expectations of wonder after wonder to come.

'We must look out for these pretty birds, look. Crossbills. The male's red and the female's green. And bullfinches – look at those pretty pink feathers. They're very nice, aren't they? We might see a sparrowhawk – that's fierce-looking, isn't it? And here's a wheatear disappearing into its hole. And look at this. "Keep an eye out for the bombardier beetle. It fires a puff of smoke, to defend itself against animals that attack it."' Michael laughed in gleeful anticipation.

Oakleas Wood was enterable from almost anywhere on its perimeter. Whichever section of road verge you chose to park on would stress to you the utter arbitrariness of that choice, in the same way as did, on Sandbay beach when I was a child, the particular patch of sand, no more, no less, suitable than any other, that we eventually chose to sit on.

'Why are we going into the woods here, Dad?' Michael asked.

'Because this is as good a place as any,' I said cheerfully, decisively and possibly erroneously, in that tone which gives children such faith in their dads until a certain age and in which one day Michael and David in their turn would convey similar hit-or-miss decisions to their kids.

We entered the wood and began walking through the bracken and dead leaves, making our way between oak trees and clumps of hazel.

'Take that book off Mum, Xav. It's very heavy.'

I did so, with ill grace, no longer able myself to stroll, as I'd hoped, unencumbered and relaxed.

Running ahead, the boys kept expressing their intention, not their hope, of finding badgers' footprints, owl pellets, hornets' nests, sparrowhawks et al, and from time to time peered touchingly at the unforthcoming woodland floor and canopy.

Soon a clearing appeared through the trees. Michael and David raced towards it. As we drew nearer I could see a lone figure crossing it at right angles to our path, a tall blond man of about forty. And what might he be doing here, I caught myself wondering with shocking injustice.

A girl and boy, in a wood, dash with joy...

The boys ran into the glade, and David informed the man in a piping voice, 'We look-ing for bom-ber beet-oos.'

The man stopped. 'Found any yet?' I heard him ask.

'Boys,' I called. 'Here. I want to show you something.'

The man looked in our direction. A plain, clean-shaven, unremarkable face, lank hair, dressed in sweater and jeans, as

I was. He could have been anybody, he could have been in the wood for any purpose you cared to think of. Most probably it was an innocuous one. But for parents, despite their knowledge that dark deeds were rare, woodland and other lonely rural spots had long since lost the inviolable innocence they once had.

The blond man continued on his way and disappeared.

We carried on with our walk a little longer, but the boys soon gave up looking for what they had so emptily been promised and more sensibly they raced around and hid. Back in the car they expressed their disappointment at not having seen one velvet foot, one crossbill, one wheatear, one bombardier beetle, etc., etc., etc. I felt for them. They had discovered that in fact what to see in the woods at springtime generally amounts to little more than an extremely large number of trees, and through this, more generally, had discovered very early on in life the great gap between tarted-up promise and mundane reality.

'A very few'

Sally and I were watching television, a new sitcom. And as on previous occasions, I found myself looking out for her laughs, willing her amusement to increase and even, to make her laugh again, occasionally repeating a payoff-line in admiring disbelief. Since, as far as I could remember, I only felt and behaved in this way in the company of Sally, Michael, David, Dean and Olivia, I could only suppose that this particular disposition was an index of love – and I suspected, even though I had never heard or seen it mentioned anywhere (in any context), it was a more common and more reliable such index than many more usually proposed. Fondly observing in this way Sally's laughter and the temporary banishing of her weariness, I felt surge through me a desire to do the very best I could for her.

Later, when Sally went to bed, I stayed up. I felt unusually alert, considering the hour and the hectic day I'd had at Mega. I switched off the television – and, as the bright picture vanished, was unpleasantly reminded once more of how a world so seemingly potent can be annihilated at a stroke. My thoughts turned to my book – that is, its fragmentary successive metamorphoses. After a while I took them out of the bureau drawer where I kept them. I reread parts of the earliest version, written before I had decided to introduce elements of the political thriller, then later still had begun to spoof this. Yet again, reverting to my original apolitical dream, I set myself to make one last attempt to think up some wonderful mystery like Master's, some ingenious plot with a conjuror's false lining, with magnificently concealed yet fair clues of sleeping beauty. The house was silent, there was no sound from outside, I had no distractions. I concentrated intently. The minutes ticked by, the quarter hours. Yet again, nothing. Nothing but variants on what Master had already done. Yet again I felt as frustrated as we do in dreams when, try as we might to walk or run, we scarcely budge, our efforts get us nowhere – or as frustrated as, in another dreamworld, one of those Kafka characters who believe that they can win through by exerting greater resolve, only to find, inevitably, that that is of no more avail than anything else. Yet again I took down from the bookshelves my by now dilapidated original paperback copy of *Mosaic*. Yet again I read those pages in which the shot-silk prose integrated puzzle, clues, atmosphere, wit, poetry seamlessly, as though by magic. Yet again I compared them unhappily with the pages I had written. Yet again I realised that Master had really got what so many of us, at moments of heightened awareness, or moved by contact with a great work, only have the illusion we possess. Or perhaps, to put it more accurately, less harshly, I realised that what it was in Master that we who loved his book sensed to exist also in ourselves existed in him to a far greater degree than it ever could in us.

I reclined in my chair and rested my head against the back. Yet again the truth that I'd glimpsed before reappeared to me, this time as plain and unequivocal as a simple geometric figure. My determined attempt to emulate *Mosaic* had been fated to fail from the start. To have created a mystery as startlingly original and beautiful as Master's, together with the equally original and beautiful clues to its solution, would have required in me the same gift that he possessed, and no amount of striving could ever have endowed me with that. It was as unacquirable as the gift of creating original and beautiful melodies. Both were 'nameless Graces which no Methods teach. And which a Master-hand alone can reach.' For too long I hadn't realised that I was no more capable, no matter how strenuous my efforts, of conceiving a mystery to rival *Mosaic* than I was of conceiving a melody to rival one of Gershwin's. Not only that. If I were honest, I had to admit to myself that there had never spontaneously occurred to me an idea for a worthwhile mystery of any sort. I was like Raymond Chandler, to whom I'd once ironically compared the hacks of *True 'Tec Tales* when he said 'I'm one writer who never says I have a terrific idea for a story. I don't get ideas.' Well, no. On second thoughts, I wasn't, with my single, piecemeal, constantly course-changing, unfinished manuscript, anything like the author of *The Big Sleep*, *Farewell My Lovely*, *The High Window*, etc.

Perhaps, subconsciously, I had known of my incapacity all along, and perhaps all those accumulated jottings in notebook after notebook ('The atmosphere of Lime Street on a smoky evening needs to be the setting for a major clue', 'In some way, I don't know how, integrate Cal as a piece of the puzzle', and all such other procrastinating entries), in which the intent, solely by virtue of being sincerely noted, seemed to do comforting, self-fobbing-off service for the attainment, perhaps they had been nothing more than continual sops to the would-be writer, a constant postponement of that emulous young man's need to face up to the painful truth, that he never would be able to write the book he craved to write.

I gazed back to that first literary intent of mine, to my desire to make of certain seemingly charged atmospheres and numinous experiences I had once known the very stuff of a mystery story, and of no other kind of book, because the only faithful and sustained reflection of them I had found was in such a story, Master's. And it seemed to me that if they were not to be embodied in a mystery, they were – in painful contrast to the myriad varied themes of those I regarded as *true* writers – too meagre for anything else. And yet, and yet, a voice from deep within me insisted, how could I call meagre what had once taken such possession of me, seemed so significant? How could I belittle what I had originally been trying to express in my book? As Kenneth Grahame said, 'it is no disparagement of the dreams themselves that only a very few of the dreamers have the power, or rather the gift, to harness their dreams with mastery.'

Well, let me not devalue those experiences, then, by calling them meagre but simply say that if in themselves alone – unMastered, unintegrated into an ingenious puzzle of this world – they provided no basis for a mystery story, neither were they enough to provide the dominant theme for any other kind of work, in particular for the standard literary novel with its emphasis on character development and relationships. Not that I had the desire or ability to write a novel of this kind. I felt I was like John Banville, who said 'As a writer I have little interest in character, plot, motivation', or like Evelyn Waugh, who said 'I regard writing not as investigation of character, but as an exercise in the use of language.' Well, no. On second thoughts, I wasn't, with my single, piecemeal, constantly course-changing, unfinished manuscript, anything like the author of *Nightspawn*, *Birchwood*, *Doctor Copernicus*, etc. or the author of *Decline and Fall*, *Scoop*, *Black Mischief*, etc.

I knew, by the way, that even if I could have found some form in which to express my sovereign theme I would have had nothing else to say, I would have been a one-book man. For I hadn't any desperate desire to achieve publication for its own sake. (Certainly I wouldn't have had any wish to attempt purely as an exercise or a way of making money – even if I could have thought up the characters and plot for it – the sort of popular novel that begins: 'Set on a rocky promontory, lashed by the salt spray of the Channel, Carleton Acres had about it, on that first morning I set eyes on it...' or 'It was late on a Friday afternoon when Dan Oblonsky laid the Rotterdam assignment on my desk...') No, I wasn't thirsting to see my own words published whatever they might be. After all, I had already seen a large number of them in print, and what's more, disseminated far and wide – I was already a published writer, and one of some versatility: 'Drop the roscoe, Smiler, I'm warning you'; 'The raspberry filling tends to be more popular than the apricot'; 'The flounder has an eye ¾in in diameter.'

But as to that sovereign theme of mine, those experiences that I had wanted to memorialise, I began to wonder afresh what *exactly* they were. Were they unique to me? If that were so, I should certainly have had no wish to describe and explore them in a book. But I knew from my reading that they were certainly not unique to me – just as I had known from my reading that the same was true for the polar opposite of those experiences, the fears engendered by settings of desolate cold. And more than that, the fact that there were others who had written about them, even if only to mention them, indicated – as certain small signs in that well at the heart of Mega House indicated what must be writ large in the day beyond, Out There – that there must be countless others who had known them without expressing them in writing, Out There.

And there was no doubt in my mind that the experiences I read about were similar to mine. As with the fears, in the particular forms they took and in the intensities with which they were felt there might be differences but in essence they were all of the same kind.

They seemed, those experiences, to have three closely related aspects. One was the promise of an apparently imminent adventure, some glorious, as-yet-unknowable adventure. In Alain-Fournier's *Le Grand Meaulnes* François Seurel feels as he comes to the edge of a wood, 'I too am on the path of adventure...I am looking for something...mysterious...' In one of his notebooks Chesterton writes 'There is one thing which gives radiance to everything... It is the idea of something round the corner.' In Sartre's *La Nausée* Roquentin walks down an empty evening street and suddenly senses, for no apparent reason, that 'at last an adventure is happening to me... something is going to happen...' Something. (A thought struck me: could it have been that my own intimations in the past of 'something mysterious', 'something round the corner', 'something going to happen' did not stem solely from what I was contemplating at the time but also, as a sort of faint pre-echo, from what was then far in the future, my contemplation of the ideal book that would express those intimations? For that book too, when I still hoped to write it, was always to seem tantalisingly on the point of revealing itself, without ever quite doing so.)

Another aspect of those feelings was the message, the hidden message that was waiting to be deciphered. In Nabokov's *The Gift* Fyodor, contemplating a scene in spring, wonders 'what is concealed behind all this, behind the play, the sparkle, the thick green grease-paint of the foliage? For there really is

543

something, there is something!' In Proust's novel Marcel has the feeling that 'a roof, a gleam of sunlight on a stone, the smell of a path...appeared to be concealing, beyond what my eyes could see, something which they invited me to come and take...' And in *La Nausée* Roquentin, leaving a park, is convinced that 'The smile of the trees, of the clump of laurel bushes, *meant* something...' Something.

Finally, there was the desire to become one with the source of that feeling, what was instilling it within you. In *Field and Hedgerow* Richard Jefferies, experiencing an almost religious communion with a carpet of wild flowers in the July grass, wishes he 'could do something more than gaze at all this scarlet and gold and crimson and green...something more than see it...make it part of me that I might live it.' Something.

I began to ask myself the same sort of questions I had asked myself when reflecting on the ideal forms of those scenes and places and things that had beguiled me as a boy and on the transcendent worlds conjured up by music. In the case of what all those writers or their spokesman characters I have cited had intuited, or, less confidently, postulated, were such feelings a true glimpse of what lay beyond the merely apparent? Were they evidence of Delacroix's Nature as dictionary, of Baudelaire's Nature as hieroglyphics, of Pope's Nature as mysterious art, all signalling something? But if so, what? If you had no religious belief – and some of those writers who spoke of that something had none – what might that something be?

Or were they all an illusion, those intimations, as baseless as certain other strongly felt intimations may be, such as the conviction of a nervous person that he is in danger when in fact he is not, or that of a hypochondriac that he has a fatal disease when in fact he has not? Were they simply moments of heightened awareness (to which the impressionable young, on whom everything – nature, music, literature, love – makes such an impact, are particularly susceptible)? Was that all that such moments, beautiful though they were, and for the privilege of whose visitation one might admittedly be forever grateful, was that *all* that they were? Did they merely exemplify what Robbe-Grillet believed to be the 'false mystery' of objects, the 'suspect' nature of their 'inner life'? Was Sartre's character right when, before he felt there was a meaning behind the smile of the trees and the laurel bushes, he was equally convinced that 'things are entirely what they appear to be – and behind them – there is nothing'? Nothing.

Something. Nothing. How were we poor lost mortals, each floundering at the heart of our allotted, defective, non-returnable consciousness, so limited in our sensory perceptions and our powers of understanding that we cannot even imagine another colour outside the spectrum our eyes are restricted to, cannot even grasp the concept either of there being or of there not being any origin or end to Everything, how were we to know – even the greatest and wisest, who truly *know* no more than the rest of us – how were we to know, at those special moments when we had that certain feeling, what the truth was, whether what we apprehended corresponded to any reality, or not?

Well, whatever that truth might be, I must, anyway, forget the literary dream that had flowered from that feeling, the dream that, encouraged by Modigliani's injunction, I had tried to preserve for so long.

Into the flames

After smouldering for some time, the bonfire, suddenly revived by the wind, crackled and once more burst into flame. A stronger gust, and the smoke dipped, made towards me, enveloped me, stinging my eyes. It was late on a cold spring afternoon and I was at the top of Lil's garden. Over the previous year I'd let my regular work on it lapse and it was now badly overgrown: grass knee-high in places, nettles invading the planted areas, bindweed festooning the fences, ivy rampant in the old apple tree. A sense of duty had brought me back. That, and another reason.

The north wind, moist with impending rain, whisked up and scattered some of the dead leaves I'd gathered for burning, and in the crown of the apple tree it set the ivy shivering. The fire, glowing at its heart, was blazing away now. I reached down and took from a carrier bag a bundle of papers. This was the other reason for my visit. I was burning the manuscript of my book. Self-consciously aware of a certain unwanted melodrama in the act, I threw the pages into the flames. As I did so, I experienced a sense of mingled comedy and tragedy: irresistibly reminded of Wodehouse's line, 'The unpleasant, acrid smell of burnt poetry', I couldn't help smiling, almost laughing, yet at the same time I was understandably sad at seeing the dream that had sustained me for so long during uncongenial working days at Lea & Lyle, at *True 'Tec Tales*, at *The Swiss Roll Maker*, at Mega Books, literally going up in smoke. I could of course simply have thrown those pages away at home. But burning them in that garden was for me, as burning his rhymes was for Chesterton's Adam Wayne and burning his pocket-book was for Waugh's Guy Crouchback, 'a symbolic act'. The frustrated, buried artist in me felt at some deep level that since it was in that garden many years before that I had first decided to write my own special book it was symbolically right that it should be there that I destroyed it.

Memories of that garden in the past returned to me. Waiting eagerly by the fence to receive that week's *Knockout*; standing at the top late on Christmas Day afternoons, with not another soul in sight; lying in the long grass on warm sunny Easter days reading *Dandy*; later, sitting beneath the apple tree, lost in, entranced by, *Mosaic*...

I took from the bag the notebooks I had accumulated over the years, romanly numbered on the front in imitation of Master's, and threw them too into the heart of the fire. As I did so, I was aware of a certain ambivalence towards them. On the one hand, I would miss them. After all, whenever a thought had struck me as to something I must do in connection with the book (though rarely accompanied by any idea as to how I could actually do it), it had given me pleasure to take the latest notebook from my pocket and jot down in it that earnest intent: reinforced by my knowledge of similar reminders addressed to himself by Master, they had fooled me into thinking I was laying the groundwork for the tour de force to come. And that had given me that satisfying commitment to a particular purpose that, over and above our everyday responsibilities, impels us forward in life. On the other hand, even though I would now miss that sense of purpose, I felt a partly compensatory sense of relief. No more of that self-imposed task of jotting down all those reminders, no more of dropping everything to fetch my notebook when I was without it, for fear I would otherwise forget what it was I had decided I must do. With that relief, I now understood what Gide meant when, to a young would-be writer troubled by his impulse to abandon the struggle, he responded along the lines of: You have the opportunity to quit, and you hesitate? But even so, I suspected that this new feeling of freedom would not last. I suspected that the frustrated longing, the thwarted ambition, the bitter disappointment lay deep and that, like poignant memories of a lost loved one, from time to time they would resurface.

I watched my abortive work burn, blacken, disintegrate, release fragments of itself that fluttered up and away on the wind. The first drops of rain fell. I turned back to the house.

Cathedrals

One Friday morning in April I finished reading my last batch of page proofs. My work on the Gardening book had come to an end. Flint and Simon, soon to move into a smaller office to leave the large one free for a new project, would 'put the book to bed' (journo-speak that Plumpford had introduced); the rest of us must await our fate.

At midday I received a call from McStutt. He would like to see me that afternoon, at four. With so many delightfully free hours ahead of me, all the more relishable after months of hard graft, I realised I could for a change have a long leisurely Flintian lunch break. And since the bay trees and brickwork and windows in the central well told me that the spring day outside was one of true splendour, I decided I would take my time off as a long leisurely walk to Hyde Park – by a roundabout route, heading away from Knightsbridge, towards Belgravia.

Belgravia, late Georgian, spacious, decorous...listless according to some, but to me, as maligned suburbia had been when I was a boy, replete with a dreamy charm on such a day as this. Soon I found myself strolling down sunswathed balconied streets and cobbled mews, inhaling that smell characteristic of certain classy urban residential areas on fine days of spring or summer: the faint, subtle, warm, dry, ever so slightly pungent smell of sunsoaked stonework, pavements, evergreen leaves, planted urns. The warmth, the scent moved the creatures blessed by them irresistibly to express their delight. A Jack Russell, happily believing today that it was a greyhound, raced flat out down Beauchamp Place. An office worker, wondering whether he should perhaps have been..., flicked with sobershod foot and striker's aim a pebble down a distant drain. A whistling youth startled himself with his melodic brio.

As I meandered on my way, my sighs of pleasure at my

release from Gardening, at the halcyon scene around me and at the merest whisper of a breeze that was fondling my hair submerged any apprehension I felt about my next task at Mega.

Sloane Street. Cadogan Place. Belgrave Square, with its lofty neoclassical piles, its porticoed embassies and institutes, dressed by haze and sunlight in a powdery blue gauze appliquéd here and there with diamanté where windows and parked cars flashed in the sun. Halkin Street, where outside a Regency mansion the black iron casings of the lamps atop two gateposts were painted by the light a golden grey (like that I remembered lying in contented oblongs on the black worktops of Bexcray post office), while over this soft luminosity there lazily, gratifyingly played, beneath the branches of an overhanging plane tree, an intricate pattern of black-restoring shadows, a mobile notation of the tender song that fine days sing.

At Hyde Park Corner I gazed across at the great bronze group that crowned Constitution Arch: Peace in a Quadriga. A winged boy in a chariot drawn by four horses. The day had resculpted the group: the surfaces it lit up on Peace, his extended wings, his wreath held aloft against the clean blue sky and his heavenward-straining steeds, and the sharp dark shadows it cast on them together modelled in a new depth and detail the faces, muscles, plumage and drapery. And, too, although the charioteer tried as usual to hold the team in check, he seemed today less able to curb them, for, as they caught sight of some dazzling white cumuli moving across the blue towards them (blue and white that in its purity recalled the sky and primary school walls in Kingsdon St Mary on perfect summer days), they became a team no longer simply striving upwards but actually, supernaturally, airborne, like Pegasus, bearing their angelic driver aloft with them, flying – in an Einsteinian demonstration similar to that also provided by the gliding moon on a night of driven cloud – at an even, purposeful pace, dramatically, gloriously, towards the seemingly motionless silvery white ahead.

I entered Hyde Park. Inviolately cathedral-like in summer (as I liked to picture it to myself in mental words and paint), it was now having to begin restoration work on its roof and chapels after the ravages of winter. This budding activity, carried out by so many unseen forces, burst gently on my eyes – as, so it seemed, might equally have burst gently above me what appeared to be so many large bubbles hovering on high but were in fact the glass globes of the park lamps. Set off to perfection, those cool crystalline spheres, by a backcloth of warm, dull, indistinct orange, plum and grey velvet – the buildings beyond seen through hazy bare trees – and perched on top of slender, ornate standards, they seemed to have been blown into existence through these, to be hovering there, still attached, and, but for their metal casings, to be about to break free and float off into the sky, like those fragile glistening pink-gold-and-green orbs that Danny and I as boys used to watch sail over the rooftops.

I lunched in a restaurant overlooking the Serpentine, observing with pleasure how the branches of some planes overlaid with lacework the blue and white silk above, while lower down, where their trunks had shed irregular flakes of old bark, they were dressed in more homely style, in close-fitting coats of vari-coloured-pastel patchwork. As I sat there, I consciously savoured during this unusual lunchtime that man-of-leisure existence so brazenly led by Flint all the time.

At last I made my way back to Mega House. Leaving the bright day behind, pushing through the swing doors, crossing the vast shadowy foyer, I felt in my innards that familiar unpleasant old lurch of return.

Exiting from the lift, I turned right as usual down a familiar corridor with a familiar ox-blood carpet but one whose tread-muffling now seemed to possess a sort of hushed ominousness. At the crossroads I turned left towards an office that was my temporary billet. Barney Potts, in cream and chocolate today, was at the drinks machine. Forever, as a creative writer, bitching to anyone who would listen about the 'cultureless' nature of his tasks at Mega, forever more or less demanding of Fate a windfall, he was on this occasion, most unusually, no longer frowning, querulous. In response to my perfunctory greeting, it was with a happy grin that he peered at me over his 'man of distinction' half-moons.

'Guess what. I've been given a lovely job at last, a *lovely* job.' He had, he told me, 'moved on' from the *Conservatory Companion* (but I knew that the troubleshooter on the book, Chris Alexander, was more responsible than Potts for this 'movement onward'). He was now working on the *Book of Britain*, and his latest assignment on this, he said, was to write a piece on every English cathedral. He smiled with cat-at-the-cream contentment, a look that reminded me of when he used to return from yet another stationery store foray. 'They thought it was right up my street.' Of course. Potts' mysterious reputation for expertise in all things cultural. 'Masses to do,' he said, 'and it's needed in a rush as usual. But never mind. Such a lovely job for a change.' He was one of those for whom any form of High Art, or anything closely associated with it, was, no matter what its actual quality or how little they really knew about it, automatically, without question, hallowed, important, laudable, and for whom by extension any job connected with it, no matter what its quality or how unfitted they were for it, must by reflection be equally hallowed, important, laudable.

'How are you producing these entries?' I asked, as though I didn't know.

'How do you mean?'

'Well, where are you getting your info from?'

'Guide books. Pamphlets. The usual. They've got everything you need to know. When such-and-such a tower was built, who carved the misery-cords, that sort of thing.'

'You have to watch the plagiarism of course, reorder all the facts, twist all your sentences around, to disguise your sources.'

'Yes. Bit of a bind, that. Difficult, too, sometimes.'

'You haven't visited any of these cathedrals yourself recently,' I said pointedly, unfairly.

'No, of course not.' He looked at me as though I'd lost my reason. 'When would I have time to do that? Anyway, as I said, it's not necessary. The facts are all in the guides. That's all Debbie Gradd wants. And Willie.'

For sure. I heard in my mind's ear that precise Scots croak: 'We certainly don't want any romantic descriptive guff, er-heh-heh, er-heh-heh.'

I had of course no difficulty in understanding that, as usual, Mega Books wanted only facts, facts, facts, and of the starkest kind ('The chapter house dates from 1147', 'In the south aisle is a figure of John Donne by Stone (1631)', 'The cloisters contain elaborate vaulting'). Fair enough. That was their bag. But what I did have difficulty in understanding was how anyone could repeatedly and delightedly describe the clerical accumulation and regurgitation of already paraphrased lists of those dry-as-dust facts about buildings he had for the most part never set eyes upon, combined with the tedious exercise of constantly rephrasing the perfectly acceptable, if say-nothing, statements that presented those facts, how he could describe this chore as 'a *lovely* job'. Why, to me it was scarcely distinguishable from what, apart from my creative work on the plant-feed section, I had had to cobble together on Orchids. I couldn't even see that, as a tiresome task, what Potts was doing had much over adding up grocery prices at Lea & Lyle.

'I must get back,' Potts said. 'This afternoon I've still got to do' (he ticked them off on his fingers) 'Coventry, York,

Canterbury, Winchester, Worcester, Lincoln – er, Coventry and, er – what is it now? – oh, yes, Norwich...' I tried once more, resolutely but unsuccessfully, to comprehend this strange being, with his tropically deep complexion and white-strawy hair, his cream suit and tie and chocolate shirt. 'God,' he exclaimed, 'if there were only more jobs here like this, I might be more of a happy bunny.' And he hurried off, his coffee slopping in its plastic cup.

I gazed after his receding figure blankly.

Ugugug

I looked at my watch and saw that in a few minutes I was to learn my fate. I was nervous. Ever since his elevation to the managing editorship, McStutt, who had seemed to me when I'd worked in the same office with him simply a pompous twerp, had now acquired, solely by virtue of occupying at the far end of a long corridor an imposingly large office all his own, on whose door one always had to knock, even he of all people had now acquired the capacity, which I hated to acknowledge, to make one tense up, to become slightly breathless, as one approached that door.

'Ah, there you are,' he said as I entered. 'Take a seat, er-heh-heh. Give me a couple of minutes and I'll be right with you.' He proceeded with implausible rapidity to finish scanning and 'gutting' a substantial sheaf of copy. 'Young Eileen King's pieces on steam engines, iron working, spinning mills, etc.,' he eventually informed me. 'Room for some improvements, er-heh-heh. But too late now. And it will pass muster, I think.' Then he canted his head back and sighted me along a nose that new loftiness had tilted now almost to the horizontal.

'First I think I should let you know about an important new post I'm creating now that Gicbog is nearing its end. Deputy

Managing Editor. It's to take some of the heavy workload off myself, er-heh-heh. Fortunately, a very capable person is available to take up the position.' He paused. 'A very capable person, er-heh-heh. Chillingford. When he's finished putting Gicbog to bed in the new office, he'll move into that one.' (He indicated a small room adjoining his own.) 'And Bunty, who's been far from happy since Bob left, will move in too, as his secretary. Actually, Chillingford, who'd spotted how snowed under I am, was thoughtful enough to suggest this new position to me himself, er-heh-heh. I followed it up, and Vin has given it his blessing, er-heh-heh.

'The others' – he referred to them dismissively – 'are being dispersed here and there, wherever they can slot in.

'And now I expect you're wondering what's in store for you, er-heh-heh. First let me say how impressed all of us have been by your grasp of practical matters on the Greenhouse section of Gicbog. As a result, Chillingford and I think that you're the ideal person to take charge of a major project we shall soon be embarking upon in the Allotment, er-heh-heh. It's a most exciting challenge. The *Ultimate Guide to Greenhouse Gardening*. As exhaustive as those two old warhorses, the *Ultimate Guide to Wallpapering* and the *Ultimate Guide to Lawnmowing*. But, of course, because of the subject matter, considerably longer. Three volumes, er-heh-heh, er-heh-heh.'

I had over the years, as the reader has gathered by now, acquired considerable poker-player's mastery over my features and my voice. So there was no way, I think, that McStutt could have had any inkling of the wave of horror that swept through me at his announcement. But that control, that ability to prevent myself screaming 'No. *No. NO!*' was only of limited help to me in dealing with the situation into which I had now been thrust. Confronted with McStutt's shocking proposal, I found I was bereft of any sensible reply. I just stared at him and said nothing, feeling myself revert to that catalepsy I'd experienced years before in a deserted concrete storeroom and more recently when first setting eyes on Bark-Chipping's Orchids copy.

'Each volume will make about eight hundred and fifty pages. That's about two thousand five hundred pages in all, er-heh-heh. The schedule is nine months for each book, so we're talking about two and a quarter years for the entire project.' Confronted with my continued silence and lack of expression, he added, 'You would of course be rewarded with a higher salary, commensurate with your increased responsibilities, er-heh-heh.' And still receiving no immediate response, he felt impelled to conclude: 'I realise Ugugug is going to be a considerable undertaking, a considerable commitment. So I shall quite understand if you want to sleep on your decision until Monday.'

I seized this temporary lifeline. 'Yes, yes, I think I would like to sleep on it.' Monday morning. More than two whole days away. I felt some of my senses slowly returning. But far from completely, for on my way out of the office I bumped against the door jamb and in the corridor collided with Manny Van White, who, instead of smilingly accepting my apology as he once would have done, directed at me another of his latter-day looks of detestation.

'An exciting challenge'

Sleeping on it. Friday night. Saturday night. In considering what my life would be like *if* I were to take on the terrible taxing new task, one positive aspect kept recurring to me. I would at least be free, wouldn't I, of what had always racked me before: the awareness that all the tremendous amount of time and energy I was giving to Mega was at the expense of my book. Now that I had given up my dream, I would no longer fret that...

And then suddenly, at one point, there flooded through me, brief but intense, a painful return of the desire to be working on that literary design of mine as I'd originally vaguely conceived it, idealised it, a pain as anachronistic, in view of my recent destruction of everything I'd written, as the ache an amputee sometimes feels in a phantom limb. Once more I seemed to apprehend, in solution, what was needed to realise the dream. Once more I sensed within me the power to precipitate it, to materialise it in the form of a book. But once more, almost at the same moment, I realised that that power was illusory, that the *sense* of possessing it was far from the *truth* of possessing it, and that, like so many others, I had allowed that feeling to lead me astray.

For all these years – apart from brief musings on possible creative alternatives – I had considered my 'true' life to be writing my book and my 'false' life to be working in one uncongenial job after another. Now I realised unhappily that all along I had got it the wrong way round. Writing had been my 'false' life, and those jobs – the nuts, bolts and washers, the bacon and dog biscuits, the 'tecs, the swiss rolls, the fish eyes, the greenhouse shading paint – had actually been my 'true' life.

How disconcerting that realisation. It was like that optical trick of the Necker cube. You looked at it and for some time you saw it in only one particular aspect, until suddenly that vanished, replaced on the instant by another completely different, of whose existence you'd previously been completely unaware…only in this case, unlike that of the Necker cube, what you had seen originally would never come back.

On the Monday morning I went to see McStutt in his office.

'I've thought about your proposal very carefully over the weekend,' I said. 'And I've decided that I'd like to take on Ugugug.'

McStutt showed his satisfaction by combining a head cant, a smile, some 'kisses' and an 'er-heh-heh' all in one.

'It sounds like an exciting challenge,' I said. 'I'd like to get cracking as soon as possible. When do you think the Allotment will be free?'

Epilogue

We had spent the afternoon, Sally, the boys and I, shopping in Bexcray. Our car was in for repair – at a garage run by the swarthy mechanic who long ago had replaced me, and then himself been replaced, in the extended, intrepid sexual odyssey of Linda Lorell. Having failed to obtain a cab, we stood now in the High Street waiting for a bus to take us home. The light was fading, and that strange heightened atmosphere of a town at approaching dusk was upon us.

It was two years since I'd taken on the three-volume Greenhouse project. The schedule had proved punishing, tougher even than that of the single-volume Gardening book. It was only through a reluctantly donned and uncomfortably worn ruthlessness that I'd managed to get the first two volumes produced on time – just. But now, with the third, I was really struggling to meet the daunting deadlines that Sharpes, McStutt and Flint demanded we stick to. I regularly worked late – so that the boys were usually asleep when I got home – and I even, when I felt I had no other choice, went into the office on Saturday mornings, and got others to do the same. And since design was still paramount at Books – in fact increasingly imperious with each passing year – and since my efforts as a project editor to revoke its more outrageous decrees were constantly overruled from on high, I was forced to insist the subs carry out tasks that were even more maddeningly absurd than those that had once almost deranged me. At meetings, I echoed the references by my superiors to various 'exciting challenges', I laughed at Sharpes' crude quips. At lunchtime in the pub I installed myself at the centre of the group instead of, as once, at the periphery. My look and my voice became more masterful than ever, my handshake firmer, my simulated amazement, disappointment or delight more convincing. In short, I entered fully into what Wilhelm Reich saw, in such circumstances, as our unacknowledged agreement with everyone else not to notice that we are not living a real life.

Sharpes and McStutt had gone from strength to strength. At a ceremony at Hampshire House they had been presented with the Bronze Owl award for best illustrated reference book of the year: the *Book of Britain*, 'this exuberantly wide-ranging and magnificently produced volume'. Which I now supposed was not an inaccurate description really. In fact, I had rather come to admire its stuffed-with-this-and-that fruitcake quality.

As for Flint, he had, in that position of Deputy Managing Editor he'd engineered for himself, achieved his ideal: having himself taken on an assistant, he had ensured that his own workload was so patently light that no one could have questioned with any justification his many absences from the office. And these were even more numerous and lengthy than before: he was to be seen on most days and at all hours strolling nonchalantly on his way out of or into the building, pipe clenched between teeth, from around the stem of which he might deign to acknowledge you with a cool, barely audible drawl. He had become a sort of hero to me.

Simon had moved on to the *Great Book of Motorways* and was now obtaining sustenance from even more electrifying alarms, disasters and escapades. And Barney Potts had, in an unprecedented manoeuvre, been shunted by Flint off Editorial on to a hapless new Product Development department.

Mike Mallarmé was at Patten Paige, doing much the same kind of hackwork as he'd done at Mega. From time to time I met him for a lunchtime drink, when we would swap stories about our travails. These were, natch, anomie-soaked – but even so, I noticed a change in him. He didn't rage as much as he'd done in the past against what he saw as the idiocies and injustices of his work and he'd filed down the extravagant jagged foul-mouthedness to a more normal level of cursing (whether all this had anything to do with his settling down with a woman he'd met at Patten Paige and becoming a stepdad I don't know). He was also working on a novel set in a giant publishing organisation he called Colossus.

Sally's father had died suddenly the previous year. He'd been felled by a stroke one morning as he got up from the breakfast table. Mrs Banks was shocked, confused, lost, and Sally and I dealt with the funeral arrangements and probate. Soon afterwards, at her request, we sold the house in Blackwell, and she went to lodge temporarily with a married sister in Bexcray until she could move in with us into the house we were buying in Dulwich. An enlightened Sally was soon to start studying for a degree in modern languages now that both the boys were at school and her mother could collect them.

Lil was a pensioner now and had aged considerably. She had acquired a 'boyfriend', a retired lavatory attendant and widower, seedy-looking and with some horrific form of skin disease, which obviously did not remind her too disagreeably of her preferred terms of abuse of earlier days, 'scabby-faced' and 'poxy-faced'. She boozed with him at the Cat and Powder Monkey (the Prince Albert that was), where she had long since given up her cleaning job – and apparently he was about to move into 33 Danehill Road.

Dean had twice been shortlisted as a prospective parliamentary candidate for the Labour party but had failed at both selection conferences. He received the tacit message that all the work he'd done for disadvantaged youth couldn't offset his electoral baggage as prosperous ex-publisher (scarcely an encumbrance today). But I'm sure that, in what the ingenuous would have seen as a paradox, it was his talk of redistribution of wealth, higher taxes for the rich and the abolition of private education that actually did for him. Now he and Olivia, retired from schoolteaching, were planning to sell the Rectory and move to Italy.

Finally, Danny. He had, almost unbelievably to me, struck gold with the children's story he'd based on our old fantasy world, which, taking up my half-hearted suggestion, he'd renamed Kaleidoland. Macmillan were publishing it, the paperback rights had been sold and a sequel was already being asked for. And Danny had not unreasonable hopes, he said, of further rewards: an adaptation for children's television, an animated feature film even.

The dusk deepened. I gazed down the High Street, past Sam Sports; past what had been The Rendezvous coffee bar but was now the Choozie Floozie boutique; past Smart Feller men's shop, W.H. Smith and the chemist's that had once been Gowdy & Simpson's with its flasks of red and green but was now just another Boots; past the library, which over the years had so richly nourished my imagination but had now cleared out most of its treasures to make way for the ghosted lives of soap stars in duplicate and videos of schlock movies in quadruplicate; past the traffic lights and neo-Gothic Barclays and Lloyds at the crossroads; down the long vista of King Street, past the Regal, Court's the bookshop, Pergolesi's ice cream parlour and what had been Valentines disco but was now Bexcray Property Services (through which we were currently selling our maisonette); past the main post office; past assorted stores and shops beyond; to eventually, in the distance, houses, schools, churches. The darkening double line of rooftops converging in perspective formed an indigo V that made the sky look by contrast paler than it actually was, a luminous sky of a peculiar yellow-green, which, suffused ahead with purple cloud, had thus the coloration of a bruise and called to mind that similar sky in a key scene in *Mosaic* which Master, sending such a frisson through my young self, had described as 'unearthly'. At one point, where the dark rooflines dipped and made more room for it, the yellow-green and purple contusion provided a delicious backdrop for the juicy orange globe of a crossing beacon, ripe as a harvest moon, while street lamps, along the arms of the indigo V, decorated each edge of the sky with a string of white diamonds. At a lower level further, assorted jewellery: shop lights, traffic lights, tail-lights, Regal neon, in the deep blue velvet display case of the darkling road. I caught a whiff once more of an old incense, traffic exhaust. And permeating everything – the green vault above, the embers of the dying day, the fumes of the dying day – was the volatilised essence of something indefinable. In it I seemed to catch the last smouldering traces of the past, the pure pre-infection past, the past of Bexcray and myself as we once were, when I would sometimes have the feeling that...

Involuntarily, my hand moved towards the pocket in which I used always to carry a notebook. Until it remembered – and fell away.

Putting my arm around Sally, I drew her close.

I looked down at Michael and David. They were gazing at the magic of the dusk stretching away before us. Their lips were parted, their expressions rapt.